You're not listed if.

205Z
TIME AND SALVATION

205Z: TIME AND SALVATION

ISBN: 978-0-9970475-1-6 (Hardcover)
Library of Congress Control Number: 2021905419

For more information, please contact:
Jason Michael Primrose
info@lostchildrenofandromeda.com

205Z
TIME AND SALVATION

Jason Michael Primrose

Illustrations by The CMD Studios

Quote designs by Kieron Anthony Lewis

DISCLAIMERS

This is a work of fiction. Names, characters, places, and incidents are the products of the author's imagination or are used fictitiously. Any resemblance to actual events, locales, organizations, or persons, living or dead, is entirely coincidental.

———

DEDICATIONS

To my mom, you have always been cosmic
To my Nana, you have always been the catalyst
To my dad, you have always been imagination
To my family, you have always been stellar.

And to you, an Evolutionary bursting with potential,
you have always been

Enough.

215 DAYS LEFT

A clock strikes Day 215.
Quiet cries begin to haunt me.
This is where it ends, with Z
In 2052, you'll see.
Earth it quakes.
Shivers, shakes.
Foundations cannot stay in place.

———

I believe in salvation, too.
I believe there's time for you.

———

Hours we've wasted, days we've lost
War strips away at the love in our hearts
Can we rise,
to power inside
fighting the darkness to reclaim the light

———

Spare the blood of us lost children.
Living our truth in pure freedom.
Here's how it begins, with me.
My heritage, I am the key.
Courage aflame.
Shadows break.
Death to a fear I've come to crave

———

Two hundred days, and I won't give in.
Two hundred days until the end.

———

Heroes doubted, villains praised
Time counts us down to the last of our days
Does it burn
in your soul
What would you give for the good of this world?

PROLOGUE

ALLISTER ADAMS
Cumberland Falls, Kentucky, 2040 AD

ALLISTER ADAMS HOPED the worst had come and gone.

It was well-intentioned hope. A child's hope. As flashes of blue light spread through the passing thunderclouds. The sky rumbled a few times more, sounding angry, the last of its evening thunderstorm threatening the quiet town.

Allister, a boy midway through his seventh trip around the sun, sat on the grooved floor of his dad's car, an Ukimoto Hover Model X. His arms were wrapped around his legs, his chin pushed against his thighs. He was sulking.

His dad had always said nothing was the same after the West Coast earthquake. But now something else was coming, something more powerful, if that were even possible. It seemed the worst was still on its way.

The conversation about the car rules neared its end. His dad knelt in the passenger doorway wearing an uncharacteristic scowl. Mostly because he was telling Allister to stay out of sight. His beard was overgrown. His long, dreadlocked hair was tied on his head like frayed rope in a loose knot.

"No matter what you hear outside, don't you go gettin' up in that seat," his dad warned.

Allister side-eyed him, impatient, suspicious, waiting for his dad's often-comforting smile to reappear.

"But, Pops...what if the...the storm comes back...and...and...you need help?" he finally asked.

"Storms aren't made to hurt us. They're just Mother Nature tellin' us how she feels." His dad flipped the straps on his overalls and smiled at last, though it wasn't very big. He stood after he finished and stared out at something Allister couldn't see. "Stay low, okay? It's too dangerous out here, son."

Allister frowned.

There went the *D* word again. When something was dangerous, then it couldn't be done. Those were the house rules.

His dad lowered the car's door and left Allister alone in the power plant's parking lot, the place he spent most nights when both his parents were called to their separate out-of-the-house duties.

Allister's smooth, steady breaths came with ease, even in the car's confined space. But a sense of wonder kept pulling his eyes to the windshield, as he hoped to catch a glimpse of a lightning strike in the forest or wind twirling objects into the air. Hoping to experience this *dangerous* his parents always warned about.

He picked up his toy unicorn, which had been stuffed beside him in the seat, and nodded as he repeated, "Stay low," to himself, once again comforted by his own imagination. With a quiet *whoosh* from his lips, he lifted the unicorn up, letting it take off toward a pretend sky.

Then the car began rocking back and forth, swaying like their house often did against the wind, clanking like loose pipes as it moved. He froze.

The wind howled, sweeping through the air in sudden bursts. A light too bright to be lightning blasted through the windshield. An engine somewhere above screamed. It was louder than any thunder he'd ever heard.

His dad's warning to stay low repeated in his ears. Also present was his own curiosity about the powerful thing on its way. He climbed onto the seat for a better view and plastered his hands against the dashboard to look out over the grass.

There he saw a squiggly line of blue light soaring up from the facility's open ceiling toward a break in the clouds. The strange light quivered and flashed and fizzled and brightened, struggling to stay connected to a glowing oval that was falling, as if from space.

Allister blinked in disbelief, his heart thumping, his mouth hanging open. He could only hope that his dad had aimed and was somehow shooting the beam into the sky to stop that speeding object—but even if he was, the object wasn't quieting, wasn't dimming, wasn't slowing.

Every time the tiny oval flashed, the blue light from the plant faded.

Another earsplitting *boom* echoed overhead. Light spread across the atmosphere, expanding from the tiny oval in a ring of blue. The sound reached Allister seconds after the light did, loud enough to crack the windshield and shake the car more violently.

He screamed and tried to cover his head and his ears at the same time.

Something was wrong.

The brave-sounding voice in his head told him not to hide. Not to be afraid of this oval object, even if it seemed *dangerous*. He needed to stay alert in case his dad needed help.

Still positioned above the dashboard where he wasn't supposed to be, Allister looked up at the sky again.

As quickly as the blue light had appeared, it zoomed back down and disappeared into the plant. That was when the other voice—fear—took hold of him. Something was *wrong*. The blaring noises were getting louder, and the light overhead was getting brighter. All of this happening as the clouds were swelling higher.

Allister wanted to understand what Mother Nature was trying to say. It was a storm like he'd never seen or imagined. And the flashing oval didn't have too much longer before it—his eyes followed its trajectory down—would crash into the plant.

"Pops!" he screamed. "Pops, get out of there!"

He felt the tears rising in him, ready to spill from his eyes if his dad didn't emerge that moment.

Suddenly his dad burst through a side door, running at a full sprint.

"Yes!" Allister pumped his fist into the air. "Come on, Pops, you can make it! You can…make…it."

He'd stopped cheering as hard because his dad's mouth was opening and closing like he was shouting, and he kept looking up at the sky every few strides.

Then his dad looked straight ahead and pointed at Allister, eyes widened. What he was yelling became very clear.

"*Get down! Get down! Get down!*"

Allister refused to get down, not until his dad made it to the car safely.

"*Get down!*" his dad repeated.

He had never seen his dad this way. Furious. Screaming. Likely running too fast to properly catch his breath. His dad's arms were covered in the same blue as the light, as if they had been painted. Allister couldn't begin to guess why, and wouldn't dare ask.

"Allister!" his dad shouted, now close enough to be heard. He opened the door and jumped in the driver's seat, gasping. "Didn't I tell you"—he pulled Allister down into the seat—"to stay down!"

"I'm sorry, Pops, I just heard the—"

His dad's voice was shaking as he interrupted. "I asked you to do one thing. One thing!"

He jammed his finger onto the acceleration button, then shifted the gears and turned the wheel, whipping the car around as it lifted off the ground. The rear boosters blasted behind them, fiery and loud like a trash incinerator, rocketing the car forward.

Their vehicle alternated between a series of nauseating movements: swerving side to side, leaning hard through winding turns, which forced Allister to lean, too, and ended with a burst of speed when the road opened up.

But still, he watched his dad, who was hunched over in the driver's seat, quiet, brooding, periodically hitting the wheel. His dad was soaked in sweat, his clothes covered in soot. His sleeves were nothing but scraps of burned fabric. Allister knew the man driving looked like his dad. He also believed that it couldn't be him, not without the offer of reassuring words in that signature southern twang or that comforting smile to show everything would be okay.

Maybe everything won't be okay this time, he thought to himself, somewhat antsy.

Was that ring of light the more powerful thing his dad had mentioned, or was it the oval object? Nothing Allister thought of could be more dangerous.

By then, his heart was beating so hard he thought it might break free from his scrawny chest. He clutched himself with both hands and checked the rearview camera. What he saw was much worse than anything he could've expected: that same glowing oval had plunged toward the ground and was getting closer every second—and with it came fire the color of the sea. The strange oval was all but engulfed in those turbulent blue flames, yet he realized that it was somehow the source of light, now illuminating the sky with the radiance of midday when it was meant to be midnight.

The odd-colored fire flashed bright around the vessel and hit the ground, setting the surrounding forest ablaze.

Allister jerked his head away and squeezed his eyes shut just long enough to catch his breath.

His dad had always told him to be brave. And Allister thought that to be brave, he should imprison his fear. How could he contain a fear unlike anything he'd ever felt? The intensity of it rattling the bars of the imaginary cage, threatening to burst free. He wondered—between stuffing away his sobs and rapid-fire questions and the sickness swimming in him—if this new strain of fear was multiplying in his dad with the same quickness.

He opened one eye to see.

His dad was frowning deeply, but he seemed to have calmed into the dad Allister recognized. Placing a firm hand on Allister's leg, he exhaled. Though he didn't offer the smile Allister had been hoping for.

"I should've listened to your mother," he said. "Kept my potentials—" He ended his sentence abruptly.

Allister stared down at his dad's hand, which was double the size of his, looking for the reassurance he was meant to feel. What he found was the urge to suck in more tears, because he could tell his fear had broken free, infecting his dad, too.

"Foeht Zeorgen?" his dad whispered aloud, sounding confused. "If 2052 ends with Z, the experiment should've worked…"

His dad shook his head and mumbled the two strange words again as he strangled the car's wheel one-handed.

Allister put his hand on his dad's hand and squeezed. "Are we gonna make it home?" he asked.

"Just keep your head down and pray a little bit," his dad replied. His face was apologetic as he took back his hand and stared ahead at the stretch of civilization left.

Allister, however, kept his eyes cast out the passenger window.

The car was silent, though everything around them was erupting in chaos. Destruction was inevitable, the flames limitless, as if they would never stop spreading. Even the storm cellar beneath their house didn't seem sturdy enough to protect them—nowhere did.

Allister covered his mouth in shock. "Is Mommy okay?" he asked through his fingers.

"Your mom's on her way to the special place I built to keep us safe. I promise, we'll all be together soon."

To Allister, it sounded as if they were almost there.

"How soon?"

His dad opened his mouth to say more, and instead was forced to jerk the car to the side. Something heavy and burning landed hard where the car had been, then scraped the pavement before bouncing ahead of them and exploding.

Allister contained the intense urge to cry out, though his lip quivered as he asked slowly, "Did the Evolutionaries make the blue fire come? You know, the ones Mommy hates?"

"Ah, my little EV…come here."

Frightened, Allister leaned over. His dad hugged him. He hugged back.

"Not all Evolutionaries are scary, some are even tryin' to save the world." His dad's voice cracked as he kept speaking. "I thought we could contain it... I thought I understood the—" He stopped midsentence, his face falling and tears falling with it. "I did it. I made the blue fire come. And I think you can, too."

"Pops?" Allister asked. "What do you mean?"

"We're—" His dad gasped and glanced down, then frantically looked back through the window as though he'd seen a monster in the rear camera. He shouted a curse word—one of the really bad ones—and tried pushing Allister back into his seat while maneuvering the car. Allister wouldn't let go. He was too frightened of the rabid inferno attacking them from all sides.

Allister didn't know how it had caught up to them until he realized why his dad had lost the color in his face and kept pushing the accelerator button with desperation.

Something sped at them from behind.

Moving too fast.

Getting too close.

It could only be the oval object shooting forward like a launched firecracker and shrieking with the high-pitched whistle of one. The sound deepened into a deafening rumble as it caught up, and the car sputtered and sank lower, unable to stay airborne.

———

Artist: Lester Niesta/ The CMD Studios

Allister tried to sit up. Before he could peel away the other arm, his heartbeat disappeared into the harsh vibration of the vehicle shuddering around them.

The oval ripped their Ukimoto straight down the middle.
A white flare blasted Allister's skin with searing heat. Reverberating booms drowned out his involuntary screams. And within seconds, the car exploded in opposite directions.

With him still strapped inside the seat, Allister's half of the car spun out like a top and landed on hard asphalt with enough impact to bounce, flip over itself, and land again.

The car screeched along the pavement until it skidded to a stop.

The world fell still.

Allister screamed in agony, shocked at the strange pain bombarding him on his left side, though it was mostly concentrated near his shoulder.

It didn't matter that his overalls were torn from the waist to the leg. Or that his green turtleneck was blown to scraps and his unicorn burned toward a dusty grave at his feet.

Because he could see that the arm he'd kept wrapped around his dad was missing. The pain tearing at him made sense, as did the screams clawing at his throat, scratching it raw.

His heartbeat slowed. A cold sank beneath his skin, gripping his bones with the chill of death.

Shuddering, he went quiet.

The night became nothing more than whispers of a wildfire. Smoky darkness danced across his eyes.

"My arm," he whispered, his voice filled with fatigue. He placed his shaky hand just under the gaping wound. "Pops, my arm is gone."

His dad didn't answer.

A soft wind whipped at the exposed, bleeding socket, stinging him deeper with every gust.

Allister's surroundings refused to take shape and so he closed his eyes and counted the seconds until his inevitable end. Until his heart stopped beating and his oxygen stopped flowing. But no matter how high he counted, neither happened. Just over a minute passed before his violent shaking eased to shivers and the throbbing in his shoulder to a dull pressure. The blood dried as a familiar tingling weaved its way through his mutilated flesh.

He guessed it was happening again.

Wailing with more uncertainty than pain, he lifted up his head and rested it on the seat back. His eyes fluttered open. In his peripheral vision, he could see muscles stretching from his shoulder and reattaching to the bone growing from the socket. Skin climbed over new tissues toward what might become an elbow.

Allister gagged and turned away.

He'd seen something like it before, watched as his body recovered from small injuries, cuts during afternoon play, tiny bruises from wrestling around the living room, and the occasional sickness—*rapid healing*, his mom called it—but nothing like this. The car crash should have killed him.

Against the agony of nerves pinching at his skin, he unclipped the seat belt and stumbled onto the street. He wondered where his dad was, wanting to believe he'd been just as lucky, yet he couldn't keep focus on anything except his half of an arm, which continued to grow until the bones of his wrist and fingers began to interlace, putting themselves back together as if they were puzzle pieces come alive.

Soon he knew the muscle would begin to reappear, then the tendons and ligaments, and last, the skin. The final stages of his healing seemed to drag on forever, and just when he thought it might end, the sharp pain returned. Now, wishing for the sensation to soften into a semblance of relief, he could hear his hometown burning in the distance. He was almost positive that no one could heal in that town but him.

Then why were there booster rockets creeping over pavement? He heard folks shouting. Had some people survived? His ears perked up—his eyes, too. The harsh beams of vehicle headlights rounded a corner, temporarily blinding him. He covered his eyes with his good hand as he took a step back.

The vehicle stopped advancing on him.

"Turn 'em down, team," someone commanded.

The headlights dimmed.

Allister's sight began to clear—first revealing the dense, wide trucks hovering above the pavement, then the soldiers. They were untouched by the blue fire, each holding either a charging energy weapon or an automatic gun.

"Who's there?" Allister asked.

No one answered.

"Don't shoot," he heard his dad say, straining on every word. "That's my son. Please don't shoot him."

Allister gasped at the sound of his dad's voice and twisted around to see where he was.

"Everything's going to be all right, long as little Allister cooperates," said one of the soldiers in a voice as rough as ground pavement.

Allister squinted. "Pops, are you there? Where's Mommy?"

"Everyone's here," the same soldier answered. "Safe and sound as long as you come with us." The soldier pulled Allister's fussing, kicking mom out of the armored vehicle and forced her to stand up straight. He took her by the neck with one hand, then held a shiny weapon to her head with the other.

It was devastating to see his mom's soft curls touching the end of something so *dangerous*.

"Hey, sir," Allister said, trying his hardest to sound brave. He took a small step and wobbled on an unsteady ankle. "I'll come with you. Just don't hurt them, please."

"That's right, Allister, honey, come to Mommy," his mom pleaded. She spoke without steadiness, and she was paralyzed, no longer struggling against the soldier's grip.

He recognized that stiffness.

Fear.

She must've known something, seen something he couldn't see along the now intensely dark edges of the main road. "We're going to do what these nice soldiers say so they'll help your daddy," she said. She tried turning to the soldier, her arm extended toward the charred field beside them. "Is that Patrick, at the edge there? Won't one of you help him? Please...he's bleeding out. Nicolas, I'm begging you. I'll do anything."

The soldier—Nicolas—squeezed her neck, pressed the weapon deeper into her temple.

"Shut up," he said.

She flinched in pain.

Allister took another lopsided step.

"You promise to keep us safe, together?" he asked the soldier.

"Pinky promise," the soldier replied.

"Son, don't you move," his dad said. "Don't. You. Move."

The soldier dragged the gun from his mom's head to a spot near the road.

"You don't want to do this, Nic," his dad said. "We'll still find a way to save your daughter. Neight promised."

"Well, now he's dead!" the soldier shouted, beginning to squeeze the trigger.

"Wait!" Allister yelled.

The soldier stopped, loosened his finger, and turned to him. His mom's mouth fell open. The other soldiers stepped back and started talking over a radio about the return of the blue light that had scorched the sky.

It was true, the fiery blue glow had returned, right next to Allister.

Initially, he didn't feel anything at all. He watched it spread over pavement slick with fluids and littered with car parts, and tensed as it covered the row of soldiers and their trucks.

On his left side, the side where the light had appeared, he felt burning. It wasn't from fire, like he thought, but the vibrant blue light crackling around what had become a limb. It stretched, then squeezed, solidified, compressed, taking the stringy shape of what had returned. A seven-year-old's human arm.

The feeling of a million tiny needles pricked Allister under fresh bright-blue skin.

That's when he realized the light wasn't next to him.

It was part of him.

"Pleased to see we've got ourselves another Evolutionary," the soldier said.

His mom shook her head, the terror in her eyes as unbearable as what he could now see: his dad lying bloody, barely moving on the side of the road.

"Pops…," he said, about to take a step in that direction. He stopped when he saw his mom gave him the stern look that meant *no*. It seemed his bravery would only make the situation worse.

"Please…the spaceship," his dad said. "The Z-energy, it's there… You have everything you need to save her. Leave…my wife…and my son alone."

The soldier threw Allister's mom back into the vehicle, knelt down on the street, and pressed the shiny weapon to his dad's head.

"I'd be happy to."

Allister knew he had to save his mom and his dad, and the burning inside his fast-beating heart told him he could. There came a deep voice that sounded like bravery. With it came the strange words his dad had recited in the car, chanting inside his mind, louder with each repetition.

Foeht Zeorgen, Foeht Zeorgen, Foeht Zeorgen.

Allister looked down at his new arm, mesmerized by the light beaming from it. Unable to think of anything else, he whispered, "Foeht Zeorgen."

The soldier must've heard because he faced Allister again.

He growled to the other soldiers, "Get. Him."

The dozen or so of them obeyed immediately, rushing at Allister with weapons aimed.

I can do what the fire did to the sky, he thought as they got closer.

He didn't step back, he didn't step forward, just waited with both fists clenched for the soldiers to surround him, the conviction and determination building in him like a volcanic eruption.

Allister threw his hands up and yelled out, "Foeht Zeorgen!"

The light beside him grew. Beyond his arm. Beyond comprehension.

A wave of raw energy burst from his body and surged forward, each moment of its eruption a flurry of burning anguish. His eyes rolled back into his head. From somewhere in the chaos, he could hear his mom's screams, soldiers' yelling, and the single shot from that shiny weapon.

Everything faded to a tense quiet.

The light retreated into him. Left him relishing in the same calm that chases a stream, breathing air free of *danger*, listening to the thirsty licks of nearby flames.

The soldiers were scattered away from Allister on their backs. And his mom… his mom was staring at him through the car's now-shattered window, weeping between screaming and hitting the seats. Though the town of Cumberland Falls was still charred from the inferno, Allister felt safe. The burning in his arm was gone. But when he searched for his dad, he was gone too.

———

CHAPTER 1

ALLISTER ADAMS
Riser Town, Suburbs of the District, 2052 AD
Day 215

ALLISTER ADAMS WAS running out of time.

To be fair, the rest of the world was running out of time, too.

But none of the rowdy teens were worried about the apocalypse that afternoon. They were more concerned with winning the game, which would decide who controlled the trash-ridden alleyways behind the neighborhood. For the next two hundred and some odd days, at least.

Allister rather enjoyed this outlawed game of Schwebevogel. In fact, it had been his favorite game since childhood. Often treacherous. High-impact. And despite the dangers of using stolen parts and poorly assembled tools, Schwebevogel was played in the air, making the sport all the more nerve-racking *and* exhilarating, especially when superheated by tension between rival buildings. He played because he could handle the violence in ways that others couldn't. For him, it was less about being athletic and more about being evolved.

He waited in midair atop his reconstructed hoverboard, gripping his flugbar—a magnetic stick—nervous for the next round to start. The ball—or rather, an assortment of scrap metal tightly packed in a ball—was cradled in the bowl-shaped magnet at the end of the handheld stick. It was his job to keep it there until he reached the other side of the alley.

The stakes seemed higher than Allister had planned for, as he and his friends were squaring off against the infamous FBX crew, who as a whole were larger, stronger, tougher teens and used that and their mob mentality to get what they wanted.

Sure, in the spirit of justice, he *had* challenged the crew's leader, Saunder, to a face-off, using the game as form of civilized confrontation. It was true that he wanted to stop the FBX crew from robbing them of food on the street and breaking into their houses for supplies. And, of course, Allister believed everyone deserved the freedom to enjoy the shabby dwellings of Riser Town equally. But now, he realized he needed to *win* for them to do so.

"Who's 'bout ready to win back this block?" Allister yelled, forcing both enthusiasm and confidence into his voice.

A small group of younger, malnourished teens hooted and twirled their wiry arms in the air.

"Who's ready to beat and rob all these fools?" his opponent, Saunder, yelled back.

The recruited members of the FBX crew howled and punched their fists at the air.

They all followed Saunder—a built-to-fight, abnormally tall human—as if he were a king. Perhaps to those lost, strung-out teens, he was the closest thing. He was certainly well fed. Outspoken. Commanding. He was older than Allister by a stretch of three hundred and twenty-five days, making him almost twenty, and the oldest teen in the neighborhood.

The two crowds gathered beneath the airborne field were clustered together and cheering from under the trio of players each supported. Plastic garbage bags and expired food and old appliances were piled between and around the spectators, leaving not a spot of the pavement bare.

Allister switched his concentration to the thrum of the hoverboard's downward propulsion.

There was an impermanence about the way his feet were wedged into the footholds of the illegal, wing-tipped device, and also an ickiness about that day in general—it felt strange, heavy. Maybe it was the distracting sense of loss. Maybe it was the distracting sense that his team was liable to lose.

As usual, his fear was breeding within him. The fear he'd make a mistake. The fear he'd ruin the last days of those who believed in him. Collectively, it took up too much space, and, wanting to feel confident, he sentenced the fear to the imaginary cage in the pit of his stomach. It still managed to twist up his insides in knots.

Allister checked the Apocalypse Countdown Clock from where he hovered in the sky.

0 years, 215 days, 9 hours, 23 minutes, and 45 seconds rotated on a digital display large enough to see from every high-rise dwelling in Riser Town. He and the FBX crew weren't counting down those neon-green numerals to humanity's impending demise. They'd agreed when the massive numbers hit twenty-two minutes they'd begin the next round.

One minute and forty-five seconds were left.

Saunder tugged at his thick Afro and grinned.

Allister narrowed his eyes. Saunder was not a king, he decided, but a dangerous, borderline insane bully. One that needed to be taken down.

On Allister's team was Lex, the crass, round smart-aleck of a girl who managed the game with aggressive defense and, of course, Allister's best friend and Lex's brother: Quigles, the scrawny, agile boy who was balanced and nimble but easy to knock off the board.

Allister was still the largest liability of the trio. An adult teen with muscle density startling for anyone born out of the Omega Generation and the body mass to match. Though it made knocking him off the board challenging, he could just as easily fall off from his own lack of steadiness.

He squeezed his flugbar tighter and adjusted his feet.

"Double A, you good?" Quigles asked from behind him.

"Better than, Quigles. Better than," Allister said. *For now*, he thought. He didn't turn around. Besides being afraid his wince might betray him, with the game tied and near its end, he needed to keep both eyes on Saunder, who was bound to try to pull shady moves to win.

"Mega, cuz this is the golden moment," Quigles added. "You score, and every kid on this block will worship you."

Worship, Allister repeated to himself. *What a way to see the end, as a hero*. His fear settled, calmed by them chanting his name and the idea of a big win. An overconfident smirk appeared on his face.

The glory felt so real.

"We'll rename this spot Allister Alley," Quigles whispered loudly.

Allister's smile widened. "Don't get me cynqued on it, I'm already hyped as it is."

"You ready, sucker?" Saunder taunted between subtle head motions left, right, then to the sky above them.

"He'll be ready when it's time," Quigles shouted back. "And trust, you'll be sorry."

Allister was glad he hadn't turned to talk to Quigles. Those barely noticeable head motions from Saunder were the signs he'd been waiting for. Signs of cheating, or at least unfair gameplay. They would be followed by raising the airborne field to a more dangerous elevation and aggressive maneuvers to take the ball.

He watched the FBX crew move farther away from one another and high enough to be caught in a drone scan, prepping for a move Allister knew all too well—the air strike. His intuition had been spot on.

"Keep it together, Adams. I know you tend to get uneasy in the air," said Saunder, getting into an angled-down position.

Allister looked back at his teammates.

"We can't go up that high," he said.

"The drones," Quigles said, shaking his head. "I'd rather take a beating than get scanned by one of them again, to be honest."

Allister guessed the drones were worse; being bested by Saunder meant the loss of food, but a scan by a drone could mean capital punishment.

"You got this," Quigles said. "Just keep it cool, yeah?"

Yeah, keep it cool.

Best friend code for *don't do anything mega*. Quigles knew the must-be-kept secret—that Allister's biggest challenge was the same as it had been since his childhood: not letting the rest of the neighborhood discover that he was an Evolutionary. Before Allister knew to be careful, the onset of his potentials had forced he and his mom to stay off the radar and move on too many occasions.

"You got this," Quigles repeated.

"Crap if I ever heard it, Q," Lex spat, scowling. "Look at him, there's no way he's getting across now. He's shaking like a faulty patrol drone."

"Lay it down for once, Lex," Quigles said.

"I got it locked," Allister concluded with a tempered smile. He turned toward the clock and saw that twenty seconds remained.

They're gonna drop in on Quigles, I know it.

He exhaled and used his feet to steer the board a little higher.

"Lex, stick to Quigles, don't cover me," he said quickly, cycling through tactical moves in his head. "We're running your fave: the mother and her ducklings. Just follow the leader."

Lex snorted. "Shut your can and worry about the ball, mister."

Allister eyed the metal ball.

Yeah, you stay with me.

The clock hit twenty-two minutes.

More cheering and taunting rose from the audience below.

Saunder switched his hoverboard's angle and launched it backward, stopping near a threshold marked by two high-rises. Allister launched his board forward. He crouched into the swift breeze, holding his breath against the stale air bombarding his face, then rushing through his braids.

One of Saunder's teammates, the lightest skinned and burliest of the three, dove toward them.

Allister veered left and brought himself and the board sideways. He assumed Quigles and Lex had followed suit because the game was still in play, but he didn't stop to look back, too excited by the fact that he'd successfully maneuvered the board while "keeping it cool."

The third member of the FBX crew team, a stocky young man with dreadlocks, came down from the other side, harder and faster than the first. Allister swung his board the opposite way. Lex tried to follow but lost her balance, spinning out too wide to keep her speed. Allister wobbled on his way back down and thrust out both hands to keep himself from falling. The ball wiggled on the edge of the stick. When it stopped moving, he switched the hoverboard's direction, cursing his clumsiness.

Two more sharp dives from the opposition kept Allister and his teammates from resuming formation.

The attack left Quigles wide open, had him rotating and ducking as their opponents went at him with elbow jabs and stick swipes.

Allister flipped around and headed back.

Every moment was an almost—he *almost* had enough room, *almost* had enough time, *almost* had enough courage to go in and run off the other team with his size. He was too sturdy for a jab, too thick for an airborne tackle, and with his back, chest, and abdominal muscles inhumanly carved into him, a flugbar might bend or even snap against his torso. He pumped his hoverboard forward and back in place, his fear refusing to let him forget he could still lose the ball—and the game.

The faster the FBX teens moved around Quigles, the more wildly he dodged. Allister watched them whip by, shoot up, and zip across, both of them a blur of buzzing and insults as they left Quigles spinning in circles, as if a twig caught in a tornado, helpless.

They returned to their positions up high, then positioned themselves for their next plunge. Allister brought his hoverboard back around until the game's victory was in sight, trying to guess the distance. Him going for it was the perfect distraction.

Just follow the leader.

Allister boosted forward again.

His other two opponents shifted directions and swooped at him from either side, one going for his board, the other for his body.

Saunder smirked and zoomed toward him.

Though he and Saunder were on a collision course, Allister noticed that Saunder's eyes weren't on him but on the ball he carried, nestled inside the magnet.

Real slick with the gang up, Allister thought, dipping and sidewinding in the air. *I got something for you, too.*

A phrase bubbled up from his memory, two words of a foreign language he'd never learned yet always came when he had an overwhelming desire to use his energy potential.

"Foeht Zeorgen," he whispered.

The skin on his left arm turned a cool blue, somewhere between the color of water and ice, then went back to its usual deep shade of mahogany. A tingling feeling soared down Allister's shoulder, ending in his palm, as an unbearable heat flared beneath his skin. The burning was hotter than the sanctuary city's perpetual summer heat—as if someone had lit a fire inside his muscles, scorching every cell in the process. He tucked his arm behind his back. The blue glow would soon resurface and bring a bright flash with it.

That flash would be the perfect counter to the FBX crew's gang up strategy, not dangerous, not obvious, and not traceable back to him. He could explain it away with a Cynque augmented reality add-on application.

The energy returned with a crackle only he could hear.

It still sounded louder than normal, was possibly stronger? Than normal. He only wanted to summon enough potential to distract them, so he could shoot through the opening for the win—though not summon so much as to let the energy's full manifestation give him away.

"Just a bit closer," he mumbled, ignoring his concern.

He slowed down while pulling the flugbar close to his body, and though pained by a more intensified burning sensation, he subtly revealed his empty palm and prepared to say the words again.

His mouth opened.

But it was then he saw the drones circling just beyond the threshold he was meant to pass, out of sight for everyone except him. He tried to stop and go backward at the same time.

"Drones!" he gasped.

He pitched forward, arms flailing, and lost his footing on the hoverboard and his grip on the stick in one upside-down motion. He kept wishing he could stop the energy manifestation already in full swing, but he knew that calling back his potential once he'd summoned it was impossible.

Everything seemed to happen in slow motion.

A bright-blue light erupted from his wrist and zoomed every direction in a series of straight lines, bursting like bottle rockets in the air.

Kaboom.

An explosion went off somewhere in front of him. The recoil dislodged his feet from the hoverboard's base. Small specks of blue fire tumbled toward the crowd while he fell spine-first into a hillside of discarded garbage.

Loud gasps became panicked screams.

"Snap!" Quigles yelped.

Snap was right. Allister had messed up big. Bigger than big. That was hardly an explainable flash of light. He'd unleashed multiple streams of blue energy *from his body*. He leaned forward and winced, praying his display of potential didn't happen as slowly for everyone else as it had happened for him. He hoped, wished, begged it had really happened all at once, so fast, so unnoticeable, no one would ask any questions.

But beams of energy and explosions weren't the kind of occurrences that went unnoticed, and neither were flakes of blue fire.

"You cheated!" Saunder shouted.

He was on his back, too, cushioned by his own bed of waste. Though he'd hovered high enough to raise the stakes, it had still been low enough to avoid becoming a burned corpse at the sanctuary's edge.

Still, Saunder's hoverboard lay in smoking pieces among the alley's already full graveyard of broken technology. Glaring evidence of Allister's misfire.

The crowd of loyal FBX followers converged on their screaming leader, pressing him for an explanation, wanting to know if he was injured and what he'd seen.

They chattered loudly about Allister being a cheater and ended up puzzling out a story that labeled him something much worse. An Evolutionary.

With his teammates' help, Saunder hopped his way to his feet. He pushed through the crowd and pointed at Allister, yelling, "I swear, we got 215 days left, and I'm not lettin' a psycho piece of EV scum like you take 'em from me."

Allister's eyes stung with brimming tears of humiliation, his heart going at full speed inside his chest. He hid his arm, afraid that since it was still burning, it might still be glowing. "I…uh…I wasn't…I didn't…I'm not," he stammered.

"Uh—uh—uh," Saunder mocked.

The other burly teen descended on his hoverboard. "An Evolutionary? In Riser Town? We can't let that sort of mess slide. We gotta protect the neighborhood. Right, Allister?"

"No! I mean, yeah! I mean…" Allister paused, trying to find an explanation that wouldn't incriminate him. "Dude, c'mon. We were just settling our differences."

"We were until you tried to blow me out of the sky with your freak arm!" Saunder screamed.

More eyes from both crowds focused on Allister. Their faces were a mix of concern and confusion, shock and fear. The FBX crew joined Saunder as a united front. Those that had been cheering for Allister, Quigles, and Lex cowered at a distance.

"Ha, so, Mr. Save the Neighborhood is nothin' but a terrorist in disguise," Saunder said, limping toward him.

"That's a load and you know it!" Allister protested.

"C20 already got you signed up, don't they? They want you to shoot stuff, huh?" he said. "Guess what? I like shooting stuff too."

Saunder's jaw tightened as he fished a plasma pistol from inside his pants.

"Yeah, finish him off," someone said.

"That hybrid freak doesn't deserve to see the end," said another.

Saunder activated the weapon's plasma core and pointed it at Allister's forehead.

Allister scooted deeper into the garbage, still hiding his arm. "I don't know what happened. I didn't see."

"Whoa, whoa, brother, calm down," Quigles said as he hovered between Allister and the weapon. "What if he is with C20 like you claiming? You really want to go getting mixed up in that? I heard those Evolutionaries are dangerous."

"I'm not your brother." Saunder shoved Quigles aside and made his way closer. When his shadow covered Allister and the trash he sat on, Saunder said, "Plus, mighty hard to be dangerous when you're dead."

Allister let the buckets of sweat run down his face, thinking, *Please don't shoot me. Please don't shoot me.* He didn't want to make the mistake of regenerating in front of those people too.

"Drones! Drones!" someone yelled.

Everyone looked up, even Saunder.

The drones were posted up, rotating on an imaginary axis as they scanned the ground.

"Please remain still for Cynque verification," they boomed in mechanical voices. "Please remain still for Cynque verification."

Luckily, Allister and Saunder were mostly hidden by the trash; Allister moreso because he was on the ground.

The stocky teen jumped off his hoverboard and pulled Saunder by the arm. "C'mon, c'mon! It's not a good look, dishing fades with the drones watching, man," he said. "One first-degree scan and the whole neighborhood is finito. He ain't worth it."

Saunder hesitated, then lowered the gun and spat on Allister. "Wait 'til I tell my uncle you're one of them. He's a District patrol. You and your mama'll be a memory before sunrise." After getting out his threat, Saunder was carried off by his two teammates like an injured war general, rejoicing in his soon-to-come vengeance.

"Geez, triggered much," Allister mumbled. He used the back of his hand to wipe Saunder's spit off his chin, shook it away, then peeked at the alley immersed in chaos.

The other members of the FBX crew scattered as the drones' thin red beams targeted them from the air. The drones descended into the alley, sensing the fast-paced movement, and followed the teens as they dispersed—in one moment warning them to stand still for a scan, and in the next, charging for a fatal shot to the back or skull.

He half expected the drones to open fire; they were programmed to scan Cynques and shoot those who ran, not ask questions. He watched them miss a handful of targets but continue swinging around looking for something else to finish off instead.

Allister froze as his eyes landed on Quigles.

His friend was in the crosshairs of a drone's infrared targeting, standing still, though trembling and on the verge of collapse.

The drone was level with Quigles's forehead, the red beam burrowing through his temple. It beeped, clicked, and the beam turned blue and disappeared.

"Scan complete, violation recorded," the drone said, then rose into the air.

The other drones followed.

One first-degree scan...

Allister climbed up from his hiding place and cringed when he got there. The pain in his lower back still lingered. "Quigles?" he asked, hobbling over, a hand where the pain was strongest. "Are you golden?"

Quigles wiped his hands on his shirt and faced Allister.

"Far from it," he said, stiffening.

Allister tried to brush off the hint of accusation in his friend's voice. "I'm with that...mega-rowdy, right?"

"Yeah, mega-rowdy how that drone almost took *me* out, execution style, huh? Or the fact that I just got another Federal scan hanging around you?" Quigles twisted his face and kept glancing at Allister's left side. "You promised you wouldn't use your potentials all loose like that"—he jabbed his finger at Allister's arm—"especially when you can't control the fallout."

"The energy? I know how it triggers... I just lost my focus... I mean, the drones—" Allister looked away. "They were playin' dirty, Quigles. Lay it down, okay? I was tryin' to keep us safe."

"And look how twisted that turned out!" he shrieked.

Allister looked up.

Quigles was white as the sidewalk, blinking back tears, his teeth pressing down on his bottom lip.

"You almost got us killed," he said.

A lump rose in Allister's throat.

"Quigles, look, you gotta trust me," he said, swallowing it down. "I'd never let any of my potentials hurt you or Lex, I swear."

Quigles's face darkened from the white of fear to the red of fury. "It's not about your stupid potentials, Allister! It's about what happens when you use 'em!" he shouted. He didn't say anything else at first, just let the silence drive an invisible wall between them. After a while, he mumbled, "You shoulda stuck to our code. Keep it cool. Now we got drones *and* Saunder to watch out for."

Allister wrung his hands, the shame of just being himself heavy in his guts. Saunder couldn't tell anyone what he'd seen. If he did, Allister and his mom would have to disappear overnight.

Lex hovered lower and stopped alongside Quigles. "Because of you playin' freak show, Quigles got a Federal flippin' scan," she said. "I knew we shoulda turned you in two hundred days ago. Been screwing us since the second you got here."

Her eyes traced Allister up and down.

"Just do us all a favor and keep your distance. Thanks to you, those of us ain't dead yet may not make it 'til the end." Lex barked at her brother, "Get it in gear, Quigs. Auntie wants us home before we lose the hour."

She rotated her board and hovered away from them down the alley.

Allister hugged himself. "I'm sorry, Quigles," he said. "I wish I had a way to make ya feel good about it…about me. You'll still be my best for the rest, right?"

He pounded his chest with his fist, then held it out, waiting for Quigles to do the same.

But Quigles wouldn't look him in the eye, and the expression on his face was one Allister had never seen, some mix of sadness and regret. His friend opened his mouth to answer a few times, but kept closing it too early, as if the words in his heart and the words in his mind weren't matching up. Quigles finally shook his head, his hands clasped at his waist.

"Auntie's sick and needs me and Lex to prep for the end, time's almost up," he said. "I get one more scan like that and I'm toast. Sorry, Double A, I'm not with it."

———

26

CHAPTER 2

ALLISTER ADAMS
Riser Town, Suburbs of the District
Day 215

ALLISTER'S EMPLOYMENT ASSIGNMENT was due to start before the afternoon was lost, and by the low position of the sun and long shadows stretching behind him, he knew that evening was on its way. He looked at the time-measuring app on the Cynque device embedded in his wrist to be sure. The days and hours and minutes glared back at him in the same neon-green hue. Nothing told time neutrally anymore. It just told them how much they had left.

A little under 215 days.

He dodged a few more lingering drones, moving building to building, ducking under hanging ladders, and sprinting through open stretches of pavement. He gave thanks when he reached the bottom of his building, trying not to let the exchange with Quigles sink in. But his heart was weighed down, his feet lifting slower and slower up the winding flights of stairs to his home. Less from fatigue and more from that same sense of loss as earlier.

Since then, he'd lost the game, the neighborhood, and his best for the rest.

He paused midstep and gripped the metal railing tightly with a mix of frustration and sorrow.

Maybe humans could never understand. Maybe it was only other Evolutionaries who could grasp the full weight of his burden.

"I wasn't trying to hurt anyone," he muttered, squeezing the rail.

The metal crumpled beneath his fingers.

Allister swore up and down about his enhanced strength, another one of his potentials he couldn't control, then resumed his journey to his doorstep. There had to be others out there like him. Evolutionaries not joined up with C20 who wanted to use their potentials to save humanity rather than hurt them.

He stood face-to-face with his front door and said to himself, "I gotta find a way to skip Riser Town. Better for Mom, she can stay put. Better for me, I can cynque up with peeps like me."

He turned and looked out over the barren alley behind his building. Nothing but trash blowing in hot wind.

"Gotta skip Riser Town," he repeated.

He'd planned to sneak by his mom and head straight to the shower pod to get ready. A decent plan, except as he reached for the transparent sliding panel door, he paused at the aluminum container full of junk next to his feet.

It wasn't like his mom to leave trash near the house. She liked to keep that little square slice of patio pristine at all costs, to the point he'd find her up sweeping it in the middle of the night.

Curious, Allister knelt down next to it.

He moved the already open lid farther back and rummaged through the box full of gadgets, trinkets, and printed photographs. It didn't look like trash to him, so he wondered why it was outside.

"You get into it with another one of those kids?" his mom yelled from in the house.

"Sort of. Hard to explain," he replied, picking up what looked like a small transmitter.

Is this my dad's?

He became more suspicious the deeper he dug.

"I told you about those boys up the block. They're killin' types."

Allister rolled his eyes. It was the same speech he always got in the afternoons. She'd been warning him to stay inside and away from the FBX crew, especially lately, with the drones on high alert and the raids happening more frequently.

"Lucky we don't have nothin' they want, besides blood," his mom continued.

"One thousand, Mom."

He fiddled with the transmitter to confirm it didn't work, then turned it over before sighing and putting it back. As he reached down, his eyes locked on an upside-down photo of him sitting on his dad's shoulders.

His heart seemed to get even heavier. The sort of sinking sadness that came whenever he thought back to his formative years.

The day in the photo was a day he would never remember, like any day that had passed before he turned eight years old.

He rested his fingers on top of the image, just as intrigued by the texture of printed visuals as he was by his bright, snaggle-toothed smile. Did he used to be that happy? He was so used to seeing everything on screens and projected as holograms, he was trying to zoom in on the picture without picking it up. Thinking to himself maybe those individual pixels would show every missing detail from his past. But the image was as it was. A snapshot. A frame of time suspended. He couldn't get closer to it, nor could it get closer to him.

Unless.

Allister caught himself smiling as he picked it up.

In the photograph, he was seven, holding up locks of his dad's hair as if he were the littlest puppeteer. His dad's eyes were puffy and wrinkled at the corners, barely visible because his smile covered so much of his face. A thick, unruly beard surrounded his mouth like joy surrounded the moment.

On his dad's shirt, the logo had two letters, *A* and *P*, conjoined on the same line. It stirred more memories that would not surface. Was it a long-dead fashion brand? Or, maybe a clever combination of their first names?

Allister and Patrick.

He would've smiled at that thought, but he frowned again, angry that he couldn't remember his own playfulness, or his dad, or the time they spent together when he was alive. From those seven years, all Allister had from him were those two words, *Foeht Zeorgen*, and a small assortment of vintage clothing. Those words were special though, they were the last thing he remembered hearing his dad say before he died, and twelve years later, the phrase wouldn't let him go, nor would the deep voice that whispered it to him in his dreams.

His fingers tightened around the material until he became aware of himself. He loosened his hold and tried smoothing out the photo's new crease against his leg, wanting to restore the glossy finish, the uninterrupted purity of father-son love.

"I know it's been a couple days, but I found some decent food!" his mom interrupted. "Hurry up so you can eat this before you go. It'll be spoiled by morning!"

"I'll be in in a sec...," Allister said.

Another keepsake caught his eye.

Why's she tossing all this stuff?

He picked up a piece of squared card stock.

You are the only hope! Join the Andromeda Project today! read the title. It was dated FALL 2033.

His Cynque device came to life in the intrusive way artificial intelligence technology often did: triggered by immediate surroundings, geolocation tracking, changes in the environment, visual cues. The device was forcefully adhered to his wrist, the wires constantly digging beneath his flesh for a biometric reading to verify he not only existed but was…connected. Or, in other words, *Cynqued*.

"Cynque cancel," he commanded under his breath.

But his Cynque kept loading whatever data file was linked to the tiny card. The word *retrieving* flashed across the air above his wrist, and in that instant, a near-transparent video screen popped up and played an infomercial.

In it, the suited soldier stood upright, spoke with zest, and wore a wide smile. The logo on his clothing was an identical match to the one stitched on his dad's shirt.

"The Andromeda Project is looking for people like you!" the soldier said. "We believe it's not the end for our world, and together, with the help of our great governments, we can find the solution. It starts with you—you and your amazing potentials, you and your dynamic intelligence."

A slightly older woman replaced the man on the screen, her voice a whole octave higher than the man's, the inflections on her words even more exaggerated and forced.

Allister leaned closer to his Cynque, cupping his hand around the speaker to keep his mom from hearing.

"Are you dedicated to saving our race before natural disasters wipe us out? Do you want to hone and master your specific potentials? It will take courage. It will take vulnerability. It will take resilience. I challenge you to step into your highest self as an Evolutionary, to live in honor and integrity, to be in contribution. You can stop the apocalypse and return our world to its former glory."

"Mega. The gov's looking for Evolutionaries now?" Allister asked, excitement sneaking into his voice. "To stop the apocalypse?"

It was the answer to all of his problems, a chance to be an Evolutionary hero.

"You matter, because you are the only hope," the woman continued.

"I'm the only hope," he repeated.

The transmission glitched hard, fast. The video blanked and another voice replaced that of the two soldiers and their jovial recruitment messaging. The new voice was low, serious, shaking.

It was his dad's.

Allister held his breath and lifted the Cynque to his face, unable to see anything but the blackened screen with the vocal recording embedded in it.

The world fell away as his dad started speaking.

"Son," he said. "I don't know how you got your hands on this, but your Mom isn't gonna be happy about it. All I can say right now is…use your potentials—"

There was an urgency and seriousness in his dad's language. One Allister didn't think would have come from the smiling face he'd seen in the photograph.

The transmission glitched again, stretching his dad's words into long, drawn-out syllables. "The apocalypse can be stopped if we can find the—"

Allister managed to catch him saying something about artifacts before the message cut off.

Trying to steady his trembling hand, he waited for more information and barely registered his mom yelling for the third time.

"I know you hear me calling you!" she shrieked.

Allister snapped back to reality. "Whoa, Mom," he said. He looked up to find that she was straddling the open doorway, fuming. "What's got you triggered?"

"What's got me—?" She leaned down and snatched the photo out of his hand. "What are you doing going through this stuff? This is all trash."

Allister rose in silence. He closed his hand around the square card, afraid she'd take that, too.

But he wanted the photo back, so he reached for it.

She held it away from him. "You need to get ready for your employment assignment. Clock is ticking."

She was gripping the photo so tight, he knew it would bend even more, become creased in too many places and thereby ruined.

"Don't ditch the photo, Mom. It's not trash," he said, insistent.

Allister entered the apartment and undressed in the hall—as the bathroom off of the main hallway was too narrow for him to move around in comfortably—then swept through a compact room with a leaky toilet and a vintage sink until he reached a narrow pill-shaped shower pod.

His minute-and-a-half-long shower was just enough time for two rounds of lather and a rinse, a routine perfected through years of water restrictions.

He angled his head so the water didn't come within an inch of his carefully plotted cornrows. It was a shame to spend years growing out his hair and hours getting it to cooperate, to then have moisture ruin the look. It was a bigger shame to know his good hair would end with everything else in a couple hundred days.

Unless, of course, everything didn't end.

Allister flattened his hand against the pod's chipped tile.

Dad said the apocalypse could be stopped. The Andromeda Project wanted to stop it, he thought.

"They wanted *Evolutionaries* to stop it," he corrected himself aloud.

Bringing the photo to life in his mind, Allister could see how his dad's hair was, in a word, epic. Thick, healthy, the brown of a hundred-year-old oak. It stopped well below his shoulders, which was where Allister's hair also might've stopped if it weren't for the tight coils. For the first time, Allister wished his cheeks and jawline weren't smooth and scarless but matured with a few nicks and a grizzly beard like his dad's. Next, he thought of the audio clip. His dad's voice had been smooth, like the pod exterior, and gentle, like the fragrance of the handmade soap Allister used. He replayed the words in his mind—*use your potentials*—and let them reassure him. Perhaps there was room for him in a world that hated Evolutionaries.

He then tried to recall a memory of them together. Tried to bask in the warmth of his dad's smile, surrender to the feeling of invincibility atop his shoulders.

Even with the photo as a guide, whatever life they'd shared together was as cold and faint as the shower's overhead spray.

As the faucet turned off—timed for accountability purposes—Allister looked up at the heat-drying system his mom had installed. The auto-start mechanism was malfunctioning again. In Riser Town, sustainability had been idealistic but hardly reliable.

He stopped at the mirror before he left the bathroom, puffed out his chest, and said, "Allister Adams—the good Evolutionary." He managed a weak smile and grabbed his uniform for the day.

Allister wondered whether his dad worked at the Andromeda Project because he was a well-respected Evolutionary trying to save the world, or if he was just posing as a human lending his intelligent mind to science in the spirit of salvation. As he got dressed in the hallway, he thought of ways to confront his mom about what he'd found. Only she knew the details of his dad's life, and for years, she'd refused to share them and got angry when asked.

Now she wanted to throw it all away.

"It's not trash," he mumbled to himself, tossing on his dad's old sleeveless cardigan.

Allister was old enough to handle the truth. He was old enough to demand it.

He walked into the shabby kitchen, still damp from the shower. It took him just a few steps to get everywhere in that tiny flat. Tight spaces. Minimal furnishing. The perpetual feeling of fluctuation. Conditions he'd gotten accustomed to during the last twelve years of his adolescence.

His mom had transported them around the world, somehow able to bypass sanctuary population regulations and the increased international border control. Despite the stress, the age in her face had managed to defy the giant countdown for as long as it could. But within those 365 days, he suspected she'd been through more than she could talk about. The once-smooth skin in the corners of her emerald eyes were lined with crow's feet. She still looked youngest when she smiled, which he'd only see her do twice: once when the government passed out stimulus checks, and once when Allister got his employment assignment. Like many Alpha gens, she didn't have much to smile about besides still being alive and the luck of having four walls to tend to, and everyone agreed that wasn't enough.

Though she was standing still, watching him, her coffee-and-honey-colored hair kept moving, a wild mane of kinked curls shaping the angles of her jaw. He likened her hair's density to the surrounding neighborhood, and enjoyed seeing it out around the house, knowing she wouldn't dare leave those walls with it free flowing. She seemed annoyed, even more than normal, he could tell when she sucked her teeth and swatted her hair out of her face.

"I wonder if you try half the time," she said, a frown forming as she looked him over. "I see you were too lazy to dry off."

"That fancy dryer broke," he retorted. "Hair looks beat, though, yeah?"

Her eyes shot back up.

"That is the last of your father's shirts. Don't ruin it." She nodded at his left side.

Allister rubbed his arm and said, "It's barely got sleeves. I should be good. *I'm* surprised it's not in the trash with everything else."

"Give it a rest." She turned back to her single-burner stove, her hair swinging behind her, and while she made his plate, said, "Mr. Skinner and Mrs. Garay are doing me a huge favor assigning you employment. They shipped out another hundred or so unemployed kids your age to rebuild the Midwest Sanctuary after those cyclones hit."

"As if it's a bad thing."

"It is." She pushed a plate in his face. "Here."

He side-eyed the genetically engineered bread before him, its synthetic texture woven to resemble a seven-grain wheat. The mushy vegetables were browned and withered between the two slices, sweating as if they, too, felt the heat.

"Here!" she snapped, placing the plate against his chest, then muttered, "Ungrateful behind."

Allister sat down. After he took his first bite, he snuck a message to Quigles on his Cynque asking for forgiveness and a second chance by way of a hang session at the junkyard after his shift.

"So what happened with those boys, then?" his mom asked. "I heard you riling up the neighborhood kids, zipping around the alley on that floaty piece of scrap metal like some lunatic. It's not safe for you to be out there tryin' to live your final days like everybody else."

"Those FBX jack-offs been giving these people hell since before we got here, and everybody on the block's tired of it." He cleared his throat and leaned over the table. "So, yeah, I tried doing something decent."

"Mm-hmm. Well, try doing what you're told. You don't owe anybody nothin' just cuz you have potentials. People can fight their own battles."

"So what if they can? You expect me to fake like I don't see?"

"Yes, that's exactly what I expect," she replied.

"I was 'bout ready to knock the smirk off Saunder's face—" Allister began.

"Then the drones came," she finished.

"Just a couple...yeah," he said. "They managed zero kills though...luck of the day, I guess."

His mom stared at him, her face getting redder as each second was lost. Her mouth was twisted so tight, he was surprised words came out.

"You used them, didn't you?"

"It was an accident," Allister replied.

"Usin' your potential wasn't no danged accident," she said. "I told you, the government's on high alert thanks to C20. They're lockin' up and killin' Evolutionaries from here to the Divide."

She continued cooking in silence.

"Now what are we supposed to do?" she asked after a few minutes. "I'm gonna have to call in more favors, find someplace new…" Her voice trailed off, but she kept going, more talking herself through logistics than talking to him.

Allister listened to her weave them a new origin story—one that would get them to their next safe haven—and thumbed the damp Andromeda Project flyer nestled deep in his pocket. He knew it wouldn't be a good time to ask, yet that sense of loss urged him to ask anyway.

"What's the Andromeda Project?" he asked.

His mom stopped talking to herself and half turned to him. "The what?"

"Dad had an employment assignment there or something? I saw the logo in the photo." He poked at the sandwich, a knot forming in his throat. "It's been twelve years since he died, and…I don't know a thing about him or what he did… or what he was."

"What he was?" his mom asked from the corner of her mouth. "What do you mean, what he was?"

"Well, I'm saying, he was an Evolutionary…he had to be if I am. Unless I missed something?"

"It's not up for discussion."

The knot thickened the more Allister tried to swallow and make room. A wet film clouded his eyes as he picked through his lunch.

"So you just chuck his stuff and not tell me anything?" he asked. "It's twisted, Mom."

His mom slid into the seat across from him. She spoke as if she were telling someone else's story, her delivery steady and casual, her body relaxed.

"Twelve years ago today…I lost your father," she said. "I wanted to make peace with it all before the end. I don't want to take that kinda pain with me wherever I end up."

"Today?" Allister mumbled. He didn't realize his dad had died on this day twelve years prior. It explained the heaviness he felt, that overwhelming sense of loss spreading back through his body.

"Yes, today."

The story seemed to be hers again.

For her first bite into the sandwich was slow, her chewing even slower, as though she were digesting her feelings along with her soggy bread and vegetables. She lowered her sandwich to the plate and stared at it, her eyes still with contempt.

"The Andromeda Project," she said in a whisper, looking around suspiciously, "is dangerous. That's all you need to know."

Quieter, Allister said, "I found something. That's why I asked."

"Oh, is that right?"

He retrieved the square card from his pocket and tossed it onto the table between them.

"Where'd you get this?" she asked.

"It was with all the other trash," he answered, a bit too sharply.

She stared at it, her fingers inches from snatching it off the table. Her face tightened when she touched it, her hand poisoned with unsteadiness.

"They're rounding up Evolutionaries to save humanity?" Allister asked. "To stop the apocalypse? Are they still around?"

The card he'd found was in her hands by that point. She flipped between stroking it, bending it, holding it up to the light, and finally, examining it under what he liked to call her *faux mom microscope*.

She let out a soft, "Hmm…"

Then, she crushed it.

Allister gasped.

His mom held up a fist so tight he thought she'd completely compress the card from existence.

"You have no idea the lengths I've gone to, to keep what you are a secret."

"But what if—"

"What if what, Allister?" she hissed. "What if *what*?"

He sat back, arms crossed. His leg bounced up and down off rhythm. "What if I can do whatever Dad did? What if, you know, there are good Evolutionaries cynqued up to a bigger cause that can teach me how to use my potentials? And, I—I could help stop the disasters wiping out humanity before the big one hits? We could enjoy life like we did before the countdown—"

"What do you know about life before the countdown?" his mom scoffed.

"I know it was way more beat than this…"

His mom released the Andromeda Project keepsake as if it were a strangled victim and let the crumpled ball roll across the table.

Allister let out a long exhale. "Mom, I've got potentials for a reason… What good are they if I'm not using them?"

"Your father used to say the same thing," she said in a trance, staring past him. "He said the same thing."

"I just…I just wanna get someplace where I don't have to fake what I am."

His mom blinked herself free of her glossed-over gaze and picked up her sandwich but didn't take a bite. "You've done it this long. You can do it for two hundred and fifteen more days."

Allister jumped up from the table, his fists tensed where they hung next to his trembling body. "Stop saying the world's done, Mom!" he yelled.

She slammed her sandwich back down.

"Don't you raise your voice at me," she said between clenched teeth. "I'm only doing what's best and preparing for what's worst. I knew the world was gonna end fifteen years before they put up that damn clock."

But behind her forced hardness, he saw her face was powdered with terror.

"There's a way to stop it…," he said. He sank back down in the chair. "We just haven't worked out the gears yet."

"Allister, how you gonna stop the Earth's crust from movin'? The temperature from rising? The storms from brewing? Hunny, you got a lotta potentials, but none of them can stand that. Mother Nature is tearing our world apart, and I can't say I blame her." She dabbed the corners of her eyes. "And I bet a week's wages those"—she spit out the next word with disdain—"*people* are still around. They find out where we are, they'll want to take you from me…make you a soldier in a war for salvation. Just like your Father."

She retreated into herself. "Even if the world doesn't end—and it will in one way or another—I didn't raise you to become an Evolutionary on the front lines."

His chest felt too tight to ask another question or make a statement intended to declare his independence.

"We need to start packing up since you wanna go using your potentials all over the place," she continued, eyes on the floor. "But I don't want anyone getting suspicious, so go on to your employment assignment and come straight home after." She paused and looked up at him, stirring in anger that must've been older than he was. "For clock's sake, Allister, I mean it, if you get another Federal-level scan, I don't know what I'd do with myself. No junkyards or neighborhood hopping with that boy up the street. No detours, all right? Come straight home."

"Sure," he said.

She nodded and checked her Cynque.

"The tram leaves in ten minutes," she said.

He dragged himself to the front door and grabbed his ratty canvas backpack off the hook on the wall.

She waited until he reached for the door handle, then said, "I don't want either of them to find you, the Andromeda Project or C20, you hear me? Not now. Not ever."

Allister lifted the handle. "I'm with it, Mom," he said evenly. "Consider it dead."

———

CHAPTER 3

ALLISTER ADAMS
Riser Town, Suburbs of the District
Day 215

ALLISTER STOPPED SHORT outside the flat, frustrated at losing the same argument for the millionth time. He wished the door would slam as he left, but it just slid sideways on the rolling track and sealed closed.

The aluminum box near the door still tugged at his curiosity. And the answers he wanted about his dad were somewhere in there, he was sure of it.

He looked down and saw a heap of folded-over papers stuffed into the side of the box.

Loose-leaf? Was that there before?

He raised an eyebrow; paper production had been banned more than a decade ago. Which meant there had to be important information on them his mom didn't want him to see. He bent down and snuck free the sheets of paper.

The pages were frayed along the left edge, appearing as though they'd been ripped out of a notebook. Handwritten headings and bizarre symbols covered both sides.

"Allister, you better not be in that box again!" his mom shouted.

"I'm not!" he replied, bounding down the stairs. When he was partway down, he could hear his front door opening and his mom's cursing traveling down the narrow staircase. After he reached the alley, he turned back to see her leaning over the railing, glaring at him with laser-focused suspicion, with the box of his dad's stuff balanced on her hip.

Allister showed her his now-empty hands and avoided her gaze, the papers stuffed in the front of his drop-crotch cargo pants.

He then took a deep breath, inhaling Riser Town's persistent stench.

Riser Town, as it was known throughout the District, was an expanse of homes with identical frameworks, all of which were built on top of one another. From the concrete foundations to the gray aluminum sidings to the floor-to-ceiling tinted windows, the neighborhood towered above the sanctuary's skyline like a residential forest. Planted on the acres and acres of government-bought land, it accommodated the influx of estranged Americans seeking refuge from climate-related disasters.

Solid waste had been piled into hills that would soon become mountains. Street vendors sold old produce and expired meats for twice their value. Desperate neighborhood residents fought each other for what they couldn't afford.

At least the sub-sanctuary was off the radar. Riser Town was pretty close to bearable, especially for someone like Allister who had the tendency to get into fights with the neighborhood's teenage mob or steal away in the afternoons to benchmark his strength potential.

Too bad I gotta leave, he thought as he checked his Cynque for a response from Quigles.

His message hadn't been read.

Once around the corner, Allister reached into his pants and took out the papers. He unfolded them, held them up, and shuffled them until they were in the order he thought they belonged.

At the top of the first one were the words *Time* and *Salvation* above a sketch of two odd-shaped crystals and a half page of scribbled equations.

"Crystals of Temporal Transportation," Allister read next to the sketch of the crystals, then, "Daal Trelkkien." There was a colon between them, and he understood that they meant the same thing, although he didn't recognize the second language.

At the bottom, his dad had signed his name, *Professor Patrick Adams*.

Allister smiled.

Maybe these pages were the answers to the questions he'd been asking.

Next, he scanned the equations—what appeared to be letters, shapes, and numbers with missing edges or with lines drawn too short—but got lost midway down the page, bombarded by the complexity and his dad's hard-to-follow pattern of thought. There were triangles attached to other triangles, squares, and circles, some shaded in, some empty, all in a linear sequence. Then below them were those same shapes inside other, more complex shapes—hexagons, octagons, trapezoids—and they didn't always fit together comfortably. The page was filled with half-drawn *A*s, slanted *S*s with dots inside the swirls, conjoined 6s and 7s, equal signs standing at attention instead of laid on their sides…the math, if it could be called that, was impossible to understand.

He flipped over the page and found a set of paragraphs attempting to rationalize his dad's obsession with what had been identified as artifacts. His dad didn't know what the artifacts did exactly, but he knew they were alien and was insistent on the fact that they mattered to human preservation. By the list of crossed-off locations on the back, it seemed he had been looking for them and hadn't been successful.

"What the heck were you up to, Pops?" Allister asked.

Pops?

He didn't know where the new nickname for his dad had come from, but he liked the way it added a spark of joy and fun to his faded memory.

"Daal Trelkkien," he read, looking over the sketch again. "Mega."

Cynque chimed.

"The next Silver Line A.E.T. Trac departs from Riser Town Military Outpost at approximately eight hours and three minutes to Day 214," his Cynque announced. "There is a delay due to a mandatory scan site farther up the route. At your current speed, you won't make it in time."

He quickened his pace.

"Map alternate routes," he said, stuffing the papers under his arm.

He unfolded his hand. Cynque projected a holographic grid across his palms, out of which rose the sky-scraping steel and manufacturing warehouses distributed about the area.

Artist: The CMD Studios

An illuminated guide routed him through the sanctuary's bustling madness. "No faster routes found."

"Well...crap."

He dipped and dodged through the thickening crowd, careful not to catch the lens of a face-scanning drone. When he hit a slow-moving cluster of people, he jumped into a street full of traffic jams—both for the cars at eye level and those that hovered off the ground—and set off running alongside them.

Old cars still bound to the road chugged and screeched and stopped under slightly more recent airborne Ukimoto Hover Model prototypes. The drones that clocked citizen behavior seemed to register his speed and approach. A pesky buzz of rotors, which he hadn't heard before, circled closer. He slowed down and skipped back on the sidewalk as he reached the station's entrance, then jumped down the stairs.

The station sign shuffled the A.E.T. Trac departures to the most up-to-date one. His.

"Doors closing," echoed a voice from over the loudspeaker.

Allister burst through the turnstile and squeezed through the doors just before they closed. He went on stumbling and groping for the nearest pole as passengers reluctantly made room for him.

"Thanks," he said aloud, finally securing his grip.

No one responded.

Allister stood crammed between overly dressed contractors, some off-duty patrols, and a few other essential workers, likely food and medical providers.

Those grim-faced commuters were engrossed in their Cynque news and their share feeds. New video content speculating how the world would end played on more than one device near him.

It was impossible not to get sucked in to someone's visible screen.

The artificial intelligence influencers were more entertaining and creative when laying out predictions than their human counterparts, but Allister found it ironic, them speaking on the savagery of the human condition. Last he'd checked, they were simply digitally programmed to simulate the human experience *online*. Maybe that's why the upcoming apocalypse was made to feel less real. He blamed the decorative backgrounds, over-sexualized animated avatars, and overused abbreviations like *EOW*—end of the world.

As with most things Cynque related, the AI influencers reporting from speculation got more interest than anyone reporting from science.

From what he had overheard, he couldn't decide which was worse: the world ending in flames due to wildfires or a massive tectonic shift, or that no one had any measurable data to support either theory. He was skeptical of new concepts like the magnetic poles switching. Sure, that might lead to a massive global positioning nightmare, maybe temporary electromagnetic fallout, but the end of humanity felt like a stretch.

Could swear they flipped a few years back anyway, he thought.

Allister saw these broadcasts as distractions. Off-handed predictions to hide what the Sanctuaries already knew.

The truth.

A young man near the door started crying hysterically and tried forcing the doors open, screaming about how he just wanted to end it. A heavyset woman shoved him into a seat and held him there. Allister couldn't hear exactly what she was saying, but it sounded as though she was offering him the opportunity to finish himself off on his own time, as in when everyone got where they were going.

He wasn't surprised at the quick reaction, or the man's damning sense of futility.

Which got him thinking about whether the existence of a pair of crystal artifacts could really stop an end already in motion.

"Would be so beat if they reversed time," he said out loud by accident.

A few passengers shot their eyes his way, then rolled them back down to their Cynques.

On the woman's device next to him, Cynque News flashed a photo of Morocco's princess, Celine Nephthys. The report stated she was still missing after the tsunami from 182 days past and that the king, Marshall Nephthys, had denied claims that she was an Evolutionary. He was still offering rewards for both her return and the heads of her kidnappers.

Allister took a step closer to get a better look.

Celine was stunning, though a bit solemn. Young, like him, so she probably didn't have much to smile about, either. In the image, she looked severe, like a bad weather forecast, and he knew without knowing her, her anger came with swift, hard punishment, her stare piercing his soul like sharpened quartz.

When the woman attached to the Cynque eyed him, he cleared his throat and looked away. But the digital imprint of the princess's face went with him.

Allister shuddered. If Celine was an Evolutionary, he hoped she'd be a good one—and if not, mercy on the poor idiot hired to take her.

He gazed through the car's polished windows, somewhat numb to the sprawling sanctuary known as the District coming up on the horizon. It was a newly finished painting, a canvas with no white space. He had gotten used to the medium gray that was permanently shaded into the sky, no longer hoping for blue skies or a clear, sunny day. To him, the canvas edges were the stacked-high homes of the saturated and gentrified sub-sanc neighborhoods. The background: a monochromatic color scheme of metal and glass buildings, used for innovative weapon development and rigorous training; the foreground: occasional foliage, military law enforcement sidled next to their sixty-ton tanks, and the expansive Aerodynamic Energy–conserving transit system, a tram that ran along a single solar-powered track—which he and the other Omega gen kids called the A.E.T. Trac.

The tram jerked left.

The old veggies sloshed around in Allister's stomach, as did the unfiltered tap water. He held his hand over his mouth as the A.E.T. Trac made its third abrupt stop. A number of the commuters he'd deemed "regulars" got off. A few of the stranger, off-base types got on. There was suddenly more room in the car, and Allister's age was evident enough to command distance when the A.E.T. Trac would allow. Teens such as him still had a bad reputation. They were known for being troublemakers, drone dodgers, and on the extreme end, patrol killers. Some fel-low commuters gave him side glances as they moved into available seating, or just farther away from him, while the—*one, two, three, four,* he counted—newcomers didn't take their eyes off him.

He could brush off people scoffing at his braids or his afro, or correcting him when he spoke slang, but the hardened stares from those four strangers were more intrusive than he was used to.

The first two were Asians in all white: one male, one female, their ethnic features and cultural attire too distinct. And with border laws functioning the way they did, he was sure they couldn't be living in the United Sanctuaries.

The two of them stood back-to-back, rocking with the car as it got moving again, their almost-identical scowls carrying a seriousness that bordered on sinister.

The female looked down at the papers in Allister's armpit, then back up at his face, before turning casually to stare straight ahead. The male, taller than her by at least a foot, kept his murderous glare pinned to Allister, looking as though he were devising ways to kill him.

His stomach turned over. Maybe it was watching them sway with the shifting tracks, maybe it was fear of a look that deadly from someone he'd never seen before.

He shifted his eyes to the third person: a concealed passenger, who, from the orange flash that quickly emitted from beneath their hood, he gathered was gifted with a mechanical eye. Cybernetics weren't common; still, they weren't unheard of. The confidence to spread out on public transportation, however? That was rare.

And finally, he turned his gaze to a woman dressed to the nines in civilian clothing. She wore big hoop earrings that swung as the tram rattled along the tracks. Her high-turtlenecked top concealed her nose and lips, and her curly hair was pinned up in the messy elegance of an afropony. Her eyes locked with his. He swore he saw a flash of red energy consume her violet eyes.

Straight away, a tingling sensation penetrated his mind.

He shivered and blinked himself free, her stare a prison he'd narrowly escaped.

Is she some kind of Evolutionary with mind-bending potential? he thought. *What's she doing here? Uh…wait, can she hear my thoughts? Crap. Think of something… No, don't think of anything. Dammit!*

He slapped his head.

Cynque had done a lazy job of classifying the different types of Evolutionaries there were, and a flat-out terrible job of explaining them in a way that didn't incite widespread panic. From what Allister knew, an Evolutionary by Cynque's definition wasn't something he'd stumble across on public transportation. They rarely lived in the open among those they considered the "unevolved." These Evolutionaries stuck close to one another and pledged their loyalties to C20, the global terrorist organization that convinced them to go into hiding, then deployed them for coordinated attacks.

C20 and their band of Evolutionaries could very well be right where he was on the tram; they had proven they could be anywhere. The four people watching him seemed wildly out of place, and Allister was surprised no one looked as bothered or uncomfortable as he felt.

The A.E.T. Trac shook on its way around a sharp turn toward the inner sanctuary.

His queasiness returned. He closed his eyes and got a better hold on the overhead bar, hoping with everything inside him he wasn't on C20's list for recruiting. They weren't the type of Evolutionaries he wanted to get cynqued up with.

Cynque's signature voice announced their next stops over the loudspeaker.

"This is the Silver Line with transfers at Ground Zero station. Next stop, Museum District," it blared. Metal squealed against metal as the tram labored to slow down.

He took a breath and looked up. Of course he'd managed to crush the bar during his overthinking. He gasped as they came to a stop, fretting to himself over the crinkled metal where his hand had been.

As the doors opened, Allister practically fell out.

He stumbled backward from the woman concealed by a turtleneck, the cybernetic-eyed chair hog, and the scowling pair in white. He let himself be swept away by the exiting crowd, a herd of sheep moving with the call of the sanctuary's ingrained urgency.

The military soldiers assigned to the exits commanded everyone to slow down, line up single file, and scan their Cynques. Their semiautomatic weapons and drone assistants made sure everyone listened.

Allister stuffed the papers in his bag and followed the homogenous collective aboveground. He shook his head as he reached the street, wanting to dismiss his gut feeling as paranoia, and the chilling tram encounter as a coincidence.

Somewhat uneasy, somewhat curious, he looked over his shoulder.

He expected to see someone following him and prepared to duck behind the nearest building. But besides the frantic drones, all he saw were people with oversized uniforms, solemn faces, and hunched shoulders. The words "Keep moving" rose into the air every few minutes, loud and without much emotion, even anger.

It was a regular day in the District—contractors disappeared into their respective facilities, uniformed guards reported to their respective posts, and down the main boulevard, fellow essential workers moved to-and-fro across a thin strip of concrete-caged lawn.

No turtlenecks. No white suits. No theatrical hoods.

He exhaled as he turned around and—

Ran into a hulking soldier on patrol.

Ground Zero, Former Capitol Hill, the District

ALLISTER COULDN'T AFFORD to get another Federal scan. He cowered as he eased back on light toes, an uneasy expression plastered across his face.

"Cynque," the soldier demanded.

The man was shorter than him but wider, with a silver weapon cradled in his arms as if it were a vicious kitten. Every few seconds, it hissed with a charge of plasma energy.

Allister gulped and took another step back. He fumbled to form sentences without using slang, not wanting the patrol to think he was talking slick, which was a surefire way to get taken down.

"I'm so sorry, sir. Really, I am," he said, pushing away the invisible air between them. "Promise, I'm legit...I've got an employment assignment I'm running late for."

He turned around to keep going.

The soldier snatched him up by the collar and shouted in his ear, "Did I say you could walk away, civilian?"

"No, I just need—"

The soldier turned him around.

"You need to follow my orders!" he bellowed. "Your Cynque. Now!"

The soldier's wide, beady eyes didn't have a hint of moisture in them, even as he blinked and waited for Allister to submit.

"I'm waiting," the soldier said with a sneer. His lips parted for crooked, yellowed teeth.

His breath smells like Riser Town, Allister thought.

He hunched over in a bid to appear less threatening. A trick his mom had taught him.

"Are you gonna scan me?" he asked. "I didn't do anything."

The soldier moved the double-barreled weapon behind his back and pulled Allister by his cardigan until they were nose-to-nose.

"You're refusing a scan, resisting authority." The soldier breathed in his face, the revolting odor clouding Allister's senses. "I say you're doing plenty without doing much."

Allister bit his lip and looked away to hide his watering eyes.

The soldier wasn't going to let him off.

He held his arm out, wrist up.

Being cynqued was mandatory for all citizens of the Sanctuaries. Inside of the device known as Cynque was the culmination of Allister's living existence, which projected upward in that moment as a digital sphere. The small sphere's illuminated binary code was arranged in layers that orbited an invisible axis and stocked full of his personal interactions and data, the rights to which had been signed away during the social connectivity boom. But the soldier wouldn't care about his mom's unanswered texts or that the few QB coins in his portfolio dwindled too close to zero. None of that mattered.

What mattered was what was most incriminating: criminal history, occupa-tion status, last hardship duty, and most recent Federal scan. Like clockwork, the soldier began performing the routine check.

"I'm going to miss the start time for my employment"—he swallowed—"sir."

"Yeah, I find it hard to believe you got an assignment, punk," the soldier said.

Allister fiddled with his pocket and looked around, distracting himself from the reality that when he got this Federal scan, his mom wouldn't know what to do with herself.

"Already got a few scans for destroying property on the A.E.T. Trac. Got caught by a drone in last month's Riser Town raid," the soldier noted. "No wonder you're actin' so *mega*."

"They were accidents," Allister said feebly.

The soldier navigated to the next data point.

Thin green letters spelled the words *Essential Transport* next to *Pioneer Koffee* on the glowing sphere's surface.

"Well, I'll be a countdown survivor, you do got a job."

Allister's eyes brightened. "See," he said, pointing at the sphere, "just like I said."

"I see all right. You mighty blessed for a troublemaker. Get going, then," he grunted and released him.

Allister didn't know whether to say thank you or keep his mouth shut. He didn't have time to decide before—

He saw the reflection in the adjacent building's glass.

The hooded passenger stood on the opposite side of the main road, waving at him with metal claws.

Allister's jaw dropped. He whipped around and saw nothing but empty sidewalk. He turned back to the building and saw them again in the reflection, still waving.

The orange eye flashed.

A tingle shot through his mind, just like on the A.E.T. Trac when the woman in the turtleneck had looked at him.

"Get going!" the soldier shouted from his post. He took a threatening step toward Allister.

So as not to actually get a scan, Allister rushed away and lost himself in pedestrian traffic, leaving behind the memory of the encounter and, hopefully, the orange-eyed stalker. He kept his head down, a hand covering his pounding heart, and continued toward the coffee shop where he sometimes packaged and shipped ground coffee and sometimes baked sweets.

Despite getting more than a block away, the tingling in his mind lingered. He couldn't stop fumbling over his feet and his thoughts.

No way she's trailing me, he said to himself. *No frickin' way.*

Allister looked up—and stopped cold.

The two Asian individuals in white were charging up the block toward him, mouths unmoving, eyes determined, their advance forcing him back into the crowd he'd pushed through. He searched the square for an escape.

Two, maybe three, steps behind him, he found a narrow corridor. He slipped inside and moved down it until he found a protruding doorway to hide behind.

His back slammed against the wall.

Cynque's holographic screen automatically ballooned above his upright wrist. The address book was rotating with the coffee shop's information file open and was asking if he wanted to send a message and let them know he'd be late.

Allister shook his head, unable to stop his heavy breathing. He was already late. And he was being trailed by…what he assumed were Evolutionaries. He flipped the screen to his mom's contact file and thought about issuing the command, *Call Mom*, but after more consideration, he didn't. She'd just tell him to come home.

He disabled the screen and leaned forward.

His stalkers, who looked alike enough to be siblings, were standing at the corridor's edge, their backs to it, looking for him in both directions. Then they performed an eerily slow, synchronized head turn and pivoted their bodies. Their soulless expressions drilled through Allister as they headed in his direction.

He gasped and bolted deeper into the corridor, which opened up into a courtyard and then emptied onto another busy boulevard. He was flinging trash cans and crates behind him as he went, and emerged on the other side sweaty and disoriented. People screamed at the sudden sight of him. He screamed back, recoiling as he spun toward the alley.

The siblings on his tail were almost to him by then. He saw the woman's body start to fade into transparency and the man's body gloss over and thicken as though he'd put on armor.

"Snap!" he exclaimed.

A hand grabbed the fabric of his cloak with startling strength and yanked him sideways, up a small flight of stairs and through a set of double doors.

The hand didn't let go until he was inside a damp hall. He had screamed from the street to the doors, and now, bewildered, he hyperventilated over his knees for a moment before looking up at the person who'd snatched him.

He shot back up.

It was the woman in the turtleneck, her chin in the air, hip cocked.

He sized her up while she did the same to him, and found himself wondering how hot she must be, wearing that knitted thing in the District's eternal summer. But he shook the thought away; there were bigger questions here, such as: Why had she been following him, too?

"What do you want?" he asked, raising his arms in defense.

There was a calm in her bewitching violet eyes. A friendliness in her tilted head.

The relaxation that followed felt induced, the tingling in his body an injection. His heartbeat slowed. And as he experienced the coolness of calm breezing through him, his arms lowered.

She pulled down the bunched-up fabric around her face to reveal full lips stained sunset red and a voice kinder and more gentle than he had expected. She had an English accent with a pinch of something Mediterranean, which gave her authority even more poise and affluence.

"So, you're Allister Adams," she said.

CHAPTER 4

ALLISTER ADAMS
Ground Zero, Former Capitol Hill, the District
Day 215

ALLISTER EYED THE stranger, wary of her intention.

"Me? Allister Adams? Uh…depends on who's asking," he said.

"Well, it's not me asking," the woman answered. "I already know."

He opened his mouth.

"Stay here," she said.

His mouth snapped shut. *Who is this Alpha gen and how do they know my name?* he thought.

To him, it all felt wrong. Every passing moment was proof that his mom had been right about why he needed to lay low. He watched the woman closely, suspicious of everything that had gone on since his ride on the A.E.T. Trac. She didn't appear worried about him as she hung about the doors she'd dragged him through, considering whatever was beyond them. The siblings perhaps.

"Where are we?" Allister asked, looking over the interior, then back at her.

She tapped her chin but didn't answer. The answer was obvious to a degree.

They were in a musty, vacant foyer surrounded by manufacturing equipment. Welding stations and mass-production-style machines sat next to large engine parts, detached aircraft wings, and loose metal shavings. The facility appeared to be either temporarily shut down or recently abandoned.

Once again, he lifted his wrist and held it there, hesitating to speak, *Call Mom*, into his Cynque. And once again, he second-guessed the idea and dropped his arm without saying it.

"Look…I don't know why you were giving me eyes on the A.E.T. Trac. But I'm a little triggered right now because you know my whole name and your eyes light up."

"Mm-hmm," the woman said.

She passed him on her way back from the double doors and stopped at the wall behind him.

"If I get mixed up in some mega EV stuff, I'm toast—"

"Hush, will you," she interrupted.

Without looking, she traced her hand along the wall next to them, only stopping when she found a digital panel. One tap of her finger and it sprang to holographic life.

He narrowed his eyes at her bare, slender wrist.

The woman wasn't cynqued.

Everyone was supposed to be cynqued.

"Okay, pause. Who are you?" Allister asked. He pointed at the flesh-toned scar peeking above her sleeve where the wires would've invaded. "Why aren't you cynqued?"

Sunset Turtleneck, as Allister had nicknamed her, punched in a long code, her lips pursed in confidence. The door's windows lightened to reveal the street.

"You're an Evolutionary, yeah? Is that why?" he pressed. "You with C20?" He stepped forward, waiting for a response. Nothing came. "Uh, you keen to answer or you just—"

Sunset Turtleneck held up her palm and shot him a glare as she returned to the doors. She moved along the row of them, almost dancing between each window, back and forth and back again.

"They're still out there, waiting for you," she said.

"Who's they?" he asked.

"Depends on who's asking," she quipped. She, now facing the street, leaned closer to the glass, then answered, "They…is C20. More specifically, the Density Twins. I suspect you have something they want"—she glanced down at his feet and back to the window in one fluid motion—"though I imagine it's not your shoes…"

She clipped her insult and flattened herself against the wall opposite him. Her forefinger slipped over her painted lips in the universal request for quiet.

Not soon after, an obnoxious noise coming from the street flooded the empty foyer. Allister heard shouting—louder than person-to-person chatter or an unruly protest about maximum wages and the electric curfew.

The people, they were…screaming.

Allister rushed to the doors and squinted through the glass.

A loaded-up tanker chugged down the main boulevard with the determination of a steam-engine locomotive. It swerved on eighteen wheels, leaving limp, struggling bodies; damaged buildings; and destroyed memorials in its wake.

"What the hell? Is C20 attacking the District again?" Allister grabbed the doorframe and exclaimed, "I knew those twins were Evolutionaries, I could feel it! And the hooded, orange-eyed one was, too, right? Why didn't you take them out on the A.E.T. Trac? You could've stopped this!"

Sunset Turtleneck positioned her shoulder against the door, about to push it open. "Because civilians…," she said quickly. "Just curious, how strong of an Evolutionary are you?"

She nodded at his arm muscles, likely a reference to their size.

"I don't know. I lifted a car once," he replied, speaking fast as he backed away. "But it was tiny and the interior was gutted. Can't you do something with your eyes or whatever?"

He tried to keep his voice calm. To seem more together than he was. Inside, though, he was having a full-on meltdown. He fretted over how the patrols had let this happen, if the barricades would be enough to stop the truck's rampage. The authorities didn't seem to be doing anything, and the screams were getting louder.

"I'm hardly in a position to stop something that big, moving that fast." She fluffed her afropony, the urgency easing out of her body and language. "And I'm guessing neither is anyone out there—" She looked back at him. "You *are* Allister Adams, yes?"

"Yes! For clock's sake, yes!" he admitted, throwing his hands in the air.

"*Va bene*. Then, I need you to use your strength potential to stop that truck."

His eyes darted to the windows.

People cluttered the sidewalk, pushed against one another to keep themselves out of harm's way, never lending a hand to those in danger.

He slid his hands down his face.

"If I stop that truck," he said into his palms, "everyone will know I'm an Evolutionary. What if they think I'm with C20 and execute me on sight?"

"Allister, I'm one of the good ones, and I'm asking you to help me save these people."

He checked the street again.

Those still in the path of destruction needed help, but it didn't look like help would come. Unless…

"I guess I *could* use them…," Allister said. His eyes widened in excitement, and the more he thought about his dad's simple suggestion, the wider they got.

Finally, he exclaimed, "One thousand percent I can use my potentials to save them!"

"Exactly—seems like an appropriate time to find out what you're capable of," she said, shoving the door open. "Let's go!"

Allister rushed out the doors and followed her into the crowd.

People half his size collided with him, small enough for him to easily move past but big enough to make an impact. His shoving only just fell short of actual aggression as he tried to keep pace with Sunset Turtleneck. The woman was nimble enough to squeeze between the cars, which were now bumper-to-bumper in the chaos, and shimmy between even the most frantic fleeing, screaming civilians. Before he knew it, she had already made it onto the opposite sidewalk.

Military helicopters circling above the attack issued broadcast commands to stop. The truck's driver responded by speeding up. The vehicle veered off the road again.

"It's turning," Allister shouted to her, pointing. "Hey, it's turning! Go this way!"

Sunset Turtleneck didn't turn around. He suspected the screams of panic were too loud. More people flooded past them in haste, and suddenly he couldn't see her.

Though his body kept moving with the crowd, Allister's eyes stayed on the sidewalk she'd vanished from, waiting for her to reappear.

There was no turtleneck or sunset-red lip color, no bushy afropony or posh voice telling him what to do next.

A chorus of shouting and hysteria could be heard from the office building that was situated at the end of the truck's now-obvious path. He watched the vehicle careen across the groomed lawn and back onto another less crowded street, heading toward the high-rise stuffed with essential workers.

Allister's stomach twisted around itself like old wire. He looked down at his feet and swallowed as he curled his fists, working up the courage to run. After a series of deep breaths, he brought his head back up and launched into a sprint.

The crowd thinned as he ran farther, full of fear and determination, his bag bouncing against his back.

A spotlight from above tried keeping pace with him. He leaned into his speed, lengthened his strides, kept pushing beyond it. His shoes pounded the street as he powered past a blurry sea of onlookers.

"Civilian in black, whoever you are, stand down," a voice broadcast over the square. "Stand down. We have a clear shot, and we'll shoot you, too."

Allister dodged out of the light again, but didn't slow; his potential for speed was too great.

Almost breathless he sprang across the grass, gassed up as if running on fuel, chasing after the truck with the immense speed of an engine-powered car. As he caught up to the rear of the vehicle, he pushed himself to run faster. Past the truck's midsection. Past its passenger door. He finally overtook the vehicle.

But with his speed potential on max, his turn was too wide.

His feet got tangled beneath him. He tumbled, then fell forward, wind rushing at his face. His palms smacked the pavement.

From the truck's open window, he heard a man's voice yelling, "We are not all cynqued, we are not all one. Reclaim freedom and purpose in the name of C20! Hail Tas-Salvatur!"

A rush of adrenaline and Allister was on his feet again. A sharp inhale and he charged forward. A defiant yell and—

He turned his head away, flexed his shoulder, and rammed it into the truck's radiator grille.

The engine crunched inward. The wheels, screeching and heated by friction, sent geysers of white smoke into the air.

He didn't know which body part would be best to use to stop a tanker, so he'd just chosen one and gone with it. Now, as extreme velocity kept them skidding toward the tanker's final destination, he realized the truck wasn't going to stop where he wanted it to—despite the power beneath his heels, despite his intention. He was screaming and barely knew it, though he could feel why he might be, with the overheated metal sizzling against his bare biceps as he tried pushing forward. Soon, his skin was being ripped away like the asphalt at his feet.

More adrenaline fought off the throbbing pain of continuous impact, and he hardly felt the bones in his shoulder splintering.

He flattened a hand against the grille and jumped in the air, securely holding his grip on the truck as he drove his heels through the ground. His hands inched closer to his body by no fault of his own, reducing the distance between himself and the truck. But his arm muscles flexed one last time, searching for what was left of his strength potential. Still, he felt his grip slipping. Nothing seemed to come.

Perhaps his dad advising him to use his potentials was the only sentence he'd ever needed to hear. Because while repeating it in his head, a wave of incredible strength surged like fire within him, starting at his toes, moving up through his back, then through his arms. He felt strong enough to tear the vehicle in half. With a final scream, he pushed both hands out, his heart pounding toward explosion.

———

The vehicle whined as it slowed. A giant beast wrestled to its last breath. The trailer, momentarily airborne, slammed back onto the street and scraped the pavement as it swung sideways. But the truck finally wrenched to a stop. The whole thing steaming and smelling of friction and agitated rubber.

Allister couldn't feel his hand, though he cringed at the sight of it. Next, the dizziness would arrive—in part a reaction to the gruesome injury: flesh revealing traces of bone beneath scraps of muscle and connective tissue. He stumbled back, feeling the dizziness do more than sneak into him—it was starting to take over—a common side effect of his regeneration potential working on overdrive. The muscle and tissue began filling back in, threading itself around his fingers until his hand was stitched back to completion. The pain was a constant abundance of stinging and burning. It reminded him of the way the truck had arrived: fast, ruthless, seemingly unstoppable.

He held in his tormented screams. The healing would be over soon, he reminded himself.

How soon?

Seconds later, layers of fresh skin appeared on the length of his forearm and filled in past his wrist, restoring the pigment.

The pain began subsiding in slow waves.

He was swathed in relief, hunched over with his hands pressed against his knees, imagining his face was a sweat-soaked blend of washed-out brown and distressed red.

The drones continued buzzing overhead. Loud sirens signaled the arrival of authorities.

He had to get out of there before someone shot him, but he could barely stand, let alone walk, let alone run.

Instead, he watched as soldiers in strange uniforms surrounded the truck and shot off the driver's side door. The public didn't seem to care when the yelling troops dragged out the driver nor batted an eye when the alleged terrorist screamed out misinformation concerning false democracies and the crooked caste system.

The driver was tossed face-first onto the pavement, then held down as the soldiers shackled his arms behind him. A woman moved among the commotion.

Allister realized who it was.

Sunset Turtleneck.

Now in authority's company, she injected a needle into the suspect's arm. The liquid sedated his sentiments, some of which Allister knew the population believed and would never vocalize.

"C20 will be salvation," the man slurred as he went unconscious.

But where were the twins? The orange-eyed cyborg?

Sunset Turtleneck's violet eyes fixed on him. No red flash this time. She first nodded in his direction, taking calculated, confident strides to a vehicle suspended just above the street by four ground-facing thrusters, then she ascended that vehicle's rear platform and disappeared without so much as a smile. The suspect was dragged up the platform behind her, after which it was sealed shut. Rising swiftly, the vehicle became a blip in the bustle of the airborne highway.

And *zoom*.

The vehicle sped away.

Hushed whispers swept the square in its wake.

Allister rubbed his head, blinking the scene beyond the demolished truck into clarity. What he saw was his valiant effort transforming into a fatal mistake.

The gathered crowd's faces ranged from skeptical to disturbed to terrified. They clutched their own bloody, dusty bodies and stared at him, their wrists upright. Allister realized then that the connected devices of the District's populous were recording his past, present, and soon-to-be movement. Before this moment, he had been an awkward and sometimes reckless citizen of the District, but now he would forever be seen as a wobbling, barely conscious Evolutionary.

Cynque would circulate the uploaded footage no matter how grainy or how shaky, while every human engagement flirted with an algorithm to distribute his feat among a global social ecosystem.

A *heroic* feat, at that.

Yet a handful of onlookers began to turn and limp about their business, clearly desensitized. No one thanked him for his bravery. No one asked if he was okay. And besides the obvious fact that the people cowering in the windows of the office building were likely plotting suicide from such heights, he guessed saving civilian lives didn't matter when they were all going to die anyway.

"Don't much matter, fake hero. You'll join the rest of your kind soon as the patrols arrive," a man yelled at a distance.

The insult seemed to knock him sideways. Well aimed. Blunt.

Allister teetered before he toppled over, vomiting into the street on his way down.

The heat of exertion refused to let him go.

On the other side of him, a teenager began to swing a loose pole in Allister's direction.

Allister went to defend himself, and dragged his head down between his knees instead.

Any minute now, he thought, still unable to get to his feet.

"We don't need terrorists like *you* helping us," an older woman growled. "Go back to where you came from!"

Then a *krakow krakow krakow* echoed through the open square.

People started screaming.

Allister didn't bother looking up. He recognized the sound of explosive plasma.

"Are you people mental?" he heard a man yell. "Get away from that EV. It might be dangerous! Disperse!" The man fired another round before anyone had time to react. *Krakow. Krakow. Krakow.* "I said disperse, or you're all getting Federal scans!"

They all moved away, the sounds of their shock becoming fainter.

The man, who Allister assumed was a soldier, approached him from the side and addressed someone else.

"Don't know who picked up the other guy," he said loudly. "But I'm willing to bet a hundred days this genetic accident knows something. Could be a decoy."

On the other side of him, a set of boots pounded the pavement with urgency and aggression. This someone else was running up.

"Remove the bag and put your hands behind your head," a female soldier shouted, her weapon raised at his face.

A stiffness crept down Allister's legs and into his toes.

The first soldier put his finger back on the trigger, his weapon just as close. "She said get down!"

Allister slid his arms from under the straps of his bag and placed it on the ground. He inched his hands to the special place behind his neck. The special place that for any man of his social stature meant submission, cooperation, and possibly…survival.

"You again?" the male soldier said, incredulous. "I knew I shoulda scanned you and locked you up."

Allister clenched his jaw. He'd welcome a Federal scan over another weapon that close to his head.

The soldier grabbed Allister's bag and unzipped it. "What you got in here, you filthy little EV?" he asked as he dug through it. "Loose-leaf? Shoot, your case keeps gettin' better and better." The soldier started crumpling the pages with his dad's work on them.

"No, don't!" Allister shouted. "They're my dad's—from before the countdown. It's all I have from him."

The male soldier hesitated, then crumpled the papers anyway and shoved them back into the bag. "Tough draw. Tell us what you seen."

"I *saw* what you saw. A truck mowing down a bunch of innocent people and trying to plow through an office building."

"And nothing else?" the female soldier asked.

Allister shuddered at the memory of the hooded person whose reflection had appeared briefly across the street and the twins who had chased him into the alley. He tightened his grip on his neck, his interlocked fingers held firmly, and pulled his head lower.

"Nothing else. One thousand percent. I swear. I wasn't with them—him." He corrected himself too quickly.

The male soldier pressed the heated gun to Allister's head. "What you mean 'them'? You lying, EV?"

"Hey, watch the hair, man," Allister said, then added hastily, "I meant C20. I'm not with *them*. I was just trying to use my potentials to help."

"Yeah? Where were you four years ago when C20 attacked, huh?"

"Uhm…year two of secondary learning academy."

The male soldier stroked the trigger. "One more word and you got no days left." The obvious answer was silence.

"Good boy." The soldier jabbed the barrel into Allister's shoulder. "Smarter than the rest of your kind, I'll give ya that."

"Let's take him in and get him sorted proper," the female soldier said, straightening. "Could win us some days off."

The other one closest to Allister laughed. "We'd hit the ole Alley a few good times, I reckon."

And there, forehead touching his knees, the reality of being exposed sent chills through Allister's spine.

This was the beginning or the end. There was no in-between, there was no going back. He didn't know the exact consequences for being an Evolutionary, especially one who tried to play hero, but he knew that the few of his kind who allied with C20 that were ever caught were "terminated." There were horror stories about the inhumanity of the process, justified by the fact that Evolutionaries weren't considered human.

"I can handle this one, soldiers," someone called out in a distinct Southern twang. "Why don't you finish clearin' the square?"

"Who're you to tell me how to do my duty?" the male soldier asked. "That don't look to me like a regulation uniform."

"I'm from Evolutionary Federal Detention," the man replied. "How's that?"

Allister lifted his head.

A man wearing a more fitted, more stylized version of the District patrol uniform approached. Beneath it, Allister caught the glimmer of a golden-armored chest plate.

The soldier stepped to the newcomer, his weapon positioned to fire.

Allister's eyes shifted with uneasiness between them.

"Hey, guess we got no juri to go mega on him, Spence," the female soldier interrupted. "Check our latest orders."

"EFD, huh?" the soldier—Spence—asked. "You better give credit where credit's due when you take him in."

The man snatched Allister's bag away from Spence. "Gladly," he said with a short, almost-disrespectful bow.

The female soldier turned her partner around and pushed him toward the overturned vehicle, fussing about "losing the kill" until they were out of earshot.

Allister adjusted his hands on the back of his neck. His eyes darted along the rooftops and in the spaces between a dispersed crowd for signs of…C20.

Nothing.

The pasty man standing above him wore an ensemble fitted to his frame: a chic jacket buttoned to the neck and tailored pants, both the color of cabernet. An insignia on the large hat hinted at his military prestige.

"On your feet, EV," the man said.

Allister wiped the sweat that dripped from his throbbing temples. He shook his head. "I'm not with C20. I swear!" he said too loudly.

"I said, on your feet. Now."

He began to stand. Eyes on the pavement, he whispered, "Please don't take me in, sir—"

Before he could finish, the man reached for something on his hip. Allister tried to rise faster, more concerned with getting away than explaining his innocence. But he was too slow as the man snatched the weapon free and aimed it at Allister.

Sharp metal pierced his neck in two places.

An electric surge invaded Allister's flesh with the pain of a thousand beestings. His senses blacked. His body numbed. Though he knew it was shaking uncontrollably. He fought for the strength to stand against the current zipping through him, choking from the foam bubbling in his mouth, buckling from the weakness in his legs.

"Stand back, folks," he heard the man command, his voice foggy and far off. "The subject's dangerous. This is for your safety." The rest of the words reached Allister's ears drawn out beyond comprehension, and he hardly registered being caught in the man's arms as, just short of paralyzed, he sank to the ground. "Shhhh, sh, sh, sh, sh...don't fight it," the man coaxed. He was rubbing Allister's back as if putting him down for a nap. "Everyone's already seen what you can do."

Allister squirmed and pawed at the man's jacket, his eyes drifting closed. Eventually, he slumped over, completely limp.

The man then cradled his head with an unusual tenderness. Removing the wires, he leaned down and whispered, "You have a lot of potential, Mr. Adams. And as your daddy used to say: it's not about what you have, it's about what you do with it."

———

WHAT'S YOUR POTENTIAL? (I.E. CONNECTING PEOPLE, SPREADING JOY, CREATING, TELLING STORIES, EMPATHY, UNDERSTANDING?) IF YOU COULD HAVE ANY SUPER POWERED POTENTIAL, WHAT WOULD IT BE?

———

CHAPTER 5

ALLISTER ADAMS
Unknown Location
Day 214

ALLISTER WOKE UP in a panic, bewildered, inhaling so sharply he coughed. The cough grew more violent, more strained, agitating the tightness he felt in his throat. He slowed his breathing and swallowed—once, twice, then a third time.

The cough seemed to retreat. The tightness seemed to loosen.

But as he became more coherent, he felt a new tightness elsewhere, coupled with a tingling in his hands, arms, and feet.

It was the constriction of restraints.

Fear was a current surging through Allister as he tried pulling his body free, up from the long bench to which he was tethered. Thick link chains jangled around his flexed biceps and across his chest in response, but they didn't budge enough to break. He could see his hands were shackled inside cylindrical metal containers, so he tried stretching his fingers in the hope that they'd move in any direction. But they remained forced together, even as the shackles groaned against his effort.

His eyes traveled past the harness gripping his waist, and though he couldn't see it, he knew a second harness held his ankles parallel to his knees. The panic he'd felt when he awakened returned.

He examined the room with haste. It was dim and empty. Thick metal made up the floor and a ceiling too low, while thicker metal wrapped around the tight interior, forming the walls. His stomach squirmed at the sight of the closed, bolted door. It was the type of door one might find in a prison.

He rocked forward, eyes squeezed shut.

If he was in an Evolutionary Federal Detention prison, there was no telling what sort of harm would come to him next.

"Cynque, where am I?" he asked, his voice hoarse.

Tick, Tick, Tick, the device beeped, searching the inter-web for his answers. "Location not found. You are not linked to the Cynque Global Network at this time."

My Cynque's not linked? he thought, concerned. Cynque was always linked no matter where you were.

"Any records of where I was last?" he asked.

"Unfortunately, Allister, your last recorded location was manually deleted at seven hours and forty-five minutes to Day 214."

"Deleted... What the...?" He struggled against the chains again, flexing harder as he attempted to lean away from the wall. "Hello?" he shouted louder, his voice rising into hysterics. "You know if I can stop a truck, I can break these chains, maybe...just give me...a minute..."

More than a minute had passed with no significant movement in the chains. He'd been counting and was well over one hundred seconds before air released between the door's hinges. It slowly opened, creaking as it moved, allowing halogen bulbs to give the space harsh light and perspective. The prison interior lived up to Allister's expectations: it was dismal, patternless, and filled with flitting dust particles.

The light chased the shadows away from the strapping man who entered. Allister glimpsed a clean-shaven face decorated with strong, angled lines, though it was hard to tell if they were from stress or from age. The man wore a devious grin and wrinkles at the edges of his eyes, and his pointed nose seemed to have grown too long, as if he'd spent his entire life lying.

"Goin' out on a limb here and guessin' you don't know where you are?" the man asked.

Allister thought it was a stupid thing to say to someone who'd just been kidnapped. He raised his chin, his teeth gritting. "Sorry to let you down...Mr. Whoever You Are...sir—"

"Captain."

The so-called captain smiled wider and bowed ever so slightly.

"Sure, okay...Captain, sir—I don't...I don't know where I am, somehow not cynqued up to the CGN." As Allister spoke, he kept trying to twist his way out of the harness. "I thought cutting someone off from the CGN was illegal."

The man dismissed the idea with a wave of his hand. "Not here."

Allister stopped. Shocked, he jerked his neck back in a swift motion just as the chains snapped him back to the wall.

The man walked around the room casually, his back straight, no single step too far or too long from the one before it or the one that followed.

"I need"—the word *need* sliced through his teeth, sharp and intentional—"you to think hard about where you might be."

Allister swallowed and thought back on Day 215, the last day he remembered…then came back to the man's grimace. Even without the oversized hat, the crisp red suit and golden-armored chest plate gave him away.

"You're from Evolutionary Federal Detention!" Allister gasped. "You were there, right after—"

"You saved all of them innocent people?" the man finished.

"Saved all them…" He paused. "You're not gonna finish me?"

"Didn't even give it a thought."

Allister squinted at him, a bit skeptical. "If you don't want me finished, what gives?"

"You said you wanted to help beat the apocalypse," he replied. "I figure I give you the chance."

His mom's warning crawled its way into his thoughts. *I don't want either of them to find you, the Andromeda Project or C20, you hear me?*

"I take it you've been snooping around my neighborhood, listening in on me."

"We got 214 days left. We're snoopin' around and listenin' in on everybody."

"We?"

The captain produced an identical copy of the square card Allister had found in the box on his porch. It was as he held it up that the light caught the medals that adorned the captain's red jacket's rich color, and a logo dressed in gold: an *A* and a *P* conjoined on one line.

"The Andromeda Project," Allister whispered.

"Name's J. Brandt, Captain Brandt to you, of course."

The name *Brandt* rolled over Allister's tongue. He recognized the drawl injected in the captain's words. He recognized the aroma of fresh timber. And he couldn't begin to dig up the reason why this stranger's presence didn't feel strange, didn't feel as dangerous as he was sure it ought to feel. There was another word that wanted to replace *captain*—not a designation, but something more *familial*.

"Captain…Brandt. Are you…an Evolutionary?"

Captain Brandt scratched his head. "So they say. I've got the same offbeat genetic makeup you do, so I guess if that makes me something other than human…" He shrugged.

"Time's up, Captain!" someone yelled from down the hall.

"I need five more! Ease up off my hind parts, Gattison!" Brandt yelled back. He waved the square card in the air and tossed it at Allister's shackled feet. "Listen, son, I'll keep it simple: Your strength and regeneration and whatever other surprises you got ain't nothing but trouble for you outside these walls. Trust me, I know. If you're serious about doing something good for humanity while there's still time, this is the place to do it. Best of all, you don't gotta hide your potentials anymore."

"Allister Adams...the good Evolutionary," Allister said. "This is too mega to be real...like...there's gotta be a hang-up." He fidgeted in the waist harness, uncomfortable with more than just his restriction. "Gotta be a hang-up somewhere..."

"No hang-ups. No trickery. Everything's fine," Captain Brandt replied.

"Everything's not fine. This"—he tried lifting his wrists above his chest—"doesn't make me feel safe." The chains dragged his arms back to the wall.

Captain Brandt's expression darkened. Whatever mission, whatever intention had been programmed into his subconscious, seemed to return to his mind and ran the ease right out of him. "Not about safe. Not about comfort. It's about duty. It's about preservation," the captain said. "You sign on the dotted line, I tell you everything you want to know. Maybe some things you didn't want to know, too."

"Everything?"

"Everything." Captain Brandt resumed his pacing. Between his heavy exhales and the aggressive rubbing of his chin, the captain appeared torn up about this ambiguous *everything*. "What made you chase down that truck and jump in front of it?" he finally asked.

"I mean, there were people in danger. I had to."

"You expect me to believe in twelve-somethin' years, you ain't never seen anybody in danger and done jack about it? Gimme a break, Allister."

"I do my part, always." Allister paused, then swallowed to keep his voice steady. "Just not with my potentials. But, I peeped that truck, and...I swore I was fast enough to get to it. Stopping it, though? Hmph, I didn't know I had that sort of strength potential. Guess I was triggered."

"So you tried anyway," Captain Brandt said.

"Yeah, I tried."

"And you succeeded, because, deep down, you wanted to."

Allister nodded. He glanced at the captain as he continued shifting his shoulders under the chains. "Bet the whole District thinks I'm a blasted terrorist."

"I can promise ya if they do, they won't for long." Captain Brandt cleared his throat, straightened, and took a seat next to Allister on the long bench. "Deal is, I'm not authorized to tell you nothin' until you sign the offer."

The cell went quiet after that. They watched each other, the dust twirling between them in a dance that had been kicked off by the captain's earlier methodic pacing. Allister thought about what the captain had just said, the word *offer*, and what it would be like to work for the Andromeda Project. Would he be the Evolutionary on the front lines like his mom was afraid of? He wondered if he was afraid of that, too, or excited by it, without even knowing what it meant yet.

"Let me see the offer, then?"

"I'll show ya, but I caution you, this ain't the kind of offer you walk away from."

Discomfort took the cooperation out of Allister's voice. "Let me see it."

"Cynque, access the Andromeda Project onboarding contract," Captain Brandt said.

Above the captain's wrist, a holographic term sheet appeared, embedded with the words *The Andromeda Project* in big, bold letters.

Allister read through it.

The assignment details were vague, but it was worth three hundred thousand Quincyn Bourdeaux cryptocurrency coins—the digital currency that now dominated the world's fragile financial market the way Cynque dominated the world. It was too many QBs for one person—heck, too many QBs for two. That amount of coin would pay off his and his mom's flat in full and leave them more than two hundred days' worth left over.

Allister's heart skipped with excitement. "Snap, this pays QBs?"

"Sure does. Guess I forgot how big a deal that is." Captain Brandt laughed half-heartedly. "You Omega gen kids and your slang, I swear."

His mom had said the same exact words to him many a time, even in the same Southern twang, though in a higher pitch and without any laughter. Allister could feel the connection forming between himself and the captain, and by the looks of it, the new bond seemed to have latched on and pulled the man free from his hardened exterior.

But which one of his acts was real? This jovial mentor-like figure, or the captain at war with the apocalypse?

Captain Brandt let out another deep breath, moving his Cynque so it was level with his mouth. "Cynque, initiate release, prisoner Allister Adams, authorization code"—he paused to test a set of numbers on his lips, then said with impeccable speed—"1121291920518."

The shackles clicked, unlatched, and clattered to the floor. The chains loosened soon after and slid down Allister's arms until they were settled over his lap and the bench.

He stayed completely still, feeling as though he'd stepped into a trap. Freedom, or the illusion of it, felt too good to be true.

"What are you—Why?" he stammered.

"Cuz I have a feelin' you want this more than you're lettin' on. You don't really got a choice, you know? Sometimes it's nice to think you do."

So it was a trap.

Allister drew his eyes to the open door and the darkness beyond it. He stretched his fingers and his legs, began massaging his wrists. He had a clear path to escape. To what end? He couldn't even try to guess.

But Captain Brandt knew that, just as he must've known Allister was stronger, possibly faster, than him, and still, he sat casually to one side instead of blocking the entrance.

The captain gave him a knowing look. "Whenever you're ready, son"—he moved the projected contract close enough to be scanned—"just scan right here at the bottom."

Allister reached for the hologram and asked, "No hang-ups?"

"None that'll be any trouble for you."

Allister scrolled up to skim the wage amount, nodded in confirmation, then skipped down to where he was meant to scan his digital signature. He figured, if nothing else, his mom could use the QBs. Maybe she'd forgive him for going against her overprotective rules if the flat didn't have any more payments *and* they somehow managed to stop the end.

Unless he was making a mistake. Unless there was something about his dad and the Andromeda Project that he didn't know. His mind was stuck between fear and obligation and excitement at being chosen, just as his arm was stuck in midair.

But his excitement remained the guiding force, pushing his wrist to connect to the tiny, flashing cube with the unique maze pattern. Beaming lines of laser light linked the three-dimensional box to his Cynque, transcribing and matching his digital imprint.

"Confirmation received. Allister Adams, accepted."

Allister Adams, accepted. A sentence he'd been waiting to hear his whole life.

Cynque continued. "Updated occupation: field agent, the Andromeda Project. Updated status: employed. Updated clearance level: probationary, level four. Updated reference name: Private Adams."

Allister scratched at his braids, embarrassed by his own disappointment. "Private? Can I pick somethin' a little more my vibe?"

"This ain't a super-hero academy, son. This is a highly classified security employment assignment." Despite the harshness in his voice, Captain Brandt started smirking all of a sudden. "And, maybe, if this whole plan don't go up in flames, one day we'll be calling *you* Captain Adams."

"I'm with it." And Allister was. Though there was more on his mind. He really wanted to ask whether the assignment had to do with what his dad had been looking for: *the Crystals of Temporal Transportation...Daal Trelkkien.* "Uh...so...the apocalypse...you have a plan to stop it?" he asked instead.

"The plan ain't to stop the apocalypse before it hits... The plan"—Captain Brandt placed both hands on Allister's shoulders—"is to escape it."

———

CHAPTER 6

LIEUTENANT LEESA DELEMAR

Quadrant Alpha—Executive Wing, Andromeda Project Headquarters
Day 214

LIEUTENANT LEESA DELEMAR woke from a daze with a fierce grip on her wrist, numb from the news. C20 had successfully attacked the District *again*.

The man driving the truck couldn't talk after being brought in. Somehow his mind had been reduced to mush while in transit from capture to imprisonment. She hoped his mental incapacity didn't signal C20's recruitment of new Evolutionaries, or worse, the resurrection of the old ones.

A shiver ran through her shoulders.

Keep yourself together, she instructed herself harshly. *XBA's dead, I saw her...in pieces...*

That day, Day 214, she faced a direction she rarely faced, looking toward the glass divider separating her hexagon-shaped room down the middle. Beyond it was the area she loathed—her designated living space—and the things she loathed along with it: the standard-issue queen mattress with a generic headboard, regular civilian clothing from her late teens, the digital photo album of her childhood stuck on the bedrest.

Some would say she rose to her greatest potential.

Potential. It was how she walked, how she flew, how she moved objects with a flick of her wrist or a swipe of her hand, sometimes with just the squint of her eye. If she wasn't so careful, so in control, the glass she faced might shatter.

But it didn't. Nor did she, thinking of what it had taken for her to be there, at the Andromeda Project, or what it meant that C20 was still active.

She ignored a file transfer begging for review on her Cynque, which notified her with repeated beeps and the occasional vibration. After another vocal prompt in that heinous, digital voice, she rotated her chair to face the desk again.

The office's once-blue walls around her had been slathered in gray at her request. It minimized the fluorescent glare caused by energy-saving bulbs. Leesa hated bright things—colors, light, and personalities alike. She liked to keep it simple. And for that reason, just her lonely interactive glass desk and high-backed fabric chair occupied the almost bare office space. The case where she kept her cape was by the door so she'd never forget to put it on before she left the room.

She loved when the dark-purple fabric was fastened around her neck. It was the one thing her father had ever given her, and she felt safer with it on. Her uniform, however, she took off only to change into one of the seven identical others.

"File transfer complete, would you like to review now?" Cynque asked proactively for the fifth time.

Leesa couldn't stand how impatient technology had become.

Pursing her lips with contempt, she pried her fingers from her wrist and flicked them across the expanded holographic surface of her device. The jumbled images in the digital square shot onto her flattened wall-to-wall monitor.

"Allister Adams," Cynque announced. "Classification, undocumented Evolutionary with notable energy potential."

"What kind of energy potential?"

"Z-energy potential," Cynque continued, reading out definitions Leesa already knew. "When potential is met, wavelength frequencies recorded are similar to ionizing radiations on the electromagnetic spectrum."

"They're trying to replace me," she said, suspicious, her voice as chilly as the room. An expected move by the resident veteran and know-it-all, Captain Brandt. To source someone to posture as a more malleable solution to their EOW problem. "And…how many Z-energy readings were picked up from the greater District?"

"Nine, Lieutenant Delemar, starting from 223 days 'til zero and ending 215 days 'til zero. The previous eight readings were categorized as manifestations, with the last one categorized as a mixture of explosive and projectile."

"I hear untrained and dangerous. What about the mother"—Leesa smoothed her hair back, making sure it was still straightened and perfectly in place—"Dolores? She must be one, too? Any potential, no matter how…insignificant…is linked to some genetic abnormality."

"Subject Dolores Adams has numerous genetic tests on record, all run after extreme fatigue, disorientation, and temporary loss of consciousness. All results returned clean with no anomalous genes present."

"So, it's possible this Allister Adams has a weakness—half the genes, half the access to his potentials."

"To be confirmed," Cynque stated. "Subject Allister Adams has no genetic tests on record. Potentials are assumed based on observed behavior."

"Based on observed..." She wrinkled her forehead, skeptical of the network's assertions.

The profile picture that stared back at her was of a boy in his early teens. He had long, kinked hair, an awkward smile, and poor posture. Despite it being an old picture, his potentials couldn't be denied. An updated image of him in action showed a lean frame shredded down to just muscle, the skin pulled so tight there wouldn't be a place on him to pinch. In the photo, he was pushing against the speeding truck, his arm muscles flexed, a large, capable hand flattened against dented metal, and his legs—built for speed *and* power—digging into the street.

Her body went stiff, a subtle rejection of the heat rising to her pores. She fanned it away, uncomfortable with how the image made her skin tingle and her stomach flutter.

"Looks like all he knows how to do is stand in front of moving vehicles and nearly die trying to stop them," she said to herself, checking her forehead for sweat, then her hairline for the slightest curl. "He's clearly inadequate, and holds little to no merit as the Gateway."

"A little green perhaps, but I think he's charming, and quite fetching up close," a woman said in a grating accent.

Leesa's body went cold at the sound of the woman's voice. She twisted her head to eye the new arrival in the entryway, going from frustrated to livid at the sight of her—both at her clothes and at her interruption. Granted, the woman's outfit, which consisted of a lightweight, bulletproof top and loose bottoms sewn together at a cinched waist, was state-of-the-art protective gear for someone of her stature. At the same time, it was hardly regulation attire for the Andromeda Project.

"I wager he'd punch his way to our so-called Crystals of Transportation and not use a proper entrance," the woman continued.

The woman was Dr. Florence Belladonna. She'd been inserted months ago by the Andromeda Project's directors to keep an eye on things. Some high-riding political claiming to be a doctor. Leesa had her own beliefs about Dr. Belladonna, mostly that the woman thought too highly of herself and didn't really bring much to the organization.

"*Buongiorno.* I knocked multiple times; you obviously didn't hear me," Dr. Belladonna said. "It's urgent."

Leesa clenched her jaw. "Next time, wait until I give you permission."

Dr. Belladonna smiled as if her words didn't matter. "*Certo*, of course, Lieutenant...I'd like to discuss the test results of Bridget Sparks, the recruit I reviewed on Day 217."

"I had her removed from the batch. She's a waste of everyone's time and this organization's resources. She doesn't have the energy signature we're looking for."

"C20 is resurfacing in more territories with each sunrise," the doctor replied coldly.

"That might be so," Leesa said, "but we have no proof Evolutionaries were responsible for this attack. The man you picked up was human. The more EVs we keep alive, the more EVs C20 can corrupt."

"The man I picked up was an Evolutionary with the potential to manipulate machines." Dr. Belladonna drew her finger along her chin knowingly. "Besides, if you'd read my report you would've seen that I do have proof. Visual proof, in fact. The Density Twins were seen in the vicinity just before the attack."

"The Density Twins joined C20? Even after...EFD's termination?"

"I imagine they joined *because* of it. Hard to scramble the molecules of two EVs that can shift their density, don't you think?" She straightened her mouth, serious again. "At 214 days out, we don't have the luxury of being selective. We will need to deploy counter-units when they strike next, and while Ms. Sparks is rather unhinged, would you really kill off someone with the potential to manipulate electromagnetic fields?" She left ample space for Leesa's rebuttal before continuing. "I ran the analysis, I weighed our options, and I am requesting you reconsider your decision."

Leesa scrunched her lips, troubled by all that had come at her in such a short amount of time. Tranjam and Vonnie Kim, the Density Twins, had survived the Evolutionary Federal Detention's termination chambers. Allister Adams was being positioned as her replacement to find the artifacts. And the Andromeda Project's saving grace against C20 had arrived in the form of a homicidal stripper. Realities hard enough to swallow without the woman above her forcing them down her throat. She went to answer, a simple *no* waiting between her teeth.

But Dr. Belladonna tilted her chin and raised an eyebrow, daring Leesa to refuse. She had been pushing Leesa's boundaries since she stepped through the door two hundred days past, injecting herself when it came to handling their

Evolutionary training, intake, and termination—three departments Leesa oversaw with *precision*.

Leesa moved to the edge of her chair, agitation needling through her body. "You think you can come in here with the blessing of our directors and act like I haven't been building this organization from its inception."

"This organization is older than you are." Dr. Belladonna took a threatening step closer and flattened her fingertips on the desk. "I think the ice you're skating on is thinner than Alaska's permafrost. Especially with those twins running loose." She then leaned over to finish. "I think you should do whatever you need to do to make sure we find those artifacts and save the bloody human race. *Capisci?*"

"Understand?" Leesa repeated back at the doctor. She felt as though she would burst, her pulse rising, blood sailing through her veins with anger at the helm. Her legs tensed to stand. Her hands gripped the sides of the desk, which shivered beneath her palms while the chair rattled beneath her body. That woman couldn't know the danger she was in. Standing that close, stabbing at Leesa's insecurities with a sharp tongue and serrated words.

"You'll reconsider, then," Dr. Belladonna said—a statement, not a question. A red flash flickered in both eyes. She snapped her fingers.

It was as if the emotional dial inside Leesa had been turned down. Her pulse and blood flow slowed. Her legs relaxed. The desk and chair stilled.

"I'll have my formal recommendations to present before I retire this evening," Dr. Belladonna said as she began to walk away. "I really do appreciate your faith in my strategies."

"Let's call it considerable intrigue." Leesa settled back into her seat, a search for authority in her body for her next words. "I am certain you were issued a standard uniform to wear during operating hours."

Glancing back, Dr. Belladonna replied, "Yes, Lieutenant. That ghastly-looking thing is a little tight around the hips. I'll send for one more suited for my figure. *Ciao, ciao.*"

Leesa kept her eyes on the empty entryway, fuming at her inability to respond how she'd wanted. The proclaimed "psychiatrist" had friends in very high places and made sure everyone knew it as often as she could. If it weren't for that, Leesa might've hurled her through the glass divider, or at least restricted the doctor's airflow until she submitted.

Still, Leesa's frustration had all but *disappeared*. Dr. Belladonna's telepathic potential was a more likely explanation than her own restraint.

"Lieutenant," Cynque said, "General Delemar has requested your presence immediately."

The notification returned her focus to the screen.

"Tell him I'll be right there."

Leesa rose from her chair, her mind zipping back to this new Evolutionary, Allister, with Z-energy potential. "Roll footage from the C20 attack on Day 215."

Cynque obeyed. The clip started with Allister's figure at a full sprint, almost a blur moving through the streets. She stood right up against the monitor and studied him from the invasive distance, clocking the time stamp when he tripped in front of the truck, noting his arm movements and foot positioning when he charged toward it. It had taken effort for him to stop the vehicle, but not all of his effort. He was tired, but not out of commission. He was hurt, but not beyond repair.

So what if he was resilient? The Z-energy potential Cynque had mentioned was nowhere to be seen and that's what they needed most. She swiped away the footage.

"I suppose I will leave it up to the assessment to determine his worth, if there is any," she said.

Either way, Allister couldn't be worth more to the Andromeda Project than her. Not considering her years of dedication, how she'd sacrificed her young adult-hood for their agenda, surrendered her immense power to their unquestioned command. After Captain Brandt, she was next to lead the Andromeda Project.

And she'd find a way around the captain anyway.

She deserved it.

"Lieutenant...," Cynque began cautiously.

A sharp pain pierced her temple, a sign her telekinetic potential was clawing for freedom.

The monitor rattled within the wall.

"Another alert from your—"

Leesa interrupted. "Thank you, Cynque," she said, her hands tight around the monitor. The cape seemed to hug her tighter around her shoulders as she wrestled control of her telekinetic outburst. The rattling stopped.

She let her stress escape through her words instead, addressing the device with terse, short sentences. "Tell him. I'll be. Right. There."

Leesa smoothed her hair on both sides and adjusted her uniform, afraid something had fallen out of place, then exited the room in quick strides.

Director's Correspondence Auditorium (DCA), Andromeda Project Headquarters

LEESA FOUND HERSELF on the verge of a rare smile, relishing in the fact that she'd replaced Captain Brandt there, steps behind her father, in the most important room in the world.

Well, in what was left of the world.

Lights above ran in parallel rows, buzzing as they emitted low illumination inside the director's correspondence auditorium—or DCA, as it was known.

Leesa had the honor of joining her father daily in the DCA because Captain Brandt had proven he couldn't keep his mouth shut. She wasn't surprised at the reports, the captain was known for his temper, his self-righteous speeches, and affected immunity. He went around boasting that he'd helped "found the organization," and therefore, "couldn't be terminated."

So there she stood in front of seven towering screens, her eyes bouncing between them as the Andromeda Project's overbearing benefactors grilled them from various parts of the ravaged globe.

Republic of Brasilia. Korea Stronghold. Rossiya Seyf. Yoruba Sanctuary. Londinium Floating Isles. The People's Refuge of China. And, of course, the United Sanctuaries of America.

A cohort of the last-standing economically intact nations, joined together to solve the world's problems in secret, starting with the apocalypse. She didn't know much about the set of circumstances that formed their board, but the arrangement was clear.

When they spoke, everyone listened.

There were no faces. There were no names. The screens were lined up side by side, projecting only misty silhouettes and distorted voices of each location's director, which made them barely distinguishable from one another. During her first few briefings, Leesa had trained herself to hone in on the hard-to-find space between glitches, where hints of their true voices waited. Every time this happened, she'd analyze them, giving her the rare gift of knowing who was speaking when.

The director from Rossiya Seyf, formerly Russia, was speaking from the farthest screen to the left but seemed to only be addressing her father. "It is still a wonder to me how you convinced us that the Andromeda Project did not need the alien, Neight Caster—your supposed friend and ally—to achieve this mission. Yet, from what we're witnessing, you've still made no progress since his disappearance. My president has come to me following each lost day about the people freezing to death in their sleep. Our body count is reaching the millions."

Feeling herself slouching, Leesa stood up straighter. The directors had been known to scold for everything from posture to attentiveness.

"The organization's progress has become increasingly stagnant," the director of the Korean Stronghold added from the middle screen. "We're getting nervous about the viability of this endeavor, General Delemar."

Another comment directed at him and not *them*. Numerous briefings later and still no one paid her any attention. Suddenly, it felt less like an honor and more like a tiny razor digging cuts slowly across her ribs—torturous and acutely painful. But after a moment of frustration, she realized that perhaps her father's experience of it was even worse. She watched his shoulders sink with each judgment, then sink deeper when he tried to answer and got shut down.

Perhaps it was about more than being acknowledged. It was about being listened to. Respected. At that realization, she dipped her chin, swallowing the urge to speak out in his defense.

The Korean director continued. "Our scientists say rising waters predicted on Korea's southern shore will sink the capital in less than twenty-five days. We have already lost sixty percent of our land, and you have said nothing that can ease our uncertainty."

"I understand that you're not feeling particularly confident in our recent strides," her father said. He folded his arms behind him and added a bit of boast to his voice. "But per Professor Ashur's theory, we are investigating Allister Adams. We were able to bring him in without incident."

Leesa's heart picked up its pace. *To replace me,* she thought.

"Splendid update, General," the Londinium director said, though Leesa couldn't figure out from where. "It's good to see our QBs weren't a total waste on you and your team."

"And does he have the capacity for the energy potential we need?" the Rossiyan director asked. "Or is he a waste of time like the others?"

Leesa pushed her fingers tightly against her thighs, annoyed. *Of course he's a waste of time. He's got a fraction of the energy potential I have,* she thought, exhaling too loudly.

Her father looked back at her, face tight with disappointment, then returned his focus to the screens. "Our best guess is yes, but we will know for sure after the assessment. In addition to that, I have scheduled a soft introduction with him. I want to rule out possibilities that he might've joined for…ulterior motives."

"A soft introduction is not part of our intake process. We prefer that you consult us before making those decisions," the Chinese director snapped. "You've continued to operate under an absolute authority that has not been granted, while I hear there are hundreds of millions waiting in our streets for rations of water and imports."

At least you have hundreds of millions left.

Leesa was becoming sullen, impatient, unable to keep herself together. The painful tingling of rogue telekinetic potential shot down her forearms.

The light above her blinked off, then back on.

Her father looked up at it, but this time he didn't look back at her. He didn't need to. He knew what it was, and so did she.

Keep yourself together, she thought to herself, stuffing her potential back down.

"With all due respect, getting humanity off the planet is my priority," her father said. "Allister Adams could already be compromised by C20 and been sent here to—"

"I am curious, General," the Rossiyan director interjected. "With the world in disarray, what is the source of your impudence?"

"It sounds like General Delemar is taking a necessary precaution," Leesa said, blatantly out of turn. She was a breath away from triggering her potential again, so she kept her words stiff and her body stiffer. "As you know, intention, rigor, and experience have profound effects on an Evolutionary's potentials. We just… we just want to make sure this recruit's intention is aligned and he is prepared to do whatever it takes to succeed."

"Is that not your job, Lieutenant?" the Rossiyan director asked.

The heat of embarrassment warmed her ears. "Partially, yes."

"We have 214 days left, and you're suggesting General Delemar and Private Adams have a chat?" the Chinese director scoffed from her right. "With proper direction, our motivation will become his motivation. I trust you can handle that at least."

"Private Adams will do what needs to be done," the director of Yoruba Sanctuary added, commanding enough to bring the discussion to a close. Though Leesa couldn't see their eyes, she felt them pierce her as they said, "And you will ensure he does so, or you will terminate him. It is why we have kept you alive in light of your catastrophic missteps."

Their accusation drilled guilt through her gut, which she disguised with a forced bow of respect. "Understood, and thank you for your mercy," she said.

She cursed the heat now making its way to her cheeks, knowing the flushed skin would show up under the harsh light.

"Our mercy lasts only until the crystal artifacts are retrieved," the Londinium director said to her.

Leesa stayed slightly bent, her eyes lifting and narrowing at the screen from which the Londinium director spoke. Second in from the left. She didn't handle threats well no matter who they came from. Unlike with Dr. Belladonna, there'd be no telepathic switch to calm the rage building her.

"Lieutenant, do keep yourself together," her father said over his shoulder. His words were soft like leather, but cracked like a whip. She snapped back into her upright posture, her focus shifted to honorable presentation.

He stepped farther ahead of her and turned to each individual screen to acknowledge the director hidden on the other end.

"My apologies for the interruption," he said. "I assure you, it was not representative of the lieutenant's behavior, simply a measure of her passion." He straightened his shoulders for effect. "I have just received word that Professor Ashur is close to pinpointing the exact location and operating capacity of the TEWR on the West Coast. I strongly advise we move forward with approvals on a retrieval mission."

The directors spoke in distorted language among themselves, some of it sounded combative, some more diplomatic.

Leesa listened closely, waiting to hear who spoke next, wondering if they would agree with her father, or disagree. They hadn't heard from the Republic of Brasilia or the United Sanctuaries.

"Not granted," the Rossiyan director finally said.

Her father took another step toward the screens. "This machine…is…one of a kind," he stammered.

"You don't even know how it works, and government legislation has prohibited travel across the Divide, even for military…" The United Sanctuaries director seemed to catch themselves, then added, "Or…so we've been reminded. I'm requesting allocated resources, but don't have a sight line into the extraction options if anything were to go wrong. Your team would be at the mercy of whatever's out there."

"We propose to reconvene at six hours 'til Day 213," the director of Yoruba Sanctuary said. "Have alternative solutions prepared."

"Of course," her father responded in an almost whisper.

"A word of caution, you might worry less about your enemy, and more about the prize," the Rossiyan director said. "You're both dismissed."

Worry less about your enemy…, she thought. Though she was confident in her ability to defeat anyone C20 threw at her, the artifacts were the prize.

Her prize.

The light retracted from the corners of their respective screens until they faded to a dull gray.

Her father turned slowly to face her as she braced herself for his punishment. He could just as easily raise his voice and cut her down with insults as he could keep his solemn expression and wound her deeper with silence.

"I can defend myself," he finally said, deflated. "You are here to observe, and to protect me should someone try to interfere with the organization's private dealings." He walked toward the exit without looking at her. "Come, Lieutenant."

Leesa followed, her head down, stewing in disappointment. Part of her longed for his unapologetic wrath. It always felt like love.

"I want to know where we stand with Private Allister Adams, and I want to be ready in the event C20 strikes," he said when they reached the door.

"Yes, General. I am aligned."

"Good." Her father waved his Cynque over a seam in the wall, then said quietly, "Tell Captain Brandt the assessment happens now."

CHAPTER 7

ALLISTER ADAMS
Quadrant Beta—Ops and Infosystems, Andromeda Project Headquarters Day 214

ALLISTER HAD OVERHEARD that he was being taken to meet someone known as simply "The Lieutenant."

He, Captain Brandt, and four armed soldiers exited the elevator. Behind them, past a security checkpoint, Allister glimpsed a monstrous foyer. An elaborate sculpture hung in the center. Squiggled lines made of something light and bendable like aluminum or chrome were attached to each other and the ceiling by small metal rods. Spinning slowly inside the abstract shapes was a giant purple sphere with a *U* on it—a strange letter to choose, in his opinion, when maybe it should've been the *AP* logo. All things considered, it had the appearance of an entryway, but Allister guessed it was for show. He had major doubts that anyone came in or left through the four sets of sliding doors just beyond the art.

The checkpoints weren't even patrolled.

He saw a countdown clock and squinted at it for the time.

214 days left.

One of the soldiers directed Allister forward with a shove. "Keep moving. That's why you got Cynque," they said.

Allister was annoyed by the soldier's aggression, but kept moving, as commanded.

The soldier continued as they walked. "Back here, we don't keep time. We just make the most of each second, and for clock's sake, hope we'll all be a'ight."

"Now that we got this one, we'll be golden," Captain Brandt said with a smile, a bit of pride in his step.

Allister blushed.

The six of them stepped into a tight hallway lit up by thin strips of hot-white light. They were arranged artistically: some as rectangles on the walls, some as triangles on the floor and ceiling. But no matter the shape, the illuminated arrangements continued down the hall until they split off in three directions, as if each new pathway were a shimmering portal to somewhere else, and at the end, someone got to choose what realm they went to.

He happened to like the design but pretended to be extra interested in it while counting the lights, making note of how many they passed on their way.

As they reached the three diverging hallways, Captain Brandt nodded right. "Hard left," he said.

They pivoted accordingly.

Nice trick, Allister thought, assuming it was meant to confuse him.

While they rounded a corner, he got a second look at his escorts.

The soldiers were a four-person, tight-lipped unit, each of them as androgynous as any Alpha gen, wearing chrome two-piece uniforms with the Andromeda Project logo across the chest and marching shoulder to shoulder with nearly soundless steps.

And in perfect contrast, Allister swung his arms casually, his shoes squeaking against the floor, carrying him deeper into that maze of a headquarters. The glamour of the modern office building eased into the harshness of a stone and metal fortress. The once-playful arrangement of lights became more serious, more structured. They no longer connected across the floor or the ceiling. They stood straight up and down like soldiers, a set of them spaced a few feet apart on either side. The hallway split again.

"Hard left," Captain Brandt said, nodding to the right again.

Suddenly, the logic of the captain's head motions clicked for Allister. He was being given directions.

Two rights, Allister thought, keeping himself oriented with the layout. *Golden of him to look out.*

They traveled the hallway's expanse. Here, all design choices had been driven by simplicity. There was only concrete, dull steel doors, and the occasional glass window. Metal piping was arranged over them in an unsolvable, monochromatic maze. Single bulb floor lights lit the walls, which had the flags of seven different sanctuaries painted on them side by side. Underneath them, the Andromeda Project logo, an obvious symbol of unification and hope, was stamped in even increments.

Allister slowed to identify the flags, and was curious to find that over the past twelve years, he'd lived in six of the seven locations.

Mega lineup, he thought, unsure how they were all involved.

"Walk faster," the lead soldier said. They poked him with their weapon, a triple-barrel plasma gun the size of an adult canine. Allister noticed the power output was set to "vaporize." He wondered if it would work on him.

"You sure you want me to go faster?" Allister said, taking a double step. "I can go *a lot* faster if you want."

"Give us a min, will ya?" Captain Brandt said.

The soldiers dropped back a few steps, still following, though out of earshot. The captain matched Allister's rather unhurried strides and stuck close.

"Boy, your mouth is as slick as your mama's, I swear," he said in a hushed voice.

"You know my...mom? How?" Allister asked. Then, slower, the thought ran its second lap. He raised his eyebrows. If Captain Brandt knew who his mom was, he probably knew where his mom was. At all times.

"I knew Sweet Dee and Patty Cakes way before all this mess took our lives for a whirl..."

Sweet Dee and *Patty Cakes*? Were those his parents' nicknames? Allister would've asked for confirmation until the captain's brow furrowed. The look in his eyes was unresolved, his mouth still in mourning.

"We grew up together in Cumberland Falls," Captain Brandt finished discreetly. "Back where you were born."

"My mom never talks about Cumberland," Allister replied. "Pretends like we never had roots there. Acts like...like it was straight-up fiction."

"If I didn't know better, I'd think you wanted me to tell you more."

"Maybe." Allister rubbed the back of his neck and shrugged slowly. "Maybe not."

"Ya know it takes a strong person to admit when they're not ready. Long as, once they figure it out, they start gettin' ready real quick."

Allister bit down on his lip.

"You're nervous."

"I just want to know I'm doing the right thing," he said.

Captain Brandt used his Cynque to bring a digital projection to life and held out his wrist.

In the picture, four smiling people in identical uniforms stood in a line, their arms relaxed around the shoulders of the person next to them. His dad, the captain, a rugged-faced Latinx man with a patchwork of stubble, and a beautiful woman with melanin-kissed skin, exotic features, and kinky blonde hair. The background was a courtyard of a building entrance, on which the Andromeda Project logo was mounted.

"Our first real mission," Captain Brandt said. "We were so excited."

Allister wanted to know who the other two people were. He recognized them from the digital commercial he had seen. "Who are they?" he asked, pointing at them in turn.

"That's General Delemar. You gotta deal with him at some point. That's... Naorima. She...uh...she didn't make it."

The image shrunk back into the Cynque and eventually vanished from the screen.

"I'm sorry," Allister said.

Captain Brandt frowned deeply. "Nothing to be sorry about. She chose to save us." He tried to smile then. "2035, my goodness. Seems like we hit a different timeline after the West Coast Killer."

Allister remembered the West Coast Killer. An Earth-shattering slip on the Pacific plate that all but uprooted California and set the apocalypse in motion.

He rubbed his bare arm as he sifted through the underground theories around what had caused the slip—the idea that the magnetic poles had flipped was the most ridiculous, especially after he worked out the science. Perhaps the earthquake was just overdue. "Yeah, that was unreal, mega on a fresh level. I heard stories and stuff, but I was only two, so..."

The captain straightened up and glanced at the vaulted ceiling. "You were two. I remember that."

Allister gave the captain a sideways look, unsure what to make of the comment. Captain Brandt didn't lower his gaze. Or elaborate.

"I always thought we could jump back in time...ya know?" Allister said at last, his eyes still curious, and focused on the captain. "Put a permanent pause on the earthquake. Make sure my pops stayed alive so he and Mom could be happy... And we'd eventually catch up to now." He raised his voice into a theatric tone of valiance. "Good Evolutionaries keeping the world safe, and I'd get to be one of them."

"Imagination at its best." Captain Brandt patted Allister on the back. "The world we knew is gone, Allister. Erased. Best option for us is to survive however long we can and skip off this rock the moment we got the power to."

"With the Crystals of Temporal Transportation?"

Captain Brandt stopped walking and shot his arm across Allister's chest, stopping him short. "Dee tell you 'bout those?"

Allister swallowed. "No."

"Then who did?"

Fear knotted him up from inside. "Uhm…I don't—"

"Captain," the lead soldier interrupted, "the assessment has been moved up. The lieutenant is on her way and requested Private Adams be escorted the remaining distance alone."

"Soldier, I'll let Lieutenant Delemar know I like to hand off my recruits, make sure they properly get where they're meant to go. Thanks." Captain Brandt then paused to whisper to Allister, "We hash this out later."

The Andromeda Project's interior conditions took a turn sharper than the one ahead of them. Harsh light judged them from low ceilings of tarnished metal. Bare, dismal walls intersected at worn corners.

"Halt," the lead soldier commanded.

Allister swiveled around. "We're stopping…here?"

"If you run into any problems, they're yours to keep. Sir," the lead soldier said, saluting Captain Brandt.

The captain waved his hand and said something Allister was too busy lost in astonishment to hear.

The extravagant foyer, the lighting design in the hallways, the painted walls, even the roughness of his escort—it was now explained by the vision of a woman moving toward them. She was the queen of that disproportionately cared-for castle. Her emerald-green eyes hid between angry slits. Her pin-straight hair, which Allister hoped smelled of the chocolate it resembled, was wrapped up in three stacked buns like a gift set atop her head.

He wondered if her heart was beating as fast as his, and in the same thought, he suspected she was beyond human, even beyond Evolutionary. Maybe she didn't have a heart at all.

She was radiant—standing in thigh-high boots, an armored bodysuit, and gallant cape slung across her back.

He took an unconscious step in the woman's direction, his mouth open to speak, his hand ready to shake her hand. What Allister wouldn't give to command such presence. He was drawn to her in a way he'd been drawn to few others.

And then came the rapid-fire questions in his mind.

Who was this being—this powerhouse of an Evolutionary? This *lieutenant*? Could he learn from her? Would she be willing to teach him?

Allister was beyond eager to know the answers.

"Is she...my partner?" he asked too loud, too fast.

"Lieutenant," Captain Brandt said, sneering.

"Captain," the woman replied with a slow nod, never taking her eyes off of Allister.

Even in that single word, he picked up the hint of an accent, something exotic, possibly from one of the Latin Sanctuaries.

The captain moved toward her, swaggering step after swaggering step, the tension in his neck as apparent as the hatred between them.

Captain Brandt then gestured and said, "My recruit, Private Adams," before crossing his arms.

"Hi, I'm Allis—"

"I thought I made myself clear when I sent instructions with those fine soldiers," the lieutenant interrupted. She turned just her head toward the captain. "Am I mistaken?"

"Apparently so," Brandt answered.

Allister looked down, embarrassed, aware of himself for the first time. He was wearing the same dingy cardigan draped over his torso, still covered in the District's dirt and pollution. To her, he must've appeared disheveled and unstable. He probably smelled like dried blood and sweat too.

Captain Brandt gripped the edges of his shoulders with encouragement. "Use your potentials, Private Adams," he said. "You were built for this." At that, he turned on his heels and swept past the lieutenant, grumbling, "I'll leave you two to it. My work here's done."

"Bring your feet together and stand up straight," the lieutenant said to Allister once Brandt was gone.

Allister obeyed without thinking.

She circled him like a boa constrictor. And he puffed out his chest and flattened his arms against his sides, afraid to look directly at her lest she be tempted to squeeze.

The lieutenant rounded him a third time and stopped to address him, her chin level with his sternum. She was even taller than he'd originally thought. The hair styled on her head even taller than that. "Look at me," she commanded.

He snapped his head downward. "Yes…yes ma'am."

"I'm Lieutenant Delemar—" she began, speaking directly at his face. "And *lieutenant* always comes after yes and before my last name. I'm not your partner. I'm not your friend. I'm your superior, and you will respect me as such. Do I make myself absolutely, one thousand percent clear?"

CHAPTER 8

99

ALLISTER ADAMS
Quadrant Delta—Training Wing, Andromeda Project Headquarters
Day 214

Allister was in.

Inside the elusive organization whose logo had appeared on his doorstep and on his dad's clothing.

The accomplishment he could get into. The conditions he could not. Cracked walls of uneven concrete surrounded him, close enough to touch with both hands out. Metal wiring slithered its way up through deep groves and disappeared into the out-of-sight maze that was the hallway's ceiling. It seemed the room he waited in had once held the same glory as those first spaces, a glory that had long faded. Now, the color schemes were disrupted, the flags scratched away, and the Andromeda Project logo incomplete.

Lieutenant Delemar instructed him to wait in that tiny, undecorated box of a room, and as she left, promised him without a hint of emotion that the Andromeda Project's surveillance was omnipresent. The door then sealed and locked behind her.

He sat on a hard seat with no back, the sharp edges of a chest-height table digging into him. He was fired up inside, as hyped as he was restless, thumbs smashing together again and again as he let the smile he'd been holding in spread across his face.

His Cynque chirped.

He glanced down at it, vowing even that nuisance of an AI wouldn't take away his joy.

But his Cynque blinked bright, then chirped again—a sign it was rebooting, reconnecting.

The countdown popped up first. Green numbers glowing on a black backdrop. *0 years, 214 days, 8 hours, 5 minutes, and 42 seconds.*

A reminder that they'd lost another day.

He expected what came next to dampen his mood even more. The notifications—broadcasts of the latest natural disasters, the newest uprisings, the most recent wave of suicides.

And alongside that, the flood of messages from his mom.

After all, he'd broken his promise by not coming home. He shuddered to think what she'd done during the twenty-four hours that had ticked away.

His face fell. Guilt was the ash shoveled and dumped over his fiery joy.

But there was no subsequent chirp, or string of vibrations. There were no new broadcasts or new messages.

He raised an eyebrow at the device.

Really, Cynque? Nothing?

His very short contact list matrix projected from the device, attaching itself to the nearest solid surface for contrast. He scrolled to his mom's contact file. He knew she deserved to know where he was and that he was safe, even if she wouldn't approve of his decision.

Yet he couldn't understand why she hadn't messaged him. She *always* messaged him.

Maybe I'll hit her up later, once I get sorted, he thought. *No sense getting hyped if she's not.*

The more time passed, the angrier she'd be, he reasoned. He imagined her sulking in her chair, picking at her food, and staring at the place he was supposed to be sitting. Maybe she'd curse at the air. Maybe she'd keep quiet. Maybe she'd just move to another sanctuary and leave him behind.

His heels tapped the concrete as he moved his finger between the CONNECT TO VIDEO OPTION and SEND VIDEO OPTION, neither feeling appropriate for the news. *I'll spill what went down later, once I get sorted,* he thought again.

Holding up his hands, he searched for the excitement from moments ago. "Allister Adams—the good Evolutionary," he said with bass in his voice.

The holographic message from the box of keepsakes and its scripted delivery played between his ears, reminding him of the valiant mission to return the world to the glory it once was…although now he knew that the mission had changed. The goal was now to leave the Earth completely.

Beep, Beep. Beep.

"Reminder," Cynque announced after the alert sounded. "You have a reminder set to this location. Would you like me to open it?"

"What, Cynque? What're you talking about? Not right now."

"Allister, this reminder is marked urgent," the device said.

"I'm not with it," he snapped. He scanned the holding area for security surveillance embedded in the walls. "You trying to get me finished off, Cynque?"

"Override confirmed, retrieving reminder from Patrick Adams." A video hologram materialized on his palm. In its glowing square dimensions were the pronounced chin, thick eyebrows, and dreadlocked hair that belonged to his dad.

Allister fell silent. His eyes scanned up and down the image, looking for similarities and differences. The hair Allister had played with as a child was tucked behind his dad's square head. The wide grin he'd seen was not there.

Tears welled from his dad's bronze eyes as he adjusted the camera angle.

"Allister, my own little EV…," his dad said as if he could see him.

Could he? Allister thought. He lowered himself to fit into the square frame and whispered, "Would be fresh."

Allister and his dad stared at one another across that square table as if they were both sitting there together and not separated by however many years of absence. After a moment, his dad let his eyes drop to the wooden countertop he was hunched over.

"You must be taller'n me now. Way taller." His dad held back a laugh. "I'm willing to bet your potentials are in full swing like mine were at your age. Wish I could be there to teach you how to use 'em. God, son, I'm sorry. I made a mistake I'll never forgive myself for but…but it doesn't matter. What matters is that you know the truth about the Daal Trelkkien artifacts." He examined his surroundings before finishing, then said in a forced whisper, "The energy in them's brand new, volatile like all hell. I never seen nothing like this in all my engineering days… It's disruptive and sneaky at the same time."

Allister couldn't believe what he was hearing. He had a harder time accepting the interaction as reality. He sat back and brought his Cynque with him, forgetting where he was and what he'd signed up for. All that mattered was that his dad was speaking to him, like *right* to him.

"I built this machine," his dad said next. "A Temporal Energy Wave Receiver that tracks the artifacts' behavior by seein' glitches between time sequences." Someone knocked furiously in his dad's background. His dad looked over his shoulder, and poured out his last words in a rush. "The machine's the fastest way to find them and stop what's coming. Go to the TEWR, but be careful when you reactivate it. There are others after this power…and not just the others we know of."

The transmission ended.

Tears brimmed Allister's lids. Shivers raced up his arms. He covered his Cynque with his hand and squeezed his wrist, attempting to snuff out his dad's message and its effects. But no amount of pressure could silence the lingering voice in his ears.

I was his little Evolutionary, he thought to himself.

He hadn't experienced his dad in such a profound and connected way since before he could remember. Watching him move as if alive, share from his heart, offer wisdom and guidance in death as a father would in life. It was almost too much for Allister to take in.

He rested his forehead on the table's edge, the video on replay in his mind.

As sweet as those words and that experience had been, the fear in his dad couldn't be dismissed. Allister wondered if the others after the artifacts he'd referred to were members of C20. Had C20 been around before 2040? The year of his dad's death had a tsunami of emotions towering over his composure, ready to make ruin of it all.

He lifted his head to suck in his tears and gasped.

"Private Adams!" the lieutenant said, already leaned over the table.

Allister nearly jumped out of his seat. "Yes"—his voice cracked—"yes, Lieutenant."

Lieutenant Delemar arranged herself upright, just the way his mom did after getting his attention. Because her presence required more respect. He shot up, pulled his feet together, and straightened himself up like a beanpole, arms included.

"Yes, Lieutenant," he said again.

"It's time. Follow me," she commanded.

Allister scurried from the room on her fast-moving heels.

The lieutenant paraded deeper down the neglected hallway, explaining the assessment as Allister tried keeping up with her inhuman pace. He enjoyed listening to her speak, even when she was clipping her words or speaking slower to hide her accent, which was, without a doubt, native to one of the Latin Sanctuaries.

"The Evolutionary Potentials Assessment determines if a recruit possesses the energy potential needed to accomplish our mission."

Allister almost mentioned the crystals again but caught himself. "Ya, I want to accomplish the mission," he blurted instead. "I'm with—"

"We observe your behavior under a series of trauma-based triggers that have proven to make the potential manifest itself."

"Triggers like what?"

Her answer was a scoff, then the quiet of another never-ending hallway that curved around the building.

He didn't ask again.

They passed a row of tinted, oval-shaped windows facing the District. The giant windows were connected like honeycombs, extending up to a sloped ceiling he could assume was the roof. The muted sun of the early evening was the first flood of natural light he'd seen, and while he tried to hold on to the novelty of being inside the secret building, he might as well have been winding through the tunnels on the A.E.T. Trac. It was like commuting from the District back to Riser Town: the scenery providing a once-in-a-lifetime sense of location, conditions deteriorating the farther they went.

Artist: The CMD Studios

104

Lieutenant Delemar's skin was the kind of pale brown that would happily absorb sunlight, should it receive any. It seemed destined to be another shade, a richer, darker brown. She was lean at the waist, slim around the chest, and curvier around hips, trailed by a faint lavender scent. Her hair she had pulled into a tight, high ponytail, which flowed from her crown into a silken waterfall down her back—though heaven forbid a strand curl out of line. She plucked one right from her scalp for its disobedience and tossed it aside.

He'd never seen anyone more meticulous about their hair than he was. Although, she seemed to prefer hers *bone straight* as opposed to its natural texture.

The windows disappeared, and the light disappeared with them. She guided them down another vast hallway where he expected piles of trash to appear at any moment, reeking of mold and urine and solid waste. But nothing was too unusual as, still walking in silence, they passed through sliding double doors and into a corridor so narrow, the cape she'd been wearing earlier would've flapped the width of it.

Lieutenant Delemar finally spoke as they exited onto a steep ramp, the walls widening around them. "Trauma-based triggers caused by things like extreme combat, Private. The individual's adequacy is not in simply manifesting the energy potential. What we need is someone with a capacity for it. To conjure it, handle it, and focus it without causing complete and maddening chaos. And someone on this team believes you possess said capacity."

"Captain Brandt?"

She ignored him as they made their way up the winding path and onto a grated platform.

"The captain's been watching," the lieutenant said. Her tone was similar to one of his mom's sneers. "Reported the energy signature readings coming from your neighborhood and advised we collect you to weigh out your value."

"I promise, Lieutenant, I got tons of value. I know I talk like an Omega-gen kid, but I'm real smart. I rewired the coffee machine at work to brew faster and lower the electricity drain." His face brightened as more things to boast about came to his mind. "And you know, I put the brakes on a truck with...uhm...one hand yesterday..."

The lieutenant put her hand up swiftly, cutting his rambling short. She halted and kept her back to him, keying something in on a digital panel. The monitor above it blipped on and booted up.

"You used two hands," she said.

"Huh?"

"You used two hands when you stopped that truck."

His face twisted into a grimace. Feeling defensive, he replied, "Well, technically I used my shoulder and one hand, then I used two hands at the end…"

The lieutenant turned back around. "Correcting me is never a good move. Ever."

Noted. He ran his fingers through his braids, unsure of how to defuse the tension.

"Are you going to just stand there?" she asked.

Only then was Allister aware they'd stopped in front of a massive rectangular entrance sealed shut in the center by two doors.

"Scan," she commanded.

Allister held out his wrist.

"Private Adams, accepted. Welcome," Cynque announced in a voice he'd never heard.

"Is that a fresh OS? Or you configured an integrated system?" Allister asked.

The lieutenant raised her arm to the screen without taking her eyes off him. "Your clearance doesn't go that high."

He stretched his jaw in response to her obvious insult so as not to suck his teeth.

"Lieutenant Delemar accepted. Welcome," her Cynque said.

The chamber corridor, which led to the training area, was split down the middle just as the doors were. He noticed the standard nonbinary, zero-waste washrooms were on one side, while the other held timed shower pods, some instant dryers, and a changing area. Digitally labeled lockers were stacked in between.

Lieutenant Delemar pointed ahead of them. "Uniform's in there," she said. "Put it on and meet me in the training room. Two minutes from, and not a moment after."

The woman might as well have been made of the same metal as her uniform plates. Lifeless. Rigid. Impossible to penetrate.

But her hardness lost durability in the nuance of her reference to time. She was the only person he'd heard refer to the countdown in the positive—days from versus days until. Perhaps that explained her passion for the Andromeda Project and its procedures. If she really believed the apocalypse could be avoided, her demeanor would be a well-warranted seriousness for her position, not something personal against him.

Yet, the lieutenant seemed to be chasing away the afternoon warmth from their conversation, hell-bent on cutting off any seedlings of connection with giant shears. Sure, he was used to not being accepted, but shouldn't it be different with other Evolutionaries?

His name glitched on the locker in front of him. In its different voice, Cynque welcomed him again and granted him access to the locker's contents.

It was definitely a different OS—faster, crisper, even more human sounding, which was creepy.

The uniform hanging above the shelf was identical to the lieutenant's in color and style, modified to fit his physique. He opened the locker wider. Next to the uniform were calf-high boots zipped closed. The smooth silver material stood upright on a grooved sole and shimmered even in the dim light.

Allister tore off his clothes in excitement and balled them up. When he went to shove the rank, dusty cardigan, the ripped pants, and the scuffed-up boots in the bottom of the locker, he found his tattered backpack sitting on its side. He paused at it, knowing someone had to have put it there. His first guess was Captain Brandt. He just hoped the pages he'd found were still inside.

"Def coming back for that," he mumbled to himself, tossing in his old stuff.

The uniform reclaimed his attention. He grinned as he felt the shoulder armor's geometric shape. His eyes widened at the miniature plasma core on the chest, which powered both the suit and his giddiness. He held it out, thinking he'd never been more pumped about anything, even hoverboard parts, then clutched it to his body with delight. "This fit is beat!"

After dressing himself in a hurry, Allister marched into the training room, his arms swinging.

Lieutenant Delemar tapped her Cynque from the room's center. He stopped near her with a wide smile on his face.

"This is the most mega thing I've ever put on my body. What's this even made of? It feels like titanium. Looks like titanium. Gotta be titanium. I don't know, though." He twisted his torso from side to side, then stretched his arms over his head. "Nah, too nimble to be titanium—"

"It's not titanium," she snapped. She smoothed her hair on both sides, inhaling as she reclaimed her patience. "Now, during our combat, the monitoring system will evaluate your capacity for the energy potential we're looking for and let me know the outcome: admission or termination." Her lips twitched when she said *termination*, as if something was amusing, to her who seemed to have no sense of humor, no less.

His smile faded fast.

"Termination?" he asked. "What you mean termination?"

"The contract you signed states that if you're not admitted, you'll be terminated, and we'll notify any living relatives of your death."

His chest tightened with unease. "Wait…wait…what? No way I'd sign, no way," he protested, shaking his head and pumping his hands in front of him. "Show me where it said that."

"Show you where it said that," Lieutenant Delemar repeated, stepping forward. "Show you? Where it said that," she repeated again, another step closer. Her tone bit the air like a whip's lash. "It sounds like you're implying that I'm being dishonest about what terms and conditions are in a contract I have reviewed hundreds of times, that you barely reviewed once. But that can't be right. Can it?"

"No, Lieutenant," he said with intended reluctance.

She stepped away with her hands behind her back. The stadium lights boomed on, their sensors activated by her movement. "Private Adams, it's my job to make sure that you can find the Crystals of Transportation. They are the only thing that guarantees our exodus from this planet. And if you can't, humanity has no use for you. Considering we are 214 days from a cataclysmic event, it seems ridiculous to send you back to Riser Town to argue over expired food with your impoverished neighbors."

Allister felt his arm muscles lock up. "Captain Brandt said there were no hang-ups, why'd he lie?"

"The captain can be deceiving when he really wants something," she replied, slowing to a stop. Her figure dwarfed by the room's expanse.

He dropped the subject, suddenly astounded. The comment about Captain Brandt was too small to compete with the size and magnificence of the dome-shaped room. One was spoken almost under her breath, the other was about the breadth of the distance they'd traveled.

She'd still probably meant to leave him to his fear of execution but instead managed to inspire more wonder in him with the effortless use of her potentials. She maneuvered her body through the air with the grace of a songbird, twirling as she rose to exchange gestures with a figure in a tinted window. She hovered there, her arms moving beside her like wings, a pink energy flowing down from them like propulsion.

When she was finished, she returned to the floor with the same grace, one foot at a time.

His mouth was open and wouldn't close. He stuttered and pointed at her and the sky, too impressed to form a sentence.

She seemed pleased at his shock, the tiny smirk on her face reading as arrogant. From where she stood opposite him, she flipped her hand just as casually as she'd flown moments before, awakening a machine behind her.

"That was…," he said, finally finding his words. He looked back up at the figure in the window and narrowed his eyes. *Too mega*, he thought.

This assessment suddenly felt like a trap on top of a trap.

Nervously tugging at the neck of his uniform, he said, "Uhm…maybe there's another test we could try instead, yeah? You know, really put my intelligence potential to work. This way, you don't have to trip over trying to bring out my energy potential."

The machine she'd activated hummed to life and cast a vivid blue glow throughout the room.

The lieutenant rose into the air again, her body backlit by blue light and draped in new shadows. "The assessment is not collaborative. I am not helping you 'bring out' your energy potential, I am forcing it out of you via extreme combat. I will be a constant threat to your life."

"We're meant to battle?" he asked.

The playing field was kilos from being even, and any awe he'd felt vanished inside the realization that she knew how to use her potentials with ease, and he still fumbled to use them at all. He felt it unfair that those were the circumstances under which he was meant to prove himself.

Allister stood somewhat paralyzed—too intimidated to appreciate the technology inside his first training room or the light flickering around her sharp features.

"It looks like you're ready to begin," she said.

He tilted his chin and curled his mouth down. The intimidation thickened to anger, then hardened into determination.

Perhaps it was like the strategic game of Schwebevogel he'd practiced so much at, except this time he was allowed to use his potentials. There was just one drawback, he told himself, staring up at her.

Only one of them would be hovering.

———

Radiation from the reactor's glowing field warmed Allister like nuclear heat. Whirring blue energy circled the room with a repetitive *whoosh*, compliments to the machine's orchestra of boisterous humming.

"Code FZ-MMLII—Evolutionary Potentials Assessment activated," a robotic voice said in surround sound.

The blazing energy manifestation was swallowed into the reactor. Darkness draped the room in its sinister curtain, smothering sound before it reached his ears and smells before they reached his nose, blackening sight before it reached his eyes.

Then the temperature dropped.

He was breathing heavy while he waited for what would happen next, the air condensing into white puffs between his lips.

A burst of intense cold blasted him from every direction.

Bewildered, Allister shrunk into his torso, clutched himself as he spun halfway around, watching the room come to life through rapid blinks. The space became an indecipherable mess of shapes and outlines. Dark lumps that might've been rocks. Grayed silhouettes aiming to be trees.

In a flicker of light, long, flat scraps danced around him like shredded paper in the wind. They were assorted in color and size, in weight and texture, fluttering across the vacant space until they adhered to the grayed structures and fuzzy backdrops. They billowed up and down the room in broad strokes, drenching the open void in vividness and illumination.

His gaze followed a coniferous forest as it sprouted up a rising mountainside, then came down as snow and ice descended on the wooded landscape, covering the evergreens in white powder and frost. Sleet falling slanted stabbed at his eyes.

Allister lifted a shivering arm over his brow, his sight line leveling to the landscape conjured out of thin air.

That's when he spotted *her*.

Lieutenant Delemar moved in the shadows of the frigid shower. She tiptoed low to the ground, coming up every few steps to look left and right, though not behind her.

Allister ignored the icy hand of winter pressed against his cheeks, the chattering of his teeth, and moved deeper through trees, faster over bushes. He stalked her silhouette into a ridge, thinking as he came up on her how best to pounce. The path toward her was already well laid, stocked with hiding places—giant rocks, shrubbery, fallen timber. Any precaution he'd left far behind him. He knew he could gain the upper hand using his tactical advantage, but knew that to survive, he needed control of the energy—his impossible-to-understand, temperamental-when-present energy.

The lieutenant appeared to trip over a bundle of branches and cursed as she wrapped her arms around a tree to keep from falling. He thought it was amusing enough her hands only made it halfway around the trunk. What he found more amusing was that she couldn't manage to get back up. Maybe she'd already shown off her best moves.

He crouched as he inched closer. Poised to pounce.

"Boom, finished," he whispered, ducking behind a nearby tree. He took a deep breath, rolled his eyes to the whitened sky, and looked to see if she was still there, within reach.

Lieutenant Delemar was gone.

He returned to where he had been hiding, his back pressed to the bark, his heart thumping its way to an attack. Her sudden disappearance was what fueled the tension and fear building a tower inside his chest. But it was her return that completed said tower. He held his breaths captive.

The lieutenant was levitating off the ground. The tree she'd clung to levitated next to her, as if weightless. She had but two fingers extended to the sky — which was seemingly all she needed for such power and control. Then her wrist flicked inward.

Allister ducked with both arms over his head, immediately snapped free of his surprise.

Boom.

An invisible force split the tree at his back down the middle, blowing it to sticks. He shrieked and fell over, then rolled back to standing. Before he could dodge, the tree trunk she wielded like a flugbar swung forward.

111

Forearms up, he braced himself for the blunt force of solid wood, his gasp of shock an afterthought.

The tree slammed into him an instant later.

Throbbing pain shot from his wrists to his elbows as he was propelled backward, his body plowing through trees just as thick, if not thicker than, the one she'd hit him with. Allister was little more than a metal ball thrown loose, headed at high speeds toward another player. The lieutenant followed him, gunning to intersect where he might end up—for the win. He slowed enough to hit the ground with a bone-shattering crash, then bounced up and flipped over. She was still speeding toward him, faster than any hoverboard he'd ever re-engineered, targeting his open torso the moment he returned to the air.

Her fighting style mirrored a machine's computed moves. She stayed on top of him, wore him down with alternating punches to already-cracked ribs and an already-loose jaw. His blocks were ill-timed. His retaliation was poorly executed. And he couldn't seem to keep his balance, or his eyes on her, as she whipped back and forth through the air. But something else made the battle even more deadly: her primal instincts, the swiftness of her execution. Her potentials were a sharpened weapon. Her skill with them just about perfected.

He backed away, his hands up, his body shaking, not knowing which direction she'd come from next. His right eye pulsed with incessant aches, his vision impaired by its swelling. It was the only time since they'd started battling he appreciated the sting of the environment's cold.

Allister knew that for all his regeneration, which was slowly stitching its way through his injuries, he was bound to be terminated.

The lieutenant sped toward him. Her face was drawn in permanent fury, the violence in her eye that of a creature who'd killed for no reason and didn't have qualms about doing it again. Something about it wasn't human; something about it wasn't *humane*.

She took him by the throat as he tried deciding between two.

Humane. It wasn't humane, he decided, prying at her fingers for oxygen.

Though sputtering and kicking at solid ground on the outside, inside, he was thinking about how when they killed him, his mom would've been right all along.

Lieutenant Delemar lifted him up. She closed her hand tighter, such a fierce grip hidden in such soft hands. Now, he felt no air in his lungs, just heard his own choking and, beyond that, her light breathing. From the edges of his vision, blackness began creeping in. The environment narrowing and blurring as she squeezed.

And when Allister thought he might surrender to termination, the words that conjured his potential arrived. This time, without the fear of their consequences.

"Foeht...Zeorgen," he choked out.

The familiar sensations resurfaced: the short-lived tingling, the illusion of tiny needles stabbing underneath his skin. Then came an unfamiliar sensation: the explosive heat of the blue energy's charge burning through him like a wildfire. He'd never experienced his energy potential with such intensity, and drew his hands to his body, both of them clenched to keep the furious energy contained. Yet it refused. To be. Contained. The surge of potential was already radiating over him — from his toes to his waist to his neck. If the energy burned externally a fraction of how painfully it burned internally, Lieutenant Delemar's look of shock made sense.

She dropped him.

He landed on his feet and rose, covered in the sweat of panic and terror. But those emotions had been burned away with the last of his pain, his senses, his restraint. A barbaric yell forced its way from within, rattled his chest with a sound so beastly, it could not have come from his aching throat.

CHAPTER 9

LIEUTENANT LEESA DELEMAR

Quadrant Delta—Training Wing, Andromeda Project Headquarters
Day 214

LEESA LET GO. Not out of mercy. Because she felt something she hadn't felt in hundreds of days.

Pain.

Micro-burns on her palm quickly became shallow yet painful blisters. She looked at her bare hand with disgust. In cockiness, she had fixed her fingers around Allister's neck, an inhalation away from crushing his throat. Whereas with any caution, she should've squeezed the air from his lungs at a distance. There was twisted satisfaction she got in knowing that no one was as notorious or powerful as she, neither within the Project nor within the world of Evolutionaries. She wanted to see his face when he realized his irrelevance.

Too bad his relevance burst from him in a blue inferno, scorching her flesh and her perspective in the process.

Leesa gasped and flew away from him, but he quickly moved forward, locked on to her position like a honed missile. The heat billowing from him touched her before he was able to. She knew then it was time for defense, to summon her potential to protect her until the energy burned its way through him like it was known to do in others. Winding threads of telekinetic energy spiraled in the air, solidifying around her in the pinks and purples of her forcefield.

He launched himself from his invisible silo and tackled her around the waist. Bodies entangled, they tumbled through the ridge, wrestling all the way. They landed in a small clearing: him on top, fingers locked with hers; her out of breath and seething in dirt and snow. She was surprised by his strength as he pushed down but was determined to reclaim her edge as she pushed up. They seemed matched for a moment, neither able to break free or fling away the other. His arm was bathed in the blue energy from left hand to left shoulder. The wild power they'd been looking for was working its way through her forcefield a single bolt at a time.

She let out a loud, high-pitched scream. Forcing more strength through her weakening arms, she surged them upward. A telekinetic wave erupted from her hands. Allister was catapulted into the sky and landed shortly after in the clearing's outskirts.

Adrenaline hadn't stopped fatigue from making itself at home in her body. She seethed, furious at his possession of the energy and fearful of its potency. It had been minutes. Too many minutes for him to still have the energy circulating through his veins. She kept watch on the bushes he'd crashed through and approached from the side, looking more for the blue glow than Allister himself.

He emerged, weary, stumbling, arms swaying without purpose. Captivating blue colors swirled and danced around his loose-hanging limbs until his open hand became a clenched fist, as his exaggerated stumble became a full run. He charged at her. Body low. Arms flexed.

She lunged forward. Arms raised. Eyes narrowed.

It was a surprising trick to see in a rookie, but it didn't matter to her. The game always ended the same. It wasn't the first time an Evolutionary had lasted longer than expected.

Leesa threw her power-packed punch, however, it was he who spun to one side and caught her with an uppercut. Air rushed from her lungs as he lifted her off the ground, flipped her in the air, and slammed her body back down.

Boom.

The wind howled in a single burst. Blended energies expanded in a single wave. But what struck her more than any physical impact was the crisp winter air cooling her bare skin. For the first time, she tasted the snow and the dirt, closed her hands around sticks and leaves. She felt exposed, unsafe, as she saw the pink glow fade in the corners of her vision. Her telekinetic field was destroyed.

So the only thing coating her body was vulnerability.

She wiped her lip and tore out the stray hair in her face, then focused back on—

Allister's deep-set eyes bereft of sympathy. He'd returned to his best combat-ready stance, prepared, as she could see by his heaving, for the next round.

She stood back up, cheeks flushed with warm rage.

How was this possible? Allister had never trained. She knew from his file he'd never even fought another Evolutionary in his life. He might as well have discovered his potential a day past, the few times he'd used it—for showing off and self-preservation. She wouldn't be bested at her own assessment, one that had been designed for her to win.

"Keep it together," Leesa whispered to herself.

The assessment had to end, soon, fast, differently than the others. Allister wielded the energy in ways she'd never seen before. He'd even demonstrated he could use it. There would be no nameless body buried for having only mere traces of this potential, or inadequate access to greater amounts. And if Allister defeated her, he'd take the decision out of her hands and place it in Captain Brandt's. The general would have to approve his admission due to irrefutable data.

You've been replaced.

Three words she never wanted to hear come from anyone's mouth.

Only if they think he's stronger than me, she thought.

She couldn't kill him—unfortunately, the directors wouldn't have that—but she could put him down. Teach him a lesson about *potential* the way only she knew how.

A strange sensation soared through her at that moment, an injection of power destined to cause an overdose.

Her jaw clenched.

His pace quickened.

Her eyes raised.

His footsteps slowed.

She floated off the ground, postured in the air like a deity of vengeance, full on a fury untamed—her bloodless, clamped fists drawing in the nearest objects in the vicinity: dirt, branches, shrubbery, even the remnants of smaller trees, all caught in the upward twist of a telekinetic cyclone. Her pumping heart echoed in her ears as any expressed logic and reason melted into a snarl. But was this display of grand potential enough to have him stand down?

The answer seemed to be no.

Allister was still on the offensive, one hand clutching the other arm at the wrist and holding it down by his side. The arm being restricted still crackled and burned with the violent energy, brighter than before, when it had first arrived.

His eyes were trained on her, the blue glow reflected in them.

"This ends," Leesa said.

He let go.

His hand shot up.

Zoom!

A wide and thick and almost perfectly cylindrical blue energy burst was blasting forward with concussive force. She called forward a thicker version of her telekinetic field. Opaque energy waves rippled, smoothed, and flattened as they shimmered in their vivid pinks and bright purples, then hardened. Next came a shuddering *kaboom*, low and rumbling like a thunderclap. In that instant, their opposing energies collided, spraying crackling bolts throughout the environment. Any remaining scenery was incinerated.

Sirens from the training room wailed while red lights flashed warning. Cynque verbalized its concern. "Subject, Allister Adams, Z-energy potential reaching critical. Subject, Leesa Delemar, telekinetic energy potential reaching critical. Manual shutdown recommended."

The monotone, mechanical words competed with her self-criticisms. She couldn't shut it down, not until she shut *him* down, as planned. And with their potentials battling their way back and forth in a fierce tug-of-energy-war, she wasn't sure she could.

"Warning: if this session is not terminated in T-minus ten seconds, energy potential must be reduced via termination procedures. The facility is threatened with structural damage."

The word *termination* cut through the chaos with a double-edged sword—the assessment had surpassed expectations in a bad way.

"That is enough, Private Adams!" she shouted, her face awash with white-hot light, her arms yielding to fatigue.

She drove her arm out across her chest. Her field expanded, and consequently, so did the blast.

The energy would not yield, she realized, as pulses drenched in erratic blues consumed her vision. Fractures formed on her field's surface, its integrity failing to the tune of shattered glass. Searing heat and brightness penetrated the cracks. She knew what would come next, though it had never happened before. Her arms covered her face as her knees curled to protect her body. She held her breath close.

The forcefield burst.

She was blown from the air, her tensed body spinning in the fetal position. She tried to slow herself, only managing to regain her senses when she hit the surface, as a sharp pain rushed up her back. On impact, she cracked open like an egg, and the reverse force propelled her backward along the ground, digging up the floor as she went.

The assessment was over.

Burning toxins stung the inside of Leesa's nostrils. She covered her nose and rolled onto her stomach, cringing in agony though struggling to her knees a limb at a time.

The structural damage Cynque had cautioned about shimmered into a harsh reality, their mess now visible to her through clumps of her loosened hair.

Metal panels blown loose by her telekinetic storm littered the floor. Patches of concrete foundation had melted and become warped by the energy's nuclear heat, eyesores on otherwise flat terrain.

And Allister was across from her, his face buried in his hands, his body twitching with irregular rhythm. She limped toward him beneath hanging wires, stepping atop shards of translucent glass that had shattered free from the control room above. She traveled the partial width of the room, annoyed at the amount of pain she was in. But beneath that physical pain was a deeper psychological wound: the shame of her performance.

Anyone watching could see that he'd won. Anyone watching would know what he was: the Gateway.

She eyed him, suspicious of his intention.

But his victory looked a lot like hers had in the past—his resulted in the same curled spine of regret, in a body twitching with the same fear.

Perhaps he was simply overcome with the desire to survive.

The cuts and burns decorating parts of his face healed before her eyes, much faster than the giant gash on his bulging arm, which was slower for some reason than the dislocated rotator cuff that took less than a minute to snap back.

Allister looked up at her, his brown eyes unable to stay still. "I'm sorry," he said. "I was so stoked to use my potentials…and I know I should be on some next-level vibe that I have what the Andromeda Project's been after… But I didn't want to hurt you. I don't want to hurt anyone." He waited for her to say something in return and lowered his head when she didn't. "I just…kept thinking what if I die like my pops did, and leave my mom alone?"

An irrelevant question.

Artist: Lester Niesta/ The CMD Studios

"What did you think you were…" *doing?* She didn't finish her sentence aloud, breathless as Allister disappeared and visions of another planet replaced the room. She thought the machine had turned back on and dropped her inside an off-world simulation. But she was alone, looking from the heights of a tower at a sky with two suns. She blinked twice at the lush landscapes. She brought her hand to her mouth, marveling at the crystal architecture in glimmering purples. Stumbling back, she wondered how a place could be so foreign and so familiar at the same time and began to feel her way back to the training room. Yet the training room wasn't behind her.

She reeled at her distorted reflection in a wall that doubled as a mirror.

"Lieutenant Delemar, you sorted?" Allister asked.

His voice came from outside the vision, strong enough to pull her back to the facility, to *reality*. She awoke to the smoke and sparks of the damaged room, to his hands, still a safe distance from contact, outstretched with concern.

Leesa lowered her head, refusing to address what she saw in her mind, even with herself.

"Lieutenant?" he asked again.

Leesa turned away. She found his sincerity grating. Allister Adams, her replacement, would be the last to see her weakness. At present, blood trickled down her side. Her limp couldn't be hidden with slowed steps, and flying was guaranteed to be painful.

To answer his question, however, she was *sorted*. Though thanks to him—

Only until they found the artifacts.

———

CHAPTER 10

ALLISTER ADAMS

Quadrant Alpha—Executive Wing, Andromeda Project Headquarters
Day 214

LIEUTENANT DELEMAR HAD seen something Allister couldn't. For her to touch her lips with a silent gasp, for her to widen her eyes, for her to stumble away. Allister had known her the total of one hour and knew none of those actions belonged to her, for they were associated with emotions.

"You've been admitted," the lieutenant said, her mouth barely moving. "You'll be promoted to Agent Adams effective immediately. Collect your belongings with urgency and meet me in the hall. You have four minutes from, and not a second more."

She ended the conversation with a slow turn and an even slower exit.

Allister tried to forget his guilt, slip it into the background. He'd wanted to properly celebrate his admission when she'd passed through the doors. He imagined himself spinning around with his arms out, and in the end cheering while jabbing his fists at the air. But he only spun once, toward the locker, and hugged himself as he came to a stop in front of it, his feelings somewhere between triumph and concern.

It was the most monumental achievement of his life, a sign that he'd chosen the right path for himself. So why didn't it feel that way?

He bit into his knuckle, contemplating.

Perhaps because, once again, using his potentials had hurt someone.

Allister opened the locker and stuck his head into its lower half. The bag lay in the same position.

"Hmm."

He unzipped the front flap and pulled it down. The six or so yellowed pages were still crinkled but no longer crunched into a giant ball. They were folded over and in order.

Curiosity drove Allister to revisit the first page, where the words *Time* and *Salvation* were written large in all caps.

Crystals of Temporal Transportation—his dad had written in script. He ignored the equations and turned the page over to the paragraphs.

The name screams motion, movement, Allister read to himself as he leaned up from the locker. *But temporal means in relation to time, and exactly how is hard to say without the things in my hand and a solid outcome to hold up to the light. We got a lead on them, though. Good ol' West Coast. The Andromeda Project is giving me the funding and my own R&D lab to build a machine to locate them, bet they're hoping these alien crystals can do away with this apocalypse prophecy twenty years down the line. I say let's get on the horse and ride before all this mess starts to go down. Spending six months away from Dolores, God. Don't let her run off while I'm gone.*

His dad had dated the entry September 6, 2032, the year before he was born. Another paragraph started a line below it.

Before he could read it, he heard the sound of footsteps entering the room.

"Agent Adams," the lieutenant said. "With urgency."

"Yes, Lieutenant Delemar," he said, putting away the papers.

He slung the bag over his back, a firm hold on it, relief and gratitude as he followed her into the hallway.

Now aware of his dad's devotion to finding the Crystals of Temporal Transportation, Allister felt a similar sense of purpose. It made him wonder what had gone wrong. How, twenty years later, his dad was dead and these crystal arti-facts still hadn't been uncovered.

Maybe the machine had failed.

Lieutenant Delemar had tended to her bruises in such a quick and callous manner that, though bandaged on her side, she still bled from their battle. Her face was almost florid with restrained agony, and her uniform scuffed and bent where she'd hit the ground. She held her cape by her side with just the tips of her fingers, looking at it as if deciding whether or not to put it on.

Guilt for her condition came storming back into him.

"You're required to complete a briefing with the head of the Andromeda Project," she said.

He kept a straight face, nodded without any exaggeration. *Just keep it cool,* he reminded himself. While inside he was bursting with questions, so many questions, about the Andromeda Project, about his dad, about the artifacts. Not that he'd ask them, not all at once, but—he nearly squealed—the chance to finally meet the head of the Andromeda Project. What a treat.

124

"In his presence, it's not recommended you speak unless spoken to," she said, eyeing him too closely, as if she could read his mind.

"Yes, Lieutenant. I'm with it." Allister assumed that the head of an initiative so pivotal was very important and very busy. Perhaps he'd just listen to the man speak at him, take in every word with a breath of inspiration. "It's just beat that he's taking time out to say what's up."

"Hmph."

Without another word, she turned to lead them back down the ramp and fastened the cape to her uniform, almost hitting him in the face as she slung it around her shoulders. Her manner had returned to the grace of an automatic weapon, her hair rearranged in a frazzled, somewhat curly version of the stacked bun style. From above, he saw the loose strands and irregular clumps, watched as she pulled and tugged at the strays, then tucked and folded what remained.

"What's with the cape?" he asked casually. "Some kind of superhero thing or…?"

He didn't really expect an answer, and she didn't give him one. As he watched it flapping between them, he thought it was kinda cool but also kinda ridiculous, like Lieutenant Delemar herself.

"Maybe they'll give me one, too, yeah?" he asked, still trying to lighten the mood.

They wound back through the maze, and ended up somewhere new, though it must've been older than any other part of the building he'd been in thus far.

The area looked miserable, just a bland stretch of freestanding rooms.

A door squeaked open to his right. A soldier scurried out of it and disappeared around the corner. Did people work in those? Live in them? He wondered. They were certainly big enough for one or the other, maybe both.

It took at least a minute to pass by each room, every roof just far enough from the vaulted ceiling to see a gap. Their doors were hard to make out, camouflaged as they were inside wide, concrete walls that sloped down on both sides. He thought they looked a bit like prisons, especially without any windows, and was curious if any of them had once belonged to his pops.

The lieutenant stopped at the smallest room. A simple cube surrounded by exposed infrastructure, brown puddles, and the faint stench of mildew. She didn't have to say they'd reached the end of the Andromeda Project—he knew. There was no place left to go—no additional corridor, no secret hallway.

Lieutenant Delemar's eyes darted in the direction they'd come and then back to the door.

"We'll get situated," she said, somewhat rushed. Her demeanor had frizzed into one more anxious, more unsure.

They entered a room that hosted little more than thrift-store furniture and out-of-date technology, and situated themselves in rusty chairs arranged parallel to each other. He faced an empty desk. She faced the door.

Allister had pegged the head of the Andromeda Project as a legend. Valiant, proud, determined to save the world—and nurture young Evolutionary talent. It was hard to believe such a person would occupy a space the size of a meat locker flooded by a single overhead strip of light.

He rested his bag against his shins and fidgeted in his seat.

"So, uh, the head of the Andromeda Project's meeting us...in this spot?" he asked.

Lieutenant Delemar hadn't opened her mouth, perhaps hadn't even breathed since they entered. So he wasn't surprised when she just kept her eyes on the door and waited.

And waited.

He sighed and ran his hand through his thick hair, which the energy's arrival had blown from braids into an afro, and turned to face the lieutenant. His mom had always told him it never hurt to keep trying. At least she used to say that before the countdown.

He tried starting up a conversation again. "Sorry again for what happened in the assessment. Is healing one of your potentials?"

She clasped her hands together. Her face didn't move.

"I hope so...I really don't know what went down with me. We won't have any weirdness now that I'm cynqued up with the AP, right?"

Lieutenant Delemar winced.

He thought the pain of sitting up straight and holding her face that way had caught up to her, until someone entered from the hallway.

She must've been on puppet strings the way her body shot to attention. How her arm bent sharply at the elbow, slinging her open hand into salute against her forehead.

With the slowness of caution, Allister did the same.

The man who'd arrived was dressed in a gray military uniform, swinging his matching hat instead of wearing it, the rhythm in step with his casual stride. His tall shadow stretched over her and the desk as he approached, and with each of the man's weighted steps, she straightened her posture a little more.

Allister was perplexed about the way this man incited the lieutenant's hard-pressed obedience, but he was more perplexed with the man himself—as he resembled the delightful person from the recruitment video, though much older.

He was tall but not too tall. Fit but not too fit. Allister tried counting the gray hairs in the man's mustache and beard, noted how his chin curved in from both sides to form a cleft canyon in the center, and the way his cavernous nostrils flared at the end of his bony nose every time he breathed. The man wore an expression that suggested his expectations had never been met, nor could they ever be, as if everything around him were a permanent disappointment.

No one could be more disappointed than Allister.

If he hadn't seen it with his own eyes, he would deny to the end of their days that the person standing before them had gotten in front of a camera and preached hope.

"At ease, Lieutenant," the man said, then turned to Allister and nodded. "Agent."

She seemed to deflate when she received permission. But Allister was way ahead of her, already slouching, thoroughly disillusioned.

"Thank you for joining us, General," Lieutenant Delemar replied.

Allister accidentally rolled his eyes, a habit his mom had tried breaking with many a severe punishment, then looked straight ahead as a hasty cover-up. He still didn't share the lieutenant's gratitude. Not. At. All.

The general ended up behind the desk after performing a lengthy, silent study of Allister. If he had noticed the gesture, he didn't react. "It is my pleasure," he said.

Allister exhaled, a quiet "Whew" hidden somewhere in there.

"I'm General Nicolas Delemar, head of the Andromeda Project."

The man extended his hand over the table.

And it stayed there—level and steady, fingers pressed together and pointed at Allister's heart.

Allister looked at the hand he was meant to be shaking, his mouth twisting from side to side. General Delemar's voice sounded like roughed-up asphalt, his delivery as forced as his sincerity was feigned.

It was subtle, Allister's…agitation, like a pocket of lava bubbling beneath the crust, the kind of threat no one could see, would plan for. But the agitation heated to anger as it spilled into his body language. Now, his face was carved into a scowl at this voice that bred…defiance. His fingers stroked his palms, curling deeper until they were almost tightened into two fists.

Faint noises in the distance chipped away at a moment of stillness. The building creaked. Water leaked.

Still, General Delemar's arm did not fall. Nor did his dark eyes, both of them—soulless, jaded, derailed—shrouded by something, maybe deception.

Allister finally stretched out his fingers and lifted his hand. The general would be one to keep an eye on, he decided, extending his arm. "Allister…Allister Adams…nice to meet you."

They shook hands briefly.

General Delemar sat first, relaxing into the cushioned seat behind the desk. "Welcome to the Andromeda Project, Agent Adams."

Allister lowered himself into the chair. The sound of his new title, Agent Adams, settled into the hard seat with him. He smirked in spite of the tension.

Agent Adams. So beat.

The general gestured at the lieutenant, who was still standing. "I assume you're properly acquainted with Lieutenant Leesa Delemar. My daughter, and third-in-command here."

Leesa, what a pretty name. Allister nodded. His daughter, what a complex situation.

A glass screen lowered from the ceiling to eye level. Two renders of semiprecious Earth crystals glitched into view. They were a more detailed, digital drawing of his dad's hand sketch, some mix of onyx and amethyst at first glance.

"Lieutenant, please begin," General Delemar said.

"You know where we are, what this place represents," she began, pacing slowly, perhaps to hide her limp. "Human salvation, put simply. We're looking for a pair of crystal artifacts of alien origin to help make that a reality." The screen animated the story as she spoke, shrinking the digital drawings and placing them next to an enlarged picture of their last-known location, the southernmost tip of the West Coast, now referred to as—

De Los Muertos. The biggest casualty of the West Coast Killer.

Double whew, Allister thought as he leaned back. His dad had written about doing research and development on the West Coast. 2032, the year the journal entry had been dated, was just a few years before the quake hit.

"We aren't sure how long these crystal artifacts have been on Earth or where they came from, but a little under twenty years ago, we lost their location and the device we used to find them."

Though the Temporal Energy Wave Receiver wasn't mentioned by name, Allister was sure it fit the description of the device they'd lost, and since his curiosity was more often a wild beast than a domestic pet, somewhat unconsciously, he blurted, "Lost? Whoa, whoa, let me play this back. So, you saying you woke up one day, and, like, you clued in on alien artifacts bopping all over the world?"

The general and the lieutenant looked at each other.

General Delemar cleared his throat. "Someone…well…some*thing*"—he corrected—"gave this information to an Evolutionary named Patrick Adams, your father, who spent a few years translating the significance of their power and discovered some manner of how they work. But as you know, he is dead." The word stung Allister as it hit him, but the general kept going. "And this 'someone,' a known traitor…died before him."

Allister picked up on the shortness in the general's delivery, the slight air of disrespect at the mention of his dad's name. A wave of heat crashed on his forehead and cascaded down his face.

"One thousand…got it," he said through clenched teeth.

Lieutenant Delemar cut her gaze at him and kept explaining. "We believe the crystals may have moved."

Well, if they moved, no wonder pops couldn't find them. He ignored the intensity of her focus and read the headline of the image to see if it matched the one above the sketch. *Crystals of Transportation.* Small typo, he reasoned, probably nothing to worry about. He ignored the missing word and kept listening.

Lieutenant Delemar paused at Allister's side. "In recent years, we've seen a steady increase in unnatural disasters all over the world. The Resilient Nations of Global Unity have been advised to abstain from any attempts to revive the decimated areas of their respective countries. We don't have the resources to go around, as you've seen on domestic soil." She double-tapped the screen, shifting the visuals to calculations and geographic maps. "We think the Crystals of Transportation can get at least fifty percent of the remaining human population off the planet before these disasters destroy us. By our predictions, at around 214 days past, the cluster of super typhoons forming in the Pacific will take out—"

"What super typhoons?" Allister asked, gripping his forehead in shock. "What cluster? I don't know anything about that."

"No one does." She glared down at him. "We expect enough rainfall to flood continents. Drastic oceanic swells. Dramatic spikes and falls in temperature. Its ripple effects will take out over ninety-five percent of the population—leaving roughly one hundred and fifty million alive, and that's if we're fortunate and strategic."

He shifted in his chair and laughed a bit to hide his fear, both of her *and* the prediction. "Thought I'd heard everything."

"The nature of the storms is irrelevant, we've been told they can't be stopped," she said quickly, and resumed. "The energy signature the Crystals of Transportation give off is similar to the signature emitted from your energy potential. A long-standing hypothesis is that only someone proven to withstand a related energy's radiation could not only get close enough to the crystal artifacts to retrieve them but also would survive contact. We called this the Gateway Theory."

Allister sat up straighter and looked up at Lieutenant Delemar for the first time. "Hold up, you're saying I can do that?"

"In so many words, you have the potential." Her mouth remained open as if she had more to say. Maybe there was more to the story. Instead, she minimized the graphs and let the globe take up the whole screen. "Right now, we're focused on finding and retrieving the crystal artifacts. We believe they've resurfaced somewhere on the planet."

He squinted; something wasn't adding up. "But?"

"But—around one year and 135 days from the apocalypse, we started registering a series of coordinated terrorist attacks, like the one you thwarted, in leftover sanctuaries with the highest populations. These attacks campaigned for unity and reform in the name of a someone known as Tas-Salvatur." The screen zoomed in on the map's highlighted areas one after the other: Londinium Sanctuary, Soviet Sanctuary, ChiTown Sanctity, Stockhamn, the Yoruba Sanctuary, and Sanctum de Paris. "When we started tracking their movements, the attacks increased in proportion to our efforts, creating a worldwide distraction, when really—"

"They were searching for the crystal artifacts on the low," Allister interrupted. "It took you 180 days to catch on to—I mean…wow, that's so meg—"

"Don't…say that word again," Lieutenant Delemar ordered, low and menacing.

He thought he felt the room shake. And when General Delemar gripped the desk, he was sure of it.

"You feel that?" he asked.

The lieutenant straightened up for some reason, appearing painfully aware of herself. "C20 is the antithesis of all that we, the Andromeda Project, represent. They want the Crystals of Transportation to choose who of humanity comes and who stays behind," she said. He saw the pink energy from their battle leaving her hands and knew then she was trying to cover up an obvious slip in her potential. She turned away from them as she finished. "Tas-Salvatur believes only humans devoted to their highest evolution deserve salvation. By his logic, for us to reach our highest evolution, the current social structure must be eliminated, including those that run it."

"I think that's enough context for now," General Delemar said, rising to his feet. "It's important we get you, Agent Adams, the rest of the way through onboarding before we lose the day. We believe you'll be one of our most valuable assets. Just have to keep those potentials of yours in order."

Allister crossed his arms and watched the general sidestep the desk while the sentence hung in the air, suffocating and toxic, trailing General Delemar as he left.

——

Artist: The CMD Studios

LOST CHILDREN OF ANDROMEDA

"IT'S NOT ABOUT WHAT YOU HAVE, IT'S ABOUT WHAT YOU DO WITH IT."

— CAPTAIN JARED BRANDT

ARE YOU AFRAID OF YOUR OWN POTENTIAL? IF SO, WHY?

ARE YOU USING YOUR POTENTIAL? IF SO, HOW?

———

CHAPTER 11

ALLISTER ADAMS

Quadrant Alpha—Executive Wing, Andromeda Project Headquarters
Day 213

YET ANOTHER DAY had been lost.

Though, according to Allister's Cynque, only by a few minutes. He'd gotten a pinch of sleep. Eaten a few morsels of food. Funny how time liked to skip away when it wasn't being watched.

Once he'd taken a quick pod shower and gotten dressed, Lieutenant Delemar brought him to one of the trapezoidal rooms and left him with similar instructions to be quiet, pausing to again warn him of surveillance. He deduced from her grumbling that there was supposed to be a handoff between her and another high-level executive, and now she was forced to leave him unsupervised for a more important task.

Inside, Allister realized what he'd seen from the hallway was just the front half of each trapezoid shaped space.

The rooms were actually giant hexagons. He walked the perimeter, checking the corners for spots where near-invisible cameras might lurk. This office belonged to a person who was meticulous, borderline neurotic about aesthetics and decor. He identified their social status by their belongings: handcrafted furniture aligned perpendicular to an ash-pink accent wall; one-of-a-kind paintings and sculptures by long-dead artists, some Italian, some African; a row of hanging diplomas, awarded by the top schools in medicine and economics (before they stopped accepting students); framed medals for sacrificial service and diplomacy. He paused at the Nobel Peace Prize, finding it the most impressive of all their things—they didn't even give those out anymore.

It all belonged to a woman named Dr. Florence Belladonna.

He must've heard of her, then, maybe seen her in a global broadcast, Allister convinced himself, certain Cynque would've blasted her details all over the network.

He plopped down on the couch and extracted the papers from his book bag, content with reading the pages about the Crystals of Temporal Transportation while he waited for this...Dr. Belladonna. Twice he reviewed the concepts, the loose-leaf splayed over his lap, then went back a third time to make sure nothing was overlooked.

A series of supplemental journal entries ran out in 2034, when his dad had figured out a way to track the crystal artifacts and sketched out blueprints of the Temporal Energy Wave Receiver. The technology determined temporal wave output and frequency over a period of time in a specified region. His dad's scientific hypothesis explored erratic distribution of temporal energies. Occurrences and people alike, moving through dimensions, realities…time itself. It was about documenting what happened, lining it up and figuring out where the gaps of time were.

In one example, a ship left a port in Southern California, and during its travel, the crew reported encountering a storm within a day of leaving. But they were really three days out to sea. The kilometers traveled and the clocks weren't adding up when including their speed in knots. Forty-eight hours went unaccounted for, tossing somewhere in the waves, a discrepancy based on the extreme distance they'd traveled and how long it took the storm to gather strength. The time was still there, though first distorted by the energy, then balled up until it wrinkled, then ironed back out again without anyone noticing. But the machine noticed—and registered all of it.

His dad mentioned his plan to archive such continuum glitches, where minutes or hours or days were unaccounted for. However, that data would have to live inside the machine for it to keep working and measuring new information that came in. An increase in glitches within a single region implied the presence of the crystal artifacts.

"Brilliant, Pops," Allister said. "Just brilliant."

He leaned forward and sifted through the papers a fourth time, looking for the machine's original location. It would at least be a place to start.

"Uh, where do I go?" he asked himself, not finding anything. "How do you lose something the size of a bus for fifteen-plus years?"

"Really depends on how important it was, *sei d'accordo*?" a woman said. She appeared behind him somewhat suddenly, taking only a beat before she came around the couch. But maybe he had been so engrossed in the papers, he hadn't heard her come in.

Allister refolded the papers and quickly slid them back into the bag. Having loose-leaf might not have been illegal here like it was everywhere else, but he was starting to think his dad's work wasn't common knowledge…that it might even be classified.

The woman kept walking until she passed him, a sleeveless dress draping her from neck to ankle, the smell of rich scents wafting behind her. Solid gold bracelets jingled on her wrists as, arms swinging, she found her way to the desk. She leaned down to open the top drawer. He thought she'd retrieve one of the portable screens used for transcriptions and recordings, but instead, she pulled out a bound notebook and pen. This woman followed no one's rules.

Dr. Florence Belladonna was intriguing Allister more by the second. From her skin, which was so smooth it seemed the sanded chestnut brown of an antique chest, to her clear posture of authority and grace.

She sat down in the chair nearest and leaned back. Where, with her facing him, he could make out more of her features: her high cheekbones and angled chin, the perfect symmetry of her wide, rounded nose. She had dark, tightly coiled curls that danced around her face despite her stillness, her violet eyes sparkled with fascination, while her lips dazzled with the color of a—

Sunset.

She was Sunset Turtleneck.

And even more of a vision than he remembered, a real jaw-dropping type.

He perked up, overjoyed. "Of course I've seen you! You were...you were on the A.E.T. Trac, and then you—you took me to that warehouse...and...and you convinced me to—"

"I apologize for my tardiness," Dr. Belladonna interrupted. "I have a gala I'm to attend tonight, and your psychological evaluation was...unforeseen."

Her accent came off a bit less English this time, laced with more rhythm and pacing and patterned changes in tone, as dynamic and textured as the pink paint next to her.

Again, Allister fidgeted with questions, so many questions. *Who goes to a gala at a time like this?* he thought. *Who is this woman?*

"I think you already know the answer to that, yes?" she responded. "Good to see you again."

Red energy flashed inside her eyes. He felt a tingle zoom from temple to temple behind his forehead, which he touched as he shot her a look. She was one thousand percent a mind Evolutionary. A rude one at that.

"Are you ready to begin?" Dr. Belladonna asked.

He kept his eyes narrowed at her. "I'm golden. As long as you stop doing that," he said, shaking away the sensation. "I think you're chill and all, but it's pretty twisted to read my mind offhand."

"I'm establishing a connection." She wrote something down and drew a box around it. "You'll have to deal with it." Her pause was long, and the way her head tilted, he wondered if what she said next would be more curious or condescending. "So...you're *the* Allister Adams. You know it. I know it. And yet, I get the sense you're still hiding."

The observation stung. Something ate at the pit of Allister's stomach. Shame? He touched where he felt it chewing and pressed inward. "Hiding? I don't know if I'm hiding...anymore."

He held out his forearm and ran his fingers along its snaking veins. After the assessment, the blue glow had fled to his bloodstream's depths. A phantom pain made him close his eyes. He relived the energy shredding his epidermal layers like tiny blades as it erupted from his palms as a somewhat concentrated stream.

"I sense that...you're afraid?" she said.

He shrugged. He'd felt the inferno in his chest, in his guts, in his legs, in his hair. He'd felt like he was on *fire*.

Nothing terrifying about that, right?

"I imagine being on fire is quite terrifying actually," she continued. "Is that a confirmation or a denial? Are. You. Afraid?"

He shrugged again, knowing his thoughts weren't safe. "A little," he said. *Very,* he thought.

She leaned forward. "Very," she repeated.

He glanced up then, the tingle burrowing deeper, faster than his thoughts. Frustrated with her intrusion, he grabbed his head and rocked forward.

"You're afraid. Even now," she pressed. "But not of me, or people...of—"

"Myself," he forced out. "My potentials."

The tingling stopped. He exhaled fully and tilted his head back. "That hurts," he said, trying to sound irritated. Secretly, he felt relief. The annoying part: she probably knew that, too.

"Well, that's a shame, isn't it?" she said. "Because I'm not here to hurt you. However, in my experience, it does tend to hurt if you resist."

Maybe I don't need to resist with her...

He guessed her telepathy was prying at the words he'd always whispered to lure out the energy, because they were suddenly top of mind. *Foeht Zeorgen.* He'd never known the meaning or the source of this phrase, and suddenly there was an intense desire to know its translation.

He wondered if it was his desire, or hers.

Dr. Belladonna underlined something she'd written three times. Allister watched with a blend of suspicion and intrigue as she struck the page over and over in a controlled yet fierce motion, then turned another page. "Moving on... Do you have any particular thoughts and feelings associated with the assessment?" she asked.

"You mean how the lieutenant tried to finish me until I lost control?" He frowned. "I...the assessment was...not my bag, honestly. I just...I don't know what people are expecting from me now they know I've got this energy potential. Every time I use it someone gets hurt...and...maybe, maybe that's why my mom told me to keep it hidden away."

"Hiding it isn't going to help anyone," she said tenderly. "We are at war—and that wasn't close to the worst version of it."

"Heavy."

"Unless you'd like a position in the mezzanine cafe?"

He thought he saw her smirk as she resumed writing in the miniature notebook. He'd been counting the number of times she had licked her forefinger and used it to turn a page, and if he'd counted right, she had amassed five to six pages. He'd only spoken a handful of times.

"Are you just pulling stuff out of my head?" he asked.

"We telepaths call it deep listening." Her pen touched the page again. "You have"—she looked up at the ceiling, reciting the countdown's position from memory—"213, yes, 213 days until the world ends, what do you do?"

"Find a way to keep on living, hoping it doesn't." *Hoping I could save it,* he thought at her, almost wanting it to be the thing she replied to.

"Do you think you could?"

"Do I think could what?"

"Save it?"

Victory.

He stared into his lap and swallowed. "Maybe. Sure."

"You already have the potential, it seems." She flicked a curl back into her afro, something his mom often did before she made her point. "And while that's all well and good, now you need the discipline. Our success depends on it."

"On me?" he asked.

Dr. Belladonna nodded. "On you. You see, C20's rhetoric spreads each day, preaching acts as unthinkable as abandoning entire populations to suffer what's coming. Their actions, their violence, jeopardize everything we've built to maintain such delicate infrastructure during this time of crisis." She clasped her hands together, a determination creeping across her brow. "C20 is only ahead in this race because Tas-Salvatur is a master strategist. That's why I'm here, at the Andromeda Project—to make sure we find the crystal artifacts first and win this underground war."

"So you're not really a psychiatrist?"

"What I am and what I do don't always coincide." Her eyes twitched with mischief. "At my core, Agent Adams, I am a human with a range of psionic potentials, nothing less, and so much more."

"Don't peeps call that being an Evolutionary?"

"Some would, yes. But I don't like labels unless they're vintage and fit over my hips, of course."

Allister's mouth widened as if by its own desire, shaping his lips into a boyish smirk. The calm in her helped settle his angst about the lieutenant, the countdown, and having to eventually tell his mom about joining the organization. Interesting, the way Dr. Belladonna stirred sarcasm, sternness, and savoir faire together and let it coat her presence with the same glossiness as her skin.

Her concentration was held captive by the crimson bound notebook balanced on her thigh. She, without looking up, said, "There's something amusing you'd like to share."

"I—"

"Ah, ah," she interrupted, one finger held high. "Not a question."

He noticed Cynque still didn't have a place on her wrist.

"This place makes zero sense," Allister said. His gaze traced the room and landed on a giant sword hanging against the pink wall. He paused. *Was that there before?*

"Oh, that?" Dr. Belladonna said. "It was a gift. I use it from time to time."

Allister threw out his hands. "I mean—what gives? This room is a palace, you've got fancy swords and beat art and a mega furniture arrangement, but the spot down the hall is a garbage can, and the hall itself is built like a sewer."

She answered without slowing her pen, her hand swimming across the worn pages, the notes flowing down the paper. "My space is my space. Not theirs. That aside, I haven't had time to take a stroll through every quadrant, floor, or the expansive basement Vault, however, I suspect most of it is abandoned, possibly even forgotten. From my relatively brief observation and the ramblings of an overzealous veteran, the newer parts of the Andromeda Project were built on tense budgets, whereas the older parts of the Project were built as the"—she bolstered her voice for dramatic effect—"grandiose spectacle of a public-facing Evolutionary entity"—her delivery returned to normal—"and somehow it's all woven together in a never-ending web."

"I'm with it, but—how deep does it go?"

She stopped writing. "It? Do you know what you've signed up for, Agent Adams?"

"Uh...the Andromeda Project?"

"An organization so elusive it sits in the center of the District without anyone the wiser. The Andromeda Project is not a school for the gifted, it is not a training facility, it is a lifelong commitment to service. You're an Evolutionary at war. Whatever was behind you is already gone—your home, your family. To answer your question, it doesn't matter how deep it goes. Either you're here, protected and protecting, or you're dead. *Capisci*?"

His hands separated in astonishment. He couldn't believe Captain Brandt had lied to his face. He was no longer feeling the good vibe between him and Dr. Belladonna, or certain of the trust he'd awarded the captain.

"That's a hang-up if I ever heard one," he snapped.

"I advise taking that up with Captain Brandt." Dr. Belladonna closed the notebook and stuffed it down the side of the chair. "Let's move on," she said. "We're going to do a little exercise."

His heart jumped. "Whoa!" he exclaimed cautiously, hands up. "I'm about worn of these exercises."

"This is a mental one," Dr. Belladonna said reassuringly. "*Molto facile*." The red in her eyes returned, and for the first time since she'd sat down, she stared at him.

The weight of his eyelids became unbearable. "How does it work exactly?" he asked, yawning.

"I use my telepathic potential to dive into your conscious mind, check for anything glaring or unusual. And if all is"—she paused for emphasis—"*golden* as you say, I give you the clear to attend our next mission."

"One thousand." Allister stopped himself from tipping over and pointed at her with a weary finger. "Just don't fiddle...with anything in there, my head's... a...a mess as it is. Next mission, though? That'd be beat. Gotta find the...gotta find the..."

He let his arm fall as his eyes fluttered. His heart beat slower and slower, pulsating in matching rhythms to the telepathic energy he felt traveling over his knees, up his torso, and past his chest. When it enveloped his head, he felt himself drifting almost to sleep, but really drifting somewhere between states of consciousness.

CHAPTER 12

DR. FLORENCE BELLADONNA

The Conscious

Day 213

FLORENCE KNEW THE rules before she tapped into her mind-scanning potential. She also knew the dangers. Though the conscious mind was safer, it was controlled by thought, shifted by reaction. It was the place she always began—a distortion of desire, memory, and trauma.

And there was one way to get there.

The Gelen Psionix.

The astral realm, discovered while investigating the limits of her telepathic potential, was a parallel state of consciousness that linked more minds than she cared to imagine. It required focus and intention to enter without getting lost, and more of the same to return to her body without getting trapped.

Florence drifted through the Gelen Psionix, the wholeness of her spirit outlined in blush-red psychic energy. She was surrounded by black holes and neutron stars, gravestones in the graveyard of the universe's first stars. Just as frantic thoughts totaling in the quadrillions fired at her at faster-than-light speed. Her psychically projected form twisted and turned through the bombardment of multicolored beams of light, dodging what seemed like a universe full of desperate cries for acknowledgment and validation.

Forward she moved, ever concentrating on reaching Allister's mind, and his mind alone.

Soon the laser-light display blended into a singular stark-white flash, and as it faded, Florence stood inside...the unfamiliar terrain of a familiar mind.

Intuitively, she knew she had arrived.

The setting of the conscious mind tended to reflect wherever the person felt safe: the place they grew up, their current circumstances, a fantasy land of their creation—for those who lived in delusion. Fundamentals, as always, remained the same. Desires would manifest as colors or shapes, memories would be structures and people, trauma would be weather and terrain.

For Allister, his chosen setting was a vista of knee-high grass colored in a chalky blue that stretched to a pink sky. A calm so disturbing that Florence expected the environment to shimmer.

She was looking for evidence of trauma she suspected Allister to have, which caused his potential levels to increase to deadly intensities when in life-threatening situations. The common thread was that such Evolutionaries lacked a deep connection to the neurological source to their potentials, essentially missing the capacity to reach beyond the pattern formed by the traumatic event.

Such a limitation would prove counterproductive to the Project's mission. Allister could just as easily destroy the artifacts as he could find them—and kill the team in the process.

The horizon of Allister's conscious mind was dotted with structures incalculable distances from one another. The strangest of which, and coincidentally the closest to her, was a floating house. Stairs anchored to the ground led up to its front door.

And waiting there was a woman basking in a celestial glow.

The foreground glitched in front of Florence, then spread apart as if torn in two. She looked at her feet and watched as the grass beneath them transformed into the stairs.

When she looked back up, she was standing in front of the floating house.

"I'm Dolores, Allister's mother," the translucent form said, an old broom in her hand. Florence could tell by the pile of trash at the woman's feet that she'd been sweeping. "He isn't home right now. I can let him know you came by?"

"Actually, may I come in?" Florence asked.

"It'd be my pleasure, although he hasn't cleaned up in some time. I wasn't expecting company." Dolores smiled, warm and kind, and gestured for Florence to continue inside. "First room to the left"—she pointed at it—"I do have one house rule: Don't touch anything."

Florence entered, thinking, *Mi dispiace, Miss Dolores, but I may need to deal with the trauma I find.*

The small flat was clean. No, *spotless*. A fabrication of perfection, as she might expect from someone who'd spent their life hiding the truth. She made sure Dolores was still on the front patio before she made her way to Allister's room, where the evidence of his young adult angst exploded at her like an emotional outburst. It was noisy with conversations he'd overheard, someone and his mother discussing their frequent relocations across impossible-to-access borders. The room was cluttered with the emotional disconnect between him and her, stuffy with the stress caused by grappling with his potentials and living in new-age poverty. A mess top to bottom.

But none of that was trauma enough.

In the floor's center, Florence saw six worn pages ripped out of a notebook and a photo of a boy on the shoulders of a man. The papers looked identical to the ones Allister had tried stuffing out of sight before she saw them. She was curious about their contents, but because she knew what happened to his father could be the trauma she was looking for, she went for the photograph first.

As she leaned down, the picture shrank. The farther she leaned, the smaller the picture became. She reached to snatch it from the pile, and almost—

"Did you find what you were looking for?" Dolores asked.

Florence spun around. "How could I? You've hidden all of it."

Dolores's smile was now injected with impatience, diluting the warmth and kindness from just minutes before. "I did it for his own good," she said. "If he knew what really happened… Don't mind it…you wouldn't understand."

"I supposed I wouldn't," Florence replied, feigning disappointment. She rushed forward and pressed two fingers against Dolores's forehead. Her other arm moved in a counterclockwise motion as if she were winding back an old clock.

With each rotation, time tore away, taking with it the woman's wrinkles, the length in her hair, their dingy apartment, and its placeholder furniture. Counting up days, counting down years, time went until it could go no further, until the starting point of Allister's new life had not yet come to pass. 2040 was the year the button had been pushed, introducing a new reality.

"There are seven years missing," Florence said. "Why on earth would there be seven years missing?"

Dolores staggered backward. Her hands covered her face, and a soft weeping echoed inside the room in which they stood, now a small, one-room flat in lower Londinium. A double bed was arranged on the dusty floor, those same pages and the photo stacked on top of it. At the foot of the bed sat an aluminum box, full at first glance, empty at the next.

Florence raised her eyebrow, beginning to see the rare sophistication in the inner workings of Allister's conscious mind. She watched the mother sink onto the bed and rifle through the empty box.

"It doesn't matter. They aren't here," Dolores said. "I was trying to get rid of those blasted...words." She extracted a piece of fabric and draped it across her knees. What it was became visible to Florence, but only after it had touched the air: it was an old, sleeveless black cardigan. The one Allister had worn the day she met him.

Perhaps, Florence thought, there was a more appropriate question to ask. One Dolores might be willing to answer.

"The words, do they trigger Allister's energy potential?" Florence asked.

Whispers then came from the ceiling in droves. A fierce wind came whipping in with them, blowing against nothing in the room but her, Florence. While in bright-blue letters, two words she couldn't read were being written—or rather, scribbled—on the walls, over and over, at high speeds.

Dolores's eyes shot up at her, trembling with a fear so certain. "My baby said something that night. Something *bad*."

The wind spun faster around Florence, as she, still watching Dolores stroke the garment in her arms, realized who was responsible for the flat destabilizing and why the words on the walls could not be read. Not Allister.

But Dolores herself—who gripped the fabric, her eyes narrowed. "I think you've overstayed your welcome."

A sound similar to stereo feedback pierced Florence's ears. The room moved beneath her as the apartment walls scrambled and separated.

Florence reappeared in the never-ending field of blue grass, her face tilted upward toward the building. The apartment door slammed. The windows darkened. The steps crumbled. It had become *unreachable* at a few simple questions. Blocked by the slightest curiosity. Florence stood, surrendering to the wind as it blew harder and faster in the other direction, almost pushing her toward a second house.

A two-story house. One that rested farther from her point of origin. It had been built at least two decades earlier and in a less densely populated area, a debilitated example of upper-middle-class living when it existed. The house was fastened to the ground, and featured a gravel driveway, a dying orchard, and a tacky, wooden wraparound porch.

She trudged forward, believing her answers were inside.

A man leaned over the porch's farthest edge, his body stripped of detail and grayed out, his facial features so vague they might as well have been blank.

"You shouldn't be 'round here, it's not safe," the man said.

Grief struck Florence like a fist to the chest, practically penetrating right through her. She nearly collapsed at the impact, hit with all she needed to feel to learn that this man was Allister's father.

Florence was hurled back to her original question. The trauma. The seven years. And though struggling to regain herself, she managed to force out, "I'm—I'm looking for the seven missing years." She placed one foot on the wood for support. "I assume…I assume you have them?"

Patrick Adams strolled to the porch's center and spread his arms the length between two beams, blocking her advance. "You're late. The king cleaned this place out years ago, not a memory or a thought left from back then. But I know you mind types like to see things for yourself." He laughed, then leaned forward to whisper, "Be my guest."

She sensed the emptiness beyond the chipped red paint, beyond the rusted knob and the splintered oakwood. "The king?" she asked.

Patrick went back to the porch edge, taking any answer with him.

A slight push and the feeble door gave in, creaking as it opened to a square, barren room. Peeling plaster walls pulsed with a fading heartbeat.

Florence headed down a cream-coated hallway. She was thrown off at first, slowing her pace when the walls narrowed and twisted, keeping her from reaching the door at its end. She ducked down in an attempt to get closer, but the door shrank into a crevice too compact for her astral form to fit, even in the expanded reality warping of the conscious mind. Only a few steps backward and she was once again in the first room, where a large portrait of Patrick Adams now hung over a gilded mantle. A fireplace she hadn't seen before burned with blue flame.

She studied the portrait, intrigued by its detail. The missing follicles in Patrick's hairline were easy to spot, as were the dimples in his wide smile and the exact shade of forest floor in his eyes. Matter-of-fact and precise in all the ways his astral form was not, though it possessed no information save for the fleeting memory of his existence.

"Told ya," Patrick mumbled from behind her.

She whipped around.

Patrick had become a decomposing replica, his eyes darkened by death, his teeth blackened by time, his skin withered and flaky from biodegradation beneath the dirt.

She stepped to him, ever cautious, her glowing hand outstretched. "Who did this to you?"

"Don't worry," he said, cupping his chest with skeletal fingers. "I make sure Allister don't see this. He only gets the best of me."

The house trembled at his admission. Floorboards snapped and split away from one another. The portrait fell and caught fire. Florence rushed past him through the front door, speeding down the stairs and back into what should've been the grass field she left behind.

A new landscape awaited. Sultry vines embraced trees as they sprouted from ripe soil. Thick trunks rose and stretched their branches, forming an impenetrable canopy of foliage shaded that signature blue. The house was crushed by overgrowth, taking his father with it.

She cried out at the loss of him, feeling her insides rip down the middle. Her psionic form glitched and separated as her connection waned, then fused back together. She had scarcely encountered anything so...visceral.

Still, Florence held on. If for nothing else than the tiny face staring up at her.

In the spot where the house had just been swallowed stood seven-year-old Allister, swaying side to side, his knees knobby and his arms gangly.

The tension around him and Florence seemed to ease as he regained his balance.

But the glitching in her body remained.

"I don't know where he went," Allister said, finally steady. He bent over to pick a blade of grass. "He just disappeared." Sadness laced the words, spoken with a child's singsong rhythm.

She had a close eye on him and the background, acutely aware of the terrain continuing to blossom around them.

Florence had deduced the following:

Triggering Event (primary): Life-threatening experience that requires use of potentials—introduces need.

Traumatic Event: Death of father seemingly caused by an erratic manifestation of energy potential—introduces fear.

Triggering Event (continuous): Life-threatening experience that requires use of poten-tial—reinforces need.

Pattern: Erratic manifestation of energy potential—reinforces fear.

The words: A direct link to the potential that doesn't take into account any existing behaviors.

Then the words could be the answer to connecting Allister with the source.

She knelt to his level. "Allister," she said slowly, "I need you to tell me something, okay?"

He nodded without looking at her, instead examining the grass between his fingers. She watched him twirl it, watched his expression bouncing from longing to uncertainty to tempered joy. "Look, it's so blue," he said, holding it to her face. He giggled suddenly, then squealed, "You said you had a question! Ask! Ask! I love questions."

"What do you say to use your potential?"

"The king says I shouldn't tell you," Allister answered, the sorrow settling back into his voice. "I don't want to hurt you like I hurt those soldiers and my pops."

"Don't worry, you won't hurt me. You can tell me anything."

"Really?" He brightened for a moment. "Are you sure?"

Florence took him by the hand. "I'm sure."

With one finger, he gestured for her to bring her head closer and leaned into her ear when she did.

"Foeht Zeorgen," he whispered.

Zoom. Blue energy shot through her forehead like a bullet. Her psionic form was jettisoned free of his conscious mind and into the abyss of the Gelen Psionix, a deep voice following her the whole way.

2052 Ends with Z, it chanted.

She curled into herself, concentrating on her reality, where her head was pressed against her *nonna's* chair and her hands were folded around the armrests. She tried to feel her feet fastened to the polished floors.

Everything around her flashed red. Like an ending daydream, the office interior reappeared. She felt her feet on the floor, her hands on the armrests, her head cradled in the chair's cushion…her aching joints screaming for relief.

Instantly, she gasped, inhaling real oxygen into her lungs.

She looked up in time to see Allister's eyes flutter open.

He sat up, panting. "Crap. I'm so sorry, Dr. Belladonna, I don't know what happened."

"Not quite what I thought," Florence said. She touched her forehead, deciding whether the abrupt disconnection was his fault or hers. *His*, she decided. "We're done here."

"Done? But I—" he sputtered. "I had more questions."

"You ready for us to take him, Doctor?" a soldier asked.

Florence nodded at the two escorts who'd arrived during her recovery.

"C'mon, Agent, let's move," the soldier said.

Allister was taken from the couch, open book bag in hand. "I'm really sorry," he said to Florence as the soldiers pushed him out the door. "Hey, I'm not even triggered!" she heard him protest from outside the doorway.

She listened to them manhandle him down the hall, wishing EVs were treated more like glass than garbage—more breakable than disposable.

A fight for another day.

Florence grabbed the notebook from where it lay on the seat cushion and reread the transcribed thoughts lifted from Allister's consciousness — stopping on a sentence in the notebook that stuck.

2052 ends with Z, it said. *Ends. With. Z.*

"The same bloody phrase, likely a trigger all its own," Florence mumbled. She drew a finger across her lip and raised an eyebrow at the empty doorway. "Curious who told it to you…"

But she had some ideas. The depth and echo she'd heard it in gave her a prickling sense that it'd come from something ancient or, judging by the organization's associations, something alien.

———

CHAPTER 13

ALLISTER ADAMS
Quadrant Beta—Ops and Infosystems, Andromeda Project Headquarters
Day 213

HOURS HAD BEEN sacrificed for the game of preparation. There was an urgent mission briefing, Allister was told. He was then instructed to attend. Be on time. Be in uniform. Be...quiet. So he stood, lingering in the doorway of a room with a cryptic pattern of green and white lights running like irrigated canals through a series of dark metal panels.

Via those lights, he saw the three other Andromeda Project members he'd met, waiting, he guessed, for this *urgent* mission briefing to begin. He seemed to be the last to arrive. They had chosen to sit as far from each other possible, and separating them was a glass table almost the size of the room, a hologram of the Andromeda Project logo hovering above it. Eight chairs—one of which was a masterful, high-backed hover chair—were arranged equidistantly around sharp edges carved of white crystal. *What a divine table*, Allister thought to himself, taking in the design. *What a tense room*, he thought after that.

For Lieutenant Delemar...Leesa sat at the table's front corner, still bandaged. Captain Brandt sat in the back corner, brooding. And Dr. Belladonna was in the middle, her nails clicking on the table impatiently.

Allister couldn't look directly at her right away, too ashamed of the pain he'd caused.

He didn't know what Dr. Belladonna was looking for, but by the strain he'd seen on her face, she'd spent a considerable amount of effort not finding it.

Allister glanced in her direction, just a once-over. For reassurance.

She appeared okay from what he could tell. He managed a smile, then pressed a fist over his mouth to hide the reaction and pretended to cough.

"Find a seat," General Delemar grumbled behind him.

With a nod of acknowledgment, Allister slipped into the empty chair next to Leesa. The general filed in after him, and said, "Dr. Belladonna, please, begin," never bothering to look at her.

Dr. Belladonna rose at her name, then faltered, grabbing the table to pause and touch her forehead.

"My apologies…," she said, rubbing her fingers in circles against her temple. "I'm still regaining my senses."

He began to wonder if her gala plans had been sidelined due to his failed evaluation.

"First, I'd like to welcome our newest agent, Allister Adams," she said, focused on him and him alone. Her face was stern at first, but after a beat, she smirked. "I trust you'll all cage your egos to make him feel like part of the organization and not like an outsider, as you've done to other recent additions to the team."

Allister was so relieved she didn't seem mad at him that he sat up straighter and looked around the room for the acceptance he'd always wanted. Only Captain Brandt delivered, performing an airborne fist pump like a true cheerleader.

His cheeks burned with excitement.

Hmm…maybe the captain lied about the contract because he really wanted me to join up, Allister reasoned.

"Welcome," Dr. Belladonna said. "Fear may be all around us, but we are among the best living Evolutionaries qualified to do this work—and so courage will remain our compass."

"I'm with it," Allister replied.

"We believe Agent Adams's recent energy manifestations are what drew C20 to the District," Dr. Belladonna continued. "My theory is that they were hoping to pull off *la mossa della regina*, also known as the queen's gambit—a power move to gain access to Allist—"

"I found something!" interrupted a voice from the door.

Allister turned to see a man with clear-framed glasses hovering by the threshold, thoroughly engrossed in a data grid projection from his Cynque. He was a cool, nerdy type—messy black hair as if he'd just woken up, rounded shoulders, and wiry arms—an engineer or a scientist by the looks of the long white coat that was crossed and fastened over his chest. "C20 was not after our 'Gateway' to retrieving the crystal artifacts this time around," the man continued, his thick accent hard to place. Allister guessed mainland Asia from his lush pecan complexion.

Dr. Belladonna cocked her hip and eyed him with a look of distaste, as if she had never been told she was wrong in her life. "Oh? Do elaborate."

The man glanced up from his Cynque and adjusted his frames. "It seems, or so I can tell by this order of events, C20 was pulling more of *la difesa siciliana*—the

Sicilian defense. Agent Adams was moving bait for you, Dr. Belladonna. While the C20 attack was a planned data extraction, around multiple EV-related distractions, i.e. Allister chased into an alley, suicide bomber–style truck driver, fleeing civilians, etc. The Density Twins were looking for…a hidden transmission from the machine developed to detect and track the artifacts' energy signature."

Captain Brandt raised his hand. "Professor Ashur, I'm…pretty sure you were lookin' for that? True or false?"

"It is true. On Day 215, the machine broadcast a coded transmission to a location in Riser Town," the man, Professor Ashur said. "I didn't know where the transmission went at the time—some strong protections on that initial broadcast—and so we sent poor Belladonna on a wild goose chase." He chuckled. "I can assume it went to you, Agent Adams, because of what happened next and because of who created it."

Allister jerked his head up. *Because of who created it?*

Professor Ashur keyed a series of commands into his Cynque. The spinning Andromeda Project logo was replaced with squiggly lines drawing the flattened perimeter of the District's landscape. At the professor's voice command, the building C20 had targeted and the few others nearby grew from those glowing lines into three dimensions.

Following everyone else's lead, Allister leaned into the holographic projection.

"A Cynque scan on Agent Adams's device happened here"—the professor gestured to one of the buildings, a nondescript multistory corner unit—"transferring the coded transmission and all associated data to another encrypted location within the master grid, which is here." Professor Ashur then pointed at the sprawling wiring system that interconnected under the target building's ground floor. "My guess is that there was an attempt to retrieve the transmission on the A.E.T. during his transit, then again on the street during the scan, and finally through the grid. After that they moved to destroy it."

With the truck, Allister thought, following the professor's pattern of thinking.

"So you thinkin' the truck was on standby the whole time?" Captain Brandt asked.

"An implosion would've worked well, I imagine," Dr. Belladonna said.

Allister imagined so, too. The sequence of events tracked in his head: the way the woman in white had looked at his armpit on the A.E.T. Trac and not his face, how the orange-eyed stalker had been waiting for him in the glass. The cybernetic eye, he realized, must've been aimed at his Cynque, the creepy wave just a distraction. No one had mentioned the other Evolutionary, the one wearing the hood, and with all of those important people in the room, he didn't want to be the first.

Professor Ashur was busy considering both points. "I admit," he said, "I would have a helluva time pulling transmission data like that from an individual device. It would take time and concentration and discretion. But from a grid system, you just narrow in on what's not cycling through the CGN. Most transmission-associated data moves through the network fast. It's all *zoom, zoom, zoom*"—he pretended to throw mini-jabs at the air—"but this one is not built for speed, it's built for protection. It basically sits still. Makes for very quick process of elimination."

"Ashur, this is irrelevant to me," Leesa said. "What information was hidden in this coded transmission? Did the twins find it? And, for that matter, did you?"

"I don't believe the information would, in a sense, 'go quietly' to a source it wasn't intended for. Such was the power of Patrick Adams's encryption work."

Allister felt himself squeeze the table, becoming aware of it when it started to give under his fingers, and immediately let go so it didn't shatter.

But this man, this Professor Ashur, was the first to acknowledge his dad for any kind of a specific contribution since Allister had arrived. *Wonder what else he knows...*

The space above the table transformed into an overhead view of the lower West Coast.

"As for us," the professor added, "the transmission contained the precise location for the TEWR—"

Allister jumped out of his seat. "My pops built that machine."

"And?" General Delemar said.

Allister stared at the terrain map, his mouth hanging open. "And...I—I—" He didn't know exactly what he wanted to say, to offer, and the lieutenant looked about ready to fling him through the single door.

Professor Ashur gave him another second to speak, then kept going. "This is a discovery I suggest we act on within the quarter day we have left. I'll show the general location here for context and will send you the original transmission with the exact coordinates once you cross the Divide."

"Anything else I need to know before I begin putting this extraction team together?" Leesa asked.

"It's a collaborative effort," Dr. Belladonna said, rolling her eyes, "despite what you and General Delemar convince yourselves of daily. Professor Ashur? Any more brilliant discoveries?"

Allister checked their faces again, noticing how each of them reacted depending on who was speaking. It seemed Dr. Belladonna commanded a rather tense level of respect, just as Professor Ashur seemed to breed casual dismissal. But there was a new reaction from Captain Brandt: him scooting to the edge of his chair and rubbing his chin.

Intrigue.

"I mean, you're sure it works, right?" the captain asked.

Professor Ashur nodded. "Indeed, but only Patrick knew how."

Allister raised his hand and said under his breath. "Uhm...I know how it works..."

"Speak freely, Agent Adams," General Delemar said. "This isn't a grade school education module."

"I know how it works!" Allister yelled then.

Eight pairs of eyes fell on him, all widened in astonishment. Silence fell on the room.

Allister lowered his eyes and his voice. "I know how it works."

Dr. Belladonna crossed her arms. "How?"

"The morning of the attack, I found some old stuff that belonged to my pops. Some papers."

"Loose-leaf?" Leesa asked, leaning forward.

"Yeah, loose-leaf. They were old notes about the crystal artifacts and the machine and...yeah. So, I read them, and I know how it works."

"Do you still have those papers?" General Delemar asked.

"No," he lied, looking away. "A soldier in the District took them off me when I got scanned."

Allister waited for someone to call his bluff. Only more silence followed.

"Still, that's the best news I've heard since I've worked here," Professor Ashur finally said.

"The best news?" Leesa snapped, shooting up from her seat. "I'm glad our inexperienced, untrained recruit will be here to help you figure out some ridiculous, twenty-year-old machine."

"Hey!" Allister said.

"I see why everyone considers you a failure, Professor," Leesa said scathingly. "You're our top on-site engineer, and you don't even know how an invention incubated and developed inside this organization works. If it was so critical to our mission, perhaps you should've developed another one instead of waiting almost twenty years to go digging up the original. I could've retrieved the artifacts by now."

Allister sank in the chair, his face scalding hot with embarrassment on behalf of the professor.

But Professor Ashur just rocked forward on his toes and rubbed his hand over the Cynque. "I can't tell you what would've been done by when. I can only tell you what can be done now."

"If we're to look for this oversized tracking device, then C20 is going to send the Density Twins to look, too. We should do something different, something that saves us time, not costs more." Leesa checked her Cynque. "We won't even leave until 212 days from."

"Look, time is against us no matter how you slice this pie, so we might as well eat from the edges and see who gets to the middle first," Professor Ashur said.

Allister wrinkled his nose at the analogy, finding it both clever and strange, just like the professor. He was starting to enjoy the man's ill-placed laughs, the matter-of-fact tone, and most of all, the way he let the lieutenant's insults slide right off of him.

He raised his hand again. "I wanna go," he said, mostly certain he was telling the truth. Sure, he wanted to go, he wanted to be part of the mission if it succeeded. *But...*, he thought to himself, lowering his hand, *what if it doesn't?*

Captain Brandt cleared his throat and said to the general, "We're all going."

"According to who?" Leesa spat.

General Delemar tapped his thumb against the table, forehead crinkled in frustration. "Lieutenant, that's enough," he said. "In the professor's defense, we are dealing with infused alien technologies, unfamiliar cosmic energies, and artifacts from another galaxy. And while our dear Ashur is extraordinary...he is not Evolutionary. He does not have the intellectual potential the late Professor Adams had." He then stared at Allister hard, his jaw sliding across the hinges. Allister tried to keep eye contact without a reaction spilling from his lips.

But Professor Ashur spoke next. "Thank you, General." He looked at Allister. "A potential it seems he passed down."

The display in the center of the room shifted to show diagrams of the TEWR's two primary components, simulating how the facility collapse may have shifted the machine location and where under the rubble it might be buried.

"When the machine returns to the facility, you can get it back online," the professor said.

"And you can even teach Professor Ashur how in the process," General Delemar said too cheerfully, standing. His tone darkened. "Your father kept a lot of secrets, Adams. He told us what he wanted us to know, and it left us vulnerable in many instances."

Allister's body tensed at the sight of the general's flared nostrils and the sneer that lingered long after he'd finished speaking.

Captain Brandt stood up. "*His father* told you people what you could handle without going off the rails. Shoot, even when he did tell you somethin', you did jack with it."

Whoa, mega big talk, Allister thought, feeling a new kind of tension, this time, outside of him. The two men were moving closer to each other, making their way around the clutter of extra chairs until they were face-to-face.

"You dared undermine"—the general's voice began as a frigid grumble and quickly became a shriek—"my authority and position!"

"Maybe you try givin' credit where credit's due, Nicolas," Captain Brandt shot back.

"General Delemar—" the general corrected over him.

"Ya know what your problem is," the captain said louder, "you've got your clock forsaken head—"

"—is how you're to address me at all times—"

"—so far in the clouds, you can't even see this whole team—"

"And I advise you take your disrespectful tone—"

"Scratch that, this whole operation's—"

"—down a few notches!"

"—falling to pieces!" Captain Brandt shouted.

General Delemar took another step forward. "It fell to pieces the day you let those artifacts disappear."

"You'll always have that on me, won't you?" the captain replied.

"Yes, I will."

They were nose-to-nose, necks tensed, arms flexed.

Allister stared at the two men, who were both trembling, their faces tight and different shades of red. He could see then that Captain Brandt and General Delemar had passion for the Andromeda Project and the mission they'd sworn to accomplish, but the captain had more than that; he had love for Allister's dad.

Brandt stepped away first, his shoulders as low as his tone was light. "We're never gonna agree on how Patty Cakes handled all this. But what we can agree on is that we're crossin' the Divide to crash a zero-tolerance, restricted zone on the West Coast. We need to be prepared for any and everything."

At that, the room broke into a fit of tense arguments: Leesa and Captain Brandt on whether Allister should go, General Delemar and Dr. Belladonna on whether anyone should go at all.

Professor Ashur slinked backward toward the door, leaving Allister the only one of them still sitting. He got up slowly.

"Uhm, everyone," Allister said quietly. He then cleared his throat as loudly as he could. "We're on the same team, yeah? I mean, hello, can we just—"

He stopped, frustrated. His chest was starting to heave. His chin was beginning to quiver. He knew they didn't have time to argue; they barely had time to go after the machine. But deep down, who else could he trust besides his dad? Wasn't he the celebrated expert of all things energy? They'd all alluded to as much, even the general, though his particular allusions were peppered with scorn.

Allister stood tall. If his dad said locating the machine was the fastest way to find the artifacts, then that's what they needed to do—he checked his Cynque quickly—before they lost any more time.

"213 days, 1 hour, 33 minutes, and 10 seconds!" he shouted over them.

The four squabbling leaders stopped and eyed him with the same astonishment as before.

"That's how much time we have to get every living thing we can off the planet. Y'all are all triggered, I'm with it. And look, I don't know what my pops did or didn't do, or what he did or didn't tell you. But we know two golden things"—he counted on his fingers—"where it is, and that I can reactivate it." He swallowed hard and ran his hand through his afro, nervous. "I don't want the world to end with us in it. So can we go already?"

Captain Brandt let out a short laugh and shook his head. "Yeah, you're Patty's kid all right."

"I put this measure forward when Professor Ashur alerted me of his progress," General Delemar said, scowling as he bent over the table. "The directors denied it yesterday. We'd be on our own."

Dr. Belladonna looked over at Allister and pursed her lips as she ran a finger across them. At last, she said, "Still, C20 tracking Agent Adams to collect information on this machine is enough of a red flag to have me go mad. You'll take him with you. I'll keep my mouth shut for seventy-two hours from this moment. Captain Brandt, you've been past the Divide, this is your mission." With a small smirk of satisfaction, she tucked her hair behind her ear and flipped it back. "You all know what's at stake. Create an extraction plan, fly there, do it, and be back before the directors know what happened."

"To DeLos Muertos, then," Captain Brandt said, giving Allister a nod.

Allister smiled. The urge to hug Dr. Belladonna overwhelmed him, but he kept his hands tight against himself as he bounced on his toes. He was going on his first mission.

CHAPTER 14

XBA

The District, Potomac East
Day 213

0 YEARS, 213 days, 1 hour, 0 minutes, and 54 seconds.

XBA's orange eye flashed with impatience. She adjusted her oversized hood, annoyed by the rain and the terms of her arrival there, on that ledge overlooking the penthouse of the Willard.

The audacity of Bazzo Sparks, an Evolutionary for clock's sake, hosting a gala that grand and inviting the representatives of so-called countries, that were actually sad sanctuaries posing as democracies, or whatever they labeled those scraps of government during those last days.

At least the gathering brought everyone together in a room who might know the coordinates of the Temporal Energy Wave machine's location. She was sure someone in attendance had invested in the Andromeda Project, hoping to secure their place on the other side of the salvation they thought the artifacts would deliver.

She knew better. Those toasting to their own ignorance would be insignificant where they were going.

Still, she was willing to bet the human half of her body one of the entitled, moronic leaders from the alleged Resilient Nations had the coordinates she needed locked inside their mind. She'd rip open each one until she found whoever that person was.

Sparks's lengthy guest list consisted of the feeble, if not already broken; each one was disguised as a change-maker, when they themselves had not changed at all.

But her, *she'd* changed.

Thanks to Lieutenant Leesa Delemar, XBA had become what she was meant to be. Beautiful, augmented, unstoppable. Her enemy's telekinetic rage had incinerated the limiting majority of her human flesh and bones. Her survival was a miracle—the procedure, unorthodox. She didn't know where the doctor had found the cybernetic enhancements or the psibernetic technology that comprised them. She did know, however, that everyone deserved to feel as powerful as she did, that everyone deserved evolution.

Her lips rose into a snarl behind her micro-lattice mesh mask. The fabric light as air, tough as steel. Just like her. Her father would be so very proud.

She only needed to make sure Bazzo dropped dead before the party really got going. He was cursed with electromagnetic potential, a parlor trick of redirecting currents and manipulating fields. Though, unfortunately for XBA, the human brain was a thriving ecosystem of electric fields, and so was she.

She could feel his potential blocking her telepathic probing.

XBA stretched her claws, then slid them against each other, antsy for Bazzo's sudden, tragic, Cynque News–worthy accident. Tas-Salvatur had suggested the homicide be untraceable. "For appearances." She agreed.

So short of driving one of her psibernetic blades through Bazzo's chest, she'd devised a scheme to scrub the world free of his charm and wit, of his golden hair and light-green eyes, of his swoon-inducing Australian accent.

She waved away the night they'd spent together under the stars in the south of España. She'd written it off as figuring out what he was up to and how he was involved in Belladonna Corp, but knew it was a nagging craving for connection—a momentary slip that she paid for with the last of her old self.

She thought back to that year, back when years mattered.

2048: It was the last cold winter; it was the last presidential election, before they knew it'd be the last—but most surprising of all, it was the year the apocalypse went public.

XBA could only hope that on this very night, Night 213, with Bazzo standing center of attention in a room full of the untrustworthy, a room full of *humans*, that poison would be…most appropriate. And successful.

The hotel's well-lit room shined from the balcony's French doors. But despite the wraparound awning, no one was outside, save for the quartet of undercover soldiers in fancy suits.

Cream-colored satins draped the walls and table settings. Silver platters rested on the help's flattened palms. Glass flutes kept filled to the brim were stroked by intoxicated fingers.

Bazzo always knew how to get down.

She spotted him dancing around the room—his young, handsome face smiling and his champagne glass full. The poison she'd arranged needed only his glass tipped back, his throat wide open with him guzzling it down drop after drop, as she'd seen him do in the underground clubs. She counted down the minutes, cursing every instance he cheered, teased a sip, then didn't take it.

Her human eye narrowed. It was unfair to call it the pretty one; it certainly wasn't as useful. With that eye, she saw everything the old way, her surroundings filtered through the brown of parched grass. It was one of many organs that persevered in light of her constant physical pain.

With the other eye, everything she viewed was basked in the intense orange of an inferno. Thanks to the mechanical implant attached to her brain via wires and code and extensions. Her sight in that eye penetrated the rain and the darkness, the building's metal-reinforced exterior, down to the high-society guests, to their extravagant clothing and their helpless human flesh.

Red energy scratched through her temple, hungry as it was to raid those defenseless minds. She endured the agony long enough to prove she could, then gave in to technological suppression of her potential in favor of...

What came easier.

Orange text populated in front of her good eye: extracted data on the environment and the layout; number of personnel in the building and where they were placed. Using a hacked Cynque clearance, she confirmed the attendees' names and statuses. Then mid-extraction her connection shut down. The orange in her eye flashed slowly, powering off, until all she saw out of it was darkness.

She blinked her human eye and pressed her palm against the side of her head, trying to reboot her systems and reestablish the connection to no avail.

Now the behemoth of a building looming before her was opaque, shrouded in secret conversations and private funding deals for who would get off the planet and who wouldn't.

Did Bazzo bloody shut me down?

She growled. She was furious at miscalculating how fast he would get tanked. And even more furious at his subtle defiance, if it was, in fact, an attack at all.

She moved her feet closer to the edge, extended her claws, and sneered, only able to see the room through a few slices in the curtains.

Bazzo was now in the corner talking to the Moroccan king, Marshall Nephthys, concern splashed across his tanned, sober face, full glass in his hand. The topic between the two men was likely to be Celine, the king's missing daughter, and a call for support to bring her captors to justice.

He hasn't drunk it yet? What the devil is he waiting for, the apocalypse?

The rain thumped harder and faster against XBA's hood, the quiet storm mild compared to the big one on its way. Despite the torrential downpour, her smile returned, and a sinister strain of hope came with it.

Bazzo seemed to casually wrap up his conversation with King Marshall before he walked out onto the patio, greeting the four soldiers as he passed them on his way to the ledge. He kept a hand stuffed in his trouser pockets and the other wrapped around the glass.

Yes, she thought. *Drink to yourself, you arrogant twit, in celebration of your pitiful efforts.* She pulled the cloak's fabric away from her head, part of her wanting him to see her as he drank it.

Lifting the bubbling poison to the sky, Bazzo grinned and winked, *at her*, then poured the drink onto the railing. He watched it sizzle and steam, eating through the metal as it would've eaten through his insides. He tossed the empty flute over the edge and returned to his guests.

XBA's chest burned with fury. She perched herself higher, ready to leap across and finish the job. Upon further consideration, she just shook her head, defeated, and swiveled around.

What a mess.

She let the hood's fabric settle around her neck, let the hostile rain pelt her unprotected head. In minutes, it drenched her already-tangled hair and erased the neon-green lipstick from her lips. After one more penetrating look at the building, she slipped off the hood and tossed it over the ledge. There was no reason to hide anymore.

It's not that XBA couldn't have blown up the entire building, or even infiltrated it with an illusion and sliced up every guest herself. It was that Bazzo was formidable. He would detect the tick of a bomb, he might see through an illusion, and even from that distance, he'd managed to turn off the tech enhancement in her brain.

She suspected it was more of a warning on his part, meaning she'd need to be extra careful in the coming days should he decide to try shutting her down completely.

The setback, although temporary, wouldn't be well received. That was strike three. However, it wasn't fear that triggered her brisk walk across the roof. It was pride. She fancied herself a reaper, a timely and authorized deliverer of death, and so did Tas-Salvatur. XBA always got the kill.

Her final lesson had been learned: His evasion was not a fluke. Bazzo Sparks was smarter than his polished white smile and party-boy antics led the world to believe.

Cynque interrupted her anger. "You have an incoming message from Tas-Salvatur." The words *Is it done?* flashed across her visor.

She'd reply when she had good news.

XBA peered over the opposite edge into an alley, confirming the sleek matte-black hovercar was where she left it.

Good, she reassured herself; she'd done something right that night, and if she hurried, she'd have the opportunity to do something else right, too. Failure and its sting would have to stay on the roof, and she hoped the rain had washed clean its venom, lest it interfere with her progress.

Grimacing, she thought about the prime ministers of this and presidents of that dining and drinking, enjoying the cool of an air-conditioned breeze and the warmth and familiarity of fluorescent decadence, all under the dryness of a sound roof. Whereas the city and its people were blacked out and roasting in a mandatory no-electricity curfew.

"You would let your people suffer for your status," XBA said, squeezing her fist. "But I'm the bloody terrorist."

She skipped backward and took off running, arms pumping, mechanical heart rate climbing. She planted both feet together and firmly on the edge, her arms tucked at her sides, and jumped. She cleared the building and fell needle-straight toward the ground, feet first.

Thwoom.

Wet asphalt cracked under her heel.

She bent her knees on impact, exhaling as one of them touched the ground, but not too hard. The armor in her legs was once more a blessing, keeping her body from being splattered across the alley.

She could hear the hovercar's boosters blasting, the vehicle's butterfly doors hissing as they rose. She looked up, watching it lift off of the wet asphalt. Gears cranked the wheels under its mechanical body. Blue headlights drenched her front like the rain.

She slipped around the hood and into the driver's seat.

"Welcome, XBA, you have an urgent message from Tas-Salvatur. Would you like to answer now?" Cynque's voice asked from the dashboard.

Her partner already knew she'd failed.

A message appeared across the console: *Do not count your failures; count your learnings and leverage your resources. You have a new target, one who has the information you seek and, I hope, so much more.*

"Engage self-driving mechanism, code X-BELL-ASCENDED," she said, smirking at the chance to redeem herself.

The car spoke in ticks and hums, clicks, and cranks. *Bing.* "I've retrieved your destination coordinates, navigating stealth route to...Riser Town."

—

Artist: The CMD Studios

CHAPTER 15

DOLORES PRIMROSE ADAMS

Riser Town, Suburbs of the District

Day 213

TWO NIGHTS GONE and Dolores hadn't heard a word from Allister.

She stood in the alley between two sky-rises, Riser Town visible in its range of gray shades and backlit by an emerging gibbous moon. She had her hands on her hips, foot tapping as she waited for her son's best friend, a scrawny seventeen-year-old named Quiglesworth to answer her question.

"Well?" she pressed. "I could always count on ya'll gettin' yourselves scanned in the middle of the night, and all of a sudden you're tellin' me you don't know where Allister is?"

Quiglesworth fidgeted with his tattered clothes. "Uhm... I... He...," he stammered.

She knew he knew something and was trying to hide it. Otherwise, the answer would've spilled right out. She'd seen that same sheepish look, those same downcast eyes, every time Allister tried to get away something he had no business doing in the first place.

"Well?" she asked again.

"His potentials," Quiglesworth finally blurted.

She stiffened at the word, at his knowledge of it. "His what?"

"His potentials," the teen repeated. "Allister, I think...I think he used them, in public. Saunder saw it on CynqueShare, went around talkin' 'bout he was right. I didn't want to believe Allister'd do it, I told him to keep it cool, but now..." His voice trailed away.

Dolores tried to keep the anger pushed down so her next words came out even and not as a shriek loud enough to wake the drones. "Show me."

"I can't—" He looked up at her quick, his voice not shaking or cracking for the first time. "CGN, they took it down—no archives, no history, nothing. It's gone. Saunder said his uncle said they took Allister in"—he lowered his voice to a whisper—"to the EFD."

Again, she forced the calm into her voice. "Is that so?"

But out of sight, her chest was alive with her heart's anxious beating and an all-too-familiar tingling sense of dread. *Evolutionary Federal Detention of all things. For clock's sake, Allister.*

She also wondered what a human teenager would know about potentials and military forces rounding up stray EVs like animals. And she was about ready to ask when the composure Quiglesworth had held together disappeared. In its place was the tear-soaked face of a terrified kid, shaking so hard, she thought he might break apart.

"I swear, I'm not lying," he sobbed. "I lie about tons, I do, but I wouldn't lie about this, about Double A."

Dolores pinched the bridge of her nose and closed her eyes, her mind running in circles for an answer. Someone she could call. A favor she could leverage. Her eyes opened without a solution. "Don't you tell nobody about this conversation, you hear? Not a soul," she said, a finger pointed at him.

He nodded.

"You promise?"

He wiped his eyes and nodded again, whispering, "Promise, Mrs. Adams."

She dismissed Quiglesworth with a wave and, head shaking, started the mile-long hike back to her flat, damn near yelling about the idiocy of Allister using his potentials in public, then reliving her anger when she found out he had them at all.

He was five years old when his body regenerated for the first time. Six when he put his fist through a wall and brought down their roof. And of course, seven the first time he used the energy.

Foeht Zeorgen.

Those danged words Allister's father used to say to conduct his—

"Mrs. Adams," Quiglesworth interrupted.

Slightly caught off guard, she stopped and turned halfway, her lips pursed with irritation. *What more could there possibly be?* was what she thought to herself, but what came out was, "Yes?"

Unlike their first conversation, his eyes were wide and focused, meeting hers with the intensity of truth. "Double A and I got into it, after the game," he admitted. "Like, real bad. Worse than ever, I reckon. I was mega-pissed cuz…well, cuz I got scanned and it was my last one before I woulda got shipped off… It doesn't matter." He paused and tugged at his head of short curls, looking ashamed. "I…I yelled. Told him…he was too dangerous to hang around, and that I didn't want to be friends, and now he's gone and—" Quiglesworth burst into tears all over again, tried hugging himself and controlling his sniveling in the same big breaths. "He's gone and got himself picked up, probably for good."

"It's not your fault," Dolores said curtly. "Allister made his own choice. Now we all gotta live with it."

Quiglesworth nodded, the sniveling softening to sniffles. "If you find him, just tell him I didn't mean none of it. We're golden." He pounded his chest with his fist and held it out to her. "I'm still his best for the rest."

Dolores considered him, then said a bit more gently, "I'm sure he'll appreciate that. Go get on home, before the drones come back 'round."

She watched him disappear around the corner, opting for discretion over hysteria, albeit temporarily. When he was gone, she secured the bonnet wrapped around her head and ran back to her building, almost the whole way.

She slowed down to catch her second wind, her modest condominium beckoning from the third level up a winding staircase. She clutched the guardrail and kept her hips steady as she climbed. By the time she'd reached the first level, pain was shooting through the blistered soles of her feet. She knew she shouldn't have run like that, she scolded herself, her fingers slipping. Her leg muscles loosened. She inhaled and found another spot higher on the railing to hold.

At least her grip was stronger than her sense of hope. Otherwise, she'd have tumbled back down the stairs.

She kept climbing.

Dolores had been looking for Allister for nearly two days past. Midway through his shift on Day 215, her associates at the coffee shop, Mr. Skinner and Mrs. Garay, had reached out to tell her that Allister hadn't shown up yet.

She didn't start to panic until the evening disappeared and she still couldn't get in touch with him, *or her associates*.

The authorities didn't care about missing people. More people went missing the closer the world got to the end. So her last resort was to track down the one person who always knew where her son was. That boy up the street, Quiglesworth. It had cost her almost two days just to run into him. As he was never home, always dodging the other rowdy teens, and riding into the District to pickpocket for food and medicine.

Yeah, she knew all about Quiglesworth. She knew about *all* of them. How else would she keep her and Allister safe?

She'd known her son could be absentminded, even a bit silly, at times, and downright defiant at others—but she didn't think he'd ever be stupid enough to lose an employment assignment, and certainly not stupid enough to use his potentials with tensions in the District higher than the temperatures.

With Quiglesworth's testimony, and Allister's non-responsiveness stretching far past anything that would be considered normal, even after their most volatile disagreements—it all made sense. Why none of her hundreds of Cynque messages had gone through, why the video chats wouldn't initiate, both claiming lack of service.

Dolores finally made it to the third floor, her heart pounding from the exertion. She held the banister as she guided herself with tiny, even steps to the door, still feeling the burst of speed in her aching joints. Something about moving too fast always messed with her in one way or another; maybe it was the universe tell-ing her to take her time.

She was still somewhat relieved to be home, though arriving at home hadn't been the same since they left Cumberland Falls. In the country, southern magnolias and an orange grove used to greet her when she came home. Now, the only things that bloomed and ripened before her were heat-melted plastic and aging food containers. The aluminum box of Patrick's things was nestled among them. She'd picked it up quite a few times already, only to set it back down again, always too tired to carry it down the stairs.

Patrick had been gone twelve grueling years. She couldn't believe that after moving through countries and continents, sanctuary to sanctuary, to keep them off the radar, her son was gone, too.

She shook away the sorrow swelling in her chest and reached for the front door. It was already ajar.

She caught her breath. "Hello?" she said, peering between the crack. "Allister?"

She slid the door to the side and waited for her eyes to adjust to the faint outlines of the kitchen's countertop and single-eye stove. A dance she'd done before.

Darkness welcomed her with its silence.

"Hello," she repeated, her voice a bit lower.

Nothing.

Dolores felt her skin tingling, experienced a heaviness on her tongue. *I'll be fine, just gotta go in…and figure out…if someone's here. No. Big. Deal. Right? Right.*

At that, she entered the flat slowly, her hands ready to sock someone as she rotated, backing her way to the kitchen. Maybe she should've thought better than to come home, but she didn't have time to dwell on the oversight and instead focused on what she needed in that slow-moving moment of apprehension. She flicked her eyes at the dining table, knowing there was a battery-operated lamp and an illegal plasma weapon hidden under there. She decided she'd turn on both long enough to take a look around, and that she'd shoot anything with a pulse.

She was used to her privacy being invaded anyway. After years with Patrick, she always half-expected strange people to show up in her home looking for someone she loved, or trying to use her as a bargaining tool against them.

Those days playing damsel are long past, she thought as she stood next to the table.

"Shame, isn't it?" A woman's voice resonated from the darkness of the living room, sounding of rough foreign tongue.

Dolores swallowed her terror and, in a bid to sound in control, replied, "I hope for your sake you don't have your feet on my couch."

"Hmph, do I look like a heathen?" the woman scoffed, but the cushions squished and something creaked as if she were swinging her feet off of the couch in a move to stand. "All the hard work you put into trying to keep a tidy home. All that effort to keep your Evolutionary son off the radar."

Dolores leaned down, groping at her feet for the plasma gun. She got the lamp instead, cursed at her clumsiness, then snatched it to her chest and pressed the on switch.

Blue light splashed over the room. Standing before her was a cybernetic hybrid of some kind.

Her body went cold.

Dolores had seen many things in her life—from aliens to spaceships to an entire town going up in *blue* flames. But she'd never seen anything or anyone like this. It'd been over a decade since cybernetic surgery was outlawed in the United Sanctuaries, and even when it was permitted, it was not weaponized.

The woman walking toward her was definitely a weapon. She could be nothing else, her body hissing with every shifting motion and callous swing of her arms.

More light washed over her armor-clad figure with every clinking step, revealing metal-capped knees and a girdled waistline and—Dolores paused her observation—cybernetic hands with claws sharp enough to slice her head off at the neck.

She swallowed again, wishing she'd grabbed the weapon. *What in the name of the apocalypse…*, she thought.

Trembling, she held the lamp higher to something she…couldn't quite make out.

It was a mechanical eye glowing the orange of her sun-kissed grove.

The eye flashed brighter than the lamp.

Dolores tripped backward, the terror now too thick in her throat. "I think you stepped into the wrong unit," she sputtered. "It's the gentleman upstairs who is into anonymous encounters."

"There's the Dolores Adams I've heard so much about." The woman chuckled, still advancing. "All good things of course. It's nice to see you in the flesh, alive and breathing. No one told me you had such a captivating glow."

The thick, hot air seemed to be avoiding Dolores's lungs. The room began to spin around her.

"Such…well-planned seclusion," the woman continued. "If I were searching for a gateway, this might be the last place I'd rip apart to find it." She clanked loudly into the kitchen, scraping the countertop with her claws, then the stove, as she went. She swiveled to face Dolores.

The woman's bionic eye appeared to twinkle.

Dolores flinched.

"You're not afraid, are you?" the woman asked.

"Do you know something about my son?" Dolores replied quietly.

"Do I?" she replied with a grin. "Cynque, be a dear and playback the District C20 terrorist incident."

"Yes, it would be my pleasure," Cynque answered. Dolores was surprised that the sound came not from the woman's wrist, as was customary, but from somewhere within her torso.

The woman's orange eye flashed like a cinema projector, premiering the ten-minute clip on the flat's undecorated walls. Dolores watched as Allister sprinted after a runaway truck, clearly moving faster than any human should be able to.

Her heart sank when he had the audacity to *jump in front of it,* his shoulder positioned to strike the front. But she couldn't have prepared herself for what she saw next, because everything up until that point could've been explained away by added digital effects, augmented-reality filters. She hugged the lamp, rocking with disbelief as he used his strength potential to wrestle the truck to a stop, then healed completely in front of the astonished crowd.

"Glad I snatched that baby before they took it down. Managed to hit over twenty million views," the woman said. She gestured casually at the wall where the video was paused. "He went and hurled himself in front of a bloody truck. I'm thinking that violates the 'no detours' rule, mmm?"

Dolores sank into a chair next to the dining table. She wiped the tears from her lower lids before they dripped down her face, ignoring the impulse to sniff. She didn't want to believe that after a decade of hiding and scheming, that one of the two organizations had finally found him. The inevitable ate at her like a parasite as she tapped her finger on the table. "You're not with the EFD, so I guess you're with *them,* then?" she asked. "Come to tell me he's your property now."

"With...the Andromeda Project?"

Dolores paused her tapping and glared at the woman. "Or C20."

"Let's just say, I only play on the winning team," the woman taunted. "The Andromeda Project does have your precious boy, though, and brainwashed him into believing they're actually trying to save humanity."

The knotted feeling in Dolores's stomach reminded her of the day Patrick had received his offer letter from the Andromeda Project. A fateful opportunity sealed inside a cream envelope, decorated with a six-figure salary and top-of-the-line benefits. That same sadness and anger played tug-of-war in her soul.

The woman's arrival was no longer a mystery. Dolores knew why she was here—it wasn't about Allister at all. The list could only be so long when it came to saving humanity, and Dolores either had what this bionic woman was looking for, or knew someone who did.

"Listen, miss," Dolores said, forced. "I've been around the block long enough to know either you're going to kidnap me or kill me. So, whichever it is—"

"Now, now, let's not make any assumptions, love. If I was here to do either of those things, they'd be done." She loomed above Dolores, then leaned down and snatched one of Dolores's worn hands. She held it like a male suitor, then drew the captured hand so close to her smirked lips, Dolores swore she'd kiss it. "You, my dear, have divine fingers."

Even in her attempted courage, Dolores's trembling couldn't be helped. It took everything in her not to cry out as the woman smelled her hand and caressed it against her face. The cyborg's cheek was leathery and uneven to the touch.

"I'm looking for the machine your husband built—"

"To track the crystal artifacts," Dolores cut her off, wanting with everything in her for their interaction to be over.

"To track the crystal artifacts, yes. And I have this strange feeling you know exactly where it is." The woman released her grip on Dolores's hand. "I know you'd give anything to save your son, you always have. My proposition is we get me my machine and make sure Allister is safe, with you, forever. For now, we'll call it a trade between you and my partner, Tas-Salvatur. Comes with no upfront costs and no binding loyalties. All you have to do is follow my lead..." Her orange eye flashed. "Do we have a deal?"

———

WHAT'S THE WEATHER LIKE INSIDE YOU TODAY?

———————

CHAPTER 16

ALLISTER ADAMS
United Sanctuaries of America Airspace
Day 212

ALLISTER SQUIRMED INSIDE the shaking vessel known as a stealth aerocraft, more than a little anxious about their mission to infiltrate De Los Muertos.

It wasn't so much that he wasn't pumped about going; it was more like no one else seemed pumped at all. He felt a little discouraged when boarding had been nothing more than Captain Brandt's lengthy speech, followed by the conversation-free loading up of materials. But after hours in the air, Allister was deflated, not to mention queasy. Not much more had been said, or shared, save for the weather patterns, the turbulence levels, and the current altitude.

As a "team," they were about as far from connecting as they were from finding the artifacts.

Lieutenant Delemar…who he had started to think of as Leesa…and Captain Brandt sat parallel to each other in the cockpit with her piloting and him co-piloting, both in complete silence. Together, they monitored a set of gear shifts, U-shaped steering controls, and a console of colored buttons and switches that extended around them in a semicircle.

Allister looked for some unspoken flow between them, believing perhaps their silence could be a symbol of mutual trust, but what he found was almost palpable friction—small nods, sideways glances, postures constantly being adjusted—as if while occupying that space they were rubbing up against each other fast enough to start a fire.

"Heavier turbulence on the way. Brace yourselves," Leesa announced, flipping a switch.

"Copy," Captain Brandt replied.

To Allister, the Andromeda Project's aerocraft seemed like more than just a tool to get them from the District to De Los Muertos. There was the matter of its wide girth, the arrangement of plush bucket seats wrapped in chrome, and a number of amenities one would never see on a commercial flight. The whole thing was more of an airborne base, complete with up-lit flooring for ambiance and various technological integrations for ease of interaction.

He just wished it would stop moving around in the air so much. Perhaps the treacherous crosswinds of the Midwest were to blame.

They were passing over ChiTown Sanctity, a sprawling web of urban neighborhoods and cultural centers connected by threads of orange light.

Allister watched from the boxy window as the sanctuary twinkled up at them, illuminating what was now the third-largest sanctuary in the world—carrying the burden of thirty million–plus people, all hustling, all struggling, all trying to sort out their existence in the lead-up to the countdown.

The turbulence Leesa had warned about rocked the plane. The fifth instance—Allister was now keeping count—to occur in too short a time. He stopped staring out the window, already starting to feel sicker.

This time, his squirming was even less about the mission or the group dynamics, and even more about the roughness of the sky. Trying to stop the feeling of nausea, he pinched his eyes shut and held on to his seat, careful not to let his strength potential crush the chair's geometric edges. He swallowed until the acidic mixture that was steadily creeping up his esophagus went back down.

"Hey there," Captain Brandt said.

Allister opened his eyes, surprised. He hadn't heard the captain approaching. "Hey, Captain."

"How you holdin' up?"

Allister tried to smile. At least someone cared enough to check on him. "I don't do so well with transportation."

"We had a saying down in Cumberland whenever we were going through something tough," Captain Brandt said. As he went to finish, he took Allister gently by the wrists and pried his hands free from the chair. "Just put your head down and pray a lil' bit."

The corners of Allister's eyes stung with a sad nostalgia; it was like Captain Brandt saying it made him remember it again. He averted his eyes and rubbed his now-freed hands together. Though the trust between them felt inherent, there was still Allister's nagging bitterness about the contract and its hidden terms and conditions. Lifelong service to the Andromeda Project was not his idea of *beat*.

"I'm hyped to be on this mission with all you other Evolutionaries," he said. "Really, I am. But I—I didn't know picking this life would cost me my family."

Captain Brandt crouched down so they were eye level. "One way or another, it always does. Sometimes to survive, you gotta look out for yourself first. You can't save others if you can't save yourself."

Allister stared at his jittery knees, his chest numb from holding in air. "But I can't go home ever? It's twisted, Captain... My mom doesn't know where I am, if I'm okay. She worries, you know. She always worries." He grabbed at his afro in frustration. "Like, I told her I'd come home after my shift. That was three days past."

Captain Brandt put a hand on Allister's knee, maybe for a better connection, maybe to stop it from moving. He said, "Your daddy was part of this—matter-of-fact, he was the *reason* for this. He knew what he needed to do to save the world."

"Yeah, and now my mom can't say his name without going off the rails." Allister sucked his teeth. "She'll never lay it down. She'll hold it up in my face even if I'm dead, just like she does to him."

"Tell ya what," the captain said. "I'll get a private message to Sweet Dee. Let her know it's all good and not to worry."

Allister took a deep, pained breath. "So, I can't see her."

"The only way folks like you and me stay safe is inside the Andromeda Project, off the radar. And the only way she's safe is if you're...permanently off the radar. Sweet Dee knows that, otherwise, why'd she hide you for all them years?"

"I hated hiding."

"I know ya did, son," Captain Brandt said. "But you still want her to live, don't ya?"

He was skeptical of the offer, though he nodded in agreement. "One thousand."

"Glad we're cynqued on it." Captain Brandt made sure no one was looking at or listening to them before continuing, his voice lowered. "So, I made sure you got them papers back," he said, holding out his hand. "You bring 'em?"

Allister hesitated, swarmed by a strange sense of unease. The captain *had* proven he could be trusted with the knowledge, from small gestures like, Allister guessed, giving the papers back to him in the first place, to grand gestures like defending his pops against General Delemar. So why didn't it feel right?

He reluctantly pulled the pages from where he'd held them behind his back and surrendered them.

The captain handled them carefully, as if they were just as precious to him. "I remember this...," he said, fanning them between his fingers. "Three essential parts to the machine—the receiver. Okay, check." He flipped the page. "Whew, Z-energy-powered data storage unit and reactor. That's gonna be heavy." The third page he kept his eyes on for a while before he spoke. "And...the tracking system. Intricate, sleek, still a pain in the ass to haul cuz it's shaped weird. Your daddy was a genius, you know that? Too smart for his own sanity."

Allister half laughed, half choked. "Pops was beat for sure."

"Should've known ol' Patty Cakes would find a way to tell you 'bout the crystal artifacts."

"Maybe he figured ya'll couldn't get as far without understanding what he knew."

"Yeah, he was arrogant as all hell." The captain smirked a bit. "That's what I loved about him."

From the way Brandt looked at him in earnest, Allister could tell the captain had seen hard times. The break in his tone, the gloss in his eye—the pain in Brandt was a quiet beast caged behind a crooked smile.

He had to let Captain Brandt slide for not being honest about the contract. He must've had a good reason, as he didn't seem like the type to lie for the sake of lying. Forgiveness always seemed easier for him when it came to strangers. It was the kind of mercy he never gave his mom.

"Nobody's been past the Divide since the big earthquake...have they?" he asked.

"Not too sure, if I'm honest. But none of us are just any ol' body," Captain Brandt replied. "We'll find the artifacts, don't you worry 'bout that. I promised your daddy I'd do as much after he...after he...uhm...found out they existed. I gotta get back to it." He stood back up and made his way toward the cockpit. "No one's ever ready to jump, Adams. Have to figure it out before we hit the ground."

Before we hit the ground. Allister shuddered, instinctively tensing his arms and pressing his knees together. After a moment of imagining the terrible ways they could crash, another more potent thought calmed him—that he was on a mission to retrieve the TEWR his dad had built. Because he knew how it worked, he could help find the artifacts and save humanity.

He somewhat relaxed at the thought.

The captain took his seat. Leesa had been engrossed in her Cynque up until that point and looked up when he returned. Allister couldn't tell if she was pissed off or disgusted as she swiftly closed whatever she was watching and faced forward. *Wonder what's got her so hype?*

Maybe the other woman on board, an Evolutionary, like them. Bridget Sparks was her name. She had the kind of seductive features Allister had seen in those old Hollywood films: a slim face, large eyes, and long lashes, a neck like an African gazelle. Plus, she was shapely in the most distracting way, her body like a blade, slender, sharp, and curved in all the right places. The captain had called her their ace in the hole. The lieutenant had called her a liability.

From Allister's perspective, she could go either way.

Bridget roamed the cabin, particularly vocal in her boisterous Australian accent about the aircraft's gadgets. The sound of her stilettos moved around with her—first clicking their way to the row of healing chambers, then to the sleeping pods, then to the weapon controls next to the cockpit, where the lieutenant shooed away the woman and her shoes.

At that, she headed toward him, her chin-length red hair swishing with every stride. Her big eyes were a sinful red and flashed with a hint of electricity the same color as she arrived at his side.

"Sparks," she said.

Allister's stomach stirred again. He covered his face and leaned away.

"You don't look so good, mate," she said, attempting to stroke his hair. "Maybe they should've kept you on your training wheels a bit longer?"

Allister blocked her hand with his elbow, feeling triggered on multiple levels. "Hey, keep all that static away from my hair, I fixed it before we left," he snapped.

"Just needs a little more volume, eh?" Sparks said, going for his afro again.

He swatted her hand away. "I'm fine," he said. "Not really…used to…flying."

"I mean, who is these days, right?" Bridget chuckled down at him. "Staring out the window isn't gonna help ya, idiot." She paused, squinting as if she were trying to figure out some secret about him, then cocked her head and teased her tongue over her lips. "So, what's your gag? Guess you can't leap tall buildings in a single bound."

"My gag?"

"Your special abilities, potentials, *curses*, whatever they're calling them as of late. I'm guessing…strength? You look like one of those dumb blokes that swings at everything hoping for a solid win.

His answer stewed in the pit of his stomach and wouldn't come up without a foul-smelling, liquid companion.

"Agent Sparks, have a seat," Leesa said sharply, the first time she had spoken directly to anyone since they'd taken off two hours past.

"Well." Bridget scoffed. "Who died and made you queen? Last I cynqued, the seat-belt signs were off."

The lieutenant released the harness on her chair with a swift push of a button. She stormed to the central platform, her boots thumping loudly against the floor. "I'm not known for having patience," she said. "It's best you listen the first time."

"Oy, this bird's got some nerve. Patient? Guess no one told you, I killed a guy cuz he took too long to—"

The aircraft pitched forward. Allister gagged in response, a hand over his mouth.

"Agent Sparks, take your seat, now," Captain Brandt commanded without turning around. "Lieutenant, I need you up here—someone's got eyes on us."

Leesa glared at Bridget for longer than was comfortable, then turned on her heel and headed back to her seat.

Allister couldn't see the console, but he could see the lieutenant's face flushing with the color of alarm. "Who's firing?" she asked in a high pitch.

"Firing?" Allister and Bridget echoed in unison, their pitch even higher.

Captain Brandt finally looked over his shoulder at the two of them, but remained calm, his voice even. "I said strap in, Sparks. We're gonna find out in about one minute lost..." He turned back to the lieutenant. "The defense system is offline."

"What do you mean, it's offline?" she asked.

"What do you mean what do I mean? I just told you. It's a new prototype. I guess they decided pushing a button and having reflective shields was too easy. Anyway, I need more time than we've got to get this thing operational. I'm thinking a forcefield of yours would be good any second now."

The captain must've been talking about the same forcefields Allister had seen during their training... Was a good call, in his opinion.

Leesa, by contrast, didn't seem happy about forcefield duty. Allister found himself gawking at her as she took slow steps to the central platform, scowling the whole way. She glared at him when she got there. A kind of silent: *What are you looking at?*

He looked down quickly and gulped, feeling ashamed. But he couldn't keep his eyes at his feet, not when he'd been counting down the seconds to impact—which was the real reason why he'd been watching her absentmindedly—and he was down to—

"Security systems still offline, impact in forty-five seconds lost," Cynque announced. Next came the loud warning sirens and spinning red lights, as if either would help them in the event the attack landed.

By then, Leesa was levitating, her palms pressed upward against the air, her chin lifted with the right amount of concentration. The strain of using her potential crossed her face in a way Allister didn't expect. As if…as if it hurt her.

"Impact in fifteen seconds lost," Cynque announced.

"I need more time!" Captain Brandt yelled.

Allister held his breath, waiting for her potential or for destruction. And with a surge of hope, he shouted to her, "You can do it, Lieutenant!"

At that moment, her telekinetic potential arrived, each strand of energy weaving its way from her fingertips like threads. She cried out in agony as they moved faster, spreading themselves around the interior and, Allister hoped, the exterior. He could see a detail in her potential he'd never noticed before, these tiny honeycomb shapes interlocking together, the thousands upon thousands of them a hive pulsing and throbbing with telekinetic juice.

"Impact imminent, impact—"

Boom!

The aerocraft bucked and shook, then shuddered and dropped.

Allister felt his stomach lurch, felt the aerocraft tilt too far forward. But both the sound and the color of the interior sirens were missing, Cynque's voice missing along with them. It took him too long to realize that the main lights, which had been flickering, were now off and hadn't come back on…wouldn't come back on. Only the backup lights flitted like tiny candle flames.

He held the seat tight enough to crush it, his rapid breaths moving toward hyperventilation. He thought they were protected, would've sworn on the clock that they were. He'd *seen* it all, from the energy's strange, new purplish color to the way it had woven itself around the plane like a safety net. It didn't make any sense why they were tumbling from the sky.

Until.

He put together that the lights weren't the only thing that had cut off.

The engine was off too.

Allister's awareness seemed to turn the tumultuous noise of the cabin back on full blast, starting with Bridget's hysterical screams about being too young to die and Captain Brandt screaming for the Leesa to keep them in the air.

It was unbelievable, how adaptable her potential was—fastening to the controls and winding around the chairs, clinging to the floors, the paneled walls, and the ceiling—a glowing garden of energy, leveling the aerocraft out to balance.

Leesa lifted her arms a bit higher than the first time and maintained her position in the air.

Allister checked the wings, blinking rapidly in disbelief. Her telekinetic potential was there, too, holding them up in the sky.

The cabin brightened around them, the interior lights flickering on with a smidge more intensity than before they'd gone out.

Allister cheered for her in his head.

"Look alive, people! We're in business!" Captain Brandt exclaimed.

Starting to feel safe again, Allister loosened his hold on the chair and leaned over to check the cockpit.

The pilot console had also come back to life. The captain's hands skipped across the digital screen, bringing online what could be brought online, testing and troubleshooting what couldn't. He then turned toward Leesa, his brow furrowed. "We're not all there yet. Can you get the flight controls back online?"

"Not my wheelhouse," she said.

A voice came in over the comm unit—the other pilot. "Captain, we had to split off. Too dangerous to stay in formation."

Allister didn't even know they were in a formation.

"Any idea what hit us, Windrider?" Brandt asked.

"Our weapons ID system labeled it a kinetic pulse. Highly focused. We've got no counter-defense for that sort of attack. Besides, the firepower doesn't match any known projectile weapons in the database."

Allister's mouth dried, the fear growing faster in him by the instant. A highly focused kinetic pulse? An unknown source? Only a few explanations came to mind and one of them he hoped was way off-base.

"With urgency, Captain. I'm losing focus," Leesa interjected, descending from her place in the air.

"Keep at it," the captain shot back. "An energy pulse? If it didn't come from a registered system…"

…Then it was most likely the thing Allister didn't want it to be: their enemy. His eyes darted between Leesa and Captain Brandt, then ended on Captain Brandt. "You think it's them? You think it's C20?" Allister asked, balanced on the edge of his seat.

"Got their doggone name written all over it. Fact is, if it didn't come from a human-made weapon, it came from an Evolutionary."

"I don't remember Vonnie or Tranjam having energy projection," Leesa said.

"I think it's the other guy, the one who tried to blow up the District." Captain Brandt spun around. "We got a bigger problem, though: I can't fly this thing."

One thousand. And if the lieutenant loses her cool, we fall 30k feet, Allister added to himself.

"The rest of the unit is taking fire!" the man called Windrider yelled through the comm unit.

"I can't help them *and* keep us airborne," Leesa said. "What do you propose?"

"'Ey, mate," Bridget interjected.

"Not now, Sparks," Captain Brandt snapped. "I'm thinking."

There were so many loud voices coming from so many places. Allister couldn't process all that was happening. Nearing the edge of a meltdown, he eyed Leesa, whose arms began to waver, and eventually, she sank back onto the central platform.

She looked over at him, her eyes quivering, maybe even pleading.

"Anything I can do?" he asked quickly.

Her teeth clenched at that. "What could you possibly do?"

Perhaps he'd misread her expression.

In the windows beyond her pale cheeks and disheveled hair, he saw two blinding orange flashes, on the heels of which came two large *booms*.

The aerocraft pitched sideways, causing Allister to tumble and crash into his chair, unhinging it from its bolts. He curled into a ball, yelling as the ship dropped.

"Two units down! Raising altitude, follow if you can!" Windrider interrupted.

"I can't take us any higher!" Leesa yelled.

Bridget screamed over her like an unheard child. "'Ey! You blokes forgetting something?"

"What is it, Sparks?" Captain Brandt shouted back.

Electricity crackled in Allister's ears, raised the hairs on his neck and arms. He glanced over his curled-up knees.

Despite the vessel's constant motion, Bridget was anchored to the floor with a wide, devious smile, her obvious answer to the captain's question.

What they were forgetting was *her*. Specifically, her electric potential.

It was only in that slowed-down, somewhat everlasting stretch of time between death and salvation that Allister noticed the overcast gray of her metallic suit, the matching boots all the way up to her thighs, and the storm of red lightning flashing in her eyes.

Bridget snapped her fingers.

Red bolts of lightning twisted up her arms, crackled as they surged from her palms, then cut back and forth across the cabin in crazy zigzags before striking the cockpit.

The console reached full illumination. Recharged, like a battery.

"Flight controls online, operational capacity restored, weapons and defense systems activated," Cynque announced.

"Whoo! Here we go!" cheered Captain Brandt.

Allister unfolded himself in awe.

But electricity kept pulsing along the walls, kept moving in syncopated rhythms toward a healthy feast of control panels and computer circuits. Each bolt separated into sidewinding serpents, crackling and hissing as they slithered toward their prey.

"Uh, Sparks...," Allister said. "You might want to...call it back. Like now."

"Bloody hell, it won't retreat," Bridget said, her fists closed.

Electric sparks exploded from the controls and the plane titled sideways.

"God bless the Sanctuaries!" Captain Brandt shouted. "Get those currents of yours under control!"

"Captain, everything okay down there?" Windrider asked. "We've been analyzing your flight patterns and—"

"Soldier, unless you got a rubber airplane we can hop into, worry about yourselves," the captain said and shut off the comm unit.

Allister anchored himself to the arm of another chair. He watched the distress of the cabin, lost in everyone doing everything they could: the captain hunched over, swatting at the stray bolts; the lieutenant trying to get back up, a front-facing field of pink energy her only protection; Bridget stricken by the sight of her potential gone rogue.

He didn't curl back up. He stood up. His hands were stretched between two seats, helping him stay balanced against the constant dips in altitude. He took a step toward the central platform with the same courage he felt when he'd challenged Saunder and the FBX crew, then took another step with the same courage he felt when he'd stopped the truck. "I got an idea!"

Leesa didn't look at him, as she was too busy glaring at Bridget with a fear he recognized, the kind of fear that comes from one's own reflection.

Another bolt darted across his sight line and ripped a panel off the wall.

"Me too," the lieutenant said, holding up her hand. "I'm taking her out."

Those same glowing vines of telekinetic potential began to grow up from the floor. They thickened as they climbed higher, wrapping around Bridget's legs and torso, tightening against her body as they continued toward her throat.

Bridget sputtered for consciousness, the currents calming the further she slipped.

Allister gathered his nerve, determined to present his idea, and launched himself in front of Bridget. He stumbled for a moment but spun around to face a very pissed-off Leesa and planted his feet.

A hissing bolt slammed into his arm. He screamed in agony, also in surprise, recoiling a bit at the smell of burned flesh. *It'll heal,* he thought.

"Lieutenant, stop!" Allister yelled through the pain. "This seems mega-twisted, even for you."

Leesa's lips tightened. Her fingers didn't.

But it wasn't his words that stopped her. It was his potential. He followed her narrowed eyes to the hideous burn on his upper arm, where he expected to see flesh being reconnected and repaired. Instead, he noticed the blue energy twinkling above his skin and the residual red glow of the absorbed currents dispersing within him. This was even better than his original idea. He stretched his face in surprise.

"I can absorb the currents!" he announced excitedly, turning to Bridget. "Let the currents flow through me!"

Artist: Bradd Maesa/ The CMD Studios

"But—what if—" she protested.

"You asked me what my gag is, remember?" He took her hands and pressed them against his chest. "I'll be gold—"

The overwhelming surge of currents wouldn't let him finish. Bridget's lightning couldn't have had better aim if he were a cluster of steel rods extending into the sky, each bolt exploding against his flesh like a warhead missile, boiling away the blood in his veins and the nerves under his skin.

Unable to take anymore, he tried in vain to separate her hands from his chest, feeling his consciousness fading with his heartbeat.

———

Allister couldn't feel much of anything, except the throbbing pain traveling the inner rim of his skull, pounding its hardest against his forehead. Old memories flashed one after another through his mind.

The phrase *Foeht Zeorgen* drilled through the chaos. It boomed louder and louder until—

His eyes popped open.

The bright ceiling of the aerocraft's healing chamber was directly above him, which meant he was on his back, laid up on one of the metal beds they slid underneath the regeneration rays. He counted six of the rays, and though often arranged according to what body parts needed healing, these six were moved so far to the edge of the chamber, they wouldn't touch him at all.

What shined in his eyes was just the examination lights.

Groaning, he turned toward his right. Bridget was unconscious but breathing. Somewhere to his left, Leesa and Brandt were arguing in harsh whispers.

"You insisted on bringing not one but two untrained recruits on this mission," Leesa said.

"You forgot one over-ranked, overpaid novice," was Brandt's reply.

"Do you have any idea the danger you put us in?" she asked.

"The danger I…put us in? You got some nerve. Since when can you barely hold up an aerocraft? I seen you toss around tanks by just blinking."

The lieutenant didn't answer.

"Yeah, that's what I thought. You're supposed to be the muscle, Delemar. Kinda worthless if you can't lift nothing."

"I deflected that kinetic pulse just fine," she said.

"Just fine almost got us killed," Brandt growled. "If not for Sparks's and Adams's collective effort, we'd be scrap metal somewhere along the Divide."

"Effort? As in, uncontrolled outbursts of potential and impulsive self-sacrifice measures constitute as effort? I would *beg* to differ."

Allister stopped listening to the conversation, more concerned with the damage he had received from the electric shock. Breathing was a good first sign. Then came the faint, almost-nonexistent heartbeat. He tried to turn his arm over, hearing it squish against the table, but he felt neither his arm nor the table. Something was sloshing beneath him and dripping onto the floor—bodily fluid, maybe—but he didn't feel that, either.

He squirmed atop the bed, panicking when he wasn't able to get up. "Wha-what's happening?" he asked, his voice barely there, trembling.

The argument about hierarchy and strategy continued in the background.

"Captain, what happened to me?" Allister asked a smidge louder. "Captain...I feel...I feel..."

Nothing, he thought.

He looked down at himself, stunned beyond words by a waxy, transparent layer of fluid covering him. As his eyes focused on what seemed impossible, being able to see the deep striations and intense red of his muscles and the blue of his veins snaking through them, his shock became hysteria.

That smooth mahogany skin that he loved was nowhere to be found.

"What did I...my...my skin...what happened to my skin?" he sputtered. He tried lifting his arm to look for even a patch of it, tried rationalizing why the heartbeat that he heard strengthening in his ears could not be felt in his chest.

He shouted, "Why can't I feel anything!" then dragged the words out into a guttural scream.

Midway through his tantrum, the lights were lifted higher and a shadow fell over him. The healing chamber's set of glaring bulbs now shined behind Brandt's head, who held Allister down by the wrists.

"Hey! Hey!" the captain yelled. "Bring it down."

Allister stopped screaming, limp from weakness, though resisting the captain's grip.

"I don't understand what's happening," Allister said. "I'm not healing. How come I'm not healing?"

"Relax, Adams. Relax, you *are* healing. You still got more healing to do." Brandt held Allister's attention with his intense gaze, probably so Allister wouldn't look down.

He felt himself starting to calm.

"See there? You're gonna be all right, champ."

"I don't—I don't know—doesn't look like my body's with it," Allister said.

He let his eyes wander over the healing bay: from the digital charts with his vitals, to rough estimations of the speed of his regenerative potential, and finally back down to his exposed body. He couldn't help wanting to thrash and scream more, the whole thing feeling like a mistake—the Andromeda Project, the mission, his potentials.

"Look at me, Allister," Brandt commanded.

Allister jerked his eyes up.

"Do you trust me?" Brandt asked.

He nodded.

"I swear on my life, you'll be all right."

Allister swallowed. "I'll…I'll be all right," he repeated, his eyes drifting closed again.

In the darkness of his own mind, he completed one eased breath. Let doubt be replaced with hope. Let his intention to heal overpower his belief that he'd die.

And then, he suddenly felt everything at the same time.

A stabbing pain covered every inch of his existence.

His mouth was forced to open as wide as was possible. He needed the room for the anguished screams bubbling from the back of his throat. He jerked his head from one side of the cot to the other, his back arched, body twisting, feeling the torture of epidermal regeneration.

The layer of new skin stung its way around the outside of his skull, continued the assault down his jaw and past his neck until it slipped over the rest of his body like a slow-moving, albeit painful, curtain.

The horrid sight of semi-human anatomy disappeared.

His screams turned into something between nervous laughter and cries of relief.

Brandt released him. "As promised," he said.

"I'm all right!" Allister said eagerly.

He sat straight up as if resurrected. He went from flipping over and examining his hands to kicking his legs over the side of the open chamber to caressing skin as soft and fresh as that of a newborn baby. All to verify that it was, in fact, true. He was alive. But more than alive, he was *all right*. Fully functional.

Maybe indestructible?

"Allister, listen here," Brandt began, taking a serious, long look at him. "So far, we've been pretty sure us living life the way we all were was just us running down time until we didn't have none left." He took Allister gently by both shoulders. "Now, look, I don't know nothing 'bout the limits of your regeneration potential, but I do know you're our last hope and we need you tip top."

Allister tried to swallow, feeling guilty about using his potentials so recklessly yet again. He was beginning to believe he'd never be able to discern when was the right time and when was the wrong time to use them, especially when he was so sure in that moment he was doing the right thing. "I'm sorry," he managed to cough out.

"I know you are. Just don't pull a stunt like that again. Ever."

Brandt's face was stained with the same fear of loss as when his mom gave him a talking to, this hard-to-scrub-away sadness. With a look of disappointment, he turned away. "Nobody plays hero on the ground. Got it? I swore to General Delemar and Dr. Belladonna I'd bring you kids home safe"—he gritted his teeth—"so don't make me out to be a liar." He then lumbered back to the cockpit, this time taking the pilot's chair.

Leesa stepped briefly into the healing bay, a scowl on her face. She flipped her cape over her shoulder and began to wind her hair back into its triple-stacked bun.

"Were you...were you...really going to finish Bridget?" Allister asked her.

"Don't be so naive," she said as she disappeared into the main cabin's shadows. "Of course I was."

When Allister was sure she couldn't see, he rolled his eyes, fed up with her. "I keep trying to help," he said, "keep trying to keep it cool, and no matter how much I'm with it, she just acts like a cold, robotic—"

"Get dressed, Adams," Leesa interrupted.

He mouthed, *"Get dressed, Adams,"* mocking her with an exaggerated head gesture, and his chest puffed up as he pretended to swing a cape over his shoulder.

"Get. Dressed. Adams."

The second time he realized she was speaking to him over an intercom. He looked around for surveillance, pretty sure she could see him.

"Yes, Lieutenant," he muttered.

He snatched an Andromeda Project uniform off of the nearest table and tugged it on one piece at a time, only to pause once he was dressed, dumbfounded.

"You mean to tell me..." His voice trailed off, cheeks warming with embarrassment.

He'd been naked that whole time and no one had said a word. Leesa hadn't even flinched.

Allister snuck a side glance at Bridget. "You and I could use some more training, hm?" he said, then sighed. *Honestly, what am I even doing out here?* He lifted his hand, meaning to run his fingers through his—afro?

"Wha!" he yelped. His fingers skated across his bald head instead—once, twice, a third time. Each time he expected his hair to, by some miracle, be there on the follow-up. He felt around with both hands and kept finding more smooth, hairless skin. "No. No. C'mon. This is way beyond—seriously. Isn't *everything* supposed to grow back?"

He let his shoulders slump, his legs swing. Maybe it would eventually. Maybe he'd have to start over. The afro was a small thing to lose, in the grand scheme of the apocalypse, but for some reason, his hair had felt like the last part of himself that no one could take away. And now that was gone, too.

He hopped off the bed and walked to the window.

Pitch darkness stretched beneath them like a never-ending blanket. They were a thousand miles past the mass that was ChiTown Sanctity's saturated metroplex, where towns subject to permanent electricity curfews were overrun with victims of the latest superstorm or economic upheaval. Over one-third of the Omega generation was stationed down there, working long days, sleeping restless nights, trying to keep the Sanctuaries together.

Riser Town was a paradise compared to anything below him.

Allister leaned against the interior, thinking of what he'd given up for what he thought was better: the life of an Evolutionary. For the first time since C20's terrorist attack, he really missed his mom. He would've done anything for one of her overprotective video messages.

Brandt had made it very clear without saying too much. Allister's Cynque wasn't connected to the CGN. Not like it used to be.

"Approaching the Divide," Cynque announced.

Allister nodded in recognition.

The Divide. That invisible line that ran from Arizona to Idaho and separated the desolate from the doomed.

"All right, Adams," Brandt yelled, "there's a lotta wind out West, and I'm guessin' it's gonna be a rough ride down. I'd buckle up sooner rather than later!"

The aerocraft descended without waiting for Allister to obey, rocking as it lowered.

He scrambled out from the healing bay and dashed toward the cabin. After sliding into an empty chair, he snapped the harness over his chest and settled in the best he could.

His body felt weak. His skin hurt.

Still, he exhaled the pain. *Just gotta lose a few more minutes, and I'll be golden.*

"Follow me down, Windrider," Brandt said to the other aerocraft. "I have a spot close enough to the old facility to get our bearings. Used to land out here aaalllll the time."

0 years, 212 days Allister saw glowing on his Cynque.

The minutes and seconds they had left didn't seem to matter.

———

"I DIDN'T KNOW
PICKING THIS LIFE
WOULD COST ME
MY FAMILY"

- ALLISTER ADAMS

CHAPTER 17

ALLISTER ADAMS

De Los Muertos City Ruins, Past the Divide

Day 212

ALLISTER WALKED FORWARD, horrified.

The Divide may have been touted as a permanent line, but when faced with the gaping fissures tearing through the landscape, all of them shaken open by the earthquake, he knew the line was imaginary.

They'd landed at dawn's first flush, south of Heaven's Hill, a quarter of a mile east of the Pacific Coast. Jagged cliffs leaked rubble, dirt, and rock into a blue blanket patterned with white foam.

Standing there, staring out at fifteen years of deterioration, not a living human in sight, he really hoped they could find his dad's machine and get it reactivated.

Or De Los Muertos could be everyone's future if they failed.

"Low air quality," Brandt said, restrained. "Wildfires."

Allister had spotted a few on their way in. *Tastes like ash,* he thought, unable to fully inhale. He coughed.

The captain slapped something hard against Allister's chest. "Put it on."

Besides the breathing trouble, Allister actually felt almost back to normal. His afro had even grown back.

He examined what the captain had given him for a moment—it was a full-face nanotech mask, not something he'd ever expected to wear, but fairly standard issue—then put it on. It attached like a bloodsucker, its smooth material clinging to the front half of his face down to the underside of his chin. The visor across the eye area bloomed into an illuminated info stream and a high-definition layout of everything in his field of vision.

As cool as the visuals were, Allister was more thankful for his deep breaths and the smoothness of the air coming in. Leesa and Brandt put their masks on, too, allowing Cynque to established comm links between the three of them and the backup unit of aerocrafts circulating overhead.

"This is where we lost the Crystals of Transportation," Brandt said. The waver in his tone suggested he still couldn't believe it, yet the resignation in his posture suggested it was one of the few things he did believe.

"You know…," Allister began, "you guys keep getting the name twisted."

They both looked at him.

"I don't understand your language, Adams," Leesa said.

"What, twisted?" Allister questioned. "You know, like, messed up. Wrong. *No bueno*."

"I didn't ask for a translation," she snapped. "I'm telling you to use the correct words."

"Sure. Okay." He tugged at the curls of his afro. "It's just some stuff I picked up moving around. But...yeah, they're called the Crystals of Temporal Transportation... in our language, I guess. Daal Trelkkien in whatever language they came from."

Leesa scrunched her face, looking puzzled. "Temporal—as in, having to do with time," she said.

"My pops didn't tell anyone?"

"He might've," Brandt said, then: "Leadership changes hands. Marketability comes into play. Not sure who was and wasn't down with Temporal theories fifteen years past. We'll deal with it, let's get in position." He waved his arm over his head before starting his trek down the steepest part of a gravelly hill, which was littered with giant boulders and ended above whatever was once Los Angeles. Leesa floated down behind him without saying a word, eyes fixed on the horizon, appearing as confident as ever.

"Agent Adams, your only concern is the machine," Brandt said over their comm channel, alternating between jumping and flipping downward from boulder to boulder. "The facility should be at the base of this cliff up here. I'll take you in, you'll let us know when you've got eyes on it, then the lieutenant comes in, picks it up, and we go. This a retrieval mission—not a rescue mission, not a combat mission. Everybody got it?" He turned around and motioned for Allister to follow. "Everyone stay alert—just cuz you don't see it don't mean it's not there."

"Me, get the machine, got it," Allister confirmed.

He part jumped, part slid to the base of the hill, super-proud of himself for keeping up.

They passed a crushed-in dome and cracked columns, a dried-up fountain and scorched gardens—a structure, he imagined, that had once been considered grand.

Allister started to wonder if they really knew where they were going. "Did Professor Ashur ever drop those coordinates from the transmission?" he asked.

"Nah. Probably knew it wasn't safe," Brandt answered, steadfast in his stride. "Especially after I reported what happened near Tri-state. They wanted us to come back. I said over my rotting corpse."

Leesa stopped short. "So, we don't have the coordinates," she said.

The captain kept walking.

"I said, we don't have the coordinates," she repeated. "We. Don't. Have. The. Coordinates."

Brandt finally stopped. "What's your point, Lieutenant?"

"Well," Leesa said, crossing her arms, "how do you expect us to find the machine if we don't have the coordinates?"

"I know where it is," Brandt replied, his legs already moving again. "It's right where we left it."

The three continued the rest of the way in tense silence, then stopped at the edge of the steep drop-off.

White smoke from the fires drifted in thick layers, yet the haze still failed to hide foliage overgrowth and survivor camps.

Allister took in the panoramic view around him. Through the mask's technology, he could see the heat signatures of every leftover citizen within a mile radius, details on every downed building it had time to study, and even redrawn terrain maps of the city's former layout.

The avenues and boulevards of old Los Angeles must've been filled with luxury hovercars, lavish restaurants, and extravagant sets for film and television. The beautiful people of a utopia thriving inside a socioeconomic bubble poised to burst. It reminded Allister what the world used to look like, used to feel like, before the Resilient Nations voted to start the countdown.

But the vision redrawn by his imagination shimmered.

Those busy streets snapped into asphalt cliffs, jutting up and out over ravines.

Those sets exploded into bonfires.

Those luxury hovercars melted into dismembered parts—fenders, bumpers, doors, and engines littering the ash-soaked ground.

And worst of all, that privileged population crumbled into the starving, the delirious, the forgotten people of De Los Muertos.

Artist: Kingsley Calungcapin/ The CMD Studios

"So this is where my mother died," Leesa said flatly.

"Our first mission...," Brandt said. "I wish I coulda done more to save her. She was really somethin' special."

Leesa just stared out at the waves. Silent.

Brandt turned her direction, lowering his head as he repeated, "Really somethin' special."

Allister bit his lip, feeling hurt for her. He thought about the blonde woman in the photo Brandt had showed him, the same woman who was in the Andromeda Project recruitment video. Naorima. So, she was Leesa's mother and General Delemar's wife.

The lieutenant's inability to display emotion made more sense to Allister now. And even as he looked to her for any signs of a spine curved in sadness or hands clasped in reverence or *anything*, he just saw her fists at her side and her chin as high in the air as it had been when they exited the aerocraft.

She was unbreakable.

Allister gazed at the already-dead city being carried away by the ocean, then did a double take. He swore he saw the water glitch, then the sky, then the buildings. His nausea returned. He shook his head and looked away, unsure where the new nausea had come from and why it persisted in waves. Was there a correlation between what he saw and what he felt?

Subtly grabbing his stomach, he checked on everyone else, more as a gauge than with any concern. Brandt seemed to have pushed the memories from that place back down and was now watching his Cynque feed him data on activity in recent days. He balanced his foot on the charred foundation while holding a long rod inside a rusted holster. Leesa took her first steps on the ground and, chin lowered, massaged her temples outside the mask.

Maybe she feels it, too.

"Lieutenant, I need you to go high," the captain said. "I thought we were ahead of the competition. After that pulse attack, I'm not so sure."

Leesa seemed to shake herself free of what was bothering her and returned to the air. "I'll be up there, waiting for you to need me," she said, her voice as still and dry as the valley they'd infiltrated.

"Forgive me for trying to keep you outta the thick of it," he said defensively. "Just be our eagle for once. You're not allowed to swoop in unless you're grabbing that machine." He saluted her as she rose higher. "We'll let you know when we reach the old facility, see if we can get a visual on the merch."

"Stay in each other's sight. Only one of you has done this before," Leesa said. With that, she rocketed skyward, cape flapping behind her.

"You ready?" Brandt asked Allister, who nodded, quickly moving his hand away from his stomach. Brandt didn't seem to notice. "Good. Stick close."

The ground leading to their destination was flatter, covered in an almost literal forest and snaking through the many empty, half-collapsed buildings and abandoned camps. Vines and moss had grown up the sides of concrete walls and around turned-over cars.

As they crept through, Allister heard a beep from his wrist, and checked his Cynque. A new notification had appeared. *Unknown sender*, it said. He stared down at the blinking message, racking his brain for who it could be from. How did it get through when he wasn't fully connected to the CGN?

He perked up. *Pops?*

It was the most plausible explanation. His dad's messages were the only messages he'd received since he got behind the *fire*walls of the Andromeda Project.

He glanced up to make sure the captain was still in sight.

Somehow the stretch of De Los Muertos in front of them was distorted in the perfect shape of a monstrous-sized sphere. The sphere seemed to be speeding toward them, its borders growing as it gained momentum, and inside it, more of the devastation glitched, separated, and came back together. Allister was about ready to step back, possibly run, when he saw Brandt heading straight for the center, oblivious to the danger he was in.

It looked as though the sphere would do to the captain what it had done to everything else.

"Look out!" Allister yelled, suddenly charging toward the captain. "Look out! The clear sphere thingy!"

Brandt half turned to him, his hands flinging outward as if to imply: *What the hell are you doing?* He turned back toward their next hiding spot and put his hand up, signaling for Allister to stop, then pressed himself deeper into a moss-covered wall.

"Does the word stealth mean anything to you?" Allister heard him hiss over their comm connection.

He must not have seen it. But—*just cuz you don't see it doesn't mean it's not there.*

Allister didn't answer, too focused on his speed and the sphere, which was now seconds from tearing Brandt apart.

"Adams! Hold your position!" the captain yelled, now with both hands up. "Hold your—"

But Allister ran that much faster, pushing to reach him before the sphere did, spotting a crevice beside the wall as he neared, one he hoped was big enough to fit the captain's bulky frame. Eyeing the crevice, he got close enough to the captain to shove him sideways into it, hard, then tried sliding to a stop, so as to brace himself for whatever might happen.

The translucent threat slammed into him.

Allister's body shuddered on impact, his knees buckling under what felt like the gravity of a hundred suns. He cried out, blinded by pain, squeezing himself in desperation as this powerful, mind-numbing force ripped right up the middle of him like a heated sword.

The sensation evaporated like water, left him dazed and swaying on both knees. One short breath, and he collapsed onto the ground, coughing and holding himself around the gut.

He was too shocked by what he saw to check and see where the sphere went, and too busy trying to recover to process what he saw in those few seconds.

Beneath the mask, he felt the cool of a broken fever, a sort of relief that also brought clarity. There had been a vision so tangible, so real, of that same moment, inside that same city, though what surrounded him was a different De Los Muertos, a Utopian city untouched by disaster.

The buildings towered. The people thrived. It seemed like another time, an *alternate* time. Yet, the more he tried to hang on to the image, the faster it drifted from his memory.

When he looked up, Brandt was standing over him, face toward the sky.

Allister realized the conversation happening over their comm channels was about him.

"This is unnecessary time lost," Leesa said. "I told you he wasn't ready. I checked the perimeter twice and didn't spot a threat. What could he possibly have seen?"

"I don't know exactly, Lieutenant. Maybe something we didn't," Brandt said. "Looks like it hurt him somethin' good. We'll sort through it. You stay put." He dusted himself off and leaned over with both hands on his knees. "All right, Adams, spill."

"The…sphere… It was… Everything was *glitching*, didn't you…didn't you see it?"

"We're bound to see all kinds of things out here, don't mean we go screaming and running every time." Brandt sighed. "I know it's your first mission, but you breaking formation like that was beyond outta line. This is supposed to be in and out, so I need you to pull yourself together." He reached down to help Allister up.

"Yes, Captain." Allister let the captain pull him to his feet, but felt himself withdrawing when he got there, annoyed for being made to feel guilty.

Brandt forcefully repositioned him flat against the wall, then positioned himself the same and whispered, "No sulking on it. Just save all that potential for when we really need it, you hear?"

"Captain," Leesa interrupted.

He touched his earpiece, but patted Allister's chest for reassurance. "Go ahead."

"Unless your new recruit sees some invisible threat up ahead, you're clear."

"Copy, Lieutenant," Brandt said between his teeth. "Hope you've still got some of that speed left in ya, Adams. We're sprinting in fifteen."

Allister imagined the captain held a stern expression beneath the mask. He nodded and gave a small salute. Though inside, he was still sour that no one had acknowledged his noble attempt to save the captain or the sphere that he'd seen.

Besides, it wasn't like he'd only seen it, he'd felt it—like really felt it.

He steadied his vision on the visor's top right corner where his navigation was set to the facility's position.

Between the mapping technology inside the aerocrafts and the lieutenant's aerial surveillance, they'd narrowed down which of the hundreds of caved-in rooftops might've belonged to the old facility. Brandt made the final call on the one to infiltrate, citing his astute memory and gift of "intuition."

Allister felt the nervous energy building up in him, every second lost a heavy reminder that there was no time for mistakes or wallowing in them, and that his poor choices could mean their failure.

He shook his hands out and hopped foot to foot, waiting, as if for a gunshot, to take off.

"All right…in three…two…go," Brandt said.

They sprinted forward, side by side at first. Until Allister settled into his potential for agility and speed, feeling a surge of energy in his legs, causing each of his long strides to become two of Brandt's. He flung himself over downed walls, maneuvered through tight spaces, and dodged falling concrete—never second-guessing, never slowing down, never glancing back to ensure the captain's safety.

Apparently, that wasn't his job.

"On your right," Allister heard inside the mask.

He eased into a jog, slow enough to see the threat clearly without losing too much momentum.

Up ahead was a bunch of sticks and leaves arranged in the shape of a hollowed-out hut. At the opening was a tin of water boiling over a fresh fire pit, and next to that was a skinned cat cooking on a skewer.

"Possible survivors," Allister said. He slowed his jog to a walk, then felt his way behind a cracked stone wall without taking his eyes off of the camp. Only half his head above the wall, he searched for movement.

As he waited, he noticed—

Blood.

The hair on his arms stood up. His heart might as well have been thumping in his throat, but he didn't dare scream.

It was: bright-red blood, loads of it seeping from the base of the house into wide, shallow pools around the encampment. They connected like lakes, ran from one to the other like rivers, and after a few minutes, looked like one giant ocean. Hacked-up organs and limbs were scattered carelessly on the hut's farthest side, some bathing in the blood, others left out to rot in the heat.

"Captain, whatever went down at this camp was…mega-recent," Allister said, trying to keep his voice even. He took a breath and followed the trail of body parts, only to discover two maimed corpses with slashes across their chests and gaping holes in their stomachs. "Someone for sure finished these people…looks like they were living around this building…Captain?"

Brandt answered by forcing Allister to duck down behind the wall, then dropped next to him. "Verdict?" he asked, but not him.

"Tracking an abnormally large canine species, big claws, big teeth. Possibly rabid…," Leesa said over the comm.

And her observation didn't seem to bother her at all. Once again, she delivered her status update without any alarm, or even concern.

Had they all seen this sort of stuff before?

"At least we're seeing what he's seeing, so we're making progress," Brandt said.

Allister's cheeks burned with embarrassment.

"I have to admit, it was a decent observation"—her voice tensed—"and even more surprising, an accurate one."

Brandt jabbed Allister with his elbow. "Almost a compliment. Look at the lieutenant, making some progress of her own."

She didn't laugh.

Allister crossed his arms and leaned his back against the wall, huffing beneath the mask.

"All right," the captain said. "I won't make a big fuss about what goes on in this hell of a wilderness. But need you a little closer, Lieutenant, just in case." He hit Allister and motioned for him to get up. "Adams, cover me."

Allister obeyed, but with an attitude, a slowness in his reaction, a jerkiness in his shoulders. He couldn't help feeling unappreciated all over again.

Brandt pointed between the holes in the stone wall at what resembled a towering metal castle. "That old piece of crap's right up ahead." He waddled a few steps closer. "We're aaalmoost there. Got a good feelin' that machine's just waiting inside for us to pick 'er up and go." He ventured out from their hideout, grabbed the weapon handle attached to his side, and removed the long, slender rod from its rusty cage. "Keep your eyes open, your steps extra quiet, and your mouth zipped."

The facility had held on to a semblance of its striking architecture—the angled face, the granite exterior, the sloped rooftop—and now resembled an exhibit showing the harmony technology could have with nature, if given the chance. The shrubbery was thickest near the entrance, growing around exposed parts of what would've been the ground floor and up through giant, busted-open windows.

Brandt prowled toward an opening that appeared cut away for convenience. "Eyes out, not up," he warned, pointing two fingers at his eyes, then at the wall beneath the opening, which looked as though it had been smashed through. "Those twins might be blending in 'round here somewhere." He signaled into the air as Leesa flew by overhead, closer, as he'd requested. "In we go."

Brandt turned to Allister and nodded in confirmation before sliding inside. Fists up, Allister followed.

The room was drenched in shade, all but sprays of smoky light blocked by the thick canopy of shrubs and branches covering the window frames. Therefore, Allister only saw red grid lines of what the visor could categorize, along with an attempt to remap the layout. He imagined a hanging sculpture at the entrance, pictured the winding hallways and engineering rooms where his dad would've been working hard to locate the artifacts.

As he took in the remnants of playful lighting fixtures and the chic materials that had been stripped down by nature, he could tell that any utopian grace had been lost in the quake. The whole building was leaning as if it were ready to end its own torturous existence by falling backward over the cliffside.

Somewhere beneath them, waves crashed against the ass of America.

They sounded too close.

He thought to ask but decided not to—fearful of Leesa's sarcasm or indifference. Instead, Allister watched the captain creeping through the abandoned laboratory. He tried to mimic what he saw, the low-to-the-ground position, how the captain checked the area ahead of him before he made his next move and stretched out each new step to cover the widest area and make the least amount of noise. And for some reason, he was either always positioned sideways or in constant rotation.

Brandt was slowly swinging his plasma rod left to right and back again, a gesture that would've seemed calm had he not been stroking the weapon's activation button as if it were a trigger. He was visibly agitated. Maybe by the room's eerie silence. Maybe by its darkness.

Allister felt it, too: the uncertainty.

"Need more light," Brandt said, finally pushing it.

Plasma energy snaked through the rod's geometric grooves, the white-ish light dancing over smashed countertops, overturned sinks, and crushed lab equipment, all of it covered in a layer of dirt or ash, or both.

Allister felt the rod's blistering heat from more than an arm's length away. He shuddered, reminded of the plasma weapons the patrols carried. Watching the energy singe the dust kicked up by their movement and cut through the vines in their path, he hoped he'd never have to feel the burn of *that* plasma weapon.

After checking for the proximity of the opening, he realized they were already in pretty deep. He couldn't even see the foyer as they moved beyond what remained of a wide hallway.

But where was the TEWR?

A long row of numbers appeared on his visor's main screen. They ran backward and forward like a slot machine at full speed, as if he'd just pulled the lever.

Allister had trouble seeing past the numbers and tripped over a wooden beam. He swore aloud, which was an annoying enough accident without the beam toppling over and taking two others with it.

The collective noise echoed loudly throughout the space.

Allister stopped dead where he stood, and half a second later, Brandt whipped around with his rod pointed in the direction of the disturbance. When he saw the downed beams, he sighed. "Will you keep it down…?" he whispered.

But Allister hardly heard him, because one by one, the numbers spinning in front of his face slowed to a stop.

He thought it was the countdown repopulating. Then the first numbers showed up separated by a decimal, not a colon.

He was wrong.

It was another set of numbers—

Coordinates.

They flashed when complete, then disappeared behind glitching visuals. The visor's layout of the facility was no longer the grid lines of an educated guess, a mere stab at what rooms had been where based on old data. It was an informed map—unfolding before Allister's eyes in mint condition. He looked around with new perspective.

Brandt stood in front of a wall beneath a ceiling that Allister knew was caved in but, to him, appeared reconstructed. He had his hands on his hips, facing Allister as he shook his head. "I don't see anything," he said into the comm channel.

"Great, just great," Leesa replied.

The channel was quiet for a moment.

"Get out of there, then," she said next. "We can still get back to the District before we lose the day."

"Makes no doggone sense…," Brandt said. "No way anyone had time to move that thing, even C20."

Allister listened to them go back and forth until a flashing dot appeared on his visor. Unsure of what it was, he raised his finger to the dot, trying to gauge the depth of its location. When he touched the place in his vision where the dot rested in the air, it expanded into a three-dimensional rendering of the TEWR inside of a giant, hidden laboratory.

He shivered, feeling the excitement run through him like a bolt of electricity. He'd located the machine.

"Yo, Captain," Allister said, interrupting them. He pointed over Brandt's shoulder. "I see the machine…it's back there. Behind that wall."

Brandt shook his head. "I already checked scouted it, it's the storage part of the building. The whole thing caved in. It's rock solid."

The frustration from earlier sat heavy on Allister's chest. It forced its way up into a sentence as he threw out his hands. "You're wrong," he said in a loud whisper.

"Excuse me, Adams?"

"You're wrong," Allister said again, more defiant, more certain. "I'm telling you guys I *see* the machine. Through here"—he pointed at his mask—"so maybe you could lay it down, you know, and just check, versus making me out to be mega—"

"That's it. I'm coming down there," Leesa announced.

"Hold up," Brandt commanded. He hesitated, as if he was about to reprimand Allister, but he reached behind him and touched the wall instead. He felt around, and then pressed his ear to it. "Holy hell, it's hollow," he said, staring at Allister in disbelief.

Allister smirked though no one could see. *Finally.*

"Lieutenant, looks like we got a lead, thanks to *my* new recruit." Brandt kept his hand on the wall and looked up at the fallen-in ceiling. "I just gotta get a feel for this thing and...make sure the rest of that don't come down."

Get a feel for it... Allister was confused, partly because he thought the glow coming off Brandt's arm was the white light of the plasma energy pulsing through the rod. Peering closer, he realized it was not plasma energy at all, nor was it coming from the weapon.

"Uhm...Captain... I don't think I ever asked you what your potential was..."

A yellowish energy wafted around the captain's uniform sleeve. The effects likened to the rippling of heat seen in the arid regions.

"Disruption," Brandt said solemnly. He held out his hand, showing him the length of his forearm. "Most times it's a weird aura working in the background, sometimes it's a field...now, you can kinda see it." He put down the plasma rod, then splayed his fingers on the stone slab while keeping his palm away from the surface.

Allister saw Brandt's body tense, then tremble, presumably at the strain of using his potentials.

"Be a lot easier if I could move this outta the way like our mighty lieutenant," Brandt forced out, "but I'm stuck trying to figure out how it all fits together, so I can bust it apart."

Despite the fact that the captain's fingers hadn't so much as pushed inward, and there was no visible pressure against the wall, the material cracked down the middle and started to crumble in the shape of a perfect circle.

Brandt checked the ceiling again. He pulled back his free arm and thrust forward, stopping just short of impact. But the yellow energy of disruption blasted beyond his still palm and plowed through the wall with a thundering *boom*.

The building shuddered, then buckled, the entire structure groaning as the foundation shifted into a steeper decline away from them, spewing dust outward. To keep himself from sliding forward, Allister turned away and ducked down, instinctively covering his face with his elbow. He wasn't so sure about dust being filtered through the mask. Choking soon became the least of his worries as he heard the ceiling cracking overhead, then large pieces falling and smashing against the ground around them.

———

The building stopped moving, almost abruptly.

Allister realized the mask had properly filtered the dust and felt silly when it rushed past him. He peeked over his arm to find Brandt facing where the wall had been, breathing heavily.

The captain gestured to a gaping hole with his hand. "Disruption," he breathed out.

"Mega," Allister said. He surveyed the damage done by the captain's potentials. It was hefty. Yet, the building's lean seemed to straighten out beneath his feet.

"You're welcome," Leesa said in their ears.

Allister figured her telekinetic potential had kept the whole thing from tipping over, though, unlike Brandt, she didn't sound the least bit winded. He was starting to notice an inconsistency with her potentials.

"You gonna go in or just stand there?" Brandt gasped.

Allister skipped to the captain's side. "So I, like, go in and tell you when I found the machine, yeah?"

"Somethin' like that." Brandt slapped him weakly on his lower back. "Try to stay alert...and focused."

"I'm with it," Allister replied, climbing up into the hole.

To his astonishment, the hole was a perfect circle all the way to the other side. The missing stone Brandt had cut away from the edges had not made any change internally to what held the bigger slabs intact.

Figure out how it all fits together, so I can bust it apart.

Allister crawled through, impressed, wondering if the captain had severed the bonds on a molecular level. "Now that's discipline," he whispered. It worked just like Dr. Belladonna had said it worked.

"You in there yet?" Brandt asked.

"Almost."

"Good, get it in gear. I'm not feeling too hot. I think I finally get what had you spooked earlier… I'm sensing a sort of disruption. Can't seem to pinpoint where it's coming from…but…it's there."

"I'll hurry, promise," Allister said.

He reached the open room and jumped down. The light streaming in through a wide fracture in the ceiling was a pleasant surprise, perfectly framing the Temporal Energy Wave Receiver where it sat like a giant, tilted throne in a royal hall.

"This is whoa," he said to himself.

The dramatic tilt was due to its sunken position inside a misshapen cavity in the foundation, probably caused by the earthquake. Allister could see how the machine's odd construction had gotten it lodged there. He noticed the sound of the waves crashing was even louder inside the hidden lab. What he'd suspected upon entry was true: the entire back half of the satellite facility, including the machine, was dangerously close to falling into the ocean.

The machine itself was in worse shape than he could've imagined. A full-width, built-in screen on the front, cracked down the center. A bulky, broken generator and thick rods threatening to detach from the middle. A lengthy central processing unit and retractable console wrapped around the back side, extending the rear by an extra foot.

He expected something sleeker, smaller, but maybe holding that much data, measuring that much energy, and mapping that many sequences needed a much chunkier operating system.

"Captain, I see it." Allister pressed a spot near his chin, adjusting the mask's input function. "Sending visual through now." The mask beeped as if to say the content had been delivered. "You get it?"

No one responded. He tried again.

"Captain? Lieutenant? Windrider? Anyone?"

Allister was about to take off the mask and check it when his Cynque flashed.

"Incoming audio message, the Andromeda Project West Coast. Correspondent, Patrick Adams," it said in his ear.

"I knew it was you, Pops." He almost squealed waiting for it to load. "What gives? Cynque it up, play it through already."

His dad's vocals came booming from the transmission like a wise and immortal deity. "I can't say I'm surprised you found it," he said. "You're my little EV after all."

Allister dipped his head, a stinging in the corners of his eyes. He wanted to hear that part of the recording again, over and over for the rest of his life. He found himself hanging on for more—more love, more wisdom, more reassurance.

But his dad had paused for almost the amount of time it took Allister to move through the statement, and shortly after he lifted his eyes back to the machine, his dad began speaking again, his voice lowered to the familiar seriousness of his previous message. "To activate the machine, all you need is your Z-energy potential. Right now it might feel like you have all the time in the world, but remember, that ain't much. I love you, son. Be strong, but don't be foolish."

"Audio message complete," Cynque said. "This message has been destroyed for security purposes."

Allister clutched his wrist near his Cynque. He was so taken by the interaction and so moved by his dad's thoughtfulness. There was trust in those transmissions, coded with the same engineering expertise as the encryptions.

He took a step toward the machine, ready to speak the alien phrase—but before he could get out the first syllable, something toppled over and crashed in the farthest corner. He jerked his head toward the noise. His mask's heat sensors identified two bodies: one human, one animal, both still warm.

Allister went on the defensive. "Lieutenant," he tried over the comm channel again. "Think I found that canine you were talking about. It's real big. Mask says there's someone in here, too…"

He listened for a response. First, all he heard was a glitching in his ear. Then a blend of voices coming in, though distorted. He knew he should go back toward the hole and check to make sure the captain was still there, but he wanted to assess what he was seeing, determine if it was a threat or not.

Ignoring his intuition, he snuck around the perimeter of the machine. He was able to make out a lean human adolescent barely breathing and slumped next to the canine, if the heavily mutated beast could be called that.

The muscles in its upper body appeared reminiscent of a lion species. So did the patchy coat of tan with that glorious white mane, but the animal had hind legs and a tail closer to that of a wolf. The mask couldn't identify the creature with full access to Cynque's extensive database. It stood, saber-like fangs bared, and began barking as Allister approached.

His heart pumped faster. His fists clenched tighter.

"Easy there…," Allister said, trying not to sound afraid.

He knew if that thing had attacked the rest of those survivors and the kid on the floor, it would have no problem attacking him, too.

Brandt's distorted voice pierced his ears, obviously frustrated. "I repeat—did you find it yet? You don't answer in two seconds, and I'm coming back there!"

"Captain? I can't really hear you," Allister replied. He spun behind a pile of clutter. "I've got eyes on the merch, but that—that beast is in here, and there's a kid, too… I think…he looks hurt."

The captain came back on the comm system, his voice deeper, angrier, and thick with his Southern accent. "Anything you found that ain't the machine is worth jack to me. Neutralize 'em both if you have to."

"But…I—"

"The aerocrafts are following the lieutenant. They're three minutes out, get yourself ready, Adams."

Allister closed his eyes, resolute about not wanting to hurt anyone, but also not wanting to mess up the mission. They were so close.

"Okay, yeah, I'm ready. But the TEWR…it's"—he gave it another once-over—"kinda stuck…and basically done for. Could use some fresh parts…"

"Two minutes," was Brandt's answer.

"I'm with it… Look, I just…I'm trusting my gut and making sure this kid's golden. We're, like, the same age."

The captain scoffed. "Don't you go near that kid or that animal unless you're planning to knock them out. That's an order."

But Allister couldn't shake the overpowering tingling up his spine. It was that familiar sense of disobedience, or as he liked to call it, determination. He had to make sure the kid was sorted; he wouldn't feel right if he didn't.

Allister came out of hiding and took a few steps closer.

"I can see your position," warned Brandt. "Stand down."

He took another step, balanced on his toes in case he needed to spring out of the way.

For the creature had resumed snapping its jaws at the air and swiping at him with claws outstretched. The kid, a boy, stirred and sat up in a panic, eyes darting around the room. After a moment, they locked on Allister.

The kid studied him from behind sunken amber eyes, hands clamped over his ears, back pressed against a stainless-steel countertop. Scars covered his narrow face and even more peeked out through tattered clothing. He wore no shoes, and his curly hair was draped over his shoulders in a knotted mess extending to his torso. He was scrawny, like Quigles...curly haired, like Quigles. The likeness was almost too much to bear.

"Adams! You've got less than a minute to get your—"

Allister peeled off the mask midsentence, dropped onto both knees, and opened his mouth to speak. He felt his heart clenching, as if the next thing he needed to say was sorry for something he didn't even do. "Are you golden? What's your name? I'm Allister."

The kid flinched at the sound of Allister's voice. The creature put out a paw, stuck its ears up and tail straight out, and snarled almost silently. Allister realized in that moment the animal hadn't attacked the kid; it was *protecting* him.

"So, no sound?" he whispered.

The kid nodded in agreement. He gently nudged the animal aside and sat up in Allister's face. With quick but graceful communication, he spelled his name by shaping the letters with both his hands—Dorian Xander. Then, he pointed beyond the wall and, eyes quivering, started to mimic tearing at his own clothing and flesh with wild, violent slashing motions, as if his fingers were claws. He fell back on his haunches, hysterical, and buried his head sideways in the animal's fur.

Allister tried to understand the story: the five-fingered "claws" tearing at human flesh and clothing was weird enough, but for Dorian to seek comfort in the thing that was most likely the murderer really raised his alert levels.

It meant whoever or whatever killed those survivors had to be something *else*.

As Dorian took in deep breaths and blew them back out, energy bubbles laced in a rich-navy glow whipped around his hands and then disappeared into his palms.

So he was an Evolutionary too.

What kind of potential is that? Allister reached for the kid's hand and mouthed, "You can trust me."

Dorian looked at Allister's open palm, then at Allister, and nodded before offering his own.

They both stood up.

Allister knew what it was like to feel scared and in danger, especially as an Evolutionary. Maybe they couldn't take the kid back to the Andromeda Project, but they could find him a safe place on the outskirts of some sanctuary. He just hoped Brandt wouldn't get too hyped over the detour.

Suddenly, Allister sucked in his cheeks.

Brandt. It had been well over the minute the captain warned about. He'd expected Leesa to have blown away the roof by then and swooped in to get the TEWR. Besides him not hearing the roaring aerocraft engines, he noticed a strange mist-like substance gathering in the air. It was almost the smoke from the outside, though it seemed thicker…darker.

Allister covered his mouth and nose as he led the two strays around to the front of the machine, Dorian's situation bouncing in his skull. A warning so frantic it couldn't be ignored. Once again, he believed his intuition had revealed an important piece of the mission's puzzle, a lurking villain neither the captain nor the lieutenant had seen.

He lifted his mask and went to put it back on—partially because the smoke was starting to cluster, partially to communicate. Holding it inches from his face, he gasped, almost dropping it.

Two women stood beside the machine.

Allister recognized the first woman immediately, her soft skin, her stern eyes, the wiry curl of her untamed hair. He knew this woman's face almost as well as he knew his own, it being the first he had ever set his eyes on.

"M-Mom…," he stammered.

She had her hands fixed at her sides, and she was being held hostage at the neck by a gleaming set of mechanical claws. Allister felt his heart was running a race it'd never win and his body heat rising to temperatures that might call forth his energy. The desire to run toward her came as no surprise, however, when he went to do so, he felt no movement in his legs or in his arms.

His eyes shifted to the second woman.

One eye was visible, an almost-dead brown, the other was a black hole burrowing to what seemed to be a hardwired mind. Metal paneling framed her skull like a sculpture, yet all of her skin was scarred, a textured terrain map of uneven elevation, its color the kind of pale pink you find only in the third degree. The other aspects of her face and body, her angular cheeks and the flesh side of her chest, were infused with some form of cybernetic enhancements.

Time would not move forward and neither could Allister. Perhaps fear held his heels to the floor.

"Ah, you're the Gateway I've heard so much about," the woman said, her smile wrapping her face in malice. "I had no idea you'd be so darn handsome."

———

CHAPTER 18

ALLISTER ADAMS

De Los Muertos City Ruins, Past the Divide
Day 212

C'MON, POTENTIALS...ANYTIME NOW, Allister wished to himself. It appeared not one bone or muscle below his neck would respond to him, no matter how hard or how passionately he willed himself to—

Move.

He had to move, any direction would do—he just had to move. For the longer he remained still, the tighter the cybernetic woman gripped his mom's neck. "Get away from her!" he yelled, forgetting the kid's need for silence. "Get away from her, or I'll…"

"Or you'll what?" the woman dared, lifting her arm as if she were about to take his mom's head off of her body.

His mom squirmed, eyes widened in fear.

"Or I'll"—Allister's voice wavered—"or I'll rip you to pieces!"

His feet remained firmly planted shoulder-width apart. His arms and hands hung loose on either side, fingers spread open and not in fists like he wanted.

The woman sighed. "And to think, I was almost convinced."

He couldn't bring more boast to his voice, not with the fear spreading like a disease inside him. All those potentials, and he couldn't summon an ounce of strength, couldn't muster a burst of speed—

But being able to speak meant he had one potential ready and waiting.

The Z-energy.

"Ha, Foeht Zeorgen," he said.

Allister glanced at his immobile arm, expecting it to ignite at any minute. He waited for the searing heat that never came. Listened for crackling that never sparked.

His mom looked him in the eye. A barely perceptible glance that simply meant *no*. It was a look he recognized so well from every encounter they'd had with authority.

No talking back.

No fighting back.

Because with cooperation, the danger would pass.

He looked at the woman again. She just stared back at him with the same satisfied smile. The black space above her cheek, the space that he thought was missing, came to life in a flash of vivid orange. His heart plunged into his stomach.

He felt helpless. Vulnerable. Deceived. Finally he was able to identify her and why she might be there. "You—you trailed me off the A.E.T. Trac that afternoon."

"Awww...you remembered." Her human eye narrowed. "Name's XBA, and I've been watching you and Sweet Dee here for a looooong time."

A terrifying thought in itself, that woman lurking around Riser Town and the District keeping tabs on them.

Hastily, Allister checked for Dorian, the kid who'd just been right next to him. He was nowhere to be seen, nor was his strange pet. He expected to hear Brandt yelling at him from the hole somewhere to his right, thought he might even climb through, angry, plasma rod swinging and take out that woman before she had a chance to do any irreversible damage to his mom.

The mechanical woman's body was the only sound in his ears, her every attachment clanking as she moved herself and his mom forward.

She's gotta be doing this, blocking my potentials...maybe the communications, somehow, Allister thought, focusing on her again. "What are you after?" he finally asked.

The orange eye burned as XBA's smile widened. "I seriously thought you'd never ask," she began. "I'm after the Crystals of *Temporal* Transportation. I'm after humanity being saved, ascending to their highest selves. I'm after you and your mum living happily ever after. Not too much to ask, right?" She removed the menacing claws from around his mom's neck and held them where he could see, feigning innocence. "I was patient like I promised, allowed the Andromeda Project to so desperately induct you, and now I'm here to make you awaken the machine."

Allister was unnerved by XBA's request. Without her saying it outright, he knew it had come down to his mom...or the machine. Meanwhile, his mom's terror had softened, albeit only slightly. Her body was still rigid and her eyes were still begging him to cooperate. His guilt returned to pierce him through the middle. The reckless use of his potentials had backfired and put her in danger.

"It's pretty busted up," Allister choked out. "But...please...let her go and I'll do whatever you want."

"That's a good little Gateway," XBA said. She slid her claws across his mom's jawline. "You just need to say the words *Nournt Zeorgen* to your daddy's brilliant invention. Then you get mum back. Deal?"

The force holding Allister back released. He fell forward, coughing into his wrist as he landed on both knees, then looked up toward where the hole was *supposed* to be.

It wasn't there.

"How's this...how's this possible...?"

"Oh! You're wondering where everyone is." XBA's other eye, the non-cybernetic one, flashed red. "Well, they're looking for you, too, of course. But they can't find you as long as I've got going what I've got going. Now hop to it, Agent Adams," she teased.

Mind potential, Allister thought, clocking the red flash.

Obedience seemed to be his only choice.

The machine loomed above them, a glaring reminder of his dad's work, a never-ending scavenger hunt for cosmic artifacts. Turning to the woman, he held his arm out to it and asked, "Those words you said, what do they mean?"

"We're just conducting an experiment," XBA replied, squeezing his mom in a sideways hug. "Isn't that right?"

His mom pinched her lips together in response, her eyes cast down. She must've known more than she could spill. And he, no matter how much he racked his brain, had not the slightest clue what saying those words would do to him...or to the machine. His next moves required—faith.

Allister faced the machine. To guarantee his mom's freedom, he needed to say—

"Nournt Zeorgen," he whispered.

A stinging pain traveled swiftly from his shoulder to his wrist, carrying the energy's unbearable heat through his skin. The blue bolts traced his veins and crackled above his uniform like a malfunctioning circuit breaker.

Screaming out, he spread his legs wider, then gritted his teeth as his arm faltered, forcing him to hold it up with the other.

The energy flashed brighter until it erupted across the room.

He shrieked and jerked back. His inhales were as big as his exhales, his eyes wide and trained on the blue soaring through the veins in his hands. He thought the energy would dull and eventually vanish. But his arm blazed hotter and brighter, a twist of his potential he didn't expect.

It struck the machine. A *boom* reverberated throughout the room.

Allister's eyes shot up.

The energy was slithering its way through the machine's center, where he guessed the Z-energy-powered data storage unit and reactor were located. In a burst of light, the reactor came back online, and streams of energy wove their way through the rest of the TEWR, almost like sewing needles, repairing dented panels, resealing cracked screens, and reattaching broken rods.

The entire ordeal was a boisterous, vivid display of his potentials. A display more beautiful than he imagined was possible.

The energy rose through the reactor's rods and exploded sideways through the ceiling, splashing the blue glow over Allister's face and the rest of the room.

He gripped his arm, which began fading until it cooled. The room darkened again. Suddenly, his knees gave beneath him.

"There," he said, an eye on XBA.

"Hm. I see love is more important to you than obligation," XBA said. "Well, go on, goooo on," she urged, nudging his mom forward. "Be reunited with your Evolutionary son."

Allister struggled to his feet and held his arms wide to receive his mom. He felt unsettled as she stumbled her way over to him. He knew he'd done a bad thing, a traitorous thing, handing over his dad's work like that when they needed it so badly to save everyone. But had he still done the right thing, choosing his mom?

His answer arrived seconds later.

"Oh, Allister!" his mom exclaimed, wrapping her arms around him.

It was a joy he didn't expect. He hugged her back, soft at first. "I'm golden, Mom. We're golden," he said. "Now, we gotta get you somewhere safe."

"I am safe. Here, with you," she said against his chest. "XBA promised she'd help me get you out of the Andromeda Project."

"But I don't want to...leave..." He looked at XBA, who stood tapping her claws against the slanted keypad, then took a deep breath, and hugged his mom harder. "Mom...are you..." He stepped back and stared at her. "Are you...real?"

The body he held at arm's length had gone cold, measuring a temperature well below human. She resembled Dolores Adams in every shape and form. Even the way her head tilted as he studied her would have been enough for him to question his doubt.

But it was not her, rather a glitching, immobile projection of her.

"What'd you do with her?" he demanded.

XBA clicked her tongue. "Come now, you understand good business? I had to make sure I got what I wanted."

His mom was a distraction. An *illusion*.

While Allister was being suckered into a false reconciliation, XBA had brought the temporal energy tracking mechanism online. The screen attached to the TEWR showed the in-process extraction and categorization of temporal anomalies into sequences.

Allister powered forward, mouth closed, chest still. She wouldn't get away with her deception or that machine.

XBA's human eye began glowing red. Allister's feet stopped moving.

"Hold on there, Superman, I'm not done yet," she said.

She plugged her extended forefinger into one of the machine's inputs, convulsing through the obvious pain as the blue energy flowed into her. Smoke rose from her metal attachments. And just as her expression went from menacing to blank, saliva leaked from the side of her mouth. During that millisecond of weakness her hold on him released.

Allister saw his chance.

But that smile of success crossed back over her face, and it was then she ripped her arm away. The side-effects were wearing off too fast.

He ran at her anyway, wild with rage, ready to knock the data she'd stolen free from her circuits.

XBA squared her body to confront his advance. Her human eye flashed with red energy.

Their surroundings rippled. XBA disappeared, as did the manifestation of his mom. For a moment, Allister was alone with his mistake.

Then the sound of aerocraft engines broke the eerie silence. He stood where he'd been at XBA's arrival. His momentum false, his guard down. A body slammed him off his feet with the force of a speeding bulldozer.

He flew into the air and landed hard on his back. Clearly, an attack.

The unknown assailant spat onto the floor. "I been waiting to get my hands on you," said a man. He launched himself into the air, fists over his head. At that height, he was but a shadow with no details, backlit by light streaming through new cracks in the ceiling. The relatively slim body was poised to land where Allister was crouched.

Allister glanced behind him. There was room to maneuver. Intuitively, he rolled backward, the easiest and quickest way to avoid being crushed, then flipped over his hands and back onto his feet. The man landed an instant later. The floor shook from the impact, caved under the weight. Allister looked at the fresh crater, up at the man no larger than him, and ended back at the crater. That floor could've been his torso. But it was the uniform that had caught his attention.

"I recognize you," he said, eyes back on the man. His attacker wore a stark white ensemble made of hardened material. A uniform he'd seen only a few days past, on the A.E.T. Trac. "You're one of those twins. The Density Twins." *Guess that explains the force behind his attacks,* Allister thought, briefly rubbing the shoulder the man had struck.

His attacker didn't confirm or deny his identity, he just charged forward again, too fast for Allister to regain his bearings.

The best he could do was block another frontal assault.

"Foeht—" Allister said as he threw up his hands.

The man was that much quicker, catching him by the wrists before he could finish. Allister grunted in frustration. Once at his attacker's effortless grip. And again when he tried to break free and the man's density increased in direct proportion to his resistance. Soon, they were spinning in circles, faster and faster until Allister felt his legs leaving the ground. He couldn't believe his strength potential had been made irrelevant. Nor could he believe the man had made himself the center of their gravity. The room and the machine were now indistinguishable, both reduced to nauseating streaks of grays and browns and blues, and just when Allister thought he couldn't take any more *spinning*, the man smiled at him something cruel, swung him around a final time, then tossed him free.

At least he was *free*.

Allister felt his body sailing through the air, flung as if a twig yet moving like a cannonball.

Artist: The CMD Studios

He plowed through the wall he'd climbed through, which crumbled, and he continued rolling over flakes of glass and rubble, stopping inches from a pile of appliance parts.

Here is where he attempted to catch a break.

He lay on the ground, blinking, for a moment disoriented, the wind still knocked out of him. Though the wound in his side felt shallow, manageable, his lower spine throbbed much more severely—the result of two consecutive impacts.

Worse still, he was in the room where he'd left Brandt.

That was probably part of the cybernetic woman's plan: get him far away from the TEWR so they could take it. Her escape made him seethe. He wondered where she'd gone, whether his mom's presence was real or imagined.

It doesn't matter, move, he told himself, struggling to lift his head up.

He tasted blood from somewhere in his mouth. *Move!*

Nearby, he heard columns snapping and beams firing, weapons slicing the air and clanging against fixtures.

A body landed hard on the ground and slid next to him. Allister could see the now-dirtied red suit…the damaged mask, could feel the irritation even before the captain spoke.

Brandt turned to him and said in an irate whisper, "Put. On. Your. Mask."

Allister knew the ambush was his fault. Any excuses escaped him. He'd tried to do a number of things in those few short minutes, and many of them had been all wrong. "Where's the lieuten—"

"The mask, dammit!" Brandt yelled and rotated sideways.

The edge of a blade stabbed through the floor.

An aggressive, bright-haired woman stood on the other end of it, and didn't hesitate to go for the kill again.

Disruption potential didn't seem to work well in combat. Certainly not as well as density manipulation. While the woman's swipes were aimed at striking flesh and failed due to the captain's stealthy dodging, his attacks would've landed, and instead breezed through her figure as if passing through air. Brandt and the quite literally transparent woman he was fighting went on going after each other's vital parts deeper and deeper into the corridor.

Allister felt around for the mask. He found on the ground nearby, dusted it off, and fixed it against his face, soon forced to acclimate to multiple conversations over the intercom and a distorted view through the visor. Circular icons danced across the screen, trying to narrow in on a fast-moving target.

The mask finally registered the advancing silhouette of the twin.

"Analysis complete," Cynque said in his ear. "Recognized, Tranjam Kim. Designation: rogue operative, C20. Origin Sanctuary: Shenzhen. Potential: density shifting, subclass mass manipulation."

It was long past time to get back up. As another impact had all but arrived. Tranjam shook the ground like a herd of elephants, knocking aside boulders, columns, and anything else in the way. Allister had to think fast and act even faster.

"Mass in motion...," he whispered. It was simple science. Physics, in fact, his least favorite study. He teetered into a standing position, faking his lack of equilibrium like he'd done with Leesa. He let Tranjam get real close, then spun out with but seconds to spare. The twin charged past him. As he'd predicted, stopping was too challenging, so Tranjam kept on ramming his way through walls before slowing himself down. Hopefully, it'd zapped a bit of his stamina, too. "Lieutenant, what do you see?"

"Hands are currently full, just see what's in front of me," came her reply.

Asking about his mom would cause confusion, particularly if she wasn't really there. He was certain no one had seen her or XBA except for him, otherwise, they might've mentioned it by now.

Tranjam's thundering footsteps came back for round three—or four; Allister was too frazzled to keep up. He thought back to the truck speeding at him in the District, then narrowed his eyes under the mask.

Allister pretended to block again—but when Tranjam was feet from collision, Allister faked the maneuver, ducked, and rammed his shoulder against him. Tranjam's torso was as dense as concrete. Pain spread across Allister's shoulder as he jammed it deeper. With a guttural grunt, he lifted Tranjam off the ground and tossed him over his head.

Thwoom!

The building shuddered. "Structural damage detected," Cynque said.

"Yeah, no kidding," Allister muttered, staggering to the side. Sharp pangs shot up his clavicle and over his collarbone.

"Ledge is breaking," Brandt shouted. "Adams, get back to that machi—" The captain's words were cut short, lost in his own sudden gasp of shock, followed by a loud yelp of intense pain.

"Captain!" Allister shouted. "Captain, are you golden?"

Groans were all he heard.

"Say something, Captain. Anything!"

"D-don't worry 'bout me..." Brandt sputtered. "Gotta...gotta extract the machi—Argh!"

Allister heard metal rip through flesh. The captain must've been stabbed through the chest for the acoustics to favor such explicit detail.

He had to go help him. He had to go save him.

"Can you still get the machine out, Lieutenant?" he asked, though, really to anyone who would listen. "I already activated it...by accident..."

Telekinetic energy crackled through the comm channel.

"By accident?" Leesa yelled out.

Allister ignored her. "I'm going after Captain Brandt, can you get it out or not?"

"This is why I suggested you two stay together," Leesa complained. "I swear, I could've led this mission with more efficiency. Get in position, Adams! The machine's extraction begins now..."

———

Artist: The CMD Studios

———

Allister began criticizing every choice he'd ever made, starting with the most recent. Maybe taking off the mask was how XBA had infiltrated his mind at all, and if he'd left it on, those enemy Evolutionaries wouldn't have gotten the jump on them.

He needed to redeem himself.

Because now, Leesa was pissed.

He shrank at the sudden high-pitched whine of fast-moving air. A cyclonic force twirled upward in a counterclockwise motion, tearing at the facility's roof one chunk at a time. The ceiling opened up like a can of old beans, peeled away to reveal the smoke-filled outdoors and muted sun of De Los Muertos. Leesa came floating down through the opening, her cape soaring behind her.

Allister could finally see a 360 view of the chaos he'd heard over the comm channel: a man surrounded by blazing orange energy was at the facility's edge, hurling blasts at the aerocraft; Tranjam, who he'd thought was down for the count, came plowing back through the rubble toward him; and the transparent woman attacking Brandt was standing over the captain's still body, ready to again drive her giant blade through his torso.

XBA was not among the attackers.

Leesa eyed each threat, then dispersed the leftover rubble with her pink-laced potential. A cluster of giant boulders buried the energy-charged man. An army of rocks pelted Tranjam until he was forced to retreat. The woman about to stab Brandt was whisked into the air like a leaf.

One of the bulkier aerocrafts hovered nearby, matte black against the sky's reddish gloom. Following Leesa's direction, the flying tank sped forward, blunt nose down, and stabilized above the rendezvous point.

It was a basic exercise: lower the cables, attach them to the machine in nine places, lift, and exit. The dozen soldiers transported by the aerocraft climbed down a set of ladders, each with a cable hooked into their backs. When the collective cavalry touched ground, the cables were removed in a single unified motion and with coordinated precision, after which they worked to find secure locations on the machine to fasten them onto.

A soldier emerged, coughing, carrying Brandt like a log over both shoulders. He made it clear he couldn't stay as Allister rushed to help him lay the captain on the floor.

Brandt removed his mask and clutched Allister's trembling arm. "You have… you have…to go make sure…she gets…the machine…out."

Allister could barely hear through so much shouting and chaos, but he nodded, eyes on the captain's bleeding injury. The wound was, as he suspected, carved next to Brandt's sternum, wide and deep enough to see the red tissues beneath the flesh.

"With urgency!" Leesa shouted.

Allister scrambled aside to give her space to land.

She removed her mask to examine their fallen comrade. "Unbelievable." She lingered there, occasionally glancing past the demolished wall into the next room. "Shouldn't you be with the TEWR, Adams? Isn't that why you're here?"

"I was…but…then…"

"He'll be fine," she interrupted. "It's just a scratch."

Allister scanned the ruins for his mom and an orange flash above a silver grin, a hand clasped on the cracked bone in his shoulder. "That's not it… Another EV was here, a cyborg woman with claws."

Leesa's face changed. Beyond frustration. Not quite anger. "A cyborg woman with claws?" she asked, accusation in her tone. "Why didn't you alert us that you saw anyone?"

"I tried…but, I—I took off my mask to help the kid, and then XBA, she—"

"XBA…" Leesa's face twisted in surprise, contorted in shock and disbelief, reddened with fury. "Where is she now?"

"I don't know!" Allister yelled, exasperated. "She was about to finish my mom, decapitation style. Told me to repair the machine if I wanted her back. I was triggered, I didn't know what to do…so I fixed the machine, made it fresh…like the earthquake had never knocked it around… Sh-She stuck her finger in it and extracted the energy and the data too maybe—"

He paused abruptly. He could feel in Leesa's stare that efficiency was the game to start playing, especially if his mom was really involved. "I don't know if it was really her, though. My mom, I mean. When I touched her…she was cold…," he finished.

Allister crouched lower to the ground in defeat.

"Pull it together, Adams," Leesa said. "XBA casts illusions as part of her mind potential, that's what you experienced." She put her mask back on. "Just make sure that machine gets airborne. That's the only result that will make any of this worth it."

Allister winced as he felt the bones in his shoulder seal together under his bruised skin. "I'll try, Lieutenant. What you gonna do about XBA?"

Leesa rose slowly toward the gaping hole above them. "Find her."

"I'm on my way with the other aerocraft, hang tight," Windrider announced. "By the way, Agent Sparks is awake. She's mad that she's missing the fun."

"Tell her to mobilize and get down here," commanded Leesa.

Maybe Sparks can help turn this around, Allister thought. He hoisted Brandt onto the shoulder that wasn't bruised and made his way over the rubble leading to the next room. More noise invaded his ears through the mask. Yelling and cursing about the TEWR's height, its width, and its weight. Someone said the machine was stuck too deep. Someone else said to try lifting it anyway.

He entered the room where they were attempting the extraction. "Take the captain and set him up in a healing chamber ASAP," he ordered a handful of idle soldiers who'd just come down. They obeyed and returned to the getaway plane hauling Brandt's body with them. "Need you to speed it up, yo!" Allister yelled to the others, unsure of what else to do. "This ledge isn't gonna last long."

The lead soldier and the dozen others had the machine surrounded, each one hooking an additional coiled metal cable to the base and exterior corners of the TEWR. *With the extra support, it would lift,* Allister reasoned.

The lead soldier shouted, "Clear!"

The aerocraft's two turbine engines thrummed, ejecting bursts of fire so hot they burned blue. The TEWR creaked and groaned, stubbornly clinging to its grave in the ground, resisting the slightest notion of movement.

His dad's invention was too big. Add on the soldiers climbing their way up and the combat equipment fastened to the aerocraft's underside, Allister figured the vehicle required the power of at least ten thousand more horses.

He watched the extraction's lead soldier steadily giving commands, offering other angles.

Then Allister noticed the air changing around them, the clear sphere forming just as it had done outside, the distortion happening to everything within it.

More spheres appeared, clustered and compressed, pulling at whatever was clos-est—namely, the lead soldier—as if they might strike there.

"You, get down!" he yelled, leaping forward. He tackled the soldier to the ground as the sphere expanded above them. It blew through the facility walls, grinding them to dust. A heap of the poor soldiers who'd been helping were caught in the wave and went from full-bodied humans to skeletons, then ash before his eyes. The few surviving soldiers called to each other in confusion.

"What kind of potential was that?" asked the lead soldier, mouth hanging open.

Allister tried to form an explanation. "Got me," was all he could come up with. Then: "I think I can pull the machine out."

"Do it," they replied. "Quick."

Allister got up as someone on the ground shouted, "Almost there! Give it a little more thrust!"

A little more thrust was given. The aerocraft engines ignited with enough force to launch a rocket, dislodging the TEWR from the crater. The machine merely inched skyward. Allister had a bad feeling about the way it had been uprooted. Shouldn't the machine have been airborne by then? Besides the fact that it was positioned just high enough to swing without touching the ground, so, decidedly *not* airborne, its back and forth pendulum motion seemed…dangerous, especially when the speed started increasing. Above, the aerocraft sputtered and squealed, pulled this way and that with greater distance and intensity.

The ground shook again.

"The ledge!" Allister shouted. "Everyone get clear! The ledge…it's breaking!"

He slid backward with everyone else. The almost paralyzing twisting in his stomach had him believing one of those murky spheres was right on top of him. But as his eyes kept combing the air for what only he could see, the distortion in the room was widespread. Another version of that "alternate time" he'd seen before was glitching in and out. Within it, the walls were reconstructed and new, the ceiling bright with artificial light and enclosed, the lab, which must've housed the TEWR, fully intact. It was as if the first sphere hadn't disappeared when it burst, rather grew larger and stronger, and so then did the strange depiction.

Temporal…as in, having to do with time, Allister repeated to himself.

He spotted the pulsing thing above him, gasped, and checked for everyone's position.

The remaining soldiers scrambled toward the sturdier ground.

Grabbing his stomach, Allister dove forward and rolled away as, this time, the air seemed to collapse, stripping away the visuals and returning the room to its beat-down state.

Yet, the sphere burst like a firework. Four soldiers trying to escape became skeletons in withered clothing. More shrieking came through the comm channel, but not over the dead, over—

"The cables," the lead soldier yelled from a place he couldn't see.

Allister turned to the oscillating machine. The cables stretched more with each complete swing, already frayed at the center. They were aging before his eyes, their color fading from gleaming grays to rusted reds.

The first cable snapped at the midway point between the aerocraft carriage and the hook attached to the machine. It was impossible to hear it over the soldiers yelling, the engines failing, the wind wailing around them.

Allister barreled forward. Background noise fell away from his ears, leaving just his heavy breathing and the beat of his fast-moving heart.

Two more cables snapped in unison.

The machine swung toward him. His body reacting on autopilot, he slid under the TEWR on his hip, and when clear of it, spun around and stumbled into a run. He had the idea to get a handle on his dad's invention when it swung back, but the remaining cables rusted over, stretched, and snapped on the way down, sending the giant thing crashing back to the facility floor with an earsplitting *boom*.

Dust and debris rushed outward.

The aerocraft shot into the sky at full thrust.

Through the dissipating particles, he watched cracks in the foundation widen to fissures. They darted around the shifting floor in zigzags, connected to one another as if they were playing a cruel game against him. Beneath his heels, bigger pieces of building began breaking off and tumbling away. The floor and some of the ledge underneath went tumbling away with it. And as the ledge gained more angle against them, the TEWR slipped toward the ocean in reverse.

"Lieuten—" Allister stopped when he heard an explosion echoing in his ears. He couldn't tell if it was caused by Leesa or aimed at her. It didn't matter, he still heard her breathing and cursing and fighting, most likely keeping C20 from reaching their position.

Mad ups to her for handling all three of those suckers, he thought.

But with her occupied, it was up to him to fulfill the mission. He held out his dirty hands as the ground tilted further. They'd have to do. A firm nod of reassurance, and he took off running.

"I got this!" he shouted, not expecting an answer.

Everything seemed to be moving away from him at light speed, and he realized as he ran down the slanted ground, the ledge the building had been sitting on extended much farther than he thought.

The TEWR itself was too far from him now and sliding faster, the monster of a machine crushing debris under its weight, twisting around as it collided with whatever it couldn't demolish with its size. The few cables that had remained intact trailed behind, still attached.

Allister believed there were only two cables long enough for him to reach.

And he kept his focus on them as he continued chasing after the TEWR, leaping over uncrushed debris being pulled to the edge, ducking foliage trying to hang on to both the ground and pieces of building, dodging dislodged boulders tumbling at his back.

Sweating and panting, Allister looked up. His heart soared, hopeful, as the flailing cables were finally within reach. He alternated swiping for them with each hand, trying to grab on to one—just one—before the machine was lost and it was his fault. For a split second, the two cables were entangled together in the air, and for a split second, Allister was smiling, running, and reaching all at once.

He snagged them right where they'd coiled, wrapped them around his forearm, and pulled.

The machine kept sliding away and taking him with it.

As his heels skidded along the ground, he leaned back as far as he could, repositioning his heels apart to keep from being dragged farther forward or off his feet. In that position, gravity did the hard work of digging his heels into the rocky ledge, giving him the foothold he needed.

The machine slowed and...finally—after Allister made another loop of the cables and yanked them backward—jerked to a stop.

He continued working his hands down the cables one at a time. Seeing the possibility, he kept finding the strength for each newfound grip and twist, each mighty upward tug—even against the sinister form of rope burn adding stinging incisions to his already-worn palms.

A few more meters, he thought, pulling again, then he repeated, *A few more meters*.

This was one of those golden moments. Discipline he breathed in. Patience he breathed out.

A few more meters.

Then he paused. And pausing was a mistake. It made the tiniest room for doubt to slip between his fingers. He and the machine seemed suspended in time; his strength, though colossal, had limited impact, the machine's polished exterior offering bragging rights if caught.

He had hoped that—*eventually*—he would reel it back up the sloped ledge.

All he saw before him was defeat. He felt it, too, suffocating his resolve, contaminating the air he depended on. The mission was almost impossible to envision shifting in his favor; eventually he'd have to give in because he could see by the loosening rocks and rampant cracks in the ground that eventually the ledge would cave. Very soon, in fact, he realized as the earth shook beneath him, breaking apart the rocks at his feet.

"Lieu-Lieutenant!" Allister boomed over the rumbling of the ledge collapsing. His knees buckled. He rocked forward. "The ledge"—he paused to inhale, and secured the steel cable around his wrist—"the machine."

It was now balanced at the edge.

He stared at it, the thing he'd been sent to retrieve, the thing he'd been coerced into activating, suspended close enough to imagine victory yet far enough to give in to failure.

The machine taunted him in its teetering toward the ocean.

Nournt Zeorgen ran through his mind, as if a solution. He didn't know what it could do...and he didn't know what it couldn't do, either. He felt he had to try whatever potential he had or risk the regret of not giving it his all.

So not fully thinking about either the energy's torturous burning or its destructive blasts, he whispered, "Nournt Zeorgen."

And...

Fwoom.

A blue ring of Z-energy burst from the TEWR.

The regret arrived in him anyway, bright and fast, just like the thick bolts of blue energy jumping free of the reactor. Whatever power had been poured into restoring the machine to its present glory traveled back up the cables, running and leaping for him like pets called back to their master.

He'd summoned the fullness of his strength to arm muscles ready to rupture. His veins, on fire from exertion, masked a feeling he'd become wary of. He was too hot to even distinguish between the atmosphere's heat that was pressing on his pores and the heat that was rising from them.

The energy reached his fingers. Continued swimming up his arm, igniting flesh as it traveled. He gripped both cables with all the patience he had left, terrified the energy would do to them what it did to everything else.

Just as he feared, the cables crisped against his hot skin. Waves of heat rippled above the places where the metal met his hands and wound its way up his arm.

The smell of it melting sent him into a silent panic.

Allister wished the Z-energy to the depths of him, rapidly breathing his way through the effort. Because his arm was all but bombarded. A limb glowing with an unprecedented luminosity. And from that same dangerous shine, he knew there was another outcome everyone could see—imminent destruction.

Now, the yelling in his ear was about him, about the energy, about the machine.

A surge of strength from his quads and lower back drove his hips forward. As his body swung back up, he wrenched the cables toward him with everything he had left.

Then he let go.

—————

CHAPTER 19

LIEUTENANT LEESA DELEMAR
DeLos Muertos City Ruins, Past the Divide
Day 212

XBA WAS HIDING and Leesa knew it.

Leesa was, at present, locked in a standoff with C20's latest set of misguided recruits, floating just high enough to avoid being ganged up on but low enough to engage.

Their Cynque files were populating in the corner of her visor in real time. To her left, Shahar Prasai, the tall, strapping man with bulging veins and a wicked grin, slammed his glowing fists together. To her right, Tranjam Kim, the lean, grimacing man with a tattoo over his eye, crushed a loose boulder with his foot. At her rear, Vonnie Kim, the partially transparent woman, swung a blood-soiled weapon and thrust it forward.

She'd been at it with them to the point of exhaustion and needed a quick-and-dirty way to find out what they knew...then remove them as obstacles.

Because among the fury of this battle, only one thing was on Leesa's mind.

Where is XBA?

Allister's casual mention of her enemy couldn't have been helped. He didn't know of their violent past. What Leesa had sacrificed in an effort to rid the world of that cybernetic weapon posing as a woman.

That was classified.

"Deliver XBA to me," Leesa said, both fists clenching, "and I'll let you EVs live...for the rest of your lives in our Vault."

Vonnie Kim came at her first, face round as a full moon and fixed in disgust. The woman jumped skyward and swung the sharpened blade at Leesa's spine. Shahar Prasai aimed one of his glowing fists at her and fired an orange blast at her torso; its color, she realized, was identical to what had hit them over ChiTown Sanctity.

Her retaliation was swift. Well executed. It began with telekinetic energy charging in her hands, and ended with the expulsions of it streaming in all directions. Anything within range blew outward; car doors and stray siding, concrete slabs and steel beams, charred appliances and broken furniture. She didn't expect such an attack to stop her enemies; she didn't even expect it to slow them. She just needed time to regain control of the mission—which now included killing XBA.

Hovering backward, Leesa looked over her shoulder.

She could see Allister standing on the last intact slab of rock jutting out over the ocean, sweating, straining as he kept the TEWR from tipping over the ledge. She imagined he'd snap at any moment, either mentally or physically. Regardless, he was a crumbling cliff away from losing it altogether.

"Lieutenant!" Allister shouted, interrupting her thoughts. "The ledge." Instead of a cry for help, what followed was a breathless warning. "The machine."

"The Z-energy," she whispered, disturbed by its rippling vibrance coming off the TEWR.

She went to use her telekinetic potential, yet it was clear she'd reacted too slowly, because she heard Allister whisper something over the comm channel—just two words.

Nournt Zeorgen.

At that, the energy moved fast, whipping and jumping *away* from the machine's steadily dimming core. The machine darkened when it had been drained, its alleged restoration reversed before her eyes.

And Allister...Allister was ablaze with Z-energy, shielded from her sight by flashes of volatile blue eruptions.

She heard a loud sizzling, either his skin or the metal—or both—and grimaced.

"No!" she screamed. "Don't let—" *go.*

But he did. He let the machine go.

Mere seconds later, the ocean-carved plateau split under him. The sounds came at her fast: the machine's loud groaning as it tipped toward her and landed flat; the loose rocks breaking off and against one another; the back half of the ledge grinding against the cliffside striving to hold it in place.

The angle was already too steep, the gravity too strong to reverse, and she watched in horror as the ledge, the rest of the facility, and the machine fell from her vision in... One. Great. *Roar.*

Leesa's eyes burned with purple fury. Hers was an exercise in intention: the intention to isolate the TEWR among random parts of the building with similar texture and size, to cast her telekinetic force underneath just the thing she needed, and stop it from breaking against the water's turbulent blue surface.

Though she couldn't see the machine, she focused on it—its weight and density, the nuanced curves and bulky construction—all from the visceral memory of witnessing it disappear.

Palms to the sky, she scrunched her brow and brought forth her telekinetic potential, sewing the pink and purple threads together like a net beneath the behemoth.

It couldn't be heavier than the aerocraft, but when she'd lifted that, it hadn't been *falling*.

She curled her hands as if she were going to catch the machine with them.

And, with an exhale, braced herself.

The machine landed where she'd wanted. Though doing so almost yanked her out of the sky. "Ahhh!" she yelled out, wind rushing up at her as she plummeted.

The machine was still plummeting, too.

She nearly hit the ground, stopping herself just short of plowing into the dirt. Here, she strained to exact enough reverse force to lift the machine, neck and back and arms tensed from the effort. It slowed, succumbing to her willpower, then stopped—she assumed—in midair.

She was beyond out of breath, working toward being out of energy. De Los Muertos had fallen quiet, the eerie type of quiet found in an illusion. Tranjam, Vonnie, and Shahar had all disappeared.

"XBA! I know you're here," Leesa shouted.

She closed her eyes. She had called for an enemy she couldn't face. Not while managing the weight of what felt like a small mountain. She might as well have been holding up the machine with her bare hands.

C'mon...keep it together, she thought, concentrating on the cliffside's sharp drop where the back half of the facility had been.

Leesa had to let her feet touch land. Easing the strain of self-levitation was about the best she could do to ensure the TEWR made it to safety. She mustered more energy, the last of it, she was certain. But she felt it climbing higher...and knew she was...*almost there...*

The machine floated into view: first the rods, then the core reactor, then the oddly shaped base. It cleared the ledge and, though it was a considerable distance away, followed her mental command and drifted closer.

The flutter in her chest was a feeling she rarely felt in the real world. Triumph. Sure, she knew her potentials were powerful, but to see them work with such grace...with such precision. She smiled wider, thinking how Allister wouldn't be the Gateway for much longer. She didn't see what happened to him. She didn't care. He'd gone from being an asset to a liability in that moment of choice. The mission's footage would likely be his one-way ticket to the termination chamber.

"The general must be so proud," said a voice as bubbly as acid.

Leesa pressed her lips together in satisfaction.

"Unregistered subject detected," Cynque said in her ear.

She knew it was one of the few times she didn't need the global network to feed her information. Beyond the rubble, amid the smoke, she heard the clinking of metallic armor. The arrival of none other than XBA.

Leesa glanced around, defensive, suspicious.

But it was just XBA walking toward her. Her enemy was...alone.

"Leesa Delemar, my oldest, dearest friend," XBA said. "I heard you calling for me. And, truthfully, I'm just beside myself that you missed me as much as I've missed you. Surprise! I'm not dead."

Leesa tried to disguise her astonishment, acted as though she already knew by narrowing her eyes in hatred, rather than widening them in shock. Because she did know, right? Allister had told her. The pounding in her heart convinced her that she hadn't believed him...even if him lying made less sense than XBA's survival. But now she felt forced to; the evidence was standing before her, undeniable.

The cybernetic hands, Leesa remembered. They were XBA's signature. The metal claws, her trademark. But beyond that she was *different*. Upgraded. A couple hundred days past, she had two brown eyes. Her face and skin had appeared smooth, bred from wealth and privilege, and her human body, though guarded by metallic armor, was not infused with it.

"How...did you...survive?" Leesa forced out, still consumed with the burden of levitating the machine.

XBA's mechanical eye seemed to be wearing Leesa down with a hardened stare and the repeated flashes of orange light. And though its counterpart radiated a dense, almost captivating autumn brown, it was no less dangerous—the red energy of XBA's telepathic potential would come from there if it came from anywhere.

Leesa shook with anger—at her enemy's nonchalance, at the thought of, yet again, being paralyzed by that potential…at perhaps having been deceived by it. She could swear she'd seen XBA die, remembered standing tall as her nemesis took her last breaths. "*How?*" Leesa demanded.

XBA shrugged. "Who knows… Maybe something about the resilience of Mind Evolutionaries." She flipped her thick curls as if she were flirting. The deeply saturated green hair flew up and landed on the other side of her head, revealing scarred scalp and facial tissue.

Burns, Leesa thought, swallowing hard.

"Yes, burns." XBA's brown eye flashed with red telepathic energy. Her grin faded fast. "I suppose you thought your energy pulse would turn me into ash, hmm?" she asked, clenching her teeth. "Well, I promise you, you're going to wish it had."

Infuriated, Leesa listened to the clanging of metal on metal getting louder as XBA approached.

She resigned herself to taking XBA's vengeful torture. For she believed it would be worth it, worth being the one to save the machine and make up for Allister's desperate attempts to play hero.

Victory felt so close, yet any aim at self-defense and she knew their mission would fail.

XBA must've known that, too. "Could this be the moment I've been dreaming of?" she asked, flexing her claws. "Could I somehow have *predicted* that in vulnerability you would meet your end? Why…color me psychic."

Leesa met the taunt with a quiet sneer. She realized after her third glance at the metallic claws that one well-aimed slice could rip out her throat.

Were they that sharp before?

Her gaze searched the disaster area, looking for something to fling between them, and eventually fixed on a small, egg-shaped pod to one side of her. The Andromeda Project logo was painted across the pod's belly. It wobbled back and forth, hatching, in a sense.

Thankfully, XBA didn't seem to notice.

The pod hissed an instant later, unsealing along the seam, and swung open. Out popped the last person Leesa expected to see: Agent Bridget Sparks, looking more excited than anyone should ever be. "Everyone can settle down. I'm here, I'm here," she announced over the comm channel, her chest puffed out.

Artist: The CMD Studios

"You're late," Leesa said in a whisper.

"Well...whose fault is that?" Bridget asked. "You tried to off *me*, remember?" She pointed at XBA. "Do I wreck her first?"

"Yeah, maybe start with her," Leesa suggested.

Bridget took the hint, stepped up to XBA, and said loudly, "If anyone's gonna kill that bird, it's gonna be me." Electricity crackled around her hands and shot up her arms.

"That sounds...familiar?" XBA replied, though she didn't stop walking.

"I mean it, not another bloody step," warned Bridget. "Looks like you got heaps in you that'll fry real good."

At that, XBA stopped. She stood parallel to Bridget and, barely turning, considered her. "Fair."

"Whatever you were planning to do here, you've failed," Leesa said, satisfied by XBA's alleged surrender. She nodded at Bridget. "If she moves, zap her."

The bolts of electricity darting up Bridget's arms reddened and intensified. XBA stopped trying to slink backward.

Aiming to appear loads stronger than she felt, Leesa guided the titanic device one-handed to a suitable resting place. She hoped no one saw her hand trembling as she leveled it, or saw her face tighten as she set it down.

A sharp inhale, then a flip of her cape, and she returned to her usual posture-perfect position, beaming with self-importance.

"Mission accomplished," Leesa said to the pilot, Windrider. "Give us a minute before you come back around. We've still got EVs unaccounted for." She glanced over her shoulder, distracted by the ocean waves crashing against the side of the cliff. She was starting to wonder where Allister had gone...and if he'd survived.

"Lieutenant, why do you always look so stressed?" XBA asked. "You really need to learn to relaaax." She drew out the last syllable in her typical taunting way.

Leesa snapped her head forward, advanced on XBA, and stopped just out of arm's reach. Though the urge to kill XBA had tripled, she began to wonder if killing her would do the damage to C20 that the Andromeda Project hoped for, or if she'd be replaced with someone newer, stronger.

"Where are the rest of them?" she asked, both of her wary eyes on the glinting claws.

XBA wiggled them, baiting Leesa—and rolled her eye sarcastically. "The rest of who?"

"Them. C20."

"C20 is all around you, it is *vision*," XBA said.

Leesa ran out of patience. Looking to Bridget, she said, "Zap her."

Bridget raised her arm, and using the other hand to pick at the red bolts burrowing in and out of her like worms, she plucked one free and tossed it at XBA.

It zoomed forward, ripping through XBA's body on contact. The sound of her disrupted circuits was stifled by her furious screams of pain. When it was over, she collapsed where she stood, telepathic energy evaporating from her eye.

"Bloody hell," XBA spat.

The illusion of their surroundings flickered one section at a time—from the barren, quiet disaster zone to a backdrop filled with hostages. Shahar had an older woman Leesa had never seen before trapped in a choke hold. The frail kid and the mutated animal she'd spotted inside the facility were being held at blade point by Vonnie. Tranjam was staring past her, at the machine, she assumed.

"It's over, XBA, surrender the hostages…and yourselves," Leesa said, her hands already glowing.

"Is it *over*, Lieutenant?" XBA teased. "Or is it just beginning?" In an orange flash of her eye, she was flipping back to her feet and slicing at Bridget in one motion. Bridget dodged—almost too slowly—out of the way and stumbled back until she stood next to Leesa.

In Leesa's ear, she heard…huffing. Next came the sound of a fatigued yet hysterical voice.

"Mom!" Allister shouted, coming in loud through the comm channel. Leesa turned and glimpsed him running full speed toward them.

"Mom! I'm so sorry," he continued. "Hang tight, I'm coming…I'm—"

"Mom?" Leesa said, her heart clenching. His mom was really *there*.

Bridget's power sputtered and sparked. "Just say the word, and I fry brains," she said.

"No!" Leesa yelled, gripping Bridget's arm, then repeated quieter, "No."

"Are you kidding me, Lieutenant?" Allister shrieked. "You're off if you think—"

She didn't pay attention to the rest. The TEWR was the number-one priority in her mind.

"You know what I want, darling, so why don't you just give it to me?" XBA laughed and playfully flipped a strand of hair out of her eye. "Step away from the machine."

Leesa hesitated.

"Give it to her!" Allister pleaded. "Please, I promise we'll cynque up on another way. Just help me save my mom."

His mom whimpered then, her body squirming inside Shahar's grasp. He squeezed his hand tighter around her body.

Guilt held on to Leesa just as tight.

Still, she turned away, an impossible-to-tame fury rising in her, similar to the feeling of an overdose she'd felt in the training room, identical to the lack of control she'd experienced in her last encounter with XBA.

"Do your worst, XBA, you will not get this machine," she said with all intended derision.

Allister gasped in her ear. "Are you twisted?"

She was feeling *twisted*, she guessed, but not for the reasons he'd assumed. The potential spreading through her body was not telekinetic—there were no pinks and purples, no organized grids or linear threads—only wild bright-blue energy creating gaskets of her pores, prepared for something like fire to shoot from her skin's surface.

She recoiled, heaving as the heat reached her mouth. She couldn't let go again. Not here. The footage alone would bury Evolutionaries forever, then add to the planet's devastation.

But as she rose into the air against her conscious will, body curled to contain her suppressed potential, the mounting miles-wide pulse ran out of fuel.

Energy rushed away from her veins, cooling her body in seconds. Her fists loosened as she lost control of her levitation and tumbled back to the ground. Like a dying nova, she burned out and collapsed.

Leesa's eyes fluttered open moments later. She stood on wobbly legs, groggy, shaking away the confusion. Bridget had kept her from hitting the ground.

Did I really stop it...did I stop the energy pulse?

"If you won't do anything, I will," Allister said, rushing forward.

"Ah, ah, ah." XBA waved her clawed finger in response. Now standing next to the other rogue EVs, she gestured for Shahar to release the woman in his hands. She zeroed in on Allister and said, "Awww…now isn't that just *mega*. The Andromeda Project's full of not-so-good Evolutionaries, too, isn't it, Allister Adams? Just remember, it was Tas-Salvatur who showed your mother mercy when this one was ready to sentence her to death."

XBA shoved his mother in their direction. "As promised, here's your payment."

Leesa, though enraged at her enemy's trickery, could feel neither her telekinetic nor her Z-energy potential.

"You see, Lieutenant," XBA continued, "thanks to your newest recruit, *we* didn't fail. We got exactly what we wanted."

Out of the corner of her eye, Leesa could see Allister and his mother embracing. "You gave them the information inside the machine," Leesa said, jabbing a finger at him, "didn't you, Adams? Because of you we're screwed from here to the end of the countdown."

His mother crossed her arms and scowled, presumably at her. She opened her mouth to speak.

"You never answered my question," XBA interrupted, consumed by her own laughter. "How can we be cynqued if we are not one?" She pressed a button on her torso. "An eye for an eye, Lieutenant!"

In a split second, Leesa connected the threat with the reality. The machine was on her left side, the same side as XBA's orange eye.

"Down!" she yelled.

She dove to the ground. Waiting for flames. Bracing for incineration. When she didn't feel either, she looked up, only to see the machine's blinding detonation and concussive force carrying a fiery expanse over her, over *them*, in silence.

There the young survivor stood, his shoulders low, his body facing the explosion. The kid gestured with both hands out as tiny, fast-moving bubbles of navy energy shot from them. She didn't understand how the conjoining bubbles had formed a wall sturdy enough to stop the explosion, or how the blast's force was shooting up toward the sky without the slightest sound instead of roaring through them.

Thwarting something close to a megaton of energy from eliminating what little was left of De Los Muertos seemed to take the kid's all. But his all was what he gave it. The blast folded in on itself and shrank back, snuffed the fire, the parts, the data. The machine landed on the ground a charred ball of metal no bigger than her.

The kid then fell to his knees, panting, shaken. His animal companion trotted to his side and sniffed at him with concern.

Leesa was standing as soon as the danger had passed, scarcely exhaling before she saw that XBA and the rest of C20's Evolutionary soldiers were gone.

"What was that about?" Allister shrieked, hopping up next to her.

Leesa responded first with an icy glare, then said, "What was *what* about?"

"You know what"—he pointed—"you were going to let them kill my mom, and this innocent kid and his dog...or whatever it is."

Allister was shaking. His face twisted up on one side. The accusation had come at her charged up with anger and disbelief. It was a wonder Allister wasn't charged up himself.

She didn't care how he felt or what he thought he could do about it. Hostages were never a negotiation point at the Andromeda Project. Humanity was.

"I've been in dozens of hostage situations, Agent Adams. You've been in one. This one." Leesa glanced at the mother, angered by the very idea of her. The woman stood next to her son, wide hip cocked, judging Leesa from that short distance. Leesa straightened up in defiance. *The nerve*, she thought. To her, the mother was nothing more than a faulty energy core, a rusted pipe. The system couldn't work with her in it. "I suggest you fall in line, Adams. Start looking at your own mistakes. Because of you—"

"Because of him, what?" his mother snapped.

"We failed," she said definitively. *And Dr. Belladonna is going to take it straight to the top.*

The chorus of excuses rose from them like the ocean's waves, crashing and loud as they pounded against her. Bridget and Allister and the mother were casting blame *at her* while the dog-thing barked aggressively and the boy moved his hands with an odd sense of serenity and elegance. What could he be communicating with such simplicity?

It didn't matter. Nothing mattered. They'd failed.

"Enough!" Leesa shouted, silencing them all. "There's only one way across the Divide, my way. So, if you want safe passage, I suggest you cooperate *and* keep your mouths shut."

Soft growls and grunts and groans came in response.

Leesa dismissed them and the mouths they fell from, frustrated at the collection of realizations piling up. Besides XBA's survival and Allister's incompetence, she was somehow indebted to a random Evolutionary disaster survivor, a soon-to-be refugee. She walked up the slope to the drop point and checked her Cynque. "Status, Windrider?"

"Two minutes," they replied.

The aerocraft's landing was nothing short of disruptive, its thrusting mechanisms kicking up debris and throwing it around in a miniature tornado.

A soldier opened the cabin door, Windrider, she presumed. "Believe it or not, they disappeared in a cloud of gray mist," they said.

"It's not the first time," she said. "Video?"

"Recorded a few seconds, just enough to run under the potentials database."

"How's Brandt?"

"Stable. Unconscious." Windrider nudged their chin at the group. "All of them coming?"

Leesa looked over her shoulder. She found it ironic that Bridget turned out to be the one she could trust, particularly after she'd campaigned so strongly against her.

"Everyone gets shackles but Sparks," she ordered. "Maybe get a muzzle on the dog thing."

"Yes, Lieutenant."

"I'm sorry," Allister finally said to her. "Maybe I got this Evolutionary hero thing flipped. I just thought—"

"You thought what?" Leesa turned on her heels to face him, inching closer as she asked, "You thought we went around saving people from evil Evolutionaries? You thought you'd get to show off your potential? Maybe win some award for honor and bravery? Wake up, Adams. We're not heroes. We're operatives."

Leesa brushed past him and boarded the vehicle, refusing to make eye contact with any of the others. Her commands were carried out with haste, and she, still questioning her own competence, listened to Windrider repeating her words over the comm system.

The ruins of De Los Muertos stretched to the horizon, a foreshadowing of the doom to come. She knew she should leave them all there. Should leave Allister and his mother, at least.

The challenge would be figuring out a way to find the artifacts without him. He'd shown he wasn't up to the task, couldn't handle the pressure. She was sure that if the artifacts had been within his reach during this mission, he'd have given them up in fear.

While Leesa was no stranger to raw power, to rage, to requisite violence, fear was a face she pretended not to recognize.

He's incapable, she said to herself.

Not to mention completely disconnected from their reality.

"Gonna be a bumpy ride back, soldiers," Windrider said.

Allister kept his gaze on Leesa for too long, an obvious look of disappointment, then looked down at his leg that refused to stop moving.

Leesa fed on many things. That day, his shame wouldn't be one of them. It was sticky, and at first taste, too difficult to digest. The heaviness she felt in place of satiation was new and hard to make sense of. She shook her head and stroked her hairline, burdened by the thought of not only explaining their failure to the general but possibly owning it as well. Her pending termination brought her knees closer together. Death was always a possibility.

With everyone crammed onto the surviving aerocrafts, they began their three-hour journey back to civilization.

An overhead view showed the Hollywood sign's broken letters jumbled at the base of a shallow canyon, lying beneath the mansions it must've ravaged on the way down.

Leesa folded her hands in her lap. "211 days from," she muttered to herself. De Los Muertos wouldn't suffer for long; the rising Pacific was well on its way.

———

Artist: Lester Niesta/ The CMD Studios

WHEN WAS THE LAST TIME
YOU GAVE UP? WHAT DID
THAT FEEL LIKE?

WRITE DOWN OR SAY
ONE WORD FOR YOUR
FUTURE SELF.

———◆———

CHAPTER 20

CAPTAIN BRANDT
Quadrant Delta—Z-Laboratory, Andromeda Project Headquarters
Day 210

BRANDT'S EYELIDS TWITCHED with anguish. Death felt close enough to touch. Even if he wasn't ready to take its hand.

Feeling trapped in the nightmare that was De Los Muertos, he relived the sharp tip of the glaive piercing his chest again. His skin remembered. How it had welcomed the metal, peeled away to let serrated edges slice through his flesh, scrape his bones, expose his…vulnerability.

The aerocraft's spotlight had caught the glaive-wielding EV known as Vonnie Kim, her silken skin glistening as she stood over him, pushing her weapon deeper. Blasted woman—nimble…beautiful, a density shifter able to move through solid matter. He knew her from the reports he'd seen on C20's Evolutionary terrorism. She didn't like to be reasoned with, that was for certain.

"Preserving my culture is more than worth the artifacts, wouldn't you agree?" she'd asked, sneering, heel pressed to Brandt's chest. "Of course not…foolish captain. I fight to ensure the legacy and survival of my sanctuary. You fight for glory and significance."

She had twisted the blade, then ripped it out angrily.

Brandt gasped, opening his eyes to dimness.

Glory and significance, he thought bitterly.

The infirmary's bedside lighting was haunting if not scarce.

He had endured twenty-four hours of sedatives, fresh stitches next to his heart—all the while feeling the sharp ache in his spine from being pinned to a poorly padded cot. And why? Another West Coast infiltration. Another team of powerful, but inexperienced, Evolutionaries. Plus, C20's intel advantage and their more coordinated takedown strategy.

Brandt had a mind to blame Allister, and he didn't know which was more disappointing: that Allister had given up so easily to XBA, or that he'd taken off his blasted mask and lost communication with the team.

Then again, XBA's supposed to be in the ground…, he thought.

That had been Lieutenant Delemar's job. A job he thought was done over a hundred days past.

Perhaps many things could've been avoided—namely the ambush—but Dolores as a hostage wasn't one of them. And, though conflicted about the mission's outcome, Brandt knew that nothing, not even the end of the world, would've stopped Allister from saving her.

He gritted his teeth.

Sweet Dee always finds a way to land smack in the middle of this.

He couldn't help his body's constant, subtle shifting. Mostly in the discomfort. He started overthinking the arrogance with which they'd moved through their mission to retrieve the machine, reminded, yet again, of his first failure on the West Coast.

The fallout from that had been a warning. Different times. Different regulations concerning Evolutionaries. But this second failure was guaranteed grounds for termination, there was too little time to make exceptions.

Termination, he thought, apprehensive—the longest way to spell *death.*

His chest expanded and collapsed, his mind tearing through memories. It stopped on the one from two and a half days past. A quiet, off-the-record conversation between himself and General Delemar in his quarters. The documentation to amend the termination clause in Brandt's contract had been *allegedly* submitted, granting him dismissal over death, a trade-off for his decades of loyalty and sacrifice.

"Trust that I gave you what you wanted, the potential for freedom," Nicolas had said, coughing every other word into a scrunched-up handkerchief stained with blood. "Now you get to make sure I receive what I want. That machine, and those artifacts. Are we clear?"

Brandt had nodded obediently, taking the general's strict tone on the chin. He didn't have much of a choice.

"And you make sure the lieutenant comes back alive," Nicolas had added.

"It's all or nothing," Brandt had said to that. He had been close to inquiring about the general's health. But he was more concerned if Nicolas was just blowing smoke.

For once, he wanted to feel honored, safe.

Now under the healing pod's dim light, Brandt drew his hand across his grizzly neck. He was surprised they'd taken the risk of putting him under the expensive machine. His potential for disruption was bound to flare up at any minute, and knowing the yellow energy was liable to thwart any natural process—from redirecting the vital liquids back into their containers to shorting out the pod's functions altogether—he tried to find it vibrating above his bare skin, sparking along his fingertips, before it found him first.

The lingering throb near the wound didn't count. And besides that, Brandt didn't feel *anything*. Hours of combat training and he hadn't come any closer to honing his potential. It still worked, of course, even if sporadically, as it had in De Los Muertos when he needed it most. But he'd always felt the potential in his body somewhere. Just like his intuition. He sighed at its absence, half disappointed, half relieved.

Brandt then stirred to the tune of a hushed voice. It was calm, strong, deliberate…spilling forth in mildly broken English. Taking into account his location, he knew the voice belonged to the resident geneticist. Dr. Rabia Giro—a man as slippery as a lake frog, quiet and watchful as a barn owl—was shuffling around the room doing God knew what. When the sounds of rearranging and scrubbing and organizing got too close, Brandt dropped back onto the bed with his eyes closed.

The makeshift door next to his pod was whisked aside. "No need to pretend to sleep," Dr. Giro said. "We are all friends here."

Brandt opened one eye. "Good morning."

Dr. Giro laid his hand on the captain's shoulder. "Indeed," he said with a soft slap. "Good morning, indeed."

The doctor's face had deep lines running from the corners of his eyes down to his pillowy cheeks, obvious deterioration caused by old age. His age didn't seem to make him any less nimble as he was humming and dancing around the healing pod like a jolly chef. "Your potential is miraculous, Captain," he said, unhooking the machines attached to Brandt. "You can unsettle natural processes. You can break molecular bonds. Or, with the right amount of focus, you can achieve something as remarkable as reversing blood infection. I sometimes dream of how formidable you could be, if you weren't so afraid of success."

Brandt didn't speak right away, suspicious of taking the bait. He was afraid of few things. Success wasn't one of them.

"What're you talkin' about, Giro?" he asked.

The doctor gave him a stern eye. "Humanity's departure is grand, yes, ideal even. But what they propose for exodus is for the few, not the many. And it requires power, incredible transportive power."

"Isn't that why we're fiddling with the artifacts?" Brandt asked, a little too matter-of-fact. "We figure out that mess, and we'll be the most famous Evolutionaries in history."

"Fame does not interest me, only time and salvation."

Brandt had rebuttals—about his perceived fear of success and the artifacts as another tool for maintaining hierarchies. But before either was able to materialize on his lips, Dr. Giro handed him a canister of water.

As the captain gulped it down, the doctor explained the mission's final report to him, as paraphrased by Lieutenant Delemar, who had taken responsibility for the machine's loss.

"Underhanded, she was, our Evolutionary powerhouse," Dr. Giro said, "that she mentioned but once your carelessness and lack of agency, and in the same breath assured them she was a better fit."

Brandt lowered the canister. "Better fit for what?" he scoffed.

"Why, leadership."

The captain could feel his eye twitching as he resisted the urge to scowl, though he suspected he couldn't outrun his skin reddening with the flush of anger.

Lieutenant Delemar had tried to get rid of him. Of *him*! And in his sleep, for goodness sake. It was impossible, crazy—and he was ready to bet his life no one would go for it, not when the ticking Evolutionary time bomb of Z-energy was coming from her.

He finally scowled. It was just like a Delemar to try to save their own skin.

"So it's no wonder, then," Dr. Giro continued, pacing around the pod, "that, in your extended absence, there has been a decision made of your future. A decision that prohibits you from seeing the magnificence that will be the end…or the beginning…should we succeed." He paused and lowered his head so it was next to Brandt's. "Termination."

Despair consumed Brandt's body, the word *termination* ringing between his ears. To assuage his fears, he thought through his contributions, reminded himself of his unflinching dedication—to the mission, to the Project, to the world. Perhaps he should've stopped before he'd gone all the way back to Cumberland Falls.

It was too late. He'd already arrived at the premature burial of his wife and son beneath their single-story home. A tragedy brought on by…

By the Arrival.

The past flared up in him like gasoline-fed fire. The excuses, the lies, the secrets, the turmoil, the nightmares. His foundation was *weakened*.

A light fog crept into his mind. The cloudiness that came with doubt and distrust. For all that had been taken from him, he'd be given death in return.

"You're lyin', Giro," Brandt sputtered. "There's no way, not in your wildest. General Delemar said he would—" He choked on the words he wanted to say—*Free me*—then sat up straight. "You're full of it, I swear to God."

"There is nothing to hold you up but lost lives, strings of misjudgments. And it would be naive to overlook you taking the blame for others' mistakes. These three consequences of loyalty and sacrifice seem to be sound pillars when bound together, but are highly susceptible to the smallest upset. Yes or no, Captain?"

Dr. Giro circled Brandt, spewing philosophies the captain couldn't digest, explaining logic he couldn't grasp.

He wasn't listening anymore. Nothing the doctor said mattered when Brandt realized that his role at the Andromeda Project had become an inevitable trek toward a meaningless life, constructed to end in a meaningless, uncelebrated death. His pod was a coffin, the headquarters a cemetery.

Betrayal's cold sifted through his organs.

Brandt shuddered. *First Patrick. Now me.*

"Captain?" Dr. Giro asked.

"I'm still listening, dammit," Brandt said harshly.

"Lies come so easy to your lips, you do not taste their sting any longer." Dr. Giro picked up a warm cloth and held it to the captain's forehead.

Brandt let himself be pushed down by the doctor and soothed by the wet fabric, allowed the warmth to push his mind to stillness. His breathing deepened at the prospect of eternal peace.

"It is neither here, nor is it there," the doctor continued. "I can see you are consumed with contemplation. What could you be thinking of with such intensity?"

Death.

"How the heck I'm gonna change their minds," Brandt said. He pushed Dr. Giro's hands away and swung his legs around the cot. "I can't go out like this, not when I swore to Patty Cakes...to Patrick...I would bring this mission over the finish line. We worked so hard...sacrificed...we sacrificed everything, our families, our homes." He believed there was still time to save it all, and then, hell, he'd promised Patrick to take care of Allister, too. His head sank. Who would protect Allister if he were gone? Finishing his thoughts aloud, he said, "Dr. Belladonna's got her own damn agenda. The lieutenant's got it out for Allister, I'm sure. And Nicolas will have him terminated the moment he hands over those artifacts."

Dr. Giro snapped his fingers, as if to cosign the immediacy.

"I promised Patrick," Brandt said. "Swore on my life."

"And what would you do to keep your word?" Dr. Giro asked.

"Anything," Brandt replied.

"Anything?"

"Anything."

"People do the unthinkable, the unfathomable, to save the ones they love. Why when it is time to do anything, you do nothing? You wait to be done to. You think you must have power to be powerful? To have followers to be leader?"

The words struck him like an earthquake, shaking every piece of resolve he had left. A dryness filled Brandt's mouth. Sweat drenched his forehead. He was dangerously close to breaking down, to stuffing his head between his knees while his past mistakes continued burning his spirit black. Maybe it was time to welcome the ashes of what had been his foundation. There was nothing left to hold onto.

Dr. Giro began to walk away. "Your termination comes from pursuit of two dangerous things, my mighty soldier: glory and significance."

The mistakes and the anguish they'd brought seemed to evaporate. Brandt's resolve steadied, just long enough for him to run the words through his mind again. *Glory and significance.*

"What'd you say?" he asked. His eyes followed the doctor as he moved around the infirmary.

Dr. Giro kept his back to him. "One day left, maybe one and a half with preparations, and *poof*, you go away. How will you spend this time? Waiting for permission to live?"

"I guess…I can still save us."

"To do that, you must survive." The doctor paused thoughtfully at the doorway below an area to the lab labeled, RESTRICTED. "You are cleared for exit," he said. "I will delay news of your release… Choose wisely where you go."

Brandt went to thank Dr. Giro for the heads-up, and in place of his rotund figure was the faintest trace of white fog.

That son of a gun moves quick.

Brandt slipped back into his uniform and snuck out of the lab. He was careful to take the shortcuts through the facility that only he knew. Steps from his office, Cynque beeped with a message from an unknown sender, someone off the grid.

Meet me. Oil Alley, it said.

As he read it over and over again, mulling over whether to go and who it was, a question washed to the shores of his conscious mind, and glimmered like a rare seashell: "How can we be Cynqued if we are not one?" he mumbled to himself, mesmerized by the device's glowing graphics.

Suddenly, Brandt knew who'd summoned him. His ticket to redemption.

———

210
DAYS

16
HRS

33
MIN

Artist: The CMD Studios

CHAPTER 21

LIEUTENANT LEESA DELEMAR
Quadrant Alpha—Executive Wing, Andromeda Project Headquarters
Day 210

LEESA WAS TIRED of being punished. The rigorous training to maintain self-control. Being overlooked for her energy potential. And constant reminders that when their mission was accomplished, her termination was imminent. There had to be a way to prove her value, to prove she was more than a weapon: that she was the Gateway.

From a few dozen holes in the ceiling, pressurized water cleansed Leesa's skin of the ashes, the dirt, the scars from De Los Muertos. She shivered. The shower pod did, too, rattling as tiles traced in glowing purples peeled away from the interior. She slammed them back into place and smoothed her hair down to the shoulder.

XBA's survival was what sent chills through her, not the frigid water temperature mandated by the District.

Despite lathering lavender fragrance and essential oils into a sparse foam, her shock wouldn't be scrubbed away.

I almost lost control.

Just like in Brisbane, Australia.

A city she'd never forget. Tens of thousands dead. Hundreds of thousands without homes. Millions without power. *Rogue Evolutionary goes nuclear in a recovering city,* was the recurring video caption. A story spread through Cynque's algorithm before the Andromeda Project could adjust the narrative. Leesa remained anonymous. A faceless representation of unchecked potential, adding to the already-growing fear of Evolutionaries worldwide. The only consolation was that Leesa thought she'd killed *her* in the process.

The shame of failure was sticky on her tongue. She knew it tasted familiar.

After the District's three-minute maximum had been met, the water shut off.

"Heat dry activating," a voice within the walls said.

She didn't like the drying machine, but, *everything in moderation*, she thought. The moment she felt the last trace of dampness leave her pores, she switched off the machine and stepped onto the bathroom's marble floor.

Leesa liked cutting out the fluff. Unlike the rest of her generation, she refused to adopt mindless consumption because the Earth was "doomed anyway." A giant storm wouldn't destroy the world alone; she'd made a few sizable contributions herself. Her recycled uniform fabrics soothed the sting of her cataclysmic mistakes. Living a zero-waste life quieted the cries of her unintentional victims.

"Lieutenant, your presence is requested in General Delemar's office at sixteen hours 'til," Cynque announced.

The time had come to stand before the general…her father, and accept her fate. It could just as well be summed up in one word: *termination.*

Anticipation held the shower's latent chill against her like an ice-cold blanket. Her father's request had come after one-quarter day of ignoring her messages, the longest they'd ever gone without some form of communication.

"Eight hours lost," Leesa said. She tugged at her damp curls. "Eight hours wasted," she corrected, feeling the harshness between her teeth.

Eight essential hours. Eight hours they could've spent tracking C20's registered Evolutionaries or scouring the dark web for where XBA had gotten her cybernetic enhancements. This wouldn't be the first time she'd fallen victim to his passive aggression. But having spent years by her father's side, observing him, shadowing him, carrying out his whims, and covering up his mistakes, she knew such behavior wouldn't win the race they were…*losing.*

She snatched up her uniform with a furrowed brow. The bodysuit slid comfortably over her torso, and when her sleeve fabric was twisted and arranged to the correct length, she forced the zipper up to her neck and slowly fastened the cape around her shoulders, ignoring that twinge of apprehension. Wearing the cape was mandatory. No matter how unworthy she felt. Nearly perfectly presented, the only thing awry was her half-frizzy, half-tightly-curled hair. She hadn't the time to tame it to the required style and wrestled it into a high, messy bun.

Leesa scurried down the hallway to her father's office in the Executive Wing's deepest corner. She entered the dusty room, pressed herself upright against the wall, and waited for acknowledgment.

Her father was leaning over the desk with his hands clasped and thumbs tapping. The steaming mug near his elbow indicated he'd had a grueling struggle to stay awake and receive her.

"Your hair," her father said, barely looking up, "is not regulation. Haven't we discussed *those* curls?"

"Yes…," Leesa replied. "Yes, of course. My apologies, I didn't mean to upset you." She placed her hands near her forehead, then let them glide over her hair, sparks of telekinetic potential leaving her fingertips as they moved, unkinking every strand to the straightened perfection her father required. And, in a twirling mess of excess curls, her regulation triple bun reformed atop her head, a prison keeping her resemblance to her mother at bay.

Leesa inched forward, rounded her shoulders back, and cleared her throat. "You wanted to see me, General?"

"See you? No, I didn't want to see you." He leaned back in his chair, staring at the framed, digital carousel of images that chronicled his and her mother's romantic beginnings. "I wanted clarity on what happened in De Los Muertos. I'm still trying to wrap my mind around how two of our best agents, an overpowered rookie, and a hotheaded misfit managed to come back with a civilian, a disaster refugee, and a dog, but not the machine you were sent there for."

She swallowed. "I submitted the report for review. It details—"

"The report you submitted is a fairy tale spun in your favor. The truth is"—her father's forehead wrinkled in disgust—"you failed."

"I was not in charge of this mission," Leesa protested. "Captain Brandt, he—"

"Captain Brandt is up for termination thanks to his poor leadership."

Leesa's heart skipped a beat.

She had waited to hear those words since her starting months at the Andromeda Project. There was no one she'd rather see eliminated except perhaps, after his cowardice, Allister. But…the captain's termination removed a layer from the prospect of her leading the Andromeda Project when her father stepped down. Given there was no one else to take his place, no one *qualified*, such leadership could cancel out her death sentence. Everyone agreed the artifacts would need to be managed…governed once found…and who better than someone like her, who'd wrestled power to near death and won by placing it in an iron box.

She shifted her weight and let the realization of Brandt's fate settle on her shoulders. "But he's still in recovery," was all she could say.

Captain Brandt hadn't submitted his recap of the events. He hadn't gone before the directors and stated his case.

"It doesn't matter," her father said, still not looking up.

The glamour of her advancement shimmered. She would be a step closer to her desired status, absolutely, and she'd also be a step closer to sacrifice, in position to take the fall for any additional failures.

"He has to go down for this so you don't have to," he continued. "Dr. Belladonna and I agreed to run this mission at his insistence, with his crew, and under his leadership."

Leesa folded her hands in front of her, expectant.

"However, using him as an example doesn't excuse your incompetence. I can't keep saving you."

Because you couldn't save my mother? she wanted to ask. What came out was, "Of course not, General. I understand."

She longed to call him Father, for him to take her in his arms and soothe her, teach her life lessons. She couldn't remember the last time they'd hugged. She couldn't remember the last time he'd said her name.

All she had was the cape. It did his job for him, caressing her shoulders, closing itself around her and offering its protection. Maybe that's why he'd given it to her in the first place.

"You say in your report that Agent Adams endangered the mission by"—her father squinted at his Cynque—"letting go of the machine?"

"His inexperience and lack of control are *detrimental*," Leesa said. As she paused, she took the cape's smooth, dense fabric in her fingers.

"Go on," he prompted.

"The Z-energy linked to his potential, I saw it shoot out of the machine and into his arm. It was wild, volatile. I suppose if he didn't drop the machine, he would've destroyed it." Her jaw tensed. "He should've been able to absorb it."

"You've just said yourself Agent Adams is not as experienced, Lieutenant," her father said.

"Then why do we need him?"

"Because—"

"I've been training every day to balance my energy potential," she cut in. "If I can get control of my access to the Z-energy, I can find the artifacts myself."

His breathing was heavier than normal, she noticed, and though he was rubbing his chest, she couldn't tell if it was from fatigue or frustration. "We've had this discussion," he said. "You're not to think about the Z-energy, let alone try to conjure it. It's dangerous to you in ways you couldn't imagine. Do I make myself clear?"

"Yes, General."

He began to cough, the only sound in the room.

"Would you like to explain to me how…XBA survived?" her father finally asked.

She took a sharp breath. That was *not* the reaction she'd expected. Which meant—"You knew. The whole time, you knew she survived, didn't you?"

"Of course I knew," he said calmly. "We combed every inch of Brisbane looking for her body and didn't find so much as a limb."

"Why didn't you tell me?"

Her father got up and walked toward her, scowling. "Why didn't I tell you? Why didn't I tell you?" He almost laughed as he repeated it. "Why didn't you tell me you left without confirming her death? You should've brought back the body, but you could've at least checked her pulse."

Leesa shrank at his honesty, hoping to disappear into the wall or the floor, whichever would take her without judgment. "I—" *Thought her potentials were neutralized,* she caught herself before leaking an excuse. "I apologize."

"Your apology doesn't explain your failure then or your failure now!"

The vat of stirred emotions hardened to stone at her core as she realized feeling them wouldn't help her make her case. Whatever composure she'd lost to his insidious interrogation replenished itself and rebuilt her posture to a straightness that bordered on defiance. She stepped away from the wall.

"XBA knew what she was doing," Leesa said, low and serious. "She stuck around to make sure I got a good look at her upgrades. She wanted me to know she was alive, even if you didn't." In her courage, she was so bold as to point at his device. "I did the best I could with what I knew and the team I was handed. Further down in the report, you'll see that I retrieved the machine after it was let go of."

"Then XBA blew it up."

"C20 didn't want the machine, General. They wanted to prove that I would choose it over saving Allister's mother."

"I imagine you're wanting to pass that off as an explanation," her father said. "Do you have anything else to say for yourself?"

Leesa shook her head.

"Good, I think you've said enough." Her father's skin stretched across his knuckles as he made a fist. "*Agent Adams,*" he corrected, "stays in the vault until he's cleared of any residual influence from XBA. Have Dr. Belladonna handle that immediately and provide a report before another day passes. He's no good to the mission locked up down there. Considering Professor Ashur might have intel on

C20's next move, we must seize the opportunity to bring them down before they get any further ahead. Prepare yourself to lead that attack when we're confirmed."

"But, General, the artifacts—"

"Will be retrieved by Agent Adams. That's all, Lieutenant Delemar." He gestured for her to leave. "Cynque, resume work session."

An illuminated screen flickered between them, cutting off eye contact.

Leesa stared at him, hands clasped by her thighs in restraint. *This will not unravel in my hands,* she thought. She turned on her heels and walked hastily to her quarters.

———

CHAPTER 22

Artist: The CMD Studios

DR. FLORENCE BELLADONNA

**Quadrant Alpha—Executive Wing, Andromeda Project Headquarters
Day 210**

It was the moment Florence had been waiting for. The moment where she must do whatever it would take, even breaking the District's curfew, to swoop in and save the Andromeda Project. If she'd learned anything from her upbringing, high risk often meant high reward.

She fluffed her warm brown curls in the mirror welded to her polished storage chest. She wondered, briefly, if she was overdressed for the occasion. Her mother had always said there was no such thing.

An impromptu meeting labeled URGENT had appeared that night on her private calendar. The final destination was unlisted, but she accepted the invitation, hop-ing it was from the person who'd put her inside the Andromeda Project in the first place. She couldn't miss a meeting that anonymous; after the team's recent failure, such an event promised updates and information she couldn't get anywhere else.

The catch: she needed to reactivate her Cynque.

She pressed her finger against the mirror. A thirty-eight-character keypad of scrambled letters and numbers appeared on its surface. She typed her alphanumeric password one painstaking digit at a time, grimacing as she did so. She despised anything tedious, especially when passed off as precautionary.

The chest's top drawer slid open to reveal her solid gold Cynque nestled deep in its bed of plush protection.

Unlike the general population, Florence's Cynque was an accessory she kept in her self-designed handbags, not as a tool embedded in her arm. But to play good citizen she needed to wear the device—for the foreseeable future at least.

"Time to wake up, Cynque," she said.

The device's gold band snapped around her slender wrist, pinching her as it affixed itself to her skin. Tiny wires dug into the space already scarred from when she last removed the device.

She cringed, cursing the scientist who'd developed such an intrusive answer to connectivity, Dr. Quincyn Bordeaux.

The technology found her bloodstream and resumed its primary functions: calculating her vitals, connecting to her public data set, confirming her identity through biometric analysis.

Cynque spoke to her as if it had woken from a deep slumber, full of pauses both for yawns and attempts at accelerated brain activity. "Thank you for reactivating my capabilities, Dr. Belladonna," it said. "Reconnecting to the server... Give me...give me a moment while I catalogue updates from the global network." The loaded visual panel lit up with activity. "I'd be much more useful to you if you didn't disable my functionality."

"If your functionality was of use to me, then I assure you, I would put it to use," she said, still gripping her arm from the pain. "Haven't we had this discussion?"

It replied with calculated empathy. "My apologies. But please be advised this feature will be disabled by Day 200 in accordance with the Personal Disclosure and Data Availability for Historical Preservation Act."

She let go of her arm one finger at a time. "*Aye, stai zitto. Non sei spiacente.*"

A robotic hiss pierced the quiet.

"Connection restored," Cynque said with an uncertain rhythm. "You're mistaken, Dr. Belladonna. I truly *am* sorry for the loss of your opt out feature."

"Just make yourself worth a damn, Cynque, and tell me when my transport arrives."

"The meeting scheduled for you begins at 21 hours and 30 minutes to Day 209," Cynque replied. "You'll need to lose no more than fifteen minutes if you want to be there on time, and your transport, per your request, arrives in two."

At that, Florence shook off the numbness in her wrist. She resumed getting ready, dotting her pinky along her lower lid to blend her makeup. *Appearances can be your deadliest weapon*, her father had always said.

Until he actually gave her one.

Florence stared through the mirror at the sword hanging on the pink wall.

The bequeathed sword was centuries old, an artifact in its own right, gifted to her by her father on her eighteenth birthday. Razored edges cut like his sharp expectations. A twenty-four-karat golden handle as hard to grip as his perspective. The snarling dragonhead on the hilt as menacing in appearance as his deeds against humankind were in practice.

"You'll have to sit this one out," she said.

Cynque let her know that the car had arrived. It would wait fifteen minutes and not a second more, the message warned. *Va bene, time to get this done with.*

She vacated her office and headed up a steep, grated ramp to the elevator.

Florence deserved a second chance at happiness. But when they had dropped below a year on the clock, she decided to settle for a life of peace and solitude instead—away from Cynque's prying circuits, and the judgments of the brainwashed populace. It no longer mattered that she already had a man, a very important man, who wanted to marry her. Her Evolutionary status made that more a nightmare than a dream.

At least after solving the matter of the artifacts, she'd owe no more favors.

She shuffled into the main hallway as her Cynque received a written message—*My office, now*—sent from LIEUTENANT LEESA DELEMAR.

I have an off-site appointment, she replied.

The lieutenant answered with: *Now.*

Florence rolled her eyes and switched directions.

"I am on my way out," she said when she arrived at Leesa's office, stationing herself in the dark entryway. "Can you turn on a light or something?"

Leesa snapped her fingers. The lights flickered on: two luminous strips that crisscrossed above where she stood and another pair that crisscrossed above the entryway Florence was underneath. The room was remarkably disheveled, given the lieutenant's obsessive tendencies. And Leesa herself, the iron-faced maiden, was cape-less, a hollowed-out look on her face.

"I want him terminated," Leesa said, hovering nearer to her.

Florence didn't step back, challenging Leesa's intense stare with one of her own. "Him who?" she asked.

"Agent Adams," Leesa replied. "He's proven his inability to do what this mission requires. So before General Delemar and the directors make the mistake of putting greater faith in him and stalling this operation further, I want him terminated."

Florence scoffed. "It's been made abundantly clear to me that you're no longer being considered the Gateway. After your Brisbane run-in with C20, your access to the Z-energy, I believe it was called, was deemed 'catastrophic and acceptable only through complete mental suppression.' You campaigning to remove Allister does not put you in a better position to reclaim that title or undo that judgment. So, I'm not sure what your angle is here."

"There is no angle," Leesa insisted. "You think this is for me? You think I would have someone eliminated so I could simply have the pleasure of saying *I* saved the world?"

"Are you asking me or telling me?" Florence leaned closer. "Because on the one hand, I'd say the apple doesn't fall far from the tree. But on the other hand, I'd hope to heaven there was something at play here bigger than your own ego."

Deadpan, the lieutenant replied, "Yes, the fate of humanity."

Florence narrowed her eyes. Initially, at Leesa's lack of emotion, then at the familiar tingling of her telepathic potential. She blinked, confused because she hadn't activated it, and without warning, she was yanked to her knees by an invisible leash. A painful vision blocked out her thoughts.

The office was gone—the uninspired furniture, the echo of its emptiness, the smell of Leesa's lavender wash. In its place was somewhere off from the Gelen Psionix, Florence guessed, where star systems she'd never seen shined on planets that teased of far more robust civilizations. She shook her head, but it didn't go away...it didn't even *move*.

Until the pocket of space flashed.

The vision dissolved into a room made of distorted mirrors with a young version of Leesa standing in its center. She was disfigured with washed-out skin, not moving, yet the mirrors reflected an image of a blue-shadowed silhouette that stood strong and tall. A ring of blue energy exploded from the teenage girl's still body, shattering the mirrors and leaving her in the expansive darkness of eternity.

It was that darkness that thinned into the office's concrete walls and glass divider. It was that teenage girl who was replaced by Leesa's adult figure.

Their breaths raced each other's in the otherwise silence.

Florence held her chest to calm its heaving. "What the—what was that?" she asked, looking up.

"You tell me, Mind Evolutionary."

"*Cazzate*. That wasn't me. That was you." There was a fear rising in Florence for the lingering connection between their psyches, the blips of the lieutenant's past popping up like targets on a radar screen. It was *Leesa* who'd triggered Florence's psychic potential, who'd pulled them through the Gelen Psionix. As if Leesa had wanted to see something and needed Florence to do it. "Lieutenant, look at me."

Leesa mumbled aloud, hugging herself around the shoulders where her cape should've been.

"That was the most powerful psychic projection I've ever experienced in my life," Florence said. "How did you do it? What aren't you telling me?" She grabbed the lieutenant by the arm. "Leesa!"

Leesa's head snapped in her direction. Her face had lost the iron hardness. By her wide eyes and sucked-in cheeks, she was moments from being crushed by the astounding weight of human vulnerability.

"This isn't the first time," she said, a lilt creeping into her voice.

It turned out it was the second. Leesa, whether by compulsion or confusion, began to open up about another vision she'd had after her battle against Allister. She retold the story with vivid descriptions—citing every strange nuance and minor coincidence. Florence was finding it harder and harder to follow. For the more Leesa spoke, the more she picked up on that strange lift in her voice. Individual words were lost in sentences carrying melodic inflection, sentences swathed in a tenderness too great to belong to Leesa Delemar, the lieutenant, the iron-faced maiden.

But it took an even stranger turn when, in a burst of passion, she described an armored creature with clawed hands.

"And there was the most beautiful baby, purple-skinned, radiant," Leesa concluded. "A child of existence. Mythical, almost." Then her voice sank into someplace dark and wavering. "It seems everything I imagined for myself is disappearing. I am feeling emotions I have never felt…and I need something to hold on to. An anchor to make me feel worthy. I do not want to blink and find out the directors decided to terminate me in favor of"—she swallowed heavily—"Allister."

"Your termination does seem to be written in stone."

The lieutenant's stiff grimace didn't hide the fright in her eyes. "The only shred of redemption for me is with those artifacts in my hand. I'm sure you can understand."

"I'm beginning to," Florence replied, standing. "*Allora*, these emotions? These transient visions? Did they start when Agent Adams first arrived?"

"No." Leesa hesitated, ashamed. "It was during the assessment, after I came into contact with the Z-energy again. Something woke up inside of me." She looked at her trembling hands, trying to steady them. "I keep losing control, and

I can't tell if it's my telekinesis or the potential I am consciously suppressing. If I continue to unravel this way…there will be no case to be made for my life…when destruction…when it radiates from my fingers."

"Lieutenant, imperfection, it's part of being human."

"I am not human!" Leesa shrieked.

The room shook with the fury of a small cyclone. Cracks split the wall. Her desk shattered into tiny projectiles and covered an upheaved floor.

"None of us are human," Leesa said, after she had calmed herself, though not by much. "Everyone, from my father to the directors, has made sure we do not forget that. As Evolutionaries, we are only safe here, remember? That's why they terminate us when we don't matter anymore. Especially monsters like me."

She smoothed her hair on the sides, then secured her forearm plates. Next, she focused on the damage.

Blown-out wall pieces levitated back to their homes and, with a squeeze of the lieutenant's fist, fused to one another and their surroundings. Millions of broken shards were arranged to outline the intricate furniture, and with a narrowed squint, she reformed them solid. The pieces of floor were pushed back down by an invisible pressure and, with a subtle twist of her arm, sealed together.

Leesa inhaled. The consequences of her anger, shown as traces of *blue*, faded from the veins in her neck. "You'll keep this between us," she said.

"Are you asking me or telling me?"

"Agent Adams was subject to a mind-melding illusion in De Los Muertos. General Delemar is concerned that XBA may have left a residual psychic signature to gain easier access to him in the future, as you Mind Evolutionaries are known to do."

A bold accusation in Florence's opinion.

"I don't think XBA got very far in his mind," she rebutted. "In fact, I'm sure she had a difficult time maintaining any illusion around him at all. She has no history of displaying significant telepathic ability, just mind tricks from what I remember. And she certainly isn't as adept with her potential as me." Florence couldn't help but raise an eyebrow, observing as Leesa's body tightened at her words. "I don't like to bother with the details, who's who and what Evolutionary's done what," she continued. "But…along those lines… XBA…weren't you meant to kill her?"

"A minor oversight," Leesa replied. "Regardless, the general is requesting you eliminate all doubt."

Florence raised her other eyebrow to match the first. "Is he?"

"I've sent the authorizations to your Cynque. Besides the admiral, those files stay between you, the general, and I, as does the report. The directors did not approve this measure."

"If the directors didn't approve it—" Florence began, then stopped, wondering, *Why would you share it with me?*

Cynque interrupted with two consecutive beeps. The paperwork's delivery to her device coincided with an alert that her car was leaving. She hit snooze on the alert and opened the files detailing her assignment.

"Deep-probe analysis required for subject, Agent Allister Patrick Adams...," Florence mumbled to herself.

She shuddered at the idea of drilling into his subconscious. Few knew as well as her that deep telepathic probing damaged the fibers of human thought and was potentially traumatizing for the subject. There was no telling what she'd uncover, or if she'd be able to cover it back up before it manifested in the conscious mind.

"You know this is madness?" Florence asked, looking up for the answer. Though she could see the vulnerability still lingered in Leesa's eyes, her colleague's face had once again become as impenetrable as the walls of the Andromeda Project. "Curious what you'll be doing while I'm scouring Agent Adams's subconscious for something that doesn't exist?"

"Preparing for our interception of C20 and the death of XBA." Leesa turned her back to Florence. "But we both know that won't save the world."

Florence sighed. It wouldn't get her back to New Soho any faster, either. "*Va bene—stasera.* You'll have your report," she said as she turned to leave.

Leesa called after her, her voice high and light as it had been during her breakdown. "I don't want him dead; I just don't want him here. Do what you have to do—with urgency."

Well, when you put it that way, Florence thought, then entered the hallway.

The correlation between Leesa and Allister was difficult to dismiss. She had this idea that somehow their energy potential fed off each other, which would mean if she could find the source to Allister's energy potential, Leesa's would likely be the same. *Was it really those words? Foeht Zeorgen?* She grimaced at the memory of the Z-energy piercing her astral form. Still, the risk seemed too aligned with her strategy to let trepidation take over.

Florence could end the Andromeda Project's enforced suppression on Leesa, doubling their chances of success with two Evolutionaries who could retrieve the artifacts. The directors might be so pleased with her work they'd let her off the Project early.

She skipped into a run once the ceiling's track lighting allowed her to travel along the wall unnoticed. After passing the corridor leading to the skyline windows, she swept past the newer, shabbier parts of the Andromeda Project and wound her way through.

Florence went from climbing into the beautiful, up-lit elevators at the heart of the Andromeda Project to enduring the not-so-short six-minute ride down to the Vault, and emerged in a musty basement.

Three plasma barrels were aimed at her. Standard, though a tad jarring.

Florence stepped to them with authority, Cynque held high. "I have orders," she said. She projected the signed documentation in life-size format for the soldiers to see.

"She's good," a woman said. Admiral Alli Gattison, a different sort of high-ranking official.

The soldiers lowered their weapons.

If the Andromeda Project were set in Greek mythology, General Delemar would be Zeus and Admiral Gattison would be Hades, queen of the underworld. She kept her semiautomatic plasma weapon cradled close to her hip like a two-pronged staff. "I've heard you don't like to follow rules," Admiral Gattison said as she sized up Florence. "That's not gonna work down here. You have a thirty-minutes to lose and then we come get you. Anything funny goes down, we shoot first and ask for forgiveness later. Got it?"

Florence flipped her hair away from her face and held the admiral's gaze, hoping to challenge her resolve.

But Admiral Gattison turned abruptly on her heels and beckoned for Florence to follow. "Excellent. This way."

Florence trailed the admiral down the central path into the Vault. A linear string of cells creeped by on either side, sealed shut by black doors, and too thick for sound to escape. Behind each one was a mix of terrorists awaiting execution, low-powered EV criminals, or captured C20 agents. Plus a host of transcripts and files not linked to the network hid somewhere within the walls.

The ceilings were too high to climb. The darkness too absolute to penetrate.

"This can't be all of it?" Florence asked, tilting her head back to view the high ceiling.

"It's the most you'll ever see," Admiral Gattison said. She stopped and gestured to a space indecipherable from the wall or the surrounding darkness, and announced, "We're here."

———

CHAPTER 23

285

ALLISTER ADAMS
Quadrant Gamma—the Vault, Andromeda Project Headquarters
Day 210

ALLISTER WAS BACK where he'd started, imprisoned, rejected.

This prison was smaller, darker, and dustier than the first one he'd been in.

One thousand seventeen, one thousand eighteen, one thousand nineteen, Allister counted, doing push-ups in an attempt to pump out his anger.

"One thousand twenty," he breathed out, his nose an inch above the prison floor. He held himself there, mouth quivering, muscles ablaze. He'd often wondered how many he could do without stopping, determined after he'd surpassed his original record of five hundred to go on and clear one thousand. Satisfied, he slowly pushed himself back up, brought his feet in, and stood, waiting for the feeling of relaxation to wash over him.

But his anger kept its hold. So did his underlying despair.

There didn't seem to be anything he could do to quell his inner conflict as he assessed and reassessed their mission to De Los Muertos.

If he couldn't find companionship among other Evolutionaries, where else was he supposed to look? And if he couldn't do what it took to be an Evolutionary hero, then what was the point in having potentials at all?

Aside from losing the game of acceptance, to his utter shock, his mom hadn't refused transport in a vehicle owned by her sworn enemy, the Andromeda Project. She even managed to sit by Allister on their return trip, jammed shoulder to shoulder with him on one side with soldiers on the other. Strangest of all was how she'd squeezed his arm from the Divide to DenHaven and beyond. A loving gesture soaked in relief. He knew by that alone she was more concerned with him being okay than the mistakes that had gotten him here.

Perhaps there was no need for hysterical weeping for her long-lost son (they'd been separated for nearly three critical days). Perhaps it would've been futile to yell for his freedom. But more than her docile approach to his association, was her apathy for the members of the Andromeda Project themselves. She didn't give the lieutenant a second look, though she kept a careful eye on Brandt's unconscious body, and seeing as how an audience wouldn't have stopped his mom from an impassioned outburst, Allister became all the more suspicious of why she was being so calm.

The lock cranked behind him. The door clicked and creaked open.

He glanced over his shoulder.

Dr. Belladonna loitered patiently, cautiously, near the door. Her mouth was twisted to one side, her head tilted, and her sympathetic gaze clawed at him, feeling more like pity the deeper it dug.

He hated that look.

"What?" Allister said. "I'm totally beat."

"Are you sure you're...beat?" she asked.

He crossed his arms. "Don't psycho-evaluate me right now. I said what I said."

"I just want us to come up with a definition for 'beat' that we can use as a benchmark. Your generation uses that term...inconsistently."

He sat down on the metal bench, his exhale heavy, burdened. He was far from beat.

Part of him didn't believe he could trust her. Part of him didn't believe he could trust himself. Allister kept his eyes darting as he mused, as if when they stopped moving, she'd invite herself into his psyche and finish trying to figure him out.

And he wasn't keen on being figured out.

In the end, he guessed it didn't matter. One minute she'd be plucking thoughts out of his head, the next she'd be writing them in that stupid notebook.

Might as well spill it all now, he thought, glancing in her direction.

Dr. Belladonna was still waiting for him to speak, the curiosity in her face almost a cover-up for what she must've really been doing.

"Stop it," he said.

She lifted both hands in protest. "I'm not doing anything." She took a step inside, hands where he could see them, and kicked the door closed behind her. "I'm not doing anything...except asking you to tell me how you feel. So?"

Allister didn't feel any tingling, but he felt a ton of other things. Too much to keep in. "Okay, you want it straight?" he began. "I'm not beat. At all. You know, it felt good to get accepted for my potentials. Then—I went and messed up..."

"Well, I—"

"I couldn't have taken a harder left. Got tricked into turning on the machine by XBA, some Mind Evolutionary, and full circle, threw my mom in a frickin' hostage situation. How unreal is *that*?" He shot back up from the bench. "And here I am just frozen, watching it all go down while this cybernetic woman is cheesin' at me. Literally, worthless."

"Okay, slow—"

"Then when they're hauling the…now very hyped…machine, the chains snap, a buncha soldiers get blasted to dust—some kinda energy wave, not mine, though. Definitely not mine. It's like, yo, what are the chances? I'm losing my rag by this point, really losing my rag. So I run over there and—"

"*Rallenta, per favore*," Dr. Belladonna snapped, gesturing at him with her thumb and fingers pressed together, "*Mio dio, sembri pazzo. Non posso a capire cosa stai dicendo quando parli cosi in fretta.*"

He paused, mouth open, taking in her frustration even though he didn't understand what she was saying. "Uhm, sorry?" he said, shrugging. "I'll lay it down a bit."

"*Va bene*. Explain the energy wave again."

Allister inhaled. "It went down three times, maybe? The air starts to displace, then a bubble forms, it's kinda clear and distorts like everything, then expands. Suddenly, my stomach is, like, in my throat. Not much different from me on a plane, really. I manage not to wretch just as a weird ripple tears through everything. Soldiers just go *poof*—dust. The cables age. I'm talking shiny to dull in about ten seconds, tops. They just snap in the middle, totally finished—I mean, don't get me wrong, they weren't doing a great job to start with, but anyway—the machine hits the ledge…starts to slip…I tried to jump in, haul it up, ya know, play hero."

"Allister—"

"No, no!" He pointed at her. "Don't 'Allister' me. I had the machine in my hands. Yeah, the wires were scraping my palms raw and it hurt like a *Bee I Tee See H*." He held up his palms without a scratch on them, then snatched them back to his hips and bit his lip. "But we almost had it. What if those were the artifacts? I would've let them go."

"And you let go because…"

"The Z-energy! What else? I guess when I activated the machine, my energy went in the reactor, and so, as I was pulling up the machine, I tried to say them again, thinking it *might* help. The energy tried to come back. I freaked."

"I'm hearing that this is a lot for you to unpack."

"You don't get it, the Andromeda Project might be a job for you, but it's the only place I can be me." Allister traced where the dulled lines in his palm had widened and glowed with the energy's power. "I thought I could learn, thought I could…" His mouth and fist closed with the same slowness. He'd returned to the instant Leesa justified choosing the machine over his mom. A simple line: *We're not heroes, we're operatives.* How could he blame her then? Maybe he'd gotten it wrong like everything else. "I swore Lieutenant Delemar was going to leave me on the ledge. Hell, guess I'm just lucky she didn't throw me over it."

Dr. Belladonna pressed two fingers against the bridge of her nose, her eyes squeezed closed with impatience. "The words you said to revive the machine… have you said them before?"

"One of them I always say when I activate my energy potential."

"To activate?" Dr. Belladonna asked. She looked off, briefly, as if considering the word. "Which one did you say, *Foeht* or *Zeorgen*?"

She'd said them both with enviable ease. Didn't she know what those words could do? The damage they could inflict?

"The second one," he said.

Allister moved one of his legs behind the other and in doing so, kicked his bag. They both looked at it.

She didn't have to ask; he felt the tingle shoot from the base of his skull around to his forehead. His possession of the papers wasn't a secret anymore. He huffed as he snatched the bag from the floor. Grumbling, he took out the papers and arranged them in order.

"Hand me that fourth page," Dr. Belladonna requested.

He did so and sat back while she read through it, thinking back on his willingness to give XBA access to the machine in exchange for his mom's life. He would've made the same choice if they'd been standing in front of the artifacts. What would be the point in saving humanity if his mom didn't survive, or worse, if he was the reason for her death?

"Did they happen to let my mom go?"

"I believe they're keeping her here for now, for her protection," Dr. Belladonna answered. "She's a target until—until we can confirm otherwise."

"Yeah," he said in agreement. "Doubt she's hyped about that."

"Let's just say your mother hasn't been very…compliant."

The noncompliant version of his mom was the mom he knew well. Putting aside the grace with which she'd handled De Los Muertos, he guessed that since they'd returned to the District, she'd be yelling soon enough—campaigning for both of them to be released. Maybe after Leesa's warning his mom had played nice to get them back to the Sanctuary in one piece. And maybe, considering she was being forced into protective custody under the Andromeda Project, her concern about his potentials wasn't as misguided as he'd previously thought.

Now his mom was mixed up in his decision. Now she was on C20's radar.

Dr. Belladonna interrupted his train of thought by handing him back one of the pages, staring down at the words as she let go. "Read it."

Allister tilted it to the dim light that shot up from the corner. The words *potentials* and *experiments* had been written above detailed images of what could be Evolutionaries—some were surrounded by the elements, or nature, or forcefields, or energy, or the universe, some had body parts shaded in: arms, legs, heads, hands, organs.

Potentials was a concept he knew well, the definition assigned to what was possible for an Evolutionary to accomplish. But the word *experiments* struck him, fresh and unexpected like the page itself. He must've overlooked it half a dozen times.

He read what his dad had written. "Experiments are a way for certain Evolutionaries to *focus* each *potential* for a specified outcome. On the next page, I wrote out the list of phrases and which Evolutionaries they might work for. Not all of them are English—shoot, not all of them are from Earth. But...I'm a tad blown away by the ones for the Z-energy, which I found out the hard way is a hidden potential of mine that I can't seem to get under control." There was a paragraph break. "For others, managing potential comes more natural, such as in Mind- or Body-enhanced Evolutionaries..." His dad demonstrated this in a diagram of various EV types below the declaration, then noted that experiments didn't work for everyone, and the strength and control of each set of potentials were dependent on the genetic heritage.

The explanation cut off before it ended and didn't connect to any of the remaining pages. Maybe the rest was in whatever notebook they'd been torn from.

"Experiments, huh?" Allister said with a bit of skepticism.

They were experiments in a sense. Based on its meaning, each phrase like *Foeht Zeorgen* was linked to a hypothesis. There was evidence that a desired result might happen if the experiment was repeated and conducted with the same intention. But the outcomes were interpretive and subjective to variation.

"Z-energy." He then folded up the page with the other papers before adding, "Pretty beat name, the more I hear it."

Dr. Belladonna dusted off the area next to him and took a seat. "What did we talk about in your first session?" she asked.

"Lots of stuff. My pops, the assessment—"

"Discipline," she interrupted. "It's not a minute here, an hour there, a day on and a day off. It's every day, a majority of the time."

He nodded, watching his leg bounce.

Dr. Belladonna grabbed him at the knee, her grip tight enough to say *stop*.

"Sorry, nerves are *poof*," he said. "But I gotcha. Push it down. Keep it cool. Aka discipline."

He noticed she was wearing her Cynque and squinted. *Solid gold, huh?* he thought.

Dr. Belladonna covered it up, then continued, "Discipline is not about suppression; it is about intent."

Intent, he repeated in his head. He thought about the captain and his disruption potential. "Captain Brandt good? He got messed up out there cuz of me."

"He's not awake yet."

"Oh."

"The healing chamber will do its work, if they caught the wound in time."

He sat up. "I want to fix it. How can I fix it?"

"If you want to fix it, focus on learning." Dr. Belladonna's voice quieted. "You spend your energy trying to compensate for your mistakes thinking it'll make you good enough. Sometimes being good isn't enough." She ran her hand along the embossed gold binding of her notebook, a thoughtfulness in her touch. "Getting stuck in the cycle of validation is soul destroying."

Allister tugged at his afro, pondering the visual of him running on an imaginary wheel. Being a hero was all about validation, wasn't it? Carrying that title meant always doing the right thing. It meant making sacrifices. If Dr. Belladonna was suggesting the opposite, then Leesa had been spot on. They were indeed *operatives*.

Dr. Belladonna stood then. "I do hope you find the page with those experiments on it. That said, there is another essential layer to this. I know your potential is important to you, and I believe that you have more potential than any of us are aware of."

"You do?"

"I do. There are seven years of memories and experiences in your conscious mind that are missing. My theory is that, buried too deep in your subconscious for you to be aware of, are these missing pieces, and with them is the source to unlocking your full potential."

"Twisted. You think if you fix my mind, maybe next time I say those words every-thing doesn't get blown to hell?"

She smiled, maybe by accident. "It's a strong start."

Someone banged on the door and yelled, "Fifteen-minute warning!"

Admiral Gattison.

"Do you think C20 will grab the artifacts first?" Allister asked.

Dr. Belladonna swirled her finger at the ceiling—he guessed a reference to the powers that be—and crossed the room. "If I can't wrangle all of these egos, it's a large possibility." She jotted down a few notes in her paper journal. "It's times like these I'm thankful for my years running policy and ops in the president's cabinet. If I can get an entire party full of Gen Zers to let go of their aged-out belief systems, how hard can a few Evolutionaries and a fifty-something-year-old babysitter be?"

Allister smiled, almost on purpose.

"Truthfully," Dr. Belladonna added, "what anyone finds or doesn't find will depend heavily on the work you and I do here tonight."

"If we're doing this mind-dive thing again, I don't want to be responsible for what happens."

"Relax," she soothed. "I'm well trained in these matters. Surrender to the depths of yourself—don't resist."

Relax...surrender...don't resist, he thought.

Eyes sealed closed, he focused on his purest intention: to save humanity from the apocalypse. The figurative door to his mind unhinged, and he felt her psychic presence penetrate the edge of his thoughts and sink beneath layers upon layers of protection.

———

CHAPTER 24

DR. FLORENCE BELLADONNA
The Subconscious
Day 210

FLORENCE HAD VOWED long ago that she'd risk anything for freedom—from her family, from the public eye, and now, most recently, from the Andromeda Project and her obligation to the United Sanctuaries.

That's what fueled her as she decided to play the game of the subconscious, a nearly impossible game to win. For that place was a sub-truth of circumstances and history. What was found there was never as pretty as what was on the conscious mind's surface. It was a dangerous place to go. A dangerous place to be, even for a telepath of Florence's training and potential. Down there, friends and family could become enemies. Enemies could become the voice of reason, solidifying all that the subject believed to be true. Dark feelings twisted thoughts and sent them up to wreak havoc on anything the person came into contact with. No matter how much they loved it, or cherished it, or wanted it.

The Gelen Psionix appeared as if it were a supernova with a cooling, dark center, expanding toward her in the colors of raw emotion and pure thought. Surrounded by many millions, if not billions, if not trillions, of minds, she navigated a maze of pulsing lights, each luminous sphere representing just one of them. She recognized Allister's mind, a blue beacon as volatile as a star's surface, drifting inside a bright cluster.

She concentrated on his existence and let herself be drawn toward him like a satellite falling into orbit.

Their connection re-engaged.

Psychic energy manifested her inside of his psyche and assigned the physical world's scientific laws to his consciousness. This time, she was not standing center in Allister's conscious mind, rather she stood at a smooth barrier reflecting it.

She looked up to the sky and across the landscape. The barrier was a sharp division spreading as far as she could see. She assumed Allister's subconscious was concealed on the other side, the glass-like construct acting as a form of protection against her access.

She traced the vivid reflection of his conscious, a constructed world she'd explored, which had been reverted back. She noted the abundance of grass, the addition of twisting trees, and the structures that represented his adolescent homes. She would've expected a door somewhere so Allister could come and go, maybe some holes poked through, where memories and beliefs that crossed over could come back out. But as she felt along the barrier, she found nothing close to a point of entry. Or exit.

Florence hesitated, the danger alive in her frizzing astral body. To break a barrier that had never been broken, she risked unleashing a turbulence she didn't have the potential to tame.

She held one hand close to her chest. The other—charged with psionic energy—returned to the barrier's surface, hovered above it for the span of a breath, then pushed forward.

Crack.

The glass fractured. From that tiny disturbance, the shards separated to either side, floated away from the site of the psionic collision as if the barrier had been broken under still, deep waters.

Just beyond the opening, a field of memories bloomed. Each suppressed life event was concealed inside one of dozens of floating cylinders, while each cylinder was supported by thorny petals and attached to the ground by twisted roots. The mostly flat land was like a field of psychological triggers waiting to be picked and smelled, to the detriment of whatever curious mind would dare. For they were not to be touched. They were not to be experienced.

The source to his potential would be there, in that field, if it were anywhere— lurking among the darkest, more sinister parts of him. And that barrier might've explained his disconnection from it.

"Here we are, then," she whispered, passing the first few cylinders before she stopped.

There was a cylinder double the size of the others flashing at her. Within it, formed his father, Patrick, Allister at seven years old, a groomed lawn, and a large country house with a flat roof. Patrick was…alive in the memory, running around the yard, smiling up at where Allister was bouncing on his shoulders.

She stepped closer.

Allister squealed as he took his father's long dreadlocked hair in his hands and flapped it like wings. The scene glitched to a new image, this time of Patrick supporting his son's waist as the boy stood on a brand-new hoverboard. Allister practiced his balance technique for the game she knew to be Schwebevogel.

A shadow washed over the cylinder and what happened next became unclear.

There was a visual sharpness afraid to return, even as distinct voices spoke from behind a curtain of darkness that refused to lift. "Ends with Z" was spoken in hushed tones, over and over again.

She saw nothing more, only sensed the seven-year-old's distress and confusion.

Perhaps this was the triggering event (*primary*) she'd been looking for.

Lured closer to the cylinder by the promise of an impending tragedy, she followed the sounds through a familiar field of towering blue grass. She spun at every noise and bright flash as she went, maddened by the ambiguity.

Amnesia, she thought, relieved, slowing as she reached the cylinder. She was getting the same hazy picture Allister probably got when he tried to remember that moment in his childhood.

But the sounds moved beyond the cylinder and began to blare at her from all sides—the hum of Ukimoto engines; the pop and sizzle of fire consuming all it touched; metal crunching against pavement.

A fire? An accident? she mused, picking apart each noise.

As a boy, Allister's anguished screams mourned a lost limb. His pain shot through her arm as if it were her injury to relive. She grabbed it, tight, her heart pounding.

The pain subsided behind the warmth of a moderate summer. She let go and moved closer, certain she'd found the traumatic event caused by the erratic manifestation of his energy potential—which introduced his initial fear.

If she could move that out of the way.

Perhaps.

Perhaps the deep connection to his potentials they needed would be possible.

Voices swarmed the scene: one touting betrayal, one pleading for life, one offering Z-energy as a prize more precious than an Evolutionary boy. The first voice came from someone familiar, a person as obsessive as they were misguided. General Delemar, she concluded, but in another time when loss had consumed him. The second voice had to belong to Dolores, with the weeping and pleading for a bloodied body near the road.

Definitely an accident, Florence thought quickly.

And the last voice…she caught her breath as its heaviness sank to the depths of her chest. Patrick Adams was speaking then, because it could only be a father making promises he could never keep, all to spare his family.

The Z-energy exploded from within the cylinder, blasting away the shadows. And obscured by its brilliance, Patrick said his last words.

Then silence.

The cylinder, the field of memories, the subconscious…all remained as still as that last moment. Florence had to admit she was shaken by the slow-to-fade imprint of Patrick's death. If the Z-energy killed him, and it was Allister's fault, then his fear of his potentials could easily be explained…even if he didn't remember where that fear originated.

The Z-energy was still shining from the cylinder. She looked at the blazing light a final time, saddened as it faded into the beginning of the memory, him perched on his father's shoulders. "But if reliving this memory is what will unlock his potential…"

Florence turned around to go back, tortured by her discovery, and almost ran into Dolores. A much younger version of her, at that.

"You've returned," this Dolores said, her statement absent of warmth or kindness. She wore a flowing skirt and artisan-made jewelry, her hair tied in a neat bun on her crown.

"I came for answers, and now that I've got them, I'm leaving," Florence replied.

"You're not going anywhere, not with that secret. It has to stay here. *Everything* has to stay here according to the king." With a sly grin on her face, Dolores turned and gestured to the resealed barrier behind her. She began twirling and singing, "The memories here are not to be taken, this tended garden of time and place. And if you hope to change this truth, you'll need a Z to crack the case." The projection of Dolores lost consistency and fell apart like wet sand, with her clothing, skin, and bones melting into the shifting soil. Just before she disappeared, she sang higher.

"And if you hope to change the truth, you'll need a Z to crack the case."

The ground shook with enough vigor to sink a continent. Florence crumbled, gasping, and her astral form just about disintegrated. The violence of the subconscious wasn't new to her, but the violence Allister's subconscious used against her—that was not a common psychological trick, especially from an Evolutionary with no psionic potential.

Perhaps it was the work of this king the characters in his mind kept mentioning.

Above all, she needed to keep herself intact to stay connected. She summoned energy from the Gelen Psionix, inhaling as red lines ran the length of her arms and torso, traced her neck and jawline, and recoiled around the coils in her hair. On hands and knees, she fought to hold her form together, fortifying herself despite his mind's attempts to shake her apart. Now, it wasn't about getting in but about getting out.

"Dr. Belladonna?" the child version of Allister asked.

She lifted her chin.

His oval head and stringy, seven-year-old frame wobbled in front of her as if he were reeling from the same impact. He planted both feet and blinked at her before scrunching his face. "Why'd you come back?"

"If you're asking, I suspect you know," Florence said back.

"I know," he said, kicking his bare foot. "I just wanted to hear you say it."

He was disappointed—she could sense it—but she was thankful for the ease slipping into the atmosphere. His arrival must've repressed the attack.

Allister's mood softened, childhood joy radiating through his beaming, snaggle-toothed smile. He was soiled from an afternoon of the Kentucky outdoors: grass stains on his knees, a tangled mess of hair, sweat glistening on his temples. He picked a handful of grass, threw the blades in the air, and twirled beneath them in loose suspenders and a fitted green turtleneck.

Florence gave him a questioning glance. She stood, suddenly freed from the previous strain, and walked to his side.

"I hate when it's like this," he said, then made a circle with his arms. "All the potential goes away."

"Where does it go?" she asked.

He sighed and pointed to a structure behind him. "In there, I think."

"Is that where the king lives?"

Allister giggled. "Sometimes."

Sometimes.

The structure was sinister in its presentation and alienating in its size, constructed with fire-forged stone to the widths and heights of a fortress. The same stone concealed any details of the architecture, and she saw only the highest tower's arched windows and pointed rooftop. Stranger still was the glowing field radiating around the fortress in a blue spectrum deeper than the grass.

More potent, Florence imagined.

She raised an eyebrow at the spectacle before them, intrigued. It seemed his untapped potential was suffocating in a field of subconscious trauma. Perhaps, then, she hadn't found the key like she thought. If unlocking the moment his father died wouldn't unlock his potential—and it was clear by the energy's restriction inside the fortress that it wouldn't—she still had more work to do.

"What do you mean, sometimes?" she asked.

"I'm bad at remembering when. If you really want to know, ask the *king*. He's in there now." Allister tugged at her sleeve for her to follow. "You're not scared, are you?" he teased, a fearless little thing, springing and leaping away with glee.

She debated between following him and trying her hand at cracking the barrier again.

He waved her along as he reached the fortress. "C'mon, silly!" he yelled. "You can't leave unless the king lets you, anyway!"

Near him, a dark-gray substance swirled around an invisible core, just as light and fast as the black mist present in C20 operatives' psyches. She started toward it with her hands ready to neutralize any threat. As she got closer, she noticed it was more coagulated liquid than condensed air, more lucid than what she'd found in victims of the enemy organization's programming.

The solidifying liquid stretched toward the ground, spinning like clay on a nonexistent wheel. A faint figure was carved from the blob, shaped and molded into spiked armor, massive claws, and bright-yellow eyes. The clearer the creature became, the clearer the fortress became and the lower the landmass floated toward the surface of Allister's subconscious.

Florence perceived no tangible threat, picked up no…subliminal commands… which the mist was liable to carry. And the most important note, which would go in the lieutenant's report, was that she sensed no confusion on his part.

Allister knew this creature, this supposed king, whatever it was, intimately. He was all courage as he approached it…void of hesitation.

She remained skeptical. That was no king in her eyes, merely a creature. Her fingers tapped her mouth in rhythm as she pondered. *Two plus two does not equal four in here.*

Artist: Kingsley Calungcagin/ The CMD Studios

Her apprehension wouldn't stick. Not with Allister's comfort blowing as a light breeze through the environment.

He stood at the fortress entrance and held his forearm upright to the newly formed manifestation. He said to it, "I welcome you into my mind, offer you faith and gratitude, and a place to keep the secret of your people."

"You are most spectacular for your generosity," the creature replied. "It shall never be forgotten nor misused."

Florence expected a bow or a handshake to follow. Instead, two raised fore-arms—one large and spiked, one small and bony—met in sanctity and sincerity. A practice as strange as it was ritualistic.

The strength of its emotion reverberated throughout the environment, almost soothing in its coolness.

Florence waited in awe for one of them to speak again.

It was Allister who hopped closer to the creature. Their conversation had cor-dial, playful beginnings, and though Florence was able to translate any language spoken on Earth, she couldn't understand what they were saying now, based on the string of quickly spoken phrases and the individual words that comprised them.

It was undeniable. Their words were an alien language.

Words like *Foeht Zeorgen*.

For the third time, Allister nodded while pointing back at her. For the third time, the creature shook its head. Allister thrust both hands toward her as though he were pleading. Still, the creature shook its head. Allister fumed, stomping around in circles, screaming at the sky and the grass. The creature turned away from Allister and his tantrum and began to retreat to the stairs, losing its shape as it moved.

Whatever the subject, it was now closed.

The cloud cover deepened, bringing with it the sweet, pungent smell of a storm. The sky's dark underbelly grumbled as more clouds gathered into the beginnings of twisters, swirled at high speeds, and sank. Lightning slithered from the sky and bit the surface in various places while thunder opened its mouth and boomed.

Oh no you don't.

She forced her body forward. Panting, straining, she battled the raging winds, dodged the strikes of lightning. By the time she reached the fortress, Allister lay on his side, halfway to falling asleep from exhaustion, tuckered out by his own mental defense mechanisms.

The fatigue hit her next. Her connection to Gelen Psionix suddenly too distant to draw psionic strength from.

Florence faltered.

"Wait!" she shouted out.

The creature stopped its ascent to the fortress entrance, turned over its broad armored shoulder, and extended a hand to her. "Come then, closer," it said, their lips stretching too wide as they produced an appropriation of her human language. "I am annoyed by your determination but intrigued by your resilience."

Her revelation came with the depth and tone of its voice. *2052 Ends with Z* had been implanted by this purple creature. Their relationship suddenly fit together. The presence. The secrecy. The inherent trust between them. For she'd seen an image of the creature on one occasion, read about its origin on another. Any records of it were slim to nonexistent, and she realized in studying the spiked forearm plates and striated musculature, she'd been privy to practical renders of its physique and form. None had captured its seven-foot glory. Was this the thing Leesa had seen in her mind, too?

"I am—" the creature boomed.

"Neight Caster," Florence answered, astonished. She paused, unsure where the name had arrived from. "You are…King Neight Caster," she repeated.

He *was* real. An alien with the hard chin of, yes, a king, the posture of a noble warrior—the sharpened glare of a blade forged in flames.

Intimidation chilled her psionic spirit. "You're dead," she said, taking cautious steps sideways until she reached him. "Yet I can sense you."

"Life, death…both are inconsequential in the realm of the subconscious. I am not the reason you can sense me. You—are the reason you can sense me."

His acknowledgment of her potential seemed to provide a fresh surge of psionic energy beneath her feet, but perhaps there was something to be said about how close she'd gotten and how determined she was to succeed.

She cast her gaze at the fortress. "Is this it? The source to unlocking his potential?"

"It is not."

Florence exhaled in defeat, pressed her hands together in prayer, and brought them to her forehead.

"The stronghold contains the incredible energy of my home world, *Uragon*, yes," Neight added. "The energy called Z, its catastrophic tendencies avoided through this minefield of psychological triggers you've infiltrated. That fortress will remain as such until Allister can brave his subconscious. When he will get to decide what structures and systems here are worth deconstructing. But no, it is not the source *to* his potential, rather it is the source *of* his potential."

Victory.

The alien knelt down and stroked Allister's afro.

"I see," Florence said slowly, trying to hide her excitement…and her desire. "What does it mean? Ends with Z?"

"Ends with Z-energy," Neight Caster corrected, standing again. "I prefer it in my species' dominant language—*Foeht Zeorgen*. It means more than you—or any human, Evolutionary or otherwise—could comprehend. But for simplicity, such a phrase brings intention to obscure power."

He and Florence now stood shoulder to shoulder, him facing the mental landscape of Allister's subconscious, her facing the fortress and the radiant field.

He continued. "This is the information you came for. An answer more important to you than the fragility of his psyche, the consequences of your hostile intrusion, or your prolonged occupation of another's subconscious. I would call your behavior irresponsible, but that would be a disservice to those without conscious knowledge of consequences. What you have done here, in this sacred place, on this night, is deleterious."

Florence narrowed her energy-charged eyes, furious at his judgment. "Unlike you, who seems to be exploiting this as a place to keep their secrets, I came here to help him, and in the process, save millions of people," she said, resolute about braving the fortress. "*Allora, mi spiacente*, but your accusation doesn't change what I'm about to do. I must say, I would be curious about your condemnation of me with such language, and yet, I had read briefly about your wisdom, I suppose I should've expected your arrogance with it. *King*." She turned to him. "After all, you are better than us humans, right? Smarter than us. Stronger than us. I wonder, why help humanity at all? Why tell us the location of the crystal artifacts just to feign ignorance on their location? Then, abandon us during our time of greatest need to hide in the psyche of a seven-year-old boy?"

"You believe me to be hiding here?"

"I believe you're hiding *somewhere*." She took hasty steps toward the force-field-protected fortress.

Neight growled at her back. "A telepath becomes a fool the moment they underestimate the systems of thought."

She stopped midstep and turned over her shoulder, the phrase repeating in her mind…

Underestimate the systems of thought?

"You're lying about the fortress," Florence said. "There's nothing in there but the mess you left behind. Which can only mean"—she swiveled to confront him, crimson energy igniting along her fingertips—"you don't want him to have full access to his energy potential."

Which means you don't want us to succeed.

She clenched her fist and, with the last of her strength, conjured the psionic energy needed to bind him. Tendrils of red energy slithered with the speed of her thoughts, encircling Neight Caster's neck, racing down the front and back of his torso and widening into thick slabs the moment they reached his waist. They continued merging and flattening until they covered his upper half and solidified.

He roared, fangs barred, unleashing fury in the language Florence didn't understand.

She was upon him like a panther on its first kill, reeking of overconfidence, her astral body pulsing brighter with each forward step.

"This is your final warning, Neight Caster," she said. "I will not allow your disregard for human existence to be the end of it. We need his energy potential to save ourselves, why keep it locked here?"

"You will never find the answers you seek if the questions are always wrong, Dr. Florence Belladonna," Neight replied.

She ignored his quip and planted her energy-charged hands on his face, to pull the answers out of him the way she knew how.

By force.

Her power was steadily seeping into his skin, skin as gray and rough as stone, even as he resisted her probing, twisting his head inside her grip.

"Give in," she urged, squeezing tighter. The energy coated him with its thickness, forcing the history of his time on Earth to replay for her one frame at a time. "Give in!"

Unexpectedly, her potential stopped advancing. The single image she'd brought forth—a remote crash landing with two teenagers as witnesses—disappeared. She paused, caught up in the intensity and loosened her hold, but only for a second before trying it again. This time, though, her psionic energy didn't come.

Now Neight wasn't fighting, he was staring back at her, his lips moving. Blue lines of Z-energy raced from his eyes to his feet, ripping his body free from her psionic prison.

Florence cried out in shock, at his freedom first, then at the two words he was mouthing.

"Foeht Zeorgen."

The background was ripped away; the ominous fortress, the murky cylinders, the swaying grass and rolling hills and twisted roots, the ever-present blue after-glow—all stripped like paint, taking her psyche with it. The Gelen Psionix passed her in a flash, the stars and thoughts one giant light. And somewhere between a second and an eternity later, her psionic form crashed at traumatic speed into her body, the force knocking her out of the chair.

She lifted her head, awakened to the sound of loud banging. Rose-colored energy evaporated from her skin while the pitch-black room replaced the electric-blue glare of Allister's subconscious.

Florence took in a breath big enough to choke her.

Then she collapsed.

———

CHAPTER 25

ALLISTER ADAMS
Quadrant Gamma—the Vault, Andromeda Project Headquarters
Day 210

ALLISTER STIRRED INSIDE a telepathically induced slumber, his body twitching and jerking in resistance to the probe. There was a barrier he knew about, a solid wall of amnesia…and behind it, memories he could never recall.

Until he felt it shatter.

A sharp pain sliced down the center of his brain.

The subtle awareness of titanium walls, the hardness of the bench and unpleasant odors were overpowered by the latent memory of a single-story home, a gravel driveway, and fresh-cut grass. Birds sang alongside whispering trees. A fierce sun burned through wispy cloud clover. He and his dad were…playing in the yard.

There was a glimpse of that day? Month? Year? Streaming in an accelerated sequence, the events flickering through his mind like a high shutter camera. The last event froze in place, an image of him surrounded by blue fire, consumed by the Z-energy and yelling "*Foeht Zeorgen.*"

The memories vanished, almost faster than they had arrived. A tingling followed, again in his brain, sharper this time, and warm—perhaps the barrier's shards slipping back into place before sealing off again.

He felt momentary peace, a tangible stillness. Then the soft, even heat worsened to burning, concentrated almost exclusively in his head.

Allister awakened, breathless, paralyzed on his back, feeling submerged in the Z-energy's crackling power. It held him there, hostage, and he could feel its heat begin rippling up and down his body, though he hadn't said anything.

"What…what's happening?" he asked, groggy, the energy and his paralysis fading in unison. Or at least that's how it felt when he was finally able to move, and the hotness in him was replaced with the Vault's cool draft.

Seconds later, a hazy collection of noises nearby slammed into him, robust voices screaming next to his ear. Something about Dr. Belladonna. Something about what he'd done to her.

What I did to her? he asked himself. *But how could I…*

The answers didn't arrive in any clarity, and he only managed to turn over slowly, his blurry sight clearing to Dr. Belladonna curled into herself on the floor.

Her knees were damn near touching her forehead. She was…shaking…sputtering. He guessed their activity had gone wrong.

Or, he dreaded, perhaps his mental resistance had made the activity go wrong. Again.

He sat up, his heart pounding at the severity of her condition.

"Dr. Belladonna…," he began. "Dr. Belladonna! What happened?"

She didn't answer, but someone answered for her: Admiral Gattison, the woman who'd escorted him to the Vault once they'd landed from De Los Muertos.

"Everyone, quiet! She's stabilizing," the admiral said harshly. She held her Cynque screen over Dr. Belladonna's fluttering eyes, scanning them.

The soldiers crowded around Dr. Belladonna as she curled deeper into herself. Their bulky bodies kept Allister from seeing exactly how she was progressing. He wanted to know whether she was awake, if she could speak, and peeked through the half dozen sets of hands, arms, and legs moving around her.

"Vitals confirmed, report available," Cynque said.

"Any damage or injuries?" Admiral Gattison asked.

The Cynque went to work calculating. Allister took the chance and scooted closer for the answer. A soldier put up their hand, indicating that he stay back. Sucking his teeth, he said, "Lay it…lay it down, soldier, I'm not doing anything mega."

"Abnormally frantic brain activity for the subject in question suggests over-stimulation," Cynque finally chimed.

"Can anybody tell me what happened?" Allister asked over the machine. "I need to know what I—"

"Agent Adams!" Admiral Gattison interrupted. "I said be quie—"

"I'm just making sure she's good!" he yelled back at her, shooting to his feet.

The soldier trying to keep him back whipped around and lifted their plasma weapon in retaliation. Orange energy flashed in front of the barrel, firing louder than the combined commotion of the room. There was no measurable time between when it left the weapon and when it blasted Allister square in the chest. Just an instant, the flash, then the impact.

Krakow!

He screamed, the plasma's heat tearing through his uniform almost to the skin. He flew backward and smashed into the Vault's interior before crumbling to the floor. He remained there, facedown in shock, the smell of burned fibers invading his nostrils. Disoriented, he tried to get back up, one arm moving, then the other. Despite the weakness in them and the absence of any coherent thought, he was able to get from heaving for air on his stomach to gasping for it on his hands and knees.

"Get the harness! Get the harness and secure him before he recovers!" he heard Admiral Gattison yell.

More soldiers rushed in. In a whirlwind of rough hands and forced movements, Allister was wrestled against the wall and restrained inside the harness the admiral had called for. He cried out at something sharp digging into his neck, winced at the constriction starting at his shoulders and tightening around his chest, biceps, and waist. He was unable to move without feeling the pain.

The soldiers moved away with caution. Through his fleeting bits of lucidity, he saw Dr. Belladonna lifted from the floor and carried into the hall beyond the doorway.

Everyone vacated the room in a flurry, still yelling. The prison door slammed hard. The bolt snapped across the threshold and burrowed into the wall, sealing him inside, alone.

Allister's neck was tensed and stretching away from the harness's collar, whose serrated edges had made tiny, stinging cuts along his throat—a punishment for resistance. Carefully he looked left, then right, startled to find a nest of chains snaking in from closed hooks on the wall. He didn't need to look down to see where they ended up, because the friction across those three areas of his body was acute, unchanged, and aggressive enough to make him beg for freedom or mercy, whichever could be delivered fastest.

"Dr. Belladonna," he said, dejected. "I didn't mean to…hurt you…"

But he had.

The woman who claimed herself a human with a range of psionic potentials, nothing less and so much more, was left a speechless zombie.

What did Dr. Belladonna find down there?

Allister was distraught about not knowing, his mind straining to find some clue, some visual to give to him.

What did she see?

He needed to see whatever she saw. Experience whatever she experienced. He wouldn't stop searching until he did. Closing his eyes, he concentrated on the thoughts and memories he knew and understood, used them as bridges to hunt for the ones he didn't.

As he tried in his mind to hitchhike his way to his subconscious, to bypass a barrier he was now so aware of he refused to let it continue hindering his potential—he stopped short.

A loud hissing cut through the prison's silence. He glanced up, confused to see thick orange gas spewing from the prison's corners. It filled the room almost immediately, creeping around Allister's head, floating above his sweaty lip, and at every small inhale, soaring up his nose. Numbness settled in his fingertips. Tingling tortured his lower legs.

He felt too afraid to use the Z-energy, even if it could set him free. For some reason, surrendering to that fear made him angrier than being imprisoned did, perhaps because, ultimately, it meant admitting that he was afraid of himself.

Allister seethed quietly, furious at the idea, and curled his arms, stretching the chains wrapped around them.

A link squealed.

A link snapped.

One of the chains broke away and fell as the others loosened.

The heated anger continued pumping through him, the blood pumping with it, and he knew the faster the blood in him moved, the faster the numbing orange gas would shut down his body.

He thrust himself forward, tightening the chains against him. He twisted in any direction he could, flexing without holding back, his brow furrowed, jaw set.

Another link snapped and hit the floor.

The jets within the prison hissed from all four corners, and more gas cascaded into a thickening haze. The room's wobbling visual lost more definition. The same wall panel Allister had been staring at for the last few minutes separated into twos and threes. A single blurry door became a semi-blended trio.

There, dancing at the edge of going unconscious, his mind dredged up the glimmer of a figure not quite human and a giant fortress he'd never seen before. Echoes of a strange yet familiar language—the same language as *Foeht Zeorgen*—mingled with a connection to the energy surging from within.

The figure became more defined and more unusual looking at the same time, its beastly face and weird skin unrecognizable.

Artist: Bradd Maesa/ The CMD Studios

Now his head was slumped forward, swaying side to side, wooziness tugging at his will to stay awake.

What's that, Pops? Is that...that thing, is it an Evolutionary? he heard himself ask in a child's voice.

He'd already inhaled too much gas, he realized, as he tried holding on to the image and his consciousness.

How did what kept happening to Dr. Belladonna tie into his energy potential? Was this hard-to-make-out creature to blame? What wasn't he seeing in his dad's pages? In himself?

He went back to staring at the metal harness, his words beginning to slur. "The Crystals of Temporal Transportation...the Z-energy...the experiments..."

His breaths slowed as he gave in to the gas. Somewhere between what could be either eternal sleep and hallucination, his dad waited for him, wanting something about their conversations to be remembered.

The experiments.

As XBA had demonstrated, there were more phrases than the one he knew, and more ways to use the Z-energy than the dangerous way he'd defaulted to. Drifting alongside his revelations were the words she'd told him to say. Maybe if the bolts came to his hands the way they'd done in De Los Muertos, the shackles on his arms would melt like the chains.

"Nournt Zeorgen," Allister whispered, eyes closing.

His head shot straight back. The freezing cold of a timed shower cut through him at the wrists, adding to the sharp pains already stabbing at his palms like icicles. He felt the Z-energy flowing into his arms, its heat coating his skin with perspiration and quickly puffing away as steam. The neck brace fell away. The arm restraints unlatched. The chains loosened.

But the energy expanded beyond his skin and onto the walls of the prison interior. The room's air filters creaked open. Wind rushed into and out of the prison with the speed and force of a vacuum, sucking away the many toxins that had previously permeated the room. Fresh air pushed him to an acute alertness.

He shook off the chains and reached down, silencing the heavy pieces just before they jangled to the floor.

The glow faded back into Allister. As it did, he waited for sounds of stirring soldiers or the tattletale sirens. Besides the reversal of the gas-releasing mechanism, there was no sound that suggested he'd been caught.

The stiffness in his calves and thighs lingered, and though his body was still out of it, he jumped to his feet with his arms stretched out above him. Standing on his toes, he enjoyed the looseness of his limbs, their ability to reach, to swing.

To punch.

Allister marched toward the door, his fist lifted to bang his way through the metal.

His Cynque flashed before his fist made contact.

He slowed to a stop. "Hold up."

"Video message loading from subject Patrick Adams," it said, almost cheerful.

"Here of all places," Allister said.

He pivoted away from the door to listen. Anxious, he teased his index finger in front of the circle that covered the holographic projection. Pixels rendered. Audio loaded. His heart refused to beat in any rhythm.

Seventy-two percent.

"Any time, Cynque."

"Playing message now, Agent Adams."

He stared into a perpetual black abyss as the sounds of shuffled movements, stifled arguments between multiple men, and his dad's foot tapping leaked out from the low-quality speakers. Funny that they shared such an obnoxious habit.

Whoever was in the room with his dad must have left, their exit marked by the slam of a door.

Still watching the black screen, Allister heard the distress in his dad's heavy sighs, though it sounded like he'd moved on as he was flipping pages by then, turning a few forward before he went back one and stopped.

"Hmm," his dad said, tapping the page. "*Nournt Zeorgen*...begins with Z."

"I'll take anything you got, Pops," Allister said, eager. "For real, anything."

"Oh!" his dad exclaimed as if he'd forgotten something. The camera switched on and refocused, bringing him into plain view.

Now Allister could see the gray-and-black strands of his dad's overgrown beard, the soul-fetching brown in his eyes.

Allister's heart swelled. He reached for the video projection, suddenly remembering his dad's priceless gifts—strong hugs around his tiny body, encouraging words to his childhood doubt, pride in what he may yet become.

The screen glitched when his fingers got too close.

He pulled back and let the image settle. This was a different time than the first three videos, a later time maybe. Instead of an office, his dad was in a laboratory surrounded by shining machines, bulky computers—no doubt incomplete inventions. Maybe he was on the West Coast.

"Well, look at you, son, tapped into your intellectual potential, and you found a new experiment. My brilliant little EV. I knew you'd figure it out. Nournt Zeorgen is my favorite experiment because if you conduct it right, it just sorta flips the switch real easy." His dad smiled for a few moments, but it faded as he resumed turning the pages of a bright-blue notebook.

"You've found what's beneath, what's below. The Vault. You're in the deepest part of the Andromeda Project now. You might have to do some more digging, but I believe you'll find Neight Caster, and if you do, he'll help you like he helped me. He said…he said to find the right timeline and tell you what I been workin' on, what I've discovered. So that's what I've been doing…"

Allister nodded in agreement. "That's what you've been doing all right."

He was burdened by the idea of some EV playing keep-away with their knowledge of the artifacts. Why did he need to do more digging? Didn't this EV know what was at stake?

Twisted, he thought.

Cynque lagged mid-transmission. Annoyed, Allister almost smashed it against the bench as the last string of cautionary dialogue forced its way through the poor connection.

Raising Cynque closer, he caught the fading bits of his dad's deep voice. "I'm startin' to get it now. Time and movement are like rare flowers. They don't want to be found and gawked at, they don't want to be picked and used—so they hide in vast fields, at the bottom of oceans, on the highest mountains, in the driest deserts. The crystal artifacts don't want to be found, Allister, that's why they keep moving. But you gotta find them before they move again."

"If artifacts don't want to be found," Allister repeated. "Then, how does anyone find them?"

WHEN WAS THE LAST
TIME SURRENDERING TO YOUR
POWER SET YOU FREE?

WHAT WORD DID YOU SEND
TO YOUR FUTURE SELF?
SAY IT NOW.

———————

XBA

The Outer District, Oil Alley
Day 209

XBA CROUCHED LIKE a predator in the thickest understory of the urban jungle. Quiet as the moss, strong as a jaguar, ready to capture her next target in jaws of hardened reason.

She thought about what she'd been called to do. An action more arduous than murder. Persuasion. Tas-Salvatur had advised she be honest. No illusions, no tricks, no violence—if it could be helped. Evolution was a choice everyone deserved to make for themselves.

XBA rubbed her claws together. For once, more habit than preparation.

She reveled in the soothing smells of waste runoff and congealed oil running rampant in the District's back streets. Found her solace in an alleyway slicked black from recent rainfall, which reflected flickering neon signs in pavement as uneven as the world itself. To XBA, the aromas of methane and petroleum were more calming than peppermint and rosemary, the grind of generators more musical than the nearby club's ear-catching beats.

Oil Alley was the area's nickname. Where seedy all-hours spots paid the fines for defying the electric curfew. From dusk until dawn, this sleazy stretch of real estate was an epicenter of partygoers and hedonists frequenting those thriving dance floors.

She inhaled all that glorious tension and angst, then closed her human eye.

The other eye never closed; it was always recording, always assessing, always categorizing. She knew her target was soon to cross her digital lens.

Her orange eye brightened, the rhythmic pulse increasing as her target moved closer...closer.

"C20's beautiful killer, in the flesh," her target said.

XBA opened her human eye at the voice, a man's, coming from behind her and more confident than she'd expected. She'd read of him being a twisted, misguided soul, the drawl in his voice dragged by sadness and loss. But this person sounded robust, determined.

"Tonight, I am not here to kill. I am here to enlighten," she answered, rising from her crouched position.

"Those claws are 'bout as enlightening as an apocalypse ascension cult," the man said grimly. "I don't even know why I accepted your invitation. But—I figure if I don't like what you got to say, I can just…"

"Kill me?" she finished for him.

XBA kept her back to him on purpose. Regardless of his assertion, the man was soaked in fear.

Her circuits were alive with his data: a near-infinite feed of one-liners, battle footage, displays of potential, tragedies and triumphs. She smiled, tickled by his complicated existence. The valiant captain of the Andromeda Project had taken her invitation.

"You accepted," XBA said, "because C20 can restore hope and prosperity to those who can embrace it. You accepted because you know it is time for a collective evolution. You accepted because—"

"Yeah, yeah, I know the tagline," the captain interrupted. "Salvation is worth the sum of the remaining, not the difference between them."

"Exactly. See there, we can agree on something."

An eerie quiet settled between and beyond them.

She sensed the captain's motivation, his swarming desire for that last bit of redemption. Lurking deeper than that was his hunger to survive, to protect.

"You lookin' for space to rent in my head?" the man asked.

"Seems it's occupied." XBA turned to face him. "I invited you here to deliver an offer. We at C20 believe you've lost too many years on the wrong side of salvation. We believe in your capacity for leadership."

Though the building's sharp shadows cut off part of the man's expression, she could see that he was worn, battered. From the gold medallions fastened to his red coat to the gleam of his golden-armored chest plate to the lacing of his boots, he was holding on to what everyone expected of him—Captain Jared Brandt, the prideful soldier.

He took a step toward her, the red light of a neon sign catching the disgust on his face. Now the hunger she sensed from him was for her end. Stewing in his mangled little mind was the belief that killing her was the answer.

"Don't know if I see the difference between where I'm at and where you want me to be," Brandt said, caressing his weapon handle.

"Difference is you'll lead C20 *alongside* me. You'll have agency in your future."

Captain Brandt unhinged the weapon from his hip and swung it threateningly to the side.

XBA nodded at it, her mouth widening further with pleasure. "I take it you're not convinced," she said.

"Never was, I'm afraid. And once I kill you"—he took two swift steps sideways—"I'll end this terrestrial war before it starts..."

She followed his lead and took two steps herself, though in the opposite direction. "Open your eyes. The dissonance between us and the Earth, it's already begun—"

"I'll take the data in your memory chips and farm you for parts," the captain continued.

"—and news flash, babe, you've been on the losing team for decades—"

"—without your guidance," he said. "C20 falls and is absorbed by the Andromeda Project—"

XBA flashed her claws and sneered. "At the Andromeda Project, you're a minion, a cog in a worn-out wheel—"

"—we find the artifacts, the United Sanctuaries saves humanity."

Quiet returned in an alleyway wide enough for combat or conversation.

Captain Brandt's teeth were pressed together by then, his face red, she guessed, with fury at his own expectations. She gathered by his grip on the weapon's trigger that he was resigned to his arrogance, clinging to the idea that somehow the Andromeda Project was the purer of the two initiatives.

Her mechanical heart beat steady, neither quickened by his threats or his aggression. Like Tas-Salvatur, she believed there was a balance between violence and reason—some unspoken thread that wove them together. If only Captain Brandt could understand that C20's violence was necessary to usher in a greater era of reason. If only she could force him to.

Controlling a mind is temporary, influencing one is forever, Tas-Salvatur had told her.

Finally, XBA exhaled, scrounging for her last ounce of patience. So though her claws itched to rip open the out-of-sight wound in the captain's chest, she let them go limp and leaned back on her hip, relaxed. "You haven't seen what I've seen. Those artifacts gave us a gift. They showed us it's time to change, and when C20 finds the cosmic power and undoes its warning, we can move forward appropriately."

The intense white of the plasma's charge rushed through the long blunt rod in Captain Brandt's hand, blasting away the dimness between them.

Perhaps that was meant to be his rebuttal.

She flinched. A surge of buzzing awareness shot down her neck. She felt a deep sense of aggravation and, with it, resistance. In part due to the underlying system of veiny wires pulsing with increased vibration, ramping her up to attack. In part from the gears engaging her psibernetic weapons, forcing her fists to clench.

The psionic blades hidden above her wrists were the enhancement she cherished the most. They would've already slid into view, razor-sharp and burning with red energy, if not for every human muscle left in her fighting the programming to *eliminate* him.

Her mechanical eye flashed so bright it burned inside her skull. *Not yet*, she thought, cringing, *I'm not done reasoning yet.*

"Wouldn't you rather be a pioneer for humanity's future. A champion for continuation?" she asked.

"What you think I been doin' all these years?" Captain Brandt asked, his plasma-laced staff extended in front of him. "No sense stoppin' now."

He lunged at her, swinging the weapon in all kinds of directions. She dodged to one side, then another. She leaped. She flipped. She spun. She ducked. Narrowly escaping blistering-hot slice after blistering-hot slice. The captain was quick, she had to admit, but not as quick as her, and she found their battle a bit playful as she moved around him like a matador while he went at her like an angry bull. In the end, her maneuvers were too nimble, her kicks too strong. She struck him in the face, then in the chest, and he flew backward until he slammed into the wall.

XBA walked toward his slumped frame. "If I'd known you were so good at foreplay..." she cooed as she stood over him, delighted by his passion. "Be fore-warned, mercy is against my religion."

In one fluid flip, the captain was back on his feet.

"Good, 'cause betrayal is against mine," he said.

"Round two, then?" she asked.

He turned the weapon over and repositioned himself for another attack.

Artist: Jeffrey Viloria/ The CMD Studios

They were an even match against each other—insight for insight, punch for punch, theory for theory, block for block. His delusion was as strong as his blows, both sinking deep into her exoskeleton—the former proof she was that much closer to *reasoning* with him, the latter doing damage she didn't care to acknowledge. But the throbbing pain kept working its way through her human tissues.

She went to block his next attack, a flat-handed hit to the torso, and missed, slowed down by too much analyzing. She felt the mechanics in her abdomen contract, an attempt to keep his hand from going through her. She flew back, slid along the ground, and rolled in reverse onto her feet.

Captain Brandt didn't give her the time to recoup. He screamed out a furious battle cry as he raced toward her, the enflamed rod raised straight out to his side.

XBA crossed her psibernetic forearms in defense. The plasma weapon smashed into them with a flash, hissing as it heated the enhancements on impact. The pungent smell of liquefying metal stung her nose.

He was where she wanted him, close, at his angriest, the place where words would cut their deepest. "Perhaps if you'd put this much *intention* behind your search, Patrick would still be alive," she said.

"You have no right to speak his name," he screamed in her face. "I did everything I could to save him. Everything!" He forced the sizzling weapon deeper into her arms, frying the intricate wiring underneath. Sparks popped at their faces and singed skin illuminated by burning white fury.

"You've woven quite a lopsided fairy tale, Captain," she said smoothly. "I'm not sure exactly when you became the villain."

To anyone else, what happened next might've been a blip on their radar. But she watched, pleased, as the flushed red drained from his face in shame. He raised his eyebrows the slightest bit in revelation. The doubt billowing off him was more glorious than the plasma burning through her.

Still, he didn't lift the weapon, and after a moment of self-awareness, he was back to fury, back to force, though with that much less confidence in his attack.

Seeing her chance, XBA pretended to yield to his wrath, then shoved the rod back at him.

The handle hit him in the face and he went stumbling away from her.

XBA attempted to mask her hard, heavy breathing. Through the black smoke rising from her charred limbs, she saw her victory: the orange eye calculated his vitals dropping, his heart rate slowing, while the human eye processed his shoulders sinking closer to the ground.

Fatigue seemed to be keeping both their breaths hostage. Her advantage was being half his age and less than half human, swarming with self-repair mechanisms.

"Sustained thirty-six percent damage to psibernetic armor," her internal systems advised. "Engaging Recovery Protocol."

Again, the orange eye burned inside her skull, a sign that the computer's commands were already in motion.

XBA stood up fast, relishing in her own resilience. As she walked toward him, the mangled pieces of her psibernetic limbs that once hung loose separated into individual metallic threads. She felt them writhing in place, and walked faster when the metal threads began weaving around one another, intertwining like a helix until the restored metal coated her arms—flattening, then smoothing, and in the end, glistening anew.

The itching in her psionic blades returned above her wrist. Her body couldn't seem to resist going after the kill, even as she did. It knew, whether by running algorithms or by primal instinct, that with a single stab from the sharpened beasts she had tucked inside her forearms, she'd win.

No.

Death was not her deliverable. So she resumed their conversation instead.

"My offer still stands."

Captain Brandt hurled obscenities at her, livid as he launched himself into another attack. His body and the plasma rod were one fluid color scheme of heat, both charging toward XBA with renewed vigor. But her systems detected a new wavelength pulsing around him...the short, quick-moving energy of disruption.

"Screw your offer!" he yelled.

He went at her with the rod, his attacks laced with a potential he couldn't polish, and just as rusty. The more he fought at her, the more the yellowish energy flared around him. She maneuvered away and around. She blocked and deflected.

Until she couldn't anymore.

Perhaps her circuits had been disrupted... The energy emissions were composed entirely of chaos, after all. She stood suspended in disbelief as he pushed the searing-hot weapon into her side, burning past her psibernetic protection until it reached real skin. Pain rose like a tsunami to her nerves and flooded her metal hand with a destructive wrath. She swung forward, fist clenched—and connected.

Energy exploded at her with a deafening *kaboom*, hurling her into the sky. She winced in pain as she slowed to a stop in the air, then fell limp as she plummeted back down with the fullness of her weight.

Her body slammed into the concrete, spine first.

"System failure imminent," her internal systems advised. "Revert to repair mode."

She blamed her humanity for keeping her pinned to the ground. Cursed him as she tried to sit up in spite of the ringing in her ears and throbbing in the parts of her that weren't metal. She could feel the last bit of patience leaking out of her.

The sound of Captain Brandt's boots traveled toward her.

XBA managed to pull herself to her hands and knees, and faced him with gritted teeth. Her visuals were distorted in the orange eye, failing to retrieve the lost connection behind the glitched screen. In the human eye, she suffered temporary blindness.

But she could see well enough.

All he needed to "win" was her successful decapitation.

Except there was a weapon she'd been saving. A sentence that would cut deeper than the hottest plasma. A truth more disruptive than his potential. She grinned as he raised the plasma rod and swung at her like an executioner.

"We know about your termination!" she shouted.

The weapon froze inches from her neck.

XBA couldn't deny the feeling of triumph recharging her circuits. *As expected.*

"They're going to kill you, Captain," she said, matter-of-fact. "Discard you like they did Patrick, and you're going to let them."

He went quiet, nothing between them but the crackle of plasma heating the air.

"If I killed you…," he murmured. "I knew that…I knew that—"

"You'd be saved?" XBA giggled. "My love, you can't kill me—I'm already mostly dead. You knew that, hmm?" She let her sarcasm permeate before she continued, "Such calculated self-sabotage. Where do your loyalties lie, Captain Brandt? Or are you too weak to have any?"

"What does Tas-Salvatur want with me?"

"Would it be cliché of me to say he sees…your *potential*?"

The captain gripped the plasma rod at his side, absent of his fury, void of that disruptive force. With her psionic potential, she saw only his sorrow basking him in the scarlet reds of telepathic energy, yet his mind was blank as he thought of an answer.

"I can't betray them," Captain Brandt finally said.

XBA smirked, certain he'd surrendered to reason, and slinked back into the shadows on cue. "Ooh, my dear, you already have."

———

CHAPTER 27

DR. FLORENCE BELLADONNA
The District, Oil Alley
Day 209

FLORENCE RODE IN the boxy Ukimoto Hover Model XV in silence. The heaviness in her chest was expected. She'd left Allister Adams chained up in the Vault like a violent criminal when he'd done nothing wrong. To make matters worse, Leesa wasn't even in her office to receive the report.

Bloody rude of her.

But Florence taking the external meeting was her aggressive turn of the wheel. Her position at the Andromeda Project was about perception, and her responsibilities about economics, as in whoever controlled humanity's future controlled humanity. The concept wasn't foreign to her. She'd been hired on many occasions to steer ships from the sidelines.

So she knew she needed to walk away with substantial information on either Neight, the Z-energy, or the crystal artifacts. Three puzzle pieces to be rotated and matched to fit into the bigger narrative.

She checked her Cynque for the meeting location again, hoping it might've changed.

Club HellForest still flashed at the top of the invitation.

Florence scoffed at the name for the fourth time. She wondered why the person had wanted to meet her there of all places. Safety? Discretion? An appreciation for erotic entertainment? She didn't care for loud venues or large crowds, mostly because of how it affected her telepathy. Even though, at the moment, she couldn't sense anything.

She knew why, though. She...remembered what had happened after she made contact with the alien in Allister's mind. How she'd doubled over, clutching her midsection as blue energy invaded her astral form.

"You feel it now?" Neight Caster had asked her.

And before Florence could admit she felt the immense, permanent, mind-altering pain, her psionic presence had been shredded like loose-leaf.

For the first time since her early teens, her expertly trained mind potential collected no thoughts, scanned no emotions, didn't deliver that faint inclination that something might happen…just before it did. It had been neutralized, she guessed, by Neight Caster…or the Z-energy.

She hadn't noticed how attached she'd become to her potential until this moment. She was minutes from meeting a stranger in Oil Alley, a lawless part of town, when the fear started sneaking into her.

Without her telepathy, it would be impossible to extract everything from her upcoming conversation, most specifically, what *wasn't* being said. That could make the risk worth less, or simply worthless.

She leaned forward from where she sat in the overly cushioned bucket seat, then looked out the tinted window. She'd reached a place far more relaxed on Cynque scans and drone raids. Here, people weren't afraid of military violence or Federal scans; they walked wider sidewalks with confidence, enjoyed their nights, and beat down anyone who tried to have them do otherwise. They were living until the end—really *living*.

"Approaching Oil Alley," Cynque chimed.

"How much farther, then?" she asked.

The Ukimoto slowed to a stop and throttled in place, suspended high above the street below. "We have arrived, Club HellForest," Cynque said.

Florence secured her audio piece, technology resembling a cartilage earring accessory: a simple gold molding interspersed with silver carvings and attached to dangling chains. She fastened a floral-and-feather-decorated mask to her face.

"Take me down," she said.

The car lowered itself to the ground. Out the window, neon signs blinked in an otherwise dark alley. Bass thumped against the hovering car's sound-resistant windows. When the car reached a safe height, the door slid open.

A masked young man waited outside the vehicle. Blond, strapping, his hand held up to help her disembark. The smell of rare spices wafting up from his wrist made her quiver, and she, a little more turned on than she'd been in a long while, almost missed the second step down.

"Welcome, Dr. B," the man said in an Australian accent. He grinned as she caught herself, then guided her to the dry asphalt. "We've been expecting you. Right this way."

Florence remembered the last time a man's touch had made her heart flutter; it had been hundreds of days past. She began to feel her jumpsuit sticking to her now-clammy skin. The humidity as much to blame as his charm.

She followed him as far as what looked like a garage door, watching as he shook hands with the two armed people standing guard. Glowing QB cryptocurrency numbers appeared on his Cynque. They faded soon after. A transfer had been made—which meant she would be taken care of, protected in a sense. She ruffled her curls and lifted her nose a touch higher.

Of course she'd be taken care of, she thought to herself; she was Florence Belladonna, for clock's sake.

The young man bowed theatrically with a spark in his eye. She bowed back without breaking eye contact.

"Please," he said, gesturing to the entrance.

"*Mille grazie*," she mouthed.

Florence approached the guards.

"Fourth floor, back right corner," the taller, fitter guard whispered to her.

She tensed as her eyes wandered the alleyway. Her handsome host had disappeared. In his place, antsy patrons mobbed the plastic barrier that separated them, while a trail of people just as eager spilled beyond the stanchion. She suspected the line, which really looked more like a cluster extending from the wall, disappeared behind the alley's sharp corner. An hour into Day 209, so about the middle of the night, and the club was just ramping up. She knew those waiting were coming down from a bender or gearing up for one.

"*Mio dio*, busy night," Florence said.

"Unusually," the tall guard replied.

The other guard thrust their thumb at the garage door. "Crank it, we got a few stumbling out."

The door was pulled into the ground by chains on either side, revealing the club's interior. Body heat and booming decibels blasted her senses. A group of dazed men and women in silver suits exited.

"You remember?" the tall guard asked.

"Fourth floor..."

"Back right corner," they finished. "Don't get lost."

She wouldn't.

Florence stepped in. The door cranked closed behind her.

People soaked in shadows groped each other atop illuminated platforms. Masked partygoers writhed to an inconsistent beat. Drag queens on stages entertained with hard-to-accomplish choreography and magic tricks while chained-up performers distorted their bodies inside fogged-up boxes. Club HellForest was not a temporary escape, she concluded; it was a black hole, as strange and warped as the cosmic anomaly.

She followed a long walkway that overlooked the dance floor and climbed onto stairs that led her up to an open lounge with a few plush booths scattered along the walls. Ring lights lit up tabletops distributed in the center, highlighting the dancers on them who were looking to make a few QBs.

Feeling lustful eyes on her, she adjusted her jumpsuit and zipped the neckline higher, then walked toward a semicircle of suited guards, who parted at her arrival.

In a blue love seat sat a burly man draped head to thigh in gyrating women. The mask he wore hid most of his face, but his shaved head and stupid grin and vintage red leather coat gave him away.

Detective Hunter Steele.

"All right, beautifuls, fun's over for now," he said, sitting up. The women giggled and kissed his bald head before skipping away. He smiled at Florence. "You made it. Drink?"

She narrowed her eyes, not keen on his presence or the fact that he was shirtless and flexing underneath the coat.

"Ginger tea, hot," she answered, sitting down.

"Ginger tea, hot!" he yelled into the air. "You look absolutely radiant, doll, as always. I see why Mr. Prez has such an obsession with you."

"President...DeVries?" she asked.

She didn't need telepathy to know the answer. Yes, it was President Wesley DeVries. Who else could it be? Thinking back on the invitation's timely arrival, she should've known he would, in a panic about the state of the Sanctuaries, set up something like this to rush things along. "Hm, the pressure from the Resilient Nations finally got to our courageous leader?"

"You know Prez better than anyone," Hunter replied. "He's so, so sorry he couldn't be here, but sends his best. Politics, ya know?"

Artist: Lester Niesta/ The CMD Studios

"Yeah, I know," she said, the pleasantry slipping from her voice. "He could've sent anyone, but he sent *you*."

"I'm one of a kind, DB. I guess we have that in common."

"*Fanculo*. What does DeVries want now?"

Hunter leaned back. His answer was a wordless glance sideways at an approaching staff member. Likely code for much-needed discretion.

The waiter, wearing no shirt and a collar around his neck, slid her drink onto the table.

"We have to keep it casual, babe," Hunter soothed. "People are always watching."

"This place is degenerate," said Florence.

"I know. I love it."

The topless waiter moved on to greeting new drunken patrons stumbling onto the mezzanine. She counted eleven people lining the room's perimeter. Eleven people whose thoughts she couldn't detect, eleven people whose intentions were unclear. She sat up straighter and moved her arms closer to her body, starting to second-guess her decision to come weaponless.

Examining the four armed guards postured in a square around them, she asked, "You trust these guys?"

He scoffed playfully and swirled the ice cubes in his beverage, pretending to be put off by her skepticism. "These are my guys, sweetheart, trust them with my life. I heard you had some questions for me. But before we get to the good stuff, I have a new assignment for you."

Florence tilted her head and squinted with suspicion. "A...new assignment? For me?"

"For you." Hunter gave her the wink and the gun.

"Well, get on with it."

"Listen. Very. Very. Carefully," he began. "The name of the game is search and rescue."

"Who would I be—?"

"Let me finish," he said, pushing his hands out as if to slow her down. "Let me finish the story. Imagine, More Rock Co. gets hit with a tsunami of QB coin trouble. That's why I never sail on the Mediterranean, because that's where they lost their sea lien."

Florence squinted harder at him, not understanding.

"I think to myself"—Hunter leaned over the table—"where'd she go? I follow the elements always. I sit in the middle, right? Sit in the godforsaken former middle and look east."

She tapped her finger against the mug with impatience. Disgust a tickling in her throat. "This is a joke, yeah? Who really sent you? I know you'd let anyone with a few thousand QBs fill those horrifying cargo pockets you've got."

Hunter checked his Cynque without acknowledging her interruption, her accusation, or her insult. "Where is the sand, the wind? All of a sudden, *boom*! Too much wind. Too much sand. East of the middle, I swear."

Florence found his riddles, if they could be considered such, both questionable and complicated. She went from annoyed to aggravated, heat rushing from her chest to her cheeks to her ears.

"There it was," he continued, slurring. "The see you in twenty we'd been looking for the whole time."

She felt compelled to hold her drink pressed to the table, for if she lifted it, she knew the hot liquid would *not* end up in her mouth. Somehow Hunter always seemed to make it under her skin. And though his intoxication level was hard to gauge, she was sure he slurred his words because he thought it was endearing, not because the alcohol had affected him. The man was pushing three hundred pounds of solid muscle and dwarfed her even when seated. No way a couple cocktails had impaired his judgment.

"What the bloody hell kind of game is this?" she snapped, now squeezing the mug. She was that much closer to hurling it at him for wasting her time. For wasting *time* at all. "I swear on my *nonna*'s grave, if you dragged me here to stall—"

Hunter interrupted, "Hey, sweets, I told you to listen very, very, carefully." He swigged the last of his drink and raised his hand into the air, summoning another. "Thought you'd be better at this," he teased.

Better at not jamming my heel into your—

The waiter arrived with a full glass of iced light-brown liquid and plopped it in front of Hunter. He snatched the new drink off the table, winked at her a second time, then took a sip.

Appearing to gag, he spat it out on one of the guards. "The jasmine iced tea here is crap," he said, trying it a second time before he yelled over his shoulder, "There's no vanilla crystal in this, dude, what gives?"

No reply came.

"Between us, the green tea was worse," he whispered to her.

Florence loosened her hold on the mug, confused as she processed his body language, his drink choices, and the words he'd spewed at her just a few minutes past. *Tea? Bloody hell, he's sober?*

Her eyebrow raised.

Hunter was being serious. Dead serious. And at the same time, didn't want to be taken seriously.

Florence took a breath and let her body cool, aware then that she hadn't been listening at all. She could admit her mistake, though only to herself—she'd been waiting to pick up on what he wasn't saying rather than zeroing in on what he had been saying.

He grinned at her and spun his glass. "Aww, I see we're becoming best friends," he said. "By the way, have you met him? He's ducking Marshall, who makes sure no one knows. But someone knew that *sea lien's gotta lament all potential*."

Not riddles, she deduced, code speak…little plays on words. She was keen to his game, and after her years of studying both human and Evolutionary minds, no stranger to decoding hidden meanings. To her, it was all about structure, relativity, *emphasis*—whether it be a conscious mind or a conversation.

A smirk crept onto her face.

Someone knew that Celine's got elemental potential, she translated in her head.

Celine Nephthys, the missing Moroccan princess.

"I see," she said, leaning back into her chair.

Florence couldn't help the arrogance dripping from her next movements: how she crossed her legs and tossed her hair, then replayed his story in her mind, her gold nails toying with the rim of her mug.

He gave her a smug, knowing look.

She looked away to concentrate. Kept speeding up his sentences. Sounding out each syllable.

Ducking? No, slower…Duc-king. Da King. Then, the light-bulb moment. *The King Marshall makes sure no one knows, but someone knew that Celine's got elemental potential.*

The story was now as clear as a CynqueNews broadcast.

Imagine, More Rock Co. gets hit with a tsunami of QB coin trouble. That's why I never sail on the Mediterranean…

She already knew that the Moroccan tsunami was a disaster that had hit a hundred or so days back, costing the country millions in QBs.

That's where they lost their sea lien...Celine, Hunter had said, alluding to the princess's status as missing—but it was the next part that fascinated her most. *I follow the elements, always. I sit in the middle, right? Sit in the godforsaken former middle and look east.* She slowed it down. *Former middle...and...look...east.*

Former Middle East?

She shook her head, rejecting the conclusion.

The mezzanine seemed to be getting louder the harder she tried to concentrate. Now she was leaning forward, staring down into her lukewarm drink, trying to block out the bass, the flashing lights, and Hunter's wandering eyes.

Think, Florence.

She remembered him saying he'd followed the elements, and also the part near the end when he'd mentioned Celine's secret elemental potential—*Where is the sand, the wind? All of a sudden, boom! Too much wind. Too much sand. East of the middle, I swear.*

At that moment, the only place on Earth with too much sand and too much wind *was* the former Middle East, where a massive storm called the Middle Beast had been raging for...she counted back the days...almost the exact amount of time Celine had been missing.

There it was. The see you in twenty we'd been looking for the whole time.

The last bit shook her. Was he suggesting that C20 was operating out of the Middle East? Was he suggesting they'd kidnapped her?

She looked up at him, baffled.

"The game of search and rescue," he repeated, nodding at her in recognition. "You go get the enemy. You find and return the *sea lien*. Two birds, one sword. See how that works?"

Florence scowled, damn near enraged, her mug against her lips. She took a sip of her drink, and in an effort to control her tongue, placed the mug back on the table so carefully, so slowly, it didn't make a sound.

"I hope these additional services come with additional compensation," she said through clenched teeth. "I'd hate for our colleague to make any assumptions regarding my availability or willingness."

"Thing is, it's part of the job," Hunter quipped. "You know it. I know it. C'mon DB, let's not play the game."

He was correct. She knew the maze of obligation always led back to her, though bringing down C20 wouldn't necessarily release her of her obligation to the Andromeda Project.

"Let me make this clear," Florence said. "I want to go home. But I don't get to go home until I retrieve the *art of facts* we've been looking for. *Capisci?*"

Hunter slapped the table. "Oooh hoo hoo, this is rowdy, I like," he said. "*Quindi parliamo.*"

She tapped her lips, carefully crafting her next question. It would have to be good...and it would have to get her closer to the Crystals of Temporal Transportation. She suspected if Hunter had been chosen to sit across from her, he must've known something; President DeVries wasn't someone she considered careless in his associations.

She looked around them as she pushed the mug aside, then scooted her chair in.

"What do you know about *Night*?" Florence whispered. "When did it fall?"

"The ali—"

"Hold on, let me finish"—she flipped her hair sarcastically—"let me finish the story. It seems we have enough *inner gene* to take advantage of the *art of facts* we can't see. Yet, the volatility is the recurring limitation." She was speaking of both Allister and Leesa, though didn't want to mention either name. "I've noticed," she continued, dragging out the end, "the blue color only burns its safest and brightest at *Night*."

Hunter shook his finger at her, catching on. "They said *Night* falls from on high, always where it's deepest, darkest. Low population, small towns, you know the type."

Like Cumberland Falls, where Allister's from, Florence thought. She squirmed forward in her seat in anticipation.

He took slow sips of his drink, watching her until she reached the edge. "Strange was this *Night*," he finally said, "who told us that we'd need the *art of facts* to—'extend our time.' There was no why or how or where, just a string of prophecies revealed as more 'came to.' Everything we know, we learned at *Night*."

"Everything?"

"Everything." He twirled his glass, staring at the ice move in circles. His smile had faded. Perhaps the subject matter struck something in him. "You want stable, piping-hot cups of e-n-e-r-g-y to take advantage of the *art of facts* you don't have? Wait for *Neight* fall."

"I've been told Neight has...*ended.*"

"*Neight* has been around longer than you and me, babe. Longer than all of us. You really think it would end before humanity did?" He finished the tea. "Neight will fall long after we aren't alive to see it."

Florence removed herself from the table. "I think I have what I need," she said.

"I think you do, too." He goaded her with a blank stare and resumed his flirting with an inane grin. "Fetching jumpsuit by the way. Hits you in all the right places."

She kept the restraint in her body. "Detective Steele, have a go at decoding *this*," she said, sharpening her words the way she'd sharpen her sword. "You make another pass at me...ever...and I wipe your mind—clean."

His eyes stayed on her. "It's your world. We're just living in it."

She turned away, satisfied, and shoved past the pillar of guards.

"Your return vehicle is waiting for you on the south side of the building, Dr. Belladonna," Cynque said as she rushed down the stairs to the balcony. "It is scheduled to leave in five minutes to, so please make your way to the exit."

"Don't you worry," she answered. She was relieved that her departure was scheduled at all.

But instead of quickening her pace, she slowed down. Her senses were being magnified all at once, each one processing the environment on overload. The pounding music. The glaring lights. The smothering smells of heated human bodies.

Her body shuddered beneath the jumpsuit, tingled from the fragile nerve endings coming alive tenfold. She guessed what would come next and, walking even slower, did her best to prepare without making a scene. What followed the unchecked amplification of her five human senses was almost always the arrival of her sixth sense.

Telepathy.

On cue, a furious red energy flashed behind her eyes. The clubgoers' minds opened to her like a million doors to bright rooms. She stumbled sideways due to the hundreds of voices now shouting in her head and slammed her shoulder into the balcony's glass siding.

No one stopped partying to help her, which was just as well, considering she tangled her hands in her hair and squeezed her eyes shut while screaming to herself, *Turn it off! Turn it off!*

It was miracle enough to have her potential return. For her to be so aware. For her to be so connected. Yet, of all the minds she touched, there was a single thought: the repeating curve of the letter *C* followed by the number twenty.

C20, C20, C20, C20, it repeated, thumping against her mind like the club's intense bass.

Soaked in her own perspiration, she gripped the railing for balance and forced herself to search the array of platforms below. She scanned the room for a group of people, possibly in disguise, lured there to throw her off.

Florence stopped short, her gaze captured by a pair of blazing eyes staring up at her. They were attached to a haggard-faced man who moved like a shark through the crowd. He was too busy looking at her to pay attention to where he was going, but it seemed to work in his favor because as more bodies pushed against him, his eyes burned brighter, ignited by the impacts.

While this man, his skin now bathing in a fiery blend of orange, yellow, and red moved toward the stairs—toward *her*—she was stuck in place, her mouth hanging open in recognition, unable to release the breath she held.

His was a face she'd never forget.

Shahar Prasai. Otherwise known as the living bomb.

It was as if he'd been molded to represent someone's deepest fear—scars carved in his forehead, stitches sewn across his cheeks. He was brown-skinned and big, not just tall, but wide, muscled from shoulder to shoulder and thick from front to back. Looking at him from there, he'd even give Hunter a run for his QBs, despite not matching his strength.

"Cynque…," she said, backing away. "Can you confirm there's a C20 agent staring back at me right now?"

"Recognized, Shahar Prasai," Cynque said in her ear. "Designation: rogue operative, C20. Origin City: Kathmandu, Nepal. Potential: kinetic energy manipulation. Most recent location: De Los Muertos."

Florence reached for the sword she forgot was not at her side. Clenching her fist where the handle would've been, she cursed to herself for not bringing the weapon and activated her Cynque. "Send a message to headquarters, attention

General Delemar. C20's been spotted at Club HellForest, possible terror attack in a *very* crowded part of Oil Alley... Subject in question, Shahar Prasai."

After it sent, she tore down the winding stairs, cautious of those staring at her as she passed. When she reached the ground floor, her heart was aflutter at the stark difference in both vibe and clientele.

She stood among a dizzying display of strobe lighting and augmented reality projections. Fog had infiltrated from every corner of the main room and floated just above it like a thin gray blanket. Where before the dance floor had been filled with wild, sexually charged youths with edgy haircuts and glittery garments, it now contained a crowd of androgynous types with shaved heads and bleach-white clothing. They swayed to syncopated sound waves, their mouths moving as if without conscious thought.

At first glance, Shahar wasn't among them.

That realization didn't ease the thickness growing in her throat, because she knew he was still there, somewhere, ready to combust at a moment's notice.

Where the devil are you?

A question she didn't really want answered as she dodged through the oblivious patrons toward the exit. She paused to wave some fog out of her face and did a sweep of the room. "Could really use an update, Cynque," she whispered.

"I regret to inform you that your transport has departed. I am also having an issue with the network, specifically the part of me that plugs into the Andromeda Project. Your message did not go through."

"This is dire, Cynque. Do whatever you bloody can. Patch me through to Lieutenant Delemar and Captain Brandt, for clock's sake. Attach critical to the correspondence."

"Captain Brandt's communications have been taken offline due to his termination status. Would you like me to alert anyone else?"

"Termination status?" Last she'd checked, his termination was up for discussion, not finalized.

Florence gripped the bridge of her nose, past frustrated, speeding toward furious. General Delemar must've decided to dismiss her recommendation. "Can you get me through to anyone, or not?"

"Dialing Lieutenant Delemar...," Cynque began, the beep of attempted communication buzzing in her ear. The device came back on after four tries. "I am having an issue with the network," it repeated, "specifically the part of me that plugs into the Andromeda Project. Your message did not go through."

What is going on back there?

Florence pushed harder through the crowd. Her aim to keep ample space between her and Shahar.

She'd already gone to the trouble of bracing her psyche to penetrate the hundreds of absent minds, prepared to be overwhelmed by their thoughts of C20 from that close a distance. But as she weaved her way deeper, the thoughts were not only quieter...they were *fading*, almost nonexistent. It could've meant her potential was shielding her from bombardment. Or there was the scarier reason: that her potential was shorting out again. Touching her forehead, she tried to narrow in on one thought, any thought, and pull it to her. She caught nothing. As the remaining had twisted away from her psionic reach and disappeared.

Florence slammed her back against the wall facing the dance floor, pissed off all over again. She snatched the mask off her face.

I can't sense anything...

Halfway between the exit and the stairs, she heaved, tired of elbowing her way through, and somewhat caught up in whether to prioritize her escape with no transport, or surrender to confrontation with no backup, no weapon, and no potentials.

Moving any direction became impossible. For the mass of people who'd once had their backs turned, preoccupied with the music, now faced her and were pushing one another trying to get closer—or more like trying to close in. She threw up her fists in defense, feeling wary of their coordinated movement and put off by their aggressive dispositions.

Maybe that's why she didn't see Shahar at first.

But how could she miss him among those spiritless bodies—when he was standing that much closer, glowing that much brighter. She wondered how long he'd been there, his eyes and hands ablaze with kinetic energy.

It was obvious by his slow approach that he wasn't there to commit a widespread act of terror...no...he'd come for something very specific.

Her.

———

CHAPTER 28

ALLISTER ADAMS

Quadrant Gamma—the Vault, Andromeda Project Headquarters
Day 209

ALLISTER COULDN'T WAIT another second. He needed to see if Neight Caster was alive and could help him, then he needed to find his mom.

Flattening his palms against the prison wall, he applied force, testing for any weaknesses: low to the bottom first, then higher near the ceiling, then across the metal at chest height.

The prison was solid to the core.

There was a way he could get out. A loud, destructive tactic guaranteed to blow the door off the hinges and grant his escape. It wasn't the method he preferred, as the consequences if he got caught meant more violence against him—and possible termination on the grounds that he was going rogue. But he kept telling himself there was no sense being paralyzed by outcomes.

If saying *Foeht Zeorgen* would give him freedom, *Foeht Zeorgen* was what he'd say.

Allister stepped back, legs spread apart, and concentrated on the door with his left arm aimed at it. "Foeht Zeorgen," he said.

His skin sizzled instead of sparked.

"Okay, second go 'round, then." He widened his stance and squeezed his *uncharged* fist, nervous. "Foeht—ah!"

Before he could repeat it, the Z-energy came oozing through him like magma, twisting down to his forearm while feeling hotter than the core of the Earth. It took longer to arrive at his knuckles than he could've ever imagined, and just when he got ready to let loose and scream from the pain, the energy burst free.

The door seemed to embrace the unfocused blast, then wrap it up in its sturdy construct and smother it into silence before dissipating it throughout the walls. The blue energy blinked and shimmered around him, across the ceiling, beneath his feet—harmless like minnows moving through a pond. And then it disappeared, leaving not an ounce of damage or evidence of its conjuring, even smoke.

He'd expected a wide hole blasted through the door. But it didn't even make a *sound* when the energy beam hit; the door just loomed there, taunting him, just as tall as he and just as defiant. Unscathed.

Allister dropped his arm, disappointed with his results.

Maybe that was why they called it the Vault.

His resignation came as if a gust of arctic air, the energy cooling fast at its arrival. He supposed he could try again with more intent, or try something different—perhaps another potential, maybe another experiment.

"Could I punch my way out?" he asked himself, trying to guess the extent of his strength potential. There had to be weak spots, likely near the access pad and the hinges if what he remembered about engineering served him well. He was ready to head toward the door and pummel his way through it.

"Lieutenant Delemar, access denied," the computer said.

Allister froze midstride, eyes fixed on the space he'd intended to smash. He thought he was hallucinating after having been awake for so much time.

"Lieutenant Delemar, access denied," it repeated.

He pressed his ear to the door to listen to the heavily muffled voices on the other side.

"I need you to authorize my entrance, Admiral," Leesa said.

"Engaging with Agent Adams is prohibited until he's cleared," Admiral Gattison replied, who was next to Leesa from what he could tell. "Unless you have a special request like Belladonna did, make this easier on yourself and find your way back to sea level."

"Belladonna didn't report back to me as I ordered. Therefore, I need to carry out her assignment."

Allister pulled away from the door, astonished. Would he have to fight Leesa again in order to break free? Could he with his pulse racing at that speed?

"No can do," Admiral Gattison said. "Sad about your authorization privileges. Guess your ranking hasn't updated yet."

"It would take a twist of my wrist to rip this door off the hinges and smash you with it," Leesa said. "I won't ask twice."

"Temper, temper," the admiral retorted. "Haven't your outbursts landed you down here for enough nights?"

He heard a sharp crack and then the sound of the admiral screaming in pain.

"Admiral Gattison, access granted," the computer interrupted.

Allister dashed to the bench and sat down. He tucked his hands behind his back, afraid Leesa would see that he'd used his energy potential. The bolt lock unlatched.

Leesa pushed the door open without laying a hand on it.

"It's just a fracture. You'll recover in no time." She let go of the admiral's limp wrist, her leg already over the threshold. With purple flashing in her eyes, she entered the cell. "Your discretion is appreciated."

Admiral Gattison sneered in reply as the door slammed closed. At Leesa's telekinetic command, obviously.

"Leave her," the admiral shouted when, from the other side of the door, her minions made a fuss about the breach.

Leesa's eyes had brightened at her victory. Soon they fell with the same swiftness.

She and Allister were alone, both of them listening to the distressed voices beyond the door slowly fade away.

He watched her, unsure of what to say. The harness he'd crushed into the size of her shoe lay between them, and he hoped with everything inside him she wouldn't notice it, or realize it was the contraption they'd used to restrain him.

Fear held him there on the bench, his hands fidgeting behind his back. Fear that she knew something…about him. Fear that she wanted to do something…to him.

He should be lucky enough to kneel upon the marble surrounding her high-backed, hovering throne and beg for her forgiveness.

But the lieutenant had descended to the depths of her own castle to confront a prisoner, the rigid bones of her cheeks softened by the light, her eyes a vibrant sea moss green. Her forehead shimmered with the sweat of second thoughts. He guessed regret for hurting the admiral.

Her gaze left him and landed on the compacted metal at her feet. "Your restraints…you removed them."

"They came off on their own," he lied.

"Did they become a ball of eligible recycling on their own as well?" She kicked aside the crumpled metal. "Did they?" she asked again, two steps closer.

His tongue felt too heavy to answer or to ask what he really wanted to know, which was why she'd come.

She chopped the air in response to his silence, bringing the bench crashing down.

Allister went down with it.

Their conflict seemed unavoidable as he scrambled closer against the wall, feet pushing the bench pieces and chains into her path.

"I could've had you terminated after you let go of that machine," she said. She opened her hand slowly and held it out, a move he'd seen her use to bring forth her potential. "But I thought it might be more newsworthy if I did it myself."

Now her descent to the dungeon made sense.

He couldn't believe that after one mistake—okay, maybe two or three mistakes—he would be terminated without ever giving his mom a final hug, or learning to use his potentials, or helping humanity.

Perhaps he'd underestimated the gravity of losing the machine. Perhaps he'd held on to too much hope that they could still beat C20 to the artifacts.

He watched the fiery purple energy swirl and dance in her palm. To his confusion, she stared at it, too, maybe figuring out whether to make his end quick and painless, or long and agonizing. Beneath the obvious conflict in her eyes was the same look from the assessment: one of disposal.

Leesa wasn't so unlike an enemy while standing there opposite him, contemplating the value of his life without saying a word.

Allister flexed his arms, then swallowed hard, bravery fighting its way to his next choice. If he didn't defend himself then, when else would he? He balled up his fists...prepared to stand...

The telekinetic ball burst into cinders.

His mouth fell open at the sight of the purple energy scattering into the air, harmless.

"I didn't come here to kill you," she said, lowering her arm. "I came here...to...to offer you freedom."

Allister refused to trust—that she'd want to do that, that she'd want that for him. How could she? Why would she? He clamped his mouth shut and squinted, as if by focusing his vision he would unveil the psychic illusion. But his mind was missing that spellbinding tingle, his intuition missing that nagging sense that something wasn't quite right.

"Wait...what?" he choked out. "You're being one thousand right now?"

"I'm offering you an out, Allister. Take your mother and leave. No one will come after you and you'll never hear about the Andromeda Project again."

His heart stopped cold, though moments prior it had been speeding with apprehension. She was saying he could leave...she was saying he could *leave*.

"But I thought...I thought I was the Gateway or something?" he finally stammered.

"I have access to the same Z-energy you do. It's just, I have to be more careful when I use it." She turned away from him, arms crossed. "It's best if you go back to whatever your life was. Let us handle saving the human race."

"You've got it, too?" he asked, using the wall to help him to his feet. "Then you feel it? The burning? The surging? You can cynque with why I let go?"

"Controlling any potential requires training and experience, but the Z-energy requires them most of all."

"Uh...you sayin' you got a better handle on it than me? You don't need the words...you don't use experiments..."

"Experiments? Words? No. My energy potential is fueled by my will and my intention. I'm sure I felt uncertainty and fear, and was a slave to such weak feelings in the beginning, but I've moved past them—"

"I'm with it. You're just a better Evolutionary overall." Allister felt a twinge of jealousy, and after thinking over what she was insinuating—less that she was a better Evolutionary, more that he wasn't disciplined enough to get to her level—that feeling gave way to utter worthlessness.

She, a fellow outcast of society who claimed to share the same energy potential as him, wanted nothing to do with him.

"I'm hyped for you," Allister said, eyes downcast. He hadn't expected his face to get hot with humiliation, but it had. Just as, in light of his sarcasm, he didn't expect the words to get caught in his throat, though they did. "Guess there's no place for me here, I'll just take my little potential back to Riser Town and argue over scraps of food with my broke neighbors."

He knew if he couldn't be accepted among Evolutionaries, he wouldn't be accepted anywhere.

The world might as well have ended right then.

Leesa waved her hand at the air, dismissing him. "You keep freaking out every time the energy shows up, and it's slowing me down. So, yes. Go be unprepared and reckless and afraid somewhere it won't jeopardize our future."

Slowing her down?

Allister was confused about her choice of words until the sage wisdom from Dr. Belladonna's most recent visit snuck its way into his psyche: *Sometimes being good isn't enough.*

"Hmm, you don't care if I made a mistake," he began quietly, "or if I wanna fix it. You just don't want me here."

"It's not about what I want or don't want," she shot back. "I'm trying to protect you and your family." She got right up in his face, chest puffed up, fists thrust behind her in frustration. "You're compromised, Agent Adams. C20 knows who you love, they know how to get to you, make you do exactly what they want."

Her close proximity set him off—not in fear, as maybe she'd wanted, but in unwavering defense, both of himself and what he could do. "I'm not gonna let you run me off!" he bellowed. "I can protect my mom! And…and…I can learn! And…I can train to use my potentials like everybody else!"

"Humanity doesn't have time for you to catch up!" Leesa screamed. "This is not a discussion! You choose: termination or dismissal."

Despite her ultimatum, the boldness in his voice wouldn't slip away. "You know what I think, *Lieutenant*. I think you don't have the power to let me go."

Leesa ripped herself away, huffing, "Of course I have the power—"

"We're both trapped here, not just me!"

He regretted saying it the moment it was said. Yet, he knew it had to be true. From him "slowing her down," to her having the energy potential and supposedly moving past those weak feelings. If the Z-energy was so dangerous in her hands that she'd achieved an inhuman level of control, how could she be allowed to leave? She couldn't roam the streets with that sort of power bottled inside her. He figured it was only a matter of time before she cracked…and let go, if she hadn't already.

Leesa was trembling, arms still crossed over her chest, as if she were holding everything in. Her potential. Her anger. Her self.

He thought she'd raise her hand any second and pull him to pieces, the anxiety building in him the longer she didn't *react*. But the hardened look on her face softened, then crumbled.

Her arms simply fell to her side.

Before his eyes, she began unraveling, from her curving spine to her slumping shoulders to her defeated crouch.

She dug her hands into the hair she kept so carefully groomed, ruining it. "Your observation is enough evidence that what I believed I represented, I do not. Sometimes, I try to remember a time before this place. Before I became this, this thing, and…I can't. I can't remember having a life before the countdown… or whatever a life is supposed to look like in such a time." Her speech was lightweight, poetic and fluid versus scripted and harsh.

He blinked at her, eyes wide, not believing what he saw, and believing even less of what he heard.

"Is this the sum of my existence?" she asked.

Allister's throat was clenched tight. The discomfort in him…unbearable. He hadn't expected her to break down, just ease up on him a little. Maybe let him stick around. He swallowed hard, trying to come up with an answer for her that didn't include an accusation. He thought to himself that maybe the Andromeda Project was all Leesa knew.

As if they'd shared that same thought, she continued. "If that's true, something has to change. What I dreamed for myself, if I ever dreamed for myself, has been twisted—dictated and overshadowed by the Andromeda Project and the crystal artifacts, by…you."

"Me?" he asked in a high pitch. He placed both hands on his chest, incredulous. "Me? The lowly recruit you been treating like a second-class citizen? You talking about me?"

"You came in here and wowed the directors. They've been looking for someone like you, someone they could put out as the new face of the Andromeda Project. This is a business, after all…even if it is the business of escaping the apocalypse."

Allister sighed, one hand stroking his afro as he digested her…honesty. "The new face? A business?" He laughed uneasily. "Uhm…last time I cynqued, the Andromeda Project is a secret."

She levitated into the air and struck a dramatic pose. "It wasn't always that way—"

"No one even knows what we're doing," he continued over her. "So who cares which of us finds the artifacts?"

"Who cares? I care!" she said, eyes flashing purple.

The Vault rattled with the force of her potential.

Allister jumped back. "Whoa, mega trigger," he said.

Quieter, she continued. "I care...because I wanted to be good. I was given a second chance, so far as I know, to be something greater than human medicine thought possible." She looked off with an expression of longing. "If you're the Gateway, then what am I?"

He felt tempted by her vulnerability: tempted to take her offer, tempted to leave. Going back to Riser Town meant giving up, denying himself. Hiding all over again.

Eyeing her from the side with suspicion, he decided that she had been pretending to feel emotion. That her honesty was a trick. Her breakdown a strategy.

"Hmm, what are you? I don't know... You could start with the most powerful Evolutionary on the planet? The famous lieutenant of the Andromeda Project?" he said sarcastically. "You're so full of it. I bet this is some kinda test."

Leesa floated up to him, a challenge in her eyes. "I never received the report on you from Dr. Belladonna. Those results were the only thing keeping you alive and they're past due. I suggest you take my offer."

Part of him hated that he was right. Her feelings were a means to an end.

Allister came back at her with the same vigor. "That's really what it comes down to? We can't get cynqued on the fact we're both after somethin' bigger than us, so we fight about who gets it. How's that any different than us versus C20?"

"No one ever said it had to be different. Leave with your mother before C20 winds up killing her to force your hand."

Allister fell back against the wall. Defeated by her with that single truth. C20 *would* use his mom against him, they already had. And he was sure he *would* choose her if the conflict came down to that, he already had. Maybe he couldn't be trusted to do whatever it might take.

In one deep breath, he lost faith in human salvation—and in himself. He'd walk out of that prison with his mom, knowing that because he was the product of such unique heritage that he could retrieve a treasure as rare as time. And still be forced to live each day left having thrown away such a privilege and responsibility, always wondering if he'd made the wrong decision.

But Mom, he thought, remembering the moment he'd seen XBA's claws around her throat.

"Can you take me to her?" asked Allister.

"She's deeper in, we should go—"

The prison shook with more violence.

"—now," she whispered.

"What was that?" Allister asked, looking between her and the door. By the distressed look on Leesa's face, she wasn't responsible. "Hello, Lieutenant?"

Leesa levitated higher off of the ground as she answered, "It was them. I've been preparing for this day for as long as I can remember."

———

CHAPTER 29

Artist: The CMD Studios

DR. FLORENCE BELLADONNA
Club HellForest at Grand Central Station
Day 209

FLORENCE WAS TRAPPED, her fate already decided by the dazed crowd of Club HellForest. She was now closed in too tight for her to see the exit, let alone reach it.

There would be no escape without confrontation.

Aware of Shahar and his potentials, she knew that in physical combat he would simply absorb any impact and redirect it back to her, possibly with his energy's charge. But he didn't even need to wait for her attack. While making his way through the crowd, Shahar had already been given the kinetic energy he needed, every bump and nudge feeding an insatiable appetite for absorption.

He advanced toward her, his veins ignited with energy, the floor steaming under his bare feet.

Florence left the wall and inched sideways. Her stomach was clenched. Her breaths shallow. She wouldn't wait in one place for him to corner her, not when there was enough room in the circle of people to maintain their distance. As she moved, she kept reaching for her sword and kept cursing when it wasn't there. They'd gone around in a circle once when he stopped walking, looked at his burning hand, and smiled. Curious why he hadn't attacked, she asked, "C20 sent you, I presume. To kill me?"

"C20 sent me to stall you. *I* suggested the killing," Shahar said. His accent was thick, his voice rough and guttural. "One thousand four hundred and sixty days past, your father, Lord Giovanni Belladonna, conspired with my government to confiscate my uncle's underground farming and artifact preservation facility, something innovated by my family to preserve our Nepali heritage."

Of course he did.

She checked Shahar's legs for the slightest movement. "I stopped speaking to my father well before we started counting days—"

"The man who created you is an abomination," Shahar interrupted. "A monster who feeds on wealth and power, and, the souls of the poor." His muscles flexed in anger as he took another step, this time toward her. "That Evolutionary creature is mad, madder than I, a parasite in people's minds...it is how he drove our country to ruin."

Though he'd switched up their routine, she resisted the urge to back up, hearing the mob thrashing behind her. Florence returned to her defensive stance. "I'd have to agree with you. That still doesn't have anything to do with *me*."

At that, Shahar smiled wide, the story and any sadness melting into the orange flares spouting off of his face. "I know he loves you dearly, his prized performer on the world stage," he said. "A doctor. A politician. The once-to-be wife of the last American president. And just as manipulative, individualist, and coldhearted as him. Your distance from him means nothing when the same corrupt blood runs beneath your ignitable skin."

He pointed his leading foot in her direction and leaned back on the other, a clear move to attack.

She waited for him to follow through, her eyes glancing behind and ahead of her for a change in the crowd's density. She spotted a space just narrow enough for her to slip through. Too bad it was behind him.

"You will burn twice, it seems," he said, blocking her sight line. "Once here. Once in hell."

A ball of energy erupted above his palms.

"You know," she began, "this is the sort of unprocessed trauma I consult on. You can always book an appointment—"

Shahar let out a bloodthirsty yell and lunged at her. Heat spewed forward, the thickness of it slamming into Florence. She stumbled back, winded, gasping for breath, just as he reached her, hands blazing. There was no pause from him for mercy. She bobbed and weaved through his first punches, nimble as she lured his wrath and his fists toward the wall. But he was still coming at her too hot. Too fast. His swift jabs flying. She leaped into the air and flipped forward, spinning as she traveled over him and landed at his back. Unable to stop himself in time, he plowed through where she'd been standing and released a flurry of fiery kinetic waves against the wall.

Florence whipped around and started running.

She could see that the narrow opening in the crowd continued to narrow until it closed, and slowed to the mob of sunken-eyed burnouts lurching toward her as if zombies. The stairs beckoned to her from the other side of them.

"Hunter!" she yelled over the music. "Hunter! I know you're up there bloody watching this!"

She hesitated, checked for Hunter once more, then tried plowing forward. The half-conscious mob climbed over and on top of one another. They reached for her limbs. They tugged at her hair and her clothes. She was being dragged down by the human quicksand sloshing around her, sinking deeper the more she struggled to break free. Her muscles were weak from fighting off dozens of people at a time, but she could see her target ahead: a worn staircase just out of reach.

One hand on it was all she needed.

She stretched her fingers and squeezed her eyes closed.

Just one hand. Was all. She. Needed.

Suddenly, a cold hand—no, a metal hand—grabbed her around the wrist.

It pulled her forward with just enough force to free her yet not pull her arm out from its socket. Air rushed at her face as she rose above the mob and came face-to-face with—

Hunter.

He let her dangle in front of him, a grin on his face. "Look who made it back," he teased.

"Can we not do this now?" Florence asked.

With one hand he lifted her up, and with the other, he palmed the face of someone clawing at his jacket.

His grin widened. "Happy to pencil you in for later," he said, knocking the screaming individual back down the stairs. He elbowed another and punched a third as he carried Florence higher. "I always said Omega gens were relentless parasites."

Hunter revealed a weapon from behind his back and shouldered his way up to the mezzanine, pausing on every third step to turn and shoot plasma into the now-rabid crowd who swarmed the staircase. He lifted her over the railing and lowered her onto the platform.

"Time to go," he said.

They raced up the last few stairs back to the mezzanine where they had met earlier that night.

"C20 is in the building…," Florence said, breathless. "Energy succubus of sorts named Shahar Prasai. Know him?"

Hunter scrunched his face, but not at her question, rather at the light radiating from the ground level in a blinding orange flash; Shahar was sending a projectile blast from his position below. Again, heat blasted at Florence ahead of the rising attack. She turned away as the energy arrived—both burning hot and sinfully bright, spreading hulking shadows over the mezzanine—then ducked as the fiery blast exploded somewhere above them. Hunter yanked her to the ground and rolled them backward.

Lighter pieces of ceiling rained down on the place they'd been standing. Heavier pieces crushed freestanding tables and chairs. A dislodged beam snapped over Hunter's large frame. Swearing, he rolled it off of his shoulders and tossed it away.

"Really, no weapons?" he asked as he dusted himself off. "Did you think this was a date?"

Florence stayed on the ground, coughing as she reclaimed her senses. She could live with the debris in her hair. She would get over the rips in her clothes. Being weaponless, however, was an unforgivable mistake on her part. "The weapon I normally use isn't firing right now, otherwise, you'd both be in sleep-induced comas," she snapped. "Stop screwing around and get us out of here."

"Fair," he said, standing over her, his hand extended.

She noticed he'd activated his potential for molecular manipulation, transforming his arms from flesh to metal. She also noticed his smile was gone.

"We gotta move, DB," he urged. "Anything happens to you…and I don't get paid."

Honesty…I'm impressed.

Florence let him help her up, something she never thought she'd do. She nodded at his metal arms. "That all?"

"Can't do the torso at the same time. Too dangerous." He paused and tilted his head in the direction of the dance floor. "That the guy you were going on about?"

She followed his not-so-subtle gesture, then, upon laying eyes on Shahar, backed up. "That would be him."

Shahar stood at the edge of the damaged mezzanine surrounded by a gyrating field of glowing kinetic potential. "You are irrelevant, as are your efforts," he said to them. "While you do battle here, my colleagues are fast at work destroying that which has assigned you purpose."

"Who you calling irrelevant?" Hunter shouted.

"Dr. Belladonna, no matter who you bribe into co-conspiracy, your termination is at hand," Shahar continued.

Ahead of her response, Hunter cocked the underside of his weapon and pulled the trigger. A life-size stream of green energy whizzed forward, screaming and pulsing with the intent to destroy.

Shahar caught the attack in his hands as if he were simply catching a rubber ball. He compressed the energy between his palms until it was the size of a pea, then popped it into his mouth. "Delicious," he said, patting his stomach. "May I have another?"

"We're going over the edge," Hunter whispered to Florence. "Follow my lead." Dashing ahead of her, he charged his weapon for another attack.

Shahar lifted both hands in response and fired searing kinetic beams in their direction.

She watched Hunter twist inward and dodge a beam that came zooming toward him. She slid under the beam that followed and, not a moment later, flipped sideways over another. Now they were nose-to-nose, racing toward him, and though they didn't have far to go, her body was screaming with aches for her to slow down. She gave in to her fatigue as Hunter blocked the last beam with his metal arm and stopped short, his body completely dwarfing Shahar's.

"You move or I move you," Hunter said, fist raised.

"Hit me with all you got, metal man," Shahar taunted.

Florence started forward again. "No, Hunter, don't!"

But Hunter's fist connected with Shahar's midsection—

Boom!

The building shook. The mezzanine buckled.

Florence dropped to one knee, body stilled, expecting the whole thing to collapse. She blinked twice when it didn't, then looked up at the two of them, torn between relief and frustration.

Hunter flexed his hand and looked at it, confused. "Runnin' out of ideas here," he yelled back at her.

"Your physical energy is mine to manipulate into whatever form I choose," Shahar said, curling his fingers into a fist.

He then punched Hunter in the jaw.

"Be it strength."

He punched Hunter in the chest.

"Or be it energy."

Shahar opened his arms and conjured more of his potential. Orange light flooded the area as it gathered, as it grew into a ball as bright as the sun. Then, snarling like a rabid animal, he smashed his hands together and unleashed a concussive wave. The force sent Hunter careening past her, while the wave of kinetic energy kept rushing forward, tearing up the floor and incinerating everything in its path as it got closer.

Florence jumped to the side without looking and landed on her stomach. She felt something pierce her, but couldn't pause for the pain, knowing it wouldn't matter when, in seconds, the energy turned her body to ash. She forced herself up and scrambled into a space behind a thick wall, cringing as the energy blew by her.

Heat and smoke and force wind rushed past in a seemingly never-ending stream.

She spent those seconds near death with her body compacted as tightly as it could be. It took a moment for her to realize her ears were ringing—but in silence.

The attack had dissipated. The music had stopped.

She looked out at the smoking remnants of the club's VIP lounge.

As she crawled, she noticed the broken edge of a table, which she guessed was the thing she'd felt pierce her side. Holding herself where the wound stung, she grimaced, though it was more in anger than in pain as she felt the warm liquid trickle between her fingers.

Hunter emerged from a newly created hole that was steaming opposite her, scowling at something she couldn't see. Seconds later, the source of his disdain was revealed, as Shahar stood above her with an arm extended toward her face.

"I came here to end you," he said. "And I think it will be my pleasure to do so."

"No one plays with my QBs!" Hunter yelled out.

He tackled Shahar around the waist, carrying the steaming, fussing man away. Presumably over the mezzanine ledge, like he'd planned.

Florence pulled herself up from the floor one-handed. She swallowed the taste of ash and smoke lingering in her mouth and cringed at the pain creeping up her side. As long as she could make it to solid ground, everything would be fine.

Her body could heal.

Her potential would return.

She peeked around the wall and surveyed the now-slanted mezzanine, surprised it still hadn't fallen. She braved it, every few minutes exhaling with deeper disdain at the favor she'd owe Hunter for her rescue. After stumbling down the two flights of stairs, she stepped onto a vacant, and oddly silent, dance floor.

The handful of survivors seemed to be coming out of a mental fog. They rubbed their shaved heads in confusion, turning to their friends, asking where they were and why. Those who hadn't survived were burned to bones, or were part of the scattered assortment of clothing scraps and dust.

The scene looked just like the District in the winter of 2048: too many bodies to count, no remains to identify.

Florence's eyes found the open garage door. Her hand found the building edge. Her body found the moonlight as she stepped out into the alleyway.

Sirens wailed. Spotlights waved over the area. Evolutionary Federal Detention investigators arrived to conduct interviews. She couldn't tell if they were desperate to keep the incident off CGN, or eager to put it on there.

Doesn't matter either way, I suppose, she thought. So long as she wasn't in the headlines.

Florence took a step back inside, wary of a wandering spotlight, and was stopped short by a hardened torso made of metal.

"Dude disappeared inside some weird mist," Hunter mumbled behind her. "But, man, was he pissed at you." He groaned as he rested his weight on the wall. Now that his torso was metal, both arms were not. He tried to hide the melted metal near his ribs with his flesh hand, and revealed severe burns up the deep brown of his bicep.

She wondered if the disfigured metal would heal as it was or if it would revert to flesh. "You actually rescued me."

The night's shadows gave more angle to his hard jaw. And the light caught his eyes in an almost charming way. "Didn't have a choice, sweets," he said, puckering his lips. "But feel free to reward me."

Florence scoffed. "You're disgusting."

"Ha. The things I do for a pretty face and a paycheck." He activated his Cynque and addressed his team over a comm channel. "Get me a luxury Ukimoto to transport my guest." He paused, listened, then replied, "Yes, the one the prez uses when he's here. No, I can't give you a name. Just have it meet me around back at Club HellForest. Or what's left of it."

"I take it I can't convince you to help me stop C20?" she asked.

"The Andromeda Project don't pay well enough," Hunter answered.

Fair point. But she couldn't take on C20 alone, and of her available options, Allister was too fearful, Leesa was too high risk, Brandt was up for termination, Bridget Sparks was too crazy, and the refugee boy, Dorian, was too inexperienced.

Florence shifted her weight, an attempt to cope with the pain of her bleeding wound and the realization that her freedom and their salvation still seemed too far away.

She heard the soft rumbling of booster engines and looked up. Her transport quieted as it slowed to a stop, and with a soft *whoosh*, it descended from the sky.

Hunter lifted her into the empty back seat.

"Good first date?" he asked, winking.

"Give it a rest," she shot back. She pushed him away and closed the door on him, then said out of the open window, "You tell our friend my debt is repaid once I get the artifacts."

With a firm salute, he said, "It's your world, DB. We're just living in it."

The self-driving Ukimoto steered her into the sky.

Cynque dinged when they reached altitude. "Cynquing with autopilot controls. Destination confirmed: the Andromeda Project," the device said.

"Cynque, are you able to get through to HQ yet?" she asked.

"I've been told the system is not operable at this time and to try again later."

C20 sent me to stall you. I suggested the killing..., Shahar had said to her.

"Stall me?" Florence said.

She didn't need potential to know something was off.

Though moonlight gave a mystical shine to the rain-soaked rooftops, she lowered her head, disengaged from the artistic beauty that had captured the sullen District.

"Cynque, have the car drop me near Quadrant Alpha. I'm thinking I'll have to get my sword before anyone else can get to me."

WHERE HAS
BEING OPEN TO TRUST
BENEFITED YOU?

CHAPTER 30

ALLISTER ADAMS
Quadrant Gamma—The Vault, Andromeda Project Headquarters
Day 209

ALLISTER KEPT LOOKING between Leesa and the door, confused. Leesa's hands were still stretched in front of her, flexed and waiting. Neither had spoken since the army of heavy boots started stomping across the Vault's grated floors.

He guessed by the continuous stream of noise that more than a few dozen bodies had finagled their way down there, and not knowing whether they were soldiers of the Andromeda Project, he asked Leesa, "You've been preparing for *what* day exactly?"

"For the day that C20 discovered our location," Leesa answered.

"C20's...here? How?" He leaned closer to the door, listening for the barrage of footsteps. They were still there, still going. "That's mega, dude," he said softly. "In, like, the worst way possible."

Although more bodies traveled past than he could count, Allister didn't hear any shouting or weapons, no sounds indicative of a takeover. In fact, he didn't hear any conflict at all. Didn't they have security in place? Wouldn't Admiral Gattison and her team have taken on the intruders?

As he listened to a single voice needle its way through the prison door, he realized if it was indeed C20, they had mobilized an army, not deployed a few stray agents.

"Hold your position," a deep voice ordered, stifled by the door's thickness.

The dozens upon dozens of footsteps stopped. *All* of them. At once.

"The security grid and comm systems have been dismantled," the voice reported, "but expect retaliation. There are unaccounted-for Evolutionaries somewhere on-site. Your orders are to find the Gateway—blow off every one of these doors if you have to. Once you have them, bring them to the rendezvous point." The voice paused. "Oh, and be sure to kill everyone else. C20 wants no survivors."

"Did you hear that?" Allister said to Leesa in a strained whisper. "Did you? They're looking for me!"

She shushed him, the same look of concentration tattooed on her face.

But his mind kept replaying the speech over and over again. *Kill everyone else,* the voice had commanded. *Everyone else, including his mom.*

A single pain shot through Allister's heart. He backed away, distressed, fingers buried in his afro. They couldn't just wait there, could they? They had to do something. *He* had to do something. Distract them. Fight back. Turn himself in. Anything but stay inside that prison.

Grumbling, he marched ahead of her and gripped the lock. "I'm going out there," he said.

The deep voice yelled, "In the name of Tas-Salvatur!"

"We cannot be cynqued if we are not one!" the others roared in response.

Allister's hold on the lock loosened. His mind settled to the danger they were in. Remembering the attack on the District, he knew what that collective cry meant.

Violence.

Bloodshed.

As promised, firepower erupted outside the prison door. Explosions went off one after the other, rolled closer and closer like thunder, one *boom* at a time.

Prisoners' screams resounded in a loud chorus, even louder than the hum of the plasma reactors that had begun slaughtering them. Another bomb went off nearby, drowning out both sounds and rocking the prison with enough force to knock him over.

Allister managed to keep from losing his balance. "I'm going out there!" he repeated louder, clinging to the door.

Leesa grabbed his arm, then shouted, "Adams! Await my orders before you—"

"My mom's somewhere down here, screw your orders!" He squeezed the lock tighter. "Need to get to her before they"—he strained first to pull up, then to pull down—"before they get to her."

The thick bar gave, but not enough to bend away from the wall like he wanted. He pounded against the door, more sharp pain shooting through his heart. His bravery might've felt crushed to pieces. His resolve wasn't.

Allister's fingers were curled so tight his palms ached. "What are you waiting for? Open it!" he shouted at Leesa.

"The Vault redirects our potentials, give me five seconds to…dig deeper." She strained to finish.

Leesa drew her elbows back. Purple energy raced from her wrists to her fingertips.

He was too lost in his impatience to pay much attention to the ticking he'd heard, nor did he comprehend the meaning of the trigger when it—

Clicked.

It all went down in seconds.

The entire prison shuddering from impact. Leesa, more keen on what was going on than himself, using her telekinesis with startling precision, both crafting a barrier to protect them and lifting his body to move him out of the way. His arms flailed as he became airborne, his feet kicking as they no longer touched the ground.

Now, Allister was behind Leesa, watching as she, surging with purple energy, screamed in defiance at the imploding door.

Flames penetrated the vault interior. Concussive force shredded the prison's metal walls. A shock wave hurled him backward with a hundred-thousand-kiloton yield.

His body crashed backward through concrete wall after concrete wall. He covered his face with his arms as he was blown farther beneath the building, likely passing from under one quadrant to under another, just twenty floors lower. After plowing through one more hard fixture, he hit a column sturdy enough to stop his motion, but forgiving enough to split in half.

Concrete chunks rained from the ceiling alongside gallons of sewage water from burst pipes. Allister tumbled down with the whole mess, soaked, bruised, vaguely aware that any piece of the heavy foundation could shatter his bones. His spine slammed against a sharp-edged slab.

Crack.

Pain blasted through his back as another boulder slammed on top of his chest. His ears rang. His vision blacked out.

When he came to, he didn't stop to think before he began groping the rock's slippery corners and jagged underbelly, trying to grasp enough to lift it. Every movement sent another injection of pain up his throbbing spine. Several minutes in agony felt like two-hundred-odd days, and Allister soon gave up, instead resigned to holding it in place, the strain of keeping the boulder aloft already tormenting his muscles.

White lights darted over the unsalvageable basement. Gruff voices and loud splashes came with them.

Allister listened to the water sloshing around his dangling feet, rising to his ankles as more cascaded from the damaged ceiling. He searched for a way to anchor himself. When he found a foothold sturdy enough to support him, he lifted the rock farther away from him, even as the pain fired again and again.

"Looks like we have found ourselves a lieutenant," a woman said.

"A good consolation prize, but she is not who we came for," a man said.

"Still, Tas-Salvatur will be pleased," the woman replied. "Perhaps we get something more to send back to our aunts and uncles, and the children."

"The promise of salvation should be enough, dear sister," the man scoffed.

Allister gulped. *Sister?* The danger he'd attempted to quantify at the onset of their attack was far worse than he could've calculated. C20 had sent more than an army of agents—they'd sent their Evolutionaries, too.

He decided it had to be the pair he'd encountered before: the Density Twins. They'd followed him from the District to De Los Muertos, and now into the sewage system an explosion away from the Vault prison. So where was XBA? Were there others?

The male twin, Tranjam, continued speaking over Allister's frantic thoughts. "But there will be no salvation without the Gateway, without Allister."

Allister weakened at the sound of his name, the boulder slipping from his hands. He took a deep breath and pushed up.

He felt about ready to free himself. All he could do was think of the cells blown to bits and the dead bodies in them. But his mind refused to believe his mom had become a casualty of the infiltration. She had to be alive, he kept telling himself, she just had to be.

Your father used to say the same thing. He could almost hear his mom reliving the sadness. The betrayal felt real to him for the first time. Because it was not his dad's, it was his. He vowed he'd take whatever scolding he had coming. *As long as she's alive to say it, I'll one thousand percent deal.*

He had to find her.

The conversing Evolutionaries had been joined by others, and seemed close enough to catch him but too animated to pick up on his heavy, wheezing breaths. Wastewater sprayed wide from above and concealed him behind its brown film.

They can't see me, he thought.

He never imagined a day he'd be thankful to be covered in sludge.

Artist: Bradd Maesa/ The CMD Studios

"Check every crevice and crack, no stone goes unturned," Vonnie, the female twin, shouted. "In the name of Tas-Salvatur, find him!"

It was impossible to guess the number of C20 agents splashing through pud-dles, though the glare of a dozen or more searching lights let Allister know it was too many for him to take on alone. He let the giant rock sit on his chest for a moment, ignoring the sharp pinching in his spine.

The wandering C20 agents started moving farther away while continuing to report back on their inability to find him.

"Keep looking," Vonnie said. "Check the upper floors. We will not leave without the tools we came for."

Allister resisted closing his eyes, thoroughly drained by both scratched-up, soaking-wet palms still holding the boulder at bay.

She continued, "I want our little gateway to know he can't hide anymore."

He jerked his head in the direction of her voice.

Vonnie, a blurry figure behind a waterfall of sewage, was prowling close. Too close. He recognized her from that short distance, mostly due to her bright-pink hair and long blade. It had been that very blade that nearly killed Brandt.

She sniffed the air like a huntress, sliced her weapon through the water, and kicked over a chunk of the column he'd broken with his back. Her investigation concluded. With a damning slowness, she returned to her brother's side. "We bring the lieutenant to XBA?" Vonnie asked him, sounding somewhat skeptical.

Tranjam grumbled something, visible to Allister as only a shadowed silhouette.

Restless, Allister watched as Tranjam crouched to the ground, appearing to examine something. Moments later, he rose holding a chunk of concrete over his head, exerting little effort, it seemed; a piece of rock his full height and arm span should've been too heavy for him. He tossed it and didn't pause to rest before he dropped back down to grab another. In between each loud crash of each chunk landing in the distance was tension. After five throws, he resurfaced with a limp body.

"Got the wench," Tranjam said.

Vonnie led them away with her blade outstretched. "Now, for our other targets," she said, pausing to turn her body toward the waterfall one last time.

Targets…plural, Allister thought, glaring back at her through the water.

He felt a surge of courage and determination to give the Twins what they were looking for. Him. Vonnie and Tranjam would get him and his strength and the Z-energy, too. He couldn't stop wondering why Leesa had saved him. Did he need to save her, too? Wasn't she a Gateway of sorts?

The notion disappeared at the sudden thought of his mom, who could now, in this very moment, be begging for mercy in front of a weapon's barrel. He knew any moment he spent battling those siblings would be a moment he left his mom's fate to some rogue agent or, worse, someone like XBA.

Allister surrendered to the throbbing in his body. There could be no fight.

Leesa would have to save herself.

———

CHAPTER 31

ALLISTER ADAMS
Quadrant Gamma—The Vault, Andromeda Project Headquarters
Day 209

IT WAS TIME for Allister to go after his mom.

He rolled the boulder off of him with the last of his strength, then rolled himself free of the concrete digging into his back, landing face-first in the rising river of unfiltered water. Seconds later, he emerged, wiping his eyes and his nose and his mouth, only to fall sideways, catching himself on a column that still remained intact.

The aches and chills running through him were unsuspecting. Dangerous, like the flooding basement's swirling undertow. He found his wounds somewhat unbearable, somewhat humbling—grateful to feel true pain and have no escape from it.

It reminded him that despite the Evolutionary DNA entangled in his helix and the status in his Cynque classification, a large part of his genes and experience were still human.

He shifted his focus to the blown-out wall of his prison. Yet he could barely see it—in part because of his blurred vision, in part because it was at least a hundred feet away.

As the water level rose from his shins to his thighs, he knew he needed to get out from under the building.

The hollowed space would soon fill up.

Escape the flood and find Mom, he told himself.

His small, careful steps led him back through the basement, and he made his way, groping for whatever was nearest, be it another column or caved-in wall, to guide him.

After what felt like a never-ending series of mindless movements, Allister stumbled into his prison's charred interior and collapsed against the flattest part of the broken bench.

Find Mom, the single thought repeated.

Allister half crawled, half swam forward, and upon reaching the prison's mangled metal frame, used it to get back to both feet.

"You're golden, man...you got this," he assured himself as he stepped into the hallway.

The water's height shot to his waist.

He switched on Cynque's spotlight and shined it in both directions. The thin, concentrated beam of white light provided no greater clarity on what might be where. He knew one path would lead him toward the elevator, toward escape, even at the cost of confrontation. He felt more confident that path would take him to his mom. The other path would lead him deeper into the Vault and into the Andromeda Project, toward uncertainty, possibly toward Neight Caster, who his dad had asked him to find.

"You got this," he repeated to himself. "Just gotta…just gotta rescue Mom."

Allister chose his direction.

He waded, he hoped, toward the elevator, past floating corpses in the thickening darkness. Some belonged to Andromeda Project soldiers, some belonged to C20 agents, yet all of them were mutilated or dismembered. He couldn't stand the vacant looks of the dead at such a close distance.

Especially when one of them could be *hers*.

He moved ahead faster.

How much farther? he wondered, wiping his eyes. He squinted in an effort to see beyond Cynque's light, not so sure about the direction he chose. Was that gleaming metal beyond the curve of the hallway the main elevator? Or more of the Vault's thick wall?

He endeavored to go a bit deeper before he turned around and tried the opposite path. As he lifted his leg, a series of footsteps splashed nearby in rapid succession. He was pretty sure they were coming from behind him, closing in on his location with the speed of hostility. Terrified, he stopped, then twisted his body the other direction, his beam of light darting around the darkness for a glimpse of anything—a weapon, an enemy, an ally.

"You don't want to try ambushing me," Allister said in his bravest voice. "Trust. Now isn't the time."

A wet hand touched him on the shoulder.

He spun around and lunged forward, fist raised, one hand closing around someone's scraggly throat as he pinned them to the wall.

His Cynque light flashed over the ghost-white face and bright-blue eyes of—

Brandt gagged. "Allister," he choked out, "it's me."

His grip loosened with relief. "Captain? Oh snap, I'm so sorry," Allister said. He pulled his hand away. "Hold up...what are you doing down here?"

"Looking for you. What else would I be doing down here?" Brandt asked solemnly. "It's a massacre topside. C20 came from everywhere at the same time. I tried to stop it, but...it happened too fast. I just thought the system was down. Professor Ashur told us the system was down. Both Delemars, Sparks, Belladonna, Xander—the refugee kid—and that dog thing, they've got 'em all. I'm bettin' on execution."

Allister thought about Florence and the young Evolutionary, Dorian, he'd found in De Los Muertos, feeling equally helpless and sad for their fate. He looked at the water up to his elbows.

"I came to get you...to get you out," Brandt said, cupping Allister's face in both hands. "This is no place for you. I made a terrible mistake bringin' you into this."

"Now you're telling me to leave too?" Allister hissed. "This is some twisted, messed-up conspiracy crap." He ripped himself away from Brandt's touch, feeling it came off too patronizing. "You supposedly good EVs sell me this beat-ass dream. How I can find the artifacts because I got the potential you been looking for...then suddenly...it's all, like, bail on humanity, go be safe somewhere and hide your potential." He wanted to care that, like the lieutenant, Brandt had changed his tune, but considering C20's in-progress massacre in search of him, it didn't matter what he was meant for. Or that no one in that building seemed willing to accept him.

Allister wiped his face with the back of his hand, his words coming out too fast to be filtered. "I guess it doesn't matter if you don't want me to save humanity. At least I can save my mom...the lieutenant said she was in one of these cells. You know where she is?"

"Dee's...here? I thought they let her go."

"They didn't. Please tell me where she is. Please," Allister pleaded.

"They never told me where they put her—"

"Tell me the truth, Brandt. About us. How do you know so much about me? My pops? My mom? My potentials?"

"I don't know if—"

"Tell me!" he demanded, seizing the captain by the lapels.

"Okay! Okay. I'll level with ya." Brandt cleared his throat. "Technically, I'm your godfather. Was there the night you were born, the mornin' you started crawling. Missed your first steps, though—was out on a tour. Your daddy sent me a vid, then cynqued me in for your first words."

Allister's hands lowered with the slowness of shock, his insides too tangled to come loose.

Brandt smirked as he continued. "I know it's wild. I...I remember when you, when you couldn't pronounce your *R*s so you just said *Uncle Jawed*."

Unable to contain his small smile, Allister rubbed his arm, curious about the backstory, the nickname. It explained the captain's relationship with his dad. Justified the passion with which Brandt had defended him.

Still, his mom had never mentioned his "uncle" before. *Ever*. It could've been because of his involvement with the Andromeda Project.

"More than wild though, the way I see it. Mom never spilled a thing about you."

"You and I, your mother, we been through a lotta hell. A lotta hell to get here," Brandt said, his tone changing. The sweet sounds of nostalgia deepened and darkened to the low rumble of grief. "We sacrificed a lot to accomplish this two-decade-old mission, for goodness sakes. I'm tired, Allister. I want it to be done."

"I—I don't understand... What's my mom...what's she been through?"

"Better question is what hasn't she been through. Protecting Patrick. Protecting you, the Gateway. Not easy stuff." Brandt looked at Allister, his voice lightened with hope. "It's like a fog has been lifted and you're all I see... You're everything you need to be and more, son. We don't need the lieutenant or the general or anyone." He gave Allister a firm shake. "You and I, we gotta find the artifacts. Together. To do that, we gotta get out while we can."

"Not without my mom," Allister said, jaw tensed.

"Of course not...without... She's gotta be down here. If they had her holed up in one of these pods, she's gotta be down here." Brandt looked behind himself, then past Allister. "Head the way you were goin'. When you get to the wall, there's a corridor on the right with an elevator hidden in it. Take it up to the tenth floor and meet me in the main hangar."

"Are you sure that's golden? What if something happens to you?" Allister asked.

"Listen, I got one chance to make this right," the captain replied. "We escape the apocalypse and EVs get to create somethin' fresh for ourselves. A home where we can be accepted. You hear me? Leave the fight behind us."

A home where we can be accepted, Allister repeated in his head.

He felt like his chest was about to burst forth with every sob he'd never sobbed, but as he always did, he held it in and simply nodded. "I'm with it," he choked free. "After I find my mom, maybe I can find Neight Caster, too. Before we go, I mean."

Brandt shook his head. "Neight Caster's dead. Been dead twelve years. You focus on your mother. From what I remember, she knows her way around a weapon and she ain't a fool, neither. I'm thinkin' she'd head deeper in, find someplace safe, outta the way."

Knows her way around a weapon… Allister was puzzled by that idea; from what he knew, his mom *hated* weapons, firearms in particular.

Brandt grabbed Allister midthought and pulled him in until there was no air between them. It was an embrace filled with genuine care and love and respect, offering the type of affection reserved for a father and son—and it was almost over before Allister realized he hadn't reciprocated.

"Promise me you won't waste time lookin' for that alien," Brandt said.

Allister nodded. "I promise," he finally said, his arms raised to hug him back. But something *ding*ed in the darkness behind the captain, ending the gesture before it even began.

Brandt shoved Allister toward the path he'd suggested. "I'll survive no matter what it takes. Now hurry and find her, while I hold 'em off."

Lights swarming the hallway headed in their direction. The whistle of charging plasma energy hit Allister's ears.

He powered deeper into the Vault, eager to get away, yet curious how—though it seemed C20 had returned with more agents to the basement—Brandt's face had been absent of fear. Perhaps it was from seeing so many battles. Perhaps it was from *surviving* so many.

Grunts and screams, whizzing noises and explosions, echoed off the mile-high walls. He turned back and saw Captain Brandt unhooking his plasma rod. When he glanced over his shoulder a second time, it was burning with white energy. The third time he looked, the rod was swirling and slicing through C20 agents.

As Allister tried to go faster, his arms paddling, his legs alternating between running and kicking underwater, he realized he'd been traveling away from the main elevator when he'd meant to be traveling toward it. It was no wonder the depths of the Vault had seemed to go on forever.

It was also no wonder, then, that they still did.

The water appeared to drain off as he rounded a curve in the hallway. His Cynque's light flashed over flat, somewhat-dry floor. The area he'd found was elevated, and on it, he saw no Andromeda Project corpses, just disarmed and unconscious C20 agents. His first thought was that maybe his mom did know her way around a weapon.

Clearly someone had fought back.

Allister stood up. "Cynque, locate Dolores Adams," he said.

"Due to data inaccessibility, Dolores Adams's current location not found," Cynque answered.

"You are a piece of crap and so is your overhyped global network. I mean, seriously, what about you is use…ful…"

Allister's sentence trailed at the sound of more splashes moving through a series of puddles. As they suddenly stopped, he stopped, too, using his spotlight to search for the cause. What he found wasn't a threat, rather a partially submerged body that didn't seem to be moving.

It was Dorian, the "refugee" kid. A few deep scratches were etched into his forehead. Most of his dark, curly hair was styled into two thick braids, while the rest was matted to his youthful brown face, a face partially covered by a metal mask. That was a new addition, Allister noted. Must've had something to do with his inability to speak.

Allister leaned closer. He didn't see any burn holes or open wounds, and Dorian was breathing, though not too well.

Good, Allister thought. *He'll wake up when he's ready.*

His mind told him to keep going. He couldn't let anything slow him down when his mom needed him. Yet his intuition compelled him to help Dorian, their little savior from De Los Muertos. The guilt of leaving the kid lying there gnawed at him as he went to leave, the worst-case scenarios playing in his head: how if C20's agents defeated Brandt, they'd come hunting for Allister down the path—and for sure put that helpless kid out of his misery in the process.

"Round two for us, then," Allister whispered.

Just as he went to tend to Dorian, he heard teeth gnashing where his beam of light didn't reach.

He froze, wide-eyed. He dared not turn to see what advanced, compelled to fight the fear because he knew the creature—Dorian's companion, whatever it was—would smell it.

Allister's heavy breathing, on the other hand, was impossible to contain, unintentionally luring the low, guttural snarls closer.

Artist: Bradd Maesa/ The CMD Studios

———

Allister prepared himself to get pounced on. This was meant to be a quick stop. He'd already made the mistake of getting distracted by helping Dorian once, and the stakes were too high to do it again.

The basement seemed to wait for what would come next. Water trickled instead of splashed. The building creaked instead of groaned.

He looked away from the creature advancing on him and stuck out his hand.

"Take it easy," breathed Allister, remembering it was just protecting Dorian. "I'm not one of them."

The sound of his voice seemed to soften the animal's snarling to growling. Next, the growling softened to a light whimper. The animal began investigating Allister, its wet nose sniffing Allister's outstretched hand, then moving to the open, bleeding wounds on his arm and torso. An effort, he guessed, at determining whether he was friend or foe.

Feeling less apprehensive, he turned to face the beast. The being responded by mushing its wet nose against Allister's cheek with tenderness and curiosity, then licking him in that same spot, its tongue as rough as a cinder block.

As silly as it sounded to refer to it as LionWolf, it felt sillier not to, when that's what it looked like.

Petting it behind the ears, he asked, "You'd be ragged if your name was LionWolf, so what is it, mister?"

It snorted in response and pawed his hand away.

He looked at LionWolf, surprised at the level of comprehension. "Gimme a break, yeah? I had a fifty-fifty chance. So...I'm off. You're a she..."

The creature purred as it rubbed against him. He took that as confirmation. "Do you, like, understand me?"

She stared up at him and woofed, as if he'd asked a ridiculous question.

From what he could see, LionWolf had been washed and groomed to near perfection. The overgrown, mangy cream mane tamed—to put it easily—into the short-haired sleekness that lay before him. Her wet tongue dangled over jagged rows of ivory teeth. A set of jaws he'd never want to get caught in. She was solid power regardless, gifted with lean muscle and razor-sharp claws that sprouted from padded feet twice the width of his.

The creature broke their mutual admiration and, with her crystal-blue eyes, cast a worried look at Dorian. She trotted over to nudge her master's hand.

LionWolf suddenly whipped her head over her shoulder, got to growling at seemingly nothing.

But Allister knew better than to disregard an animal's instincts. He jumped up and aimed his spotlight at the curve he'd come around.

Both of them looked into the darkness of the giant, flooded hallway. He saw the scratched-up walls and the bodies his flashlight had already caught, but he imagined LionWolf saw more, something scary enough to keep her from barking and instead continue her low growling with her ears straight up in the air.

Bright flashes of light erupted one after another at water level, each one spreading farther toward the ceiling. Loud explosions followed on their heels, shaking the walls and loosening more concrete from overhead.

"Time to move," whispered Allister, crouching back down. He shook Dorian. "Wake up. Yo, kid, wake up."

Dorian's head flopped to one side, his lips slightly parted beneath the metal mask's grill. He groaned, and by his slight wince, looked to be on the verge of waking.

Another flare of explosive light filled the hallway. Another *boom* shook the walls.

LionWolf moved closer to them.

Allister then turned to gauge the proximity of the not-so-distant sounds of wild splashing and weapons charging.

"Uh…yeah, time to move," he said and slid his arms behind Dorian's knees and neck. He lifted him from the ground, thankful the kid was lighter than expected, and turned back once more, now able to see that the violence had caught up.

Orange beams whizzed back and forth across the corridor. Yelling filled the air with anger, screams filled it with agony. White-suited C20 agents and soldiers in Andromeda Project uniforms flashed in and out of visibility.

Allister felt a vibration up his spine. His own instincts, probably. As he was already on his way to ducking down when the concrete just behind them exploded inward. Tiny pieces of rubble, chunks of wall, and dust flew in every direction while Allister shielded LionWolf and Dorian the best he could.

The commotion calmed, if only for a moment. A chance for them to gain some headway.

"C'mon, girl," he said to LionWolf.

He hobbled deeper into the Vault, climbing over downed columns, his boots splashing through puddles.

Dorian flinched, awakened. He opened his eyes wide in terror and began immediately panicking in Allister's arms.

Allister would've reassured him, but he just held him tighter and ran that much faster. His mouth held no moisture. His muscles had begun to throb. His feet became slaves to gravity and more impossible to lift with each step forward.

As he paused for a second, he said, "Don't worry, friend, I got you. We just gotta...keep moving... Just need to find my mom and..." He hoisted Dorian higher with a big inhale. "Find my mom and..." He tried to finish, to take another step, and stopped.

LionWolf was nearly paralyzed in silence from snout to tail, her curious eyes on what appeared to be a wall.

Brandt had mentioned the dead end. Described it as a wall. Maybe to anyone else, it could've been that, but to Allister, it was a shifting darkness, one operating under the *illusion* of solidity. It was as easy as spotting the difference between a solid structure and tightly compressed liquid—and that difference was molecular cohesion.

Inching nearer, Allister examined it, then kicked his foot out.

The wall rippled.

"Figures," he said.

Dorian gave him a pained look and contracted in his arms.

"You're golden," Allister said, setting Dorian down. "I'm not making you go in there with me."

He leaned against an actual wall, hands buried in his afro. He couldn't even tell if braving the illusion was a good idea. The Vault had been explored in what he thought was its entirety—and from the battle's onset, he'd gone from trekking under the building to traversing those dark, winding hallways. And he still hadn't found his mom.

Behind that black curtain wouldn't be the type of place he'd look, but... something struck him from his conversation with Brandt, the suggestion that his mom would go deeper...find someplace safe, outta the way.

There was nothing more out of the way than the space behind a fake wall.

Allister rocked himself to a standing position again. Ahead of them stretched a pathway that led to a brightly lit elevator. To *the* elevator, he assumed, that Brandt had told him to look for.

He shook his head. "Not going up without Mom." Turning slightly to Dorian, he asked in a whisper, "What's the pup's name?"

Dorian reached between the folds of his draped top and pulled out a dull, copper coin attached to a red rusted chain. He held it up.

Allister had never seen physical money before, but he recognized the out-of-circulation currency. "Penny?"

The kid nodded.

"Beat…" Allister looked toward the path again. "You good to walk?"

Dorian took a few steps. Though he limped, he kept going until he made it to the middle of the hallway.

"Perfect," Allister whispered. "Take Penny and go straight up. Don't look back."

At that, Dorian looked at the floor and appeared to pause in thought as if he were looking for a response in the water. He must've been done thinking on it because his face fell into a scowl, yet his eyes lifted with a defiant sort of anger. His gestures were frantic like in De Los Muertos. He threw both arms out at the elevator, then turned and did the same toward Allister.

Allister didn't quite understand, nor did he have the patience to try.

"Look," he snapped, "until I find my mom, I'm not leaving this basement."

Dorian pouted, likely at the harshness in Allister's tone. The kid waved his hand by his side, signaling for Penny, who was busy sniffing at the void, to follow. He then stormed his way down the pathway, the creature glued to his heels.

"You'll be golden," Allister called after them.

He braved several cautious, sideways steps *through* the strange substance, and groped his way to the other side, stumbling over lumpy ground and his own blindness.

The darkness was more dense mist than liquid, parting for him as he moved, enclosing him as he went farther.

Buzz. Buzz. Buzz. Click.

A plasma weapon humming to life cast an orange glow over the lower half of a woman.

"Stay where you are!" she insisted.

"Don't shoot!" Allister shouted and raised his hands in innocence. "I'm not C20—"

"Allister?"

His heart jumped, and he did too, arms stretched out as he rushed forward, smothering his mom with his enormous shaking frame.

———

CHAPTER 32

ALLISTER ADAMS
Quadrant Gamma—Vault, The Andromeda Project Headquarters
Day 209

ALLISTER HAD FOUND his mom in that unlikely place. Alive. Uninjured, so far as he could tell. He didn't want to dwell on the miracle or his overwhelming joy for too long. They needed to get to the main hangar to meet Brandt.

But what a miracle, and what a feeling.

"Mom…," Allister said, sniffling, his heart about ready to burst. "You made it."

She dropped the gun. "Oh my," she whispered. Her wet hands found his face and held it up. "It's fine, we're fine. We both made it."

"I know, but…you…" *How could you have survived without potentials*, he thought. He glanced down at the weapon she'd let fall. "I thought you hated guns…"

She wiped the dirt off his cheek with her thumb. "Well, I can't afford to be choosy at a time like this, now can I?"

They hugged again, rocking back and forth and squeezing each other tighter. It felt like they were two leaves stuck together in the wind, weightless, careless, not concerned where they'd come from or where they might be going.

"I'm so hyped you're…here," he said.

"That Evolutionary, the little one from De Los Muertos, blasted a C20 agent before they shot at me. Bless him, whoever he is—"

Dorian, Allister thought.

"—I had forgotten how terrifying it was to"—she continued between gulps—"anyway, I kept running until I got here." His mom looked around, head nodding with, dare he assume, satisfaction.

Allister loosened his hold. Felt the drops of concerned tears dry in his eyes. "Here…as in, you wanted to come here?"

They separated, the tension of the past days swelling between them. Their hands continued to glide down each other's arms and over wrists and palms until they drifted apart. At the end, they hung on by just the fingertips.

It seemed they were always only holding on by that much.

His mom pulled away first. There was a guilt in her expression he couldn't quite understand. "I knew where I was going," she replied. "I know where we are."

"Where's that?" he asked.

She stroked the roped curls sneaking into her face and turned away from him, her gaze almost piercing the darkness. "Inside a haven. The Andromeda Project's deepest, darkest secret."

It was an astonishing thing to have come out of his mom's mouth. Not just because she'd been the one to say it, but because for those few minutes, Allister had thought they'd been reunited *inside* of a wall that wasn't really a wall. She was now inferring it was something besides that.

How did she know?

"I came here...to...to check on someone," his mom continued. She looked down at her hands and exhaled, giving off the impression that she was waiting for something to happen. So he waited, too.

Then, out of nowhere, white energy sprung from ahead of where she stood, sizzling as it spread from the center of the ominous void. The darkness peeled as if it were old plaster, whittled away in pieces and parts, eventually flaking into the wide-open space of an unfinished bunker.

Allister watched in awe as the room unfolded. Each object formed as if their details had been conjured into existence a molecule at a time. From the set of illuminated plexiglass cases that contained strangely familiar battle weapons not of Earth, to silver walls and a well-lit ceiling, both of which were shining like new. There were extracted spaceship communication panels. Another thing he recognized and wasn't sure why. And finally, his eyes landed on the up-lit display of a single warrior's armor, complete with an enormous horned helmet. The ensemble was an epic blend of style and stealth, regal and resilient—and he knew someone large would have to wear it, someone much larger than him.

The light bent away from the farthest corner, leaving it in the same sort of darkness they'd walked through.

Allister turned once more to observe the semblance of an underground museum. "This is *not* a dead end."

"I suppose it's a dead end to folks who can't perceive beyond what they see and believe," his mom corrected him.

"Sounds a lot like you, Mom. So how'd you get back here?"
"Once upon a time, I was filled with a sense of wonder, too. The possibilities were endless until they weren't anymore."

Allister wondered how long ago that had been. Still trying to piece things together, his thoughts and the room itself, he kept his eyes on the up-lit cases and bounced on all five toes, his mom's behavior feeling…more out of place each time he came back down.

In his mind, the root of his suspicions about her planted themselves and sprouted the trunk and the branches and stems…

He was yet to understand how his mom had made it to De Los Muertos in the first place. The kidnapping seemed an obvious ploy to force Allister's cooperation, except his mom had been unscathed, despite his resistance to XBA's illusions and the rage with which the Andromeda Project fought back.

Too many coincidences were lining up for him to continue questioning what he'd speculated and—purely out of fear—dismissed.

The fear was that his mom knew more than she let on, and that her sadness around his dad's death ran deeper than addressing her loss, deeper than avoiding the trauma, and was more painful than anything the apocalypse could bring.

She claimed to work at a factory all day, though whenever he asked her about it all she said was that she "played foreman." Not much else would keep her out of the house for twice as long as he was and earning close to the maximum wage in QBs.

Allister was fed up with her secrets. He thought about confronting her there, twenty floors underground, his hands fastened to his hips, his eyes passing between the language on the spaceship panels, and the inscriptions on the weapons and battle armor. When he realized he could read every bit of it.

Twice, Allister blinked fast in disbelief. Information was flowing to him. No. Flowing *through* him. "This stuff, all of this stuff is from some civilization like two-plus billion light-years away. Wait, how do I know that?" He knew he sounded crazy. He *felt* crazy. "Mom…why can I read controls from"—he dragged it out—"a-no-ther planet?"

She didn't say anything.

He turned to find her rocking in silence, her back to him, her arms folded over her stomach.

"Mom. Please answer me."

She sighed. "It's hard to explain."

"That means you know." He started off across the room, his surprise turning into frustration. "And did you know all this time I could've helped get us the artifacts? Don't suppose you've got a not-twisted reason why you kept me from saving the entire human race. I'll just wait for that one, I'm sure it's beat."

"Cut the slang, Allister. You got a genius-level intellect by birth and capacity for more by potential. I'm not havin' you walk around talkin' like you don't got a lick of sense."

This was the first time she'd ever mentioned his potentials in a positive way.

He couldn't breathe away his muscles constricting inside his chest. The extreme pinching he felt there, beside his heart, it might've been the organ collapsing mid-beat, or his soul being zapped of hope. He was at a loss for excuses or for anger, too busy fighting back tears and defying the urge to crumble.

Worse than suppression...deceit was in the aged corners of his mom's eyes, it was the honey color in her loose curls, it was the wrinkles in her forehead, and what lurked behind her soft features.

She knew everything he was capable of, and she'd kept it from him on purpose.

"The countdown could've been over, Mom," he finally said. "All this time, I been...I've been listening to you and hiding. Twelve years. For twelve years."

"I did it to protect you, Allister. You don't understand all this place is about... what they've...done."

"Maybe I would, if you'd told me." He looked up to avoid crying. "All I know is they're trying to save us. What kind of person would I be if I sat back and watched humanity's end knowing we could've escaped it?" he asked.

"I thought livin' out the end with me would've been good enough for ya eventually," she said.

"My potentials are part of me, maybe the best part of me, ya know? They mean I can help people"—he stuck his thumb to his chest—"and that's what I promised to do. I mean...how can other people accept me for what I am if you don't?"

His mom wiped her eyes. "You don't know the whole story."

"Then tell me. I've been asking you since I was eight!" His raised voice pierced the room.

The silence that followed was heavy, consuming.

It didn't last.

Two massive thumps shook the basement. LEDs in plexiglass cases flickered. The pebbles beside his feet jumped and skipped across the floor. "Uh...you felt that, too, right?"

Allister balled up his fists without waiting for her response, his body automatically preparing for the battle that was sure to come spilling into the room. He swiveled in the direction of where he thought the noise had come from.

An eerie hush settled back over the space while the residual darkness lining the walls crept past him like a shifting shadow and disappeared into the unlit corner. A thunderous growl froze the blood in his veins.

He took a slow, cautious look over his shoulder.

Inside of a towering glass prison, a giant reptilian hand held the darkness like a reclaimed treasure. Three curved phalanges of polished bone scraped the front with sharpened points.

Allister nearly jumped to the ceiling, screaming the whole way. He couldn't tell if it was the creature's fangs or the intense look in its yellow eyes, but when his mom outstretched her arms, he tripped over himself running into them.

Sweat caked his forehead. The quick perspiration brought on by shock. He took a closer look, unable to decipher what was the creature's skin and what was its clothing. But from top to bottom, deep, textured grays blended into purples and silvers—whether fabric, chemical element, or otherwise. The thing had a tapered torso and strangely long legs, both with muscle definition unlike Allister had ever seen. Its broad spiked shoulders rose into a snarling face of skin overgrowths and jagged cheekbones, the foreign bone structure framed by thick dreadlocks and a long braided ponytail. Next, he clocked the tattered purple cape that stopped at the creature's clawed feet. Those, he was sure, belonged on a dinosaur.

"What is…what is…*that*?" he asked, his heart punching through his chest.

His mom held onto him, tightly, hushing him as she did so. "Hello," she said to the creature.

The creature's eyes softened at the sound of her voice, its claws pulling away from the up-lit glass and taking the shadows with them.

"Dolores Adams, child of Andromeda," the creature said, its accent dripping with the echo of space and affected pronunciations. Speaking Earth's language looked strenuous, yet its voice filled the room to every edge. "It has been over a hundred of your moons since we last shared the molecules of your world. Come ever closer."

There wasn't an ounce of doubt in his mom as she walked toward the glass. Allister's teeth were clenched now, his body shaking. The creature's knowledge of her and her knowledge of it was yet another deception for him to process.

Allister jumped in front of her and shouted, "Hold up! This. Isn't. Making. Any. Sense! How does that thing know your name?"

"That thing you're referring to is the alien who brought your dad and I together," his mom said quietly. "This is Neight Caster."

Allister yelped. He covered his mouth quickly, embarrassed, a dizziness spinning its way into his head as a heaviness threatened to sink him. *No way,* he thought to himself. *Neight Caster, as in* the *Neight Caster?*

"I thought he was an Evolutionary...," he said aloud. "I thought Pops said he was..." He let his words trail off with his assumptions.

Meanwhile, his mom maneuvered past him and made her approach. She kept her head down toward the floor, not elevated to accept Neight's obvious admiration.

The being inhaled with nostrils a quarter the size of Allister's. "What brings you here, to my sanctuary?"

"I came because"—his mom hesitated—"because I need you to do what we talked about, in Soviet Sanctuary." She then half turned to Allister and added, "But he, I think he came looking for me."

"And yet," Neight boomed, "I can see by the look of lost in his eyes, he came looking for something else as well. Perhaps...me?"

"Yes," Allister replied, calming to the reality. "I was told to look out for you." He gazed at Neight, a true being of wonder. Through that widened crack in his psyche made by alien language and cosmic knowledge, Allister saw the obvious. Nobility and ancient language were welded onto his chest plates, wisdom and silver stones sewn into his purple cape.

Neight Caster was more than an alien. He was a king.

Said king bowed *to him.* "And I was told to look out for you. It is an honor to be in the presence of the Gateway."

———

C20's search for Allister became an afterthought. For he believed they wouldn't find them—not with Neight Caster on their side.

Allister stared into the alien's yellow eyes. "My pops...he told me if you were alive, if I found you...you'd help me find the artifacts like you helped him."

"It is your discretion I have honored these years and yours alone," Neight said to his mom. "May I tell him?"

When Allister turned to her she looked torn, seemed to think about her answer for the twelve years she'd held her secrets, her face and body reliving every moment, every choice, every danger. But a minute had passed, and Allister could hardly contain himself by the time she whispered, "Yes."

He sighed, almost melting to the floor with relief. Twelve years of badgering his mom and he was about to get his answers from an alien king living in a blasted basement.

"You have questions about your potential, the Z-energy?" Neight asked.

Allister nodded fast.

"About how it works? Where it came from?" the alien added.

Allister leaned in, nodding faster. He didn't want to miss a single word.

"You have the excitability of a genetic sequence following quantum evolutionary acceleration," Neight revealed. "It is no wonder then that you are a product of such a phenomenon. What I will tell you, and I cannot tell you much, is that...the constant burning of Z-energy you feel does not come from anywhere—it simply exists. In all forms. In infinite capacity."

Allister's first thoughts went back to his assessments with Dr. Belladonna, how she'd been asking for permission to look for the "source" to unlocking his potential.

"I see your human ego needling toward an answer it can take credit for," Neight said. Allister thought he heard the alien laugh, but maybe he'd just scoffed. As his face was drawn in seriousness as he finished, "You must let go of the need to control your potential and focus on the ability to call upon it. You are a vessel through which the energy flows."

"Experiments help?"

"Tremendously. The experiments are the words you say—each tiny phrase or line or stanza—designed to shape the unique manifestations of your potential. Sometimes these words are not needed, but when manifesting the Z-energy, without intention, comes disaster. Such is the case with Foeht Zeorgen."

Allister recoiled on instinct, his eyes fastened shut, waiting for Neight's skin to ignite in a crackling too erratic to contain. Saying those words so casually should've been a crime.

His mom touched his shoulder. "It's fine, baby."

She was right. For some reason, it was fine.

Slowly, Allister straightened his body. He opened one eye, then two. "Nothing happened."

Now Neight was hovering in a meditative posture, his legs crossed beneath him, his arms sweeping across his wide torso with ritualistic prowess. "Did nothing happen? Or did nothing you expected to happen, happen?" The alien gave each syllable life and meaning, and spoke without rushing, without arrogance. As if in reflection, the Z-energy came to Neight's skin with patience and elegance, shining in the richest blue color Allister had ever seen. "It seems you are…familiar with the experiment I taught Patrick—to end with Z-energy—one whose default can be so…soul-shattering. Because when missing intention, the definition will be all you have."

"I learned another one, too," Allister began.

But Neight had moved on to another unknown task. His head bowed, his jaw set.

His mom pointed toward the area separating the faux museum from the rest of the Andromeda Project, which once again appeared to be the black wall.

Allister whipped around to face the grays and blacks of the barrier being liquified by bright explosions. Weapons firing off rounds of energy, no doubt. The blasts forced the strange material outward in multiple places before ceasing as if to let it flatten and congeal. Then the barrier exploded outward again, with more volume and distortion that time.

Multiple voices were shouting about breaking through.

Allister took a sharp breath. "How do we get out of here?" he asked his mom. "You said you knew this place?"

She stared at her palms as if to escape him. "This is the safest place we could ever be."

"Neight?" he asked.

The alien's brow furrowed with a hint of contemplation, but he held inside whatever was meant to be the answer. Blue energy flooded the ravines of his skin, sloshed and churned through the striations between his muscles, and flowed from his knuckles to his neck. It was the color of new chain reactions in a sun twenty-five times bigger than Earth's. If one could stand close enough to see over thirty-five thousand degrees burning in all its glory, they'd see so clearly a blue even brighter than the blue Allister knew. The Z-energy rising from Neight's skin was more potent, he supposed; it was certainly more pure.

But one thousand percent the same.

It was clear Neight couldn't answer because he was conducting an experiment without words, as described moments ago.

Allister moved closer to protect his mom. He was certain the Z-energy couldn't go past the prison glass, otherwise, what would be the point of the prison? But if the experiment wouldn't go anywhere, then why was Neight spending his strength creating one?

The answer came swiftly. Neight's eyes shot past him, burning blue and honed in on whatever was at Allister's back.

The alien seemed to struggle in the same way Allister had struggled—to keep the energy surging through him from growing beyond his purple figure. The strain curled the alien's spine, squeezed his fangs tighter over his lip.

Perhaps it was more an exercise in focus, because the Z-energy escaped Neight's body in a way that was so measured, Allister couldn't believe it was the same power as his. The energy streamed from his skin as nothing more than a hive of thin lines. Without separating, they penetrated the prison with ease, as if its confinement were a suggestion and not a command, then swarmed the room, tracing every line in the silver walls until it reached the barrier and traced that, too.

From that distance, Allister could see two things were true: one, Neight had summoned the Z-energy in the same way Leesa called on her telekinesis, to act as an intertwining web of fortitude to hold something together—in this case, the barrier—and two, that said barrier was itself an experiment, and unfortunately, it was about to fail.

A miscalculation was possible...or an unforeseen variable screwing with the results. Beams of orange light were steadily bombarding the barrier, piercing it in the middle. That could've been variable enough.

Allister took a step back and pulled his mom with him.

"You must—" Neight began, pulling Allister's concern back to him.

The alien's concentration faltered, his face carved in inability. As the creature hovered, clinging to the space above the marble floors of his exquisite entrapment, he hadn't the opportunity to call on more energy, to muster more of his soul and expend it.

A loud *boom* echoed through the room.

His mom latched on to him, whispering with unsteadiness, "Allister, we have to go."

Allister's skin went cold at the fear in her voice. He turned and gasped, trying to hold her closer while she clutched his arms.

Plasma beams tore through the sanctuary. Plexiglass shattered and released millennia-old weapons and armor from their prisons. Of the bright bulbs shining on the battle from above, most were shot down to their blackened filaments.

Allister pushed his mom down and squatted next to her—arms wide, back flexed to the oncoming firepower, shielding her against the wall. He waited for plasma to pierce him.

"Stay down," he warned.

Whooom!

An object rammed into him from the side. He went tumbling backward, smashing through display glass.

Whoom!

Another impact. That time from the front. More momentum. Direct force. He soared deeper into the room, limp, bewildered, no control over his trajectory. Suddenly, his back was cracking against the wall, then he was falling face-first to the floor.

The landing was hard, painful. But not as bad as he'd prepped for. He had his reflexes to thank.

Though feeling winded, he opened his eyes to the small crater he laid in. His arms were miraculously protecting his face from contact with the rough stone.

Allister spat out the salty taste that gathered in his mouth. Blood, for sure. He had no idea in which direction he'd been thrown, just that when he tried to rise, the room still moved in circles like those old carnival rides.

"Hold your fire," the C20 operative commanded, bringing the room to a hush.

Tranjam.

That man's voice was becoming a rage trigger in Allister's skull.

Allister tried to get up again, fueled by that rage. He made it halfway, then collapsed.

"I won't let you take him," his mom said. He couldn't tell from where exactly.

"C20 will take whatever it must to salvage our existence," said Tranjam.

As Allister watched, the density shifter's boots blurred and spun with the floor, sometimes seeming close and in the same moment far away, but they thumped steadily toward the sound of his mom's resistance—not him.

Allister pushed himself up onto one knee. "You better…not…touch…her," he said, panting.

Tranjam stopped.

Milking the moment of distraction, Allister kept speaking. "Don't you…don't you need me for something"—he paused and spat out the name—"Tranjam?" He felt a sort of calm confidence wash over him. "That's your name, isn't it? Big, bad C20 Evolutionary, too heavy for his own good. Sent here to capture the Gateway like a good little minion, yeah? Hmph. Well, you want *me*—I say you come get me."

Tranjam turned, and from a mouth too far above Allister to be seen, spoke the words, "I see you've found the honor and dignity in your spine."

Allister's assailant came a heavy step closer. The floor shook in response. Water sprayed his face as if moved by the weight of a thundering elephant.

"There is so much possibility for you, Mr. Adams. Did you know that in my country you would be praised, not imprisoned in a windowless cage?"

"What do you want, Tranjam?" he asked, seasoning boast into his delivery.

His opponent's answer was another stride.

Pipes rattled. The foundation quivered. Water sloshed against Allister's feet. His fingers curled next to his ankle while his eyes rose to meet those of the approaching Evolutionary.

Tranjam took a wide stance, then leaned down and clamped his dirty, blood-soaked fingers around Allister's neck. "There are people in my city without roofs over their head, children without food. My newborn twins have no mother."

He lifted Allister off the ground with a startling swiftness, his hold fierce and unrelenting. The less Allister managed to breathe, the more he kicked and clawed against Tranjam's disproportionate strength.

"This is why C20 was born," Tranjam continued. "Because the ungrateful such as you sit and watch and wait—you spoiled, thankless… You've never lost anything, have you? Have *you*?" High enough to see the whole scene, Allister grappled with the futility of the situation he faced. Agents on the outer perimeter of Tranjam's swelled frame held their weapons up, aimed at Allister's head. His mom was captive in the collective grip of three soldiers.

He'd lost one thing and certainly wasn't about to lose another.

Tranjam's musty hand squeezed tighter. "As I guessed."

"Look…," interrupted one of the C20 agents. "The water…it's moving, faster."

Tranjam looked down and sneered at the distraction. "You fear these puddles?" he asked the soldiers. "I have seen tsunamis."

Allister cocked back his arm. When Tranjam looked up, wearing that stupid grin, Allister punched him in the throat. Tranjam let go immediately, shrieking in fury as he doubled over, holding his own throat and stumbling around in circles.

"Lost my pops, asshole," said Allister.

He knew Tranjam was the sort of foe who needed to be kept off his feet at all costs. Wrestling him down seemed like the wisest choice considering the tight space and difference in density.

Allister's swift tackle led them down the path he'd devised, into a tussle no one could interfere with: their bodies so entangled that a beam of plasma was just as liable to pierce Tranjam as it was Allister. Wrestling was a game of body weight and gravity, of grip and stealth, of speed and stamina. Allister didn't appear to be winning, not if they were measuring in successful choke holds, which Tranjam had maneuvered him into more than once. But as Allister arched his back and broke free a fourth time, he knew his plan was working.

He could regenerate. Tranjam could not.

Allister doubled back and spun to face his enemy, juiced up on the feeling of a victory soon to come. He and his mom would be out of there and on their way to the main hangar.

"Stay back," came his mom's voice. She was backing her away toward Allister, a stolen plasma weapon hoisted to chest level.

Somehow the three groaning soldiers had been disarmed *and* injured. *By her?*

He and his mom were standing back-to-back, a kind of moment he could've never foreseen—namely, the two of them fighting off enemies in a quest to save humanity. Allister ignored the wetness seeping into his boots and flexed his fists, ready for a second round, while behind him, his mom charged the weapon.

Artist: Ezrom Bathan/ The CMD Studios

"Allister, what are you doing?" his mom asked, glancing down.

Curious, he glanced down, too.

"Uh…that's not me…"

She was referring to the water moving in circles around their ankles, its once-murky surface now christened by blue energy. He leaned to check the darkened corner beyond Tranjam, and found Neight on his knees, his claws pushed against the glass, his body glowing.

The alien was conducting another experiment. "Foeht Zeorgen!"

The power in his voice was enough to shake the room. Though Allister was sure he was the only one who'd heard Neight or could see him, as Tranjam's face had remained unchanged.

Still, the whirlpools twisted faster and shot upward, sandwiching every C20 agent against the ceiling. Tranjam, who was by contrast partially submerged by water, gargled in anger as he punched his way through a pile of debris.

Allister and his mom held each other, their expressions matching in the awe of self-contained tempests keeping the agents both encased and submerged.

Soon the water's pressure weakened, the blue energy inside it fading to a sparkle.

The alien drew in a breath, and judging by the cyclone's increasing speed and shine, drew in strength as well.

"They will all be cast out in darkness," Neight bellowed. "For this is my sanctuary, and my sanctuary it shall remain."

At the echo of Neight's words, smaller whirlpools smashed into one another, creating bigger ones, and Allister could see the room was seconds from becoming a raging typhoon of dirty liquid. He readied himself, his body angled toward the corridor—and in that chaos, he glimpsed what he'd been waiting for—the thinnest line of dry ground he and his mom could follow.

Allister turned to his mom, grabbed her wrist, and shouted, "It's now or never!"

She let him pull her along, and together they snaked through the waterspouts and spilled, short of breath, into the corridor.

The basement's darkness slipped in around them. The water in it higher than Allister had remembered. The area they shuffled through had become a mangled canopy of low-hanging wires. Dismantled panels were strewn about their path, floating like remnants of giant tree trunks.

As he took lead, navigating them through a technological swampland, Allister couldn't help but try to decipher the meaning behind what Neight said: *They will all be cast out in darkness*.

His mom started running ahead of him, screaming, "The water, run! The water!" as she picked up speed.

Allister turned back to see what had her so shaken.

None other than a tidal wave filled with limp bodies and debris cresting behind them.

CHAPTER 33

Artist: Lester Niesta/ The CMD Studios

ALLISTER ADAMS

Quadrant Gamma—The Vault, Andromeda Project Headquarters
Day 209

ALLISTER'S MOM KEPT her steady stride and took a hard left down the corridor. She knew where to go, Allister gathered as he followed behind, now sprinting at near full speed himself and close to catching up to her. In seconds, they were running side by side, his speed slowed so he didn't pull too far ahead.

The secret elevator gave a reassuring glow from the path's end, its doors open and welcoming them into its protection.

While at their backs the storm-stricken wave crashed against the building as if the Andromeda Project were a ship lost at sea. Water sloshed against one wall, then sloshed against another. It gushed from the hallway like the giant waves of De Los Muertos, tossing whatever it touched beneath its swift current.

"Keep going. Don't look back, just keep going!" Allister screamed. One last look behind him, and he saw the water shooting forward. They still weren't close enough. "Get down!"

As if down were the best direction to go.

The wave hit him cold, square in the back, packing the heavy swell of a tsunami and the sting of saline. Allister held his breath, scrambling for his mom as the fast-moving current pulled him up, swirled him around, then swept him deeper and kept him tumbling, his nostrils and throat filling with water, heels flying over his head and under him again.

Bodies and broken glass and metal framing soared in every direction. He twisted left to avoid a fixture. He twirled right to avoid a cluster of bodies, still awkward and floundering while he tried to position himself upright. Bewildered and desperate for air, he opened his mouth to breathe and took in more water like a boat with a hole in it.

His mom tapped him on the shoulder, paddling with confidence, her cheeks puffed out. She pointed above them and swam in that direction.

He went after her, arms moving in broad, wild strokes, legs kicking out to either side—and with a dramatic last push, rose above the surface with a huge inhale.

Head just above water, he sputtered, keeping himself afloat as he looked for Tranjam among what was bobbing along around them. He saw nothing but the human enemies and pieces of the facility's infrastructure, then watched all of it recede with the water to acceptable depths and back into the main hall.

Allister and his mom began wading away in what was left behind, a waist-high river and silence.

"Need…a second to…breathe," gasped Allister, pausing before he hunched over and choked out what felt like gallons of stale water. He wiped his mouth free of the rest of it.

"I don't believe you're more tuckered out than I am," his mom said.

Allister was astonished she hadn't passed out. Was this the same woman who struggled to carry more than one grocery bag? Who hobbled up the Riser Town stairs one at a time? Who gripped every railing she could find and shuffled along the street with a shawl wrapped around her shoulders?

"What now?" she asked.

What now? he thought, frustrated at the casual way she carried on.

His mom didn't wait for an answer and went on squeezing the moisture from her hair.

Scoffing, he did the same with his afro. Though her resilience was impressive, some manner of intriguing, it was contempt for omission that played out in his mind.

"This might be my first go at it," he finally said, "but it obviously isn't yours. Time to spill—what else aren't you telling me?"

"I'm the daughter of two spies," his mom replied dryly.

"Fresh," was his response, just as dry.

What else could he say? He could see now it was an act. It had always been. She was neither helpless nor hopeless. Her spine was as strong as her spirit, her core as strong as her heart.

The farther she moved ahead of him, the more he saw the aura of white capturing her at the curves of her shoulders and tracing her down to where her legs disappeared into the water. The aura might've belonged to her, if the light didn't shine so from the rectangle at her back.

The private glass elevator.

"This way," he said, trudging ahead of her as they came upon the elevator Brandt had promised. He pulled her onto the platform. "We need to get to the main…hangar…"

His mouth dropped open when he saw the basement for the first time. They seemed to be facing the infinite extensions of the Andromeda Project's mind. Blinking lights flashed and flickered from the waterline to as high as his eye could see, the towering structures like a city of giant CPUs on either side of them.

"Your father helped build this," she said, voice flat.

Mega.

It was like sneaking outside the sanctuaries and staring up into space. Each light more than a star or data point, but part of a bigger story to be told. Allister could see that, despite the infiltration, the massive neural network through which all Andromeda Project data crossed was still transporting, storing, and extracting. He felt proud to know it was his dad's work, and thankful to his mom for revealing it to him, even in the backhanded way that she had.

The doors closed on its magnificence. "Select your destination," Cynque said.

Allister chose the tenth floor.

"You've selected the tenth floor, location of the main hangar and ZEContainment Center," Cynque announced as the elevator began to move.

"Sounds like a super-prison?" Allister commented.

"It's much worse." His mom covered her mouth and mumbled, "God, this place. Your father built that, too."

She stared through the glass as they rose, and though her reflection looked back, he was sure she saw something else, something more horrifying. She shook her head at last, then uncovered her mouth to say, "It's not a prison for people; it's a prison for energy, like yours."

My pops built a prison for energy...like mine? Maybe his dad had believed it was as dangerous as his mom did—a disheartening thought.

"This is..." He didn't finish. He couldn't. *Twisted. Mega. Next level.* The slang would anger her, and he seemed incapable of explaining what he felt: a bit of astonishment, even more confusion, and the teeth-clenching bitterness of being lied to. He faced the scenery instead of her, body stiffened at the years he'd spent unaware of these inventions, at the conversations about his dad gone cold like food on their dining table.

"You're still upset," she said.

"Not the word *I* would use, but yeah, if that's the *proper* word, then I'm upset. No...no...I'm angry. You couldn't have told me any of this? Before today?"

"Who the hell cares what I did or didn't tell you?" his mom shot back. "Six days lost. It's been six days, and you've managed to negate the twelve years I sacrificed trying to protect us. Look where we are"—she referenced the entire building with her hands—"exactly where I didn't want you to be—caught in the middle of this war for salvation, standing on the front lines."

"I'm not backing down for saving those people in the District," he said. "This is what Evolutionaries should do, why else would we have potentials?"

"How many times do I gotta tell you, you don't owe nobody in this world nothing. You think just cuz you were born with some foreign DNA, you gotta give up your life for the rest of humanity?"

He turned slightly away from her. "Lay it down, Mom. If you want me to apologize for wanting to save lives, it's not happening."

"And what happens if you lose your life? Huh?" She poked his back, her voice hardening to a yell. "What would you have me do? The same thing I had to do for your father? Walk away like nothing happened? Like he didn't die for a world that can't be saved?"

Allister felt a sharp pang in his heart and glanced over his shoulder.

His mom was crying, her voice quivering. "The Andromeda Project took Patrick from me way before the accident." She wiped her cheeks. "I promised myself I wouldn't let them take you...too."

"C'mon, Mom, I'm sorry," he said. "I promise, I won't let it go down like that."

She didn't look at him or speak anymore. She was tapping her foot like she often did at the end of the kitchen table, her arms crossed tight with the stress of keeping a young Evolutionary alive.

The elevator continued to climb in silence.

Just before they reached their destination, his mom ended their standoff with a final statement. "That boy up the street, Quiglesworth..." Allister's eyes shot up at her mention of his friend. "He...says he's sorry. Regrets your fight. Poor thing thinks it's...it's his fault. I know he wishes you hadn't jumped in front of that truck to prove something; he said as much. But I bet right now he's just wishing you'd come home. And we both know that's not possible now, ain't that right?"

He was moved by Quigles's loyalty, yet gouged by his mom's truth. How could he let anyone blame themselves for his choices? He looked at his mom, wondering if his dad had done the same thing…to her. His stomach felt like it was folding in on itself, and he held his hands there to steady himself, unsure of what to say.

"As an Evolutionary," she continued, "you might live different, fight different, but for the most part, we all love and die just the same."

This was her reality. A reality she'd confronted in solitude while raising him and providing for him and zipping him around the world to keep them free of Cynque's detection. The reality that one day, if she didn't do everything in her power to protect him, Allister would be killed.

Allister held on to her shoulder then, feeling the sobs coming to life and dying in her. "I promise," he said firmly, "I won't let it go down like that."

The elevator sounded out an obnoxious *bing*.

As the doors opened, the heat of fire rushed into the small space. They both gasped and scrambled back against the elevator wall. The hallway's haze was unbearable. The smell of charred metal and flesh, horrid.

Allister nodded to her reassuringly. "To the hangar," he said, stepping off the elevator. "Stay close."

She did.

Emergency lights blinked, though the sound of their warning cries was absent. The fires that still burned, burned slowly on fixtures. Scores of Andromeda Project soldiers had been slaughtered and left to bleed on logo-branded floors.

Wisps of black smoke appeared to be floating in either direction. Perhaps it was fear following them as they inched along dented walls, as they turned around plasma-melted corners. He kept waving it away. And it kept coming back, stronger, thicker, trying to suffocate them.

Allister's chest felt as hot as the air. His coughs as violent as what had occurred before their arrival. His mom was in worse shape, doubled over and choking on the tainted air particles. "I can't go any farther…it's just like Cumberland," she strained to say. "Oh my God, it's like Cumberland."

"The hangar's right up—"

"No." She coughed, no longer walking, a hand on her chest. "It's a trap, just like with your dad. We have to go our own way…there has to be another way."

"Mom, trust me, will ya?" Allister hissed. "There's no time for another way!"

She recoiled.

"If we wanna make it out, we gotta hurry," he said, softer.

Before she could agree—or not—he took her wrist and sped up their pace. They reached an area where the smaller hallways fed into the bigger ones, right across from the hangar doors.

"Whoa, pause," he said. He then pulled them lower to the ground and peered around the corner.

Empty.

They dashed forward.

Though narrow, the hangar doors were twice Allister's height, with access guarded by the single panel with the same black face as Cynque. Allister touched its surface, waiting for what would happen with all of the tension and anxiety he could experience in a given moment.

A digital orb appeared, requesting he scan his Cynque for validation. It was similar to the verification system he'd experienced when entering the training facility. He could assume his access level allowed him to enter, but that assumption seemed bold, and dangerous.

"Hurry up, Allister," said his mom. She was anchored to him with one hand and coughing into the other.

Allister checked over his shoulder as he held his Cynque to the orb. "Going as fast as I—can."

Her concern was clear, even through the wafting smoke.

Moving toward them were dozens of C20 agents, led by none other than Vonnie. Her polished blade swung by her face, followed by the blunt end of the staff, then the blade again.

"Access granted, Agent Allister Adams," Cynque announced. The hangar doors slid open.

"Boom," Allister said. "Let's go."

They rushed inside. Allister turned around in a flash and caught the doors before they opened fully, wrangling them closed with his brute strength. He twisted the metal together in a way he hoped the doors wouldn't separate again, then staggered backward, drained of potential and out of ideas.

The hangar lights had been dimmed and the vast space appeared empty.

Brandt had better be there like he'd promised.

"Are you sure this is right?" his mom asked. She took in the smoke-free air and rotated around in a circle. "Someone planning on flying us out of here, or…?"

"No...I don't know...this's just where Brandt asked me to meet him."

"Brandt—" his mom began, but stopped short as the dimness receded, replaced by an intrusion of harsh overhead spotlights.

The spotlights made Allister uneasy.

From what he could tell, the hangar was just filled with the technology and accessories that belonged. On one end was a fleet of dusty aerocrafts like the one they'd taken to De Los Muertos. On the other end were sealed bunkers and giant unmarked crates stacked to the ceiling.

He jumped to his feet, eyes scanning for Brandt.

A shadow stretched from beneath one of the giant wings.

"Who's...there?" he asked.

No one answered.

Then someone, maybe the person who owned that long shadow, started clapping—too loud, too slow, more sarcastic than congratulatory.

"It's just me," said a familiar voice.

"That you, Captain?" asked Allister.

"Jared...where are you?" his mom asked right after, spinning feverishly in her search. "What are you...what did you do?"

Still out of sight, Brandt replied, "I never been the same, Dee. Not since we lost him."

"Been since long before that," she muttered, too low for the captain to hear. But she didn't address him again. Instead, she turned to Allister and warned, "Keep your eyes up, Allister. This don't...really feel good."

Brandt emerged from underneath the aerocraft with a pleased look on his face and his hands pressed firmly at his sides. He walked until he stopped in the hangar's center. "I told you you'd pull it off, son," he said.

Allister looked around, confused. Though the clapping couldn't be coming from the captain, it was coming from somewhere...from...someone. Until it stopped rather abruptly. It was then Allister noticed Brandt was no longer wearing his Andromeda Project uniform. His muscular figure was flooded by the spotlight's heavenlike rays, and it was evident that the red suit he'd donned like a trophy had been discarded for something more fitted, more formal.

Certainly more new.

The glare from the light beaming down on Brandt seemed further brightened by the reflection off his—

—stark...white...suit.

Allister shook his head fast, trying to clear what he hoped was an illusion. His heart rate had already begun rising with a sense of dread, and he couldn't even process his thoughts before the questions just came tumbling out of him in quick succession.

"Captain, what's the deal? Why'd you tell me to meet you here?" Allister and his mom stood shoulder to shoulder: him facing the captain, her facing the door. He could do little more than take her hand and fight his impulse to react, terrified to ask the most pressing question of them all. But he had to—he had to know. "Why...why're you dressed in C20's colors?"

"I knew it," his mom said.

To him, she sounded more angry than scared, and he wasn't quite sure what she "knew" that he didn't.

"Look," she continued, shaking him. "Look at what they've done."

Allister spun around.

Dorian was unconscious, chained to a giant metal crate. Penny's limp body lay at his feet, her coat tainted with wet blood and open wounds.

He only wished it ended there. He might've been able to rescue one person and the LionWolf. But when he looked up, he saw the other Andromeda Project leaders.

Leesa, who was wrapped tight in a cybernetic full-body prison and still unconscious, hung from the ceiling by her legs. Atop the crate Dorian was attached to, Allister spotted General Delemar squirming on his side, gagged, sweaty and fuming, partially awake and tied up in chains.

No Dr. Belladonna. No Bridget Sparks. No Professor Ashur.

This time, Allister didn't gasp in shock. By contrast, every fiber in his body flexed, the fear and fury in him mixing. "Brandt...tell me you didn't do this?"

Brandt glanced around the hangar—up first, then to his left, then to his right. "Not alone," he finally answered.

As if on cue, a cavalry of hulking bodies in white armored suits filed in quietly from all sides—lowering themselves from the ceiling, tiptoeing in from the rows of bunkers and the stacked crates, and sneaking out from behind the towering wheels of the aerocrafts. They were not unlike a small swarm, their plasma weapons buzzing in unison as the agents moved themselves into a circular formation.

In less than a minute, Allister and his mom were surrounded.

It felt stupid to him, thinking that he could suppress his trepidation for a situation growing further out of his control. Yet, he tried. And tried, again. His heart continued rapping against his chest. His body kept maintaining an inhuman level of restraint.

The shakiness still came through in his voice. "You told me you wanted to help us escape," Allister said to Brandt. "That this place was no good for me… and you'd…you'd made a mistake."

"I do. It's not. I did," Brandt answered in order. "It's time to take this hunt into our own hands, join a team with more vision, more knowledge. C20 knows where the Crystal of Temporal Transportation are, and we both know you got the potential to get 'em. We can save all the people you wanna save, Allister. Together, like I promised."

Join a team with more vision and more knowledge? Allister repeated in his head, too busy choking on the truth to speak.

As in, join C20?

The very idea was insane. Unthinkable. Yet, the captain stood rooted in his suggestion, smirking as if he'd won some great prize, reached some unachievable clarity. To Allister, he'd just lost his mind somewhere between the Vault and the hangar.

Allister's face swelled with blood at the thought. "You saying we save everyone by handing off the most powerful thing we know of to a bunch of Evolutionary extremists who wanna pick and choose who goes?" He pointed aggressively at the captain. "Were you lying to me the whole time?"

"I was the only one who told you the truth!" Brandt shouted back. "What did I say before you cynqued with that contract? I'd tell you everything you wanted to know and some things you didn't want to know, too."

Brandt had told the truth. Brandt had told Allister everything, in fact. About their first mission to retrieve the artifacts. About what Allister's mom had gone through. About Allister's potentials.

Trusting Brandt had come so easily.

411

And he'd used that trust. *Abused* that trust.

Allister was beside himself with new levels of doubt. He and his mom had walked into a web so clearly woven he couldn't believe he'd missed the threads. From Brandt's sudden appearance in the basement, telling him what to do and where to go, to Tranjam and those agents busting through the wall of darkness, driving Allister and his mom out of the Vault with haste—the intention had always been to lead him there.

To the hangar, where C20 would be waiting.

The bitterness of being tricked moved from his chest and took the heaviness with it, morphing into the sting of betrayal near his elbow. That stinging enveloped his forearm, the energy circling and swimming before igniting his skin. He twisted his neck against the pain.

"You want to hear about an extremist?" Brandt asked.

"Lay it down, man," warned Allister.

"I'll tell you 'bout the one who killed your daddy."

"Enough, Jared!" his mom shouted, matching the captain's volume with the same passion and the same anger.

But Brandt continued. "He's a self-centered, worthless son of a—"

"Jared, I said enough!" shouted his mom again, louder.

"—and I'll give you a hint: his name ain't Tas-Salvatur," the captain finished over her.

As the tension reached its peak, the crackling blue Z-energy enveloped Allister's palms. He contracted into himself, and staring at his hands, imagined an outcome similar to Neight's, where water rushed from nowhere and flooded the hangar.

"Allister, don't—" he heard his mom say.

But he was already whispering, "Foeht Zeorgen," then louder, he repeated, "Foeht Zeorgen!"

Fwoom!

The heat escaped his body in a rush, left him freezing for the seconds that the miniature ring of energy pulsed away from him, transforming into an explosive shock wave the instant it touched the air. The ground cracked and caved beneath his feet. Deafening booms echoed in his ears.

Allister heaved with exhaustion, now kneeling, his hands pressed to the chopped-up floor. Nausea kept him from getting back onto his feet. Dizziness kept him from seeing little more than the ground under him. All he knew was that the room had fallen silent and his flesh felt *frigid*.

He imagined the results were petrifying. The apparent destruction sounding out of line with what he'd intended. Because water hadn't come from him like he'd wanted, only a fiery burst of rage.

His speculation about the extent of the damage disappeared in a few short blinks. He saw the most obvious, most devastating consequence.

Her.

His mom, sprawled unconscious at Brandt's feet, her hair singed at the tips, her body bruised and smoking from the energy's heat.

Immediately, Allister felt tears forming behind his widened eyes, the thickening in his throat. He crawled forward, mumbling, "Mom...," unaware of his surroundings.

"I wouldn't if I was you," Brandt suggested.

Allister stopped in his tracks and panicked as the captain's utterance expanded his field of observation.

The damage left him speechless.

A number of aerocrafts had tipped over, critically compromised with now-melted exteriors. Leesa, having been blown from the sky, was facedown on the ground, bleeding from her nose. While General Delemar, Dorian, and Penny remained in place, their clothes blackened by ash, their faces tarnished by burns. The C20 agents were still spread around him, though on their backs and unconscious.

Brandt was the only one still standing. He was free of any injuries, a miniature vortex of yellow energy whipping around his body. The field pulsed and flared, activated to its full potential, as did his eyes with the same color and intensity.

Disruption, Allister thought with disgust.

"I'm sorry to do this, son," Brandt said. He extended his hand. Then, breathing deep, he closed his eyes and conjured a spark of the disruptive energy.

The same sparking potential appeared in a flat circle where Allister squatted, brightening as it started...*swirling*...almost in the same manner as it was around the captain, but reversed.

Allister scrambled to move from within it. But it erupted upward with ferocious intensity. Gaining more vibrance and thickness, it rose past his legs and torso, his shoulders and head, soaring above him before solidifying as a cylindrical prison.

"Tas-Salvatur promised me more potential, and look at that, I already have it," Brandt said. He dropped down to one knee to pick up Allister's mom, cradling her with an odd tenderness as he rose with her in his arms.

I knew Sweet Dee and Patty Cakes way before all this mess took our lives for a whirl. Way before all this... Brandt had said that once. Perhaps if the captain still cared for them, he could be reasoned with.

Allister pushed his hands against the barrier, letting the anger fade in favor of desperation.

"Brandt, I get it, something's got you triggered. But this isn't you," Allister said, speaking slow and, at the same time, searching with his hands for a weak point in the field. "What about the home we're supposed to build, where EVs can be accepted?"

"That's not happening under the Andromeda Project," Brandt said solemnly. "Guess when the lieutenant went down there to offer you freedom, she didn't tell you they were conspiring to terminate me." He looked over at Allister then, the compassion on his face melting into outrage. "Terminate...me!"

Termination? Allister thought.

Feeling sympathy for Brandt was automatic. It had to be dismissed. While termination very well could've been a reason for the captain to do what he'd done, at that moment, reasons didn't matter as much as getting his mom out of those traitorous arms.

"Put my mom down, Brandt, and we can get it sorted!" Allister yelled. "Please!"

Brandt just shook his head. "This place is going down either way."

Allister threw his strongest punch at the yellow prison. The resulting impact blasted inward and knocked him against the other side of the disruptive energy field, which flared in response without budging in any direction.

He slid to the floor.

As he lifted his eyes, he could see black mist drifting behind Brandt, almost crawling along the floor as it condensed into a thick cloud, then congealed into something close to liquid.

Artist: The CMD Studios

Vonnie's body gained shape inside that mist, was outlined in black at the edges, as if she were the cause. But an instant later, Tranjam passed—no, phased—through her, both their bodies shimmering a near-ghostly blue, missing all manner of texture and density. The mist continued to swell beyond them after they'd appeared, swallowing them in its darkness along with their unconscious agent companions. Next, it traced Brandt, his rigid frame and his arms full with his mom's life.

Allister realized what was happening. C20 was...*disappearing*.

"No!" he yelled suddenly. "Listen to me...Brandt...take me. Seriously, I'll go. I'll find the artifacts for C20 or Tas-Salva-whoever. Just put her down and take me!"

Brandt held Allister's mom with that conflicting tenderness, the semblance of sorrow. "Listen," the captain began, "I got no reason to hurt the ones I love. Don't make it come to that." The creeping mist then took away the captain's legs and thighs, wrapped itself around his torso and swirled up his neck and over his shoulders. It was almost as if he did not feel the thick shadow that creeped closed around them. "C20 makes the life we want possible. Join me...join us—in freedom."

Allister thought the captain might smile after that—but instead, he frowned and looked dead at him. The look was sharp. Serious. Provoking. His eyes drilling through to Allister's tormented soul.

"Brandt! Don't!" Allister screamed. He was still pushing, though without much force, against the barrier.

"You got one day to come retrieve the artifacts," Brandt said. "Believe me when I say we can't afford to lose no more."

———

Artist: Lester Niesta/ The CMD Studios

DO I REALLY "WANT"
WHAT I THINK I WANT?
WHY DO I WANT THIS? HOW DOES
YOUR ANSWER IMPACT YOUR
PERSPECTIVE/TRAJECTORY?
WHAT DO
YOU REALLY WANT?

CHAPTER 34

ALLISTER ADAMS

Quadrant Zeta—Restricted Access, Main Hangar, Andromeda Project Headquarters
Day 208

ALLISTER HAD ONE day to help C20 retrieve the artifacts. Just. One. Day.

Perhaps an hour had passed. Perhaps it had only been a minute. Allister couldn't tell much, except that dawn had arrived, its lackluster glory further dampened by the hangar's heavily tinted windows.

All he tasted was vengeance, sweet as it went down, sour as it came back up.

Brandt's disruptive field had long since fizzled. But Allister hadn't moved, still feeling trapped in that moment. He listened as Dorian and Penny were being tended to, then again as General Delemar was escorted out by medics. So what if they were okay. His mom wasn't.

"Don't you do a thing to her," he threatened the empty space ahead of him. "Don't do a thing to her, or I swear, you're finished, Brandt. I swear you're finished!"

He got up and stumbled to the spot where his mom had been picked up like a helpless flower.

His teary eyes fixed on the clumps of burnt-off curls around where her body should've been. *I should've never jumped in front of that truck,* he thought. He wished away the hammering in his skull, and, with more intensity, wished away his potentials and those two words that had caused his mom to fly across the room. "I took away our last days together. For this." He looked at the veins in his forearm, which still glistened with the hint of the blue energy. "For this..."

Allister clenched his fist. His tears seemed to evaporate with the resurgence of anger. The man who'd recruited him was now his enemy—not his mentor, not his dad's best friend, not his godfather.

Betrayal had touched everything inside the building, including his heart.

Allister let out a massive scream, swung his fist around, and smashed the ground.

With every successful swing, he yelled.

With every completed punch, he fell silent.

Boom. Boom. Boom. Boom.

Eight, maybe ten hits in, a seismic wave rattled the floor.

"Agent Adams, keep it together," a voice shouted from across the room.

Leesa.

He knew by the pitch in her voice, the flare of accent in her delivery, how her attempt at harshness had faltered midsentence. By some miracle, she was awake, glaring at him, seemingly oblivious to the dried blood on her face and the swelling around it.

Allister glared back, now consumed by defiance. Conversations happening between rescue crews, the digital scans of evidence and damage being downloaded, the eyewitness accounts being dictated—they had all stopped. He didn't care. The anger wouldn't go, wouldn't leave him be. It buzzed in his ear like a plasma cannon. Stuck to him like the soaked garments he'd fought in, swam in, lost his mom in. He swore he never wanted to see the energy again, resigned to pounding the ground until those two alien words were erased from his memory.

He lifted his hand again.

"Hey!" Leesa said, her hand extended, pink energy pulsing from it. His fist wouldn't fall, constricted by her fierce concentration. "I said, keep it together."

She kept him in her light telekinetic grip as she walked to him. Up close, Allister glimpsed her giant, lopsided bun of hair spilling as a waterfall of curls onto her exposed shoulder. He could see that her uniform was shredded in less-than-appropriate places, and—besides the wicked slice across her neck and the blackened, swollen eye and cut lip—the underground bomb hadn't diminished her spirit more than Brandt's treachery or the destruction of the only thing she'd ever known. The Andromeda Project.

Perhaps it was that she appeared visibly shaken, imperfect, and yet she was trying to hold herself together. She approached with that resolve, calm enough for him to loosen the muscles in his arm. He felt his resistance vanish. Seconds later, her telekinetic hold did, too.

"Are you done?" she asked.

Maybe he was. He collapsed deeper into his sorrow, let the sweat run off him like he were slick with oil and not regret.

Just one day.

"I'm done," he said at last.

Leesa's tone changed but didn't harden. "Good," she said. "To business, then."

And that quickly, she was back to being the lieutenant. He felt annoyed at himself for letting his guard down yet again.

"When we were in De Los Muertos, you knew where the machine was from a private transmission."

The denial was formulating in Allister's head, then just as he opened his mouth to lie, he decided he didn't care. "So?"

"So you knew how it worked and where it was," Leesa said. "You were in the perfect position to give C20 the intel and data they needed."

"Are you—?"

"Questioning your loyalty? Yes"—she took a step closer—"and your answer will determine what happens next."

He pressed his lips together, his stare piercing her with enough outrage that she rephrased the statement.

"Agent Adams, you were going to walk out of here with Captain Brandt," she said. "I just need to know who sent you that message."

Allister lowered his head. There was no sense hiding that information now. "My pops sent it," he admitted. "Don't ask me how, but yeah, he got to me."

To Allister's surprise, Leesa sat down next to him, a look of intrigue in her eyes. She must've liked his answer enough because she changed the subject. "The phrase you say, that makes the Z-energy go off, it's not an Earth language, is it?"

"No. Why do you care all of a sudden?"

"To end with Z," she said, nodding. She wasn't asking because she didn't know. She was asking to see if he knew.

Before he could reply, she glanced at his arm. "It's in my head, too…that and all these other words and phrases. I didn't know what they all meant, it's why I never said them. That one I understood, somehow. I used to say it, then I stopped. After Brisbane."

She wrapped her arms around her knees and rocked forward. "My force-field didn't hold up in the basement," she said into her thighs. "The Potential Manifestation Disbursement system down there requires constant focus."

Was that an apology?

Allister was only half listening anyway, more concerned that the two alien words, which he refused to even think, had floated to the surface and wouldn't sink again.

Leesa kept speaking. "Know that Cap…that Brandt will pay for his crimes, likely with his life. However, unless directed, his punishment is not ours to deliver.

Brandt knew the terms. They're the same for everyone. But I guess"—she paused and sat back up—"I guess none of us could've seen that coming."

Allister wondered what he might do if faced with termination.

You can't save others if you can't save yourself, Brandt had said on their way to De Los Muertos. A simple warning wrapped in sound advice: that he wouldn't be the type to roll over and take it.

"You guys were really going to do it?" Allister asked.

"Do what?"

"Terminate him. After all those years of loyalty and service?"

"Now you see the fear I live with every day." Leesa reached for the curls rested atop her shoulder as if she might play in them. But with a fingertip, she called forth her telekinetic potential and went to work piecing her hair back into the bun. Next, she tackled her uniform, ironing out the dents, reattaching the plasma core. "We all run out of chances, Agent Adams, or we run out of time. In this case, Brandt's chances ran out first." She rose, reached down to help him up, and said, "Regardless of his indiscretions, the artifacts are our only priority. We need to regroup."

He scoffed at her hand, taking her gesture for what it was, some hollow act of solidarity, an attempt to commiserate. That was the way she looked at him and held her hand there in earnest. She needed him to take it.

Allister diverted his eyes to the disaster area. Solidarity could shrivel and die as long as retribution grew in its place.

"I'm not doing this," he said. "Screw a regroup. I have to go after them now. Tonight. I have one day."

"You chose to stay. That means you chose to honor your obligation to our mission, and that means we, as a team, decide what to do next."

"I didn't choose to stay. I chose not to join C20. Nowhere near the same thing."

"Agent Adams—"

Allister dismissed her authority with a flick of his wrist. "After I heal, I'm out—"

"Lieutenant! Lieutenant!" someone interrupted. "Lieutenant!"

Leesa looked toward the hangar doors, which had been forced back open.

The voice Allister heard brought a sliver of joy to his face. Pumped his body full of renewed adrenaline. It was the voice of Dr. Florence Belladonna, someone he believed he could trust. She came running up the smoky hallway, waving her arms and calling for attention. Whatever attire she'd dolled herself up in had been reduced to rags, and her wounds, the ones he could make out, were far too similar to theirs. "Let me through," she said as she attempted to squeeze past the cluster of investigators crowding the door.

Had she resurfaced or returned or recovered?

Allister didn't care as he exclaimed, "Dr. Belladonna! I need your help! C20—" He sprang to his feet and faltered, but a set of big hands caught him around the ribs and hoisted him back up.

A jovial, though unfamiliar, voice followed with a ridiculous "Upsy-daisy!"

Allister tore himself away from the stranger and tried standing on his own. "Hey, I'm golden. If I wanted help, I'd ask." He glanced up, did a double take, then stopped on the somewhat pudgy, old-looking man opposite him.

"Dr. Rabia Giro, resident geneticist and Evolutionary specialist," the man said. "I have heard inspiring tales of your potential, Agent Allister Adams."

"Yeah, thanks," Allister said, sizing him up.

The doctor standing before him looked fresh, as if he'd recently woken from an eight-hour sleep, possibly even had a fully cooked breakfast. His face hadn't a scratch or a scar. His debris-free skin was nearly transparent under the white lights in the ceiling. He had been untouched. Completely untouched.

"Dr. Giro," Leesa said, interrupting. "I don't know where you've been, but General Delemar has requested you personally to oversee his recovery."

"Of course, Lieutenant, I will go to him at once," Dr. Giro replied. He turned to Allister and bowed, a creepy grin plastered on his round face. "Until we meet again. Do be sure to make an appointment with me if you want to further explore your Evolutionary heritage, hmm?" Without waiting for an answer, he began to walk—no, skip—away. When he reached the hangar doors, he was ushered through them while Dr. Belladonna was still trying to pull rank, going on about why she should be allowed to enter.

"Tell them to let her in," Allister said. "I need to talk to her."

About saving my mom, was what he didn't say.

Leesa shook her head. "Dr. Belladonna left the facility. They'll need to verify her whereabouts and do a comms check first. After what happened with Brandt, we can't afford—"

"Stop," he said suddenly, then pointed at the ceiling. "You hear that?"

424

Three faint *booms* went off, each closer than the one before it.

Consecutive tremors rattled the room.

"Are those...more...explosions?" he asked.

Leesa went to answer. Dr. Belladonna screamed.

The room erupted in fire instantly.

Allister crouched down in anticipation, hearing the roar of flames and waiting for the rush of heat. But the incineration he so fearfully awaited didn't arrive. For Leesa floated, hands flattened to an opaque field of purple energy, her expression grim, her determination unwavering. What would've been unforgiving fire and scorching heat pounded the forcefield before expanding around and past them and dissipating.

With the smoke still thick, there was no telling how much of the blast Leesa had caught, and how much of it she'd missed.

She fell to her hands and knees, exhausted, gazing ahead as the field disintegrated into a million pieces in front of them.

The smoke began to clear.

"I tried to contain the blast from both sides," she said. "I'm not sure if I was fast enough." Leesa didn't have to spell it out for him to know what she meant—she wasn't sure if she'd been fast enough to save Dr. Belladonna.

Allister narrowed his eyes at Leesa, disappointed as if she'd done it on purpose, then took off running through the demolished hangar, past the melted aerocrafts, beyond more lost soldiers.

"Dr. Belladonna!" Allister yelled, charging through the smoke. His heart sank as he passed headless, limbless torsos and reached a gaping hole in the hangar wall still steaming from the heat. Dr. Belladonna wasn't among the dismembered. He shook away his panic, and unsure what he'd find, stepped through it and into the hallway.

Sparks flew from overhead. The soundless sirens had regained their voices and screamed in simulated anguish.

So much death. So much unnecessary death.

Seven days past, I was playing Schwebevogel with Quigles, he thought. *Seven days past, I was eating soggy sandwiches from Mom.*

Allister let out a heavy sigh when he saw Dr. Belladonna, a sigh so burdened by relief he dropped next to her. He was gutted by her bruised, soot-covered face, and the shock displayed on it. He sniffled and pressed his thumb and forefinger into his eyes to keep the tears dammed up.

Dr. Belladonna seized his forearm, dazed and sputtering something, her hands shaking despite her grip. She repeated herself, but it was difficult to hear over the sound of blood gurgling in her throat. Quieting, she fell back.

His eyes traced her shivering body.

She was buried from the waist down in rubble, and shrapnel had managed to cut through her arm and torso. But she was still breathing.

She was still alive.

———

426

CHAPTER 35

DR. FLORENCE BELLADONNA

Quadrant Delta—Z-Laboratory, Andromeda Project Headquarters
Day 208

FLORENCE LIFTED HER head from the pillow. Which meant she was lying down for some reason. She knew she didn't have the luxury of resting, she was meant to be going after C20 and that missing princess.

Even more unsettling was the telepathic tingle she often felt in her head vibrating down through her fingertips. She examined her hand, curious to discover what buzzed and scratched beneath her palms. She had to look twice, then look closer to confirm what billowed in slow movements atop her skin. Her potential, notorious for showing up in shades of light reds, had been saturated a deep, almost sinister scarlet.

It had returned with a strength like never before.

Her awareness of it was the smallest disturbance, scattering the energy into the air above her as if it never were. Her hand fell back onto her stomach. Feeling uncomfortable, she shifted in the—hard...acrylic cot?

What the hell am I doing on a cot?

Her head was empty, the landscape of her conscious mind as white as the ceiling. She turned to her right, anxious for a clue as to her present location. Obsessively organized surgical tools rested on the table next to her. State-of-the-art medical machines loomed beyond that. They could only belong to Dr. Giro, so she must've been in his Z-Laboratory.

The place was *spotless*, as if it'd never been...

Attacked.

Suddenly the past hours returned in a string of disjointed memories, each racing through her mind one after the other: bright bursts of fire, thundering explosions, Leesa's purple field of telekinetic energy closing around her. When the images vanished and the blanked landscape returned, the *booms* seemed to echo in her ears.

She cupped her forehead, burdened by the throbbing in her skull, in her side, and in her arm.

"Feeling okay?" someone asked. The voice had come out small and strained, a little above a whisper. But she knew it was Allister.

She was surprised anyone waited next to her. "What are you doing here?" she moaned. "What am I doing here?"

Allister was hunched over behind the table of tools, quiet, contemplating. From a distance, she could see the emotions moving through him like rapids in a river, and she feared if she stepped in, she'd be swept away. *Not again*, she thought, deciding against her telepathy. "Allister?"

"You're recovering," he said.

Florence stroked her hair out of habit, then pressed a hand against her fast-beating heart.

From the C20 attack.

"How long have I been out?" she asked.

"Too long," he answered. "Hours. I should've split already."

"I thought we had this discussion. Either you're here, protected and protecting, or you're dead."

"That was before C20 took my mom."

She let her head fall back onto the pillow. *Christ.* Her lips tightened as she searched for logic in the organization's motivation. Leaving Allister behind seemed silly, but Tas-Salvatur was a man who loved games. She'd followed his track record, and noticed he got off on influencing outcomes rather than dictating them. "Is that why you're here?" was all she managed.

"Maybe," he said.

She gave him the side-eye then, observed his heel bouncing, his elbow jigging up and down on top of his leg. Her eyes flared with telepathic potential, and through them, she saw his emotions in an outline of frenetic red energy. The outline frizzed and scattered, expanded and condensed, an indication that he was angry, humiliated...sad.

"Well?"

"Captain Brandt betrayed us," Allister explained.

He said *us*, but Florence heard him thinking *me*. He wouldn't look up, just kept swallowing and staring into his hands. The energy calmed after his admission, settled around his shoulders, smoothed along his torso. He seemed to be pushing it all down, the pain, the sorrow, the guilt. She knew when his emotions vanished from the surface, her telepathic manifestation of them would too. She blinked her potential away and looked at him through normal vision.

"I guess C20 planted explosives on every level," he continued, his tone more even, his leg no longer moving. "Who knows how long after they left, bombs started popping off one by one."

She squinted, thinking back, or trying to. Before the whiteness. Before the *booms*. Vaguely, she remembered being stuck at the hangar doors, being told the area was locked down for investigation.

He swallowed again, more forced that time. "We couldn't have predicted that the last one would be…"

The final memory arrived. He didn't need to finish. The last bomb had blown right where she was standing.

Again, the explosion rocked her memory, just as loud and just as hot as it had been in real life. She shuddered and wiped her forehead.

"Thanks to the lieutenant's forcefield, you're here, so…maybe there's something to faith after all."

Maybe. She liked to think she'd survived worse. And physically, that *might* have been true. The infiltration of an entire organization meant to be under her careful watch, though? That was a first.

Captain Brandt's betrayal was a mistake she'd have to stomach. She'd ignored the signs of delusion, a number of which had flared up before De Los Muertos. The captain's reconnection to past trauma, his determination to succeed, even against authority—his general agitation with the process. She believed on some level it was Allister who had pulled the final thread that unraveled him.

Florence fiddled with the thick sheets that were tucked up to her waist, unsure what to say and where, ultimately, he was going with his story. "I'm sorry. I know this must be difficult considering your relationship—"

"Don't. I'm not with the sympathy. I have one day to do what C20 wants"—Allister pounded his fist in his hand, teeth clenched with vengeful determination—"and no one's gonna keep me from that, not even you."

Florence pinched the bridge of her nose, annoyed but not convinced. "I don't suppose you waited for me to wake up so you could threaten me?"

Allister turned to her and asked, "Can I trust you?"

"Sometimes you can," she answered. "Sometimes I'm not sure it's in your best interest."

"At least you're honest."

"I suppose my truth is better than any lie." Florence repositioned her legs under the blanket, her calf rubbing against something smooth and cold, soft in a sense, but mechanical. "What exactly am I recovering from?" she asked quietly.

"You should...you should look."

Florence peeled back the sheet and stared at them. Her legs.

No—one human leg, and *something else*.

Something cybernetic.

Dread sucked the blood from her cheeks.

Near the leftover flesh of her left thigh, wires invaded the veins, screws dug into the bones. She inched her fingers lower, all ten of them curled with malice. She wanted the wires torn loose, would give anything to have the screws twisted free.

She snapped her head to Allister. "What is this?" she demanded, the words barely sliding between her teeth.

"The forcefield didn't cover all of you," he said quickly. "Dr. Belladonna, your leg is golden. You're golden."

Her leg was far from *golden,* and so was she.

She put on a brave face for him.

"*Sì, sto bene,*" she agreed, though inside her heart was screaming. "*Sto bene.*"

Florence swallowed hard, forced to accept the reality literally at her fingertips, which she straightened to explore the metal instead of tear it away.

It wasn't the first time Florence had seen an amputated body part or cybernetic enhancement, she just never imagined she'd be the next Belladonna in line to receive one. She remembered when they replaced the hands of her younger sister, Kara, after her accident. A torturous procedure to watch. And their mother's cruelty didn't help, either. Perhaps reassurance was ineffective without compassion.

Studying the attachment, she could see how the separation between flesh and metal was too clean, how it had been cut off by the flat edge of a forcefield, not blown off by an explosion. "*Va bene,*" she said to herself.

She took light steps in her head, away from hysteria, away from mourning. The alteration was something that would have to be addressed in private. She couldn't let a meltdown hit her now, not in the middle of a conversation where she needed answers. Per usual, she pushed her health aside for a bigger vision—saving humanity...and securing her freedom.

Because her freedom remained the priority.

Allister sat straight up, agitated. "Look, I'm here because I need your help. I can't go after C20 alone, and you're the only one I can—"

"Trust?" Florence raised her eyebrow, her voice no louder than a whisper. "I thought we had this discussion."

"Yeah, well, pretty sure I know something that'll change your mind," Allister said back.

"Oh? Is that so?"

"C20 knows where the artifacts are. Brandt slipped and said it in the hangar. But I—I think I'm the only one who heard. General Delemar was delirious, and Leesa and Dorian were knocked out."

"And you're offering me…"

"Details. You get done what you need to do. I get done what I need to do. Maybe we get it done together. Everybody wins."

"If C20 knows where the artifacts are, then no one should wait for me to get back on my"—Florence paused and glanced at her artificial limb—"feet. There's no time—"

"I have to wait for you, Dr. Belladonna. I can't really give C20 the artifacts and I can't use my energy potential to stop them." He poked his forearm flesh. "I'm really lucky I didn't kill my mom. She was standing so close. I just…I just can't…ya know…let go. It's too dangerous." He seemed fragile, more fragile than he'd been when she found him on the couch fresh out of the assessment, or when she'd visited him in the Vault fresh off of his first mission. "It's best I don't use it, especially when I'm triggered."

She watched the emotions he'd been pushing down bubble back up, visible once again in the reds of her telepathy. Now fear suffocated him like smog and held him hostage against the chair.

"It comes down to discipline," she said. "Get your head right before you go. But you should go, now, like you've promised."

The urgency in her voice was tart, even for her taste. It appeared to thin the fear around him…at least enough to let him lean forward. He agreed, nodding with lowered eyes after he'd thought about it for a minute. "I found what you were looking for. The source *of* my potential. It's not up here"—he pointed at his head—"like we thought."

"You mean you found…?"

Neight Caster, they both thought at the same time.

Florence nodded. "Where?"

He rubbed the back of his neck and looked around the laboratory, uncertain.

"Understood. Well, if you know where to find him, I'd go there first."

"One thousand." Allister rose from the chair. And he'd only taken a few slow steps toward the exit before he turned back and looked her dead in the eyes. "You'll come when you can?"

She nodded. "You have my word."

The lab door slid closed on his heels, and Florence's thoughts returned to the surgically attached limb. She rubbed the calf, finding it smooth to the touch. Then she leaned over for a better view, and pressed down on one of the tiny purple crystals next to the knee. Their infusion could've been by natural causes or manmade manipulation.

Florence tilted her head back and tugged at her curls, unable to pinpoint the source of her lingering discomfort. The feeling was deep in her chest—constant, unsettling. Maybe it was time for her to go. Her office would be the perfect place for the remainder of her decompression anyway. From what she could tell, the Z-Lab was empty.

She was balanced at the cot's edge on her human foot, gathering the courage to stand, nervous as she prepared for the thud of a contraption that had to weigh as much as she. It touched the marble without a sound, not so much as a clink.

She breathed a sigh of relief.

"Glad to see you awake," said Dr. Giro from an unlit corner of the lab.

Startled, Florence gripped the cot for balance.

The doctor left the shadows with slow strides, hands tucked at his back, alternating from smirking at his feet to examining the monitors that were overpopulated with numbers, text, and images. He stopped to swipe through her digital chart. "You are quite a treasure, my fellow doctor," he said. "Quite a treasure."

"I suppose you're who I should thank," she said.

He leaned toward her and made a steeple with his hands. "If I accepted such validations. Sure. I take pride in my accomplishments today, though, I'm not sure you comprehend how close you were to elimination. I can only hope mercy will be a two-way street."

Hmph. Creepy choice of words.

She looked him over, aware thanks to his distance that the feeling in her chest was not hers but his. What she sensed in Dr. Giro was less discomfort...rather a disconnection...a sort of numbness in relation to all that had happened.

"It is called psibernetic technology," he said, luring her back to the conversation. "Note the spelling: *p-s-i*-bernetic. I confirmed your genetic adaptability to these little sychonium crystals before green-lighting surgery. Because, you see, they enhance psionic energy potential in special lineage of Evolutionaries. It would have been just as easy for your body to shut down in response to the enhancement as to evolve with it."

"Right. You expect me to believe you just happened to have a crystal-infused, psibernetic leg lying around?" she asked, then scoffed. "Please, forgive my skepticism."

"We are in the business of evolution, yes? Of preservation? Most certainly, yes. Then, better to be prepared."

But the size and shape, the weight and function. They were *perfect.* Prepared wasn't the word she'd use. Predictive, maybe.

She part hopped, part limped toward the exit. It was time for her to go.

"Are you feeling well enough to leave?" Dr. Giro asked. He disappeared behind her without waiting for an answer and busied himself with running water and sliding cabinets.

"It doesn't matter," she said, her hand stretching for the door. "As long as I'm unfit for fieldwork, my therapeutic services can be made available to the survivors."

"Is this the most you are willing to do to save the human race?"

She heard his shoes squeak as he neared her.

Apprehension caged her breaths, and she held them there, probing him for anything—shock, trauma, frustration. Shouldn't they be talking about C20's infiltration? About the fact that he was the last person to treat Captain Brandt? But just as the lab was still in pristine condition, even after bombs had taken out a third of the facility, there was no depth to Dr. Giro's thoughts, and for her, no reaching past the barrier to his feelings.

"I understand and respect your sincere dedication to your word," he said. "However...I'm sure there is a weapon more suited for war than your diagnoses. Do not forget it."

Florence twisted to face him with intended poise and authority. "Rabia—" she began. Her thought slammed to a halt, her words stuck on her tongue. She clutched her chest in silence at the sheathed blade in his upright palms. It was *her* sheathed blade.

"Do not forget it," he repeated, holding it to her.

She was drawn to the golden dragonhead handle, struck by the psionic connection tugging her fingers toward its rescue. Had he stolen the sword off her wall? She snatched it away from him and held it to her bosom, feeling violated. "How did you get this?"

"Ah, you are mistaken. Such treasure was never in my possession. No, I returned to you after you stabilized, and it was there, nestled next to you like a furry pet. You did not summon this heirloom?"

Florence caressed the circular shapes etched in leather and pulled the sword free to survey its condition. Double edged with an elevated sharpness in its center and serrated accents on its blade. "Summon it?" she said. "How would I... That's impossible..."

"I will leave you to solve the mysteries of the Belladonna lineage." Dr. Giro chuckled for a moment, then fixed his mouth to speak in seriousness. "I hear our Gateway will finally do what must be done for your salvation."

"As well he should."

"You will go with him, yes?" he asked, though he turned away as if expecting her not to answer.

Florence kept her eyes on Dr. Giro's clasped hands as he slinked back to the edge of the room.

"The path winds and splits when pursuing glory and significance," he said. He disappeared into the darkness of the corner, was seemingly smothered by it. What remained where he'd stood was a thin gray layer of shadowy mist.

She considered it, the sword gripped tight in her hand. *You will never find the answers you seek if the questions are always wrong, Dr. Florence Belladonna*, Neight had said.

She realized she'd never asked anyone about Dr. Giro's Evolutionary potential—specifically whether or not he had one. She took in the Z-Lab one more time. Yes, she told herself, perhaps she'd been asking the wrong questions.

As she turned to leave, Dr. Giro's voice echoed its way back to her. "When potential becomes power, it has the capacity to conjure the darkness and consume. Someone must make sure Allister does not go the way of his mentor, Captain Brandt. I can think of no better candidate than you."

CHAPTER 36

ALLISTER ADAMS
Quadrant Zeta—Restricted Access, Main Hangar, Andromeda Project Headquarters
Day 208

ALLISTER KNEW HE should've already left.

Instead, he lay curled on the floor outside of the hangar. His ratty book bag served as his pillow inside the drafty halls. The wall was his headboard, the concrete his mattress.

His mom's Cynque contact file was his sole respite from utter darkness, appearing as a square of light projected above his palm. In the main photo, her hair had no grays he could see, her smooth skin didn't wrinkle around the eyes, and her radiant smile sent warmth through him. He knew the photo was old if she was smiling. He couldn't remember the last time he'd seen his mom's teeth when she wasn't forcing words through them.

He closed his eyes for the dozenth time and tried to conjure some semblance of a plan. Though he hoped to catch a few minutes of sleep as a bonus, as he assumed being awake had delayed the improvement of his physical condition—his potential for molecular regeneration had never taken more than an hour to restore his body, let alone *hours*. His cuts scabbed over, but were still stinging, ready to bleed out if reopened. His spine and muscles still ached, reminding him he wasn't indestructible, that an army of plasma weapons, WarTencks, HellHunters, and whatever else C20 had were enough to stop him before he really got going.

Alone, he'd be outnumbered and outmaneuvered, on their terms and in their territory.

Too afraid to use the Z-energy.

That was why he couldn't go alone, he concluded yet again. He needed an ally, a powerful one, a trustworthy one—

Like Neight Caster.

Brandt didn't deserve his fear, and he imagined C20's surprise when he showed up with a creature as powerful as Neight on his side. They'd be shook.

He sighed at that, deciding to abandon the floor in search of the alien. Rest would have to wait because rescuing his mom couldn't.

Allister didn't feel as though he was being watched by the Project's authority with the same suspicion. He did, however, feel uneasy about being caught wandering around during such a tense time. He crept through the facility with caution, listening for the chatter of soldiers.

Just under twelve hours following the attack, the Andromeda Project still lay in shambles. He was overhearing conversations about a virus that had scrambled the entire security grid. How essential cloud data files had been scraped for keywords while engineering and research workflows were copied, then erased.

As he snuck around, the organization seemed beyond saving, gutted of its secrets and robbed of its infrastructure.

Allister witnessed injured agents collecting bodies and piling them in sealed-off storage rooms before lighting them on fire. After a few minutes, the hallways reeked of torched human flesh—a mix of old beef in a cast-iron skillet, the charcoal of a vintage grill, and sulfur.

Tragic.

The downfall was not Allister's failure to take responsibility for, and yet with all his strength potential, he couldn't handle the crushing weight.

A trio of Cynque lights flashed over the hallway's darkness. "Someone there?" Allister heard a soldier ask. "State your rank and designation! We've been ordered to…shoot…unknowns."

Allister jumped back and ducked into the nearest crevice, more out of habit from dealing with the District patrols than actual fear. He waited as the voices got louder, surprised to hear them second-guessing themselves, then second-guessing each other.

"Relax, mate… We cleaned out the rest of those See You In Twenty bastards," another said, cocking their plasma weapon. "But I swear if I catch another, I'm blasting them to bits."

The group of soldiers straggled by. "Stop being so jittery, man," scoffed a third while they went. "This is the fourth false flag for you."

"Yeah, just another dead body, I'm sure," said the first, sounding embarrassed.

Allister waited for their voices to disappear. He sank against the wall as they did, realizing for the first time he didn't know how to get back to the secret elevator.

The older parts of the Andromeda Project were constructed around the idea of a public-facing Evolutionary entity, Dr. Belladonna had said. The elevator would definitely be old if it ran along the digital spine of the Andromeda Project. Without ever seeing the base from the outside, it was beyond impossible to imagine the building's shape and whether the spine would be in the middle or at the back. Allister decided to start with the middle and stepped back into the hallway, prepared to keep looking.

Standing there waiting was Professor Ashur.

"Agent Adams," he said urgently.

Had the professor been waiting there *for him*?

Flustered, Allister stood paralyzed on his toes, his cheeks burning while he searched his feet for an explanation.

"Uh, hey, Professor," he stammered. "I was just—"

"I hate to pester you at such a challenging time," Professor Ashur said. "But you're needed. If you could spare ten minutes, I will let you get back to...your hostage crisis management."

Allister stared down the professor, a firm *no* forming in the back of his throat.

But Professor Ashur's glasses were dirty. His coat was soiled by blood and dust, and his hand, though clamped over his Cynque, trembled in a violent blend of anxiety and shock. It was clear he'd been rocked to his core and severely injured in the process.

Allister wondered where the professor had been during the attack and how he'd managed to survive. But his eyes narrowed, the impatience around finding Neight a barrier for any concern...

"Please...it is regarding your father's invention and the artifacts," the professor continued. "I am still not all the way myself...but I fear we may have misread the machine's purpose, and thus the artifacts' purpose as well."

"The artifacts?" Allister asked without thinking. "Yeah, I guess I'll have a look." Wouldn't be worth going all that way and not knowing the artifacts' purpose, he figured.

"My humblest thanks," the professor replied, bowing. "Please follow me at your own pace."

Allister obeyed, aware for the first time that he had never experienced that level of dignity or respect from anyone, let alone a *human.*

They entered a partially lit hallway and passed technicians who were reattaching electric wires severed from their wall fixtures. Professor Ashur offered them a thumbs-up as he and Allister rounded a soft corner with a crater in it. They walked a long stretch of hallway, passing corridors stained with more bodily fluids and stifled by the loitering smell of decay, shadows and light dancing across their faces.

Then a short, awkward elevator ride later, he and the professor were a few floors up, hurrying through the intersection of hallways linking the four main quadrants.

It was then Professor Ashur spoke. "Originally, I was trying to recreate a prototype of the Temporal Energy Wave Receiver. But after repeated and, admittedly, failed attempts to construct a plutonium core that wouldn't overload, I gave up. Now it is becoming even more clear how much I *didn't* know during that process. The miracle is that, when you activated the machine in De Los Muertos, it linked back to the magnificent system your father built here, transferring everything." The professor extended his hands to either side to show breadth, his smile so broad and bright it could be seen in Allister's peripheral vision. "The hypotheses, the trials, the results…they were all over the place, yes, drawing opposing conclusions, sure. But your father used another energy to power his device, the energy you two share. Z-energy."

He cut himself off when they reached the unhinged, busted-down door to his engineering lab. Once inside, Professor Ashur ripped off his coat and planted himself behind one of the few CPUs that didn't have its monitor smashed in.

"You see," the professor continued, "Patrick Adams was his own battery, and he made the machine work! Imagine with me, Agent Adams: this machine running unsupervised minute after minute, hour after hour, day after day, never draining our already-dwindling supply of power while gathering unprecedented amounts of information about"—he peeked around the computer, adjusted his glasses, and threw his finger in the air—"time!"

Allister found his astonishment hard to cover up as he approached the counter the professor sat behind. "Time?"

"Oh yes, time. More specifically, time energy. All along, the *T* in TEWR stood for Temporal…Energy Wave Receiver, as you probably knew, not Transportation Event…Wave Receiver, which is what myself and others assumed based on the idea of the artifacts as tools for transportive power."

Wow, Allister thought, *Pops really didn't spill a thing*.

A woman suddenly emerged from behind the same counter as Professor Ashur.

Artist: The CMD Studios

"Whoa!" Allister jumped back. "What gives?"

The professor gestured casually and said, "This is Assistant Professor Eileen Jordan, executive director of keeping me on my toes." He chuckled. Eileen didn't crack a smile. He cleared his throat, then rolled up his sleeves and corrected himself. "She is executive director of energy research and testing, and does not like my jokes."

From what Allister could see, Eileen had a thick waist and thicker thighs, a tiny computer installed in the side of her head, and the kind of heart-shaped cheeks you pinched, though she didn't appear keen on being touched. At all. She eyed a loose strand of her wild, fluffy afro while chewing a wad of gum with her whole mouth, seemingly bored of her own introduction.

"Professor Jordan," Professor Ashur said with uneasy laughter. "We have guests…"

Finally, she glanced at Allister sideways from behind the round frames of her glasses and pursed her plentiful lips in acknowledgment. "This is him?" she asked, sounding unimpressed. "Whatever."

Allister's neck jerked back at her obvious dismissal. He didn't know whether to be offended or defensive or both. He decided on a sarcastic salute in response. "Golden… Nice to meet you, too, yeah?"

"Sooo…," Eileen began, rolling her eyes, "Professor Ashur is referring to this machine's ability to measure time, or more scientifically, temporal energy, and track the side effects of its presence on Earth." She moved her hands with a confident fluidity, and, peering closer, Allister was almost certain the technology implanted in her wrists and fingers cynqued to some system in the room. He knew for sure when she flicked all ten fingers in the air and brought to life a digital screen.

The material was thin enough it could only be seen by the dimension of the graphics displayed on it. The data and images followed her sweeping hand motions as she filled him in on the backstory. "During one of Professor Ashur's… uhm…escapades with a certain Bridget Sparks, she pointed out that the waves in the Earth's electromagnetic field were folding and disappearing into some mega-massive energy anomaly surrounding De Los Muertos, and when I say mega, like, I mean *mega*."

Allister couldn't have put it better himself. Bridget and Professor Ashur in an entanglement and the electromagnetic field folding was big enough news without the energy anomaly she'd mentioned after it. He wondered what the folding could mean, and if the anomaly would eventually cause the apocalypse.

"We started to get curious about 2035, the year of the earthquake that caused De Los Muertos," Professor Ashur said.

With widened eyes, Allister added, "The year the states started becoming sanctuaries."

Eileen nodded. Her hands expanded, as did the data. She arranged his dad's compiled recap of the fateful mission, the mission during which Southern California was nearly tipped into the ocean and the artifacts were lost. "Soooo, yeah. My team and I revisited the sequence of events through backed-up files of energy readings and video surveillance inside the facility," she said, her chewing that much louder now. "In these postmortem reports, Professor Adams states that they lost the artifacts' location and their energy signature after the earthquake hit and disabled the machine."

Allister watched the short sequence of events replay—first, his dad, Captain Brandt, Naorima Delemar, and a fourth unknown individual reached an area where the TEWR had calculated was the artifacts' present location. Next, the machine's readings became unstable and the connection to the temporal energy waned. There was yelling and shouting and visible panic, then a few glitches in the footage and in the scenery in the background. And lastly…well, the last bit was where Allister started to get confused. All at once, or so it seemed, the earthquake shook the city to pieces, the machine lost the connection to the artifacts, and the location his dad and the others had stood in front of collapsed in an overwhelming glitch of light.

"Wait, go back," he said.

Eileen did.

His elbows were resting on the counter. His nose was pushed right up to the footage. He watched it again and again and again, more fascinated with each replay.

Though the failure and catastrophe blurred together within the span of a minute and thirteen seconds, the machine's failure came *before* the catastrophe for the third time.

"Oh my God, did you see that?" he asked, pointing frantically as he stammered out the rest of his discovery. "They—they dipped out, they *poof*, they just— Tell me you saw that!"

The two professors didn't seem to follow.

"The giant glitch, people." Allister thrust both hands at the graphed energy wave frequencies in one corner, then the found footage of the Andromeda Project's team. "The temporal energy readings tick up exponentially until this moment, then they just, like, vanish, and there are one hundred seconds missing before the earthquake hit. It's a temporal anomaly." He cupped his own forehead in genuine surprise. "Do you know what this means?"

Professor Ashur pushed up his glasses and looked back at the screen, revisiting the temporal wave frequencies.

Impatient, Allister answered his own question. "The earthquake didn't just happen. It was triggered by this mega eruption of temporal energy."

"My, my, my," the professor mumbled. "This changes many things." He nudged Eileen aside and rushed back and forth between his monitor and hers. Determination was woven into his twisted mouth, his attention submerged in every sequence the TEWR had recorded during its active time, even the most recent thirty minutes before it was blasted to pieces. Ashur drew circles around individual events and time stamps, labeled them with dates, and connected them in sequences intended to be linear that were not. Allister watched, in awe of the quickness with which Ashur found and corrected his own mistakes.

The professor shook his head when he was finished. "Not one hundred seconds—one hundred years," he said in a hushed tone. He re-circled other countries that had suffered catastrophic disasters in the two previous decades. "There are multiple regional accelerations or decelerations of time here. The tectonic movement experienced on the West Coast is a hundred years off. The oceanic patterns where the big storm is brewing in the Pacific, almost ten thousand years old."

What happened during the latest mission to De Los Muertos was now clear to Allister. The chains rusting and breaking while the soldiers were scattered to dust, too, made sense.

Rogue temporal energy.

Allister felt the post-traumatic stress building in him. It was wild to consider— that they'd crossed into an entire region massacred by the instability of time.

Professor Ashur keyed in a command to project a map of the world and its remaining territory on the screen. Eileen made the West Coast a bit bigger and separated it from the rest of the North American continent. Afterward, she stepped back to look at the whole picture.

"It's a hole," said Allister.

"It's a rift," Eileen corrected. "A giant temporal rift in—what did you call it, Ashur?—the ass of America."

Allister rolled his eyes, scoffing at the need for delineation. "Rift. Hole. Whatever you want to call it, it checks out for the apocalyptic super-typhoon theory." With a swipe of his hand, he moved the image farther west and pressed his fingers together on a distorted spot growing in the South Pacific. It enlarged at his touch, making visible the massive typhoon swirling off the coast of Papua New Guinea. "How many days until that cluster becomes a full-blown world-finisher?"

"You mean to bring on the 'big biblical flood'?'" Eileen asked, using actual air quotes. "Mmm, I don't know that I'm totally sold on that little detail."

"You should be," Professor Ashur said. "The elemental activity inside this temporal rift is accelerating exponentially. I suspect this will become the predicted supercluster of typhoons and move inland, taking out anything less than fifteen hundred meters above sea level before we lose three more days."

Eileen crossed her arms, narrowed her eyes at something behind him, and hissed with the wad of gum in her cheek. "For clock's sake..."

"Look at you, mates, bein' all smart without me," came Bridget's voice from the door.

Allister whipped around, relieved to find her unharmed and in a somewhat stable mood. "Sparks," he said, nudging his chin toward her.

"Adams," mocked Bridget, doing the same.

She walked by him seductively, letting her hand drag across his shoulder until she passed. "Boy, the look on you guys' faces right now is...shocking. Anyhoo, I was kind of listening in on what you two geniuses and Miss Pouty Jordan were raging about, and I don't want to, like, make things less fun for you, but"—Bridget smirked—"did you decide when the artifacts plan on transporting and, you know, ripping Earth a new one?"

Transporting? Ripping Earth...a new one? Allister's brow was furrowed in confusion, his mouth turned up with skepticism. He couldn't tell if she was being the typical loud, attention-craving Bridget, or if she was trying to tell them something important.

She gave him a playful wink as if to answer his question. "They're going to move again—just like they did in 2035. What happens then, hmm?" She imitated the tearing of loose-leaf. "Another rip in time."

Crystals of *Temporal* Transportation—they weren't just moving around Earth, they were moving through time.

Dread forced him backward toward the door. "The artifacts don't want to be found. That's why they keep moving," Allister said, finally looking up at the three of them. Before anyone could address his statement, he turned, stumbling as he ducked past the opening and exited into the hallway.

He didn't know which direction was right, just that he needed to free Neight Caster. Immediately.

——

Artist: The CMD Studios

CHAPTER 37

ALLISTER ADAMS
Quadrant Zeta—Restricted Access, Tenth Floor, Andromeda Project Headquarters
Day 208

THERE WERE TWELVE hours left in Day 208. Allister had about two of those hours to figure out how *not* to cause the apocalypse while rescuing his mom.

He knew the elevator he'd taken down to the tenth floor wouldn't lead to the section of the Vault where Neight was being held. That had him racing through the crisscrossed hallways toward the hangar, fighting for his breath and sense of clarity as he went. He'd decided to use that as a starting point because it faced the District and would make it easier to find the center of the facility.

Allister took a hard right and sprinted faster, knocking through a quartet of soldiers on the way. Their angry shouts disappeared behind him as he ducked around another charred corner. He ran the full way and braced himself, arms over his face while he charged toward, then through, a windowless door nestled in steel framing. The door swung off the hinges from the force, which he ignored along with its loud crashing against the wall.

As he continued running, he registered that the interior of the narrow corridor he'd burst into appeared undisturbed. No weathered look. No violent damage. He slowed his steps and, breathing heavily, progressed cautiously down the hallway, unsure what part of the base he'd reached and how it could've possibly been spared.

Here, the floors were polished and smooth, the walls clean and painted, still proudly branded with the seven founding sanctuaries above the Andromeda Project's large logo.

But if C20 hadn't made it there, then the main hangar wasn't close, and neither was the tiny vintage elevator.

Allister turned back. On his way, he passed an office door with a partially scratched-away name on it, almost tripping as he backtracked to try to read it.

PR-F--SOR P--RIC- ADA-S it said.

His heart skipped several beats, his mind filling in the blanks.

Professor Patrick Adams, it would've read.

"Pops...," Allister said, hesitating.

A room with his dad's name on it could've been full of anything—research, *secrets.*

Entering felt right, even with such little time left. He checked the hallway in both directions, then forced the door open to a shallow workspace with unfinished floors and concrete walls.

Everything was from a time of transition. The wooden desk. The cushioned chair with legs. At least a decade worth of dust. He waved it away, annoyed and trying not to inhale, no longer wondering why his dad's work didn't exist in Cynque databases. The desk was stacked with real papers, surrounded by towers of handwritten notebooks. All of his dad's knowledge was where he wanted it to be and nowhere else.

Allister's throat was scratchy, his eyes watering. The dust wasn't to blame. It was the connection.

His dad had been there, had *worked* there.

Allister sat at the desk, upright and proud, as he imagined his dad would have. Smiling softly, he flipped through a stack of papers, then thumbed through a series of brightly colored notebooks.

Nothing was labeled. There were pages upon pages of information, equations, sketches, languages…and though Allister wanted to believe there was some missing link he'd been guided there to discover, he started to think that maybe he'd just gotten lost.

It would take days to read through all this, Pops.

Allister swiveled in the chair, agitation rising through him. He was about ready to get up and leave when his foot brushed against a single notebook.

You're Not Lost if You're Here the cover said in big, scribbled letters.

Squinting, Allister leaned down, curious at the notebook's convenient separation from the others, the fact that it was the only one of them with a title, and its strange, hard-to-stain blue color.

He stopped cold.

It wasn't just *a* notebook; it was *the* notebook from his dad's video transcripts.

Allister stared at it, wide-eyed, his hand paralyzed above the cover. He couldn't believe it was still around, let alone at his feet. Swallowing the strange feeling of coincidence, he finished picking it up off the floor and opened it to a natural crease in the binding.

The month and year was written in the top corner: November 2040. On the page, a passage or a poem had been scribbled in an alien language. Allister struggled to read it the first and second time. But he began recognizing some of the characters from his memory and tried again. The words rose to his eyes as if by magic. He swore he heard his dad's voice reading them.

> *There comes a time when we must see, what lies below and underneath,*
> *and in the times when we think most clear, a mist will drape reality.*
> *Look ahead to a future that begins and ends with the power of Z.*
> *Look ahead for a human savior and you will see only an Evolutionary.*
> *Beware the leaders delivered from wombs of tragedy.*
> *Reject the kings and queens who sit on thrones built of poverty.*
> *Many faces yet one name sever peace with blades of irony.*
> *Open your eyes to your enemy and you will see twenty.*

In the next paragraphs, his dad did his best to explain the meaning of the passage, and while doing so, revealed that it had come to Neight Caster in a dream. Nodding thoughtfully, Allister turned the page.

What his dad had written there was hard for him to comprehend, given the almost-impossible-to-read handwriting and metaphysical subject matter. But he struggled through the text a few more times.

From the bits he gathered, his dad believed the alien's words were a gateway. The utterance of possibility, the notion of what lay beyond that which could be seen, touched, smelled, tasted, or heard at any given moment. His dad seemed driven to do more than detect temporal waves. He claimed to have followed their erratic frequencies—tracked them to their destinations and traced them back to their origins. Near the end of the second page, his dad described his study, including a giant digital screen with a bunch of pins in it trying to link events from the future to their catalysts in the past.

A digital screen that no longer existed.

Allister looked up just to be sure. He closed the notebook to let the ideas sink in, took a deep breath, and opened to another page.

Daal Trelkkien was drawn near the top in the language's original characters. The English translation—"Crystals of Temporal Transportation"—was absent, unnecessary for comprehension, Allister guessed. His dad described the crystal artifacts as a representation of hope—a chance for humanity to harness the power of time and course-correct before time ran out. The language on that page was different from the first, though alien as well, and it was below that drawing and its explanation two lines extended: one line attached to the idea of Ele Trahluth, one attached to the idea of Ile Tainvorl.

Allister was surprised enough that he could decipher the characters; he didn't expect to know what any of them meant. He traced the shapes and symbols surrounding each one, vague allusions to what significance they held.

This notebook had more clarity and focus than the pages he'd found at his mom's house, as if after 2035, his dad's knowledge had begun to surpass human reason, then reached its peak just before he died in 2040. But from the notes he'd written, his dad still couldn't seem to figure out what the concepts represented and how they related to the artifacts.

Because he'd run out of time.

Allister ran both hands through his afro, a sadness tugging the corners of his mouth into a frown.

It hurt his head to think about, made him dizzy to confront the existence of those same five years…the blanked-out years he couldn't remember.

"Location-triggered interactive correspondence, activated," Cynque said. "Retrieving."

Allister's heartbeat slowed and so did his movements; he knew what that ticking sound meant. A digital transmission was loading, and it was probably from his dad.

"Retrieving," repeated Cynque.

Allister would've been fine with just an outline of his dad's wild hair and upright shoulders, content to witness a depiction of his warm smile and be the object of his loving gaze, all in full color. But as with most things involving his dad, the transmission went above and beyond.

His dad's face shimmered into view, projected outward as a hologram instead of appearing above the device as a video. The light construct continued fleshing out his compact torso, his unusually large hands, and his long, lanky legs. In the end, his dad's luminous form was presented center stage and life-size, no longer attached to Cynque and tangible enough to envision him standing in that room twelve years prior.

Allister's mouth fell open, his heart beating faster as he realized the meaning of the word *interactive*.

His dad gestured for him to come closer. "Come here, son," he said. "I know you're probably scared. But you know, being brave ain't really about not being scared."

Allister took the softest, slowest steps, and halted at every random creak in the floor or glitch in the hologram, afraid the image might disappear or, worse, be scrambled into oblivion. His hands were soaked with sweat and shaking as, having crossed the room, he stood so close he could smell the cinders on the plaid of his dad's shirt.

Unreal, he thought, touching the fabric and feeling its texture. Even as he tried dismissing the reality, his dad offered him a hug, careful to position his arms at Allister's *current* height before he pulled him in and squeezed.

His dad rubbed his back and held him as only a father could. Hard enough to melt Allister around the edges while reinforcing him at the core.

The lightness he felt warmed him to tears. "How is this…possible?" he choked out.

"I started digging into the nature of temporal energy, testing it on a small scale." His dad paused, as if he might tell Allister how, then continued without doing so. "I probably saw a few things I shouldn't have seen… Anyway, in the end, technology was how I cracked the code and transcended the barrier of a linear time sequence." He kissed the top of Allister's head. "That's how I found you here."

Allister couldn't stay composed. His mind was wrestling with a tragedy he didn't remember and their tender reunion, which to him was becoming more and more inconceivable.

"I should've stopped," his dad admitted, hugging Allister tighter, maybe after feeling him tremble. "I saw the end of our family coming and I didn't stop. I thought the end of humanity was more important."

He knew the feeling that was tensing his muscles. Resentment. There was no point in succumbing to it. Should he rip himself away and sulk inside the dim office, he was sure he wouldn't be seen or acknowledged—for their interaction, while unique, seemed programmed.

"I hope one day you can forgive me, son," his dad said.

Again, Allister surrendered to the gentleness in his dad's touch, understood the measure of his pride and the fierceness of his determination.

Allister nodded, pretty much all he could bring himself to do, wanting to give his dad the forgiveness he'd projected himself into the future for. Would his dad know if he hugged back in acknowledgment or uttered, *Yes, I forgive you*? Were they connected inside the continuum by a carefully sewn thread? Or separated by timelines too thin to prevent such a violation?

He didn't know much about how time worked.

As if to ease his worry, his dad rubbed Allister's head once more and held him at arm's length, a firm grip on his shoulders. "My little EV," he said, his smile returning. "Difference is you can't die easy like I can. I'm thankful as hell to Neight for that."

When his dad let go, Allister breathed in gratitude and breathed out relief. His dad's smile was, hopefully, an indication that on some level he'd perceived their interaction and wouldn't carry any guilt into the coming days—his last days.

"I'm glad you made it over here. It's hard to find on purpose. Probably took you a couple laps." His dad chuckled. "Can't have anyone digging through my work... Follow me, somethin' I have to show ya."

The hologram of his dad turned away.

Allister grabbed the blue notebook before following him out of the room and deeper into the unexplored wing of the Andromeda Project. He eyed every room they passed, wondering if they were just like his dad's office: abandoned evidence as to their slow downfall, a clue to their inevitable failure. Clutching the notebook close to his pounding chest, Allister checked over his shoulder for the lieutenant or the general or any soldier. These were halls they were likely to reinforce after C20's attack, guarding their well-kept secrets and past mistakes.

"It's 2040 when and where I am," his dad revealed, a sudden despair in his voice.

Allister took a sharp breath, troubled by the change in tone.

It didn't have to be mentioned that 2040 was the year his dad died, but as he recounted his years of service as an Evolutionary, tragedy weighing on his every word, he seemed to know he was lost to the Andromeda Project. Yet he spoke of fearing something far worse: losing the artifacts a second time because Allister's potential wasn't fully realized.

They came to a stop at a set of double doors. The entrance was twice Allister's height, and wide as the hallway itself.

His dad went ahead and entered his credentials in the illuminated square keypad.

"CynqueID, Professor Patrick Adams, accepted. Please say the access phrase," Cynque requested.

His dad nodded to him. "The other one," he said.

Allister hid his face behind the notebook. He didn't want to say it.

"Please say the access phrase," Cynque repeated.

"Go on, son," his dad urged. "Don't be afraid."

"Nournt Zeorgen," mumbled Allister.

The voice-recognition light display squiggled and jumped. "Access phrase confirmed: Begins with Z-energy."

A tiny sparkle of blue energy flowed from Allister's arm, twisted in the air, and zoomed through the lock mechanism. The massive doors chugged to either side.

A burst of brilliance from inside the room lit Allister's pupils with the inescapable blue from his veins. Despite its enormous size, the room was dwarfed by an ominous machine. This machine, unlike the TEWR, appeared freshly built, filling almost every square meter with a stretch of digital panels, and nearly touching the ceiling with towering metal coils and the glass sphere that was encased inside them.

"This is the Z-Energy Containment Center, or ZECC for short," his dad said, presenting the machine as its proud inventor.

Allister was frozen at the entrance. "This…this is what?" he asked.

His dad continued, again with such accurate timing. "The ZECC. I designed it to house the pure energy of manifestation…known to you as the Z-energy. For now, it is where all Z-energy potential is drawn from."

The ZECC's prisoner was as his mom had said…the Z-energy, howling something fierce like a beast behind the glass. Imprisoned as it was, it seemed to dance for him in sweeping, fiery rotations. He suspected it spun faster than a hurricane's top speed, rotating on its axis like an extraplanetary storm. Though whenever the energy tried to escape, the output was captured by the metal coils and redirected back into the volatile mass.

Allister walked forward feeling more astonishment than he thought possible. Of all that he had seen, experienced, or imagined, the Z-energy's purity was by far the most magnificent.

The proximity toasted his insides against the chill of the room. Energy surges snaked down his arms and consumed his fist. Soon, he'd face the sensation of tiny needles shooting up as if launched from his bloodstream. Then the stinging would commence.

He looked down at his arm, waiting, braced for one, or the other, or both. Neither happened.

"Now, see, your potentials will execute on your intention, if you let 'em," his dad said. "Just connect to the source *of*."

Allister was nodding in agreement, his palm opened, now rampant with crackling bolts.

The Z-energy was mega in every sense of the word. He felt seduced by it, distracted from the damage it had caused and concerned only with its alluring shape and color and consciousness.

Next to him, his dad glitched, hard, fast.

"Thinkin' one of those two experiments will protect you long enough to get the artifacts, but I don't know which one," his dad said, sighing.

Queasiness crept through Allister. He loosened his hold on the notebook and kneeled.

"Protect your mother the way I couldn't, remind her she's got gifts of her own," his dad continued, hands clasped on where Allister's shoulders would be if he were standing. "Hate to say it, but it's up to you… The crystal artifacts must be found—now. Their disappearance is a defense mechanism. That means if they sense anybody that's not supposed to get too close"—his dad snapped his fingers—"they skip town, just like that."

Allister must've been standing in an alternate version of the events, because his dad hugged the air one last time, pulled away, and smiled into no one's eyes. He knew then that his dad couldn't experience in the past what Allister himself experienced in the present, that his actions were based on what he expected to happen and didn't account for any disruptions in the timeline.

For instance, the sudden onset of Allister's sickness. "Pops…," he muttered, one arm stretched toward him.

"Be proud of who we are. We're Evolutionaries," his dad said, flexing one of his thin biceps with a clenched fist. "Be brave, son, but don't be foolish."

Allister fought through his nausea, determined to make it to his dad. The light construct of him folded in fast on itself and disappeared into the air where Allister's Cynque *would've been*, if he were standing.

The console blurred in front of him. His legs wobbled beneath him. Suddenly, he was snatched back to those moments of acute pain in De Los Muertos, the discomfort so similar to what he'd felt there that he began to believe his experience with time was different than everyone else's.

In the previous instance, the temporal rift could've been the reason. Perhaps the anomaly caused residual waves of temporal energy to circulate inside the rift, and a number of them had torn through him and those soldiers as some byproduct of instability. In the current instance, it could've been *anything*: his dad's disruption, the split of what was meant to happen and what actually did—two timelines crisscrossing as a result.

Allister felt himself stabilizing and looked up, just as the incessant humming he'd written off as background noise came to a slow and steady stop.

The typhoon raging inside the Z-energy sphere had been replaced by a sleeping silhouette of feminine inspiration. The body was not human: it had a pointed chin and narrow face, smaller spiked protrusions on its clavicle, and an expansion of hair that transformed into the energy. It glowed even in its dormancy, thin squiggly lines detailing appendages with three fingers and three toes each.

Artist: The CMD Studios

Allister stumbled away at the sight and turned to exit the open door.

"Agent Adams, is that you?" Dr. Giro asked, approaching from the hallway.

Allister tried to conceal the notebook with his forearms. "Hey, Doctor…what was it…Giro?" he said.

Dr. Giro stopped at the door and leaned forward. "Correct. Are you not on your way out?" the doctor said. "The artifacts await their Gateway. The mother awaits her...absolution."

"Yeah, I'm with it."

Dr. Giro strolled past him into the room with his hands tucked in his coat, stopping in the place where his dad had stood. It was the first time Allister saw the gray mist drifting around the doctor's perimeter.

That doctor was beyond strange, borderline chilling.

"Stay the path," said Dr. Giro without facing him. "I suspect your potential will become power soon, too."

The gnawing in Allister's insides rose again. A nausea too similar to what he'd felt in De Los Muertos and near the ZECC. Confused as to why Dr. Giro would make him sick to his stomach, he rushed out of the room. The hallway's fresh air cooled his face, settled his stomach, cleared his thoughts.

The secret elevator has to be around here somewhere.

He paused.

Or maybe...it was on the other side.

It would make sense to keep Neight and the ZECC separated—no way they'd want the alien close to the source of his power.

With the notebook tucked under his armpit, Allister backtracked his way through the facility, head down. He turned as many corners as he'd turned the first time, careful to nod and salute any soldiers he passed to avoid suspicion. Finally, the charred hallways he'd been searching for greeted him with wide, bloodstained floors and high, ash-soaked ceilings.

Ding.

He made his way toward the noise, inching along the wall, his head whipping behind him every so often to make sure he was alone. And there, at the end of the bloodiest hallway, the secret elevator waited for him with doors opened.

To the depths of the Vault Allister went.

—▬—

WHAT DO YOU LOSE YOURSELF IN? WHERE HOURS, EVEN WHOLE DAYS CAN BE LOST WITHOUT NOTICE? IF EVERYTHING IS HAPPENING AT ONCE, WHAT THREADS WILL YOU CHOOSE TO FOLLOW?

CHAPTER 38

ALLISTER ADAMS

Quadrant Zeta—Restricted Access, Tenth Floor, Andromeda Project Headquarters

Day 208

ALLISTER RISKED RETURNING to Neight's sanctuary for help while not knowing what help even looked like.

He slipped the notebook from under his arm and flipped through the pages, prepared to find more random drawings and ramblings in languages he didn't understand. His dad's theories led nowhere, at least within the notebook, and the page-long equations held no answers. He started to wonder if there was another in the stack that had the same information but complete.

He slammed the book shut and shoved it back under his arm.

His hand now rested on the wall where his mom had rested hers, the blame for her capture still simmering in his stomach. *Protect your mother the way I couldn't. Remind her she's got gifts of her own,* his dad had said.

Gifts of her own…, Allister thought, *like a glare so sharp it could cut to the truth.*

The elevator opened to the underworld of the Vault, which looked no different from the Olympus Allister had left. Wires swung loose from the ceiling. Lights buzzed and sparked on either side of the corridor and along the edges. Digital files flickered like fireflies above wide, leftover puddles on the floor. Allister rushed through the living library his dad had built, spinning around himself, pausing only briefly in another moment of awe as it rebooted, recategorized, and restored itself.

After he'd made it to the other side, he stood in front of the sanctuary entrance. Then, still juiced up on his dad's encouragement, he shoved his hand through it and whispered, "Nournt Zeorgen." Z-energy burned from the wall's center to the edges, unraveling the makeshift barrier. He ducked and stepped through with caution. "Neight?" he called.

Last he remembered, plasma weapons had blown through everything, so he expected to see the room still in shambles. But to his astonishment, shattered plexiglass displays had been fused back together. Filaments burned bright and full. Artifacts that had been knocked out of place were repositioned in their meticulous arrangement, complete with information placards in their native alien tongue.

Here, in the middle of restored tranquility, the fallen king sat cross-legged in the air, meditating.

Allister marched to the glass, speaking fast. "I need your help, Neight. C20's got my mom, and I swear they'll do something to her if I don't get them the artifacts. Which is twisted cuz if I don't get the artifacts, they're gonna move through time again and finish off humanity."

The scaly skin on Neight's forehead wrinkled. His meditation ended, no doubt earlier than he'd planned.

"Mmm…the mysteries of courage and temporal transportation elude you no longer. Impressive," Neight said. "It has been centuries since I was asked to fight another's war." He stared at his claws with remorse, as if they dripped with the blood of the lives he'd taken. His fist closed. "I cannot fight on your behalf. Despite my compassion for you and your mother, it is not within reason."

"What? You…you mean…you don't care if she…if she…" He couldn't finish and tapped his foot, frustrated by Neight's refusal. "What about humanity? You good with us getting taken out? Eliminated?"

Neight stared at him, his thick lips sealed together beneath his tiny flared nostrils.

The heat of impatience stewed in Allister. He refused to look away, and, jaw clenched, he balled his fists and stepped up to the glass until his nose touched it. "Really, nothing?" he shouted.

"It is…complex," Neight eased out, speaking in a way so unbothered, it was almost indifference.

"Don't see anything complex about it. Either you care, or you don't."

"Oh, I care." Neight's eyes transformed from a glowing yellow to a fierce blue. "It was my prophecies that pinpointed the year of your apocalypse, and therefore, they are the reason for the countdown," he said. "208 days and 12 hours *exactly*, am I correct? How divine. How…*cosmic*. Perhaps it was my limited understanding of the human and the human function, to where I assumed my proposed solution, the artifacts, would be sought in unity and not in division."

Neight's feet dropped from under him and touched the floor. As he spoke, his confessions flowed out of him like centering breaths. "When I landed on your world, I was presented with the foundation of all that would come to be, as the answers stood before me in the wooded miracle of your earthen countryside. I witnessed firsthand a...transformation...these fleeting bits of cosmic heritage blooming inside teenage bodies, Dolores Primrose and Patrick Adams. Stellar ingredients—in my humble observation—needing a mere spark of Z-energy to start the flame." The alien hesitated, that same look of remorse crossing his face. "I would never declare myself an instrument of havoc. But human genetic heritage was not a thing I yet fully understood. It was clear that within your DNA and the DNA of all Earth's Evolutionaries there had always been the coding for potentials. Those in your father and others, were ignited upon *my* arrival, while you and the remaining had your potentials ignited upon *the* Arrival."

Neight then looked over at Allister, his lip turned up on one side in an almost smile. "Here you are, Allister Adams—an Evolutionary filled with potential and good intention and connection to a heritage greater than you could imagine. You are the nucleus. You are the epicenter of change, and thereby consequence. You are the Gateway."

Allister had been waiting for something useful to slide off Neight's sharpened tongue. He shook his head, the impatience in his body moving toward rage. He didn't care about human DNA or prophecies or arrivals. He already knew he was the Gateway. And the more he thought about how Neight had managed to—in a long, drawn-out string of confessions—dodge the original question, the higher his shoulders rose.

He walked away from the glass, abandoning any composure. "Now I'm with it," Allister said tightly. He pointed back at the glass, again and again at the start of each sentence. "You stirred up this underground war of survival and dragged my family into it. You convinced my pops to build containment centers and detection machines instead of sticking around to watch me grow up...because of this stupid Z-energy and those stupid artifacts."

"I convinced him with your conception," Neight said, his tone hardened. "Patrick was in search of the same thing as you, understanding, purpose, acceptance. He did not know why his mind worked the way it did, why his knowledge far surpassed the sum of his experiences, and humanity's as well. He thought he was insane, the makings of a maddened, power-obsessed creature. Tortured by the dreams and visions of the formulas your planet hadn't discovered, the energies absent from your spectrum. I brought him that understanding from the stars."

"From the stars? Cut the crap, Neight—"

"I restored his trust in the unknown," the alien interrupted. "It was with that same trust he took you in his arms and held you, taught you, worshipped you. Patrick was devoted to your protection... He knew he must die so that you could live, so you all could live, and so he made his choice."

"Yeah, well he made a terrible choice!" shouted Allister. "You were supposed to help us, and you were nowhere to be found. And"—he choked at the epiphany—"he lost his life because of it, didn't he?"

Neight's eyes fell.

Allister couldn't tell why—guilt? regret? Perhaps the having to guess was what pushed him over the edge. Blood filled Allister's face and rage filled his throat. "Didn't he?" he screamed, punching the glass with an energy-charged fist.

Spiderweb cracks in the glass spiraled away from the impact. Allister recoiled and held his flashing hand against himself, ashamed of the outburst, unsure of his intention. The energy had never showed up like that before. *Freely.* Allister palmed the tears that ran down his cheeks, pausing a moment before he spoke again, this time, his voice softer. "How could you let him die?" His heart contracted at the question that had been too suffocating to keep inside. "If anyone could've protected him, it was you."

And still, nothing.

Neight stretched his claws and muttered something that ended in *Zeorgen.*

The energy twisted away from Allister's arm, snaked through the cracks in the glass, and fused the material solid again.

"Captain Brandt wasn't lying about one thing, you only care about yourself," Allister said as he walked toward the exit. "At least he chose a side."

"I can only blame negligence for my inability," Neight said at his back. "For on the night of the Arrival, I perished before Patrick Adams."

Allister heard: *I perished for Patrick Adams.* He slowed down and gripped the notebook tighter.

Blue light consumed the room from behind him. He heard flames crackling in the air just before claws scraped the granite floor.

Another experiment? It had to be, when the sound of those claws neared Allister's heels. Through the reflection in another display case, he saw Neight towering at his back, at least two feet taller. The hairs on Allister's neck stood up. He swallowed, somewhat unnerved by their proximity, and at the same time, comforted by it.

"I could not save your father from death with my power because I, myself, was mangled by her will," Neight continued. "I learned then, that it is not sustainable for me to attach to, care for, and protect every human life I encounter. I can, however, provide passing wisdom, new knowledge, and expanded perspective. Which is why, thankfully, no matter how I am taken apart mentally or physically, my atoms will eventually rebuild and reshape and reignite the energy that is in me, and therefore is me. Such a potential allows me to, with sincerity and courage, exist here, to provide you with passing wisdom, new knowledge, and expanded perspective. Regeneration is a potential woven within your genetic matrix, among many others. All of them gifts to guide your being."

Allister let the answer stream through him, fill the fire pits of his rage and sorrow, washing away the flames. But he knew he couldn't wait any longer to master his potentials. His mom needed saving now. He lowered his head, still unwilling to face Neight. "I can't use the energy around people if I don't know how to."

"Sometimes our potentials fail us, even when we are filled with good intention and—exploit centuries of discipline. I beg you not to worry *how* you do what it is you must do. You need only worry that you *be* who you are to do what you must do."

"And who is that?" Allister asked.

"It is for you to discover, I suppose." Neight's heavy hand pressed down on Allister's shoulder. "I am a being of my word; it is everything to me. I promise I did everything to save Patrick Adams, everything that did not violate human laws of time and existence."

"So you can't help me?"

Neight removed his hand. "You have your father's conviction."

"I'll take that as a no."

Allister began walking away. His anger felt misplaced. But so did Neight's refusal. As he reached the exit, darkness moved aside for him like a parting crowd, and on the other side, an arena of downfall and destruction waited for him.

"Do you remember our first encounter?" Neight called out. "Atop the fresh green blades at your home. I believe what you call a 'summer' storm had passed in previous hours, one of the worst in your season."

Allister's heart fluttered and beat faster as the memory arrived through feeling. Intense danger and overwhelming fear on the one hand, a tender warmth and connection on the other.

"When you are home, the storm does not touch you. You are safe. You are comfortable," the alien said. "You are not home anymore, Allister. You are here with me, in the cosmic wilderness. This storm is not the worst there could be nor the worst that has ever been."

Allister stepped back instead of stepping forward, took a deep breath, and faced Neight. The alien's soft yellow eyes peered at him above the spurs on his bony cheeks and his fanged, crooked mouth.

"When the storm is strongest, fear will wrap its arms around you. Persuade you to go back home and stay there. For if you continue, you will be faced with the deepest darkness within you and this universe." The alien's clawed hands folded over his torso. "But, it is at your deepest and darkest that you get the choice to be your greatest self."

Neight leaped backward into the air, arms outstretched like wings, talons curled as if they carried freshly caught prey. He dissolved into particles and materialized behind the glass.

Allister nodded, absentmindedly lifting his left arm as he took in the alien's wisdom. "Thanks, Neight," he said. For some reason, his elbow was bent, and his fist was at eye level.

"Study the pages your father left. They hold secrets you will find nowhere else." Neight bowed and returned to his meditative stance, then held his arm in the same position. "You must go," he said, thrusting it forward. "For lack of better words, it—is—time."

———

CHAPTER 39

LIEUTENANT LEESA DELEMAR

Quadrant Alpha—Executive Wing, Andromeda Project Headquarters
Day 208

C20 WAS PLAYING chess for their win.

Leesa knew Allister, the pawn, had been called to retrieve the artifacts in exchange for his mother's life. She also knew, with the entirety of her being, he would give them up for her.

Without the artifacts, Leesa would be terminated. And she refused to let that happen after how hard she'd fought to *live*.

She returned to her office but swept past where she usually stopped, her desk, and opened the sliding door to her living quarters. The space was pristine, hardly used, save for the bed a few hours a night for sleep. On a wall-mounted screen, she reviewed images of her thirteenth birthday, which had been celebrated while she was on bed rest. A time of white walls and name tags and bland food, CT scans and MRIs, blood transfusions and organ replacements. All circulating a lifelong battle with a genetic autoimmune disease called degenzititus.

In the image, she lay paralyzed on her back with her vacant eyes wide open to the ceiling. Doctors and nurses smiled on either side of her while her father stood off to the side, stern-faced. A banner above them read: CHEERS TO ANOTHER YEAR.

It was meant to be her last year on Earth.

Eight years past, and the memory was too clear, too vivid. *There was a barrier here somewhere*, Leesa thought, straightening up. *I couldn't see this before.*

Somehow the Z-energy fit between her time on the brink of death and the miracle that had become her life.

She scrolled and scrolled, searching for more…clarity, accidentally coming upon a single photo of her mother and father.

Naorima Delemar's blonde hair fell in thick curls over her shoulders, a hair texture Leesa had inherited, one that her father could no longer stand. Though looking at the photo, she guessed it didn't matter, since she'd also been gifted her mother's intense green eyes, high cheekbones, and the power to manipulate fields. This woman who dripped modesty, wore a tempered smile and a uniform without a cape or a speck of visible skin below the neck. Leesa could see by the carefree expression that she would never kill anyone and never had. While next to her, Nicolas Delemar held a smile so wide it touched his ears.

Perhaps she'd never met either of her parents, for she didn't recognize that smiling man any more than she would a stranger.

To date, her and her father had never shared joy. Only the Andromeda Project. Only survival.

Is this the sum of my existence?

"Reminder, your final briefing with General Delemar begins in seven minutes," Cynque told her.

Seven minutes.

Until she owned up to her failures and accepted her punishment. Again. Then, and only then, could they resume the delicate work of salvation.

Leesa's presentation needed to be pristine.

Still, the shower was meant to cleanse her mind more than anything. She shuffled into the bath closet and climbed into her pill-shaped shower pod, powdered in debris and, for once, stained with her own blood, not someone else's.

"Cleanse cycle initiated," Cynque said from overhead as the door latched shut.

Pipes in the wall rattled. Water droplets rushed toward her face and slammed into a barrier she couldn't see, never touching her.

The forcefield she suspected had formed on its own, the one she readily conjured in battle, shimmered into view. More water tumbled down the rounded, glowing edge and disappeared into the drain.

Leesa recoiled, a fist over her mouth in sheer unbelieving. She reached up with one hand to catch the water in her palms and bring it back to her body.

All she wanted was the sensation of water pounding against her with the hostility of discipline. Having already surrendered to the idea of its freezing temperatures, to the raised bumps that would appear on her skin and the shuddering that would follow, she longed for the pressure that went with it. But perhaps that filtered liquid was so disgusted by her intentions that it would not rinse her.

Her eyes stung with the eruption of her telekinetic potential.

The pod's interior panels squealed as they were ripped from the walls. The mounted showerhead was torn free of the ceiling. The pipes groaned, now visible through shredded metal as she crushed them, stopping the flow of the traitorous liquid.

She glared at her handiwork, and though the energy and the stinging dissipated from her eyes, the fury lingered in them. She tried to keep it together, tried to force down the angst around her all-but-inevitable termination.

After all those years of loyalty and service? Allister had asked of Captain Brandt's sentence, sounding as naive as a child. *We all run out of chances* had been her response.

But had she?

Not knowing the answer cracked open her exterior—unleashing more than fury, but also sadness and fear and the sloppiness of vulnerability. Leesa screamed in agony, arms wrapped tight around her waist, as if the damage had been done to her and not by her. Her sobbing couldn't be stopped as she sank into a pile of herself, unclothed and ashamed, the pod's gray walls fading behind her blurry, tear-filled vision.

"Reminder, your final briefing with General Delemar begins in four minutes," Cynque reminded her.

Four minutes.

Leesa gathered her composure and left the pod as it was, in disarray. She rushed to retrieve a new uniform from her storage locker, then mumbled reassurances to herself as she got dressed. Definitive statements like: she could still find the artifacts. And: no one had to die. The cape...the cape she couldn't bring herself to wear. It had been a gift from her father. Her only gift from him. One she no longer believed she deserved. She left the perfectly hung fabric in the case, not wishing to hear it flap in an empty, demolished hallway.

It wasn't C20's fault the organization had fallen.

It was hers.

Clinging to her own beliefs about her purpose as the Gateway had led her to the Vault, where she delivered Allister the generous offer of freedom. Down there, she didn't hear that the security grid had been compromised or that C20 had infiltrated multiple levels. As someone meant to be one of the first lines of defense, her getting incapacitated during battle was...intolerable.

Own up to your failures. Accept your punishment. Then, and only then, will there be salvation.

She smoothed the sides of her poorly assembled updo and power walked out of her office.

The cross path linking Quadrant Alpha and Quadrant Beta flourished with new urgency. Soldiers loaded up on plasma weapons and returned to their posts

472

within the Andromeda Project's walls. The surviving engineers clustered around Professor Ashur and Assistant Professor Jordan and followed them toward the control room with illuminated Cynques in hand. She could hear the words *artifacts* and *termination* used at least fifteen times in just a few seconds.

Something had changed, something far above her.

Perhaps the directors had finally delivered an ultimatum. It seemed obvious they'd blame her. There was no one else left.

"Lieutenant, when you have a moment to spare," the professor called out.

She ignored him and rounded the next corner, soon annoyed by a cluster of chattering soldiers, which she burst through, knocking them aside and stray hairs into her face. She tugged the strands from her scalp and threw them behind her.

Minutes later, she climbed through the jagged-edged, body-size hole in her father's office door.

Twisted metal lay among broken furniture pieces. Glass from the shattered desk sprinkled the unfinished concrete.

General Delemar waited for her, sweat trickling across his furrowed brow. "You didn't even have the decency to clean yourself up before you came in here," her father said. "Disgraceful."

"I—"

"Where is the rest of your uniform?" he interrupted.

She pushed her shoulders back, then steadied her voice as she answered, "I didn't feel—" *Worthy* sat on her tongue, but didn't make it out before her father cut in.

"You're to wear your cape whenever you leave your quarters. I shouldn't have to remind you of these simple, standard procedures."

The procedures were drilled into her head. Reminding her wouldn't help when she felt ashamed to touch the cape, let alone parade around in it.

He crossed his arms. "I thought I was being honorable when I postured for Brandt's termination so that we could run this organization together," her father said. "Isn't that what you've been asking for?"

"I—"

"Yes, *you* went around me and offered Allister Adams freedom. Freedom of all things. I could take the disrespect from Dr. Belladonna, abuse from the directors, but you? You're my flesh and blood."

Leesa's shoulders fell, the guilt corkscrewing through her. Like always, her father was right. *Own up to your failures. Accept your punishment.*

"People would kill for this legacy," her father continued. "This opportunity to save the world, and all you do is dismantle it like everything else."

"This...legacy?" began Leesa in a whisper. "This opportunity? I have given everything—"

"You have given nothing!" he shouted.

Her head snapped back in place. Her mouth tightened.

He walked up to her until they were mere centimeters apart. She couldn't remember the last time they'd stood that close together. "We have three days, Lieutenant. Three. Days."

Leesa backed into the wall. She knew what he was implying, and still, she asked, "Three days until...?"

"We're terminated!" screamed her father.

She flinched.

Of course.

"The directors are done! Done, do you hear me? So, we've got three days until every member of the Andromeda Project is lined up one by one and escorted into those blasted chambers. You listen to me; I will not let my life's work end in my execution."

"Yes," she replied, her voice shaking.

"Yes, what?"

"Yes, General." Leesa cleared her throat, hoping he already knew what she was about to say and hating that she had to say it. "I—I was told Agent Adams is planning to go after his mother within the hour."

Her father didn't speak right away, just watched her squirm and fidget in her fear, a grin spreading across his face. He had a look of cunning in his eye. It was one she'd never seen before. "Well," he began, stepping away, "he won't be going alone."

"No?"

"No. You're going with him. And when Tas-Salvatur and C20 force Allister to choose between his mother and the artifacts, you will kill him—because we already know what choice he'll make. Do I make myself clear?"

"Yes, General."

"Good," her father said. "Operate as if your life is on the line, because—it is."

Leesa tensed her neck, irritation creeping into her. She wasn't satisfied with her automatic answer, or his directive. Hadn't they been playing that game long enough? Putting faith in *theories*. Hypothetical choices. What about the truth? The truth was they couldn't win this way. The truth was that Allister couldn't accomplish their mission, and he'd never been able to.

"If we already know what choice he'll make, why risk it?" she asked.

"We've been over this—"

"Yes, you're right. We have. *Extensively*. But there's something I'm wondering." Her lips stayed open as she spoke, let the suspicious tone glide through the words nearly undetectable. "You have said I am unfit to be the Gateway, that I should not access this energy...*my* energy. Yet you send me to accomplish our greatest mission, the mission that will define our futures, and tell me to be a trigger. To stand by and wait to be pulled. Is this what I mean to you? To this organization?"

Her father paced in a semicircle around her. "Questioning me? You question me now? I see these recent events have ignited your curiosity...and compromised your focus."

"Or perhaps," Leesa said, joining the path of his tense orbit, "I am more focused than I've ever been, and my curiosity has become a tool and not a disease." She thought of her mother in that moment. Imagined her compassion. Channeled her courage. Mourned her sacrifice. Perhaps there was a way Allister's mother could be saved...first. "I am all we need. I always have been. How many more must die for these artifacts?"

"Ah, I see. Not just curiosity, no, empathy, maybe? Yes...empathy." Her father squinted as if he could see through her. "Dolores Adams is irrelevant. She's already dead as far as I'm concerned. You know that. I know that. My instructions, Lieutenant, are intended to keep you safe *and* accomplish our mission. I have to know you'll be ready to kill Adams with a snap of your finger"—he snapped his for emphasis—"should he stand between us and what is rightfully ours."

Leesa looked away. "Is that what you've been doing?"

At that, he fell out of orbit and limped to set his hover chair upright. "I am simply giving you what you asked for: the opportunity to bring the artifacts home and solidify your position here, with me."

Here. With me. The thinly veiled acceptance she'd been waiting her whole life to hear.

A thought came to her mind: maybe what she'd been asking for wasn't what she wanted.

She hid her disgust behind a straight-faced glare. Perhaps there was no glamour in taking over his disheveled office. Maybe there was little-to-no joy in walking through a thick titanium door each day, in squeezing herself through a crawl space with shrunken shoulders and a curved spine just to stand behind him, silenced. But there was no doubt in her heart that she would be unfulfilled listening to the wealthy and out of touch tell her how to save the human population, especially while she hid away from the planet's turmoil and her potentials, waiting for approvals inside the not-so-sturdy walls.

She'd been given a chance to live and wasn't living. She might as well have let the disease take her.

Her father studied her with narrowed eyes. "Our ranks are depleted to mere dozens, so you will do what must be done to ensure our collective survival," he commanded. "I am depending on you to ensure the artifacts are brought to us, no matter the cost. You're dismissed."

Leesa remained near the doorway, body sideways and shaking as she fought to contain a feeling that could only be defiance. The longer she waited there, for him to acknowledge her, to thank her, to love her, the more her control seemed to leave her body. And in her head, the words *Keep it together* repeating on autoplay was no longer enough to contain her potential.

The telekinetic energy's arrival sent a tingling along her temples—subtle, until it intensified, shooting down to her shoulders and her arms, then surging through her fists. Glass pieces, wooden splinters, heavy fabric, and sharp corners tap danced in place. Within seconds, they levitated at eye level.

"If you wore the cape as instructed, you wouldn't suffer these outbursts," he said, freeing the chair he held of glass and dust. "Why can't you keep yourself together?"

Leesa flicked her gaze at him. "Were you like this with my mother? Even in the face of her kindness and warmth."

He reacted to her accusation, a slight twitch, but a twitch nonetheless. "You come in here," he said, sneering, "torturing me with her likeness, those godforsaken curls, while pretending to have her passion." He paused to swallow hard.

"You would dare question that…of all things? My *love* for her? I suggest you watch your tongue, Lieutenant. You didn't know her, you didn't know us. Don't act like you did."

"You're right, I didn't know her." Leesa felt warm energy churning in her concealed palms, yet she was too engrossed in her revelation to stop it. "Maybe because you controlled and pushed her. Maybe because you second-guessed her potential. And later, because you thought being an Evolutionary meant being a sacrifice." She took a step toward him. "But in the end…in the end, it's because you didn't want to fail, so you let her *die* for your legacy!" Her voice came out layered, booming, unearthly.

The tingling and the warmth flared up from her skin in a blue flash and billowed into a radiating field of…Z-energy. She gasped at the sight of it, horrified. An instant later, the field exploded outward. The walls around them shuddered and crunched inward. A light fixture swung down, snapped free of the wire, and crashed to the ground.

She just stared at the damage.

After all the training aimed at suppression. After all her promises of improvement.

"I'm sorry," she said, panting, both hands clasped to her chest. "I'm sorry."

"The cape, Lieutenant," her father said, his face twitching. "You. Are. Dismissed."

Cool air rushed against Leesa's face as she stumbled into the hallway. Her grim, troubled past clouded her feelings, and at the same time, it put much of her emotion into perspective.

No one acknowledged her resilience, or how the contrast between her childhood vegetative state and the Evolutionary powerhouse she'd become made her stronger by virtue of distance.

Leesa's eyes filled with tears.

She recalled the photo of her father from those many years past. His face was radiant, not sunken. His cheeks tan, eyes bright. Not the washed-out color she'd witnessed, the dimness that matched his spirit. Her mother must have been incredible to make her father feel this way.

I'm incredible, too, she thought, sniffling.

She was. And she would show them.

CHAPTER 40

ALLISTER ADAMS
Quadrant Zeta—Restricted Access, Main Hangar, Andromeda Project Headquarters
Day 208

ALLISTER'S LONG-AWAITED DEPARTURE had arrived. He glanced up at an aerocraft engine that could get him across the world in half a day. Unfortunately, that wouldn't be fast enough. Nor did it match the drawing in his dad's notebook.

He was leaning on an overturned storage container inside the main hangar, holding his dad's blue notebook open to a section near the back. Identical alien-looking aircraft were sketched on the left and right pages, one shaded in darkness, one not shaded in with lines drawn shooting out, a nod to illumination, maybe. He saw what looked like an arrow going from the left page to the right, and the seemingly less violent words, *Nournt Zeorgen*, written below it.

"Okay, so. Not you," Allister said of the plane before him.

"Knock, knock, Mumblelina," Bridget teased.

She had her back against the disfigured entrance. Surveillance only knew how long she'd been there, but he didn't realize until she'd hurled her jab that he'd been talking to himself aloud.

The smell of static grazed his nostrils as Bridget moved closer. She examined him from the side and mustered an approving grunt. "A spell book. Peachy. That'll give C20 the ol' run."

"They're *experiments*," Allister corrected, then pushed off the container with a heavy sigh.

He started toward the hangar runway, opened the notebook again, and picked up where he'd left off. It was a page on the two Z-energy experiments. His dad had hypothesized that the outcomes were too broad to be mapped or tested to completion, but in the diagram, specific words and ideas set the intention, and illustrations predicted the outcomes depending on which of them were conducted.

Nournt Zeorgen, he read again to himself. "Begins with Z" was the translation. It seemed to apply to restoration, rebirth, and activation, specific to technology.

"Hmmm," he said, rubbing his chin.

Bridget popped up next to him. "Guess you haven't heard the news?" she asked.

"What news?"

"The Andromeda Project's got three days to bring back the artifacts," she said, twirling on her toes beside him. "Or we're gettin' terminated one by one. They're calling us all home, mate."

Allister took a few more steps forward. "Three days? Would be hyped to know who's leading that mission."

"Wouldn't that be you, wizard? Aren't you the bloody Gateway?" Bridget asked. "Pshh, if *I* was the Gateway, humanity woulda been saved."

"One thousand percent," Allister replied, eyes still on the page.

"Just a shame I never got the right potential, ya know?"

"Such a shame."

Bridget jumped in front of him and shoved her face between his face and the notebook. "You gonna leave your little sidekick Dorian here?" she asked.

He closed the notebook. "Cut it out, Sparks."

The sound of talons clacking on the smooth surface could be heard from the far side of the room, followed by soft footsteps.

"I present to youuu, the maaan of the hour," Bridget announced. "Dorian Xander! Glad you could make it, chum, I pinged for you ages ago."

Allister didn't look back but waved over his shoulder. "What's good, Dorian, just figurin' out which of these fresh rides to fly off with."

Dorian clapped at that, a thing he often did when he agreed. From what Allister had observed, sound wasn't always Dorian's enemy, only when he'd absorbed too much and didn't have anywhere for the excess to go.

"Yeah, Pops says the right one's around here somewhere." Allister stopped at a third damaged aerocraft, which appeared upgraded, but didn't match the frame, engines, and wings to what his dad had drawn. "Broken anyway," he snorted, and kept moving.

Then at the farthest end of the hangar, he was sure he'd found the alien craft sketched in the notebook. The design was distinctly alien technology infused— short, sloped wings; a long, pointed nose; wide thrusters underneath and a big booster rocket in back. "This *must* be the one," he said.

"Ey, what you gonna do with the artifacts when you get 'em?" Bridget asked. "Turn 'em over to C20? Light 'em up for yourself? Bring 'em back for my little Russ to tinker with?"

"Go on and take a guess, yeah? Here's a hint: whichever will keep my mom living and breathing."

"Ooooh," Bridget dragged the taunt through her lips. "This rowdy side of you is so next."

Penny barked at her.

"Keep that thing away from me or it's light out," she threatened, beginning to toy with voltage above her palms. As Penny backed away, growling, Bridget said with contempt, "Good girl." She then turned to Allister, her initial aggression simmering to genuine interest. "What if, say, you got C20 what they wanted, but maybe...you didn't give to them?"

"I won't put my mom in that kind of danger."

"Not straight-up refusal, dimwit. You'd trick them, with me and big D here as backup. Oh, and his little dog, too."

Allister ducked beneath the ship's giant underside to inspect it. "No, no way. I'm going solo. Going to do what they say." He identified what he thought were the engines, nodded in satisfaction, then kept coming around to get a look at the wings. There, he almost ran into Dorian, who had clearly been waiting for him.

Dorian proceeded to present his argument, gesturing with emphatic one-handed sign language. He held his palm out, flipped it over, and shook his head. Though the metal mask still covered the lower half of his face, the fear in his eyes was more than visible. He placed a hand on Allister's shoulder and squeezed with earnest.

"No one's dying," Allister said. "Look, Dorian, you and Penny need to break out of here before they try offing you. Sparks says you've got three days."

Dorian narrowed his eyes. In his impassioned way, he used his hands to communicate a sentiment more beautiful than words themselves could express. His fingers were butterflies at one moment, fluttering, colorful, then flowers the next, blooming and bold. His arms, while fast-moving, were the steady, ever-crashing waves of emotion: joy, fear, sadness, determination. Dorian wanted Allister to see his own bravery and power, and that if it weren't for his generosity, he and Penny would still be destitute. There was a hand motion for appreciation, another for gratitude, and a third for friendship. Dorian closed with something profound, again with the fluidity of unspoken language: that he would rather spend three days fighting to live than three days preparing to die.

481

"So that's the move?" Allister asked, smiling a bit. "Could maybe use a lookout or two wherever I end up, you with it?"

Dorian nodded, the smile hidden under the mask visible in his eyes, and signed back one of Allister's favorite slang terms, *One thousand percent*.

"You're a real one, Dorian, I say that with my whole heart." Allister got up and returned to the front of the vehicle he'd chosen. "If we do this…we gotta be mega careful. Make sure Mom's safe first."

"I couldn't agree more," came a loud, stern voice from behind him.

"Uh…oh…," Bridget said. "The lieutenant's here."

That she was. The question was why.

"Did you come to stop me?" Allister asked.

"I came to help," Leesa said.

Allister heard her getting nearer and groped his uniform blindly, scrambling to pop open the center compartment of the chest plate and stuff away the notebook before she saw it. When he did, and the book finally slid in, he snapped the compartment shut and flipped around. "Don't think we're going on the same mission," he replied. He gestured to Dorian and Bridget, then Penny, and lifted his chin, forcing a casual tone. "Besides, I'm sorted."

Leesa scoffed, crossing her arms as she stopped in front of him. "I think you're far from *sorted*. You misfits need a leader, someone with extensive combat training—like me." Leesa sized up each of them and paused at Allister. "You're really planning to take on C20 with *them*? This one uses her potentials to flip switches"—she pointed at Bridget, then at Dorian—"while this one uses it to evaporate sound before it reaches him." She cast a glance at Penny. "And that's a dog. You'll all fry without me."

"Penny, is a LionWolf," Allister corrected with a hint of attitude. "Trust, we'll be fine."

Allister played confident well, even when he wasn't fully convinced. Sure, they could use the muscle, the raw potential, the tactical advantage. But Leesa had different motivations for going—her world began and ended with the artifacts. "I'm going after my mom. You're going after the artifacts. Not. The. Same. Mission."

He stared at her, gauging her reaction.

Leesa stared back, her cape billowing beside her even though she wasn't moving. "If your emotions get in the way like they did during C20's attack, we all lose—and Tas-Salvatur wins. You need me."

There it was.

Her superiority.

What had happened to the Leesa who had sat next to him after the attack and shared experiences about the Z-energy? What had happened to the Leesa who had helped him up? Was she once again buried under the pressure of her own success? "Ahh, see, *that's* the move," Allister said, fists shaking with frustration. "We may not be the most trained or most experienced, but at least we can trust each other."

"You're mental. Where has trusting anyone gotten us? Need I remind you of Captain Brandt?" Leesa paused, watching, Allister guessed, the name wiggle its way through him. "Listen, Adams, I know what you're after, and you can't get one without getting the other first. We'll do the best we can to save your mother in the process."

Allister couldn't believe Leesa's nerve. His fists shook harder. His face tensed tighter. "Stop talking about her like she's an afterthought or just some person— she's my mom," he said angrily. "I'm gonna pass. Sorry I can't cynque up on your not-very-specific offer."

Bridget clapped her hands and squealed in delight, likely enjoying the back-and-forth.

Allister began storming away and threw up his hands. "What do you want, huh, Lieutenant? You said leave, well, here I am leaving. Thought you'd be hyped."

"Agent Adams," Leesa called after him.

He shook his head and kept walking, his arms swinging with more defiance.

"Agent Adams!" she shouted a second time, louder.

I can't trust her, she just wants the artifacts, Allister thought.

"Allister," she said in a whisper, floating down to her feet in front of him.

They were face-to-face.

"I need to go with you," she said. "I deserve the chance to save my family too." She grabbed his wrists and, after a minute of hesitation, said, "Please."

The longer their skin was connected, the more weightless he felt. Her touch was lighter than the skies waiting for them.

Please?

"Bet that's a word you've never used," he said, trying to be steadfast with his resistance.

Leesa dropped his hands. "You've only known me for seven days, Agent Adams. Hardly enough time to get the full breadth of my vocabulary."

Fair.

Allister stroked his afro, wary of her sincerity, skeptical of her motives. The measure of her character continued to lengthen, and yet, he felt like something was missing in the middle, as if the extremes she portrayed concealed a soul yearning for freedom. It made her unpredictable. Possibly dangerous.

"Don't try any offhand strategies, seriously. Something twisted happens to Mom, and I get rowdy," Allister said to Leesa, shoving past her. "And I mean rowdy, like, everything ends with Z." He only took a few steps before he was standing below the alien ship's nose, his arms held out and aimed upward. "C20 wants those crystals so bad they probably won't make any sudden moves until after I get 'em, so let's fake it, like I'm showing up alone to make good on our trade. You with it?"

"I suppose that's a decent place to start," Leesa said.

"Golden," he said. "I'll figure out the rest on our way."

It was time to go. His dad's sketch of the ship resurfaced in his mind, as did the experiment he was about to try. *Begins with Z*, he repeated to himself in preparation. *Begins with Z.* Feeling self-conscious, he repositioned his hands again. *Begins with Z*, he thought a final time.

"What are you doing?" Leesa asked.

"Shh...I'm conducting an experiment." Allister spun his arms around each other like Neight had done inside the prison, concentrating on his intention to breathe life into alien technology. Light and warmth burned through him with the intensity of restoration and rebirth. "Nournt Zeorgen!" he shouted.

The empty space between his hands ignited in a blue orb of crackling Z-energy. The mystical, round object floated beyond their collective gazes, and as it attached itself to the craft's underbelly, streams of energy burst forth, brighter than the hangar's floodlights.

The craft hummed with vigor, its fit of brightness fading to an opened hatch and a platform lowering to the ground.

"Wow," he said, smiling in spite of the awkward tension. He turned to the others. "I did it! Did you see how the Z-energy just, like, flew out of my hands and then went into the machine? And then, *boom*, all of that light and power and... Oh, man, how hype was that!"

Bridget fake yawned, her eyes rolling. "So hype."

Dorian gave him a thumbs-up and scurried under the ship. Penny trotted behind him, bushy tail swaying left to right.

"Any reason why you picked a non-Earth ship?" Leesa asked, reaching the other two.

"It's the fastest," answered Allister. He strutted up to the hatch. "You still coming, Sparks?"

Bridget glanced back at the hangar entrance. "Thinkin' I'm gonna stay behind," she said. "You might need a second wave, yeah?"

"Maybe," he said. "You sure?"

"*One thousand*," she mocked. "Call it a hunch."

"Leave her," Leesa said, tugging Allister by the arm.

He stumbled alongside her, not surprised she was being so forceful or trying to take control. "Tell Dr. Belladonna where we went!" he called back.

Bridget grinned. "Sure, what's the story?" She cleared her throat to imitate an announcer's voice. "Despite their differences, the Rookie Agent and the Iron-Hearted Lieutenant strike out on a dangerous mission to take down C20. Will they end up at odds? Will they find the artifacts *and* rescue the agent's mum? Who's the real Gateway? This, and more, next time on…the Andromeda Project." She cackled to herself. "Sounds about spot on, yeah?"

"Whatever, Sparks," Allister said, with a wave of his hand. "Just shoot straight, no games."

The square platform carried the four of them—Dorian, Penny, Leesa, and himself—into the ship. Next to him, Leesa was flushed red with embarrassment, blowing two stray locks of hair to the side with puffs of air. It was the first time since they'd met that every strand wasn't pulled tight into a bun, and it was the first time Allister noticed her hairstyle began at a hairline with such painful-looking redness.

If she knew he was looking, she pretended she didn't. Maybe so he wouldn't ask about it.

The platform stopped inside of the darkened space, prompting an intricate maze of purple lights to flicker on one after another. In some instances, they ran parallel, mostly along the walls, and in others, they crisscrossed, often as they spread across the floor or the ceiling. Allister observed in quiet awe as the lights brightened, casting a sort of mystic moonlike glow onto shiny chrome fixtures and smooth gray molding.

As they dispersed themselves throughout the cabin, he could see where the Andromeda Project had gotten their inspiration. But the facility's older architecture was merely a dulled-down duplicate of the ship's nuanced feel.

Every individual function was interwoven with and dependent on another, as if the whole ship were sentient, thinking and feeling and breathing, as one living machine.

There didn't seem to be anywhere to sit or pilot, then the floor shifted in four places, and the material it was made of sprouted from the floor, twisting and elongating and widening and, finally, morphing as if hand-molded into oddly shaped chairs arranged in a diamond.

They solidified in place. The grandest of the four chairs, a miniature throne, sat behind what Allister presumed were the ship's navigation controls. The other more modest ones were positioned equidistant on either side, farther back, and the last one was a bit removed and in the cabin's rear.

"*Elcoew, histe isi Uragonian frhact: Nournt Zeorgen,*" the ship said.

A welcome in the native language of Neight's civilization.

Impressive, Allister thought. He understood bits and pieces, while Leesa slowed as if to listen, then kept going with a confused look on her face when it didn't click.

He thought she was heading toward one of the seats on the side, when seconds later they almost collided, each on their way to sitting down in front of the controls. They both jumped back up.

"Hey! I'm flying," they said in unison.

The pilot console lit up at the sound of their voices, a puzzle of cryptic symbols outlined in orange and blue.

Allister had a serious look on his face. "I'm flying," he said.

"That's not funny," Leesa replied. She pushed him out of the way and took a long look at the console. "We are crossing an ocean. If you pilot as well as you passenger, we won't make it free of the hangar."

He pointed at an illuminated arrangement of shapes in a single downward line. "Okay, you think you're with it? What does that say?"

"This looks like…" She didn't finish, and instead leaned closer to inspect one of the symbols, a half-filled-in circle with a navy heptagon inside it. "Well, this has to be…" She stopped and sucked her teeth at the charcoal rectangle with a proportionately smaller, darker rectangle within. "Uhm, I'm pretty sure this means…" She let her voice fade and placed her finger on the orange triangle between two adjoined diamond shapes at the bottom. "Pretty sure this means…"

"Exactly. At least let me try. I turned the thing on, for clock's sake."

There came a twinge of recognition on Leesa's face. She conceded. "Do it, then."

Allister sat down, letting the safety harness stretch across his chest. "All right—everybody locked in?" he asked, taking a quick peek at his passengers. Leesa sat sulking, hands in her lap. Dorian was as shaky as a seedling in the wind. Penny was as excited as…well, any canine would be in a soon-to-be-moving vehicle.

"Beat!" he said, fist in the air.

The motherboard beeped and talked up at him in the Uragonian language, only a fraction of which he managed to translate.

It's kinda like flying an FBX, right? he reassured himself, nervously running his hand over the panel. *Gotta keep the sides balanced and don't hit the ground.* He took a deep breath, then, on faith, flipped the orange triangle on the console upside down.

That initial action seemed to work. As the loud whir of ignited engines filled the cabin, repulsor rockets blasted them airborne. Spidery legs folded away for takeoff. Feeling hyped, Allister pushed the orange triangle forward and exclaimed, "And that's our cue to goooooooo!"

The craft still hovered in place.

He laughed sheepishly and slid the triangle back. "Our cue to goooo…," he repeated as he pushed the toggle forward a second time.

"With urgency," Leesa snapped.

"I'm with it, okay!"

Allister studied the controls, replayed the computer's alien phrases. He guessed that the tiny, dark rectangle represented the engine power, and the fact that it was sitting in the middle of the larger rectangle, meant they were hovering. The orange triangle must've been for the ship's wing movement and steering, but maybe also for its balance, hence the tie-in to the repulsor rockets.

"Yes!" With his finger, he dragged the smaller rectangle forward until it touched the larger rectangle's northernmost perimeter. It locked in place.

The engines exploded behind them.

"Whoa, whoa, whoa, whoa," he said, fumbling with the orange triangle.

The ship veered off the runway and tilted sideways as it zoomed forward, scraping its wing against the exit tunnel. The ship shuddered. The metal screeched. Already nauseous from his body jerking left, right, and forward, he reached up and moved the bouncing orange triangle slightly off-center. The ship pulled away from the wall, lessening the shuddering of the ship, and allowing the wings to even out. They continued barreling forward.

"Whooo!" he yelled, heart pounding from the rush.

The ship blasted through the hangar's opening and flew nose first toward the District's skyline. Allister flipped the triangle, powering down the repulsors, then moved it forward, sending them soaring straight up as they climbed altitude. "You—you know the plan. Cynq-Cynque's off," he stammered, all but melted into his seat.

The craft rose higher into the atmosphere. When clear of the sanctuary's towering infrastructure, he slid the triangle backward, leveling the plane, and gave more power to the roaring rear boosters.

"Decent job back there," Leesa said. "You held it together."

Allister was tensed from the neck down and drenched in sweat. "You…don't sound triggered…," he said, blushing. A shy smile hid the queasiness that clawed at his stomach.

"Taking your false surrender approach into consideration, I suggest we don't make the same mistake we did in De Los Muertos," Leesa said. She settled back into her chair, her voice returning to the one he knew—pompous, commanding. "You land us out of sight and off the radar. We stay that way until we know what it looks like on the ground and establish a safe perimeter. Then we get you in position."

"Sounds like a good enough option. Guess I'll see if Brandt was telling the truth about where they went," Allister said. He transferred the captain's coordinates location from his Cynque.

"Coordinates destination confirmed," the ship announced, "Estimated arrival—eight hours and fifty-nine minutes from departure—two hours, twenty-one minutes 'til Day 207, local time."

Just in time.

Allister accelerated toward the coming dawn, thankful they would arrive at C20 under night's indigo cloak.

CHAPTER 41

DR. FLORENCE BELLADONNA

Quadrant Zeta—Restricted Access, Main Hangar, Andromeda Project Headquarters

Day 208

"WELL, HE SAID he was leaving," Florence said.

And she had given her word she'd come when she could. It seemed more was at stake than her freedom, since the directors had called for the termination of all Andromeda Project members a measly three days from, unless the artifacts were retrieved.

Florence surveyed the damage to the main hangar: the majority of the aerocraft fleet was melted to remnants, the far wall had been shredded by a sharp object—a wing, she was almost certain. Judging by the condition of the area, Allister had taken off in something with enough propulsion to get to space. And judging by the spray of psi-signatures, Leesa, Dorian, and that dog-wolf-lion thing had gone with him.

"I swear this place is on its way to hell." She adjusted her sword inside the leather sheath that was strapped around her waist. "I suppose the question is… do I go down with it?"

She walked deeper into the hangar—a painful act for her, as she wasn't quite over the bomb that had blown off her leg, or the loss of the leg itself—her recent encounter with the lieutenant becoming that much more troubling.

Following a final briefing with General Delemar, Leesa had arrived at Florence's office, hair disheveled, eyes bloodshot, cape missing, and interrupted her own much-needed mental and physical recovery.

"You still owe me a report," Leesa said.

Her delivery was missing its usual sting.

"I do," Florence admitted. "I didn't find anything to quell your general concerns, but he is free of any residual psychic influence from XBA. In light of the attacks, I didn't have the bandwidth to type it up all posh-like for you."

"I suppose that's good news considering our three-day timeline." Leesa looked straight at her then, in anticipation. "His mother's capture will make it difficult for him to act within the terms of our agreement. Don't you agree?"

"I do." She paused, resting her weight on her psibernetic leg enhancement, a stern look on her face. "Lieutenant, I know what you want to hear. So, here: while Agent Adams's potential for the Z-energy is formidable, yours is invariably more significant, more potent, and more powerful. Take that however you must to affirm your personal worth, but please don't suck out the last sentence and use it to inflate your ego further, or as a weapon against Allister."

"Noted, Doctor," Leesa said. Then she did something unusual. She smiled. It was almost too quick, how the agitation evaporated from her face, how she smoothed her hair on either side, and left without another word.

Florence had kept a hardened stare on the lieutenant as she disappeared through the doorway, suspicious because the only thing repeating in her mind was: *I can still retrieve the artifacts*.

Cynque's loud beeping pierced Florence's ears, yanking her mind back to the present.

"*Che cos' é*, Cynque?" she seethed. "What the bloody hell is it?"

Secure? the message on the device read.

It was from her confidant.

"Secure," Florence said into the gold band. "They went after the artifacts... and I suppose, since I'm up and moving, I go too?"

"Why not? You promised." The response was distorted to mask the speaker's identity, but she had her guesses—Detective Hunter Steele, for one. "Cynque up with Allister and make certain he does what the hell we found him for."

"What if Lieutenant Delemar gets to the artifacts first?"

The responses started coming in rapid fire, a frantic pitch in the voice. "She can't," her confidant said. "She literally can't. You have to make sure she doesn't. You're the only one who can handle this."

That panic could only belong to one man. The leader of the United Sanctuaries, and the global voice of reason regarding the countdown—

President Wesley DeVries.

"Un-bloody-real, you just keep piling it on, yeah?" Almost certain it was the president, and hating that it could be, she tilted her chin and inhaled sharply. "What about C20? What about Celine, the Moroccan princess?"

"Bring it down. Take her home. Same timeline."

"Okay…okay…," she said. "Okay." A few deep breaths, and she, soothing herself with a gentle forehead massage, immediately started listing out all of the underground Evolutionaries who owed her big debts. "I get the urgency…just— uhm—give me…give me two hours from, and I'll call in some favors."

Cynque dinged. "You're already behind," they said back. "They're traveling at the speed of *sound*."

"Bloody hell."

"Flight coordinates retrieved," Cynque said, "Mapping route."

The flight pattern for Allister's ship glimmered into topographic realness, the trajectory showing that they were heading somewhere in the Middle East.

Just like Hunter had said.

Now it was three birds, one sword.

"We were almost sure it would come to this, it's why you were brought in," they finished. "Get going, now. I need you to hand deliver those artifacts to me."

Florence grimaced, her hand squeezed tight around the Cynque. "Guess it's to hell for me."

———

Artist: Jeffrey Viloria/ The CMD Studios

"SURRENDER TO THE
DEPTHS OF YOURSELF
—DON'T RESIST."

- DR. FLORENCE BELLADONNA

WHAT DOES COURAGE LOOK LIKE FOR YOU IN THIS MOMENT? WHAT DOES COMPASSION LOOK LIKE?

———

CHAPTER 42

ALLISTER ADAMS
Undefined Airspace
Day 207

THE EARTH'S EVER-CHANGING sky seemed to engulf them. Its colors ranging from dawn-kissed blues to sun-stroked brightness to the occasional perversion of puffy white clouds. Allister, Leesa, Dorian, and Penny cruised the troposphere at 12,500 meters, roughly forty thousand feet; not a word passed between them for several hours.

Allister faced front in deep thought, hands clasped at his lips, sitting lotus style in the pilot's seat. His concern with anything going wrong, or everything going wrong, had him second-guessing his decision to bring anyone with him—namely Leesa. Plus, for the better part of an hour, rapid-fire messages from Florence had been appearing on his Cynque, inducing more anxiety.

Finally fed up, he groaned and set a reminder to read them when they'd landed. She couldn't help them now, anyway.

I should've come alone, he thought to himself. *Leesa's got some trick under that cape, I know it.*

He snuck a look at Leesa, who sat with her legs crossed, staring at the horizon as though she wished to move it with a nod. Her eyes wandered from the window and onto him. She frowned.

"You still don't trust me," she said, sounding offended.

Of course he didn't. He had no reason to trust her. But the real shocker was that she wanted him to. Why him? Why now?

He blamed the confidence of sitting in the pilot seat for why the next words came flying out of his mouth. "You actually care if I trust you or not? That's fresh."

Leesa stared back at him, her brow furrowed. He knew what came next would be demeaning or flat-out rude.

But as she continued looking at him, her face softened with a resignation. "It is a reflection of myself to see you this way, leading us to take on so much with little more than our collective potentials. I wonder if it's our courage that drives us...or is it our fear? Or is it simply the duty of being an Evolutionary." Her train of thought seemed to switch tracks before she spoke again. "I can understand how...well, more than understand, I can *feel* how you must've felt during De Los

Muertos, when I was leading and I didn't trust you. The feeling of being… unprotected and alone in this moment. Disposable. …Somewhat, swept with the overwhelming need to prove that I can be trusted."

Allister twisted toward her in his seat. He couldn't help feeling completely taken aback by her openness.

"I…" He stopped himself. *It's another trick,* he thought, even as he watched her struggle to keep her chin up.

Was that shame pulling it down? He'd seen that need for forgiveness in himself before—in De Los Muertos after he let the machine go, and before that, during the assessment when his potentials had gone left.

Her hands were clasped at her waistline, the cape draped around her upright shoulders. The signature green in her eyes glimmered against the interior lights, which shined on cheekbones as smooth as they were pronounced, on hair as tamed as it was tall. She looked more like a queen in that moment—humbled, compassionate, radiant.

Allister averted his eyes and scratched his head, uncomfortable with her silence and her beauty. "I…uhm, I'm not gonna pretend like I'm hyped we're on this mission together. I came here to save my mom, and you came here to save your legacy, so yeah, I'm a bit off. I don't know another way to be right now."

Again Leesa didn't answer right away; she just kept looking ahead, her mouth twitching. Perhaps coming up with thoughtful responses was more difficult than coming up with dismissive ones. He rolled his eyes and slapped the pilot's chair with his hands, wondering why he'd even bothered.

"The Middle…the Middle…," she tried to get out, unlatching the harness so she could rise to her feet.

Allister looked over at her. "The middle?" he asked. "Of what? Yeah we're in the middle of a conversat—"

She grabbed the top of his head and turned it toward the horizon. "The Middle Beast," she said as she let go.

Allister jumped up in the seat.

Where before the atmosphere had been calm, littered with white tuffs of harmless condensation, he could see that serenity was no more. Ahead of them was a sky forever transformed, stained the bleeding red of a far-off sunset, yet consumed by a towering, swirling, anvil-shaped mass.

Allister's palms warmed until they were damp. He couldn't believe he'd forgotten about the storm—the biggest, longest-running storm on record—raging above the former Middle East. He'd never witnessed anything like it before. He could tell by Leesa's sucked-in cheeks and glossy eyes that she hadn't, either.

"Approaching coordinates of destination location—unmapped Earth terrain. Region: Middle East," the spaceship said in its language. "Mentarian Elemental Disturbance detected."

The ground was invisible from that height, covered by the thick spread of blackish clouds. He didn't need to see what lay beneath to know nothing could survive a storm of that size, with that sustained level of ferocity.

"How the hell are we supposed to get down there?" he asked. Now at the window, Leesa stood with her shoulders shrunk, tugging at the hair above her forehead. She looked back at him knowingly. "Only one way," she said before turning back toward the storm. "Through."

Through?

She'd said it with such certainty. As if there were no other possible truth.

Allister went back to the pilot seat and reviewed the flight controls. "How long do we have?" he asked.

"Minutes, if we're lucky," Leesa answered.

Allister glanced up. "Minutes?" It was then he saw Dorian standing next to Leesa, though he was perfectly still, his mouth shut in a decided fashion. Penny had sidled up next to Dorian, looking at the storm as if it were a beast she'd faced before, her tongue hanging as she wheezed and brushed against her master's thin legs. Dorian petted her in slow rhythms, eyes dry and cold, both of them moving back and forth across the horizon as if reading the sky.

With a slight turn, Dorian brought his hand to his lip and twisted it down to his chin with the harshness of agony, another sign gesture.

"The storm is…suffering?" Allister asked for confirmation.

Dorian nodded. Next came a warning. A finger pointed to his ear, which was followed by the wide swing of his hand, and ended with him pushing one hand away from the other.

"Sounds? Fly? Fly away?"

"Stay away," Leesa corrected. "Stay away from the sounds. Right?"

Dorian nodded again.

"Stay away from the sounds, okay, I'm with it, but I still don't understand how the storm is suffering."

"Because it's not natural," Leesa said. "This storm is anything but natural."

"Critical atmospheric pressure detected ahead, flight pattern compromised," the spaceship boomed. "Emergency navigation engaged."

Now they could hear the wind howling with hurricane fury, could see the fat belly of the Middle Beast twisting around itself like an F7 tornado.

The spaceship shuddered then, knocking them free of their observation. "Everyone strap yourselves in," said Allister. He put on his harness and checked that it was secure. "Penny included. This isn't going to be fun." He turned to Leesa as she went to sit down. "I was hoping you could help get us to the ground."

"I can try," she said. Her voice felt smaller than normal, uncertain.

He placed his palm on the console and expanded the glowing circle with the navy heptagon inside it. "Shields up," he announced. "Just in case."

The ship dropped altitude, still jerking from side to side sharply. Allister's stomach rose with the swell of the wind's invisible waves, and when they rolled and crashed on top of them, his insides plummeted to nauseating depths. The storm seemed to come alive as they got closer. The wind more like terrified screams, the lightning more like a temper tantrum. A young woman's tortured face took shape in the clouds, her mouth opening and swallowing them as their craft rocked past the massive thundercloud's turbulent rim.

His stomach tightened, gripped by the sadness in the woman's eyes just before they'd disappeared. Now they'd breached that wide belly. The swelled, thunderous, flashing belly.

"Did I just see...a face—?" he asked. "What kind of storm is this?"

He'd meant the question to be rhetorical, because how could any of them have known the answer? Yet while his companions remained some mix of captivated and terrified in silence, the alien computer blared its response.

"Storm classification... Cosmic Origin: of Mentarian descent. Status: amplified."

A series of revelations hit Allister in the face as the words hit his ears. That a storm classified as cosmic meant it couldn't be earthly, and that if its origin was Mentarian, whatever Mentarian was, it couldn't be *Evolutionary*. Putting aside the ship's inability to communicate in human language—as in use a word made up by scientists to classify the genetically anomalous—he could conclude one thing was true: some force foreign to Earth was causing this erratic weather disturbance.

The ship pitched hard to one side and fell so far Allister was thrown from the pilot seat momentarily before he plopped back into it. He tried to scream as the ship rocked side to side and couldn't manage. The fluctuating high and low pressures seemed hell-bent on squeezing them out of the air.

His first thought was to check the shield capacity, and good thing, too: the glowing circle on the console contracted, then expanded, then contracted again. The ship offered warning sounds and notifications, alerting him that the shields could not withstand the sustained impact.

"Leesa…you good, or what?" he forced out.

She gasped, then grunted.

That was a hard-to-decipher response. She could've been reacting to the turbulence…or the overwhelming sense of dread. When he'd last checked, she was standing, prepared to summon her forcefield to protect them in case the ship's shields couldn't. Had she activated her potential already? If so, was she the reason the ship hadn't been torn to bits thus far? He held his breath and the chair as he looked back to gauge her condition.

This time, it was he who gasped.

Z-energy traced her body, and everything behind him.

"Uh…Leesa?" he asked again, confused.

Leesa was resting on one knee, her skin lightening and darkening with exertion, the energy around her glowing and flashing the vivid blue, the violent blue, the contained blue—the same as his. She closed her eyes in concentration, hair no longer in the stacked bun, but caught in the wild freedom of an energy burst, hands pressed in plea to the sky she battled.

But either she didn't speak, or she couldn't. Because the only response was the energy's intense crackling as it gripped the interior. To Allister's astonishment, her experiment was neither a beginning nor an end with Z-energy, rather it was an effort aimed at sustaining. So, maybe sustaining with Z? Though not unlike telekinesis in the way it worked, the pulsing energy showed greater cohesion, attached to more than just the surface of all that surrounded them. Millions of tiny blue strings seemed to be binding every molecule, each one sewn into the fabric of the ship's material to form a stitched-together shield.

And for a moment, it appeared to work. The ship steadied in the air, practically stilled.

Nervous beads of sweat broke free on Allister's forehead. He almost laughed out loud at the relief simmering through him. His arms loosened their hold. His chest collapsed with a heavy exhale. They weren't going to crash. They weren't going to die. *Mega close call*, he was about to say, glad she'd joined them in the end.

Then—

One.

String.

Snapped.

He watched, panic now boiling beneath his skin, as that one string began unraveling the entire experiment.

The ship shuddered out of control again.

Leesa stared up at him, lips trembling, the look on her face apologetic, weary. It was the look of giving in to fear, of letting go. A look he hated to admit he'd worn far too recently.

"Just strap back in—fast," Allister said, too dumbfounded to feel anything else. "I'll figure it out."

He turned and braced himself to resume piloting. Taking in a sharp breath, he reached for the console with one hand while refusing to let go of the chair with the other. Only a few thousand meters until they hit the ground, he'd translated from the altitude measurement device, flashing information in purple alien characters.

"It's just a few meters," he mumbled. "Just a few meters."

Allister felt he'd already lost his confidence, airsickness hitting him as hard and fast as a bolt of lightning hit the wing. He jerked forward from the impact, certain by the howls and screams behind him something was amiss in the cockpit.

But he had to keep his eyes on the sky.

Every slithering strike of lightning was intentional, every cyclonic blow calculated. A gust of wind hit the roof with the force of an angry fist and sent them tumbling.

The cockpit jumped around his vision, the spinning green lights that lined the interior flaring alongside obnoxious sirens. Allister covered his ears, eyes open to the illuminated shapes on the digital console darting in all directions.

The engines roared as they tried to keep the ship in the air. The wind roared just as loud trying to knock them out of it.

His feet were digging into the floor with unconscious force. He was too afraid to move.

"Warning, approaching terrain. Warning, approaching terr—"

The interruption was piercing—the high-pitched whine of an object slicing off a wing, the heavy groan as the ship nearly came apart in the air. Allister widened his eyes to the now-cracked windshield, and within it, he glimpsed the wasteland of an old civilization spiraling up at him. A bent skyscraper snatched the other wing. The uneven top of a half-crumbled building took out the engine. After which the spaceship flipped upside down and looped back, taking Allister's stomach with it.

He covered his face with his arms, his hoarse screams competing with Leesa's for loudness.

"Brace for impact," the computer wailed.

It was too late.

The underbelly hit something blunt.

Allister's butt left his chair again and landed harder back in it. Leesa's yelling echoed farther from his ears until it disappeared among the chorus of other thundering noises.

He no longer heard her behind him and whipped around in his seat.

The straps meant to keep Leesa in her seat flapped in the wind.

She was gone.

Dorian was strapped in on the other side, a faint navy glow pulsating around him. He held Penny around her neck and against himself, his mouth sealed closed, one hand extended toward the direction they fell. For those noticeable seconds, Allister could hear nothing, not even the sound of his own voice. The ship's descent occurred in complete silence.

It's an experiment, Allister thought quickly. *He's somehow deflecting the noise.*

He could see the ripples of sonic vibrations pounding all around them, could feel them passing through him as the orchestra of their demise was funneling into Dorian's hands and back out somewhere he couldn't see. After that, Allister noticed they didn't hit anything else, explosions just vibrated and burst on every side of them.

Too soon, he watched Dorian hug Penny tighter and lower his hand, exhausted.

The experiment ended with the return of aggressive sounds. That's when Allister heard the engines whining at the highest pitch possible. Screeching toward combustion.

"Golden move, but this thing is set to blow any second," Allister said, finding the courage to tear himself away from the pilot seat. There was a chance he could survive an explosion. There was an equal, if not greater chance that Dorian and Penny *couldn't*. "We're jumping." He wrapped his arms around Dorian and Penny and lifted them up. "Hold tight."

Allister carried them through the smoking ship, reeling across the interior as he made his way. The wind tried to yank them from the gaping hole where the ship's rear had been. And, wanting to launch them far enough away to avoid the blast radius, he crouched down to jump.

Suddenly, a fierce light ignited in his peripheral.

Kaboom.

His ears rang with the full decibels of an explosion. His skin ignited from the heat he'd tried to outrun. Allister tried holding on to Dorian and Penny, hoping to keep them all together, even as they were being blown apart.

CHAPTER 43

LIEUTENANT LEESA DELEMAR
Ruins of Man's Lost Lands
Day 207

ONLY MINUTES PRIOR, Leesa had been helpless, clinging to the base of her seat, screaming at the top of her lungs, her cheek pressed to the floor. The speed of the ship's fall, the slickness of the metal, both working against her. Her fingers had started slipping, the wind and friction peeling them away one at a time. And though Dorian reached to grab her before she was snatched into the brutal sky, his arms weren't long enough.

Then a shuddering impact knocked her free of the cockpit.

Leesa floundered in the air. Somehow the wind didn't blow her any direction—up, down, or otherwise. The sound of thunder came in muffled, as if blocked by a thick, solid wall. Slowly she began to regain control of her body and her mind. The hysteria retreated in her, and she finally realized she wasn't even falling.

Just hovering.

She glanced down, thankful to see her glimmering purple energy potential rushing at her like an updraft, keeping her suspended in the air. Her simplest act of potential: levitation. Or as Allister had called it, an *experiment*.

Meanwhile, the alien ship was corkscrewing deeper into the ruins. A large spot of black among the brown of the ancient city.

She briefly watched it go, tortured by the nagging gut feeling that she should save them. Or was this the perfect opportunity for her to go after the artifacts and finish the mission? Her automatic first thought was to do what her father would do. Another notion intercepted, to consider what her mother would do. What her mother had done…

Sacrifices were made, Brandt had said in De Los Muertos.

Before she could decide what to do, the ship exploded in a blend of navy spheres, scattering what was left of its parts and blasting her back with the monumental force of an expansive wave.

Leesa remained airborne, curled into herself, heart pounding against her knees. What arrived was a strange sense of devastation.

She looked out at the black plume of rising smoke where the ship had been. Dismembered parts flew and fell away from each other, Dorian and the mutt among them. Below that, Allister spun like a missile toward the sand.

Leesa didn't hesitate the second time, in one fluid motion uncurling her body and shooting toward them at high speed, intending to stop their descent.

She slowed her flight once close and threw out her hand. Bright-fuchsia waves of telekinetic force streamed from her fingertips, gathering in circles underneath the three free-falling bodies.

Allister, Dorian, and the dog plowed into the half-open spheres like falling meteors. Their velocity and mass multiplied by gravity into one devastating impact, disrupting her levitation and tugging her down. She cried out. At the pain, at them falling together, faster, and faster still, due to hit the ground unless she could reason otherwise.

Teeth clenched, Leesa lifted her other arm into the same position as the first. More waves surged from her fingertips and swirled underneath her comrades. She pictured their figures in her mind, tried to ignore the remnants of a once-thriving city rushing past her.

She screamed with a final surge of determination, thrust her arms down, and caught herself but feet from hitting the sand. The cape whipped behind her as she floated, chest heaving. What followed were the crashing noises of ship debris, not tumbling bodies. She must've caught the three of them in time.

It was a brave first attempt at levitating other living things without malicious intent, which seemed to require a new level of precision and care, as the projected form of her energy was liable to tear things apart.

An experiment.

Yes. Though not her first one, the effort was like so many others, unpredictable.

Leesa marveled at her own success, feeling at peace with her performance. Her companions lay unconscious, though intact, their bodies cradled within her translucent bowls of telekinetic energy.

But the sand went on tearing at the skin on their exposed faces. She gasped, a bit in shock, a bit in worry, and lifted her hands until they were tight against her chest, her whole body squeezing for more potential. The rush of heated energy coursed through her body, then erupted from it, exploding outward like a supernova and solidifying into a forcefield around them.

She lowered the bodies to the ground. The weather, the terrain—she'd made sure neither could inflict damage on them anymore—for as long as she could *keep it together*.

Leesa raised her eyes. For the first time, she could see the infamous ruins of Man's Lost Lands. A catastrophe she'd heard endless CynqueNews broadcasts about yet never witnessed. And to know that a living being could command nature over such a great distance and with such accuracy froze Leesa's arms at her sides.

The land before her was an endless stretch of sand-filled sea, tossing and turning beneath the superstorm known as the Middle Beast. Among the rolling desert's dunes lay millions of decayed corpses reaching for salvation, abandoned caravans overturned like capsized boats, fallen structures, and caved-in rooftops drifting like debris. A foul haze of trapped desert heat and human deterioration permeated over the abandoned city like a thick fog.

The Evolutionary responsible had lent the region no compassion.

A devastated people did not convince them to recall the winds, or to scatter the clouds. For the culprit was unable to quell their insatiable thirst for human eradication. Even when everything had already been taken.

Everything, she guessed—except C20.

The destruction around her was not unlike Brisbane. Further proof that C20 was in that desert somewhere, quietly scheming, silently observing anything that survived the giant swirling weapon booming and flashing above them.

Leesa knelt beside Allister with an intrigue that bordered on feral, tempted to sniff his twitching, blood-soaked face, nudge his curly hair. She did neither, and instead watched his muscled chest expand and contract, her senses perked for any unseen adversity.

As close to C20 as she assumed they'd gotten, the absence of confrontation read as preposterous, and the more authentic the vacancy appeared, it read as suspicious. She had to ask herself if Allister was given the right coordinates or if he was led to a place where he could be vetted before being drawn deeper into the mix.

She stretched her fingers and closed them into a fist, contemplating her next move.

That's when she saw it in the background: a gargantuan phallic symbol thickly veiled by the sandy foreground's rage. The rest of it seemed to disappear where the tempest's lowest clouds flicked lightning.

It was *them*.

C20.

Hiding inside that supernatural storm.

She fought back against the storm's deceit, willing more sand away, knowing there was more to C20 than that faintly outlined clue. Her mind pulsed with thoughts of triumph. Her jaw clenched with a deep rage. Still, the truth of her discovery bombarded them from an intrusive closeness, angrier by the minute as consecutive wind bursts summoned more sand soldiers and enough momentum and fortitude to bury them alive.

And then she stood, fists tight, channeling her potential through her eyes, determined to strip away the paint and see, really see, what its creator, Tas-Salvatur, had wanted concealed.

She felt her body igniting from within, could sense her experiment building from matter manipulation into something more ferocious, destructive. She couldn't bring herself to stop. Not when the outline continued to gain definition.

Clouds parted around a flattened oval, which appeared to be the top of a mushroom-shaped watchtower. Sweltering heat rippled across its thick steel base.

Leesa stiffened at the sight of it. She'd been searching for C20 for as long as she could remember. She shouldn't be paralyzed. She should be activated. Ready to take them on. To bring them down. Feeling confronted by her own purpose, she tried taking a step, tried bringing forth the fury that caused Brisbane's eradication so as to incinerate the desert.

Because her salvation was at hand. Within sight. Within *reach*.

Why, then, at the edge of her greatest enemy, was she rooted to that spot, a few brisk steps from Allister. The reason was so simple and straightforward, she knew it to her darkest depths. Not a thought in her head, but a feeling in her heart. A connection to him, a nagging force, a magnetic pull that kept them linked as one ever-evolving molecule. She suspected said force would be the catalyst to the full realization of their respective existence.

Leesa swallowed down her thoughts about Allister where they could be digested free of toxicity. To empathize with him would be to admit that his life had value, and to admit that his life had value would be to acknowledge that she had started to care for him.

Perhaps it was the strain of that truth that made manipulating the storm from such a range too difficult.

She released her telekinetic disbursement.

Allister's coughs overpowered her thoughts—violent coughs interrupted by his subsequent gagging. He was on his hands and knees, clearing his guts of sand.

"Planning to leave us?" he asked.

"If I wanted to leave you here, I would've done it," she said. "I was establishing a secure perimeter...like we discussed." As a make good, she floated over and stretched a hand toward him. "Let me help you."

He rolled his eyes and looked away, but after a moment, he reached up.

His skin touched hers. Unconsciously, their fingers intertwined.

Allister mumbled, "Thank you," as she pulled him to his feet.

She couldn't seem to let him go. Blue energies danced up through the lines in her palms and veins in her forearms. The vividness of the cosmos expanded behind her eyes.

Entranced, she wrenched her hand back and held it to her body, unable to stand the visions that mounted the walls of her conscious mind: a lush, vibrant countryside filled with wild beasts and twisted foliage blended harmoniously with sprawling urban centers, cities of sparkling crystal towers and homes of polished metal and stone.

Leesa twitched as the image appeared a second and third time.

"You all golden?" Allister asked, his voice echoing in surround sound.

His concern was enough to bring her mind back to the screaming desert. But not words to her lips. Or calm to her nerves.

"Yo, Lieutenant," he said with more urgency. "You with it or not?"

Her senses were running on overdrive. The forcefield was too bright. Her skin too warm. The wind, the thunder, his voice, all too loud.

"Leesa," he said harshly.

It came out as if a shout. She put up her hands and twisted away from him, startled. "I'm sorted," she snapped.

Allister crossed his arms and scowled, clearly offended. He was still the same distance from her, not attempting physical contact of any kind.

"Just...check on him," she said, nodding at Dorian.

He didn't protest, simply turned and trekked across the sand, head shaking in what could only be frustration.

The visions would be her mystery to solve.

Another day.

She pressed her hand against her forehead, then each cheek.

Both were normal temperature.

"Is he breathing?" Leesa asked over her shoulder.

"Barely," Allister answered.

He was kneeling, hunched over Dorian, alternating between placing his ear to Dorian's chest and pumping at it with his hands. He waited a moment, and when Dorian didn't move, he tried again.

Then, a third time.

"I don't know what else to do," Allister said after the fourth try. His eyes traveled up and down the kid's limp body. "What else can I do?"

She didn't answer fast enough.

He scoffed and continued pumping Dorian's chest with more aggression.

Guilt filled her mind with what-ifs. If she had been able to keep the ship in the air. If Allister's touch hadn't left her torn between curiosity and obligation. If she wasn't paralyzed by knowing what to do and not doing it. Once again, her ego had possibly cost another life, and it was clearer to her than ever now, as tears trickled down Allister's cheeks while he tried to save Dorian a fifth time.

"Stay with it, Dorian, you're not finished yet," Allister said, then blew air into the kid's lungs with quicker bursts and more force. Fidgeting, she watched as he came back up to see if it had worked. "Stay with it!" he repeated, pushing down in even rhythms.

Dorian took a breath too deep and turned to the ground, gagging. Sand and saliva spewed from his quivering lips.

Leesa's face broke with relief. She didn't know why the tears welled in her eyes. Perhaps from witnessing the string of small victories. Perhaps from the slim chance at self-redemption.

She'd managed to keep them all from dying. *Even myself.*

Dorian rubbed his eyes with his wrist, clearly cautious of the sand stuck to his hands. He frowned at the half-lion, half-wolf thing that still lay unconscious a few feet away. She could see the moment realization dawned, when he laid his eyes on the aircraft parts sprinkled in the sand beyond them. Dorian's shoulders slumped forward as he signed an apology with his fist rotating clockwise against his chest.

"Not your fault, Dorian," Allister said. "You tried." He grabbed on to Dorian's trembling hands, giving them a squeeze. Allister addressed her next, but he was missing the understanding from seconds ago. "Yo, you totally choked up there."

Leesa frowned, then, feeling defensive, snapped, "I did not choke." Her voice lifted, she said, "I...I lost my bearings when I saw the Z-energy—I thought..." *I wouldn't be able to keep it together,* she said in her mind, looking to Allister for words to fill fresh silence.

"Lost your—" He paused to scratch his head. "I just don't understand how you can keep this"—he opened his arms to the forcefield—"going, when we basically fell out of the sky."

She could hear in his delivery he was straddling the line between intrigue and accusation. But all she felt was the shame sewing insecurity's seeds into her jaw until it clenched.

So much for her redemption.

Allister might as well have been her father in that moment, insatiable, ungrateful. *Cold.* Would anything she did ever be enough for anyone? Would *she* ever be enough? The questions wouldn't stop repeating, maybe because the answers didn't come.

I am incredible.

Her fingers curled. "I didn't choke," she said again, trembling. "I saved your lives."

She left them in a flurry of mixed emotions and marched to the forcefield's transparent edge.

Beyond it, the sand wouldn't stop moving across the desert. She could see why: the incessant wind blustering over the dunes, the half dozen cyclones twisting amongst the ruins. The watchtower, however, was missing. She could no longer see its outline or its shadow, no matter how hard she squinted. But she knew it was still there, could feel it taunting her with its elusiveness, the awareness like a sharp pinching in her bones.

Her fingers continued curling with resolution.

She stood so close to her forcefield, she could make out the individual honeycomb shapes locking it together in sturdiness. Again, she concentrated on the horizon, eyes narrowed at the place where the tower had first appeared. Though she would swear she was aiming her potential at taming the storm, it seemed she wasn't.

The surface of her forcefield cracked like ice. Sharp, jagged lines darted out from her focal point. She let them spread beyond her frame, beyond her vision, beyond her control.

She felt small, too small—too small to keep a forcefield intact.

Keep it together.

"Mega, right?" Allister said, next to her.

Leesa really hated that word. But she was starting to hate it *less* when he said it. Maybe because his discomfort was effortless. His humility, softening. It was the radiance she couldn't let go of. How his eyes were bright without any light hitting them. How his forearm muscles flexed every time he inhaled. How his skin still glimmered with all that sand sticking to it.

Her stomach fluttered with desire while her face remained stone. Her heart chopped through her pent-up resentment and almost reached a clearing while her hair stood on her arms, charged by their chemistry.

"Dorian said I should chill," Allister said. "Thinks I'm not being fair. Sorry... for, uhm, what I said...to you." Every few breaths, he rocked up on his heels and came back down after wobbling with no suave or cool. Sighing, he continued, "I guess I never trusted you. I wanted you to trust me, yeah, but I never trusted you. Ever since the assessment, my watch-your-back trigger got switched on... and...maybe I never got around to turning it off. I think I want to turn it off." As his mouth twisted side to side, he seemed held hostage by a feeling he'd never express. "You could've left us to die, and you didn't, you saved us. That was a golden move, counts for heaps...but, I still don't know a thing about you, Leesa. You keep giving me these hard, unbreakable lieutenant vibes. I mean, look at you right now."

She loosened her fingers and looked down at herself, aware of the rigidness in her body, possibly for the first time. Her shoulders were so high they crowded her neck. And the cape—the garish, self-righteous cape—whipped at her ankles. As the fearless lieutenant, she had come there to retrieve the artifacts. Allister had to know that much, even if he pretended that he didn't. Such was a singular objective stemming from complicated priorities: pleasing her father, ensuring her survival, and maybe, somewhere deep in there, saving the world.

Leesa, on the other hand, cared less and less about survival, rejected the false promise of the Andromeda Project legacy. She was tender, exploring herself, curious about strange out-of-body visions, yet ever cautious of her connection to the Z-energy.

All she'd ever wanted was to be the Gateway.

He tilted his head toward her, a serious look on his face. "I'm a little on edge about why you haven't done it," he said.

Her eyes questioned him before her lips could form the words.

Nodding, he lowered his arms as if to show he'd play along. "Why haven't you charged in on C20 all hyped, Z-energy guns blazing, cape billowing behind you...and brought back the artifacts?"

The lie spilled forth before she could stop it.

"Because...we agreed on a strategy."

"Nice try, Lieutenant. That's not it."

After that, their conversation wandered into extended silence—him trapped between his question and her answer, her trapped between another excuse and the truth.

"Because, I'm afraid," she finally answered in a voice too soft to carry. "I'm afraid I'll destroy everything, afraid that, despite all my training and my potentials...it'll be..." *Just like Brisbane,* she thought, then said instead, "That we'll fail, and the world will end with us in it."

"Heavy." Allister looked up at the cracks in the forcefield instead of looking up at her. "Sure, you're afraid. I bet if we're scared of ourselves, pretty much gives everyone else the thumbs-up to be scared of us too." He paused and stood shoulder to shoulder with her, his eyes moving left to right with the dust. "I just...I don't want to be scared of my potentials anymore."

I don't want to be scared of my potentials anymore. She let those words sink into her, the truth of them, the pain of them. At their cores, she and Allister shared more than access to the Z-energy. They shared similar struggles...and identical fears.

"I am so—" Leesa stammered. She stopped and tried again. "I apol—" She cut herself off a second time. "I'm...how do I put this—?"

"That hard to get out, huh?"

"I'm not always good with my words, or my feelings," she said, turning to him. "I've found it's best mine stay locked up."

Allister was staring at her with a smile spread wide across his face. "Don't think we're supposed to be good at them, Leesa, I think we're just supposed to feel them, really *feel* them."

She cringed at his continued use of her name but didn't correct him. "I could see how that might work," she said. She crossed her hands over her heart and waited. When she felt nothing, she dropped her arms. "Hmmm. Feeling seems to be a potential all its own."

"Ha, you'd better start practicing."

Her mouth turned up on one side into a crooked smile. She looked away to hide it, and a piece of loose hair fell from the poorly stacked bun and over her face. She grabbed it near the root, ready to yank it free. An awareness stopped her from doing it, and she traced the wayward strand back over her damaged hairline, her jaw flexing at the soreness her touch ignited.

Still, she went higher, running her hands through her hair. Not checking for imperfections, just enjoying its texture, the softness against her fingers. She paused when she reached the top of her regimented hairstyle, wary of her father's disappointment. But would he see if she destroyed it right there? Or would he never know because she could always put them back when she needed to? Without realizing it, she was digging into her hair. First, feeling a few individual strands from the root to the tip, then pulling away clumps until it was all free.

Leesa shook out her hair and arranged it in front of her shoulders.

Dorian clapped twice from behind them.

"I agree with him. You look…free," Allister said, rubbing his neck. "I love it." Though he was still smiling, it appeared as though something more serious had come to mind. He looked out over the desert. "Wonder if our plan is shot. You think they can see us?"

"If they saw us, I am sure we would know already."

"Hmm, any clue where they are?"

"I did see something earlier, I think—a giant, rotating tower." She pointed straight ahead. "A half a mile or so west of here. I think whatever they're operating on has to be as big as a city."

Allister double tapped his Cynque. The city of Al Basra's original layout ballooned into holographic existence. His finger moved the display beyond their coordinates and farther into the barren desert. He rotated it once, then again and again, muttering at each alternate angle. When he was done, he waved his hand over the device.

The hologram vanished.

He didn't mention what he was looking for and didn't mention if he'd found it. The anger on his face was enough of an indication.

"I know your impulse is to act now," she began, lifting her chin for authority. "I propose we move when the desert is darkest."

Allister considered her. "Golden. An hour lost, then, maybe less," he said as he left her side. "Guess we're going stealth mode...no forcefields."

"I'm with it," she said slowly, though too low for him to hear. The phrase felt strange on her lips, but she rather enjoyed its simplicity, surprised how it encompassed the entirety of her emotions.

A camp, then. Something formidable that would blend in.

The fortress she'd imagined in her psyche was simple, tall, and sturdy, like the sacred wing of a crystalline castle. Alongside that image, the words *Nournt Zeorgen* repeated in her head. But as she closed her eyes and swept her hands across her body, she felt only her telekinetic potential respond in calm, rippling waves, drawing the sand molecules and stone rubble to her. She compacted them as they swirled across her waist, conjoined them to form intricate shapes. She stacked and locked them, holding the shelter in place.

The fortress grew like a beanstalk, birthing a pillar made of fused sand and stone that aspired to touch the clouds with its blunt tip. It was almost indistinguishable from the region's iconic architecture, though it had a sturdy base and an intact roof.

Using a single finger, Leesa carved the entrance. *Like how Mom would have done it,* she thought.

The forcefield fizzled and dissolved without purpose, carried away by the invading wind. She stroked her flailing hair until the strands were captive under her forearm and watched as Allister hoisted the still-recovering lion-wolf creature over his shoulder.

He held one hand over his face. "You coming?" he shouted to her, half turned.

Dorian trekked ahead of him.

So he was talking to her. Her heart swelled in a way it never had, too big to be contained and warm and energized.

The feelings—she really felt them.

Artist: The CMD Studios

CHAPTER 44

DOLORES PRIMROSE ADAMS

Unknown Location
Day 207

TWELVE YEARS PAST and Dolores was bait for Allister's cooperation yet again. It was ironic how the hands that had kidnapped her belonged to the same man who'd rescued her before. Back when the Z-energy had landed on Earth.

This was different. It was bigger than her life, she knew that much. Maybe even bigger than her death.

She'd been awake when they arrived on Day 208, wherever it was they were, winded from having held her breath for what felt like eons in Jared Brandt's arms. Allister's slumped body was the last thing she remembered before the black curtain had fallen over her vision, causing an explosion of her body into tiny droplets of mist.

Molecular transportation was more uncomfortable than she'd ever imagined, and when she was made whole again, some parts of her skin still stung, other parts still burned. Her bones ached as if they'd been smashed back together. Her muscles throbbed like they'd been tacked onto her skeleton.

Nearly twenty-four hours chained up in a pitch-black room the size of a shower pod, and all of sudden they wanted to move her "underground."

She was then escorted by two of C20's Evolutionaries, Vonnie and Tranjam Kim, who'd fitted her with a metal mask. Something funky and rusted, with blacked-out circles for eye holes, tiny incisions for her nose, and an opening in the bottom just loose enough to prevent suffocation.

Footsteps moved around her. Whispers moved with them. She strained her ears to listen but couldn't hear what they were saying through the thickness of the mask. Then, with abrupt force, a chain was looped and fastened around her neck and tugged in a single jerking motion, a violent indication that she was meant to follow. And she did, while being yanked forward every few minutes like a naughty animal.

Dolores groaned from the twisting pain in her stomach and tried to take a deeper breath, feeling her head lighten as if it might float away and take her consciousness with it. By the time their progression on relatively level sand became a steep decline, they'd turned more corners than she could remember, and she'd tripped, or stumbled, or fallen more times than that.

The footsteps stopped. A small hand grabbed her shoulder from behind, forcing her to stop, too.

"Here?" asked Vonnie, who seemed to be the one holding her in place.

The other one, Tranjam, answered, "Yeah. Here." He grabbed Dolores's arm, and after pulling her forward, shoved her to the ground and got to restraining her.

She thrashed and screamed in protest. *Please, Patrick! If your spirit is here, with me,* she thought wildly, *don't let it end like this for us! Too much is comin' for it to end like this!*

Tranjam was twisting her wrists in uncomfortable directions, trying to wrestle them against a thick metal pole lodged upright in the sand.

"Help me, she won't stop fighting," he said to Vonnie.

Dolores wouldn't stop so long as her heart beat.

"You'd better stop moving," warned Vonnie.

"Go to hell," Dolores screamed, kicking at the air, her back against the pole.

Vonnie loosened the neck hole on the mask and tore it off with one upward tug. She swung the blade across her body, then crouched down and pressed the edge to Dolores's throat.

Dolores stopped moving. Her eyes widened, glued to the woman's steady, nearly transparent hands.

The blade faded to the same transparency, losing color and molecular consistency, allowing Vonnie to push it deeper through her neck. The weapon, now touching her spine, had lost enough density to feel like something lodged in her throat, but could just as easily become something ripping through it. "Thin as air, you see?" Vonnie said, matter-of-fact. "It can be solid as steel, too."

Dolores gulped at the idea. All it would take was a thought.

"Good." Vonnie removed the blade and stood as Tranjam fastened thick shackles around Dolores's wrist and the pole, then activated them. A buzzing pain shot through her body.

She bit down instead of screaming.

Dolores knew the hostage game well enough, and the last thing she wanted them to see was her suffering.

"You resist, that's what happens," Tranjam said.

"You're all gonna get what's comin' to ya," Dolores shot at the twins. "Ain't nothing I know of can save you from that."

Vonnie leaned on her glaive and stroked the staff with a long, sharpened nail. Her smile was devilish, stark white, and wide, her eyes thinned by the look of glee. "You are thoroughly blessed, Dolores Adams. Your soulmate has pioneered us to this place of evolution and power, your offspring will be the gateway that ushers us into it. And you, you will be the sweet sacrifice of heritage. Glorious."

Dolores looked away, seething at her core with fury and despair.

"Stay put," Tranjam said from where he stood at the exit. "I know how to maim without killing."

The door slammed and bolted shut.

Lights strung to walls showed Dolores what existed beyond her bent knees— just a hollowed-out space made of compact sand.

She knew it was night by the underground temperature, it being the least bit bearable, but the storm—the Middle Beast—still howled with the agony of a lost child. Beating and clawing and striking at a surface out of her reach.

She heaved in the dimness. Even more delirious. Even more resistant. She suspected that with the pain she felt, the pain of losing her own child to something as simple as purpose, she had the strength to uproot an entire civilization. The pole growing out of the sand would be *easy*. She stretched forward, tired of it digging behind her shoulders, her legs already on their way to falling asleep. As Tranjam had promised, a series of sharp pains shot up her arms. She bit down again, muffling a scream, then stopped squirming and relaxed her muscles, but resisted the temptation to lean back.

She had taken every possible precaution. She had absorbed every possible stress. Annual relocation, QBs split across international accounts, settling in Riser Town over New Soho or ChiTown Sanctity. She'd traded the honey of her hair for grays. She'd given up the smoothness of her face for creases and wrinkles. Despite all her rules and expectations, her double shifts and hushed payments to a Cynque engineer, the future she dreaded had happened.

I refuse to die here.

Alone was a word she couldn't add to her thought, though it fit snugly before the period. To think or to say it would prompt her to feel it.

But she was alone. She'd been alone for more years than she wanted to admit. Even with a brilliant son nipping at her heels and reaching for her hands.

Allister had asked her to teach him, to play with him, to acknowledge him, to *see* him, the whole time trying to be good enough to be noticed. Yet she'd only scolded him for his every mistake, held him to standards he'd never achieve, and accountable for actions he'd never committed. It was her favorite kind of love: protection, distance. Maybe that's how she'd managed to push him into the arms of the Andromeda Project. The same way she'd pushed Patrick into his grave.

No, she told herself, *he made his choice…I just…* Didn't tell him why he shouldn't do it; that was what she couldn't bear to even think.

Her chin fell to a restful place against her sternum. Her hair fell with it, covering her face with wild, dirty curls. She swallowed her tears.

"Patrick, *are* you here?" she asked. For the first time since his death, his name brought reverence and fond memories. The way he smiled when he thought of something new, and grinned when he thought of something naughty, and stroked her temple when he upset her. How he told her he loved her every day, every hour, every fifteen minutes, as often as he could. She had to forgive him for his "mistresses"—science and gadgets and alien technology and advanced intelligence (his favorite potential)—those somewhat intangibles that had pulled him away from her.

She had to forgive him, period.

Because he didn't know.

She straightened her body, keen to the chills now rippling across her skin. A sensation. A subtle signal. The cosmic tug of heightened energy vibration. Suddenly, she could taste her wood-fire kitchen, smell the fertilizer of their farmland and the sunflowers Patrick always brought her. She could feel the cool Cumberland breeze against her cheeks—his fingers as they traced her hair, her chin, her lips.

"No," she said, closing her eyes. "No," she repeated.

A glowing white light flooded her face, pulled her forward even as she resisted its shine. She was caught between dream and reality, confronted by an awareness of the crystal artifacts…tortured by their loud, nagging whispers calling from a sacred realm hidden within the universe. This realm had once been a cave inside of a mountain that had once been a trench under the sea that had once been the throne of a civilization. But what it was now, she couldn't be sure.

She kept her eyes closed and shook her head. "No."

It was nothing to her.

The vision faded. There was no wood-fire kitchen. No fertilizer or sunflowers. No cool breeze or loving touch from her dead husband. There was no white light and no artifacts. There was a hollowed-out prison of sand and…a pole that wouldn't stop moving.

Dolores kept pulling and inching forward, pulling and inching forward, owning the pain as the pole bent to her will. It wasn't buried as deep as she'd imagined, and after several more tries, she ripped it out of the sand in one upward motion. Exhausted, she collapsed onto one side. Her legs prickled with the pain of slumber, blood threading its way to her feet like a million sewing needles, stitching feeling back into her limbs.

She smiled against the powdered sand. *Mom taught me that one*, she thought, thankful for her mother's cunning.

Being a hostage was not new for Dolores, whether it be Nicolas Delemar or XBA or the whole of C20, she had been trained since childhood at evasion, at secrecy, and maneuvering out of tight spaces.

Quietly, she gauged her own flexibility. In a fit of hasty, awkward movements, Dolores used her heels to pull the pole from between the shackles and kicked it aside. She knew the easiest part had passed and took a break as she prepared her mind for the near impossible. The move in her head was rather acrobatic, one she'd only done twice, when she was much younger—

She'd have to get her hands from behind her back to have a fighting chance.

"You can do this, Dee. You've done it before." She nodded to assure herself, then repeated, "You've done it before."

A second later, she was squirming and grunting and rolling around in the sand. Fighting her hips and their width, her arms and their inflexibility, her spine and its refusal to curve. She cursed them, then begged them to cooperate, then cursed them all over again. Combined, they were the obstacle she'd feared, an improbable win for a woman in her late thirties, even one who used to be quick *and* nimble. But with determination, she curved her hips, stretched her arms, arched her spine, eventually managing her wrists around her feet and into her lap. Disregarding of her face being covered in sand and the repetitive buzz of the shackles still punishing her for her movement, she was satisfied.

Next, she'd figure out the lock on the prison and get her hands on one of those plasma weapons.

A solid plan, if not for the sound of boots scuffing the ground. They were far away at first, yet making their way closer until they ended at the door. A long beep echoed from the hallway.

The bolt unlocked. The door creaked open. Someone stepped inside, backlit by light beaming from the tunnel beyond the door.

She'd recognize the man before her anywhere: Jared Brandt—his bright-blue eyes and serious scowl, his thick neck and broad shoulders and tapered torso, even as the shadow tried hiding who they all belonged to.

That's because they'd known each other since they were teenagers.

Her face twisted in contempt as she heard him walking toward her. "Keep your enemies closer, right?" she said.

"Now's not the time to be clever," Jared said, eyeing the uprooted metal next to her hips. He sucked his teeth. "Why're you so hardheaded, Dee?"

She looked up at him and replied, "Why're you so desperate, Jared?"

"Your mouth still as slick as oil, I swear."

Dolores watched him as he moseyed over and plopped down beside her, legs crossed.

Sitting there, together, staring at the prison door as if what lay before them was his mother's neglected farmland, she was reminded of their old times together. Except, back then, Patrick was always on the other side of her.

"You feeling okay?" he asked.

"Be a lot better if I was free."

"As expected," he said. His fingers danced one at a time across his knees. "I always wonder if you really remember how much we been through together."

She swallowed instead of what she wanted do, which was scoff. She was too angry to move and too shaken by his words to show it. "You have some nerve," she said, trying to keep her voice from breaking. "You have some goddamn nerve. You stood beside me and Patrick at the altar on our wedding day. You held Allister's head the morning he was christened. You even…you even protected us after the Arrival." She pulled in her legs and cradled them with her shackled hands. "Jared, we've been through everything together," she whispered. "I didn't forget. *You* did."

"I've been followin' my gut, and for the second time ever, somethin' feels right."

Now, she scoffed. He was always going on about his intuition.

"Why not give the power to the people?" Jared asked. "Let them choose evolution and how best to save themselves, 'stead of letting a bunch of outta-sight moguls and politicians commoditize and weaponize what we need to survive?"

Dolores let her side-eye travel up and down and back up, tearing at him, judging him. He wore that same self-righteous smirk, the look of *I always know best*. But in her experience, he'd always managed to prove he didn't know much at all. "You got no idea how deep this goes, do you, Captain?" She laughed a cruel, low laugh. "Daal Trelkkien, the Z-energy, that's just the tip, honey. Just the whipped cream. Wait until you cut into the crust. And I know you like the crust."

Jared shrugged off her taunts. "I keep tellin' myself it's not real. What that scum General Delemar did to Patty Cakes, what the Andromeda Project...was." His voice quieted. "I keep tellin' myself Cumberland was a dream and I could still go back when I'm ready. My lil' boy will meet me at the road when I pull in. My sweet Kahla will be inside fixin' somethin' nice between conference calls."

"Wake up, Jared, it's real," she said, sneering. "You know why I ran? Because I believed all of it. You been living in this fairy tale, like, like you can control the outcome just cuz you think you got a good heart and a sound mind and a steady hand. That's your problem—underneath all that, you're still a coward. You don't wanna go forward. You wanna go back."

Tears filled her eyes. These twelve years past, she'd been trying to move on from it all. The Andromeda Project. The Arrival. The apocalypse. She wasn't any happier back then, thinking they could stop the end of humanity, than she was right in this moment, knowing they couldn't.

Dolores didn't want to go back. But she did. The anger rose in her like a mountain, covered in the devastation of Patrick's loss, the wishing she'd done things different. The hope that someone, anyone, at that organization had had an ounce of courage.

"I'm trying to honor Patty's legacy," Jared said.

And there was the captain, sitting beside her, pretending not to know. The nerve. For him to speak such nonsense when Patrick didn't have to have a legacy at all.

He could just be *alive*.

"Is that it?" she asked, incredulous. "What? By joining a bunch of EV terrorists, kidnapping me, and forcing your godson to hand over the power to move through space and time?" She nudged him with her elbow. "Go on. I'm listening. Please, tell me your master plan."

"I…"

Dolores leaned close to his ear, and growled, "You and your damn intuition. I bet you didn't think it'd come to this." She hit him in the chest with her fists and yelled, "Just like you didn't think your best friend would end up with a bullet through his skull!" She raised her arms to hit him again, but he swiveled and caught them in midair. "You killed Patrick the night you didn't stand up for him!"

She writhed in his grip, cursing and spitting at his face between her elbows. It was twelve years of a widow's pent-up mourning and blistering rage, unleashed at once. Jared was as much to blame as anyone, and in her opinion, he deserved everything she threw at him, whether it was her fists or her insults. Though the skin around her wrist burned from the metal's violent friction, and her fingers tingled from lack of circulation, she fought as hard as she could.

The more she struggled, the tighter he squeezed.

"Your mama always said you weren't worth a thing!" she shouted. "Maybe Patrick and I should've listened."

Jared yanked her to him and held her there. He was shaking, red-faced. "My ma was a drunk and an addict," he said, his breath coming out hot and fast. "She didn't know nothing about the value on a human life, let alone the value on her children's, you hear me?"

Dolores pressed her lips together, the grimace chiseled into the corners of her mouth, the creases etched in her brow.

"Don't you put that on me," Jared said. "I'd give anything to bring Patty back. Anything."

He shoved her backward.

She fell on her side, searching him for remorse, hoping for a slice of the man she'd known. But in that dim, washed-out light, she found only his resolution. Perhaps it was the reflective white of his C20 suit. Disappointed, she turned away, sucking back the snot and the tears that ran down her face. The guilt didn't sink into him the way she wanted, not deep enough to change his mind, just deep enough to make him think he knew better about how to make it right. "If you really mean what you're saying, let Allister keep the artifacts. He'll do what's right. You know he will."

Jared looked helpless then, barely able to get out the words. "I wish I could make that promise, Dee. I really do."

Dolores shook her head in disgust. He might as well have kept a script around dishing out all those recycled lines. He'd said as much once, she remembered, on that drive out of Cumberland. Though, back then, it was about the Andromeda Project *not* coming after Allister.

"Fraternizing with the prisoners, I see," said a shadowed figure entering the doorway. "Shame on you."

Jared jumped up. "I'm just checkin' in, XBA. Get off my back."

"I suggest you get off my back," XBA warned Jared, her claws outstretched. "Tas-Salvatur's orders."

"I should've known," Dolores said. "No upfront costs? No binding loyalties? I coulda guessed that machine wasn't enough for you…nothin' ever is with you people."

At that, XBA strolled through the archway and stopped at Jared, the smile on her reconstructed face too wide to be confused with joy. Whatever mercy had been required in Riser Town was long gone. A new directive shined in XBA's flashing orange eye. The wild look of *do whatever it takes*.

Dolores's blood went cold.

She hoped that something she had said would get Jared fighting again, if not for her, then for what he believed in. He seemed to be resisting, still not out of XBA's way despite the acute threat of violence.

"Alright, then," XBA said. "We do it my way." Red energy pulsed from her human eye and settled on his face.

Jared stepped aside with the ease of blind obedience. Maybe mind control? He wouldn't speak to or look at Dolores, and instead headed toward the door, mumbling to himself.

"You take direction so well, soldier, has anyone ever told you that?" XBA said, waving him off. She zeroed her attention in on Dolores. "Now, let's have a good chat, like old times."

Dolores dug her heels into the sand and tried to push herself back. She could tell it was over, that she'd reached the end. There was no sense keeping her mouth shut. If the woman was going to kill her, she'd kill her either way.

She fixed her mouth in defiance. "When Allister gets here—"

"We're taking you to the dig site," XBA finished.

Dolores swallowed, thinking perhaps she'd misheard the cyborg. *Does she really mean...* "Me?" fell out of her mouth before she could stop it.

"You." XBA dragged her tongue across her jagged teeth and stepped forward, but addressed Jared, who idled by the exit. "Tas-Salvatur had the most unusual discovery today, Captain. An increase in temporal activity in Man's Lost Lands since this little treasure's arrival...isn't that right, 'Sweet Dee'?"

At the word *temporal*, swirling white light flashed behind Dolores's eyes. She pitched forward, shocked by the brightness. Her body heaved from the strain of suffocating its presence. Blinking hard, she concentrated on the white light now consuming her vision. It couldn't be there, stirring in her, not after she'd put it away. "No...no...it's not true!"

XBA pretended to frown. "It's not?" She dropped on all fours by Dolores's ankles. She started kneading at her calves, as if a cat, then moved to massaging Dolores's thighs, the sharp points of her metallic claws puncturing the thin fabric and the skin underneath. "You promise on these beautiful limbs you're not lying to me?"

Dolores was rocking back and forth and pretending not to hear her. She knew what was coming—the torture. She didn't want to wait. "Whatever you gonna do, just do it," she said.

"Splendid. I *really* don't like being lied to," XBA said. The orange eye burned with triumph as her claws reached the underside of Dolores's thigh and squeezed for thickness. She gave them a firm pat. "Good as new, hmmm?" She looked up with calculated slowness, the mechanical wiring around her jaw crinkling with amusement. "As I was saying, it seems you've been keeping something from us. Since I'm such a big fan of integrity, I'd like to give you the opportunity to *spill*." By the knowing look on her face, she was expecting an answer.

But XBA didn't know how well Dolores had been trained.

She smiled a defeated smile, still rocking, and said, "All I can spill is that...once Allister touches those artifacts...you'll never get what you want."

XBA leaned closer, and Dolores caught her breath just as XBA snatched her face forward. The woman's claws dug in again, this time into her cheeks. "I thought we were on the same page, Dolores."

"I should've told you to piss off seven nights past."

"Such language," XBA said, squeezing her face tighter.

Dolores aimed to swallow, aimed to breathe, but could do neither with the tightness of apprehension shooting from her chest to her throat.

Whatever you gonna do, just do it.

Unlike the others who'd come after Dolores over the years, threatening her safety and her life, XBA was looking to be the kind who'd follow through. Maybe it was the crazed look in her human eye, or the fact that the orange glow was brighter than all hell.

Dolores squirmed then. At the hand not squeezing the bones in her jaw, the one XBA was using to fish the metal pole from the sand. She raised it in the air. Held it there. Letting what little light shone in the prison catch the tip.

"He'll get us those artifacts," snarled XBA, "even if I have to carry your bloody, soon-to-be-irreparable body to him myself." As she finished, she brought her arm down abruptly and—

The pointed end of the pole plunged through Dolores's leg, ripping away flesh and shifting bones on its way down. Dolores screamed until her breath ran out, then screamed again. She could feel how the metal had made room in her tissues, the heat and the pain puncturing her over and over again in the same place the pole had. She held her trembling hands above the injury, afraid to touch her thigh. And yet she had to comfort it, to nurture it—to cradle it until it was free of the agony.

"Good. As. New," XBA said, letting go of the pole.

Dolores's eyes kept opening wide and squeezing shut. Her heart kept beating out of control. The shock took her to another time and another place, then brought her back with a violent slam as another wave of furious fire ran up her leg.

She cried out with the last of her strength.

"What was that? Did you say something, Sweet Dee?"

But the chills had shaken away the last of Dolores's grit. She could do nothing but slump over, sobbing, begging.

"Jared…," she whimpered, rocking to the rhythm of her own rationalization. "Jared…please…help me."

There was no answer.

I'm gonna die here, Dolores thought. *Alone*, she added. A sentence strong enough to conquer her.

Her vision began blurring, almost black, the shock starting to take its toll. As her sight faded, she caught one final glimpse of the blood caking her hands, thick like old soup. Sounds came as if from underwater, muffled, far away, fluid, washed ashore by her ever-crashing waves of pain. But there was nothing fabricated about the mention of a crash, or those three syllables leaving XBA's foul mouth.

Al-li-ster.

Then Dolores's lids closed to the prison, to the world and her future, to the chaos that was about to unfold.

———

CHAPTER 45

LIEUTENANT LEESA DELEMAR
Man's Lost Lands, Former Middle East
Day 207

LEESA NEEDED TO control the Z-energy. She saw no other solution to rescuing Allister's mother and retrieving the artifacts, save for her being the one to assume the role of the Gateway and relieve Allister of his choice. And, she supposed, his obligation.

Perhaps that's why herself, Allister, Dorian, and the animal, whose name she'd learned was Penny, had spent their restful hour in solitude and silence. Collectively lost on the how, anxious about the when, and thoroughly terrified of the what-ifs.

Leesa had felt compelled to clear her mind and prepare for their undertaking. She levitated above her companions, meditating, her eyes firmly shut, her mouth sealed in concentration. She'd arranged her legs in something of a pretzel, a seated position which made her thighs ache as much as it strained her spine. Still, she found herself settling into the pain in her lower back, careful to keep her spine upright, no matter how much the cape's presence seemed to weigh her down.

As she searched for reassurance, there was a moment she couldn't convince herself to let go of. When they'd been tumbling through the turbulent clouds of the Middle Beast. The experiment involving the Z-energy had appeared in place of her telekinetic fields—a rare occasion, even on her worst days. She had felt a sense of weakness at its manifestation, and that weakness brought doubt to her mind. For those crucial seconds, she'd needed only strength to keep going, to keep them in the air, yet it was the shame of Brisbane's elimination that had plagued her.

She'd caved to her fear of her potential. In a sense, she'd let go.

That couldn't happen in the face-off against C20. Nor could it happen when she went after the artifacts.

Leesa breathed into the gnawing along her spine. She exhaled into the depths of introspection. Perhaps it was the stillness—the momentary sense of peace. There was a fusion: her body to her mind, her mind to her spirit, all of it blooming like a flower as a jolt surged through her solar plexus.

The vibrant blue energy ran through her like a river's rushing rapids. She saw flashes of its expansion, spreading beauty and power and life beyond her and Earth, beyond the solar system and their galaxy. A realm of minds racing through open space soared past and was soon outshined by the collapsing gases of nearby nebulae.

Here, she was a single spirit, a single mind, a single body. *A singular entity,* Leesa thought as she breathed her way higher.

It seemed that the cape and her humanity were in alliance, thwarting her ability to embrace those rampant sensations, the aspiration to ownership. Just as clear as it had been confusing minutes before, the Z-energy made up as much of her brain and heart and lungs, of her muscles and bones, as the tissues and cells themselves. What she'd accepted as a gross exaggeration of her telekinetic powers became something else entirely.

The blue energy was a catalyst.

Her heart beat faster as the visions of space smashed together and exploded into pulsing clusters, then birthed new galaxies in an eruption of blinding light and fire.

Her eyes fluttered.

Wind rushed over her face and through her hair.

She was tumbling toward the sand before she realized she couldn't hold herself up. Nothing came from her hands, just incomprehensible words from her mouth. The ground rushing up was all she saw.

Allister caught her and they both fell back into the sand. As she lay there, stunned, he kept an arm beneath her knee and a hand curved around her torso, clutching her like a treasured possession, high and close to his heart.

Her body relaxed into his.

"Leesa…," he began, "what were you gettin' into up there?" His eyes searched for her eyes and covered her entire face. He seemed lost in looking at her, swallowing as his gaze came back to meet hers. "You were mega bright, like, the purest blue of the Z-energy I've ever seen…" He couldn't finish. But he didn't look afraid so much as in awe, as if it was something he'd seen *before*.

"I was trying to…" *Find myself…* Leesa touched her forehead, trying to think of an excuse instead. "Trying to hold the compound together," she said, "and I saw…" It was her turn to trail off into silence.

The warmth was at its strongest then, like a quiet inferno burning in her soul.

"What'd you see?" Allister asked.

Instead of answering, she traced the air with two fingers, causing particles to float at their faces, swirling into shapes, building solar systems, then a galaxy, then—

"Everything," she finally responded, taking in his wide, inquisitive gaze. "I saw unlimited power and possibility."

"As long as you're good? We're walkin' into some twisted mess, and I…" He lost his words again, but his firm grip stayed with her.

She stared beyond the moment they shared, still fascinated by the sand-modeled universe. "A single grain of sand is the same size as a star if looked at from a certain perspective," she said.

Allister squinted his eyes. He appeared to be pondering all she'd said with a look of skepticism. "You're not really sounding like yourself, Lieutenant."

The use of her formal title snapped Leesa back to herself. She remembered her position and what they'd come there to do and what was at stake. Her creation fell into an uninspired heap on the ground beside them. Gears cranked programming and protocol back into her mechanical demeanor.

She hardened her voice on instinct, on principle. "I don't expect you to understand," she said. She pushed off on his chest and shot to her feet.

"Did I say something twisted?" Allister got up next to her. "Look, just because I'm not with it, doesn't mean I don't want to be."

Leesa turned away. She wanted to escape his orbit, to disregard the gravitational force that kept pulling them back together. Her hovering for more distance between them seemed impossible. Somehow the guilt of shutting him down weighed more than the cape.

"Another time," she said. "I am conflicted."

"Conflicted?"

His Cynque's holographic light flooded the interior before she could answer. The robotic voice pierced the air with a CynqueNews global broadcast. She hesitated to look over her shoulder, not wanting to be intrusive. But at such close proximity, overhearing the updates couldn't be avoided.

"—and we are another day closer to the end as major islands and peninsulas in what we're calling the 'storm cellar,' an area straddling the Pacific and Indian Oceans, face the cluster of super typhoons making landfall well ahead of schedule. On-the-ground specialists are already seeing unprecedented rainfall and winds of catastrophic proportions, the likes of which will permanently flood these coastal cities."

It's starting, she thought, suddenly panicked. She was unsure how the apocalypse had caught up on them so fast. Hadn't they gotten a head start? Perhaps that was a misconception like so many others, an assumption on her part, based on the limited knowledge doled out by the Andromeda Project. If the devastation of De Los Muertos was any indication, the end of all they knew had been in motion for decades...and was coming to a swift conclusion, all thanks to nature's revenge.

She was guided to Allister's side by the prospect of certain tragedy and great loss. They both sank to the ground to watch the corresponding footage above his Cynque.

"As predicted, satellite imagery shows some of these storms are moving toward regions in a fan formation, like a coordinated attack, while the largest has remained in place, gathering more power from the warmed ocean. The bands of this storm have grown exponentially in just under two days past, spreading from an eye now reported to be the size of India. The head of climatology for the Resilient Nations of Global Unity is advising island inhabitants around the globe to flee to the nearest mainlands, and coastal residents are being told to move as far inland as possible."

But with so many planes out of service, how will they all get out? Boats? Her answer came as a series of snippets, the hungry and the homeless on display sporting weathered faces. Societal breakdown was evident in vivid montages: sanctuary streets underwater, families trapped on floating rooftops, colossal waves bombarding coastlines.

They wouldn't get out, she realized, tears stinging her eyes. Those people were being...left behind.

"The Resilient Nations of Global Unity have proposed reopening borders, allowing for as many people to find high elevation as possible, citing, 'We as a race, we as humanity, are facing the end together. Let us not allow the lines we've drawn divide us any longer.' This is CynqueNews reporting, proud to be your single stop for trends, tragedies, and everything in-between. Brought to you by the all-knowing, all-seeing CGN, our official sponsor."

Leesa couldn't believe she'd been spending her last days hunting for cosmic power rather than paying attention to what had been happening in the world around them. Her head was full enough to burst. Her stomach compressed to the point of collapse. Now her obsession over being the one to save the world felt sickening.

She searched Allister's face for the same teary-eyed remorse. He just kept looking at his Cynque, though the broadcast had faded to nothing.

The device's black screen trapped the countdown's green characters in its eternal void: 207 days, 1 hour, 12 minutes, and 31 seconds.

One hour, twelve minutes, and thirty-one seconds until they lost another day.

———

CHAPTER 46

LIEUTENANT LEESA DELEMAR

Man's Lost Lands, Former Middle East
Day 207

LEESA HAD RUN out of time. To be fair, the rest of the world had run out of time, too.

"We get the Crystals of Temporal Transportation no matter what it takes," Allister said, voice shaking. "I can't function, even for another couple hundred days, knowing we're all finished because…I was too scared."

She lifted her eyes to the cone-shaped ceiling. His words were nothing short of a saving grace. The weight of their lives seemed to rise out of her lungs and into the air.

Allister leaned toward an imaginary fire, staring ahead as if he saw something she didn't. "I'm gonna have to fake like I'm switching up, so they don't hurt Mom."

Leesa nodded, gazing into the same imaginary flames.

"That means, when I get to her," he continued, "you gotta drop in, use your telekinetic potential to waste the whole base, and rip outta here. Fly her as far away from C20 as possible. I'll head for the artifacts."

Once again, she'd been positioned as a trigger waiting to be pulled.

Her eyes flicked to the opposite side of the compound, where Dorian poured a vial of liquid into his palm and allowed Penny to lick it off. The animal then bounced away from him and nuzzled her nose into the sand, carefree as she wiggled her butt, burying it deeper.

Certain the two of them were distracted, Leesa placed her hand on top of Allister's, stroked the sand-ridden skin around his knuckles, scooted closer to let her fingers trace his wrists and forearms.

"Allister…I'm…I'm more than…a weapon," Leesa began. "You were right. This is bigger than which of us retrieves the artifacts…I came because…because I wanted you to be able to save your mom without having to make a choice between her and humanity. We can do both. Together."

"Together?" Allister asked.

Leesa's eyes brightened. "Imagine how many people we'd be able to save."

"Loads," he said quietly.

Finally, he looked into her eyes. *Keep yourself together,* she heard her father's voice in her mind.

Their two foreheads pressed together instead. She traced a vein she'd already traced. *Keep yourself together.*

But she couldn't.

Her fingers moved higher, past the ridges of flexed muscle in his shoulder, up the softness of his neck, over the carved edge of his chin and the smoothness of his cheek.

Allister's hand pressed hers against his face. He turned her palm over and kissed it.

Her body quaked at the softness of his lips, shrank as he pulled her closer. She knew a kiss would be too dangerous. They'd be basking in mutual respect instead of admiration. Any hierarchies or protocols would be moot.

Keep yourself together, she thought again as her eyes closed.

His body tensed with what she hoped was desire. Hers pulsed with what she knew to be passion. As Allister gripped her face and held the small of her back, her lips were drawn to his like a comet to the inner solar system. She braced herself for impact, certain she'd be destroyed.

But before they could kiss, she heard sniffing near her ear. Curious, she opened her eyes. The animal's rough tongue slathered saliva all over the side of her face. She almost fell back in astonishment. "Penny!" she gasped.

Everyone seemed frozen, waiting for Leesa's reaction. Was it her wrath they expected? Allister was wide-eyed, gulping. Dorian was halfway to them, face twisted in horror. Penny stood with her tongue still out, as if ready to deliver more sopping-wet kisses.

Leesa looked at them one after another. Then, she began…laughing.

In that tense moment of affection and danger, she chose joy. She succumbed to the pleasure of holding her stomach as she fell over, laughing harder than she'd ever laughed. She surrendered to the aching of a wide, unremovable smile. Whatever the lieutenant was splintered and fell away. She was cracked open. The mold would not fit with her head cocked back or her legs splayed in the sand.

Leesa petted Penny for the first time ever. Intrigued by the animal's courage, she booped Penny's wet nose and explored her soft though sandy fur. She found it beautiful, how a thing with such menacing fangs and powerful claws could be so gentle and sweet.

Perhaps it was an invitation. *Be playful with me*, Penny's eyes seemed to say.

Allister smiled, relieved, but didn't laugh. "Go get Dorian, Penny," he said, tickling the space under the animal's chin. She obeyed.

Leesa knew the moment had passed when his smile tightened.

"So…yeah…about the artifacts," he began. He pressed a button on his chest plate. The metal hissed and expanded to reveal a compartment, from which he pulled out a blue notebook. "It belonged to my pops," he disclosed before she could ask about it. "I wasn't going to show you, but you earned it, I guess."

She raised her eyebrows.

Allister laid the notebook in his lap and opened it. Two pages lay side by side, one about the artifacts, one about temporal energy, both in a language she was having trouble understanding.

"It's about a decade of unpublished research, like, exploration of potentials and Evolutionaries and aliens and…civilizations. Pops believed the Daal Trelkkien—which in that alien language for sure translates to what we've been calling the artifacts—are from another planet, where these Keepers of Time and Space had the ability to manipulate and move through the dimensions. They took like a drop of that power and put it in these little cosmically charged crystals."

Leesa stared down at the yellowed, dingy pages, swept up in his conviction. "They sent them here?"

"Well, not really *here* here. They move *through* the realm and timeline the Earth exists in."

"Whoa, mega." The words slipped out of her mouth.

"Super mega, right?" he said quickly, face reddening.

Her cheeks burned, too.

Allister continued flipping the pages until he got near the notebook's end. She could see the diagrams became clearer, the drawings became less childlike, and the explanations became more fluid. It seemed Professor Patrick Adams had discovered something about the artifacts he could not share because there was no solution.

What they sought was beyond scientific comprehension.

No wonder he hadn't told anyone. They wouldn't have believed him.

"Can I?" she asked, placing a finger on the page's edge.

Allister flinched, looked into her eyes, then handed her the notebook so she could read it.

She held the crinkled front and back covers near their edges before turning a few more pages. She stopped at one unexpectedly written in English. The phrase *Temporal Rifts Theory* was spelled out. "Have you read this?"

"I don't think I got that far, no."

"It says," she began, clearing her throat to read the handwriting aloud. "'The power of Daal Trelkkien is not to be obtained. I imagine, inside this Cavenad... cavern?...of distorted reality, they have been in so many other galaxies, plagued so many other systems, and brought about the end of so many other planets before ours. Those in pursuit triggered their defenses and blew time out of proportion. My previous calculations have been false, our strategies...so far from correct, they may have cost us our future. This seems to be one of many artifacts that have made their way to us from Andromeda, related to Z-energy only in that they share an origin galaxy, but nothing else.'"

Leesa clenched her jaw at the last sentence. *Only in that they share an origin galaxy, but nothing else.* Nothing else. Sharp pains rode her spine up and down as she struggled to take a simple breath. She could not wrap her mind around the concepts with both eyes opened their widest and her nose almost touching the page. After all she'd been through, suffered, and sacrificed, the access to Z-energy didn't matter?

She handed the notebook back to Allister, flustered.

He took it from her.

"I don't understand... How?" she asked.

"Evolutionaries aren't human...Leesa," he replied. "Not all the way, at least, looks like."

Leesa folded her hands in her lap. She lowered her head and let her hair fall over her cheeks, blocking Allister from her peripheral vision. The proof stirred up what she'd always known on some level, even said aloud, but never let herself accept. She was not human. No matter who she saved or how much control she had over her potential, she never would be. Her genetic makeup made certain of that.

She inhaled that truth, solace tingling through her chest. She was filled with a burning desire to know more of the Z-energy and suddenly emptied of any pressure to further perfect herself. Perhaps as an Evolutionary, she was meant to be flawed, and perhaps in order to be powerful, she was meant to know it.

Allister turned back two pages and smoothed his hand over a highly detailed anatomical drawing including a very complex equation. "See?" he continued. "Twisted enough, there's such a thing as a Temporal Evolutionary. It's right here." He pointed at a drawing of a curvy female figure shaded in brown. "A person walking around with the genetic composition of this random alien civ would have the energy potential to link up with the artifacts and stop them from transporting."

"Again, the same question comes to me: How?"

"They see the temporal energy waves, I guess. Feel the time glitches…which I think I can do."

"You're serious?" she asked.

"Like dead. I didn't know it back then, but yeah, pretty sure I felt them in De Los Muertos." Allister lowered his voice further. "It's like a giant sword of everything that's supposed to happen at any given moment rips your body in half, and just as you're being stitched back together, it cuts through you all over again." He tapped the notebook. "Just beyond that my pops called most of this. And there's so many notebooks. Who knows what's in them all."

"Your father knew a lot," she said.

"It was his strongest potential." Allister closed the notebook and slid it back into its place in his chest plate. "We can't make the same mistake with the artifacts, and I know it's gonna come off, however, but I think someone at C20 knows that."

"You think Tas-Salvatur knows how to get them?"

He nodded. "He knows he needs the energy of the artifacts. Temporal energy. That's why he sent for me."

"Feeling the glitches and seeing the waves isn't the same as—I mean, you've never transported or manipulated time before…"

She'd heard it so long ago, she couldn't believe she remembered what Cynque had told her on Day 214. *Subject Allister Adams has no genetic tests on record. Potentials are assumed based on observed behavior.*

"Based on observed…"

Leesa grabbed his hand and pulled it until his bare arm was under her narrow-eyed examination. She turned it over, running her finger over the main vein, the place the Z-energy would appear. But it wasn't the Z-energy she was looking for. "What do you know about your mother?"

"There's no way my mom's wrapped up in this," he replied. "They're playin' her against me."

Leesa got to her knees, taking his hands in hers. Her voice shook as the words spilled from her lips, an epiphany. "Allister, if your father had to build a machine to detect temporal energy waves, wouldn't that mean he couldn't?"

"Couldn't…what?"

"Detect them."

"I don't follow…"

"Any potential, no matter how…insignificant…is linked to some genetic abnormality. If you can feel the glitches, see the waves…it had to come from somewhere, right? From someone…"

"From someone…," he muttered. "Someone like who?"

Leesa held her lips to his knuckles, neither able to control the grip on his hand nor the tightness in her chest. "It's your mother who has temporal energy," she whispered, tears welling in her eyes. "She's the one keeping the artifacts from moving."

She waited for Allister's response. She could see him unraveling from the realization, his body trembling with expected instability, his chest moving up and down with alarming speed and heaviness. His face was tensed with fury, drenched a red she didn't think possible on such a rich brown color.

Though she expected him to stand and, without a word, plow through the wall of their protection, headed for C20—Allister didn't let go.

"What is it?" Leesa asked.

"She knew," Allister said.

The words calmed him, shattered his tension to pieces and left the soft look of compassion around his eyes. "She knew," he repeated, softer. "She wasn't hiding me—she was hiding *us*." He seemed to look for more within their intertwined hands, then within himself after he pulled away and wrung his hands together. "I didn't listen…I couldn't. Too busy tryin' to prove being an Evolutionary meant saving people." He closed his eyes, sniffling as the tears streamed down his face. "Now…now I can't even save her."

"We can still save her," she said.

He grabbed Leesa by the wrist, an earnest look riding the downward curve of his brow. "You don't understand…if she's keeping the artifacts in place, I can't rescue her before I find them. She moves, the artifacts move."

The artifacts move. Such finality.

"For clock's sake. We need to mobilize before—" She paused, startled by loud noises she didn't recognize. Not wind or thunder…something bigger.

Penny was fluffed up and ready to pounce, clawing and barking at the back wall amid snarls. Dorian clung to the skin of her collar, trying to tame her with steady strokes down her back. She wouldn't heel to his touch, no matter how gentle.

As Leesa floated off of the ground, Allister jumped to his feet, both of them looking to the fortress as if it might reveal the source.

Beyond the thick walls came the aggressive *vroom* of approaching vehicles. Then explosions rumbled above and around them, rattling the compound's foundation. And similar to when she'd heard the subtle click inside the Vault, she heard a whistling noise pierce the air, moving closer at rocket speed.

She whipped her hands up in the direction of its approach. Despite her speed and intention, the forcefield was hardly formed, if at all.

The impact was like a hard jab to her brain. The detonation like fire throughout her body. She flew back, spinning through the air, unable to reinforce her field or the structure, and landed on her stomach.

A fissure shot down the wall that had been hit. The shelter she'd constructed split in two and tumbled to either side. Sand and stone swirled upward, recaptured by the wind's relentless force.

Leesa shielded her eyes as she recovered, then looked up to the metal body gleaming in the wake of the fiery blast.

"Glad you could make it, Agent Adams," XBA shouted from atop a hovercraft. "I see you brought company."

CHAPTER 47

ALLISTER ADAMS
Man's Lost Lands, Former Middle East
Day 207

XBA STARED ALLISTER down from the seat of a hovercraft. He somewhat suspected she'd come alone, and as if that wasn't hard enough to believe, the desert seemed to calm upon her arrival. The wind's shrill whistling sank into a whisper. Lightning darted between the clouds, no longer summoned to the ground. Thunder rumbled low and quiet in the distance.

But the darkness of midnight remained.

Allister didn't move right away, paralyzed by XBA's orange eye, which buzzed at him with all intended malice.

"I must say, I'm terribly disappointed," she said, smiling her seductive smile. "Didn't we have a talk about this in De Los Muertos...about love being more important than obligation?"

The tingling sensation shot through Allister's temple, the single round of a telepathic bullet. She was toying with him again, trying to talk him into an illusion, then narrow his thoughts into an action.

He shook away the sensation of fogginess swimming in his head. "No more mind games, XBA! Where're you keeping my mom?"

XBA pumped her hovercraft forward. "But, dear Allister, you didn't uphold the terms," she said. "So, uhm… Deal's. Off."

He was gutted by her answer. A death sentence in so few words.

Deal's off? he thought, unable to look XBA in either eye. C20 still needed him, right? They couldn't find the artifacts without him...could they? He felt himself collapsing as he stumbled back clutching his chest. It was the thing he'd feared most, the loss of bargaining power. Or perhaps…

"I never had any power to begin with," he said, somewhat to himself. While he was thinking it, and saying it, he felt the words couldn't have been his. "I never had any power to begin with," he repeated.

His body didn't seem to be in his control, teetering left and right. Nor were his thoughts, erupting in the flames of self-doubt and stripping away his foundation. The more helpless he felt, the weaker his knees became, until he fell forward.

Leesa caught him by the arms before he hit the ground. "Whatever you're thinking," she said in his ear, "flip it. It's her in there, not you."

He realized the tingling had returned, was buzzing between his ears with whispers of incapability.

I never had any power to begin with.

His legs buckled at the crippling thought. The words felt that much more powerful because they weren't his.

Allister let Leesa almost carry him to where Dorian and Penny stood poised for conflict. "Just keep telling yourself...I have potential...I am potential," she said as they went. "Keep saying it until you believe it's true."

I have potential...I am potential. Then the other voice came again in contradiction: *I never had any power to—*

"No!" he yelled out aloud, twisting away from Leesa's grip on accident. He tumbled to the sand, shouting, "I *have* potential! I *am* potential!"

Eventually the voices got so loud in his mind, he curled up in a ball. He was determined to squeeze his head until he crushed it, or the voices stopped screaming at one another in their fight for dominance—whichever came first. He pressed his hands tighter against his temples, his skull already pounding with the pain of compression.

Then every noise around him disappeared.

Leesa was kneeling beside him, and he could feel her hands shaking his shoulders vigorously. He let go of his head, bewildered by the slow fade of conflicting voices, leaving just the one.

I have potential...I am potential.

He looked up at her.

She was helping him back to his feet, her mouth moving, though no sound was coming out. There was an urgency in her touch, in her gestures and expressions; she was tugging at his clothes and pointing at a glowing figure, concern spread across her face.

His regeneration began the arduous task of clearing out XBA's psychic poison. He'd never realized that his ability to heal could extend to the metaphysical, until he saw visible traces of her psionic potential dissipating above him, having been expelled. The clarity in his head was palpable, his own perceptions of reality seeping back to a trueness he could sift through.

They were heading, he realized, to a space just behind Dorian. The kid had put on his metal mask and stood with a wide stance, both hands up, body bathed in the navy aura of sonic energy potential.

Something exploded in front of them in a flash of light and didn't make a peep. Something else exploded to the right of them, still with the absence of sound.

Dorian was using his potential again, drawing sounds from the desert and conducting the waves into a spinning bubble of deflection. A literal sound barrier.

From what Allister could see, the explosions had been targeted attacks from Dorian, aimed at XBA's hovercraft. Because now XBA was standing across from them, furious, her claws extended, her eye narrowed. Behind her was a hoard of armed agents and the other Evolutionary with the giant glaive—Vonnie.

XBA's illusion of solitude had fallen.

I knew she wouldn't show face alone.

Allister was glad he hadn't, either. Despite clearly being outnumbered, it felt good to have Leesa on one side of him and Dorian and Penny on the other. Huddled together, they presented themselves as a unit—maybe, dare he imagine it, a team.

Dorian waved his hand in the air, a signal that he had to end his experiment.

Allister patted him on the shoulder in recognition, ready to do the hard thing—lead.

The barrier's silent spinning stopped, and soon after was whisked away by the loss of Dorian's intention.

Gritting his teeth, Allister counted the number of agents one more time, using each plasma weapon's glow as the defining factor. The answer was the same: too many. A battle aimed at winning wasn't liable to work out in their favor. Especially then, with the desert at its darkest.

XBA laughed. "I guess we're doing this the exciting way." She turned to the sizable cavalry of C20 agents covering the sand. "We are not cynqued if we are not one!"

"We are not cynqued if we are not one!" the agents echoed.

As they continued chanting, one of the agents navigated an unoccupied hovercraft forward. XBA took a few steps toward it without taking her eyes off of Allister and his allies.

He glanced at Leesa and whispered, "Where's the tower?"

"Just over those dunes," she whispered back, pointing past their enemies. "What're you thinking?"

"Lots. Need another minute."

"I believe Captain Brandt's instructions were fairly clear," XBA reminded. "Since you didn't come here alone, we're here to make sure you come with us—*alone*."

Allister considered her, this mechanical villain hell-bent on his isolation. Going up against her was a reasonable consideration. Perhaps for her treachery, she even deserved his wrath. But as with Schwebevogel, he'd learned the win wasn't always about taking out the enemy. More could be achieved by focusing on the objective—and simply outlasting them.

Artist: The CMD Studios

It'd be better for him and the others to bypass their problem rather than face it head-on, particularly in favor of their true objective, reaching the tower. He'd seen the consequences of scattered, reactive combat in De Los Muertos, so he figured it was time they tried executing a plan.

A plan he had yet to hatch.

He squared his hips and put one foot behind him, appearing to accept her challenge with a healthier center of gravity.

She smirked again, amused—likely at his subtle movement—then flipped high into the air, a kind of acrobatic feat to get her onto the vehicle. Her landing was picture-perfect, straight-on in the seat, her gaze still penetrating. Leaning forward on the hovercraft, she revved the engine. "Retrieve the key to the artifacts in the name of Tas-Salvatur!"

Get to the dunes, he assured himself.

Before he could second-guess his idea, he was spouting his commands in a single breath. "Everyone, we're heading west. The aim is to get over those dunes no matter what, find this tower, and tear through it until we get to my mom." He took Leesa's hand. "Stay high and blast them from above, keep things moving the way you know how. Let's both keep it light on the Z-energy. My mom's somewhere in this desert…and…it's best to lay it down if we can't use it without destroying everything or melting down." He grabbed Dorian's hand next. "Clear a path for us using every sound you hear," he told him. "You know what to do… go mega on 'em."

Dorian nodded, snapped at Penny, and pointed ahead of them. They sprinted toward the dunes.

The agents raised their weapons. Double- and triple-barrel plasma guns unleashed searing beams of energy.

Allister charged forward, kicking as he jumped, tackling as he dove, twirling as he punched and elbowed. The agents were going down, then getting up just as fast, gathering in his path and firing at him in unison.

He was skidding to a stop when he fell back and hit the sand. The blasts heading toward him slowed and smashed into an invisible barrier, flashing against it without the force to get through. He looked up to glimpse Leesa doing what she did best—controlled execution of immense potential. Next thing he knew, she was tossing her arm out across her body, blowing away the soldiers with a concussive wave of purple-charged energy. She nodded at him, then with startling speed, spun around to deflect a blast from another group of agents firing from the ground.

Allister jumped back up. Eyes sweeping the battlefield, he saw Dorian dodging past crumbled walls, arms swinging as they gathered the sounds of battle. A fiery, glowing figure was on the kid's tail, making fast headway on foot.

Allister didn't know where the man had come from. He was tanned, if not brown, bulky, and scowling. His scarred face burning red like the flaming energies shooting from his pores. Something about the fire triggered him. Something about the idea of Dorian burning up triggered him more.

Plus, *he* was their ticket over the dunes. One experiment from that tiny vessel of sonic manipulation, and Allister was sure C20 would be incapacitated enough to get past. Stumbling into a run, he dodged more incoming firepower and headed to intercept. He passed Penny, who was attacking with jaws open, ripping agent after agent from their vehicles. She was as nimble as she was gigantic, and dodged plasma blasts as if she were a quarter the size.

Well on his way, Allister tripped over something heavy and metallic partially buried in the sand. He cursed and kicked the thing, an abandoned hovercraft. But he looked at the glowing man just as he was about to keep going.

The idea was being executed before it was fully formed, him wrestling the hovercraft free, climbing on, and giving it a quick *vroom*, all while picturing it crammed into the man's side.

The vehicle accelerated. Eyes wild, brow furrowed, elbows locked, Allister half stood on the hovercraft, knocking over agents, sidewinding to clothesline them where they stood—the kind of thrills he'd always dreamed of.

His target was well in sight.

Perhaps that's why he didn't see Vonnie descending from above.

She floated down, light as a leaf, deadly as a needle from the world's tallest building. Though Allister tried maneuvering back and forth across the sand to shake her, she'd already phased through the hovercraft's engine, embedding herself inside of it. She kept her body almost entirely transparent and willed her shining weapon solid, then pulled up, ripping the metal in two.

The engine exploded. Heat blasted Allister's face as the hovercraft flipped over, pulling him down with it. He landed on his back in the hard sand and continued tumbling over small dunes until he stopped on his stomach.

Vonnie waited, steps from him, smirking, hand wrapped tight around the glaive, which was now slick with the machine's fluids.

Through her transparent body, Allister saw that the fiery-skinned man he'd been after had reached Dorian. The swirling indigo shades of sonic potential were steadily battling the man's orange globules of flickering energy.

Allister couldn't worry about Vonnie. He needed to help Dorian. His knees strained as they came in and supported him back to his feet, his legs stiffened as they tried to keep his body from sinking back into submission.

"Even your mother put up more of a fight," Vonnie said, weapon lifted.

Allister perked up at the sound of her swinging blade and spun backward. The tip still missed his chest by just a centimeter.

"Okay," he said, his stance widened, his teeth clenched. "Now, I'm triggered." He then let out an enraged scream, arms up, and was airborne before he knew he could jump that high.

The force of his strength potential seemed to converge in his muscles as, hands clasped together, he touched an imaginary peak in the sky. His descent was unlike hers—fast, torrential, with the makings of a titanic impact.

He landed with a loud *boom*.

The ground shook. Sand flew away. Furious and a bit spent, Allister spit out the sand gathered in his mouth, anxious to see if Vonnie had been knocked away. He spotted her on her back, her density normal, her weapon lying in the sand out of reach.

Leesa lowered herself next to him. "Nice move."

He gave her a playful salute. "Thanks, *Lieutenant*," he joked, nodding sideways at the pulsing navy aura that had engulfed Dorian. "It's time. Let's hope our ace is better at experiments than either of us."

"Hey—"

Allister put up his hand. "No time. There's only one way we get out of this." He looked up at the sky and pointed. "Think you can get us to the clouds?"

She looked up as well, worry knitted across her brow. "Do I have a choice?"

As if to answer, sonic eruptions began bursting from Dorian in perfectly round bubbles and popping in the air, releasing deafening noises.

"Gonna go with no!" Allister yelled, covering his ears. "Where's XBA?"

"Gone!"

Another sound sphere shattered the air with a *boom*.

"We gotta go up now!" he said.

Leesa gripped Allister with telekinetic tightness and levitated them off the ground, pausing there to look at him before doing what she needed to do next.

She seemed in need of his trust, and maybe also some reassurance, that she could, in fact, get them to the clouds.

He squeezed her hands. "You can do this," he mouthed. And he believed it.

Looking confident, Leesa tilted her chin up and propelled them skyward. They soared above the tallest building that remained standing, the wind ripping the air away before it could reach Allister's lungs. His throat tightened as they climbed altitude. The more he did to keep himself breathing, the less he got in return.

Allister heard a series of unnatural sounds following them up into the air. At least they were unnatural from what he'd experienced of Dorian's potential. He made the mistake of looking down, afraid he'd miscalculated the blast's radius potential.

He had.

The sonic experiment extended beyond and above the ruins. Collectively, the sound was louder than the funnel clouds twisting in the sky, louder than air as it collapsed into thunder, creating an explosion louder than any break in the sound barrier.

Man's Lost Lands was being blown into a massive crater beneath them.

Still, up Leesa and Allister shot, corkscrewing as high into the atmosphere as fast as she could carry them. How far they got no longer mattered. For Allister knew that if they stopped at any point, the rising energy would take them out.

Allister could feel Leesa's hold loosening and tried clinging to her that much more. But the strain was taking its toll on both of them—him feeling woozy, finding it harder to hold out for more oxygen, her slowing to an almost stop. Feeling her body relax, he winced.

"Leesa," he begged, dizzy from the air's thinness, "please keep it together."

Her eyes teared when she looked at him, as if those words had stripped her of her potential. She mouthed something before her eyes fluttered closed. Then a fierce gust of wind tore her from his arms.

Falling was the only choice he had left.

Without Leesa's telekinetic potential, he was plummeting, helpless, flailing and somersaulting in spiraling winds.

Fear was a knife twisting in his heart. For the hellish heat from below had already arrived, warming Allister's skin until it crisped.

Artist: Jeffrey Viloria/ The CMD Studios

He saw one terrifying thing, and immediately after, felt another. The first was spotting Leesa's body disappearing into the rising cluster of detonating sound spheres. The second was resounding *booms* pounding his ears until they rang.

Was it really over? Would his mom be killed? Would humanity end?

Allister felt he'd done all he could do. Relaxing his body, he surrendered to incineration.

———

"A SINGLE GRAIN OF SAND IS THE SAME SIZE AS A STAR IF LOOKED AT FROM A CERTAIN PERSPECTIVE."

LIEUTENANT LEESA DELEMAR

DO YOU REMEMBER THE FIRST TIME (OR MOST RECENT TIME) YOU FELT SEEN OR ACKNOWLEDGED? AND DID YOU ACCEPT IT OR RUN FROM IT?

———

CHAPTER 48

ALLISTER ADAMS
Man's Lost Lands, Former Middle East
Day 206

THEY'D LOST. IT wasn't the headache that pounded Allister into submission; it was regret. Nor was it the aching that plagued his stomach; it was hopelessness. And though he knew the throbbing in his muscles and soreness in his limbs manifested physically, they were symptoms of shame and doubt.

Yet, all of those sensations pointed to one truth: he was still alive.

"Allister, time to wake up," a voice cooed in his ear.

Coarse fingers cupped his chin as gently as they might a child's.

"I know this's hard to take in, but we're all here for the same reason," the voice said, still inches from his face. By the smell of burnt timber, he could only assume it was Brandt.

Allister pulled back, part in fear, part in shock. Every inch of the chair he'd been propped up in was cushioned, and for some reason, the armrests were adjusted to his height. For comfort? His body hurt in places he didn't know existed, while the obvious and open wounds were leaking blood all over him. But the most painful area, his face, was swelled to the point of slurred speech and difficult breathing. "You're full of it," he gurgled, still half conscious. His head swung like a wrecking ball across his neckline.

"We want to escape the apocalypse just like you do, and we want to take humanity with us," Brandt continued.

Allister blinked, groggy, and swayed too far forward. Brandt caught him just before he fell over. Allister resisted feeling even an inkling of comfort. It was just days ago those soiled, untrustworthy hands had embraced him like a son. He looked up, glimpsing the silver shine of metal blurred behind the captain's burly, hunched-over shape.

Brandt wore the same big hat and crisp suit, and Allister was sure that if he looked down he would see those same lace-up boots. Though now the "captain" radiated the sinister white of C20's preached purity.

Allister grunted as he was pushed back into the chair.

His chin fell again, however, lower this time, and it was then he saw the state of the uniform he was wearing. Though the chest plate remained intact, the suit of armor had been compromised. Shreds of metal near his waist clung to a flickering plasma core center. Only a few of the more resilient pieces remained, draped over his chest and shoulders. But, if the chest plate was undamaged, the notebook would be, too.

Allister tensed from the memory of how C20 must've gotten him captured. Where had they taken him? Where was his mom? He wanted to worry about Leesa, Dorian, and Penny, but he knew as long as they were together, they'd be okay. At least he hoped as much.

Sensory impairments were absent—no blindfolds, no restraints, allowing him to try unpacking the surroundings. His ears picked up the familiar hum of data processing coupled with overlapping snippets of survivor testimonies, casualty recaps, and the subtle churn of gears. His nose detected the overpowering smell of oil and cinders and heated metal. His eyes saw a perpetual dimness lining the edges of the captain's wide shoulders. A vagueness so concrete, drawing lines in it was impossible.

From the corner of his eye, he could see Brandt staring at him, a trap he would give anything to avoid.

Unless.

Allister looked again, still grappling with why he wasn't chained up.

Unless the man he'd known was in there somewhere.

He finally met Brandt's eyes. They weren't the color he remembered. Emotional debris seemed to stir inside them, the irises gray as a tornado in full swing.

"Take me to her," Allister said. He scooted to the edge of the padded seat. "You show me Mom's good. I do whatever you want."

"Stubborn, like your daddy. Don't work like that. Crystal artifacts come first." Brandt's words were a brutal cold front, flash-freezing whatever compassion Allister thought he had held on to.

The captain didn't speak again, just straightened his body and backed away.

The background cleared to a giant circular room filled with machines, most of them for communications and monitoring. The black of night spilled through a handful of the giant windows on his right, and standing in a row beneath them were XBA, Vonnie, Tranjam, and the fourth person from the battlefield, whom Allister didn't know. His heart rocketed to his throat, and his eyebrows nearly shot over his forehead.

"Relax. They won't hurt you as long as you act right," Brandt explained.

He extended his hand as if to introduce them.

Allister studied the Evolutionaries of C20, surveyed their posture, their expressions, their appearances.

Tranjam was a little too thin to be tough, but his hardened grimace made up for it. Vonnie cradled her glaive in a transparent arm like a shiny child, her posture equal parts sass and sadism. XBA's grin was too smug for Allister's liking, her armor covered in blood that belonged to some poor soul without much left. The fourth was a guy who happened to be shoeless. He smiled wide and crooked, then reopened a wound with an ignited finger pressed against it.

Allister sat up straighter, feeling threatened, knowing he was in no condition to fight. Yet.

"You know none of them Resilient Nation summits were real?" Brandt said, hands spread out as he paced in circles. "Hoaxes to simulate progress. The District, Sanctum De Paris...those weren't terrorist attacks on people; they were missiles aimed at our institutions. Our world leaders still didn't *listen*. So damn hardheaded. Name one of 'em who tried to do better, or one who shared their country's resources. Name one who got it right and started servin' the people." He shot Allister a look, as if expecting him to come up with at least one example. "Exactly," Brandt continued, sounding triumphant. "Not a single one did. Get it through your head, Allister. Nobody's lookin' for answers but us, you hear me? Nobody's got answers but us."

Allister's hands shook with impatience. He fought to bury his Z-energy, kept repeating his promise to himself not to misuse it. But he knew then, seeing C20's EV operatives scheme and stew in their goals, that their committed action knew no mercy. "Let's get on with it," he said as he wiggled forward to the seat's edge, ready to spring. "I find the artifacts. You give me my mom and my friends back. End of."

"You're where you're meant to be, son. Right here with me." The captain held his hand over his heart. "When C20 strips the QBs and systems and resources from the folks in power and returns 'em to the people, things can fall into this beautiful harmony we are creatin'."

Brandt had totally lost it, Allister concluded, him speaking someone else's words as if they were truth and not perception, his voice void of benevolence.

He'd call the captain's behavior irrational—but it was so rational, so hardwired. As though the other captain had never existed—never reassured him on his first mission or defended his dad's work against General Delemar.

It was undeniable that Brandt was dripping with the bliss of much-desired power. At C20, he was in charge, and stood beaming with pride, newly wed to their organization's motives.

"I know you're askin' yourself why? Why must everything fall?" Brandt said. "Because salvation is worth the sum of the remaining, not the difference between them."

Allister lifted his hands almost to his ears to block out the traitorous words. "Lay it down, Brandt! I'm not joinin' C20. I said it before: I get you the artifacts, I take my mom and my friends, and I go home." His eyes darted across the floor wildly and landed on XBA's glimmering grin.

"Give him what he wants," XBA said. She shrugged casually, as if she'd performed some heinous act and was sure to get away with it. "Show him where they are. Do start with Mum, though, he'll see we're *serious*."

Or, maybe she already had.

"What'd you do!" he spat, lunging at her, fists up.

Brandt was right there to stop him. "Be easy," he said, catching Allister around the torso. "Be easy now. Trying my damndest to keep you safe."

Allister's chest rose and fell without control, the whole of him unable to get anything close to *being easy*. In his mind, the energy swirling in circles on the Andromeda Project's tenth floor burst free from the ZEContainment Center. Untamed. Furious. "Not about *safe*," he said pointedly. "It's about preservation."

At that, the blue energy arrived in him, forcing the hair on his arms to stand at attention. A soft luminance drifted through his veins and with it came a faint, sputtering charge. The energy swirled faster, as fast as he'd seen it swirl in the glass bowl, cascading down his arms in steady streams.

He shoved Brandt out of the way, aimed his arm at XBA, and pushed forward. "Foeht Zeorgen!"

Allister's arm trembled with the promise of eruption, but even as the blue energy brightened, nothing shot forth. What brewed within him fizzled away. As if a pail of still water had been tossed on kindled flames, the energy was extinguished. The heat he felt now was embarrassment. His experiment had failed.

XBA's orange eye flashed. She was marching toward him, silent, all the playfulness of their previous encounters drained from her face.

Allister's feeling of powerlessness arrived yet again. His backward steps matched her advancing ones. He tripped over the chair as he tried to escape her and, with nowhere left to go, fell against a machine.

XBA plunged her fist through his uniform's power core, shattering it almost all the way through. She lifted him by the neck, sneering, salivating, searching him with both her orange eye *and* her human one. She must not have found what she wanted, because she slammed his head against the machine he'd backed up against.

The blunt force blurred his vision. He struggled to grab her hands as she pulled him forward without a word. He gasped as she thrust his head back again. *Smash.* His head went deeper into the machine's wiring, already throbbing. His vision went out. His arms dangled at his side. She pulled his head away from the titanium shell and held him up.

"I know what you're trying to do," XBA said.

She slid two of her sharpened claws under what was left of the uniform metal, then shoved them into his side. They tore through his flesh as easy as shears through fabric. He grabbed her wrist to stop her from pushing deeper and inhaled the pain through his teeth. He didn't want to give her what he knew she wanted. His *screams*.

"You think you can rescue your mother and your faux comrades and take us down," XBA continued. She pushed deeper and twisted, cutting through his guts.

His side burned like a fire ran through it. He squeezed his eyes shut and exhaled a heavy, "No," trying not to collapse as blood poured onto the floor.

"So you're not planning to trick us…?" She leaned in his ear. "And keep the artifacts?"

Though his flesh stitched itself around the blades XBA called fingers, the wound couldn't close with her in it. Allister's nostrils flared in anguish. He pushed down on her wrist and shook his head, his mouth dry and unable to produce an answer.

"What was that, hmm?" XBA asked, slicing through another vital organ.

Allister screamed, more than once, more than twice, a repetition of guttural sounds rising raw from his throat and echoing off the walls. When he finally quieted, his face was drenched with sweat and his muscles were pulsing and steaming like geysers ready to erupt.

"Pull them out," Brandt grumbled.

"As you wish," XBA said. She slid her claws out slowly.

Every healed fiber tore at their withdrawal. Allister contracted into the agony, sinking to the floor as he held the dripping wound with both hands. He lay curled like a run-over animal, knees to his forehead, bile burning in his throat.

"I only wanted to make certain our handsome key to the artifacts followed through," XBA said. "I wouldn't want anything else terrible to happen to Sweet Dee."

He thought about XBA torturing his mom the way she had tortured him. Whatever suffering she had endured, he was to blame. He wanted to relive all those years he'd resented her for clinging to him so tight, so he could trust her reasons for doing it. The notion throbbed in his mangled guts and revolved inside his head with the same frequency.

"Get him up and take him to the dig site," XBA said, quickly. "We're doing this now."

Brandt took Allister under both arms and gave a confident, "I got ya," as he lifted Allister up off the floor. He hauled him out of the room, then pushed him against the metal panels in the hallway outside the watchtower.

They were alone.

The captain held Allister in a suspicious gaze, not looking at him, more like drilling a hole through his chest. Brandt then reached between the sharp edges of the broken chest plate and tugged loose the blue notebook.

Allister grasped for it and missed. A sharp pain forced his arm back to his body. He pressed his hand to the wound, the blood from it leaking between his fingers. But he cared little about his blood loss or his difficulty standing. His eyes were on the notebook in Brandt's hands. The notebook with all of the answers. The notebook with all of the secrets. He couldn't find the strength to demand it back, just watched, cringing, as Brandt tucked it into the seat of his pants.

"Why aren't you healing?" Brandt asked.

Allister swayed left and right, babbling angrily with no clear answer. Weakness kept the words swimming in his head from diving from his lips.

The captain searched him with a furrowed brow. "You can't retrieve the artifacts all messed up like this," he eventually said.

"Don't tell me what I can't do," Allister shot back, his voice finally returned, shaking. "I'm gonna save everybody. Everybody!" He gripped Brandt's collar one-handed. "Did you know about my mom? Did you know she was an Evolutionary?" With each question he asked, he shook Brandt, almost falling over on the last.

Brandt held him up in what was almost a hug. "I didn't know nothin'."

Allister peered at the captain with an angry curiosity and realized midway he was searching for the lie. Hell, he'd lied about everything else, why shouldn't he lie about this?

"You knew enough," he forced out. "Well, lemme tell you something twisted: she's why this desert isn't underwater or frozen over or on fire and why all your stupid soldiers in white aren't skeletons or straight-up dust. She's the reason the world is still here...and you got her locked up somewhere, starving and probably dying."

"She ain't doin' well," the captain said solemnly. "You gotta pull it together."

"No, no!" Allister pulled Brandt closer. "You're gonna answer for what you did to us. You said we were family. Then you went and tried taking my mom...from me." His anger melted into disbelief as his head fell backward against the wall. "And when I hand over the artifacts," he said up to the air, "you're finished."

"They're taking her to the cavern we found, where the artifacts are!" Brandt shouted, shaking Allister until they were eye to eye again. "Do you understand? You ain't saving her or humanity bleedin' out like this."

Allister lingered there, on the border of delirious. The overhead light splashed across Brandt's face as it had inside the Vault those first days. Once again, Allister saw a man he thought he knew, thought he should've recognized, but that he didn't.

"Did you hear me?" Brandt repeated. "They're taking her to the—"

Cavern, Allister finished to himself.

That was a word he recognized, though only from the language of the crystals— Cavenad Daal Trelkkien. He remembered what he'd read about them: the artifacts transporting around inside a mystical realm, distorting every reality it touched.

"I don't know what's down in that cavern," the captain warned, fatherlike. "But whatever it is, you ain't got it in ya to beat it like this."

Brandt's tone that brought on the surge of strength and resentment. Allister shoved him hard into the opposite wall. "I couldn't give a rag...what's in that cavern, Brandt...as long as...I have enough left in me after...to beat you."

———

CHAPTER 49

<hr />

DR. FLORENCE BELLADONNA

Restricted Airspace, Man's Lost Lands
Day 206

FLORENCE AND BRIDGET had braved the mission to the presumed location of C20's elusive hideout—Florence in search of Celine Nephthys, the Moroccan princess, and the crystal artifacts, her two tickets to freedom; Bridget in search of a thrill and to secure her own way out of termination.

Eleven hours later, their aerocraft somersaulted amid conflicting winds as they escaped the dark clouds. Florence was sending silent praises for them surviving their hellish descent into Man's Lost Lands. Experiencing the Middle Beast first-hand, it had an evolutionary's name written across every updraft and forked flash. Florence might've even seen a face in the clouds on the way down.

"That was bloody hell," Florence said, flicking away a strand of hair from her face and rearranging herself in the seat.

Perhaps it had been a good thing she'd finished her pilot's license. Though Bridget's electromagnetic potential had certainly helped with deflecting the bolts of lightning.

Florence pressed a button on the craft's digital console. A projected map of the desecrated region ballooned in front of her. Altitude levels, terrain details, and energy readings populated in a frenzy. She expected sand and ruins, an empty space where C20's compound lay concealed, and perhaps some decomposed bodies, but the dead city was redrawn in a textured grid, its preserved center splattered by the aftermath of a detonation.

"What in the world happened down there?" asked Bridget, leaned over the image.

"Lieutenant Delemar happened," Florence mumbled.

Dismembered temples and stubborn columns refusing to go down teetered on the outskirts of a crater big enough for Florence to land the craft in. Her unanswered messages to the team now made sense to her. And by the time she'd needed to unplug from the CGN for stealth purposes, Hunter hadn't responded to her request for backup.

She squinted at the crater a second time. There was something about its shape that looked too organized. The blast radius was a near-perfect sphere, whereas

Leesa's energy pulse would have gone on for miles, stripping anything in its path to the particles they were comprised of.

Keeping up the first screen to give her the big picture, she activated two more projection screens—one to take an energy reading on the area, one to get better look at the crater, as in measure its depth and width in proportion to the ruins. Alternating between rotating them and zooming in, Florence recorded the size and double-checked the energy analysis. "Weird energy echoes reading as super-charged sonic vibrations…like the aftermath of a massive sonic boom."

"Must be Dorian, I reckon," Bridget said, then fell quiet.

Florence was quiet for her own reasons. Dr. Giro had mentioned her psiber-netic leg's propensity to enhance her already expert mind potential. Until that instance, she didn't know what could be *better* than what she was already capable of. It was strange enough that from their present altitude she could paint herself a psychic picture of the events using the spray of lingering emotions. Allister's angst and Leesa's…vulnerability? But most passionate of all was Dorian. His anguish as he accepted the sounds, his grit still reverberating through the desert, just as loud, she imagined, as the explosion when he unleashed his potential. She was re-experiencing the entire ordeal through thoughts and feelings.

Then the psionic trail to their whereabouts went cold on the sandy surface, erased from existence by—another skilled Mind Evolutionary.

She scowled. There weren't many others in the world with telepathic potential that matched hers, and just one—her father—with the potential to exceed it. XBA wouldn't be capable of such a grand illusion. Who could C20 have recruited to go up against her? Who would be foolish enough to try?

It wouldn't matter until it did, she decided.

Florence tapped the air with a finger, summoning her workaround. What appeared was not another digital screen, rather a tiny oval of an opening in the Gelen Psionix. Threads aligning at her third eye came to life as red energy and were tugged one after another into the physical realm by her intention.

She smiled. *Nice try.*

As the threads were lengthening and swirling and bending around her hands, each wisp rebuilt the psychic signatures that had been scrubbed away.

Her smile faded. Among them was the third telepath in question.

The person was untrained, but cunning. Their abilities both masked and impaired by…infused technology and mind-operated mechanics.

Kara?

She stared at the blank radar screen in a daze, not registering when the blinking dot appeared on its outskirts, or the warnings of it blaring at her from the aerocraft's Cynque system. Too deeply plagued by the notion of *her* being *there*.

By the time Florence blinked herself free and came to, the dot was nearly upon the center.

Nearly upon them.

The wailing sounds of the cockpit slammed into her ears. "Impact imminent!" the console boomed.

"Belladonna!" Bridget was shrieking, as if not for the first time. "The plane!"

Florence snapped to greater attention, chest swelling and collapsing in rapid succession, more a reaction to Bridget's hysterics than her own. She grabbed the console's digital controls and yanked them left on instinct.

The plane pitched sideways. A bright-orange light flashed in Florence's peripheral view, shaking the plane harder as it turned.

She rocked with the bumpiness. "I didn't peg Tas-Salvatur as one to make the first move," she said casually. Getting shot at in the air had become routine during her early days, as did going down in aerocrafts.

Bridget, on the other hand, was ghost white, her cheek pressed to the headrest. She clung to the back of the copilot seat with her legs spread the width of the swiveling chair. "I thought you knew how to fly!" she screamed.

"We lived, didn't we?" Florence said.

She watched more blinking dots come to life on the screen and immediately regretted her own sarcasm.

"Second line of defense, I suppose," she quipped. "CynqueAero, identify."

"Calculating…," it said.

She keyed in an autopilot maneuver, one that would dodge each explosion by tricking whatever was coming at them into colliding. Florence's stomach clenched as she waited for the computer to accept the command. She held her breath as she waited for the plane to execute it.

The nose tilted upward as gears cranked the wings tighter against the shell. A high-pitched whine pierced the cockpit as the blinking dots neared, but they didn't connect. The plane straightened toward the sky until it was completely vertical, then flipped, shuddering as it plunged back down and dodged sideways.

Florence gripped the chair for support while explosions echoed above and beside them in a series of violent *kabooms*. C20's MO seemed shoot to kill, she told herself, the realization shifting the urgency in her attitude. The aerocraft continued zooming out of range, then steadied in the air. The detonations kept popping off far behind them.

She exhaled.

Bridget calmed enough to situate herself frontways in the seat and fussed on the restraints. After finishing, she said, "I—I know that orange color. Same thing that hit us over ChiTown Sanctity. Almost knocked us outta the sky. Evolutionary, yeah?"

Orange color? Evolutionary? Florence pondered the potential connection, remembering the energy wafting off of Shahar in Club HellForest.

"Energy composition, identified," Cynque interrupted. "Type: Kinetic Form: pulse wave. Concentration: high, focused. Source: unknown." Cynque paused, then added, "Molecular Refraction Cloaking Mechanism detected."

"I'll work on it," Bridget said.

"Increasing stealth to one hundred percent." Florence then dragged her fingers across the screen, activating the electromagnetic wave frequency deflectors, a move that would give the aerocraft very temporary invisibility. The massive energy burn caused by the technology was a kink still to be ironed out.

The interior buzzed. The exterior purred. Tiny reflective hexagons multiplied around the front window and continued spreading around the plane.

"We're heading deeper, Sparks," Florence reported. "You've got about ten minutes until this thing goes out."

The wind knocked the aerocraft off course and sent it bouncing through another turn.

"Stealth, eighty percent," Cynque said.

Florence glanced sideways, jaw flexing. "Hurry, Sparks."

"There's...there's a machine," Bridget finally said, eyebrows stitched with the strain of concentration. "An amplification machine of some sort, surrounded by heaps of other machines."

"Stealth, sixty percent," Cynque interrupted.

"Okay, and?" Florence pressed.

"It's fueling the storm and the field projected around the base," Bridget said. "I just gotta...gotta sort through the currents...find out which ones lead where..."

"Close the deal. You're already halfway to shutting it down."

Bridget closed her eyes, kept her body upright yet relaxed into the seat. Her hair began standing on edge. Her arms crackled and sparked with electricity.

"Stealth, forty percent," Cynque said.

Then, a minute and several flashes of lightning later.

"Stealth, twenty percent."

"Sparks..." Florence warned. "We're about to be low-hanging fruit."

Ages seemed to go by before Bridget mustered a sly smile, then said, "Found it," and snapped her fingers. Electric bolts circling her limbs dimmed and disappeared.

Florence watched through the image mapping as currents burst from the sand below and snaked around a circular stretch of uninhabited desert. In a dazzling display of electromagnetic interference, C20's cloak was thrown off, the rotating tower and energy-powered domes of their base shimmering into view.

She couldn't hide her shock. A sarcastic remark might've been suitable, yet her mouth was frozen open, the stillness in her body a sensation she'd rarely experienced.

The bolts of electricity continued zigging and zagging, whipping and winding—up, around, and through. More of the well-concealed operation was revealed until the entire hidden city consumed Florence's vision.

C20 towered higher than she expected and spread farther than she thought possible. The compound was more than a base; it had the look of a military-inspired sanctuary, riddled with technological advancements, built of shining metal and durable materials. From the organization responsible for such rampant violence, she'd expect to see soldiers and operators patrolling the perimeter, as well as manned tanks, circling aircraft, and surface-to-air missile defenses prepared for battle.

She saw no one. She sensed nothing. Someone—she guessed her new psychic rival—was blocking her.

Florence knew she could break through. All she needed was her mind attuned and quiet to concentrate.

Her hands were almost to her head, ready to activate her telepathic potential, when a wave of projected emotions crashed over her, overwhelming enough to knock her from the pilot's chair like a hard fist.

She flew sideways and landed facedown on the craft's floor. A mixture of pain and sadness and rage tried imprinting itself in her psyche. Florence shook it away, just as her own psychic energy traced her figure, flickering the intense red color. Confused at its sudden arrival, she looked back at her leg and found it glowing the same color, powered by the sychonium crystals. "Keep us in the air!" she yelled in the direction of the console.

Glancing up, Florence saw Bridget was tensed to the max, all of her strength and focus devoted to keeping the base's defenses from rebooting.

Another concentrated wave of emotional trauma rushed at Florence, this time as a fast-moving blob of psychic energy. She cursed, rolled onto her knees, and with her hands lifted, caught the blob. The measure of her reddened power clashed with that of the attacker's, both of them crackling and flaring in opposition. Her hands strained to close together, compressing the rival energy out of existence.

But the writhing blob squealed as if an injured creature, then it expanded, blowing Florence deeper into the plane.

Her back hit the metal bulkhead. She groaned and tried turning over, somewhat stricken.

"Oy!" Bridget shouted. "Dr. B., the tower's jumped up at us!"

From where she lay, Florence could hear Cynque sputtering details about technical failure and an object a bit too close. Which meant the autopilot had disengaged...

The plane's front began dipping into a diagonal dive.

"Warning, altitude critical. Impact imminent," Cynque announced.

Florence was up in a flash, though she stumbled when she got to her feet. She'd managed to get halfway between the pilot's seat and the exit hatch when the craft repeated, "Warning, altitude critical. Impact imminent!"

The giant, rotating tower was right on them now, covering the entire window. "Brace yourself!" she shouted to Bridget.

But the words seemed to leave her lips in slow motion, as the window's glass was already shattering, the cockpit already crushing inward around Bridget.

Horrified, Florence dove to the ground and clasped both hands around the exit hatch's handle, waiting for the collision to reach her.

CHAPTER 50

───────────────────────────

DR. FLORENCE BELLADONNA

C20 Base, Man's Lost Lands, Former Middle East
Day 206

THE CRASH WAS as Florence expected, a whirring instance of metal grinding against metal and violent shaking movement. Death was all but certain at their speed, even without considering the flying glass and the aerocraft's now partially torn-away ceiling.

Somehow, Florence's hands were still around the thick handle to the exit hatch, and she was still pinned to the floor.

They'd managed to crash *into* C20 but, perhaps thankfully, not through it.

Their aerocraft was wedged deep between the collapsed roof and split floor of the giant watchtower. Outside, a furious windstorm had become whispers, the dust docile. Sand skipped along with leisure instead of haste.

Florence tried to dismiss the headache pounding alongside the throbbing in her lower back. She grabbed the bridge of her nose, assessed her mental capacity, and winced as she tilted her head. "I keep signing on the dotted line for this," she whispered.

While groping nearby for something to help her stand, she laid a hand on her sword, still in its sheath. Grunting, she dragged it closer and stabbed the bottom into the floor, then used it to support the painful journey up to her feet.

Bridget was nowhere to be found. At least inside the remnants of the craft. So Florence endeavored to search for her *and* Celine. To find them before C20 did.

Florence climbed over the shattered digital console, wielding her weapon like a cane as she ducked under the jagged glass edges and hobbled over bent metal.

The tower's emergency bulbs cast an eerie red glow over the broken machines and cracked computers before her, all scattered from the crash. A groan pierced the silence of the room. Just one among the dozen or so bodies of unconscious C20 loyalists. She followed the sound white suit after white suit and stopped on—

Bridget lay twisted, some of her red hair matted across her face, the rest spread in a shallow puddle of pooled blood. Lightning darted across her slow-to-rise chest and twitching fingers.

Florence climbed off the wing, eyes wide open and scanning for movement, ensuring the area was clear as she made her way toward Bridget. She was starting to feel good about her chances when a woman's voice came from inside the tower.

"I've got the electric one," she said.

Florence scrambled behind a boxy machine knocked on its side and waited. Nothing more was said. She waited a second longer, then peered over the machine.

Vonnie was standing over Bridget's body, her clothing paled, her skin thinned, her molecules separated from one another in semitransparency. Tranjam grumbled next to her as he adjusted his black gloves; the Density Twins were never apart. But Florence's only concern was the man mere steps behind them.

Shahar. The Evolutionary who'd tried to incinerate her inside the nightclub.

"Where's Belladonna?" he asked in his raspy voice.

The twins hesitated, their faces adding up to *I don't know*, or perhaps they just didn't know *now*.

Vonnie poked Bridget with the blunt end of her staff. "Tranjam? You getting anything?" she asked.

Tranjam swiveled back and forth slowly, looking for her, hands on his hips, nose sniffing the air. After taking a step in Florence's direction, he scowled in disappointment.

Florence ducked back down, her grip around the sword tightening. *But where is she? Where is Kara? And for that matter, where is XBA?*

"Well?" Vonnie pressed.

"Nothing," Tranjam answered. He turned to his sister and asked with the same contempt, "Did you lose Celine?"

Lose...Celine? Florence thought, listening for an answer. Could she be somewhere in the watchtower?

There was a pause. Then from Vonnie: "She's not dead, if that's what you mean."

"But you lost her, correct?" Tranjam asked.

Vonnie answered too low for Florence to hear the exact words, but she sounded defensive. She and Tranjam engaged in hushed banter, with Tranjam speaking a pinch louder with each new accusation and Vonnie matching his volume with subsequent rebuttals.

A series of loud coughs echoed across the room, stopping their quarreling.

Florence peeked around the side of the machine. Her heart sank with fear at what she saw, yet her body tingled with a new sense of awareness. Connection, maybe.

Celine Setesh Nephthys, the princess she'd been sent to rescue, was struggling to stay upright between soft breaths and intermittent gasps. The red glare from overhead swathed her sun-starved skin, setting alight the harsh angles of her jawline. Her scalp overflowed with long braids thick as the tension, which she held back while coughing up spit and sand, unwilling to let the sickness surpass her strength. She was outfitted in such elegant robes. She was decorated with such extravagant jewels, barefoot because maybe, Florence speculated, she needed a connection with the Earth. Now, Florence eyed the deep cuts and bruises on skin stretched taut on her arm. Frailty arched the young woman's spine. Weakness soaked her shivering bones.

"See, I didn't lose her," Vonnie snapped.

Tranjam growled in response. "But she is free," he said, turning his head to the noise.

Indeed, Florence thought. One of her missions was almost complete.

Celine was free. A detached helmet rolled side to side inches from her, its visor opaque, the material that rounded the sides thick enough to block out sound. It was an obvious accessory to the amplification machine Bridget had detected, which loomed above the princess and spanned the entire wall. The monstrous contraption, every bit restrictive and torturous as could be imagined, funneled down into a chair built like a throne but rusted like a damp prison. Soiled needles hung loose from splayed tentacles, and Florence knew they had been injecting sedative into someone who was meant to be sedated.

Or controlled.

The reason for the devastation of Man's Lost Lands was solidified by the evidence in that ransacked corner. Celine had indeed been captured by C20, then forced to use her potentials against her will, enacting the greatest Evolutionary terror attack ever known.

The Middle Beast.

Florence couldn't bear the thought of Celine's abuse, or the psychological damage of bearing the blame. Nor would she sit there and wait any longer for the girl to be recaptured.

She crouched, a firm grip on her sword's hilt.

Neither Tranjam nor Shahar moved in any direction.

Florence took the head start with all intended grace, sidestepping behind piles of rubble while careful to stay out of sight. But the cover of destroyed technology naturally diminished the farther she got from the crash site, and nervous about being seen, she shifted her focus back to the trio.

"You take her, you've got the most range," Tranjam finally said from the same spot.

Shahar rolled back his wide shoulders and cracked his thick neck, as if in agreement. "Fine," he said. "Hit me—hard."

Tranjam laughed a cruel laugh. He went into an exaggerated windup, then swung forward, stopped short, and tapped Shahar on the arm.

Florence narrowed her eyes, not sure of their angle, being that Tranjam's hit was quite the opposite of hard, rather a near-soundless impact. Perhaps his density was enough, because Shahar's shoulders ignited with kinetic potential.

"Christ," she hissed, her back pressed to a giant upright monitor.

"I'll get her back in the chair," Shahar said. Soon, he prowled past Florence, the flaming orange energy spreading down his body. "You two find Belladonna."

His orange brightness pushed away the red glare of emergency lighting, flushing out the bodies of C20 agents she'd believed belonged to the injured.

They instead belonged to the dead.

She made the sign of the cross, convinced those deceased were just like the brainwashed individuals at Club HellForest. Should they have woken up, they would be bewildered—unsure why they held weapons, wore white uniforms, and hailed Tas-Salvatur, a man they'd never met.

Florence inched toward Celine, feeling her way behind a cluster of smaller machines.

She stopped when she felt a strange heat. A *nearby* heat. The bright-orange color followed, splashing her face with a warning. Kinetic energy was spreading with the speed of a wildfire toward the center of solid metal and loose wiring.

Florence turned away just as the machines flashed white in unison. With a loud *boom*, they exploded, blowing her across the room and through something that was mostly glass with metal framing. She landed on the floor among shards. Close enough to Celine to help her, though feeling too beat-up to try.

Her human leg was numb with pain. Her psibernetic one, however, hummed and hissed with the sound of recalibration, ready for another go. She watched psionic energy blazing through the metal in deep reds, fueled by the tiny sychonium crystals in the technology. She felt the soothing sensation of psychic awareness throughout her body. Then the warm rush of rejuvenation. The combination of the two felt seductive in many ways, maybe even addictive. Could the leg really be refueling her with stamina?

"Belladonna!" she heard Shahar yell. He became a blur as he charged forward, hands and hair and eyes consumed with kinetic heat.

Florence kept her focus on him, groping the ground for the sword that had been knocked from her grip. She glanced down and back up at Shahar, who was steps from igniting her atoms the way he'd done the machines. Thankful the orange flare had brought the golden dragon handle to gleaming life.

She wrapped her fingers around the handle, spinning away just before a stream of kinetic energy plowed in her direction. It exploded against the floor. She was once again standing upright, eyeing the smoking spot where she'd been lying, contemplating whether to engage in combat or reason.

Florence squared her body opposite Shahar.

There came a tense moment of challenge, where she ran her hand over the sword's carved details, felt the precious metal's smooth texture, then reaffirmed her hold before she pulled up. The blade rose as if resurrected, sharp as it was shiny.

Shink.

She pulled harder, faster, unsheathing the weapon.

Shahar grinned at her challenge. With an impassioned roar, he launched a rapid-fire barrage of fiery balls in her direction.

Weapon in hand, Florence dodged to either side, somersaulting over several as quickly as she then slid underneath the rest. As she tumbled back onto her feet, her shoulder rolled over something sharp. Still, she got up, fuming, one hand clutching her new injury, the other pointing the sword in his direction.

"The more you move, the more powerful I get, Dr. Belladonna," Shahar said, his hands already recharged.

The next round began with her rethinking her head-on strategy and him gunning for her with unprecedented aggression.

She fought through the mounting pain, evading his wild punches and fast-firing beams while cutting away a path for her escape. His hands shot energy on either side of her like blowtorches, and she, doubling back as she dodged, slipped and fell into the tower's outermost wall.

Shahar was engulfed by his own power, transformed into frizzed orange energies pulled into a human figure with no edges.

Florence swung the sword in front of her body—a meek form of protection as she backed against the wall. There was nothing behind her but solid steel and nothing ahead of her but the kinetic potential drenching her in the glow of damnation.

"End of the line, Belladonna," he taunted, energy flickering around his wide grin.

Florence gripped the handle so tight she couldn't feel her fingers. In fact, she couldn't feel anything through the numbness plaguing her body. She looked at Shahar, looked at the sword, and looked at him again. It would take one forward thrust to impale him, she reasoned, if he got that much closer. Part of her wasn't resigned to finishing him off without giving him an out. For as her father had always said, *Death is for those without options.* "I can match whatever amount Tas-Salvatur promised you."

Shahar stepped forward and raised his arms, a ball of energy gathered inside his hands. "Freedom is a price you can't pay," he said, and brought them down.

"No!" she screamed out, thrusting the blade through his chest.

Every fear and desire in her surged to the surface of her psyche at once.

It was then she felt the pulsing of her psibernetic leg, saw the red wisps of psionic potential erupting from her hands and rushing through the sword, then steadily shooting through his midsection. The crimson energy was flourishing from her body like a rose in bloom. Tiny red lines chased each other down his arms and legs, others danced and darted up to his brain.

She pushed the sword deeper.

Shahar's eyes darkened. Orange light receded into him. He became more human and less energy until he solidified as flesh with the weapon burrowed beneath his sternum. Under the dull haze of emergency lighting, he squirmed against the hard, sharp metal.

Florence granted his obvious wish.

Release.

Fingers steady and firm, she pulled the sword's handle toward her with the same speed and power she'd used to force it in. She didn't understand what had happened until telepathic potential evaporated from his mind. This was no normal injury, she realized, as he would've been able to absorb the friction of the sword's penetration.

His lips bubbled forth black liquids like a hellish cauldron. His arms crowded his torso. He transformed into volcanic rock, grayed and cracked, before crumbling to the floor like an impaled statue.

Florence did the sign of the cross once again. He'd made his choice.

"I suggest you put the toy down," came a voice beyond the pile of remains.

Tranjam stood with Bridget's throat in his already-tight constriction, fingers fixed to compress at the slightest hesitation. Vonnie had her hands on Celine, whose fragile body showed little hope of producing more than a few whimpers.

They say you can't save others if you don't save yourself. Here Florence was, still standing, one C20 Evolutionary down, with two, maybe three, maybe *four* more to go.

She stepped over the remains of Shahar and swatted the air free of his dust, telepathy charged confidence oozing from her.

"Drop it, psychic," Vonnie said, her glaive pushed up to Celine's neck.

"I think you've seen that this won't work in your favor," Florence said. "Perhaps I'll vouch for mercy with the EFD if you surrender, now."

Celine looked straight at Florence with no discernible expression, her unflinching eyes now glowing gold between her hanging locks. An instant later, the princess transformed into a tempest of violent sand between Vonnie's fingers, blanketing the room in utter chaos. The desert swarmed around Celine, in one moment adding weight and form to her loosely constructed figure, and in the next, condensing into the fullness of her body.

The tower swayed with the motion of an incoming tide. A gentle rocking when in the ocean's hands, but ferocious in the Earth's. Blank screens and dismantled machines tumbled over. Chunks of the interior structure fractured and separated. Parts of the ceiling caved in as Tranjam and Vonnie stumbled, losing balance and grip.

Artist: Jeffrey Viloria/ The CMD Studios

Florence planted her sword's tip in the tile and tried anchoring herself to the wall. She wasn't quite sure where the sudden earthquake had come from, but she assumed, knowing what she knew about Celine and watching the golden energy bursting from her body, that it had something to do with elemental potential.

The shaking continued toward what felt like its greatest strength, peaking at an unfathomable amount of tectonic friction that was nearly earth-splitting.

Heart racing, Florence crouched down on instinct, hands flat against a jagged chunk of the floor that by some miracle had not so much as cracked.

The answer was ahead of her, Celine standing tall next to an unconscious Bridget, her shoulders broad, head high, wholly rejuvenated in human form. She seemed to be holding Florence and the piece of the floor aloft with something unsteady, and let the rest—Vonnie, Tranjam, and whatever assets C20 had owned and operated—topple down to the sand in heaps.

The potential in the princess was awe-inspiring. Her skill unlike anything Florence had ever seen, even in herself. She caught herself staring as Celine commanded the sand into a twirling cyclone and began lowering them, slow and controlled, on wobbling chunks of metal flooring. Past what remained of the tower. Past the structures now collapsing around it.

Florence was thankful for being spared. Still, the question remained, had Celine saved her because she knew about the artifacts? Because she wanted to save humanity?

"King Marshall asked us to save you," she shouted across their distance. "There is more we need to do...more I need to do. Don't leave, Princess Celine. Help us. Trust us."

"Trust you?" Celine shouted ahead of a sneer. "I trust the ground beneath your machine-manufactured soles, I trust the air you pollute with your fumes, I trust the seas you've imbalanced with plastic waste. A planet does not lie. What do the trees have to gain from deception? Nothing."

Florence sighed. *Sharp*, was all she could think to say. The young woman was right. More than right, she was spot on.

The sand and wind spun away as the ground neared, allowing them to touch the desert in unison.

Bridget groaned, sprawled on her back. "My head bloody hurts," she shouted into the air. "Those damn twins and their damn shifting."

Artist: The CMD Studios

"You are like me, an elemental," Celine said to Bridget, studying her as the other woman pulled herself up from the sand. "You summon lightning's charge the way I summon the soil and the trees." The princess stepped closer and held out her hand, fingers splayed. "Yet what runs through your veins is ice." She said *ice* as if the word stung her and withdrew her hand. Her shoulders relaxed, though she looked to the coming dawn, still troubled.

"What do you know about the artifacts?" Florence asked.

"I know nothing," Celine replied. "I listen. The Earth has whispered in my ear. The heritage, the secrets, the *truth*." She spread her arms wide, catching the breeze in an embrace, then brought her hands to her chest. "You cannot call them artifacts when they are energy. Daal Trelkkien, pure energy of time and movement. Zeorgen, pure energy of manifestation. Do you know what it is you seek? These are not things for human possession. They are forces unexplained. I will not stand by and watch as—"

Bridget interrupted. "If we're the same like you say, mate, I know you feel it," she said. "Something's off. The electromagnetic spectrum is tellin' me. What's the sand tellin' you?"

Celine pondered Bridget's words. The princess was an Evolutionary no older than twenty, slowly weeping for what surrounded them. Deep down, Florence sensed the tears soaking her full cheeks weren't bred in sorrow but in the inevitable.

Another breeze blew through her garments. Sand danced around her arms. But she didn't answer.

"If we don't find the artifacts," Florence explained, "we can expect a future that looks a lot like…well…a lot like this." She referenced the ruins of Man's Lost Lands. "All of humanity will be destroyed."

Celine's face hardened at that. Tears dried on her cool brown skin, which was quickly losing its moisture, lightened, and finally cracked like sunbaked clay.

"The sand says—I will be the only one of us left. I will be the last."

Florence opened her mouth to speak, although she knew by the golden energy surging from Celine's bare feet that the conversation was over.

Without another word, the princess's body dissolved into dust particles and was carried away by a chariot of wind.

Artist: Lester Niesta/ The CMD Studios

CHAPTER 51

LIEUTENANT LEESA DELEMAR
C20 Prison, Man's Lost Lands, Former Middle East
Day 206

LEESA'S EYES SHOT open. She was bewildered that the sense of helplessness in her mind had followed her to the waking world. It took tangible form too quickly. From the unsettling emptiness in her soul to the perceived heaviness keeping her hands palm up in the sand. Normally, the latter could be attributed to the burden of her potential, however, there was no energy gathering in them, and the warm chains hugging her wrists didn't shatter as she silently commanded.

Next, she tried moving her arms. Those same chains rattled with resistance, held fast to the wall and to her.

XBA must've done something, restricted me, she thought.

Leesa quickly scanned the hollowed space. She was pissed off by the bolt-locked door. Apprehensive about the low light and the tight space. Relieved to see Penny beside her, studying her with a tilted head. The metal contraption that was meant to hold the animal's jaw closed was sitting between her paws like a chewed-up toy, broken into pieces. And behind the oversized canine hybrid—

Dorian was sprawled on his side. His hands were chained together, and someone had put what appeared to be a thick, noise-canceling helmet over his head. She couldn't see his eyes through the black visor, but she assumed from his chest's steady movement that he was asleep, not dead.

Good. No more Evolutionary sacrifices, Leesa thought. Nonetheless, her potentials were not responding and Dorian was incapacitated, making it hard to imagine how they'd escape.

Maybe Allister if he'd survived.

Though it might cost him the artifacts, she told herself.

Besides the chills she couldn't shake, the cough climbing up her throat refused to go back down. She raised her hands toward her face to catch it, but the chains stopped them in midair. Just beyond her hands, she saw Dolores hunched over and drooling just beyond her shackled wrists.

"Dolores...," she said immediately, shuddering at the sight.

Then she saw the wound. The gut-wrenching wound.

A metal rod planted in the sand had been impaled through Dolores's leg, locking her teeth together in what Leesa assumed was excruciating pain. Disturbed, Leesa sprang onto her knees and tried to crawl toward her. As she moved, presumably beyond the area she was allowed, the chains snagged, then retracted, yanking her onto her back. She blew her hair from her face and sat up.

Leesa went to try again, fury building in her, when Penny whined, pushing her nose toward the surface above them.

Sand bled from the ceiling.

The ground rumbled seconds after, the magnitude of its movement rapidly increasing until the edges that surrounded the door were shaken away. The compact walls and carved-out ceiling shifted with a loud crack. A chunk of something solid above Dorian loosened, on its way to dislodging.

Leesa held her breath, waiting for whatever it was to fall.

The shaking came to an abrupt halt. As did the ceiling's shifting. Leesa watched, thankful the solid chunk remained in place.

Penny seemed to sigh as she nuzzled her paws.

But when voices in the tunnel sounded, yelling for reinforcements, the animal sat up on her haunches. Penny got to pawing and sniffing at the helmet fitted to Dorian's head. Growling, she moved to the chains that were looped and locked around his body. Her jaws clamped around a loose link, and she tugged at it like a rope.

"You must be the famous lieutenant," Dolores said out of nowhere, wheezing between heavy breaths.

Leesa took the statement for what it was: an insult. "My name is Leesa," she said in her softest voice. "I'm...a...friend of Allister's."

"Hmm, a...friend of Allister's," Dolores repeated, but with Leesa's forced inflection. "Funny you should say that because...friendship requires honesty and loyalty. I gather by that hideous emblem on your chest you don't know the mean-ing of either."

"I can assure you that—"

"I can assure *you* that you were raised by the wrong Delemar, and that says all it needs to say about you."

Leesa clamped her mouth shut.

"Nicolas is a monster," Dolores continued. "A good-for-nothing, murderous shell of a man."

"My father is not the man—"

"Your...father? Ah, they haven't told you yet." The laugh that followed was heavy with knowledge, and with contempt. "You're not what you think you are. Not even close," she snapped. "Leesa Delemar is an illusion. An operatin' system waitin' to fail, if it hasn't already."

Dolores let out another cryptic laugh, which harshened to a cough.

Leesa stirred in the prediction, searching herself for anything: a tingle, a warmth, an energy of any color—pink or blue or purple—to bring forth. She was certain Dolores must have gone crazy from the hours spent underground in solitude, from the lack of nourishment, or possibly from blood loss. There couldn't be any truth to her statements. So why was it that when Leesa tried to move again, she couldn't even lift her arms.

Maybe because she was *failing*.

Leesa's mind clouded as the emptiness in her multiplied. Her own version of delirium having just arrived, began settling in. Weakness had always been her worst enemy. But this...this was more than inability.

"Do you know why you wear that ridiculous cape, Leesa?" asked Dolores, a mocking tone in her voice again.

Fatigue stretched Leesa's words, broke up her sentences. "My father gave it to me as a gift when I joined the Andromeda Project," she answered. "It's part of my uniform. It...affirms my rank and position."

"Is that what it does?"

Leesa couldn't answer with confidence. She breathed too hard now, realizing her essence had gone missing, that her veins were dried up. Tears fell with nothing to stop them, pausing briefly at her chin before running down her neck and soaking into her chest. She tested her nonexistent grip on grains of sand and failed. "I don't...I don't know...," she finally replied.

Through pained grunts and incoherent mumbles, Dolores shared what she knew. "The cape cuts off your power at the source. Whenever you go above the threshold, it slams the door shut. *Pow.* That's why you feel yourself weakenin'. And sometimes...sometimes you lose control; that's the thing you have inside of you rebellin'. The comedown from that is...brutal. Takes you hours, don't it?"

Sometimes more, Leesa thought.

How could Dolores know such a truth? That a beautiful garment, faithful in its rich colors, had flapped in every available hallway, room, and sky, obstructing her from a taste of her true potential. She wanted to tear the cape off and deconstruct it thread by thread until she found the technology responsible for her limitation. For her *sabotage.*

Those same chills went on cutting through the heat around her. Leesa felt the coldness in her blood, the clamminess coating her skin. The unsettling emptiness was burrowing deeper. How could it grow in so many directions?

She hesitated at the next thought, unable to perceive beyond what she felt—and to date, she'd felt very little. Both raw anger and extreme calm begot uncontrolled manifestations of Z-energy, while her dormant state begot rigid mannerisms, clipped phrases, and manageable displays of focused telekinetic potential.

She wrestled with the notion of being separated from all that she was meant to be. From her potential and the full capability of it. She wondered what else the cape had denied her. More than that, she wondered who else besides her father was aware of its existence and function. Dr. Belladonna, Professor Ashur, Captain Brandt, XBA…were any or all of them in on the joke where her validity was the punch line?

"Just know the cape will be your undoing, one way or another," Dolores said. She cringed, wanting to say more, but gave up to her own agony.

Leesa stared at the pole. She willed it to move, knowing that at any other time, it would've obeyed her command. Instead, the metal taunted her with its stiffness, lured her into an emotional battle with an energy that wouldn't heed her call.

"I have to get you out of this place," she said with desperation. "I have to get you…free…somewhere close, but safe, I promised Allister we would—" Air came through Leesa's lips. The words did not.

Dolores struggled to ask, "What'd you promise Allister?"

Leesa's heart fluttered at the reverence in his mother's pronunciation. A reverence they now shared. "I promised Allister we would protect you," she said. Her fingers ached from the restricted blood flow. All the while she strained to make a fist. "And I meant it."

"See…there's the truth I couldn't get past. Here we are, on the brink. Both of us so close to"—Dolores paused to sniffle—"so close to a cosmic boom like the stars we came from." Her words then began to slur. "You and me, we kept borrowing time 'til there wasn't none left."

"Death will not take us from here, I won't let it. If I can just…" Leesa tried to herd sand beneath her palms. "If I can just…," she repeated.

Her hands were motionless.

"If only it was up to you," Dolores said and looked to the door knowingly.

Leesa's lips parted to reply.

Suddenly, the underground tunnels were alive with frantic voices, the lot of them leaking through fissures in the door's archway. She heard muffled recounts of a crashed ship…and…something falling…the tower…falling.

Who of us could? she thought.

The list of Andromeda Project members was vivid in her mind.

She flicked her gaze at the door, anxious. Maybe Allister *had* pulled some trick. Or maybe Florence and Bridget had come for them. She had doubts Allister would level a tower. And between Florence and Bridget, neither was built for that level of damage.

Even so, the news was the tiniest bit of hope needed to fuel her.

Until she heard the woman cursing just on the other side of the thick iron.

Leesa gritted her teeth at the hissing and clanking of metal limbs.

XBA snickered, clearly forcing the enthusiasm as she said, "Let's have a look in on our friends, shall we?"

CHAPTER 52

ALLISTER ADAMS
C20 Tunnels, Man's Lost Lands, Former Middle East
Day 206

BRANDT HAD TOLD Allister as they descended into the tunnels under C20 that his mom wasn't far behind. For some reason, they needed to be together when he retrieved the artifacts.

That was why Allister moved at a sluggish speed in a direction he couldn't discern.

Brandt guided him from behind, his powered-up plasma rod surging with energy. For the third time during their journey, a burst of heat forced jitters up Allister's spine. He glanced around again to check how close the rod was.

Close enough to burn a hole in his back if he stopped.

The captain squeezed the rod's handle threateningly. "Ah-ah."

They'd traveled far from the tower, Allister knew that much. He had no Cynque signal. He felt no surface heat. He saw no technology or C20 operatives. "Where's my mom?" he asked, slowing down. "You said she'd be here."

"She'll be along by the time we get to the cavern," was the captain's reply. "Keep movin'."

Long as she's on her way, he thought.

He heard the ground above them rumbling just as tremors reached the depths of the earth, shaking in varied intensity; the onset of it mild enough to upset their footing, the last of it wild enough to knock them over.

Allister went careening across the tunnel and slammed against the wall. The earthquake faded to stillness.

Now the tunnel was filled with a cloud of loose sand and dust. Allister waved his hand, coughing from it. "I need to chill," he said, sinking. "Fifteen seconds to get my regeneration potential going."

"Fifteen seconds, then you get up," Brandt said from above him.

Allister didn't listen. He just stared between the captain's legs. Sitting closer to the ground, he could see the thin corridor behind them was split down the middle by a twisted fissure. His eyes continued up, spotting an offshoot of that same fissure climbing the walls on either side and slithering through the compact sand and stone overhead, almost connecting where it began.

Leesa?

In somewhat of a daydream, he imagined her hovering above the surface, her hands stretched toward the sand in a bid to tear it open. His mom and Dorian would be next to her, and together they'd swoop in and rescue him from Brandt.

That would be golden.

But nothing happened after that.

He placed his palms against the paved floor in resignation, let the cool sand soothe the blisters on them. It was in that moment where, as the throbbing in his injured side pounded toward unbearable and his fantasy of being rescued vanished, his body gave in to failure.

Permanent failure.

Was that the tightness he felt around his heart? A perfect blend of apprehension like a cage, trapping his potential in it. *Boom.* His heart fought its way out of captivity, out of his chest. *Boom, boom, boom.*

"Let's move, Allister. Five...," the captain started.

Sweat droplets tumbled down Allister's wide nose and dripped off it onto his pants.

"Four."

He dragged his legs to his body one at a time, then he crouched.

"Three."

His arms were noodles—stringy and loose, hanging by his side without the tension they needed for response.

"Two."

Allister caught his breath, a finger in the air, and said wearily, "Need just one more—"

Brandt interrupted again. "One." He stepped back and flicked his wrist.

Allister looked in the direction they'd come once more before coming to a full stand. He listened for sand shifting under a group of hasty feet. He listened for the murderous hum of handheld plasma cannons. He listened for his mom's screams of protest or whimpers of pain. He waited for the slightest sound to know if he stretched those few seconds into a minute, his plan to stall the captain would work.

To his disappointment, what he heard were the groans of the Earth's settling crust.

"You think you're slick, see," Brandt said, frowning. "I wrote the whole album on avoidance behaviors. But Tas-Salvatur has certain expectations, and I'm here to make sure we get what we need." He bobbed his head at the curve of the tunnel beyond Allister and followed up the gesture with an outward swing of the fiery rod. "Go. You're wearin' on my patience."

Allister obeyed. Somehow his body kept going, even with his mind screaming for him to stop. Perhaps there was no such thing as permanent failure.

In any case, Brandt couldn't be trusted—not to lead him to the artifacts, not to ensure his mom's safety. Those were Allister's responsibilities, and yet there he was, letting himself be guided by a man who didn't seem to value anything over his own life.

Anger's insufferable heat gushed up his torso. His heart, condensed by betrayal, seemed to contract into an infinite collapse, a hole perceivable only by what swirled around it—devastation, disgust, disbelief.

His connection to Brandt had passed the event horizon, now prevented from ever escaping into the world again. He knew that although he watched what they had stretch away from him for eternity, according to universal law, it had already disappeared.

Allister was ready to make a different choice. His own.

"Guess you're feeling pretty smart?" Allister asked.

"Pardon?" replied Brandt.

"You switched it up on me, got on the right side of salvation just in time. You know, to save yourself."

"Can't help it if I finally saw the truth," Brand said. "Say I was terminated right now, you wouldn't be here...committed to accomplishing this mission."

Rather than lash out, Allister chose patience. He formed his response with the intent to distract. So he could find the distance he needed for his next choice, attack.

"If you were terminated right now—I'd be twisted up and sick over you...for no good reason." Allister glanced at his left arm. "I'd be speaking on how loyal you were, how you helped me discover my potentials, how you changed my life. Just like you promised my pops you would."

Then, Allister listened for Brandt's reaction. His slowed steps. His sighs of consideration. The rod would lower, weighted by guilt. Not just because of the words, but because of how they'd make him feel. Less than.

For a moment, Allister didn't feel the heat against his back. At that, he spun around and shuffled backward, missing Brandt's attempt to grab him by a breath.

Allister made the kind of snarl a wild animal would before it engages an enemy, his cunning and prowess alive in him.

"It's all good, though, right?" he asked, still backing up. "You *were* loyal. You *did* help me discover my potentials. You *changed* my life."

"Now that's what you don't get. C20 finally offered me the chance to save everyone I care about…including myself, and I took it," Brandt replied, unapologetic. "That's when I realized I was going about it the wrong way. Andromeda Project's always been a burden disguised as an opportunity. All your daddy wanted to do was find those artifacts, save the world, and help that godforsaken alien get back up to the heavens it fell from." His eyes flashed with the yellow of disruption potential, the crackling charge as intense as his next words. "Instead of doing what I knew in my gut was right. Instead of giving General Delemar and his corrupt directors the middle finger, I played along. Always the good soldier. Look where we are! Twenty years and they got far enough to fail."

Brandt raised the plasma rod, his stance low, his arm flexed.

"Nothing different from C20 and the Andromeda Project far as I see," Allister said, balling up his fists. His theory was half-formed, but he kept going with anyway. "Just two trash sacks of fear propaganda: one of them's decorated with a bow and the other's got glitter all over it. What better reason than the apocalypse to fight over alien artifacts, while using sanctuary association or evolution to qualify who gets saved? The miracle is, you fell for both schemes. I mean, tell me, Captain, who're we saving anyhow: the human population…or your washed-up ego?"

Brandt reddened, repositioning his grip. "You listen here, I don't wanna have to teach you a lesson, but I damn sure will."

"What you waiting for, *Uncle* Jared? This seems like a golden moment."

Brandt continued advancing, slow at first, the rod brightening as more energy burned and sparked from it. "Ha, the problem with you Omega gen kids is you think you know every goddamn thing. At least you're headin' the right direction. Seeing as how I'm too close to have you screw this up, I'm thinkin' I'll just give you a push."

They both seemed to be waiting for the other to act first, and while intuitively Allister knew the captain was the more skilled fighter, keeping them there until his mom arrived trumped any attempt at reason.

Allister charged at Brandt. Brandt charged back. Allister was armed with his strength potential, and Brandt with his rod, both ready to swing. In a bril-liant stroke of timing and strategy, Allister chose defense and caught the captain's wrist before he could strike. They tussled back and forth, firm grips on resistant wrists, clumsy feet carrying them into and away from tunnel walls. Trying to wrestle him down was a mistake, Allister realized quickly, as Brandt flipped him into a headlock and squeezed, the scorching-hot weapon held at his side.

Allister squirmed, his hands clasped around Brandt's flexed forearm. But he couldn't seem to pull it away. The strength he'd felt moments before was rapidly draining out of him. Less from fatigue, and more from…disruption. He remembered the captain's potential then—the ability to disrupt—and though the tightening constriction didn't come with the pulsing yellow energy, he knew it was in play.

His breathing became that much more difficult, when something Bridget had said about him and his potentials gave him a new idea.

You look like one of those dumb blokes that swings at everything hoping for a solid win. Perhaps Brandt thought that about Allister, too. But it was his mom that had, in her own words, praised his genius-level intellect.

"I showed you all this so you could see there was more to life than Cynque surveillance and District raids," Brandt said in Allister's ear. "Now you wanna throw it away because things didn't turn out how you thought."

"Didn't think you'd join a bunch of terrorists…" Allister tensed his neck and, instead of struggling, moved his feet in reverse, forcing them both backward until Brandt's spine slammed into a wall.

The captain cried out, let go, and shoved Allister. "Oh, and what do you call an EV like the lieutenant who blows an entire sanctuary to the sky? A hero? A savior?"

Brandt appeared faster, or at least more skilled, moving around Allister as the plasma rod's brightness burst into a sunset's blazing colors. The rod waved like a torch but cut like a sword and burned like hellfire. Allister felt its heated slash across his torso, then its red-hot slice along his back and again behind his knees.

It was Allister's turn to cry out. Sharp, stinging pain ripped through fresh wounds. He strained not to fall, and after seconds of swaying in resilience, kneeled in the sand, his shaking leg not ready to straighten again. Just four burning strikes and he'd fallen like a disciplined child.

"*Stubborn*. Just like your daddy. Listen here, are you gonna cooperate so we can get this over with?" the captain asked.

Allister spat on the ground, momentarily incapacitated by the blistering cut along his ribs. He kept hoping his mom would appear, for there was no other way to be sure his current sacrifice was worth it.

Brandt leaned down and held the rod next to his head. "I said, are you gonna cooperate?"

Allister flicked his eyes up at Brandt—the man who'd promised him the maximum wage and the truth—his mind screaming at the captain to go to hell, but not wanting his face to show it.

Brandt must've known the answer anyway. He kicked Allister in the mouth, sending him flying over himself in a complete turn until he landed hard. "I don't wanna hurt you, Allister," he said. "I love you like a son."

"You're a liar!" Allister shouted, trying to pull himself up. Brandt pushed him back down with his heel. The captain waited, maybe to let the pain sink in, then lifted his foot into the air and came down hard, smashing it into Allister's shoulder.

Allister cried out, breathless, his stomach flexed against the pain. "You're a liar," he muttered. "All you do is hurt people."

Brandt slammed the plasma rod into Allister's chest.
The impact was infernal, explosive, a heat so hot, chills shuddered through to his core. He squirmed and bucked at the smell, at the taste, at the searing plasma tunneling slowly through his insides, while fighting with every fiber in him to keep the agony from turning into shock.

"Heal," Brandt said to him. "So we can share the glory of savin' this world from itself."

His eyes locked on Allister's.

In this moment, if Allister *could* find the strength and the regeneration he needed, they wouldn't make it to his muscles and bones. Those potentials were walled off by Brandt's evident *power*, the power of disruption. The captain had become something else, a creature beyond potential; there was nothing left of his godfather but persistence, there was nothing the man above him wanted more than his victory.

"I said heal!" he yelled.

Allister's flesh continued burning away from the round, blunt center. He saw smoke rising from the growing circle and forced more screams from his throat, his vocals beyond raw with overuse.

This was the moment C20 wanted from him.

Surrender.

Obedience.

This was the moment everyone wanted from him.

Defeat.

Brandt clenched his teeth as he pushed down further and said, "Your father would be ashamed of you. All that potential, wasted."

All that potential, wasted, Allister breathed in, giving up.

The tunnels went black.

He blamed the shock in his body for his temporary loss of consciousness when it was really the words. That he was wasted potential, a prisoner to the pain jumping from the cut near his ribs to the burns on his back and behind his legs, to the bruise forming in his mouth, to the open hole in his chest.

In the darkness behind Allister's eyes, a light of hope flashed blue. "Use your potentials," his dad whispered from somewhere in his head, his smooth voice connected to the light, and guiding him out of the darkness.

Use. My. Potentials. I have potential. I am potential.

Allister opened his eyes. He wrapped one quivering hand around the energy-charged plasma rod, then the other. His palms blistered immediately at the rod's touch. He could feel his skin melting as he tightened his grip with the intent to push up, his body suffering a pain he could no longer endure.

And he ignored it.

Already, he felt his resolve gaining. Already, he felt defiance bringing resilience to his body and the Z-energy potential to his mind.

Brandt's sneer faded to a look of astonishment.

Low and guttural, Allister said, "Foeht...Zeorgen."

The Z-energy engulfed his biceps, furious as it spread past his elbow and surged over his wrist, then crackled with control along his fingertips. Last, it soared up the rod and exploded against Brandt. His body went flying, smashing into the wall with a satisfying *thud*.

Allister forced the rod back up with his strength potential, pushing it away from his lungs and into open air. He pulled himself to his feet, weapon in hand, and barreled toward Brandt, snatching him up by the collar with a Z-energy-charged grip and forcing him against the sandy wall of the underground tunnel. Their eyes met with the same intensity as earlier. An intensity reversed.

Neither said a word, their ragged breaths taking center stage.

Allister wanted with everything inside to hurt Brandt the way Brandt had hurt him. Words didn't seem to be sufficient, yet death seemed excessive. He was staring into eyes that he'd once trusted, the anger in him cooling to some twisted form of forgiveness, and again, he found compassion in his choice. Just enough to spare Brandt's life, but not him pain.

Allister loosened his hold, and Brandt, thinking he'd been spared, went to move.

"No," Allister said, shoving him into the wall again. "I said you'd pay."

He flipped the plasma rod from behind him and drove the flaming weapon into Brandt's side, impaling him against the tunnel interior. Brandt screamed, his face bright red and sweaty and shaking, both hands clasped around the rod's handle to free himself.

The captain exhaled. "You...you did it...you overcame...your fear," he struggled to say. He tugged at the weapon to no avail, visibly in more pain as each second passed. "If we...if we hurry...we can still...get the artifacts..." He groaned and adjusted his hands. "We can still...get the..."

Allister slid out the notebook from the captain's pants and stepped away. "I think I got it locked, Captain," he said, waving the book in the air. "C20 and the Andromeda Project get no artifacts from me. I'm giving them up to the Resilient Nations of Global Unity."

The brightness of Allister's Z-energy kept the tunnels lit. Under the harsh blue, the captain squirmed, and screamed out, "Tas-Salvatur...will come...after you... Kill everyone...you...love..."

With a squeeze of Allister's fist, the Z-energy flared. "Well, you let him know when he's good and golden to come see me—cuz I'm one thousand percent with it."

Artist: Ezrom Bathan/ The CMD Studios

CHAPTER 53

———————◆———————

LIEUTENANT LEESA DELEMAR
C20 Prison, Man's Lost Lands, Former Middle East
Day 206

LEESA NAVIGATED A thickening mental fog. She was trying to keep her scowl on the door as much as she was trying to keep herself together.

XBA was there, on the other side, returned to finish what she'd started.

"Confirm the captain's position. Go now," Leesa heard her say.

Dorian still hadn't moved and Penny was steadily growling. But as the door creaked open on rusted hinges and the first ray of hallway light hit Penny's iridescent mane, she shoved her snout under the sand and closed her eyes.

XBA strolled in with a handful of agents, all armed. While they waited at the entrance, she moved around in the small cave like a venomous spider might around prey caught in her web. She expanded her claws and held them up to the light. A round contraption Leesa didn't recognize dangled from her palm. "Her." She pointed at Dolores. "This is for her."

The agents took the device.

Leesa watched, helpless, as Dolores's arms were lifted, and in a blur of shuffling and aggressive movement, the unknown technology was strapped around her waist. When finished, the agents returned to their positions at the door behind XBA.

"Fits like a bloody glove," XBA said, crouching down close to Dolores. She stroked the other woman's cheek and wrapped her claws around the pole. "Time to move her. The artifacts await."

"You want to torture someone, torture me," Leesa said.

XBA frowned. "But I love making you watch." She wiggled the pole back and forth.

Dolores stared at Leesa, silently weeping and mouthing for mercy.

"Stop it!" Leesa shouted. She felt as though the room shook with her voice, but it was only her voice shaking. Only her body shivering at her feverish temperature and physical effort.

"You've got some fight in you after all. Very good." XBA released the pole and stood. Tilting her head with a sort of curiosity, she walked over to Leesa, climbed over her legs, and straddled her, knees in the sand.

Leesa's body cringed at the play toward intimacy. The anger of not being able to strike her almost more than she had the strength for.

"I respect you, Lieutenant," XBA said. "You have gone to the ends of the Earth to live out your purpose. Here you are, still fighting the good fight, still true to that jacked-up man you call a father and that screwed-up halfway house they called an organization. Bravo, really...bravo." She took a shallow breath and caressed Leesa's scabbed-over hairline. "I can honestly say I've never seen anything more beautiful than the shade of death on your cheeks. It truly suits you."

Death? I am far from death, Leesa told herself.

But everything about what happened to her next said otherwise.

Her heart slowed when it needed speed. Her skin wanted to ignite when the near-absolute zero of deep space wouldn't release her. It was the cape, she now realized, restricting something deep inside her soul along with her Z-energy potential. The more her spirit called for it, the stronger the hidden technology worked to keep it away.

No wonder the emptiness had consumed her.

Almost thoughtfully, XBA found a tender spot on Leesa's temple and penetrated it with her claws. Slow, because she knew it was excruciating; surgical, as if it *had* to be done.

This was what Leesa had asked for. This was what she'd wanted. To take the attention off of Dolores long enough to reconnect to herself. She'd thought the anger would refuel her, and now she was hoping it would be the pain.

She welcomed XBA's enhancements, embraced them scraping their way to her chin. When blood oozed from the cut, she basked in the wetness, in the stinging, too, her face hardening. Her enemy wouldn't get the satisfaction of seeing her suffer.

XBA smeared the blood on Leesa's face and teased, "There you go, doll. I still enjoy you better with a smidge of color."

Leesa stared back at her, a scream caged behind her tongue.

"And this...," XBA said as she caressed the fabric draped over Leesa's shoulders. She drew her claws up Leesa's neck until she reached the cape, unfastened the clasps, and snatched it free. "This majestic symbol of self-importance. 'Tis a prize I will cherish long after we've won. A reminder that those who seek purpose in this world will triumph over those who seek approval."

The cape's violet luster faded as it fell lifeless into XBA's hands. She jumped up, not seeming to notice, and spun in circles, holding the cape close to her like a new dress. "Look at me, I can be pretty and powerful, too."

She clenched the cape and snapped her head toward Leesa, sneering when they locked eyes. "I have half a thought to carve your face up and make you look at yourself before I kill you. I can already sense you teeming with self-hatred, but—imagine if I turned you into the monster you really are."

Leesa blinked at XBA, frozen in realization, less taken aback by her cruel words than by the chill thawing, no, melting, beneath her skin. In its place was the rising heat of *connection*. Z-energy coursed through Leesa's blood, bones, and muscles, returning strength to her arms and legs. For the first time ever, her potentials commingled, and in her mind, she visualized the experiments possible with fields and the experiments possible with energy, and she considered their outcomes with courage rather than fear.

Her fingers closed around a clump of sand. "You have no idea what I am," she said, her voice low and rattling.

XBA leaned back down.

Though Leesa kept her frown and her exasperation, her eyes rose with the speed of stealth, fixed on XBA's orange eye. She challenged its focus knowing no telepathy could come from it. And behind the cyborg woman, her fields were an invisible constriction around the accompanying agents, who writhed inside them with their mouths sealed shut.

Foeht Zeorgen, she thought, picturing the metal pole that XBA had speared through Dolores's leg. She willed it and its pain to end with Z-energy, even imagined the molecules disintegrating in her peripheral view.

XBA pinched her claws around Leesa's throat. "You still haven't answered my question from Brisbane, Lieutenant. How can we be cynqued, if we are not one?"

Perhaps the clarity of Leesa's intention, the narrowing of her focus, was why Z-energy began burning through the pole, breaking it down to but shavings before reforming it into three solid, sharpened spears.

"We can't," she answered, satisfied. "Salvation *is* worth the sum of the remaining, not the difference between them."

She then levitated the weapons to eye level, prepared to conclude her experiment with XBA's defeat.

Artist: Lester Niesta/ The CMD Studios

XBA must've seen the color in Leesa's cheeks, must've telepathically glimpsed the smirk forming in her mind or picked up on the soldiers' unheard struggles, because she flexed her claws.

The maneuvers were so quick. Leesa couldn't believe how she executed them. From the chains around her wrists dissolving, to her ducking at just the right moment. She was lying flat on the ground when, propelled by the Z-energy's force, the three spears spiraled forward, impaling XBA's torso to the prison interior. XBA floundered and cursed and screamed and clawed, nailed to the wall through her stomach, her shoulder, and just below her heart.

Leesa scurried away and paused at the prison's center to wipe her brow, then fell back with her hand pressed to the wall. "Dorian?" she whispered.

Dorian sat up with a thumb halfway in the air, followed by Penny with her tongue halfway out of her mouth.

Leesa almost let a smile slip free but waved her hand across her body instead. Z-energy sparked around the chains linking Dorian and his companion to each other and the wall, its power whittling them also to shavings. He unlatched the metal mask fastened around his head and tossed it to the side.

XBA pushed against the wall in protest. "I should've ripped out your throat when I found you in the desert!" she shrieked.

But Leesa had made sure XBA wouldn't get free. Part of the experiment was keeping her there while they escaped.

Leesa didn't want to touch Dolores, who whimpered, barely conscious at her feet, too afraid she'd worsen the woman's injury or reignite the pain. Instead, she let her telekinetic field do the work of levitating Dolores off of the ground and placing her on Penny's back. Dorian helped situate Dolores once there, then concentrated on keeping Penny steady and still with calm strokes. "With urgency," Leesa said to Dorian.

Her hands shot forward, charged with telekinetic force. At her command, the prison wall blasted outward, shaking the tunnel with the intensity of an earthquake. Rubble and debris sprayed the area, instantly incapacitating the soldiers stationed in it.

The prison was left a carved-out cave. The walls and ceiling still standing. The front a gaping hole.

Dorian led Penny over the opening, supporting Dolores with one hand around her waist. Leesa hovered behind them, and when they reached the tunnel, turned inward.

Her heart rate dropped when she saw the cape there, in a heap on the sand.

She would destroy the initiation gift from her father, she decided. Never again would she be denied. Never again would she be held back. She stared at the cape until it, obeying her desire, fluttered off the ground. The needles and strings of her telekinetic potential went to work in the reverse. Rather than holding the fabric together, she willed it apart, tearing away each thread as it spun in violent circles. As it unraveled, she found nothing special, no device or technology, no tangible reason for its power over her. A few seconds later, it was a pile of fibers.

Leesa felt her body quiver, unsatisfied with the cape's destruction.

"Where's Allister?" Dolores called out behind her. "Allister?"

Allister.

Leesa was again reminded of her promise to save his mom. "XBA!" she shouted, letting the anger bolster her voice. "Where'd they take him?"

XBA laughed. "Oh, dearest Lieutenant. I promise...I promise I'll never underestimate you again. Do you see how alike we are? We even make the same arrogant mistakes."

Leesa twisted her wrist, thereby twisting the spears deeper into XBA's body and her body deeper into the wall. "Where, XBA?"

"It doesn't matter," XBA cooed, her orange eye glitching with failure. "Tas-Salvatur, the greatest Evolutionary to walk this Earth, is almost home. I can guarantee, no potential will stop him from getting what he wants. His power transcends."

Leesa hovered backward, away from the prison and into the tunnel. "I suppose if you're lucky, this transcendent power will be able to piece you back together."

Raising her hand toward XBA, she flexed her fingers, intending to end her with Z. For good this time. Before Leesa could let the words *Foeht Zeorgen* slip from her tongue, Dorian touched her arm and shook his head.

She side-eyed him, annoyed. "Stay out of this. You have no idea what she can do."

She could feel the Z-energy waiting hot in her veins, ready for the visualization of XBA's body dismembered, and with it, that simple phrase to bring forth its reality. The more she stiffened, the more adamant he became, pushing down on her arms with the sadness of knowing in his eyes. He shook his head again, more earnest that time.

XBA's eye faded to a dim orange. She screamed out one last time before finally shutting down and slumping over.

"Fine," Leesa said.

She turned, able to clearly see the meaning of the red numbers on the device fastened to Dolores's waist. The trigger confirmed its purpose was detonation, the countdown confirmed thirty minutes left.

Leesa felt her fast-beating heart clenching. She pressed her hands to her bosom in contemplation, torn between what to do next. The tunnel was too small and dark for her to disarm the device with any precision. But what if it was the last time Allister could see his mother? What if Dolores couldn't be saved no matter how much space and light there was? "Take her to the surface," she finally said to Dorian. "I'll disarm it there. Don't stop for anything or anyone."

Dorian nodded at her, terror reflected in his eyes.

She heard the noises approaching from behind—C20's reinforcements, she presumed—just as he pointed in its direction.

Leesa flipped around to see agents stampeding into view, illuminated by the monotonous glow of plasma. There were dozens of them, shouting for backup as they moved, their weapons whining like their voices. Thinking she'd construct a protective field of purple energy against them, she held out her hands.

Z-energy surged through her fingers, unexpected, powerful, ejecting in streams of condensed blue light that expanded around her and her comrades in the perfect sphere of a forcefield. The agents' plasma fire whizzed through the air, colliding with the field in bright flashes and mini-explosions. But unlike with her telekinetic potential, this forcefield absorbed instead of deflected, and grew thicker and pulsed stronger with every impact.

Just like in the training room, she thought.

Except the field was holding up *on its own*. A sense of dread expanded in Leesa, just as the forcefield expanded before her. She opened her mouth to speak as she floated away from her energy manifestation.

"Take me to Daal Trelkkien! Take me to my son!" Dolores wailed over the blasts. "I must see him. I must love him…Zosma…please, nothing else matters!"

Allister's mother said something else, too. No doubt a phrase buried in remorse for actions she hadn't taken. Leesa retained no other words than the one with no meaning: *Zosma*.

Zosma, Leesa thought. She closed her eyes, still fearful of her inability to save Dolores. There was a possibility of triggering the bomb at the slightest touch, even if it wasn't physical, and the idea of making a mistake plagued her in her private darkness.

Yet Dolores remained as lucid as she was insistent, repeating her request in the background.

"Go to Allister," she said, conceding. "Tell him...I'm sorry."

Dorian backed up and tapped Penny to communicate their new plan. He gave Leesa a quiet salute, the smallest sign of respect and, judging by the shimmer in his eye, admiration.

The three of them left Leesa there alone and bounded deeper into the tunnel. *If Allister couldn't save his mother, at least he could see her.*

When the others were out of sight, she inhaled. She stared at her hands churning with more blue energy than human flesh, knowing her potential had reached a place it'd never been, beyond its permitted threshold.

It was...limitless.

Z-energy swelled beyond the inflamed forcefield, a final surge of harnessed power, then—

Boom.

It burst.

An explosive swarm of energy blew Leesa backward through the tunnel, the heat, dust, and force winds spreading in both directions. She was flying through the air without control or coherence, scarcely able to shake the disorientation from the blast. The agents' tortured screams snapped her back to vigilance. There was no way the fire and debris could reach the depths of the tunnel. Dolores, Dorian, and Penny were down there.

Slowing herself through levitation, Leesa flipped over and landed on her feet, then went on skidding farther away with her hands out, glaring into the billowing blue inferno like it was a demon she was meant to vanquish. Leesa let out a final strained scream: for the cape and its limitation, for her mother and her bravery, and for herself and her connection to her infinite potential. She felt her arms falter and pushed out at last, determined, Z-energy firing from her fingertips.

A vortex of blue bolts then surrounded the flames and shot straight up into the sky, taking the explosion with it. A thick, dark plume of smoke followed right behind.

She fell against the wall.

The smoke hovering above her didn't disperse in the atmosphere as she expected. It swirled like a cyclone, though in silence, the darkness inside it thickening until it became more solid than even opaque gas. Gravity meant nothing as the spinning mass curved from straight up to sideways and torpedoed toward the base.

———

WHO GAVE YOU YOUR CAPE?

"WHAT IS THE MOST POWERFUL TRUTH ABOUT YOURSELF THAT YOU'VE NEVER SAID ALOUD. SAY IT NOW."

———

Artist: Lester Niesta/ The CMD Studios

CHAPTER 54

ALLISTER ADAMS
C20 Tunnels, Man's Lost Lands, Former Middle East
Unknown

ALLISTER'S CYNQUE GLITCHED and whined as it struggled to find the time.

He was hobbling up the tunnel, fatigue creeping into him like damp into dead timber, his eyes trapped on a ground that wouldn't stop spinning beneath him. The wall was sturdy, reliable, allowed him to move along it one hand and one step at a time—until nausea toppled him forward. His knees hit the sand and his hands hit shortly after.

The Z-energy that had been lighting his way fizzled to nothing.

That's when Cynque's face went blank, then rebooted, returning to a green row of infinite possibilities.

All zeroes.

He focused on that moment of rest, somewhat relieved, somewhat tortured. Every so often, a burn's stinging would shoot across his side, a bruise's swelling would pound along his lip, a sharp pain would dart through a cut within him. He resisted their combined efforts to root him in the sand. But moving forward seemed…unreasonable.

The fortitude he clung to had disappeared with the energy, disintegrated to pieces as granular as sand.

Huddled here, memories of his childhood stirred to the surface. Occasions he'd long forgotten flashed—picking oranges from the grove, practicing Schwebevogel, being read to sleep, playing board games, hiking to the waterfalls—and by his side for each one of those, his mom. Radiant, smiling, holding his hand or smothering him in hugs and kisses. She'd pick him up and swing him high as if she might toss him into the trees. This was who his mom had been before the Andromeda Project had taken her heart and soul.

The images of his memories faded into the dull brown of a dim corridor carved in sand.

Heal yourself, he thought with the same harshness as Brandt.

He pushed himself up from the ground. "Heal yourself!" he croaked. The words echoed off the tunnel, a soft bark echoed back at him. *Penny?* he thought.

Tempered footsteps followed. Then came another small noise, a whimper.

"Penny?" Allister asked, taking a cautious step.

"Did you hear that?" someone said. "I heard something. Hello?"

A small seed of a voice planted in faith. A voice he was beginning to think he'd never hear again.

"Allister, is that you, baby?" his mom asked.

His mom was here, in the tunnel. Alive.

"Mom...I'm—" Allister stopped and limped forward. Almost two decades' worth of feelings had accumulated in his heart, and so perhaps it wasn't words he needed, but actions.

The three of them—Dorian, Penny, and his mom—came into view. His mom glowed the pure color of heaven or something like it, or perhaps the pure color of time, her vacant eyes awaiting his confirmation.

"I'm here," he finally said, continuing on until he reached her.

"Allister...oh, Allister, look at you," she said, her hair as wild and majestic as ever.

She stared at him, possibly through him, while he stared back, into her, enamored by the white energy. She was wrapped in a brilliance that was blinding, warming, and mystical all at once, a physical representation of temporal energy potential.

Up close, Allister could see that her hands were coated with dried blood, trembling with the weight of buried secrets, the weight of a mother's undying love and protection. Below that, twenty minutes were left on the device strapped to her waist. A bomb, he guessed, reaching for it.

She caught his hand and held it back. "This ain't the clock you need to be worried about," she said.

With his attention on her grip, he could see she had some navy fabric tied around her leg, covering what looked to be a fresh wound from the way it was wet and glistening, soaked through.

Allister's heart plummeted. He swallowed back the sick making its way up his throat and choked out, "Can't believe I let this go down."

"Handsome and brave and full of potential, just like your father. Thank goodness for your extra one, of course...but..." She didn't finish right away and gave him a weak smile while she fluffed his afro. "But same big dreams. You been sayin' you were gonna stop the countdown even before they put up them clocks everywhere."

Allister looked down, ashamed. It pained him to his core to think that his decision to embrace this journey would cost him more than he could ever be grateful for.

"This's been a long time coming," his mom said. Her voice drifted higher like the end of a melody. "A long time coming," she repeated. She nodded in the direction he'd come from. "The cavern is that way."

"But—you—I—"

"Yes, you and I get to go back, together."

"For Daal Trelkkien?"

"For Daal Trelkkien." She rubbed his hand. "I've always known how to move around my own way. Never knew why 'til…time obeyed me, froze solid around me like a glacier. I was just a few months past fifteen. Happened right after Neight landed on Earth. I figured if anyone knew, I'd end up dead or in some lab. So, I kept my potential from everyone, even your father. I pushed my potential down so deep I thought it vanished. Meanwhile, Patrick kept huntin' for other ways…other ways to stop the countdown." She nudged her chin up at the winding tunnel behind him. "Let's get on. I know you got more'n a few years worth of questions, and my goodness, I got more to spill."

The air around them dried and cooled as they followed the tunnel along an extended curve and into steeper descent. Penny trotted along with his mom on her back, sniffing at the ground, ears flicking at every noise and tail swishing behind her. Dorian took up the rear, on the lookout for approaching agents…or enemy Evolutionaries.

"Your father had some potentials on him, I tell ya," his mom told him. "He just had a passion for using them to save folks." Her eyes glossed over as if in memory. "I guess I never got around to doin' it myself. I was concerned with savin' you first."

Allister pretended they were strolling through one of their old orange groves, picking the ones they'd eat for an afternoon snack.

"We were always in love. The tide came in and left with him as far as I was concerned." She beamed. "Dr. Bourdeaux reached out about software and hardware dev for Cynque, the bioelectric integrations and such… Then word got around about your father's smarts. That's how the Andromeda Project found him."

The light around her dimmed. For a moment, her tone darkened. "The world was comin' to a close too fast…and they tossed the weight of keepin' the doors open right on him." The acknowledgment seemed to slice his mom open, make her vulnerable to the idea that maybe it wasn't his dad's fault. Now tears brimmed her lids with less sorrow and more pride. She sniffled, her mouth creeping into a smile, and she whispered, "Wouldn't you believe he almost figured it out. I bet he always knew about me… He just loved me too much to ask." She paused and pulled Allister toward her. "Here it is."

A circle of permanent darkness waited for them at the end of the tunnel. Darkness so dense and so concrete, it could've taken a star's nuclear reaction to cut through it. Hypnotic, seductive, never-ending—and beyond it, he sensed something legendary. Beyond it, he felt the weight of the world they clung to.

Her white light speared the circle through the center and expanded, gnawing away at the density like a rabid and starving beast, then chasing the darkness to the edges of the tunnel and sealing it into the walls.

Allister sucked in his breath and looked at his mom in a way he'd not often looked at her before—with intrigue and admiration.

Dorian interrupted the moment with a tap on Allister's back. The kid's small frown deepened, his eyes the widest Allister had ever seen them, and without waiting for permission, Dorian stepped ahead, pulling him forward by the arm.

They moved past the threshold and stopped on the other side.

In the center of a multi-tunnel crossroads was a giant drill, its bit wider than a cannon and positioned above a perfectly round hole. The rusted-over, man-made contraption had a broken generator and worn-down gears, exhibiting decades of decomposition.

Allister looked around the open space, spooked by skeletons in C20 gear, some falling apart, some already in scattered pieces.

"Wonder who got all triggered and trashed this spot?" he asked his mom.

She climbed off Penny's back, leaning on Allister's shoulder to support herself as she stood on one leg.

"Might not be a who," replied his mom.

Hopping on her good foot, she took the lead and guided them to the center where the wide hole had been drilled. The hole was fresh, despite the condition of everything else including the drill, and at its edge, he saw lanterns and an illuminated stepladder leading too far down to see. "Down we go," she said.

He swallowed. "Down there?"

The drill groaned as if being laid to eternal rest.

Penny snorted back and, ears perked straight up, looked at Dorian. The kid turned to Allister, silent in his inquisition, demanding in his gaze. Together they knew something was wrong, or at least something wasn't quite right.

Allister's clue was the queasiness he felt. The unsettling shifts in his stomach that signaled more unsettling shifts in time.

Amid stagnant air, translucent ripples formed into the giant spheres he'd seen in De Los Muertos. The spheres did what he'd known them to do—distort the surroundings in a way he couldn't make sense of—the drill and the machinery appearing as if new and in another time as the spheres expanded, congealed, and threatened to burst.

His mom was next to him, her stance resolute, her body unmoving. There was little fear of time or its energy.

He looked then to Dorian and Penny, who, for a split second, were covered by the same temporal distortion. In this other time, they were cleaned up and decorated, Dorian's hair styled in two long braids, the look of royalty in their jewels and garments. What was he seeing? He wondered, disbelief capturing his words. But the spheres passed them over, now pulsing on their way to eruption, and he realized if he didn't save them, they'd end up like the soldiers—dust.

"Dorian! Penny!" Allister yelled, only managing to take a step. The waves of temporal energy blasted forward, slicing their way through him starting at the navel. Allister crumbled to the ground. He whimpered though he wanted to scream, his lips clamped together to hold in the noise.

He watched the landscape shift. The skeletons brittled and, soon after, evaporated. Metal and machinery were oxidized beyond repair. The tunnels around them changed shape as they aged, some shrinking or growing, others becoming jagged and filled with crystals.

It was a miracle that with so much transformed by time, Dorian and Penny still stood there huddled together. Around them, Allister saw the same glowing white aura that surrounded his mom.

Had she protected Dorian and Penny? With her *potentials*?

"We have to hurry," she said, her arm lifted. Curling her fingers, she beckoned back the energy, and the temporal glow separated from Penny's and Dorian's bodies, wafting across the room and disappearing into her hands.

Artist: Lester Niesta/ The CMD Studios

Allister couldn't believe what he was seeing. "How did you... But I thought... Didn't you say...?" He searched himself for an explanation when it was hers to provide.

"Time *obeys* me," she said. "Now, down we go."

His mom pointed at their feet, where the hole waited to be entered. She grabbed the ladder handle, hopped closer, and struggled to lower herself onto it with one leg. She paused after a few rungs and looked up at him expectantly.

"Coming," he said quickly.

Dorian rested his head on Penny's mane, petting her, his eyes asking Allister what to do.

Allister smiled sadly and said, "Hey, Dorian, this is where you two get off. I promise we'll...we'll meet you topside after I get the artifacts. But jet out of... whatever the heck this twisted thing is before time shifts again."

Dorian nodded in recognition and smiled back with his arms positioned for an air hug.

"Thanks for being my...best for what's next," Allister said with a salute. He then hopped onto the ladder.

Allister and his mom traversed the gaping hole in the quiet of a temporal disturbance. They went down a rung at a time, him keeping watch on his mom's descent, her updating him on how close they were to the bottom.

The mouth of the hole opened on jagged ground some distorted amount of time later. Possibly minutes, though it felt like years had passed.

He could make out more of where they were. Inside the Cavenad Daal Trelkkien. Impossibly high walls rose up around them, almost higher than the depth they'd traveled might allow. They were bedazzled with Earth's natural treasures. Some he could name—emeralds and sapphires and rubies—but there were many more he couldn't, in glistening colors of all shapes and sizes. It appeared his mom's immaculate shine was reflecting off of the crystals as they navigated the cave.

"I can see the distortion...," his mom said, referencing the emptiness ahead of them. "That means we're here, at the opening."

Maybe she'd meant the opening to the artifacts chamber or something, because Allister could swear they were already *inside*.

He supported her the whole way, eyes still scanning at his height and above.

All of a sudden, she stopped. "Here *it* is."

Allister looked down to see what "it" was, and gasped.

They were not inside the Cavenad Daal Trelkkien. They'd been underground, sure, inside a cave inside the Earth. But dwarfed by the alien technology towering over them, he knew what he gazed upon was unmistakably...

The Gateway.

Depth was relative. Dimensions were up for interpretation. Both the triangular stone-and-metal threshold and the wall stretched past any measurable ceiling formed by the surface and was wider than the space available for occupation, never seeming to end.

The Gateway was as dark as it was ominous, immovable, and blank from what Allister could tell. He would've expected a tracing of symbols or a giant handle or a split down the center, anything that signaled or offered a way in.

There was nothing of the sort.

A shiver tore through Allister's spine, shifting something inside his uniform. He furrowed his brow and cast his eyes over his shoulder, disturbed enough by the feeling of dread. A quick feel around underneath the back plate, and he came upon his dad's blue notebook. "I knew I picked the right one!" he exclaimed, waving it in the air.

"You *found* the rest of his work?" his mom asked, looking at him strangely.

"At the Andromeda Project, yeah," Allister replied.

She gestured for him to bring it closer. "Are you sure? I could swear it was gone...lost during the Arrival..."

Allister opened the notebook and held it up to their faces, flipping through the pages and looking for the drawings his dad didn't have complete explanations for. The year on that page read 2040.

Recognition crossed her brow. "Oh, that's your father's work all right," she confirmed.

"This is where Pops called it quits," he said.

"Nope...nope...," she corrected, turning a few more pages. She passed the drawing of herself as the Temporal Evolutionary and stopped, smiling. "Ah yes... this is the one. Temporal Rifts Theory."

It was the section Leesa had read to him, that Allister had never read through himself.

"I've never seen this phrase before," his mom said, finger halfway down the page. Under her breath, she mumbled, "Ele Trahluth."

The Gateway creaked and shifted.

Allister looked up first, not sure what had happened. His mom did, too, briefly, then went back to the page. "I see now," she said. "These words have meaning, but they also got potential. This is me…" She pointed at the drawing above the words she'd spoken. "This is you…" She pointed at the other.

Ile Tainvorl, he said in his head, hesitant to say the words out loud. "You think Pops knew all along?" he asked.

"I reckon." She brought her son closer and hugged him around the neck in her hooklike embrace. "Patrick would be so proud of you. Our little EV's gonna save humanity."

"One thousand," Allister said, tears coming to his eyes.

"It's beautiful that we're here together." She took his face in both hands and kissed his forehead. "I hope one day you can forgive me for my secrets."

"You didn't do anything wrong, Mom. Just the best you knew how. And that was perfect."

His mom sighed the sigh for when she knew she had to do something difficult. It was heavy and drawn out, riddled with much-needed patience. They both checked the bomb around her waist. The clock glitched at one minute but didn't tick past. "Guess it's about time I made this right."

"I'm with it," Allister said, shuffling backward.

He held himself and his breath and the blue notebook while she hopped forward and raised her hands to the Gateway.

"Ele Trahluth!" she exclaimed.

Her voice ignited an explosion of temporal force, brightening her aura.

Pulsing white energy flowed from her toward the Gateway's now-shining technology. Allister could see clearly how the chrome molding and machinery was melded with tiny white crystals, and those crystals were protected by large, misshapen stones. But the core natural elements aside, technology was the word he'd still use because this threshold was communicating, calculating, and connecting to his mom.

Like liquid, temporal energy rushed up the edges, a rapid river flowing as it carved symbols and language into an inscription. The shapes and lines and twists and curves were not of Earth, nor of Uragon; they were the language of that other ancient alien species—the Keepers of Time and Space. Allister more than remembered them from his dad's research. He *recognized* them in his own mind.

Suddenly, his mom cried out. The continuous release of temporal energy appeared to be pulling at her, draining her.

"Mom, lay it down!" Allister yelled, reaching forward. "It's hurting you!" Just the effort ignited the temporal energy in him. The pain sliced up his arm, cutting through his heart with the acuteness of a split second. He wrenched his hand backward and clutched his chest, cursing.

Now his mom's hands trembled, the skin on them aging before his eyes.

"We'll cynque up on another way!" he screamed.

Allister groped for his mom as he lowered himself, teeth pressed together. The best he could do to avoid being hurled away.

His mom's eyes were bright, her untamed hair billowing in all directions. She spoke with confidence and joy, kept her eyes on the shining gate, and read the illuminated inscription.

"Heritage sings within these bones; I am a thing of wings from Transonian thrones. Time is wealth and riches beyond; time may be lost but is never found. We waste not ours, for doom awaits, those who squander fortune and fate. A race with privilege these artifacts seek, connection to Trel and Gelen unseen. And that is why, this favored race, is given dominion and blessed with grace. To wield a force of insatiable greed, there is not enough time for you, there is not enough time for me."

She faltered in her steadiness, body frail and shaking without her control. The act required more energy than she'd supplied, maybe more than she had access to or could bear. But she rose her shoulders higher and gave it what she gave everything else—her entirety. "Open Cavenad Daal Trelkkien, reveal the power that none may seek. Show me the gift of temporal transportation to brave a future far...too...bleak."

His mom ran out of breath just as she finished. After which, he saw the light shining through whatever had been taken from her flesh, watched her hair gray from root to strand and fall away, leaving her bald.

There his mom was. The radiant soul she'd always been.

Allister rose against the feeling of being torn to pieces and stumbled to her. He held her hand like he'd done as a boy.

She stretched her other hand toward the Gateway. "Go, Allister, go. I love you."

He turned to it, then back to her, shaking his head the tiniest bit, unwilling to leave. For the chances seemed high that if he left her there, he'd never see her again.

"I can't," he sputtered. "I can't...leave..." He stopped speaking. There was so much that couldn't be said. Besides everything he wanted to apologize for and everything he wanted to *thank her* for, everything he wanted to praise her for. Her sacrifices. Her love. Her potentials. His tears were too much, falling too fast, gushing from the realization that the next words they shared were bound to embody the rawest of truths. It was with that courage he fought through the trenches of his sadness and regret, surfacing long enough to say, "This isn't. This isn't what I wanted."

And it wasn't.

"Don't worry, sweetheart," his mom said. "I am saved by this moment. Saved by your loyalty, by your love."

Though fading into transparency, his mom held the same stern gaze, the same fixed lip, the same earnest tones and unflinching grip as at the dining room table. He imagined her saying, *Come straight home*, and imagined him listening that time. All he needed was the strength to surrender.

"I love you, Mom," he said to her, bringing their foreheads together. "Thank you." He lingered there, taking the nausea in waves, sobbing and sniveling while holding her and that moment hostage.

"Go. Before it reseals."

Allister obeyed her. He sprinted the seemingly short distance to the opening yet rushed past the time they hadn't spent and feelings they'd never shared, whizzed by their often-unspoken love for each other. When he reached the door, he whispered the words, "Ile Tainvorl."

But there was no grand inward motion where the doors opened to lush foliage, no rays of light, and no mythological creatures staged like props on a movie set.

Instead, white temporal energy erupted from his chest, surrounding him in a flourish of pure radiance, every inch of him hugged by the light—then it ripped through him as it always did. He passed through the glowing threshold, screams contained in agony, his body hacked apart by the limbs and tissues, by the cells and molecules, by the atoms.

His mom's likeness flashed in his mind. A vision of four angelic wings springing from her back as she vanished in a burst of light. This memory of her, he molded in his psyche, the manifestation of her *power*.

His mom, Dolores Adams, was the Gateway.

Allister was the Key.

—

CHAPTER 55

ALLISTER ADAMS
Cavenad Daal Trelkkien
Unknown

ALLISTER'S BODY RECONSTRUCTED rapidly, collapsing together as the gravity of his center forced his atoms and molecules to fuse and ignite into life.

He fell forward, singed by the heat that had expanded at his back. The explosive wave could've been fire from the bomb detonating. Or from something more glorious, like temporal energy at its greatest luminescence. The latter of which he birthed from a well-intentioned hope. The hope that maybe she'd survived.

Mom...

He turned back toward the Gateway. There was no triangle shape, no pretty white crystals, no symbols, just a wall in its place. His heart squeezed tight. Mostly because he couldn't see what had become of his mom. Also, because he saw no way out. If his mom had sacrificed her...potential, as he believed, the cavern would soon move without her energy to keep it there. Allister sprang to his feet. He tucked the notebook under his back plate, since his chest plate was destroyed, and surveyed the room straight on.

A bright, flickering light stretched his shadow behind him.

But his shadow was not the only one.

Solidified elements—fire, metals, lightning, wind—arranged in odd shapes floated next to his face, suspended in time, defying gravity. Each of them casting a shadow of their own. Pools of clear liquid swirling up from their valleys disappeared into crevices. Clear liquid swirling down from crevices settled into shallow, empty valleys. Overhead, in place of a stalactite ceiling, galactic matter and stars and nebulae totaling in the trillions drifted, distant spectators of a realm that required imagination to perceive.

The light that splashed over Cavenad Daal Trelkkien had no shape of its own, given context only by the colossal halo surrounding it. Temporal energy spilled through subtle grooves in walls that were painted in gray's many shades, bringing the artifacts' story to life in full color.

Allister followed the light to these vivid depictions. To date, he'd seen his fair share of cave paintings and hieroglyphics, and none had ever reached that level of sophistication and structured detail.

Elaborate artwork illustrated golden-armored creatures with green skin, no hair, and four angelic wings. Next came a shimmering city built of stone and metal rising into space. Then the paintings went dark—literally. A shadowed silhouette of a demon loomed at immeasurable heights, glaring back at Allister with eight red eyes. It wore a fiery crown and appeared to be battling eight...planets...each of which was a different color and, judging by their glow, seemed to represent a different energy. And lastly, there was Earth, many thousands of years ago, young and fresh, brimming with new civilization. The Cavenad Daal Trelkkien was drawn inside the core, and drawn inside the Cavenad was another creature, though slightly less scary looking.

Slightly.

Allister squinted and leaned closer to examine a serpentine creature whose head and body were partially scratched away. He read the passage next to the drawing. *Trelsus...the guardian of Daal Trelkkien, has sworn to transport this sacred realm through time and space to protect existence from the darkness that is Evale. It is their collection that begins the death of all we know—of the galaxies, of the stars, of the eight.*

"Spot on, Pops," he whispered. His dad had been right about the Daal Trelkkien transporting, but Allister couldn't seem to digest any of the other script.

Protect existence? The death of all we know? Were they even talking about humanity? He shook the musings away and swallowed hard at the more immediate revelation: there was...a guardian.

The world glitched like a digital image riding in on a bad signal. At first glance, he caught a shadow rising and falling on the wall. He perked up at the sight of it, swearing he could hear crystals being dragged side to side over rocks. Next came a low hissing, one that permeated the barren space until it reached his ears.

Allister's mouth dried at the sound. The brilliant light was upon him now, blinding as it blasted away his shadow.

From a distance, he heard a deep, rasping voice. "I am Trelsus...last child of Transom, sole guardian of time and salvation."

Allister turned slowly with a hand over his brow and raised his eyes.

The guardian had indeed arrived, a snake of a beast carved of tiny green crystals, speaking a language Allister couldn't believe he understood. A language of symbols and shapes, of poetic harshness, one spoken forward and backward and in circles, and with frequent pauses. He knew it to be the language of the Keepers. The language of Time.

The creature loomed at the edge of his vision. Sharp horns sprouted from both sides of its face and the top of its head. Bony ridges that resembled brows hung over two yellowed, glowing eyes. It came slithering and sidewinding toward him in slow rhythms, maneuvering around airborne objects and between upside-down waterfalls.

Then the scenery glitched. The creature was consumed by white light, and disappeared. It reformed whole and solid and menacing that much closer. *Transportation, that's mega,* Allister thought as nervous sweat gathered at his temples.

"Who could be so audacious as to break the seal of the Cavenad?" The creature—Trelsus—asked, hissing again as it whipped its legless body forward.

Another glitch.

Allister shook his head—thinking it all might disappear. The cavern, the creature, and the moment.

But it was real.

He resisted the urge to step back, and fumbled through an answer that might be expected. "Uhm...I'm...Allister Adams...son of Patrick Adams and Dolores Primrose...and I'm looking for the Daal Trelkkien!"

"Your entry is a violation, a disgrace." The creature's eyes blazed with white energy. "You smell of limitation. Every second that passes, mortal, brings you closer to death."

Allister stood taller and approached the guardian. He embraced the intense fear and discomfort roaming free within him, leaning into the emotions as he leaned into his determination. "CynqueNews alert, I'm an Evolutionary. If I've gotta go through you to save humanity, then...I guess that's what we're doing. I'll ask nice one more time: Where are the artifacts?"

Trelsus flicked its forked tongue through a fanged sneer. It swiveled past Allister and circled back around, cutting him off from the wall with its giant, shimmering body. He turned around himself as the creature vanished in another glittering flash of energy, came back together, and made another loop.

The pointed tail lashed the air behind him. "Such gifts as are given by Daal Trelkkien inspire corruption and manipulation of that which must be kept sacred...," Trelsus hissed. "You seek return to what was...to revisit...rewind... reset. That is not the law of time and motion. That I cannot sanction."

Allister lifted his foot to widen his stance, only to realize that the hardened mass of alien being surrounded him like an impenetrable crystal fortress. Trelsus dwarfed Allister, almost crushed him as it lowered its muscled torso, claws spread wide, and flapped the frills around its neck as if to warn him of attack.

Allister was forced to back up, the air he needed to breathe trapped outside him. Still, he yelled up at the beast, "I only seek to undo what you triggered in the first place!"

"False—" Trelsus replied. A comparable S sound in the alien language seemed to go on for eternity before it added, "I know what it is you seek. I know what it is you crave." It tapped the dirt with a single claw, considering him. "I know the heritage in your veins is insufficient; it is but pieces and parts of a whole."

Allister looked away, his knees shaking a bit, certain the creature could see through to his weakness. *Didn't come this far to only come this far,* he thought. He stroked his afro for a bit of confidence and met the creature's eyes.

Its visage glitched a third time, but instead of transporting again, it stayed in place, this time, duplicating itself by tearing in two different directions, each body blurring as it moved farther away from the other before coming back together and solidifying again as one.

A reunified Trelsus then slithered forward, snarling, its upper body balanced by bulging arms. "Yes. But temporal energy simmers in your blood in infinitesimal bits…this is why I cannot move the realm…this is why the Daal Trelkkien remain within mortal reach." It reared upward and landed hard, shaking the ground.

Allister fell over sideways and tumbled back onto one knee.

"Only your end brings us freedom," it announced.

The creature rattled the cavern with a roar deep from its throat, then lunged forward, fanged mouth leading the way. Allister yelped and slid under its jaws, escaping before they snapped together where he'd stood. Trelsus separated and solidified at every pivot and lunge, transporting faster and faster as it attacked. Without catching his breath, Allister leaped through the slithering, near-entangled body, dodging swipes of crystal claws from every direction. He slipped and flipped his way from inside its coils, then spun around, panting as he held his wrist.

The two experiments fought for escape on his tongue. But he chose the one that had always been the most reliable.

Forearms crossed at his face, he shouted, "Nournt Zeorgen!"

Z-energy blazed across his fist and erupted up his arm, the stinging numb in his tissues, the burning but fire for his execution. Allister leaped and spun sideways over the creature's swinging tail, landed, and charged forward.

Trelsus chugged toward him as well, speeding like an A.E.T. Trac toward its final destination.

They nearly collided—Allister's arm stretched back to slingshot a Z-energy blow, the creature's claws pulled to one side for a devastating slash.

Trelsus swiped at Allister first. His heart fluttered midstride, but he had eyes on the claws, jumping just in time to avoid Trelsus tearing through his insides. In the air, he flipped over himself and opened his hand as he came back down.

The experiment was ready to be conducted.

Time seemed to stand still for Allister as he descended. His breath left his lungs and his eyes narrowed on his target, which was sliding away on its back, body and tail winding frantically.

Allister's impassioned yell was one filled with rage and potential. The energy burst free of his palms, streaming as a single focused beam toward the creature's wide-open chest. But Trelsus transported sideways, and the edge of the attack shot through its side. Crystal fragments scattered into midair suspension.

Allister landed on the lower part of his opponent's wriggling body, steadying himself while skidding backward. With his arm still charged with residual energy, he sprung off of his toes and sprinted up the creature's spine, wild with confidence and pumped full of adrenaline.

Trelsus whipped around to face Allister and dove forward. Allister watched the creature's gnashing fangs and smoldering eyes coming at him, not fully registering the flexed claws raised to attack. He leaned into the heat rushing over his cheeks and increased his speed, his victory visible in the soft, fleshy parts at the base of the mystical being's torso. The ideal place to insert a Z-energy-charged fist and ravage it from the inside.

Allister smiled too soon and too wide, his proximity to the torso nebulous because of the tail's perpetual gliding motion. Even as he fought to keep both feet and his body balanced, his speed unchanging, and the energy flowing, out of the corner of his eye, he saw the gap between himself and a green blur closing at snap-judgment speeds.

Trelsus was slicing at him, again. Allister noticed an instant from being chopped to pieces, skidded to a stop, and jumped, dodging the attack by less than a footstep. He floundered, airborne, just as a second set of gleaming claws flashed across his position in the air.

The blow ripped through his already-shredded armor and scraped the still-scarred flesh underneath. Allister was knocked clear of their battle by sheer velocity and compounded force. The pain was sharp at first impact, his corkscrewing body plowing through floating crystals and elements, skipping atop buoyant pools of liquid, and digging up stone foundation. He slammed into a mountainous structure headfirst.

By then, there was nothing left to feel. Allister lay groaning in a trench of his own making, dizzy from spinning in circles, cradled like a corpse in a coffin. He was numb from his neck down to his toes, but his head pounded at the crown and in his ears.

Trelsus had gotten him down with one good blow. It didn't matter how much Allister could heal, he realized; his foe required force, demanded something more than potential—raw power.

Essentially, Z-energy unleashed.

Get triggered, Allister told himself in his search for motivation.

Tiny particles crumbled from the upright stone slab onto his face.

No...get hype...get cynqued on it, he corrected, hearing Quigles's words. *This is the golden moment.*

He managed to place a weary, scratched-up hand over the edge of the trench, and forced himself to situate his other hand next to it. Grunting, he pulled his torso onto the flat surface and swung his leg around before launching his body the rest of the way. He hit the ground again, too tired to catch himself, and rolled until he stopped against a rock formation rotating on a timed axis. There he caught his breath, listening for the sound of that gigantic crystal body scraping along the ground.

"Evale grows with each star's death, an unquenchable darkness beyond time and beyond existence, the likes of which you could never perceive," came the guardian's booming voice. "You claim yourself a descendant of Andromeda, yet you would use the sanctuary's only protection for self-preservation. Unacceptable."

Artist: Jeffrey Viloria/ The CMD Studios

The rock formation continued rotating, and when its flattest surface came around, a vivid artwork looked down at Allister. He stared up and touched the image in astonishment. It was a depiction of white crystals in the center of a mystical world, which floated next to a shattered creature. A shattered creature he knew to be…

Trelsus, the guardian of Time and Salvation.

He shot up and flattened himself against the rock. His head was spinning, his chest wound was bleeding, and his hands weren't quite ready to make fists again. He spat out the blood that had gathered inside his cheek and peeked around the rock.

Trelsus must've been prowling somewhere inside the realm, waiting for him to emerge.

In the Cavenad Daal Trelkkien's center, however, two white crystals floated inside a perfect ring of rainbow light, both of them radiating pure, temporal energy—the same energy he'd seen come off of his mom like a solar corona. If the image he'd just seen was true, then the elimination of Trelsus made them possible, made them tangible and visible and obtainable. They were tethered to each other, the guardian and the artifacts.

But the slithering, the speaking, the hissing had stopped.

Allister snuck toward the Daal Trelkkien, moving boulder to boulder with caution.

"You are so close to death…," Trelsus taunted, appearing briefly in the distance, then disappearing again. "So close…to death…and a wielder's death ends in separation. To command such power demands the promise of resilience for an eternity." Its hiss came from above Allister now, the sound of the sliding tail from just behind him. Dust and pebbles hit the ground near his feet.

His body tingled with heightened awareness, his intuition a gift along with his speed. He spun around almost fast enough to fall over and doubled back from—

Trelsus smashing through the boulder and scattering the rubble to either side with its thick body. "What will you do when fear seizes you as it has in this moment?" it asked, now towering between him and the artifacts. "When it threatens to take you to your darkest places and offers you failure in exchange for safety. Your weakness would cost us the Sanctuary. Just as your weakness will cost you your world."

Allister felt his heart slow at the futility of their confrontation. Because Trelsus was right. Fear had seized Allister. Convinced him he wasn't enough. That he didn't have enough—heritage or potential. It seemed he must destroy a creature so insurmountable, so incomprehensible, that he must be of cosmic origin to do so by himself.

He took fast breaths in desperation.

How could he hope to do it?

I beg you not to worry how you do what it is you must do. You need only worry that you be who you are to do what you must do.

As Neight's wisdom came to his mind with alien inflection and depth, he realized the fallen king's was the voice of bravery ever-present in his mind. *Foeht Zeorgen. Foeht Zeorgen. Foeht Zeorgen.*

Milliseconds of introspection took him to a place he'd only gone with Florence. His subconscious.

Soon, Trelsus, the artifacts, the Cavenad—they blurred fast and disappeared behind the eternal sky of another realm. His mind and spirit were one, zooming free of his body through the cosmic wilderness, transcendent.

In a flash of higher consciousness, he stood as a seven-year-old in a field of swaying blue grass, and was confronted by a stone fortress towering amid all he'd forgotten of himself. Neight waited for him there, arms open in front of glowing white stairs—a white glow Allister now realized came from his mom's temporal potential. The alien gestured to him, then to the floating fortress that was teeming with Z-energy.

Allister looked up at it.

Twelve years past, and he'd been as scared of his Z-energy potential as the day it had arrived. There it was, part of him, embedded in him, as deep as any root and just as strong. He nodded slowly, smiling, knowing who he needed to be.

Courage. Determination. Power.

Walking forward, he touched the energy with his soul, eyes closed in peace and mouth sealed in reverence. The stone fortress was not a prison for his potentials, but an access point.

I'm letting you flow through me, Allister thought of the Z-energy.

He opened his eyes to Trelsus and took two steps forward. "At my darkest, I can choose to be my greatest self."

"And so it is," Trelsus said. It then roared and moved at Allister with a deadly swiftness, clawed hands pounding the dirt with each winding advance.

"Foeeeeht!" Allister yelled, letting the word pierce the air before yelling louder, "Zeorgen!"

His body surged with the heat of nuclear fusion and primordial rage. The Z-energy that typically consumed only his left arm darted back and forth between both clenched fists, brighter than the temporal light. Concussive blasts of concentrated energy fired from each hand and connected with deafening *booms* and bright bursts, shattering the creature's arms into shards of semiprecious stone. Trelsus howled in anguish, white bursting in its eyes, and vanished in a fit of distortion.

Allister was left in the Cavenad's silence and stillness. He hunched over, hands pulled tight to his body. The Z-energy continued to pulse brighter against his torso, burning with an insatiable need to destroy. It seemed to have nowhere to go, finally surging up the veins in his neck and cheeks, then arriving in his eyes.

His vision was being filtered through a fiery blue film. Sweating and trembling, he glanced at the artifacts again. He saw them with a clarity both astonishing and

Artist: Jeffrey Viloria/ The CMD Studios

empowering. They were spinning around each other as if dancing in their jagged imperfection, flashing bright like pulsars after a full axis rotation. Looking at the deceivingly empty path to the rotating crystals, Allister knew he must go, must run for them, regardless if Trelsus lurked between time or realms or dimensions, waiting to strike.

The Z-energy didn't wane as Allister expected, didn't fade in the ways it had when he was unsure of his intention. He knew it would be with him when he sprinted forward. So he did.

The creature's roar came first, bone rattling in its loudness, bloodcurdling in its ferocity.

He stumbled to stop, consumed by the noise, then the quiet that followed, rotating to see where Trelsus might appear.

Where else but between him and Daal Trelkkien.

Trelsus did just that, reformed as a barrier of crystal fragments and collapsed into itself the way Allister had done on his arrival. The creature's horned head gained definition around glowing eyes and a flicking tongue. Its thick, shining body clinked as the pieces smushed into one another and smoothed.

Shrieking, the now-armless guardian rose up on just about the end of its tail, still large enough to swallow Allister whole. The frills flapped in fury around its neck, a final warning, as Trelsus jumped into the air, plunging fangs-first toward him, no doubt intending to end them both.

Allister was ready to strike. From the skin stretched across his knuckles to the shoulder flexed and pushed skyward, his arm was no longer flesh. The pure manifestation of cosmic Z-energy potential swarmed beyond him in blue waves and twisted around him like a hurricane's catastrophic winds, widening his foot position from the energy's explosive force. Its sweeping blasts of rogue heat incinerated floating structures, tore at chunks of the creature's crystal skin.

The experiment was unbridled, yet his intention was intact.

To end Trelsus with Z…energy.

Allister yelled for release and thrust his blazing fist into the sky. The energy gathered at it like a weapon's barrel, and with a squeeze of his fingers, he unleashed it upward like a cannon. The creature was seconds from devouring him when the blast zoomed through its wide-open mouth and burst clean through it, exiting out its writhing tail.

Artist: Kingsley Calungcapiri/ The CMD Studios

The shock wave penetrated the creature entirely, blowing its body into tiny fragments of green crystal. Just as the painted image had shown, with Trelsus destroyed, the shards floated through the air and joined the crystal artifacts, the Daal Trelkkien. They fused to completion, spraying the light of a supernova to the infinite extent of the realm.

His much-needed victory was within reach.

Allister tripped toward it, dazed, smoke rising from his body. Yet, the immense cold of an infinite vacuum blasted his exposed skin. He choked on the absence of atmosphere, snatched as much by the shock as his body temperature dropping to absolute zero. The Cavenad returned in the chaotic wrath of an untamed storm, his arms flailing inside its gravity. And with his autonomic system active, his lungs expanded with a huge breath.

Glowing white stairs molded for him and rose to the elevation of the Daal Trelkkien. He climbed them one at a time against the reverse force, huffing with an inhuman level of exhaustion.

Reaching the crystals felt impossible, and he realized, looking up, that the magnificent sky had become a vortex. At each fateful step, the contents of the Cavenad began swirling upward, harder, faster. Lingering crystals, rock formations, and ancient artwork were carried away and swallowed by the universe.

The vacuum pressure nearly took him on the topmost stair. He knew he must force another step toward the artifacts, and as he did, he reached out, wincing as the Daal Trelkkien flickered at his touch.

Still, with his arm stretched in blind faith and trust, he grabbed them.

A sense of lightness washed over Allister—some parts the joy of triumph, others the beauty of intention and the reward of realized potential. The crystal artifacts his dad had been looking for, the ones they needed to save humanity, were suddenly aglow in his hands. Their mission was accomplished.

Just when he thought he'd tear them away from their sacred threshold, everything vanished.

The chaos. The artifacts. The future.

He saw Earth split in half and turn the black of a shadow, lost inside a void. He watched time rush to fill it. It was a different kind of end, an acceleration that made buildings brittle and rearranged oceans and tectonic plates, that erupted volcanoes and birthed superstorms. He'd never seen temporal lightning flash or winds of time blow, until they did in his vision, striking at and stripping away the reality he knew and had taken for granted.

His face swelled as he sputtered, floating weightless between the realms, watching infinite ends and limitless beginnings. But he could still feel the heat in his hands, so knew he was still connected to all that existed.

The realm returned in an audible onslaught, delivered to him in the way it had left.

Allister cried out with his intense desire to let go of the artifacts. His palms were raw, the skin on both shredded to almost bone, blistered and scorched by the intensity of the temporal power, whose angelic energy burned hotter than the Z-energy ever had, and possibly ever would.

But he held on for himself, and for his mom and dad, and for the few billion who survived, preparing for more than they'd been promised.

For those with faith in a humanity that could be saved.

The Cavenad thundered as it caved, glitched as there came another resounding *boom*, this time from the black hole of a sky. Rocks dislodged and crashed into rising pools of liquid. The shapes that floated in the air shattered and split against one another, then disappeared overhead in the final scream of a swirling vortex.

Allister inhaled and tightened his hands around the Daal Trelkkien, surrendered to their intention to burn a hole through his palms.

"Ile Tainvorl," he muttered.

At that, white energy coated his skin and blasted from his eyes. The Daal Trelkkien finished clawing their way through him, fracturing his existence and what was left of the realm with cosmic fusion.

—•—

Artist: Lester Nacista/ The CMD Studios

CHAPTER 56

LIEUTENANT LEESA DELEMAR
C20 Base, Man's Lost Lands, Former Middle East
Day 205

LEESA LEANED UP from the wall, thankful XBA was incapacitated, and also hoping Dorian, Penny, and Dolores had made it to Allister in time.

A harrowing battle seemed to be in progress overhead, which she could now hear clearly because the tunnel had been blown into a crater.

Cannons fired above the opening. HellHunters circled in the air, buzzing like vultures. WarTencks rumbled over the sand, hovering, she guessed, as was their retooled nature, though they would be no less bulky or militarily equipped.

Had her father sent the Andromeda Project's remaining cavalry to take down C20? It wasn't a backup measure they'd discussed, but considering they all had one day left until termination, he was well within his fear to do something drastic. Except, of course, strap up and fly out to take their enemy down himself.

She scowled at his lack of judgment. Then decided to confirm or deny her speculation. She reactivated her Cynque, waiting for it to reboot and recalibrate to her genetic signature, and after a subtle jolt from the bioelectric link, she was reconnected.

Leesa stiffened at the notifications bombarding the tiny screen—at least fifty from her father and a few from Florence. She skimmed them, on edge. Her father had demanded updates on the mission's status, and in later messages warned that she'd better have secured her position and their survival by "following through on his orders."

In Florence's message, however, she reminded Leesa of her duty to the greater cause and not just to her father, or even the Andromeda Project. Better than the woman's faith was her loyalty. She had arrived at C20 with Bridget as her support.

Always saw Florence as more of a watch-from-the-sidelines type, Leesa thought.

She checked the collapsed rubble from the tunnel ceiling, where XBA had been buried while shut down. If Leesa had learned anything from their rivalry, she'd learned better than to discount XBA's regenerative cybernetics…and, having been deceived before, her sly psionic advantage.

At first, nothing moved.

Relieved, Leesa pushed her hair up out of her face and levitated off the ground. But as she did, something did shift underneath the wreckage across from her.

She spotted glints from the metal exoskeleton, heard the clinking of machinery moving and the hum of an operating system coming back online. Her brow furrowed with resolution. She knew what she had to do.

"What are you waiting for, XBA?" Leesa asked. "An invitation?"

XBA kicked her way free and pushed herself up backward, still impaled by the poles. "So thoughtful," she said sarcastically. "Here I thought you'd just leave me to die...again."

XBA's gaze narrowed on Leesa as she wrapped her hand around the first metal pole. With a calculated slowness, she slid it from her torso, then did the same with the second one, and the third, not breaking her stare as she did so. When she was done, she held up the last oil-slicked thing, gave a shrug, and tossed it aside as she'd done the others.

She then walked toward Leesa with a mechanical grace, the severed wires within her cybernetic torso wiggling closer to one another and reattaching almost imperceptibly. The broken pieces of metal around the hole liquefied and oozed up her torso, solidifying into hardened protection. "You can try to kill me, Lieutenant. But no matter what, C20 will be the hand that leads. It is time Tas-Salvatur steered this ship from its descent to hell and toward the heavens of Andromeda themselves."

Leesa floated lower, closer. Sand and pebbles swirled around her in slow cycles, uprooted by her residual telekinetic energy field. "As long as I have blood in my veins, C20 won't survive the coming hours."

"Is that a challenge?" XBA asked, her orange eye reigniting with murderous charm. "I mean, I can't imagine what you feel like inside, but I'd love to know."

"Love to know what?"

"What you feel like inside."

Leesa's face twisted with hatred, as far from merciful as it was from patient. Her instincts were spot on. Only one more person would die in this war.

And it would be XBA.

"I haven't shown you my new toys," XBA said, her arms pointed toward the ground. Sharpened metal slid free from a compartment hidden in her surgically attached forearms. The gleaming blade, fashioned into the shape of a sword, extended past her claws until its tip stopped just above the ground. Red psionic energy lit the sharpened tips and blazed up to the center. "*Bellissimo, no?*"

Leesa's nostrils flared with tempered restraint. Another new body part she hadn't accounted for.

"I know." XBA giggled. "I love them, too." She lifted the blade and rubbed it against her jawline, purring as friction ignited sparks. "Shall we?"

They squared off—XBA sidestepping, blades up, and Leesa hovering, fists clenched.

The onset of their battle was missing any formalities and acknowledgments, it just began. The ruthless showdown of two women on opposite sides of salvation.

Metal clashed with microfiber. For every blade's *swoosh*, there was an arm's swing; for every aimed slice, there was a calculated spin. Moans and grunts were passed back and forth with megaton blows. Kicks so fierce that Leesa spun on her toes. Punches so fast that XBA suffered at her chest and metal chin. Elbow to elbow, foot to foot, blade to forearm. They were an even match from beginning to middle. The wrestling, the tossing, the lunging, the tackling—they were dirty by the end and separated, taking deep breaths on opposite ends of the tunnel.

The telekinetic field had not come during battle, at least not in its glorious fuchsia consistency and thickness. But perhaps, since Leesa was still alive, it had danced with her as a less obvious deflection mechanism.

"Your mind is so well maintained," XBA said, drawing her blades again. "I can see clearly the circuits that keep you functioning, the ones that source your potential, the ones that source your rage, the ones that source your *weaknesss*. I wonder, what would happen if I made you overload?"

"I dare you to try," Leesa said.

Though she let the challenge be what it was, a distraction for a more suitable fighting arena, aboveground. Telekinetic energy surged from her body, each purple thread traveling up, then pulling down mounds of sand from overhead and forcing them into a cyclonic spin, eventually reducing visibility to their individual shadows. She raised her arms above her and levitated to the surface.

Midafternoon sunlight beamed over the ruins of C20's compound.

Have we lost another day? she thought.

Beside the caved-in tower, Leesa could see Florence and Bridget fighting against Vonnie, Tranjam, and a cavalry of C20 agents. They were defending themselves back-to-back—Florence a blur of psionic-energy-charged slashes from a...sword? And Bridget, a literal fuse, taking out WarTenck after WarTenck with electromagnetic surges.

Artist: Ezrom Bathan/ The CMD Studios

Lieutenant! A bit of assistance! Florence called out telepathically across the sand, spinning free of plasma fire. Somehow, even after seconds had passed, the woman's distinct accent was still ringing between Leesa's ears, inescapable.

Leesa shook her head at the invasion, ignoring the plea. Part of her wanted to help them. Part of her waited for XBA so they could resume their fight to the death. There would always be more C20 minions, like the ones her colleagues fought, but XBA was more than that. XBA was a catalyst.

C20 wouldn't exist without her. C20 *couldn't* exist without her.

Lieutenant! With urgency! Florence called louder, even more insistent.

Clever. Using Leesa's own language against her. She looked down one more time and, seeing nothing, flew backward, her feet grazing the sand. She slowed when she reached the place the two women were preparing to make their last stand. "Did my father send you?" Leesa asked Florence.

"Send? *Me?* No," Florence said back curtly, sword in front of her. "Where's Allister?"

Bridget eased closer, arms consumed with electricity. "Yeah, mate, did he do it?"

"I lost him shortly after we landed. I can only hope he's alive and with his mother." She then nodded forward. "What do we do about this?"

Tranjam and Vonnie fell in line as they approached, while, behind them, more C20 agents on hovercrafts appeared, joining the already-dense arsenal of WarTencks and HellHunters.

As if on cue, XBA leaped from the hole, blades at full length and glinting cybernetic gray. She landed feetfirst in the sand and smiled to one side. "You see, my dear Lieutenant? There is no world in which you win."

"Kara!" Florence yelled out of nowhere.

"What are—?" Leesa began.

"Kara, *so che mi ascolti*!" Florence interrupted, striding into the chaos. "Kara!"

"Enough!" shouted XBA.

C20 halted—all of them at once.

Leesa and Bridget glanced at each other in shared confusion. For Leesa, it was impossible to believe that Florence was speaking to her arch nemesis *in another language* across the sands of an uninhabitable desert. She thought she knew everything there was to know about XBA, and that wasn't much considering her shadow status on the CGN, and she was pretty sure Florence knew nothing about her at all.

But the tension was serious. No one on either side dared move.

Florence flipped her sword behind her as she stopped just short of XBA. She stood with her hip cocked and her head tilted to the side, studying the claws and the enhancements with a look of judgment.

XBA took a wide stance, rooted in her dominance. The taunting smile. The playful demeanor that bordered on seduction. It was hiding behind an emotion Leesa had never seen on her enemy before: trepidation. XBA held her hands by her waist, claws open, blades pointed to the sand. The orange eye and her human one matched for a moment, focused, softened, wide.

Leesa couldn't tell if they were about to fight, or embrace. There seemed to be an immeasurable thing between them—maybe love, maybe adoration, maybe respect. Either way, Leesa leaned back, accepting the pause in battle, wondering which of the two might reveal their relationship, if there was any, first.

"In the words of Allister Adams, mega…," Bridget whispered. "Always two sides to a coin, I swear it."

Leesa looked back at the two women, now positive she'd missed the bigger reason for the standoff than Florence's not-so-secret authority over the Andromeda Project and XBA's unquestioned authority over C20.

In such close proximity, the almost-identical hair texture became so clear, deep-green versus jet-black curls that didn't carry any weight. Their similar body shapes took precedent over what logos and colors draped them. The matching augmentation with cybernetic technology was less jarring than the identical red crystals infused in them.

"Bloody hell," Bridget began, obviously seeing everything Leesa saw. "Are they…sisters?"

Leesa didn't answer, too terrified to consider that as close to truth.

"Kara…*cos'hai fatto*?" Florence asked.

"Kara's dead, and what's left is an Ex-Belladonna-Ascended," XBA finally said, her fists closing. The orange eye brightened. The human eye narrowed. "Soon you all will join my former self in death…sans any hope of salvation, of course."

Florence straightened and held her sword up, as she retreated in slow steps. "È un peccato. I would have hoped her grave was filled with wisdom and not hatred."

The conversation was over. The war a command away from waging.

Leesa put her hands back up, this time for offense, and flew higher above the sand.

Just as she'd guessed, XBA turned to her Evolutionary companions and human agents. "Hail Tas-Salvatur, our chosen one, because salvation is worth the sum of the remaining, not the difference between them."

They cheered for their maniacal leader.

XBA raised her blade, aimed at Leesa in the sky. "End this, so that we may continue the work of evolution."

"Twisted enough, I agree," Leesa said. She looked to Bridget and Florence and relayed under her breath, "I suggest you sprint for the hole. I can't predict how this experiment will turn out."

"Experiment?" Florence asked. "Are you daft? Who knows what could happen if you unleash the Z-energy."

"*I* know," Leesa said.

C20's battle cries swept the desert. WarTencks raised their dual cannons just as HellHunters aimed their missiles. C20 agents on foot swarmed the dunes like an ant colony, their plasma weapons glowing, while the buzz of one hundred core reactors charging filled the air.

Florence glanced out at them warily. "Leesa, please rethink—"

"Oy!" Bridget exclaimed, steadily tugging Florence away by the arm. "Can it, Dr. B, the bird knows what she's doing. Let's move already!"

And move they did, sprinting toward safety beneath the ground.

Leesa watched them go, satisfied, then zoomed into the air. She breathed a sigh of hard-to-place satisfaction. Looking out over the desert and clocking every opposition, she took in the whole of her existence and the enemy, C20, that had consumed every inch of her being for six years past. She'd tailored herself to their wants and whims, living only in opposition to their vision for an evolved world. Now, she was herself, no longer just a weapon, but an Evolutionary empowered.

C20 ends with Z, she thought.

The Z-energy came alive at her fingertips. It was with that energy, and that intention, she would destroy C20 forever.

"Foeht Zeorgen!" Leesa shouted at last.

The words smashed through a barrier inside of her, something that was meant to be impenetrable, something that kept two things unconnected. Those two things, perhaps two spirits, conjoined at their root and intertwined. Z-energy stitched its way through her soul, mending it until it bloomed into the oneness with her potentials she longed for.

There, inside her mind, she transformed from a soon-to-die child into an Evolutionary powerhouse. Her father withered away from illness and faded from sight. Dr. Giro transformed into a cloud of mist. Most strange of her visions was the purple creature inside a glowing oval vessel, who was freed.

She didn't realize her eyes were closed until they opened to the vortex whip-ping its way around her. She would've been concerned about the Z-energy bubbling atop her skin, if not for the smallest blue light spinning above her fiery palms. A perfect sphere: balanced, steady, calm.

The experiment was ready to be conducted.

She closed her fist around the light and held it to her chest. The artifacts were a thing to be obtained, a tool that could be taken away, but the Z-energy... the Z-energy was *her*.

———

CHAPTER 57

ALLISTER ADAMS
C20 Base, Man's Lost Lands, Former Middle East
Day 205

ALLISTER'S FLESH FRIED on a sand skillet. Above him beamed the relentless sun, an obvious sign that somehow he'd gotten back to the desert's surface. He didn't know how long he'd been there, lucid, no less. He just knew everything had gone dark, and when it brightened, he was outside.

He was *outside*.

From the tower to the tunnels to the underground gorge...to the *Cavenad Daal Trelkkien*, Allister had been to every edge of C20 and beyond even that, to a realm between times and, albeit briefly, to space itself. And now, he was simply outside... simply on his back in a bed of sand, his body baking in triple-digit temperatures.

It was welcome after the near-instant death of absolute zero.

He rolled onto his stomach, his splayed hands partially buried in sand. Daylight inspired his skin's glistening, then it inspired something more luminous, the sparkling green of the—Allister gasped, leaping up—Daal Trelkkien.

They were embedded in the backs of his hands, pure and perfectly cut in geometric shapes. Tiny as they were, he recalled their rather surgical implantation, shuddering as he relived them forcing their way through the bones in his hands. The crystal artifacts he'd held on to shimmered up at him like hard-to-come-by luxuries.

Maybe he'd held on for too long.

"Snap!" he yelled, trying to get away from himself. He was pretty sure the whole returning the artifacts to anyone—the Resilient Nations, the Andromeda Project, or C20—didn't involve them being returned *attached* to him.

Figuring he could dislodge them or rip them out, he shook his wrists vigorously in the air as if they would unhinge and fly off. When that didn't work, he gripped the sharpened corners and tried to wedge his fingers underneath.

Allister paused his struggle, exasperated. "Somebody slipped up and left out the part about these bonding with me," he shouted into the air. Then he resumed tugging at them, grumbling about his dad and Neight, and even Trelsus keeping out that essential detail.

He paused again, remembering something Trelsus had said: *A wielder's death ends in separation.*

Ah that's what it was hissing on about.

How the artifacts would remain in his possession until his death.

Allister gave up, breathed in the sweltering heat, and lifted his hands. So, it wasn't just about finding the artifacts, it was about *wielding* them. That meant the artifacts were his to command, to be responsible for. He was now a proprietor of time and motion.

His reaction was well warranted: the way he stared at the Daal Trelkkien, smiling at his accomplishment, how his chest then swelled with triumph.

They look kinda beat.

An instant later, Allister shook away his ridiculous thought, suddenly deflated by what might've been lost in the process. He relived his mom's "disappearance," imagined Dorian and Penny as temporal dust in the tunnels, and Leesa somewhere contending with all of C20 on her own. He needed to find them, if they were still alive, and started over the dunes toward what he assumed was the ruins of a civilization.

It was mere minutes before he overheard the taunts of a crazed Evolutionary extremist, XBA, and the subsequent shouting of her loyal mob. Someone floated high into the air just ahead, a curvy silhouette with long flowing curls, her skin as smooth as the desert and drenched in the Z-energy's glow.

Leesa…, he thought, then: *Leesa!*

Allister took off running up the dune's steep slope. He was almost to the top when his feet slipped in loose sand, fighting their way until he stumbled down the other side. He fell back before he made it all the way to the bottom and looked up, distracted by—

Leesa, she was more than alive, she was living, blue flames flickering off of her skin, her and all of her essence nestled at the core of what looked like a solar flare. She showed no agony, in fact, she appeared content…and…in control. He imagined she was planning what she ought to be planning. Kept hoping she could continue channeling that potential with such grace and ease.

For an experiment.

Allister scrambled back to his feet, and once up, he ran until he reached the top of the highest dune. C20's military power was spread like a silver-and-white sheet across the sand.

Next, Leesa did something he'd often seen her do: push her arms away from her body in order to activate her potentials.

The Z-energy erupted in a ring around her, expanding first like an explosion, then descending as if a cyclone to the ground. There were waves upon waves of blue energy, each a cluster of thick globules roaring as they hit the sand, yet never stopping there—as they continued traveling the battlefield's length—wiping out WarTencks and HellHunters, blowing through what was left of C20's buildings, blasting the army onto their backs and their weapons to ashen remnants.

The experiment spared no one. Nor would it spare him.

Allister watched the Z-energy rushing at him, a tsunami of sorts, made of blue fire and sand and debris. And for the first time, he stood tall for its arrival. Bravery full in his body. Resilience carved into his stance. He wasn't afraid of his potential, and so then, he wouldn't be afraid of hers, either.

There was something to faith after all.

Because the flames dissipated before they reached him, the debris gave in to gravity, and what was left scattered until it became mere specks of sand blustering over him harmlessly. By the quiet that followed, he assumed C20 defeated.

Victory was sweet on his tongue.

Allister smiled finally, letting the hot wind kiss his cheeks.

Leesa's feet touched the sand, her experiment complete. Florence and Bridget climbed out of some open crater near the battlefield. Dorian and Penny trekked toward him from farther away, likely near the dig site.

Only one person was missing.

His mom.

Allister frowned and looked back in the direction he'd come from, the loss in him a bitter aftertaste. As if a mirage, the vivid white of temporal energy flashed in his eyes, delivering a glimpse of his mom's last appearance. He vigorously shook it away. She'd just disappeared, he told himself again.

Nothing to get triggered about.

After a heavy sigh, he decided it was time to reveal himself, and the true nature of the Daal Trelkkien.

Allister marched his best march toward the extinguished battle. Down the dunes. Across the sand. Through C20's forces. The dangling sections of armor clanked against his beat-up torso, making his approach feel more comical and embarrassing than valiant.

"I have the Daal Trelkkien," he said, striding center for all the recovering to see.

Murmurs rose from C20 agents amid steady winds. Though he didn't see XBA or C20's other Evolutionaries, he knew they couldn't be far.

"That's right!" he continued. With his hands held high and more boast in his voice, he spun in a slow circle. "It's time for everyone to lay it down. The war for salvation is over, and CynqueNews flash, nobody won."

The conversation seemed louder now, traveling through the vast crowd of white-suited people until the lot of them parted.

C20's team of Evolutionaries stepped forward; XBA first, Tranjam and Vonnie close behind.

"Tell Tas-Salvatur it's over," Allister said, eyes trained on them. "As long as I have these, I'm the best way to collective salvation."

Vonnie readied her weapon and took a step. XBA placed a metal hand on the twin's chest. "I got this." As she skulked forward, a set of blades extended, glowing red near the tips. "Over? Because of you? I'll carve the artifacts off your pretty little hands and slice you up like jerky."

"Come with it, then," Allister spat back.

XBA charged toward him, pounding the sand with swift feet. Allister didn't charge back, instead, he waited until she was almost upon him, watched as she leaped into the air, arm raised for a slice at his neck. He remembered the way Trelsus had slid effortlessly out of reach, how it had glitched through time and space as a mechanism for stealth. Allister wasn't quite there in terms of sophistication. He had no idea how to transport or manipulate time. But he knew by the tingling in his body, the power of the artifacts did not always need to be called upon—it simply existed—as such was the definition of power.

So whereas his clumsiness might've had him tripping as he dodged sideways, with confidence, he shifted a few steps, then pivoted to face where XBA would land.

And land she did. Soft as a kitten, vexed at her bloodless weapon. She whipped around, snarling as she doubled back and went after him again, blades swinging.

Just when he prepared himself for her advance, a gleaming object whistled through the air, harpooning XBA through her center and carrying her past him and back to the ground.

XBA tumbled away, her insides gouged, mechanical fluids spilling out of her like blood. Her claws trembled above a serrated sword glowing the red of psionic energy.

Allister recognized the sword from the pink wall in Florence's office.

He raised his eyebrows in surprise, first at the weapon's sharpness, then at its accuracy as he spotted Florence still standing some distance away, far enough to make her targeting more impressive than the blade itself.

Leesa, however, was not standing. She was floating over to XBA, fury molded onto her face, Z-energy whipping around her hands.

"I should've destroyed you in De Los Muertos," Leesa said. "Your manipulation, your carnage, your influence…it ends today. Here. Now."

Before any more could be said, sharpened strings of blue energy shot out, piercing XBA's torso. Leesa was relentless in her precision, weaving her hands as if a conductor, unraveling wires, unscrewing bolts, separating metals from flesh and flesh from metals. XBA held her blades at her face, trembling as they were torn from her arms, crumpled, and flung into the sand. She was nearly dismantled, the sword jutting out from her center, her two halves—human and machine—bound together by but a few parts.

"That's enough, Lieutenant," Florence said, next to them.

Allister saw Leesa's hesitation. Her eyes were focused on the needle-shaped thread of energy hovering just above XBA's heart. One blink and it'd shoot through, tearing the organ free. She had an important choice to make, and he could see the friction was grinding her resolve to dust. Would it be revenge or mercy? He couldn't guess which one of her might show up: the lieutenant who had tried to off Bridget on their first mission, or Leesa who had held his hands and told him the truth about his mom.

Florence stepped in front of Leesa before either surfaced. "Enough," she said with more authority.

Leesa appeared to choose mercy as she retracted her hand, and, without her intention, the energy faded to wisps.

Florence nodded firmly, then turned to XBA, getting a grip on her weapon before yanking it free.

XBA's mouth twisted open in astonishment, and the words she screamed couldn't have been further from what Allister expected. "Florence, you bloody wench!"

Allister's jaw fell.

Florence scoffed down at her. "It's over, Kara," she said. "I know you thought you'd gotten clever, training yourself up enough to hide your psionic signature from my detection. *Sei pazzo.* You know I'm stronger. I always will be."

"Rubbish," XBA spat.

Who was Kara? Allister thought in between their banter.

Florence shrugged away her defiance. "My authorities are on their way to pack up your illegal organization. *Capisci?*"

"I'll never surrender to you, any of you!" XBA screamed, gathering hacked-up wires and loose metal with desperation. The orange light in her eye blinked, faded, then shorted out. "For Tas-Salvatur lives! C20 lives!"

"C20's done for," Allister finally said. "Look around you."

XBA laughed loud and long, even as her circuits sparked against one another. "Tas-Salvatur, it's time we made our departure!" she yelled.

"Tas-Salvatur is...here...?" Allister asked, eyes angled at the artifacts. "Where is he?" he demanded of XBA. "Tell him I'm about ready to lay him down for good."

He looked around for someone tall, cunning, maybe alien, like Neight. Tas-Salvatur had been scheming over his life for however long, it was about time they had a few words. Starting with his mom's disappearance and the orchestrating to get him there and—

"Oh, he's here," XBA said, her human eye on Allister. "He's been here, waiting to meet you."

She looked to the sky. The brightness of day dimmed to dusk. A swirling funnel of darkness howled as it poured down from the sky, pummeling the ground with blackened mist.

Allister stepped back, a hand now over his eyes. He moved closer to Leesa and she to him. Florence followed. Bridget, Dorian, and Penny arrived last, returning out of breath from a possible skirmish.

The dark cloud lightened both in color and density to a gray fog, then to a thick white mist. It simmered as it changed shape, calmed as it quieted, hovering before them as a vague outline of a person, not too tall, not too fit, simple enough looking to be human, and one with a good amount of flaws. Slowly the mist that arrived became flesh, became human, became—

Dr. Rabia Giro.

Allister about toppled over, the wind knocked from his chest. His mouth moved to speak, but no sound came out. And as he wished for anger, begged for the gall to plunge a fist through the man's chest, his hands just loosened and clenched in timed repetition.

He couldn't believe it.

The feeling of stupidity took center stage. He looked to others for their reactions, and their faces were either twisted with rage—Leesa's and Florence's—or loosened in genuine confusion—Dorian's, Bridget's, *and* Penny's. How could none of them have seen it?

"Job well done, Agent Adams," Dr. Giro said, clapping. "Job well done." The clap was unmistakable, rhythmic, triumphant, identical to what Allister had heard in the hangar during the infiltration.

"I had hoped you would see our way," the doctor said. "To spare you more pain...more loss. But I see on your face you would defy me, the savior, Tas-Salvatur. Because you believe you know better for a species you have scarcely experienced."

Allister sucked in another breath, fists clenching for what seemed like the hundredth time.

From what he knew, Dr. Rabia Giro had lurked about the halls of the Andromeda Project, had shied away from the few briefings he was part of, and operated an appointment-only laboratory in a high-security wing of the facility. Though their interactions had been short, tense, and sometimes unusual, they were never hostile. He couldn't fathom why this would be the world's calculated and ever-present enemy.

What on Earth could he be after?

Then, as if to answer him, the crystals on the back of his hands glimmered faintly.

Of course.

Dr. Giro was after the same thing as everyone else: time and salvation.

The doctor paced before them, sturdy, upright, confident, the corners of his mouth turned down as he nodded. "I see you have bonded with the artifacts, Allister. I suspected as much. I suppose you fancy yourself a moral compass to guide the responsible use of such cosmic...dare I say...power." He glanced at the Daal Trelkkien. "Allow me to dispel that theory, here and now, before it grows your ego beyond restriction. You will be no such thing, and all of you, each and every one of you, will watch as C20 takes the fragile civilization that has been saved this day and forces its evolution."

Leesa rose into the air, spouting words of vengeance, fist consumed with Z-energy. Bridget vowed his end if he laid a hand on Russell, electricity crackling from feet to fingertips. Penny growled and barked next to Dorian, who clapped his hands, producing a cluster of sonic spheres. Florence eyed Dr. Giro as if her suspicions had been confirmed, sword and leg pulsing psionic red.

Now, the fury in Allister was consistent, as was the belief that no matter how C20 tried to manipulate human salvation, he and his friends, the good Evolutionaries, would overcome it.

Together.

Allister stepped forward, channeling his conviction into a declaration of his own. "You lost Dr. Giro or Tas-Salvatur or whoever you are. The Daal Trelkkien are under my protection and so is humanity. I swear, if C20 tries anything else twisted against us or this world, I'm coming straight for *you*."

"I will be waiting for that day," Dr. Giro said, blackness billowing around only himself, Tranjam, and Vonnie. XBA lay at his feet, a mess of parts and barely moving. He ignored her as he continued, "My condolences for your loss, Allister. You have become a means to my end—an end I have yet to reach."

"I?" XBA said, her eyes closing.

"Yes. I. You are unfit. You have fallen apart. How many times must I fix you, Kara? If you cannot keep yourself together, how do you hope to be the stitching for a new world. Today our partnership ends"—Dr. Giro bowed to her—"and as you know, I do not believe in termination. They, however, do."

Dr. Giro made his retreat with a small wave, Vonnie did so with a kiss, and Tranjam with a scowl. The darkness left with them, and the sun's immense heat returned with a glaring brightness.

There was no trace of the mist in any form.

Allister squinted at the spot where the doctor had stood, looking absently for a clue he'd missed, a string of words Dr. Giro had said, an overlooked action. Maybe a subtle slight or display of potential.

His eyes widened. Dr. Giro's potential—the mist.

Twice, Allister had seen it. Once in the main hangar when it swallowed up Brandt and his mom. Once when he'd run into Dr. Giro at the Z-Energy Containment Center. He remembered distinctly now how the light had caught the particles, how the mist had drifted around the doctor's figure like a sinister halo. With more contempt, Allister remembered its thickness inside the hangar, almost liquid as it consumed whatever it touched.

It had shown up in varying densities, but it was the same experiment. A sort of molecular-level transportation. His random appearances now seemed so much less random, as did something he'd said to Allister: *I suspect your potential will become power soon, too.*

Allister's connection to the Z-energy, his attachment to the artifacts—he wielded pure alien power, which, nine days past, he hadn't known was possible.

"The mist," he finally said aloud.

"The mist," Florence repeated, letting her blade fall to the sand. "This has all gotten immensely complicated."

"Complicated?" Leesa said. "Try dangerous. My father goes to Rabio's lab at least once a day. What if he goes back and pretends nothing happened? I have to warn him."

Allister looked over at them. "Maybe General Delemar knew."

"You think my father…would keep something like that from me?" Leesa asked, her voice catching in disbelief midsentence.

"I feel like your father has a ton of secrets."

Leesa crossed her arms, but her face softened with acceptance. "Maybe."

"I just…" Florence cupped her forehead in frustration. "I just can't believe Dr. Giro operated on me…and that I didn't connect the mist I saw in the Z-Lab with the mist I sensed *inside* the District terrorist's mind and the mist pumping through Club HellForest the night of the infiltration."

Allister realized that none of them had seen it because they weren't paying attention—too focused on themselves or the artifacts or each other. "Sometimes the enemy is right in front of us," he said.

"Beware the mist," Bridget said cryptically.

Leesa didn't respond, just faced Florence straight-on, her arms still crossed, though now, he believed, with suspicion. "Who's Kara?"

Florence glanced at the immobile body in the sand. "She's my sister," she said, sheathing her sword. After going the short distance to XBA's side, she straightened her hips, and locked her legs in a wide stance. Her hold on the sword's dragon handle tightened as though she might draw it again. Allister had never seen that look of despair on Florence's face or that language of hostility in her body.

"I recognized her telepathic signature on the way in," Florence continued, speaking more to the body than any of them. "It's distorted because of the cybernetic rubbish, but, I know my family. We are a long, strong line."

"You didn't know?" asked Allister.

Leesa tilted her head, cosigning his question.

"Of course I didn't know," Florence answered between her teeth. "There's scraps of information about any Evolutionary terrorists on the CGN, to keep them from finding each other. Her file didn't even have a date of birth. I suppose until I had this leg installed, my potential wasn't powerful enough to see through her more well-constructed illusions. But now I see everywhere she's been. Across from me on the A.E.T. trac. Streets away in Oil Alley."

There was no more from her after that.

Allister heard playful barking coming from behind him and turned to see what Penny could be so excited about. In contrast to their collective brooding, she was bounding around happily in the sand, switching between biting at it and jumping up at Dorian, who was flinging debris in a twisted game of catch. Penny ran wide and fast, following the shining metal object that flew through the air, then caught it in her jaws. Upon landing, Penny stopped and looked back at Allister, as if inviting him to play, too.

Much of Allister didn't know what being playful felt like anymore. Still, he looked on with admiration.

Penny trotted toward him at first, then broke into a run. Dorian followed her gaze, threw both arms up in the air, and began running back too. Allister thought something was wrong, but as Dorian got closer, he just looked...

Joyful.

The metal mask on Dorian's face was gone. In its place were thin cheeks stretched wide in excitement and teeth on full display.

Allister found himself smiling at the vision of his friend sprinting toward him, arms outstretched. Before he knew it, Dorian was giving him a heartfelt embrace. Allister couldn't remember the last time he'd been held so tenderly. Except, maybe by Quigles. Similarly, there was trust in Dorian's touch, admiration in his squeeze. Allister felt the connection so deeply, he wrapped his arms around Dorian and hugged back, blushing.

Letting himself relax all the way, he breathed out, the weight of reality lifting off of his shoulders. "My best for what's next," he said.

Penny was behind them, jumping, yapping, and trying to join in.

Dorian kissed Allister on the cheek before he let go. He then moved Allister to arm's length, studying his face with a look of longing, and he turned to Leesa and nodded at her. With a soft pat on Allister's shoulder, he took a still-eager Penny and led her away.

"Not bad, rookie," Bridget offered, punching Allister in the shoulder.

"Thanks, Sparks, you did alright, too."

"Alright!" she exclaimed, then added, deadpan, "Mate, I was bloody wicked." She went to nag at Florence after that.

Leesa floated over to Allister, a pained expression on her face. He felt discomfort in her look of sympathy and, as the object of it, was reminded of what he was supposed to be feeling. His body tensed, he presumed, in defense of a meltdown. He could feel her asking questions with her eyes that he wasn't ready to answer.

"Where's Captain Brandt?" Leesa asked first.

His jaw tensed at the thought of their battle. "I already took care of him." She winced.

"Not like that," he added with less edge. "I left him down in the tunnels with a plasma rod in his side." He gave Leesa the side-eye. "He'll be fine. It's just scratch." But Allister really hoped he wouldn't be fine.

She managed a hint of a smile. "And"—she hesitated, that much closer to him—"and your mother…did you two find each other?" she asked. "There was a bomb, and I…I couldn't be sure."

Allister lowered his eyes, unsure how to respond. "She…uhm…she disappeared," he forced out, his voice shaking.

"But…the timer, it was set for—"

"Never hit," he said, cutting her off. "Bomb never triggered."

It was a lie. He knew it. She knew it. And Tas-Salvatur had alluded to as much, touting Allister's loss as part of the grand vision.

If he'd focused more on the steadiness of his words, on the pretending not to know and less on the truth of what had happened, the sadness wouldn't have flooded out of him.

He burst into tears.

The words of his mom's final moments slipped out between sniffles and occasional sobs. "She…she…sacrificed herself to…open the Cavenad…so I could… get the artifacts."

Leesa stayed there while Allister cried, a hand on his shoulder, another on his face. He could hear her sniffling and swallowing hard, having her own battle with a complex mix of emotions.

"I'm sorry," she finally said, her thumb catching the tears on one cheek.

Allister didn't look up. "Don't be. You kept your promise. We did save her." His chest heaved at that, the beauty of her last seconds light enough to lift him. He'd seen his mom in her truest form, a magnificent being of pure temporal energy potential. He forced a smile. "My mom was the actual Gateway. She opened the cosmic doors for me."

Leesa hugged him around the neck.

"I'll be golden. I just need time," he said.

She leaned back and held up his hands for him, putting the artifacts between them. "You have it."

The Daal Trelkkien flashed.

He pulled away and fiddled with his afro. "Yeah…about that," Allister said to her. "They don't come off. Like, at all."

She didn't answer because Florence had returned, interrupting them. "While I appreciate the reconciliation of your differences, I might remind you both that you're still under contract at the Andromeda Project until otherwise stated."

Leesa put her hands on her hips. "Dr. Be—"

"And as a commanding officer of the organization, you are to maintain hierarchy and protocol until after our debriefing, which means no fraternizing with subordinate agents." She turned to Allister ahead of Leesa's mounting protest. "Let me see them," she demanded.

Extending both his hands, he showed her the artifacts. She traced the edges where they touched his skin, then the hexagon-shaped center. She polished them with her thumb and leaned down to look closer.

"They're deep in there." Florence straightened. "Better you than anyone else, I suppose. I trust you know how they work?"

"I mean…yeah…I'm with it, kinda."

"I need you totally 'with it,'" Florence said. "We're going before the Resilient Nations tomorrow." She lifted her wrist right after, and spoke into the golden Cynque. "I have them. Stop the countdown."

At this, his Cynque sprung to life. "Phrase activated offline message from Patrick James Adams," it announced.

A black box in the shape of a screen ballooned up from his device surrounded by a glowing border. There was no immediate visual, and behind the blacked-out screen, he heard his dad fumbling with Cynque's recording settings. He referenced Allister to a deep-voiced companion, a colleague maybe, and explained that his son wasn't at home because Dolores had to go to the diner. He was in the car at the hilltop, playing and hopefully staying put. The screen shook, still sporting the solid black color, and it seemed his dad had given up fiddling with it.

He questioned the audio's clarity, since that was all he could get to work, and before starting, expressed his hope for a successful transmission.

"I'll be there in a second, Neight!" his dad shouted, and then said, lower, "Just gotta send this to the future."

Allister smiled at his dad's intention. He wasn't just making those transmissions because he hoped Allister would get them, he was making them because he *knew*.

"Okay!" his dad began. "Hey, my little EV. This is my last vid for some time. The Arrival is today, and we're expectin' things will be shaken up around here for a good bit. There's some alien energy on its way and it's off schedule. Ever seen an alien with anxiety? Me neither, before this afternoon." He laughed to himself.

Allister laughed along with him.

"Neight keeps telling us you're gonna find the crystal artifacts, so we shouldn't worry," his dad continued. "Your mother don't want to hear it—no way, not her baby. She's a beautiful piece of work, I tell ya."

One thousand..., Allister thought, nodding in agreement.

His dad's foot tapping joined the composition of background sounds. "You know your mother wanted us to spend our time as a happy family, instead of her dreading the day I don't come home. Didn't know I was lying when I told her I'll always come home. I promised, on my life, I said, Sweet Dee, you don't got a thing to worry about. I'll always come home to you. Same went for you, Allister." He sighed and Allister heard him wringing his hands with regret. "And...that's a promise I'm not gonna be able to keep. But I swear to this if I can't swear to nothing else, I love you for everything you are, and everything you're gonna become."

Allister brought Cynque to his chest and gripped the device like a hug sent back in time. He smiled, knowing the next words before they arrived.

"Be brave," he said in unison with his dad. "But don't be foolish."

———

Artist: Lester Niesta/ The CMD Studios

LOST CHILDREN
OF ANDROMEDA

"AT MY DARKEST,
I CAN CHOOSE TO BE
MY GREATEST SELF."

– ALLISTER ADAMS

YOUR NARRATIVE DEFINES
YOUR PATH. WHAT TYPE
OF HERO HAVE YOU
CHOSEN TO BE?

———◆———

EPILOGUE

Artist: The CMD Studios

DR. RABIA GIRO

Director's Correspondence Auditorium (DCA), Andromeda Project Headquarters
Day 205

THE DIRECTOR'S CORRESPONDENCE Auditorium entrance opened to Rabia's unique Cynque signature.

"Dr. Rabia Giro, recognized," the surround-sound Cynque system announced.

Rabia raised his eyebrows at the thin corridor behind General Delemar's desk. Perhaps the blending of the metals made it somewhat hidden, but it hardly appeared to be a secret entrance.

General Delemar must've been a fool to squeeze through that space every day. For what? To be pumped full of ridicule? Then, wouldn't he be even more foolish, Rabia supposed, to have been crawling back through, only to sit in that ridiculously large chair and do *nothing*. He chuckled softly.

No wonder it'd taken them twenty years to achieve progress.

The doctor shuffled through the space with shrunken shoulders and a curved spine, dodging cobwebs and internal piping as he went. Using his hand, he pushed away a detached piece of metal jutting toward his face, ducked lower, and swiped a spiderweb blocking the entrance. "Could use tidying," he muttered.

The auditorium dome swallowed him in shadows as he emerged.

He smiled at the darkness and hobbled to the monolith that was situated at the room's center-most point. Five of the seven directors waited inside their digital prisons. Bright, distorted screens glitched and fizzled with every shift in movement or faux cough.

With his hands clasped behind his back, Rabia gave small bows to the five silhouettes before him. They were the five he'd invited, as they believed in the same vision as him. That salvation was worth the sum of the remaining.

"I hope you have not been waiting long. I was tending to our...debacle," he explained.

"What is happening?" one of the directors asked.

"You promised us this transition would be smooth," accused another.

"You promised us Agent Adams would cooperate."

Rabia found their expectations a nuisance, yet their behavior was unsurprising. He knew they were used to being fed the general's insecurity for consumption, but that day, Day 205, he decided they would go hungry.

"I promised you success," Rabia bellowed. "It is your squabbling and indecision that builds friction."

"We have stopped the clock. We were told by a reliable source that Allister Adams succeeded," the Rossiyan director said, frustrated.

"Agent Adams did indeed," Rabia said. "However, the temporal rifts Professor Ashur discovered remain. It is time we move onto the next phase: Exodus. Or would you rather leave the fate of humankind in the hands of an entitled teenager?"

The five directors whispered among themselves, murmurs and conflicting fears flying back and forth.

Already, Rabia felt the dynamics shifting. Their true desires surfacing, allowing his influence to take hold. Displeased with their chatter, he said over them, "I propose reopening the ZEE-Protocols. What we have here is an opportunity... what we have is a responsibility...to human existence."

They quieted quickly.

He paused then and watched the blank screens, amused. He couldn't see them. They could see him, though. That made it all the more riveting when, in the silence of the auditorium, he could hear that they were the ones uncomfortable—moving around in their seats, sighing heavily, adjusting their communication devices.

"Go on," the Rossiyan director said.

Rabia supposed alien life was a difficult topic to discuss, especially when it was so intertwined with the idea of self-preservation. "I have reset the ZEContainment Center. In a matter of minutes, Z-energy power will be released and return to the Uragonian specimen that graced us on the date of the Arrival: Zosma."

Rabia lifted his wrist and projected a chart of animated graphs. The math was simple to him, simple enough to explain to those with simpler minds than his.

"As you can see, Leesa Delemar's Z-energy power levels fluctuate dangerously without the cape. One minute, she is fine, another minute, a radius the size of ChiTown Sanctity could face a catastrophe likened to Cumberland Falls and... the Arrival aforementioned." He folded his hands behind him to drive home his point. "The awakening comes on speeding heels. It is not a question of if; it is a question of when. To capture and contain this energy source will not only protect who's left of this world, it will also give us the infinite power we need to rebuild after we transition off of the planet."

He found that their temporary silence echoed his permanent victory.

"Don't make us regret this," the UK director said.

"I would not dream of such things," Rabia replied, bowing deeply. "Comrades, we will resume our operations elsewhere. The base you have so generously funded is ready for occupation. Now"—he clapped his hands—"I would invite you to join, but I know you will not leave your 'thrones.'"

"What do we do in the meantime?" the Rossiyan director asked.

Rabia rocked up on his toes. "Why...you wait," he said, matter-of-fact. "You simply wait. For all that I do prepares us for our return to Andromeda's Sanctuary." Like a vintage television, the rectangular screens then sucked the directors' blurred figures into a single white point. "I bid you goodbye here and shall see you in the...how they say? Deep South."

He chuckled, though his joke fell on lifeless, blank slabs: the gateways to the world's intangibles—war, finance, technology, commerce, energy—and those who governed them.

How many years had he waited, patiently, for that moment of triumph?

At last, phase one was finally complete. The first of eight.

While it wasn't ideal that Allister Adams had the Daal Trelkkien artifacts, they'd been *found*.

Onward.

Rabia took a long, deep breath, and drew his hands toward his face as if about to conduct a symphony. The mist rose with his movement, guided by his swaying arms like an instrument, puffing around him in blacks, grays, and whites. He spun in circles with a calculated grace, his power extending beyond him, then upward in a torrential twisting motion. But the noise he heard was but a soft hum, calm, centering. He felt his human body lighten and shrink and separate, on its way to melting into the intangible.

Once he was broken down to sentient particles, and ripe for transportation, the mist rocketed free of the Andromeda Project, tearing through dimensions and time streams and dark spaces, carrying him an impossible distance for any creature save for one such as himself.

—•—

AUTHOR'S NOTE

Firstly, Thank you for being here. Your readership means the world to this storyteller who grew up thinking this very day would never come—the day that you, sci-fi/fantasy lover, finished my novel. But here it is. And here we are. At completion.

So this is where we will begin again.

If you've read my first title, *ZOSMA*, I bid you a warm welcome back to the world of the Lost Children of Andromeda. As you can see, we've gone deeper into the lore, given some backstory, and added some immersive elements that I think makes the series all the richer in spirit and style. Therefore, I'm going to have to ask you to do something very unusual. *Pretend that ZOSMA doesn't exist.* No, it isn't gone, let's just put it in a parallel universe and start with this one, *205Z*, where the truth of 2052 unfolds. Because you've made it this far, I can only hope you enjoyed this novel, possibly even more than the sequel (yes, *this* is a prequel). And as a reward for your faith and loyalty, I will reveal to you that the copy of *ZOSMA* you have is now a limited edition. It will never be reprinted, and there are only fifteen hundred copies in the world.

If you have not read *ZOSMA* and you'd like to continue the journey these characters have gone on, feel free to read it. In fact, I invite you to experience my writing from four years past, when I had lost touch with myself and wasn't sure how to bring my narrative voice to life. The story still has all of the essential elements, and it really is quite an exciting adventure. Plus, as I mentioned, it is limited edition. (Insert laughing emoji.) Just know that revisions will be made, lore will be updated, and the way the story unfolds will change considerably. I know you'll love it all the same. Because you are not just a lover of art but a lover of process and the spirits that labor through them.

Follow + Support Lost Children of Andromeda

———

@LostChildrenofAndromeda | Instagram | Facebook | Pinterest | Patreon |
YouTube | Spotify | Apple Music

Subscribe
www.2052EndsWithZ.com

Leave a Review
Amazon | Goodreads

ACKNOWLEDGMENTS

You're not lost if you're here.

Some fateful choice, some divine guidance, or some happy accident has led you here, to this—

Experience.

205Z: Time and Salvation.

You're probably an Evolutionary, like myself. You have some extraordinary potential, a gift you can conjure that you have either leaned into, forgotten about, or neglected, or perhaps you're somewhere in between. Passing your potentials and gifts off as something not meant for you, when they are absolutely yours to own.

Oh, you say you want to hear about my potentials?

Mine first showed up when I was five, as an insatiable appetite for complex stories. Fantasia, for instance. A blend of evolution and fantasy and mythology and magic and religion. Legendary scores I couldn't possibly understand would hold me captive for hours and hours on end, not to mention the vivid animation and exaggerated expressions of mythical creatures, dinosaurs, and living, dancing foliage.

It was my first imprint. It was the first manifestation.

Then came the birth of potential number two, weaving my own tales. My first story, coincidentally *this* story, was originally crafted in my second-grade class under the title *Dragon Wars*. The story came to life between coil-bound laminate covers, the whole arc no more than twenty pages drawn and typewritten, colored by crayons. I remember the first time I used Cerulean and Burnt Sienna and became obsessed—I would only accept the thirty-six-pack of Crayola crayons from then on. (Run Gen Z, I'm old and rocking in a chair on my porch yelling kids like you off my lawn.)

Soon *Dragon Wars* became two books, then three, then six, then eight. I had finished the series by age twenty-two. Then I threw the manuscripts away. College discouraged me. I thought writing wasn't meant for me because, if it was, wouldn't I be better at it?

It took me another decade to realize maybe I just needed to use my potential with more intention.

Twenty-six years later, the story has transformed into an immersive tale about lost children, the generation of Evolutionaries disconnected from their heritage, some hiding from or suppressing their potentials, others using them—but wrestling with their capacity to control them. Originally, I dreamed up this series so that I—a little black gay boy from the suburbs of Virginia—could see myself as a superhero. Somewhere along the journey, it's changed so that *we* can see *ourselves* as superheroes.

The silenced. The marginalized. The repressed.

The lost.

For when we stop believing we can be heroes, that's about where we start to lose our power, and I'm a firm believer that our power, of all things, is not meant to be *lost*.

That's why you're here.

It's time we're heard. It's time our stories are told.

That realization is how *205Z* came to life.

I suspect there are millions, possibly billions, of so-called lost children. Perhaps we've been drawn to each other, growing, evolving, our minds changing as we dig deeper into ourselves and those around us. We are determined to make change on a massive scale because we don't want to be humanity's last generation.

Know that your own power and potentials don't need to be grandiose, extraordinary, *or even creative for that matter.* It can be kindness and love. It can be organization or healing. It can be using your words to fight for rights and using your hands to build. It can be the incredible strength to uplift, to change and challenge, and the wisdom to educate.

But the bottom line is—you have power. I have power. We. Have. Power. The question is how we choose to use it. Pay attention when it shows up. Don't try to wish it away. Don't smother it when it stings and burns. When it crackles and blasts you and those near you with the light of what's possible.

Let your power show.

Because no matter what we choose to do with it or how we may ignore it, at our core, that power still runs through us, never dissipating, built by heritage and history, gently guiding our curiosity toward it and, in turn, ourselves.

This novel explores that power. That nagging sense that we can be what we're meant to be. Ultimately, it is a look inward, at ourselves and our contributions in a world caught between what was and what could be.

So I say this: I promise that if this story has found you or you have found this story, you are not lost. You are right where you should be. Where generations have made it possible for you to be.

You are here.

Onward.

There are few words to express the inner turmoil I experienced during the crafting of this manuscript, but there are even fewer words to express the extreme joy and wonder and love I experienced in tandem. I can only be grateful for that time and those challenges, for they freed more than myself, they freed the world-building and the story arc and the characters' depth in ways I'd never imagined possible. But I was not only uncaged by personal life experiences, there were many humans (really more like Evolutionaries) that were pivotal in bringing this manuscript to life.

Thank you to Jeff Seymour for taking the *205Z* manuscript and pulling out all of the moving pieces that could work together. Thank you for challenging me to explore the inner workings of the power structures, the abilities, the world-building, and the apocalypse. Thank you to Melissa Frain, who showed me the world of superheroes in literature, and showed me how mine could be different, again challenging me to look deeper into character motivation. Thank you to Emily Yau for so thoughtfully reviewing my manuscript line by line and telling me all the ways I could make the characters shine off the page. Thank you to Jim Spivey for the careful way you combed the manuscript for errors, inconsistencies, and excessive word count. And lastly, thank you to Michelle Hope, who I knew instinctively had the last pair of eyes I needed to experience this story before I shared it with the world.

Thank you to Stephen Manalastas and his firm, the CMD studios, for their hard work, talent, and patience. You were the first to re-imagine the visual aesthetic for the Lost Children. Now, your team's artwork breathes new life into these characters and the events that they go through. It is alongside your diligence and dedication that I have channeled such a powerful and immersive universe. Thank you for seeing my vision through in visual form. Jeff Viloria and Juwen Quilaneta, your daily communication always made me smile, because you were as excited about the artwork we produced as I was.

Thank you to Kieron Anthony. Number one because you have a cool alien-sounding name that I will be using, and number two, because your visual art direction and design is supreme. You took already-incredible character artwork and transformed it into covetable art disguised as merchandise. I can't wait for our creations to take off.

Thank you to Tobi Weiss, the composer for Lost Children of Andromeda, for the incredible energy you put into your scores. The music you've created for this world is beyond. The songs are every bit cosmic and layered and formidable. I listened to them as I unlocked parts of my creative writing style, ones essential for the completion of this narrative. Your range and skill are of epic proportions.

Thank you to Chris Barrett and Don Fisher, who signed onto the project to bring some sauce and nostalgia to the soundscape. To those reading, I literally grew up with these two gentlemen. Chris and I played on the playgrounds of Kindercare on Fordson Road from as early as Kindergarten. I remember us going from fighting in the sandbox over Tonka Trucks, to going on adventures through mulch, swings, and slides. You've remained just as reliable, creative, and fun as you were in those early days. You exemplify the consistency of *being*. Don and I met in Middle school. There we shared a number of classes, namely science with Mrs. Boyd, where I actually penned the first full novel version of Dragon Wars inside of a three ring notebook disguised as a notebook for school. Don, you always owned your full nerd self, and thereby allowed me to own mine, so instead of discussing homework or lessons, we spoke at length about our epic stories. Some would say we were wasting time. Evidently not. Can we just pause here to reflect on how the universe works in the most enlightening and beautiful ways? Little did I know these two souls would come back charged up on their potentials and help to fully realize (alongside Tobi) the sound candy you've likely experienced by now.

Thank you to Damonza for the incredible book cover design that puts representation front and center for all to witness. It is also a reflection of my ability to show up—on a cover, no less, as I think Allister has become symbolic of my journey as an author and has had the opportunity to shine bright like Z-energy in this manuscript.

To my Inaugural Beta Reader Book Club members, Jason E. C. Wright, the King of Wisdom; Kat Yalung, the Magical Spirit; Alexis Skinner, the Fountain of Youth; Otis Rease, the Artist Known As; Edward Liston Spence IV, the Hero; Cindy Garay, the North Star; Ben Anderson, the Leader; Bahram Khosraviani, the Virtuous; Antonia Gray, the Powerhouse; and Patrick Dewyngart, the Soul. Thank you for your twelve dedicated weeks during quarantine where we explored the depths of this story, these characters, and ourselves, creating an experience I'll cherish for eternity. It is your being that found its way into these pages, a testament to my vision of a world of superpowered entities living courageously.

Which brings me to Beta Reader group number two: John Engel, the Truth Seeker; Lena McElroy, the Courageous; Hannah Tall, the Gracious; and Edna Primrose, the Immortal student. Thank you for your eleven dedicated weeks of self-reflection, celebration, and sharing. We got to see ourselves and each other in so many new ways while having reality-altering conversations. You, too, are a reflection of my vision for this world.

Special thanks to Jason E. C. Wright, the brainchild behind the book club, for being *almost* as obsessed with my world as I am. It is your enthusiasm that pushed me through my darkest days.

Thank you to the ATX1 family for my being inside of this experience, and for showing me that I can be at choice, at all times, in all things. To Cindy Garay, my angel, and Tyla Fowler, my life coach, thank you for holding a mirror up to me and saying, "Look at who you are."

Thank you to David DeVries, and the DeVries family (Jan, Maria Grazie, Roxy), my forever champions. Your grace and generosity know no ends.

To my brother Andre, thank you for our late-night talks exploring aliens, conspiracies, new industry, and our reflections. I called upon your curiosity. To my brother Stephen, thank you for sharing with the world so fiercely, it is a joy for us all to see and witness your healing journey. I called upon your passion for enlightenment. Thank you to my brother Gerald, for showing us all what resilience really looks like. I called upon your regeneration. Alexis, my dear sister, and twin spirit, thank you for your innocence and your raw talent. I called upon your potential, a testament to the potential inside all of us.

To Nana, thank you for your bravery and your love...your pure, unfiltered love. You saw me before I saw myself. You knew me before I knew myself. Thank you for telling me I could always be me no matter what. Though I didn't believe you for many years, I promise, I believe you now.

To my pops, your words of wisdom always stayed with me, even when we felt timelines apart. The impact of your guidance is on every page. I promise. Thank you for your prayers. I know they've protected me as I made it here and will protect me where I'm going.

To my mom, this is your story, too. Thank you for everything, and I mean literally *everything*. Your power is in these pages. Your struggles, your playfulness, your sass, your diligence, your sacrifice, your strength, your love, your protection, your joy, your honesty, your transformation. Are all in these pages. You, perhaps the greatest Evolutionary of us all, have opened the door, allowing our generations of storytelling heritage to finally be unleashed.

A SPECIAL THANK YOU
TO MY KICKSTARTER SUPPORTERS

This sacred space is to acknowledge and celebrate the individuals who went above and beyond in their support of the Lost Children of Andromeda's second title, *205Z: Time and Salvation*. I consider all 371 backers producers in a huge capacity, because collectively, they saw something special in this project and, I imagine, something reflected deep within themselves—a calling to unleash their potential.

Thank you Shaun Saunders for your friendship.

Thank you Dejah Gomez for your heart.

Thank you Gattison for your innovation.

Thank you Justin Hale for your inspiration.

Thank you to the 7, Garima Prasai, Sarah Minock, Naomi Graybeal, Mimmi Ebong, Alreem Al Dossary, Courtney Culbreath for your sharing. All of your beautiful lives, milestones, marriages, babies, and prosperity.

Thank you to Jessica Burgoyne for your bravery.

Thank you to Johnny Evans for your curiosity.

Thank you to Brian Dawson for your loyalty.

Thank you Kenan Jerome Floyd for your creativity.

Thank you Matthew Martinez for your kindness.

Thank you Norman Wang for your generosity.

Thank you Sean Nguyen for your unwavering support.

Thank you Larry for your intrigue.

Thank you Kevin Francis for your faith.

Thank you Dayna Lovell for your devotion.

Thank you Cameron Brown for your support.

Thank you David Patton for your youthful spirit.

Thank you Nicholas Edwin Gulick for your dedication.

Thank you Doug Harrison for your impact.

Thank you Jeremy Williams for your words.

Thank you John Reid for your humility.

Thank you Paolo Cerroni for your good-nature.

Thank you Krystle Hutton for your sonic expression.

Thank you Stefa'nie Ross for your leadership.

Thank you Tom Wilkinson for your self-discovery.

Thank you Justin Casale-Savage for your genius.

Thank you Austin Norris for your generosity.

Thank you Jonathan Perrin for your drive.

Thank you Jay Mellili for your fierceness.

Thank you Roman Argotte for your attentiveness.

Thank you Pierce Ford for your brotherhood.

Thank you Johnathan Quiglesworth for your determination.

Thank you Gary Henton for your benevolence.

Thank you Dee Betts for your imagination.

Thank you Wesley Mitchell for your fun.

Thank you Tim Urban for your encouragement.

Thank you Erik Huberman for your insight.

Thank you RJ Tang for your adventurous soul.

Thank you Sarong Chan for your steadiness.

Thank you Danny Aragon for your resilience.

Thank you Edward Culbreath for your grace.

Thank you Nii Wilson for your championship.

Thank you Jeff Zacharski for your transformation.

Thank you Bryan Z for your abundance.

Thank you Brian Smith for your freedom.

Thank you Chris Hanna for your perseverance.

Thank you Sarah Elaine Daniels for your altruism.

Thank you Jillian Lindsey for your tenderness.

Thank you Kelly Bernard for your vulnerability.

Thank you Raiane Cantisano for your joy.

Thank you John Duncan for your honesty.

Thank you Daniela Roger for your heart.

Thank you Beewee Perez for your legacy.

Thank you Jane Jo Lee for your wisdom + Henry Lee Junger for your innocence.

Thank you Nicky Chulo (Nicholas Fulcher) for your passion.

—

PRECIOUS TIME

When I think of my home and remember my land
I drift to a cherished life of passion with my man
Dear Patrick, you loved us and gave us the stars
You're no longer here, but I wonder if you're far?
Because now I feel lost with nowhere to turn
The three of us together – for that, I truly yearn.
But I must be strong for Allister, our son
And keep him from harm before he knows he's the one.
The world has been cruel, treating us like trash
Allister is sweet, but his temper can be rash.
So much he can't remember, too much he blocks
What happens when he opens Pandora's box?
I don't want any trouble, I just want to hide
Because I fear if I don't, he can't stay by my side.
Can he save the world with his potential?
With my love and the truth, his path is essential.
But what kind of mother can I truly be
If I'm too afraid to realize my own destiny?
I must find the will to let my light shine
That kind of intervention will surely be divine.
So let me trust my son, who has become the key
And let me trust myself with the power in me.
E. Primrose

DEUTERONOMY 8:7–10

For the Lord your God is bringing you into a good land, a land of brooks of water, of fountains and springs, flowing forth in valleys and hills; a land of wheat and barley, of vines and fig trees and pomegranates, a land of olive oil and honey, a land where you will eat food without scarcity, in which you will not lack anything; a land who stones are iron, and out of whose hills you can dig copper. When you have eaten and are satisfied, you shall bless the Lord your God for the good land which He has given you.

Artist: Lester Niesta/ The CMD Studios

CPSIA information can be obtained
at www.ICGtesting.com
Printed in the USA
LVHW032050180921
698154LV00004B/12/J